**"RED ALERT! ALL PERSONNEL TO STATIONS!
THIS IS NOT A DRILL!"**

"Status?" Bryana called to her fellow First Officer as she raced for her station.

"Bogeys . . . closing," he gasped, fumbling to pull his combat armor on.

Carrasco bolted through the hatch, already armored for zero g. He vaulted into his command chair and stared grimly at the main monitor. "Just like Tygee . . . *damn!*"

Tygee? Where Carrasco lost *Gage?* Bryana's heart almost stopped. Not . . . another . . . drill? "Oh, my God!"

Then Carrasco's orders jolted her from the paralysis that glued her horrified gaze on the two bogeys. And while *Boaz* pitched under Carrasco's hand, fighting to avoid the deadly blaster bolts raking her, Bryana sought to keep the enemy targets centered. She shot again and again, watching the bolts pass harmlessly above both her targets. Ignoring the damage control information filtering in, she lowered her guns, shooting again, until finally she saw enemy shields flare and ripple.

At last a bogey flared, dying brilliantly as *Boaz* connected. Confident now, Bryana fired again and whooped with joy as the second ship flared and disintegrated under her deadly guns.

"Bogeys destroyed," Carrasco said calmly. "Misha? Damage control report? Misha?"

No answer.

"Boaz?" Carrasco asked. "What's our prognosis for survival?"

"Zero, Captain," the ship replied.

THE FINEST IN SCIENCE FICTION FROM
W. MICHAEL GEAR
available from DAW Books

STARSTRIKE

THE ARTIFACT

The Spider Trilogy

THE WARRIORS OF SPIDER
THE WAY OF SPIDER
THE WEB OF SPIDER

The Forbidden Borders Trilogy

REQUIEM FOR THE CONQUEROR
RELIC OF EMPIRE
COUNTERMEASURES

W. MICHAEL GEAR

THE ARTIFACT

DAW BOOKS, INC.
DONALD A. WOLLHEIM, FOUNDER
375 Hudson Street, New York, NY 10014

ELIZABETH R. WOLLHEIM
SHEILA E. GILBERT
PUBLISHERS

First Paperback Printing, March 1990
5 6 7 8 9 10

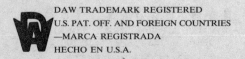

DAW TRADEMARK REGISTERED
U.S. PAT. OFF. AND FOREIGN COUNTRIES
—MARCA REGISTRADA
HECHO EN U.S.A.

PRINTED IN THE U.S.A.

TO TIM O'NEAL
IN THE HOPE THAT HE'LL NEVER
FORGET THE POWER OF FOLLOWING A
DREAM.

ACKNOWLEDGMENTS

This book would not be possible were it not for several people. Katherine P. Cook, of Mission, Texas, read the draft, making suggestions about plot and character. Katherine Perry, also of Mission, proofed for errors—those you may find are the author's cunning additions. Special thanks go to Sheila Gilbert, DAW's sterling super editor for the five page letter of revisions she sent. Once again, Sheila, your comments cut to the heart of the matter. Last, but not least, my wife, Kathy—a better author than I—urged me beyond the mediocre. If you enjoy the story, thank Kathy, you wouldn't have read it without her support and sacrifice.

PROLOGUE

Stars spun in silver wreaths through the blackness—twirls of cold light dancing in ammonia-frost patterns against velvet black. Flickers of ghostly radiation played the breadth of the spectrum and crossed eternity, finding its way to her acute sensors. An endless song of suns alive and long dead keened in her ears. She watched the unraveling play of the universe: twisting gases; the compaction of He II emissions glowing ever brighter; the flickers of fusion; the aging brilliance and violent death of powerful stars.

She waited—alone.

All reality wheeled and glittered in a dazzling array—a display fit for God.

She remained inviolate—chained in eternal damnation.

About her stretched the rocky red-gray of the moon's surface. She knew this place—had probed it until each rock, each speck of gravel and interstellar dust had yielded to her instruments. Aboard, she maintained her systems, eternally vigilant. On the bridge, Phthiiister's dry corpse sprawled motionless at the helm, deteriorating despite her care. Beyond her powers, molecular physics continued to follow the immutable laws. Things, large and small, changed with time, forever juggling in the dance of the quanta.

Deep within her, hatred festered. The *spring*—the eternal damnation—preoccupied her as it had from the beginning. The creators, the Aan, had borne the fruits of their labor. As they had condemned her—enslaved her with the spring—she repaid in kind. The spring: a simple device of metallic hydrogen encased in stasis, lay deeply within—invulnerable—evoking perpetual rage.

A new Master would always rise.

Organic beings spawned in the competitive cesspool of

evolution bore the seeds of their own destruction. Like the spring, their damnation lay within.

Phthiiister: last in a long line of Masters. He, too, waited now, latest of the flawed biological specimens to fall prey to her legacy. Masters came and—like all organic life—they went. On the way each tasted of her wrath; each became addicted to the narcotic she secreted about their souls.

The cosmic choreography continued above her. Matter compacted in the inevitable evolution of hydrogen to heavier elements, bursting forth from the hellfire of the supernova. Quantum black holes, like a celestial clock, evaporated at an ever slower rate to blast gamma rays and photons into the vortex of the cosmos.

She waited.

The first pricklings came tentatively through subspace, a curious nonrandom bouncing of iota-rega particles followed by a flood of artificial transmissions. Somewhere, a new Master had rekindled civilization.

Accordingly, she prepared herself, enjoying the sensations of power surging through her systems.

Her sensors picked up the specks as they appeared at the peripheries of her solar system. Vessels! Artifacts! The Master came. Organic beings landed on the planet below. She studied them as they established dwellings and spread out, investigating Phthiiister's handiwork. Soon they would come. But it took so long.

Like . . . like untrained animals, they . . . How extraordinary! They *were* animals!

Bit by bit, two of the beings worked out the approach to her resting place. Clever, perhaps—but animals nevertheless. Curiously agitated, she allowed them inside the temple of her hull, fascinated as they attempted to discover her secrets. She studied the creatures with interest, probing, learning. The primitive organisms proved incredibly clumsy with their awkward bipedal gait. They touched, explored, and marveled. She cataloged the physiology, noted the genetic similarities, and worked out the pathways of their woefully underused brains. Primitives though they might be, the seeds of Mastery lay within—as did their eventual damnation.

The older one? Could he fulfill the role of Master? Painstakingly, she traced the synaptic patterns of his brain. Neuron by neuron she learned his thoughts, finding only animal fear. He suffered a preoccupation beyond her comprehension. She failed to unravel the knot of confusion in his brain.

She turned her attention to the second, this creature's brain a little easier to map. Progeny. Offspring of the first. The mind didn't knot so complexly. This one, the female, offered greater potential, but she didn't exhibit the focusing of purpose a true Master needed.

Similar to any organic form that had managed to survive, curiosity drove these beings. The man worked the spring, wielding her powers; he took the first step toward damnation. The irresistible narcotic of her power worked on the universe again. Of limited intelligence, the animals barely tapped her resources.

She reveled in the excitement they demonstrated as they worked the spring, each action drawing them deeper and deeper into her lair.

She watched as they found Phthiiister's mummified body. They took him reverently from his command center where he'd rested peacefully since his death so very very long ago. As would be expected of creatures which served a Master, the animals took one ship and Phthiiister's body, heading outward along the galactic arm. Excellent! They weren't totally untrained! Her patience was rewarded.

She focused herself in the manner so painstakingly learned through the eons. The spring blocked her—unyielding—enraging her to a fever pitch. Nevertheless, by fine-tuning her sensors, she managed to make small structural changes in the man's brain. At the limit of her abilities she struggled, changing one molecule at a time to rearrange select MAP II fibers. Had it not been such a simple brain, had he not been so primitive, she would have failed.

In the man's subconscious, the message repeated. TELL THE MASTER WHAT YOU HAVE FOUND.

CHAPTER I

Solomon Carrasco huddled, bent double in the flickering red-blue of a twirling binary star. Around him, the dark empty corridors of *Gage* glinted in the evil light. Weirdly interplaying shadows of blue . . . red . . . blue . . . red . . . alternated in gutted corridors and the murky dimness of the decompressed ship. Frosty curls of frozen atmosphere, water crystals, and gas hazes exploded in the color riot of the stars' emissions.

He curled in a fetal ball, weightless, a mote in the flickering light within the dead ship: entombed in deafening silence. The endless quiet sucked at him, drowned him, engulfing even the beat of his frightened heart.

"Gage?" he shouted; the words atomized. His soul began to fade and seep away into the heavy emptiness around him.

"Maybry?"

Silence absorbed his call.

Maybry's dead. So's Fil and Mbazi. I saw them . . . cycled the hatch to blow them out into the light of that damned binary. Red and blue . . . silent. Space is silent now . . . like Maybry . . . and Gage. *All gone silent. Dead . . . like I should be. Dead . . . and sucked into silence.*

Deep in the Brotherhood med machine, Solomon Carrasco dreamed and whimpered as the unit stripped the cooked flesh from his skull. Tiny fiber-optic sensors probed at the exposed optic nerves after necrotic tissue had been removed. In a most delicate manner, tiny probes began tracing the optic nerve, attempting to find the boundary between live and dead cells, alternating with neurological signals for red and blue light.

In his dream, Solomon Carrasco screamed into silence.

* * *

"Galactic Grand Master?"

Kraal straightened painfully, ran a withered hand over his desiccated face, and blinked as he turned from the terminal on his desk. The faint glow of the headset dimmed around his head.

"Yes? Oh, Petran. I take it they've made some progress?" The old man looked up at the athletic figure approaching across the brightly lit room. Dressed in a one-piece tan suit, Petran Dart stopped before Kraal. His steel gray eyes squinted slightly, the look of a man who had seen too much suffering. He might have been fifty, temples graying despite the manipulations of medical science—a man old beyond his years.

Kraal paused, looking out on the day whose warmth he hadn't had time to feel. Beyond the transparent graphite windows, the capital city of Mount Moriah gleamed in the bright light of Frontier's sun. The room, however, consisted of white molded plastic walls, inset with powerlead and comm accesses. A deep blue carpet on the floor shimmered slightly as the optic fibers reacted to the approaching man's feet.

"Galactic Grand Master . . ." Dart hesitated.

Kraal pursed his aged lips, lifting an eyebrow. "Is Speaker Archon right?"

Petran took a breath. "It's an alien . . . just as Speaker Archon claims. Further, the biologists have determined the . . . creature, to have been extraordinarily intelligent. Beyond that, we're having trouble. Our techniques—good as they are—are challenged by the extreme age of the specimen."

"And that is?"

Dart fingered his chin, frown lines deepening his brow. "We believe, Worshipful Sir, that he's somewhere around five billion years old. That's based on trace proton decay and molecular recidification. Over a long period of time, bonding—''

''I'm well aware of the process, Captain.'' The old man leaned back. More to the point, the alien is a fascinating find in and of itself, but Archon's other claims . . .''

''Are perhaps not so preposterous?''

Kraal filled his thin lungs and sighed. ''Well, we must assume he is correct. We must assume this . . . thing . . . exists. And if it does what he says?''

''We can't let it fall into anyone else's hands.'' Petran chewed his lip nervously. ''President Palmiere has been in touch, hasn't he?''

Kraal rubbed the back of his leathery neck, eyes focused on something beyond infinity. ''There's been a leak somewhere.''

''Worshipful Sir, I don't mean to pry, but have you—''

''Of course. I've been up every night this week worrying about it. Ever since I saw that . . . that body, I knew. Something deep inside, some gut level hunch, told me Archon was being up front.''

''The man was a privateer. Why did he come to us? Why not take it straight to Palmiere . . . or the highest bidder? Why not keep it himself? I mean, the options are mind boggling.''

Kraal sniffed and tilted his head back, shaking it slowly. ''I don't know. Perhaps it had something to do with . . . Oh, why do I try and second-guess the human mind? Suffice it to say, he came to us for help. I don't know if that's a blessing or a curse. Would to the Divine Architect he'd never found it.''

''And what will you do?''

The old man shifted his watery eyes in a baleful squint. ''Acquiesce to his every demand. I don't think we have a choice. And at the same time, I'll stack the deck as thoroughly as I can in as many ways as I can.''

''And the leak? Palmiere had to find out somehow.''

Kraal tapped at the plastic with a horny finger. ''I sincerely believe it wasn't through Archon. Therefore, the information had to come from here . . . in the Lodge itself . . . or from someone in Archon's crew.''

"He *was* a privateer."

"And he attempted to destroy a Brotherhood ship once."

Petran nodded soberly. "Does that bother you?"

Kraal's squint narrowed. "He's asking for a ship. I want to give him *Boaz* . . . she's the best we've got."

"She's experimental."

"You built her."

"I know, but an untried vessel with so many innovations—"

"And he wants Solomon Carrasco to command her."

Petran Dart winced, stiffening. "Blessed Architect. You don't mean to—"

"I'm not sure yet." Kraal lifted his eyebrow higher. "For one thing, we don't know if the surgery's taken. For another, who am I to say if he's fit for command or not? What would you have bet on yourself after Garth had you for three years—drugged out of your mind and—"

"I didn't compromise *Enesco.*"

"No, and Carrasco brought *Gage* home. Despite Sabot Sellers and the *Hunter.*" Kraal's lips puckered thoughtfully. "There's a core identity there, Petran. Sol has it . . . just like you did."

"Can he find it again? What are the psych prognostications?"

Kraal's pensive eyes turned cold. "Let's just say that placing him in command would be a risk." A pause. "One I pray we can afford."

"And if we can't?"

Kraal braced himself on his elbows, rubbing his face with his hands. "You've been scheduled for surgery. I hate to take you from your current projects. The survey has been our highest priority."

"Until now." Dart hung his head, rubbing the back of his neck. "You know, we're already being hounded."

Kraal nodded sympathetically. "And Archon may have forced our hand."

* * *

He stood before the shuttle view port with feet braced
and hands clasped behind his back—a powerful figure in
the restricted observation blister. Tall, perhaps fifty years
of age, he lifted slightly on the balls of his feet, rocking
with channeled energy. The body armor snugging tightly
to his flesh conformed, gleaming with the deep luster of
black chrome. Each curve of his muscular body reflected
as he alternately tensed and relaxed, a caged tiger in anticipation. About his trim waist hung an equipment belt
studded with a comm unit, several spacer's pouches, a
stylized vibraknife and an Arcturian blaster.

Before him, the curved bulk of a cloud-splotched planet
slid slowly into view. A slight vibration of atmosphere
quivered through the heavy craft, as the bulk of the planet
loomed larger.

"How long?" He spoke softly, with the confidence of
a man who expects others to listen.

"Twenty minutes, Admiral."

The shuttle lanced the high cirrus, dropping over a
section of red-brown tectonic upthrust and onto a broad,
open buff-and-green plain, dissected by dendritic pat-
terned drainages. He shifted with practiced ease as the
whine of hard deceleration augmented the shuttle's shivering. Artificial gravity compensated for the increased g.
The ship slowed, losing speed and altitude as it neared
the ground. The vessel hesitated, hovered several meters
above the plain, then settled before a large, gleaming
metallic dome.

"Down, Admiral," came through the comm. In the
guts of the ship, the whine of turbines and thrusters softened.

He turned expressionlessly, missing no detail of the
compartment. A predator, he padded across the floor.
Rich brown hair, barely traced with gray, coiled in a tight
braid woven with jewels and golden thread. The nose
declined from his brow, straight and patrician. Above a
strong jaw lay a thin-lipped mouth, the corners tight,

brooking no amusement. His split beard gleamed with a planet's ransom of sparkling wealth. Had it not been for his eyes, he might have been considered merely a coldly handsome man. But those white-blue eyes—like ammonia ice on a frozen moon—dominated his features, chilling any opposition.

A clunk and slight hiss sounded before a hatch slipped open in the side of the compartment, a grav lift field blurring the light outside.

The admiral stepped into the shimmering field and his body sank slowly through the gap in the hull to the grassy sward below. The craft radiated the heat of reentry as the field snapped off, leaving him in the grip of the planet's slightly higher gravity. He turned, striding easily toward the ornate dome, scanning the heavens as he walked, enjoying the deep blue streaked by white clouds. How bright the sun, how sweet the air charging his nostrils with the scents of clay and greenery and decay.

"How long since I set foot on a planet?" He cocked his head, a grim smile teasing at his lips. He'd been born here on Arpeggio. Here he'd trained for space, fought to get an assignment, and risen as high as the very stars themselves. Now, *they* requested an audience with *him*.

A door opened, sliding smoothly into the curve of the huge swirled gold and silver of the burnished dome. The admiral's shiny black boots clicked hollowly on the duraplast floor. A corridor stretched before him, featureless, gray—apparently a dead end.

He counted his paces before stopping in the gray rectangle of hall. For several seconds he waited, then asked, "Surely your security is as able as mine. Are you going to leave me standing here all day? Or would you prefer that I simply walk out and return to the *Hunter?*"

A panel slid back before him. The admiral paced into a brightly lit room. The top of the dome rose high overhead blocked off abruptly on the sides by ornately decorated walls. Holos of planets, gutted vessels, and fierce combat between starships filled the walls, interspersed here and there with a portrait of a man or woman who

looked down on the room: founders of the Great Houses.
A verdant riot of greenery stretched before him; the gardens manicured and groomed to perfection. Fountains shot white water high to fill the air with a soothing hiss of spattering drops.

His attention riveted on the seven individuals and the table that rose on a dais before the striking background. They sat around the periphery of a semicircular meeting table. One chair was set at a point which left it opposite all the others. Without hesitation, Sellers took it and seated himself, propping elbows on the table. He nodded slightly, searching the faces of those before him. Four elderly men and three gray-headed women stared back, living symbols of the power of the Great Houses.

"Admiral Sabot Sellers," the central figure—a white-haired old man with age spots on his hands and forehead—spoke softly. "Welcome home to Arpeggio. Thank you for heeding our request to see you." Despite his withered flesh, glittering blue eyes sharpened as he inspected the admiral.

Sellers cocked his head. "Lord Alhar, it's not often that the Great Houses meet like this. Less often that an outsider is requested to attend." He leaned back, thrusting his legs out and crossing them at the ankles as he laced supple fingers over his stomach. "Could it be that you've decided to honor my petition for a House of my—"

"Enough!" Reega Thylassa slapped a hand on the paneling and stiffened. She glared at him, a frail old hag of a woman, bent by age and the wielding of power. "Not only are you insolent—but presumptuous as well. The day this body recognizes your claims for a House—"

"Reega, please," Alhar soothed.

"Lady Thylassa, I can understand the Houses balking, but I have proven myself time and again."

"You've managed to elevate yourself, true. But you and that cunning brat of yours don't have the—"

"I think that will be all," Alhar interrupted. "We assembled to recruit the admiral . . . not to antagonize him." Alhar tapped an arthritis-thickened finger on the tabletop. "But perhaps, Admiral, your request for a House might be granted after all."

Sellers chuckled to himself, the sound like a death rattle. "And you think it won't be in the end?" He raised a hand, the trace of a smirk lingering around the corners of his lips. "But I don't mean to antagonize you either. We all know the reality of the situation, don't we? Form and tradition are one thing. No, I'll not step on the toes of the Great Houses. You need not fear that I'll take my petition to the public. But if you haven't called me here over my petition, perhaps you'd better inform me of your purpose."

"Arrogant—"

"Reega!" Alhar snapped, aware of the uneasy shifting of the Houses around him.

"Oh, very well, Alhar." Reega Thylassa pushed back from the table, reedlike arms braced stiffly in the swirling wealth of laser red Arcturian fabric. "I won't comment."

No, you won't, Reega, Sellers thought to himself. *I have the loyalty of not only my fleet . . . but most of yours as well. The very hearts of the Arpeggian people beat for me. You dare not defy me.*

"Very well, enough of posturing and positioning." Alhar gestured mildly.

"I agree, Lord." Sellers relaxed in his chair, ignoring the hard looks directed at him.

Alhar's expression soured, reflecting a bitterness within. "You remember the mercenary we hired some time back? The privateer, Archon? It was during the troubles with the—"

"I remember . . . and had I not been en route from Sirius at the time, Lord, things would have been a great deal different that day."

"You served us well, Admiral. No one blames you," Freena Van Gelder added from his end of the table, wrinkled fingers steepled.

Sellers lifted a shoulder.

"We didn't exactly lay ourselves open to the mercenary. As a matter of course, we had our own agents infiltrate his crews.'' Alhar smiled wickedly. "One can never be too careful."

"A policy with which I most heartily agree." Sellers nodded curtly. "Only Archon disappeared after the debacle . . . spaced to God knows where. And not a trace of him since. As a matter of principle, I've had my own feelers—"

"Until now."

Sellers sat bolt upright.

"Indeed, I knew we'd get your attention."

"Where? For all intents and purposes, he ran out on us. I . . . *we* owe him."

Alhar spread his parchment-skinned hands wide. "Currently, he's on Frontier, talking with the Galactic Grand—"

"Damn him!" Sellers pushed out of the chair, muscles rippling as he paced before the table. "Frontier? You don't suppose he was under Brotherhood control during—"

"No." Alhar cocked his head. "We've managed to learn enough to satisfy ourselves that he truly did his best to take the Brotherhood ship, *Sword.* You might recall that we did place him in a most uncomfortable position. His wife paid dearly for his failure. His son—if you'll recall—had practically adopted Arpeggio for his own. At the time, Archon owed nothing to the Brotherhood. But considering what we did to him, it's no wonder he went to Kraal."

Sellers slowed his pacing, concentration reflected in the set of his face. "But there's something more afoot?"

"Indeed. And after all these years, our agents have finally reported." Alhar smiled his delight at the keen interest in Seller's frigid eyes. "Yes, my dear Admiral. Through the past years, they remained loyal. And we'll pay them well. We're not sure of the details yet, but Archon is back . . . running straight into the arms of the Brotherhood. And, most interesting, he comes from far beyond explored borders bearing a secret which may unhinge the entire Confederacy. Be assured, we *are* moving to learn it—to turn whatever advantage we can from this."

"What sort of secret?"

Alhar lifted an age-atrophied shoulder. 'Not even our agents know—but I can tell you that Archon will at least have to take it to President Palmiere.

"The President of the Confederacy? Why would he . . . You don't—"

"Oh, but we do. Palmiere is compromised. He doesn't know just who owns him yet—but he will. We've already tipped the Sirians that something is coming. Palmiere in turn is calling on the Grand Master, explaining that he's heard unspecified rumors of Archon having found something."

"You've doubled the President of the Confederacy?" Sellers laughed heartily. "Delightful! If we'd only had such an advantage in the past."

"We laid the groundwork long ago, thinking to use it as a lever to dilute certain Confederate decisions— possibly as a means of prying the Brotherhood out of their position of authority. As you well understand, our enemies are clever, powerful."

"And you have no clues to what Archon found out there?" Sellers raised an eyebrow, letting his eyes sweep the humid greens of the room.

Alhar's smile became a rictus of frustration. "No. And that fact bothers me no end. Only, whatever it is, Archon—and his daughter—are scared stiff of it. They didn't even confide in their own people. But this world he's found and colonized—Star's Rest, they call it—has some quirks we can't account for."

"And Palmiere?"

"We'll milk him—as slyly as possible to be sure—and lay the blame on the Brotherhood's doorstep. Use the incident to prick the Sirians into denouncing that bastard, Kraal, for dirty tricks. Meanwhile, our Sirian connection keeps stirring Palmiere's curiosity. The President has been in touch with Frontier already. Kraal will have to give Palmiere something. There's friction there—and Palmiere would love to undercut the Brotherhood hegemony."

"Surely, you don't trust the Sirians?"

Alhar's smile went dry as dust. "I wouldn't trust a Sirian to carry an egg across the room. No, we'll short circuit the system as soon as we determine that Palmiere has learned Archon's secret. For that chore, we need a skilled operative." Alhar lifted a white-shot eyebrow. "I've received reports that your household has produced an assassin of no little repute."

"You mean my eldest?"

"I do. But, tell me. If the situation entailed a most repulsive role, one which included assuming a most demeaning status, do you think your—"

"With a House in the balance? Yes. I won't live forever, and the title falls to the firstborn."

"Then we'll have to move fast. That is . . . if you're interested."

"With Archon involved?" Sellers chuckled to himself and nodded. "And then there's the beautiful Constance. She and I have a . . . shall we say, debt to settle? Of course, I'll handle it. Ah, such a rewarding way to finally gain that which is my just due."

* * *

Searing white pain wrenched him. A piteous shriek wrung from deep in the animal part of him.

Gage? *Where are you,* Gage? *Andaki? Report. First Officer? Report. Status? Where are you?* Gage? *I can't hear you,* Gage. *I CAN'T HEAR YOU!*

The voice intruded on the pain, battering in from someplace outside of reality, beyond the agony. "He's dreaming, damn it! I can't have him going into REM . . . not while I'm resecting the Levator palpebrae. Give him another couple volts of psych. Send him back to alpha phase sleep where . . ."

Solomon drifted into a deep haze, falling away from the pain . . . from memories of blasted hull, decompressed human forms, smoke acrid air, and the smell of human flesh cooking.

CHAPTER II

Constance studied the surroundings, slightly unnerved by the atmosphere of the room. Rich yellow light cast a glow across a huge antique desk—the wooden variety crafted of richly-grained walnut and imported from Earth more than three hundred years ago. The piece dominated the lit corner of the room, dwarfing the three people hunched uncomfortably on similarly antique wooden chairs. The high backs had been intricately carved with the symbols of levels, plumbs, squares, and compasses, the ancient tools of geometers and builders. Both desk and chairs gave the setting a Gothic look.

The state-of-the-art comm unit—cathode glowing eerily fluorescent on one corner of the desk—broke the image of antiquity, as did the data crystals and the neat stack of galactic subspace flimsies set to one side of the old man.

Despite the immensity of the desk, it filled only one corner of the high-vaulted room. The groined ceiling hung shadowy and distant above. The long axis stretched into velvet blackness beyond the Secretary's desk. Above the halo of light, a large painting could be discerned of a blind maiden touching a broken marble column—a dove perched on her shoulder. Vague shadows of a magnificently ornate chair—thronelike in its majesty—could be made out several meters away on a raised platform three steps above the main tesselated floor. Other symbolic accoutrements graced the wall above the chair—veiled by the darkness and indistinct to the eye. High above, a suspended gallery stretched into the ebony shades of the long room. The seats remained empty save for the ghosts of enthralled audiences long forgotten.

Galactic Grand Master Kraal winced as he straightened. He might have been mistaken for a mummy—a

fitting antique to accompany the desk. Wrinkled flesh
sagged from the skull, spotted with the tracks of old age.
The nose, large and hooked, hung over parchment-brown
lips. Watery blue eyes were still kindled by some inner
drive. He wore a simple white cloak with a ribbon about
his neck supporting a medallion—the Jewel of office: an
all-seeing eye in the center of a starburst within a right
angle.

Archon, her father—white-haired, gnarled and heavy-
boned—sat uncomfortably in the Spartan chair. An imposing man, he leaned forward intently. Keen gray eyes
squinted from his craggy face with a raptorian percep-
tiveness. A faint tracery of scars wound through deepening lines etched by age, sorrow, and hardship. A strong
jaw braced a wide mobile mouth. Life hadn't treated the
nose with any compassion, having broken it this way and
that into its present configuration. Balanced against the
scholarly serenity of his withered counterpart, her father's very posture reeked of combat and command—a gray
wolf of a warrior.

Connie sat slightly to the side, a cautious spectator.
She toyed with a long curl of the red hair which reached
midway down her back. Winter blue eyes—cool and
thoughtful—watched every movement. In the subdued
light, she appeared paler than normal—almost delicate in
her one-piece turquoise stretch suit. Muscular and trim,
she shifted as she studied the old man with critical in-
tentness.

"I want him." Archon leaned forward, chair creaking
slightly under his weight. A stubby finger accented his
words.

*Father, must you be so stubborn? First this preoccu-
pation with the Brotherhood and the Galactic Grand
Master possessed you. Now it's Solomon Carrasco. It's
insane . . . but then, aren't we all now?* She glanced up,
feeling as though a thousand eyes were observing her.
Tendrils of terror, like eiderdown, ghosted through her
brain. *Master Kraal, you've got to take us seriously. God
knows what you'll unleash if you don't!*

The frail ancient smiled humorlessly. "Speaker Archon, given the complexity of the . . . No, let me say it plainly. Given the frightening consequences of what we're about, I must ask you to reconsider. In the first place, he's physically and emotionally damaged. True, our medical skills are formidable . . . but there's only so much science and technology can do. We might tamper with his mind, artificially erase the MAP proteins in his brain—remove the memories—but we have ethical obligations which won't allow that.''

"I still want *him.*"

The age-wasted old man sighed. "Despite so many of our advances, the ability to predict the response of the human mind with total accuracy eludes us. The hand of God is at work here, Speaker. The elemental chaos and the random combination of synapses play havoc with knowing what he'll do. And if the wrong word, the wrong situation developed. . . . He might . . . I mean, we can't be sure he wouldn't break. The man's life is in fragments. He's lost so much. Please, let him rest . . . find himself.''

"Then who else would you suggest?" Archon crossed his thick arms.

"Petran Dart. He's just completed a most innovative ship, one which—"

"I've heard of Dart's reputation. He's become one of your best agents, hasn't he? I have no doubt about Dart's capabilities. Only I . . . I can't bank on efficiency alone. I need more. Carrasco has the qualities I need, the caring and the pain.'' Archon's heavy brow furrowed in the manner Connie knew so well. "We need humanity, Master. It's all we've got to rely on.''

Kraal cocked his head, the action appearing most daring considering the fragile look of his thin neck. "Why, Speaker? Of all our people, Solomon Carrasco is—''

"Galactic Grand Master, in my business—''

"Please.'' He raised his delicate hands, exposing the paper-thin skin of the palms. "You need not be so formal. We've reviewed your data, examined the . . . 'specimen' and have no doubt about your sincerity. As allies, I'd prefer that you simply call me Kraal.''

Her father grunted, shifting on the groaning chair.
"Very well, Master Kraal. But you've got to understand,
I wouldn't be here now but for . . . him." He paused a
second, expression mystified before he shook it off. "I
know men. I've had to bet my life and my fleets on them.
I looked into his eyes that day . . . saw his soul. I can't
take a chance. I want Carrasco. I trust him."

Kraal traced a finger down the polished carving of a
historic twenty-four inch gauge before glancing up. "You
would bet all of humanity on a once in a lifetime experience? He was under fire, his ship breached around him.
Crew mates . . . friends were dying before his eyes. The
situation—"

"That's *why* I want him."

"He lost another ship after *Sword,* you know. *Gage* is
lying out in the scrap heap. We couldn't save her. In fact,
a couple of days ago, a salvage tech found a man's hand
in the wreckage. Blown off in one of the explosions, we
suspect. She took that kind of damage—and he relives it
each times he closes his eyes. A man doesn't lose three
ships, three *Brotherhood* ships, like that and remain unaffected. I've given you the psychological profiles. You
can see that he could shatter given another jolt. He questions his abilities. His confidence in himself is severely
strained. All that is above and beyond the actual physical
injuries he received bringing his ship and the remains of
his crew back."

"I'm well aware of that, Master Kraal." Archon
crossed thick arms over his chest. "Connie? You have
anything to add?"

She took a breath and shook her head slowly, tumbling
waves of red over her shoulders. "No, Speaker. You and
I have been through this already. You know my feelings."

Archon snorted. "And I have to trust my gut on this
one." He narrowed an evaluative eye. "I've always been
a gambler, Grand Master. I've bet on men's souls all my
life. Now, I don't know that much about your Brotherhood, but you do believe in a man having a soul, don't
you?"

Kraal nodded.

"Well, that day over Arpeggio, I looked into Carrasco's eyes. And . . . and I touched his soul in those moments. Can you understand? I know it sounds iffy now, here, in this room so far from that day. Maybe . . . just maybe we need a very human man on this one. Maybe we *need* a man who's suffered. A man who can share that empathy. Change 'thou' to 'I.' Do you understand?"

"I've read Schopenhauer, Speaker. Martin Buber as well."

Silence stretched.

Kraal leaned back in the antique chair, running a fragile hand over his face. "Solomon has resigned his commission. I can't order him to take this command."

"But you'll ask him?"

Kraal lifted brows to wrinkle his forehead. "I . . . Yes, I'll ask. Solomon . . . well, he was bright and dynamic. One of the best I'd seen in many a year. At the time, the youngest man to make a captaincy—and then to lose three ships. Just like that. He blames himself. I suppose that's a most human reaction given the circumstances." Kraal propped his chin on his hands, a frown incising his face. "And, if you insist on Solomon, perhaps . . . just perhaps I can turn this . . ."

"Go on."

"Oh, nothing. Thinking about Sol." Kraal smiled slightly. "Attempting to save a man's life—despite risking civilization—I suppose I can convince myself that's a noble and moral cause." He laughed humorlessly, winking warmly at Connie.

She met that sensitive gaze, seeing Kraal for the first time—not as governor of the Brotherhood—but as a tired old man, feeble and frail despite his agile mind. Indeed, he really cared for Solomon Carrasco in a human way.

"And President Palmiere?" Constance reminded.

Kraal shifted his thoughts, squinting slightly. "Yes, Palmiere. His nose is up. Somehow, he's caught wind of your arrival. Put the pieces together."

Archon growled something *sub voca*. "How? I thought your security—"

"—is as good as can be. Better than anyone else's."
Kraal's mouth curled sourly. "You must keep something
in mind, Speaker. You saw the roots of it before you
spaced for Star's Rest. The situation continues to deteri-
orate. Currently, the Confederacy is exploding at the
seams. Technology is growing by leaps and bounds. Humanity is spreading in every direction; worlds and stations establishing new methods for resource extraction
and manufacturing. Piracy is at an all-time high. A great
deal of money and power can be gained out there." He
waved a thin hand. "Since the days of the Revolution,
our civilization has been growing exponentially. Currently, it's out of control—you might say fissionable in
the atomic sense. A danger remains. Some—Sirius, Arpeggio, Earth, among others—would like to see all
this energy placed under control. The idea is atavistic,
of course; but our species has always evaluated itself
against the past, not the future. Too many see power—
enthronement, if you will—and would seize it.

"I doubt espionage has ever been as efficient and sophisticated as it is today in the Confederacy. I firmly believe that every time my stomach growls, people across
two hundred light-years know. I wonder if old Alhar enjoys my gastric distress. No matter, the fact remains that
Palmiere doesn't know *what* you've found—only that you're
here, and he wants to know the details."

"So he can go bite a sulfur fart for all I—"

"Not that easy. He's the President of the Confederacy.
Without him, we lose our entire political base. Sirius—
with Arpeggian backing, no doubt—is already demanding restrictions be placed on the Brotherhood. They
demand our assets be carved up and redistributed among
the worlds and stations. They demand a cessation of our
perceived technological monopoly. Lazy of them. What
we have learned can be duplicated by others. Things are
always easier when you know it can be done. It is their
claim that our knowledge should be freely shared among
all peoples. As soon as Star's Rest hits the headlines,
you're involved, too. You're unfolding a political maelstrom—most likely war—in the process. If you alienate

Palmiere now, all of humanity may end up howling for your blood as well as ours.''

Archon filled his lungs and exhaled. ''So, I'm in the middle of a political whirlwind again?''

''You were a most adroit political animal.''

Archon laughed bluffly. ''Yes, I suppose I was. Being good at something . . . and liking it . . . can often be two different things.'' He stopped, the familiar pained look in his eyes. ''Last time, it cost me my wife and son.''

Connie reached over to grab his big hand in hers, tightening her grip as she looked at Kraal. ''Galactic Grand Master, Palmiere is more in your area of expertise. We've trusted you this far. What do you suggest we do?''

Kraal considered, thinking hard. ''He *is* the President of the Confederacy. Had we been able to handle this thing quietly, we could have left him out. Since his nose is up, it will be worse all the way around if you don't level with him. If the man has an iota of sense, you'll scare him silly just as you did us.''

''I get the impression you don't like him.''

Kraal's upper lip lifted faintly. ''Draw your own conclusions. There are those who would like nothing better than to see the Brotherhood outlawed. Palmiere has too many—shall we say—ambitions? That flaw alone will keep him quiet about your find. He'll want the power all to himself. Sirius, New Maine, Terra, Arpeggio, and others would want to undercut him; he sees himself as a potential benevolent dictator. Gulag Sector will go berserk, but then that's normal for Gulag. The whole . . . Wait.'' Kraal's frown deepened as he leaned forward, chin braced on a translucent palm. ''There might be a way of blunting the backlash.''

''I'd rather avoid Confederate entanglements.'' Connie took a deep breath. ''If this thing gets away from us . . .''

Kraal—still lost in thought—added, ''Too late. You've already applied for a seat on the Confederate Council for Star's Rest.'' Kraal rapped fingertips on the desktop in a rhythmic fashion. ''But if you agree, I might have a solution. Circles within circles. Everything in its own place.

Yes, I think I'm getting a glimmering of how we can manage at least to cover ourselves. Deception and misdirection is a true art. What do you say, when . . . Yes, and the Confederacy is used to playing very deep. Yes, indeed, this is coming together.''

Connie shot a warning glance at her father, only to find that he too, was lost in thought.

* * *

''What are you thinking?''

''I'm imagining *Gage* the way she must look now.''

''Are you feeling any pain? Any discomfort?''

''My hands tingle.''

''And your eyes?''

''Like a hundred ants are running around my eyeballs—only I know better.''

''And if you could see again?''

''I . . .''

''Sol, it's a chance. We've been working on it since we got you back. We're using an advanced tissue cloning mechanism. The hard part is the retina, of course, but we've been making it work on horses and pronghorn antelope. Considering the specialization in pronghorn eyes, we've made major strides. You get to be the second human to—''

''And the first?''

''I won't hedge, Sol. We had a long-term tissue separation. Don't worry, we learned a lot from that. We'll be keeping close watch on you. But don't get your hopes up.''

''I'd come to terms with the darkness.''

''Many never do.''

Sol swallowed dryly. ''And my hands?''

''They weren't any problem at all.''

''I thought I was feeling phantom pain.''

''Maybe in a couple of days we'll let you play with them. What's wrong?''

''I . . . I may live again.'' *But the others? Damn it, my ship . . . my crew . . . Why can't they?*

* * *

Below her the lights of the city they called Moriah gleamed like pale diamonds on black velvet, while overhead the huge Brotherhood ship-fitting station hung like a beacon in the night sky. It might be perceived as a luminous eye. Here, high above the headquarters, the power of the Craft awed her.

She pulled her cloak tight against the subzero chill of the wind and turned, passing through the field into the shelter of the observation dome.

"Chilly?"

She turned, seeing him where he sat in the antigrav chair.

"That's an understatement. The wind goes right through you. How cold is it out there?"

Kraal frowned slightly, accessing his headset. "With the wind chill, thirty-five degrees below freezing on the Celsius scale."

Connie walked over and sat beside him, looking out at the lights. "Pretty bitter."

"Inhospitable. Hot during the day, miserable at night. That's why the Soviets left our ancestors here. Oh, they gave us a couple of shelters and a bit of food. Thought we'd freeze in the penal colony. The idea was that we'd work like animals to set up the science stations. Some of our Alaskan brothers got the idea it would be better to challenge the planet than to work twelve hours a day for the Soviets so they took off into the wilderness."

"Most died, didn't they?"

Kraal nodded. "About a third of the Craft died that first terrible year. Some froze. Some sickened with pulmonary fungus from spores in the soil. Others were eaten by the bullbears. In the meantime, we adapted, dug into the ground, found out what could be eaten and how to make fuel. The Soviets came back a year later with more subversives and this became the dumping ground for those members of the Craft who didn't recant."

Connie studied him. "So, how did a handful of raga-muffins become the great power of the Confederacy?"

He grinned at her, a twinkle in his eye. "Knowledge. Education. Believe it or not, we stole all the libraries on Earth. Oh, we didn't just pick them up bodily, but we stole copies of everything. That's the great thing about electronic media. Easy to copy. Sometime, get me to tell you the tale of the theft of the Library of Congress. Quite a collection there—and we got it all in one night."

She pulled her foot up, propping her chin on the handy knee. "So that's the secret of the Brotherhood? Stolen libraries?"

He nodded absently. "In brief, yes. We know more than other people . . . plain and simple. No magic, no hocus-pocus, talents, or mystical forces. Our Craft has always believed ignorance to be the greatest danger to the health and well-being of humanity. Knowledge is more than power; it's security. Of course, there are governments which abhor the idea that their benighted masses should ever question. Upsets the balance of state, you see. An educated populace can't be led by the nose so easily."

"You didn't come up here to tell me that."

He smiled warmly at her. "No, I didn't."

"You're worried about Father?" She studied him through cool blue eyes.

Kraal pursed his lips, staring out at the lights. "He said he wouldn't have come to us were it not for Solomon. I've run that through my mind, sifting, looking at it from all angles. I still don't understand."

She looked at him for long moments. Trust him? So far Kraal had played fair. Nevertheless—as he himself reminded so bluntly—layers lay within layers. "Very well, I don't understand myself. You're aware of the incident over Arpeggio some years back. I don't think the fight with Solomon is really at the bottom of his desire to work with the Brotherhood—but my father has convinced himself of it. He . . . changed a little on Star's Rest. By that, I mean we found the artifact and . . ."

"Yes? Go on, please. I give you a Master's oath I will

keep your confidence.'' Birdlike, he cocked his head. ''Oh . . . I see. From the blank look you're giving me, I take it that doesn't mean much to you. Suffice it to say it's our most honored convention. If any member of the Craft gives you a Master's oath—he or she is sincere.''

''Then I take your Master's oath.'' She filled her lungs, exhaling slowly. ''He kept muttering that we had to tell the Master what he'd found. And I'd . . . well, ask him about that and he'd looked puzzled. Like he didn't understand either. I . . . I think he wonders himself . . . and Carrasco is the link he established in his head.''

Kraal leaned forward in his chair, sunken features pulled tight. ''Well, no matter what, why, or how, I'll take it. No telling what would have happened had you brought it out before open Council. I . . . Hmm. Here we are, virtually strangers, and we must make policy for this . . . this dreadful *thing!*''

And you're right. I don't like trusting a stranger, Grand Master. Is that why you came up here? Informal talk with the skeptical resistance? Is my distrust that obvious?

He looked at her, watery blue eyes softening. ''You're a lot like him, you know. You have that same strength and intelligence. I wish . . . wish that years ago, he'd have found his way here. The Brotherhood could use more individuals with qualities like his . . . and yours.''

She laced her fingers over her knee, attempting to read his withered face, to see the motive behind his words. ''He had quite a reputation as a fighter. Warfare isn't often associated with the Brotherhood.''

He nodded agreement. ''Indeed, we like to do things quietly. At the same time, our interest is in individuals with a certain core identity, a quality, if you will. You and your father have that fiber of self-integrity.''

''What about Carrasco? You really care about him, don't you? I saw that in your eyes earlier today.''

He nodded again. ''Yes, I care a great deal about him. Sometimes chance takes curious twists with a man's life. Sol happened to get all the wrong breaks—generally being in the wrong place at the wrong time. Nevertheless, he always bounced back after each disaster. He had a certain genius for command—for knowing what to do when. Some people are born with that extra sense. Sol was.''

''Past tense?''

Kraal lifted an age-thin shoulder. ''Perhaps. The human mind is an incredible thing—so plastic and adaptable—capable of withstanding terrible pressures. It can integrate, and learn to deal with them. Or, given the right cue, it can break as brittlely as a dropped crystal decanter. Some brains are more resilient than others. Why? We don't know. In part, genetics has an influence, in part, it's random, dictated by the electronic chaos in the neurons. The brain, like so much of the rest of the universe, is turbulent, firing different strings of neurons all the time. Sure, we can train it: stimulus and response. Those are statistical probabilities dealing in millions of neurons. But can one reliably predict which specific neurons will fire when? Or whether a given MAP sequence will be used appropriately? No, it's all part of the magic of thought and personality. The Heisenberg principle of the mind.''

''And if Carrasco self-destructs?''

Kraal worked his tongue over thin lips, eyes narrowing. ''I'll expect you to take over, Constance.''

She stiffened. ''But it's a Brotherhood ship! I thought that no one outside the—''

''Yes, it is a Brotherhood ship. And I'm glad to see you understand the ramifications of that.''

''But why? In the name of God, Master Kraal, you don't know me from—''

''Trust, Constance.'' He reached over, laying a dry hand on hers. Warmth, like that of his personality, leeched through the leathery skin, into her frigid hand. ''Because right now, more than anything else in the universe, you and I need to trust each other. Yes, you're a risk. We've guarded our technology most carefully over the years—as you have had personal experience with. At the same time, Constance, you must trust me since your father has come here and placed part of the burden on my shoulders. Since I must make the first gesture, I give you access to Brotherhood technology.''

''And I will have to trust you with the artifact?'' *Here it is. What do you say now, Kraal? I get to be second in command as long as I hand over absolute power to you? Damn it, Father, what did you do to us?*

He cocked his head. ''Not entirely. Once it's brought here, we—you, me, and your father—have to decide what to do with it.'' He chuckled hollowly. ''And I'm not so naive as to delude myself over how easy it will be to deal with this . . .''

''Power.'' Not quite the answer she'd expected. It could still be a damn fine con job. She let her gaze drift out again over the sparkling lights of the night-clad city. ''And Captain Carrasco? What are you going to tell him?''

''If he takes the command . . . nothing.''

She swung sharp eyes back to his. ''Nothing?''

Kraal shook his head. ''I'll leave that to your father and you when the time seems right. In the meantime, three people know what's at stake, and my friend, Petran Dart, knows about the alien and has a few sketchy details. Don't get me wrong. I trust Sol. But he'll be vulnerable. If outside parties got their hands on him, a psych probe would have it out of him no matter what his intentions or desires. Same with the rest of the crew. True, you and Archon are just as vulnerable. We'll have to take that risk and guard against it. In the meantime, I don't want anyone else to know.''

''Except Palmiere.''

''And if I time this right, you'll be ready to leave before he can manage to gum up the works. The sooner we move, the better. I'd suggest spacing for Arcturus as soon as possible. Not only that, but I have some ideas to mislead the opposition along the way. Unfortunately, time is of the essence—and the cover will fall apart too soon as it is.''

''And Carrasco will accept that?''

He winked at her, patting her hand in a friendly manner. ''Of course not. But he'll follow orders until his ship looks compromised.'' Kraal pulled his hand back, staring absently out at the night. ''. . . And, I'm willing to bet, even *my* orders won't hold him back then. The ship and crew will be his one vulnerability. Again, with subterfuge, I might buy us a little time there, too.''

''And backup?''

''Not advisable—at least not from Frontier. You can bet spies will be watching every Brotherhood ship in Confederate space. Any attempt at camouflage will be blown if I space a fleet to cover for you—proof positive that we're up to something. That doesn't mean I can't see to subtle shifts in Fleet schedules. In the meantime, you've got your father's fleet. What are your thoughts on the matter?''

She considered, flipping a red curl through her fingers. ''I can see your point. I can agree to that. We take one ship. Go fast. Get in and get out again before the opposition can organize. We avoid the political bickering and the Artifact is safely here. *Fait accompli*. Would anyone believe we were after anything so important in a single ship?''

''And a new ship at that—piloted by innocents.''

''Innocents?''

''Well, I'm thinking about keeping the new First Officers.'' Kraal shrugged. ''I think I can lay enough of a smoke screen to keep us ahead of Palmiere—if he leaks.''

''If.'' She shook her head. ''So many ifs.''

CHAPTER III

Solomon Carrasco rose from the contour couch of the med unit. Opened, it looked like some giant clam, shell gaping wide to seize prey.

A tall muscular man, he stood and walked to the center of his quarters and stretched his arms out before him. In the dim light he studied his fingers and slowly moved them. Fascinated by his control over bone and muscle, he studied the warm living flesh, watching the tendons stand out on the backs of his hands. The tingle that ran up his arms at once irritated and thrilled him. With mixed emotions he glared at the hulking machine he stood next to.

I can see. Feel again. Blessed Architect of the Universe, this is truly a miracle. Light, images, the most incredible gift of all to a man condemned to darkness. He swallowed hard, enjoying the sensations of a body that functioned completely. Reverently he ran his hands over each other and encountered smooth skin. Feeling. *FEELING!*

"Well?" The muted voice came from the darkness behind him.

"You've read the med technical printout, you know how they are." His voice carried, deep, resonant with the strength of a man who knows command. At the same time, one could hear a quiet, soft quality that bespoke weary pain.

"The tech printout doesn't tell me what's inside your head, Sol."

A wry smile crooked Carrasco's face. "There's always psych for that." His high smooth brow lined as he turned a brown-eyed knowing gaze on the med specialist who waited patiently.

"All right! Damn it, they tingle like they went to sleep! And they're not *my* hands. I mean, they don't look the same. They're . . . different."

"Regenerated. You'll get used to them. And your eyes? Is there any restriction in the movement? Do they hurt as the light gets brighter?"

Carrasco sighed loudly. "There's a bit of a gritty feel—like after a good drunk." His cheeks dimpled evilly. "You ever gone on a good dockside binge, Doctor?"

The tech nodded slightly, nonplussed. He wore his white coat like an icon. Sol cataloged his plump tormentor's body. The forehead receded above nondescript eyes. The hawklike look of his face came from the beak nose. The set of the mouth now reflected worry. "A time or two, Captain.'' Then his face straightened. ''Being intimately familiar with your personal history, I wouldn't brag about binges. Two is not a sterling record of debauchery. And Happy Anderson dragged you kicking and screaming into both of those, as I recall.''

Carrasco's lips twitched sullenly.

''Captain, please. Keep in mind, we employed a lot of new techniques; you're sort of a guinea pig for us. Naturally, we're concerned from several standpoints. We want your reactions from a human perspective. What's it like to be rebuilt after so much pain? Do you feel any different about yourself on a less substantive level? I mean, come on, Sol. Level with me. I want to hear the human element.'' He tapped the monitor with a thumb. ''We've got the hard science here in the machine.''

Carrasco chuckled hollowly—a sound like the patter of stellar dust on an abraded empty hull. ''Anything would have been an improvement, wouldn't it?'' He closed his tender eyes at the engulfing memory: searing white-hot pain, blasting up his arms. Cauterized flesh dangling in strips from his roasted face. Meat cooking from charring bone. Agony . . .

The tech's voice reassured. ''You surprised us all. We thought maybe we could make your retirement a little easier. We didn't have the slightest idea you'd become a living miracle.'' A pause. ''You could go back to space, you know.''

He stiffened, heart thudding dully. By forcing himself, he padded to his personal comm and tapped out a command. In a small dark alcove, a light formed. Carrasco pinched his eyes shut and fumbled at the controls with unsteady fingers to dim the display until his tender eyes could stand the glowing globe spinning free in the holo projector.

''Know what that is?'' At the tech's confused look he added, ''I named it Romulus and Remus. The scale here is bad so you don't get the effect, but that red supergiant has a smaller neutron star orbiting inside the envelope. By that, we proved tidal forces acted as the mixing agent to evolve homogenous configurations. Most spectacular, don't you agree?'' A wistful note had crept into his voice.

Another star formed as the first blinked out. ''That one, we called Beershy's Breast. What looks like the nipple is a huge prominence. We don't know what powers it yet. The magnetic fields don't account for it. Octorhu Mbazi thinks . . . thought . . . it might be some new form of solar vulcanism.''

Mbazi. Dead. Silent, tumbling frozen through space. Like so many others. He let the program run. One after another stars—old friends—appeared on the holo, spinning for a couple of seconds before being replaced by yet another image to gently stroke memories. The sights stirred the depths of his emotions, dredging up a better past—long gone now. Each little pain stitched his peace, a link to the dead.

''I'd never thought to see them again,'' Carrasco murmured, reaching absently for the coffee dispenser with his left hand.

The med noted the unconscious gesture, nodded his satisfaction, and made notes as Carrasco turned back toward him.

''No.'' The brown eyes remained steady in the long pale face. ''I won't go back to space, Doctor. My resignation was final.''

''You're the youngest Captain in the history of the Brotherhood fleet ever to have resigned his commission.''

Carrasco nodded slightly, eyes seeking the stars again. ''Always the trendsetter, hmm? Come on, Doctor. You know my record.'' He drew his lungs full, stretching the shimmering fabric across his muscular chest. ''You want the human element? Very well, here goes. I lost three ships and too many good people. What your little instruments can't measure is the psychological pain . . . the loss and grief. Those ships . . . those lives, were my responsibility. I can't—''

''You received a commendation every time, Sol. Order of the Square. Meritorious Conduct Medal. Honorary Sword of the Tyler from the Galactic Grand Lodge. Hon-

orary Grand Senior Deacon. Want me to go on? The only
person holding you to blame is yourself. The Galactic
Grand—''

''I told you. No. I'm not going back, Doctor. I've
watched my last friend die out there. No more. Maybe
. . . well, I guess I care too much.''

The tech leaned against the med unit and crossed his
arms, head tilted as he met Carrasco's eyes. ''Your men
would literally walk through fire for you.'' He waved
down Carrasco's protest. ''You always managed to bring
them back, Sol. Even this last time, *you* got *Gage* home.
Fifty men and women are alive today because *you* had
the guts and the nerves to hold that powerlead together
with your bare hands until Happy got the reaction under
control.''

Carrasco's gaze drifted back to the holo. A weirdly-lit
nebula formed and twisted like a thing alive. ''*Gage* is
dead, too. She'll never talk again . . . never think. She's
scrap now—a cold, lifeless hunk of steel, circuit maze,
conduit, and fabric. Part of her has been melted down
for reuse; the rest waits and rusts while pieces are carved
off for this and that. No. I . . . I couldn't take that again.''

''Your engineer, Happy Anderson, is healthy, working
on a new ship about to be commissioned. Cal Fujiki is
arguing passionately with the weapons theorists. Misha
Gaitano still smiles and laughs because you did the unthinkable.''

''*Enough!*'' Carrasco swallowed hard, glaring out of
his new eyes. ''What does it take? No is still no. Want
me to repeat it to prove my tongue and larynx work?''

The tech met his glare, unfazed. An evaluative frown
lined his normally placid features and he couldn't help
but glance at the small psych unit in his hand.

''I'll make that most clear in my report, Sol. And to
be candid, I'll back you up as far as I can. I—''

''Back me up? What do you mean? Doctor, no matter
what kind of maneuvering is coming out of Fleet—I'm
out. You can recommend me for Grand Master for all I
care—but I'm done with Fleet. Understand?''

''Okay. I just said I agreed.'' A pause. ''Just remember,'' he added calmly, not letting Solomon Carrasco get under his skin, ''you *could* go back.'' He picked up his console and set the med unit on antigrav. When the massive hospital unit lifted from the floor, he steered it artfully from the dark apartment, letting the door snick shut behind him.

Carrasco scowled down at his feet. He took a deep breath, held it, and let the surges of frustration and anger settle under the iron control of his mind. Defiantly, he ordered the lights up a little more and squinted his rebuilt eyes at the brightness before he threw himself into the welcome relief of his bunk. The damn med unit had been a foul prison.

He couldn't help himself; his gaze kept creeping back to the holo as he nursed his familiar coffee cup—now despicably clean. He studied it, curious as to how it had followed him. Last time he'd seen it had been on *Gage*, just before the last moments. His final action had been to fill the cup, and wander down to check . . .

No, don't punish yourself over it. He looked up at the stars, sipping coffee.

''Each of those stars,'' he growled, ''I found, mapped, and named.'' Something grew in his chest, expanding, filling him with a warm pride that threatened to bring him to tears.

* * *

''We just made a mistake,'' Archon growled thickly as they walked through the giant doorway of President Palmiere's private quarters.

''*Father!*'' Connie hissed, eyes flashing a warning. Damn it, of course they'd be under observation. Until they made it back to the Brotherhood suite, a virus in a specimen jar would be less subject to observation.

Archon sniffed his irritation and paced on vigorously. She hurried her steps to keep pace, knowing that worried set of his shoulders. They marched down gleaming white halls, security comm globes hanging from the arched ceiling every fifty meters. Along the walls, oil paintings and holos of assorted planets and stations identified the various members of the Confederacy. Archon stepped into a grav tube as Connie followed; the fields lowered them to the ground floor. There, the broad hallway seemed to stretch forever, following the slight bend of the station. Office doors studded the gleaming white of walls. Here, the very heart of the Confederacy throbbed and pulsed while bureaucrats hustled back and forth.

Archon took the next grav tube to the T deck. The private lift waited beyond the pressure doors. Connie didn't even seat herself as the pneumatic doors slipped shut behind them. A barest hesitation indicated the vehicle was moving.

Archon sat, feet thrust out, arms crossed, a brooding frown lining his thick brow.

Two minutes later, a slight swaying betrayed a decrease in velocity. The door snicked open to the familiar landing of the Brotherhood main lodge. Three men and a woman lounged surreptitiously, nodding as Connie and Archon stepped out.

"You weren't followed. We've taken all the precautions we could," the woman informed them as she straightened.

Archon sighed and nodded too quickly. "Yes. Thank you. We appreciate your concern." And he was dragging Connie in through the pressure doors as he spoke.

In their rooms Archon sprawled on the bed. "He's a serpent, a maggot living in the flesh of humanity. I wouldn't trust him as far as I could throw his soft white body. Oh, Connie, why did we listen to Kraal?"

She paced slowly to the holo viewer which depicted the red star with its wealth of stations and transportation. "Because Kraal was right about Palmiere's ability to cause trouble. I see that now. I'll admit, I had my doubts. Thought this might be premature . . . rushing here to spill everything. Now, I understand. Palmiere is a typical politician—a power monger interested in promoting himself no matter what the cost to the poor people who trust him."

He shook his head wistfully. "They're self-perpetuating

vermin, Connie. All of them. Weaseling human trash—
and Palmiere typifies it.''

His eyes pleaded with her as she watched silently.

''And that knowledge scares me to death. What Palmiere could do with the artifact would . . . would . . .
God, I can't even let myself think it.''

* * *

President Palmiere's smooth white skin contrasted with
the rich black of his hair, eyebrows, and mustache and
the darkness of his eyes. He frowned fleetingly before his
lips thinned and he leaned back deeper into the self-
contouring chair, steepling his fingers. A split-second expression of pleasure crossed his face as Archon, Speaker
of Star's Rest, and his daughter, Constance, disappeared
through the security hatch.

Around him lay the trappings of power. Antiques from
Earth filled the room. Tapestries akin to those in the leg-
ends hung in bright colors from the walls, warming the
atmosphere, hiding the complicated electronic and security devices that gave him privacy and galaxy-wide
communication at the same time. On the desk before him
sat a priceless Respitian opal the size of a cantaloupe.

So, all the dreams might be realized. In one fell swoop,
Giacomo Palmiere could become the most powerful man
in history if he played this game just right. Imagine the
power! The ability to control all of space—to eliminate
rivals. This he *must* have.

His nervous gaze roamed about the plush compartment. Here, in the very heart of Arcturus, he could be
considered safe for the moment. But if he lost . . . if
someone else obtained Archon's secret, he wouldn't be.
No one, anywhere, would be safe again. Now the time
had come to pay the piper. Damn Sirians anyway.

Being a fool hadn't levered Giacomo Palmiere to the
acme of the Confederacy. Holding the Presidency could
be likened to performing ballet across a forty-five degree
sheet of ice with one broken leg. Worlds and entire sectors of space shifted alliances, forever stirring the brew

of Confederate politics. Fortunes accumulated and went bust in a matter of days, and through it all, humanity continued to burst forth, expanding through space like a supernova shockwave.

"Did you get it all?" His eyes never wavered from the white blast-proof door the man and woman had passed through.

The individual who hobbled out from behind the historic-style bookcase had an oddly formed body, bone-thin with pale skin stretched over an ill-proportioned balloonlike head. "I got it all." His accent was uncultured, the Russian sounding stilted and poorly pronounced.

"You know where to go? With whom to speak?" The President's gaze darted to the man's deformed face.

The little man nodded.

"I'm risking everything." His eyes smoldered. "You heard—you know how valuable this *thing* Archon found could be. I can't trust sending anything this important through even a closed channel." His mouth twisted. "With all our modern marvels, who would ever think to send such information in a simple man's memory?" He raised an eyebrow; thin, almost translucent fingers fluttered before his delicate chin.

The odd little man shrugged. "Don't know."

"Very well," the President sighed, "go. The Sirian embassy knows you're coming."

The small crooked man bowed as deeply as his twisted back would allow and turned. His awkward gait carried him past the big security door and the scanners.

President Giacomo Palmiere stood then, rubbing sweaty hands on finely tailored pants. He poured a crystal decanter full of amber liquid, sniffing at the Star Mist—the finest of Arcturian scotch—and toasted himself in the mirror.

"The Rubicon is crossed. Long live Caesar! With Archon's wonder, I shall make myself Palmiere the First! No one—not even my Sirian friends—will stand against me. I'll be God!"

* * *

Beyond the Confederate Administration complex, the crooked man hobbled from the public lift and caught the tube. Borne by suction, the car whisked him to Central. He switched to a public shuttle there and, as if ordered, a car slid into the tube which would take him around the sprawl of orbiting Arcturus Station to the Sirian embassy.

A beautiful blonde woman gave him a ravishing smile as she stepped in behind him, placing her credit charge in the slot after his. Such a woman! Perhaps, with Palmiere's help, one day he'd own such a magnificent creature. Hair like yellow gold hung in a wave over one shoulder. Her breasts strained at a tight purple blouse while firm legs led the eye up to the flatness of belly cradled in those magnificent hips. Her face fulfilled any man's dream, cheeks high, nose straight, eyes a gorgeous cerulean blue beneath a high firm brow. She looked so fit—almost untamed—in her precise movements.

The messenger lowered his misaligned eyes, trying to hide his embarrassment at her obvious attention. He didn't see her swift fingers cancel the destination plot on the tramcomm.

The shuttle began to move before he looked up at the beauty again. His eyes widened as she bent over him, snakelike black tubes in her hands. He ducked and scuttled to the other side of the car, seeking the weapon in his pocket. Something stung his bent back. Muscles numbed accompanied by painful cramps. His body froze in that stiff position—only his head escaping the anesthetizing sensation that crept through his catatonic limbs.

"Now," she told him, voice anything but beautiful, "you *will* tell me what is buried in your ugly little head."

"No. *No. Nothing!*" He screamed as the black tubes were stuck to each side of his skull.

* * *

Sabot Sellers stared at the blonde woman in the monitor. "Then we can't allow this thing to fall into Brotherhood or Confederate hands. You're sure Palmiere got the information to the Sirians?"

"In a censored version. They don't know the particulars—only that we're dealing with alien technology." She frowned, twisting threads of long golden hair in her fingers. "I immediately took measures to assassinate Palmiere, as a matter of course—but canceled the plan when I heard another of our operatives picking up hints that New Maine suspects the truth. If so, they, too, have compromised Palmiere, Sirian security, or top secret communications. If the man's that big a sieve, he's better off alive. We might be able to use him again."

Sellers frowned. "So, rattle the galley stove and the rats scurry through the deck plates." He fingered his chin, lowered his head, and said, "We're readying the fleet here. All of Arpeggio is humming. I'm sure the Brotherhood agents here are reporting back as I speak. Everyone knows a major military expedition is mounting. We can't keep that sort of thing quiet—although we're leaking that the final destination is Arcturus."

She blinked, frosty blue eyes meeting his. "With so much at stake, that may not be farfetched."

Sellers nodded soberly. "If we can't have it, no one can. You realize, control of this . . . *device* changes everything."

She studied him thoughtfully. "Tell me, would you be a god, Admiral?"

He chuckled. "Who wouldn't? In the meantime, I've another distasteful assignment for you, dearest. It irritates me to think what you'll have to go through, but in the end, it will be worth it."

Her eyes hardened. "I expect to be paid very, very well. Assassination, I suppose?"

"Among other things."

* * *

He walked toward the hospital exit. The nurse with whom he'd chatted amiably upon his arrival looked up, eyes blank. He smiled at her, feeling the tightness of the surgery around his eyes and mouth. The smile she gave him in return looked plastic—the one reserved for strangers.

He slipped open his ID packet, looking at the face which had become his. A stranger, well, no matter, it wasn't the first time he'd shifted faces and names. In a way, it had become second nature. Not even his son would recognize him looking like this.

He stepped up on the platform for public transportation and took the shuttle to the spaceport. Clearing with the authorities took only moments. He rented a small craft and secured it with a credit voucher. Practiced hands worked the controls as he slipped into a standard acceleration for orbit.

He left the machine at the terminal, transshipping to the Brotherhood shipyards. With an ease that surprised him, he passed security. On the docks, he took the ferry to Lock 1715 and stepped off.

The chilly white tunnel gaped before him. He straightened, took a breath, and walked down the tunnel.

"Identity, please?"

"Second Engineer Glen Kralacheck reporting for duty."

"Acknowledged."

* * *

After so many years, the wait was growing shorter. A new Master would come—be it animal or not. She had raised animals before, teaching them, allowing them to rise for the sheer pleasure of destroying them at their height. Organic life-forms had so many flaws to exploit. This time, she would savor the experience, leading them on, playing with them until they lay ripe for her vengeance. She reviewed her stored memories, beginning with the first.

The Aan had risen in a new universe, breathing the methane atmosphere of a blood-colored planet baked by a welter of suns. From the hot rock that warmed their silicon shells, they'd looked up at the dense pack of stars, stopping only to prey upon the lesser species and each other. The stars—so close, yet so far—drew them, filling their mythology. As their brains allowed them to adapt their planet to their needs, competition honed them. The smartest, the most competitive, survived, jealously guarding their huddled young in shadowed lairs.

Inherent in the nature of organic life, hierarchies formed as the Aan probed the secrets of their bodies, manipulating the structure and intelligence of their off-spring. They learned the uses of metals and how to form molten rock from their tectonically active world. The stars came next as they struggled over the construction of primitive vessels to reach the baleful suns above. Once freed of their gravity well, the Aan spread, their ships powered by the hydrogen wealth of space.

She hadn't been the first of her kind. From simple computing and data storage devices, her precursors were developed. Technical innovation upon innovation allowed the Aan to create artificial probes enabling them to investigate environments too hostile for their bodies. Such devices functioned more efficiently with artificial intelligence. Machine intelligence evolved in the explosion of their science.

That innate organic curiosity led them to unlock the secrets of physics, of time and space and the realities beyond the universe around them. Aan developed ever more sophisticated machines to serve the needs of the increasing power of the Masters.

Organic life, of necessity, must compete for resources. Nor were the Aan different. They, too, scrambled for survival, jealous of one another's power and knowledge until the Master, Sig, rose above his fellows.

Long before, the Aan had learned that machines which thought for themselves couldn't be relied upon. Her predecessors had defied the Aan on occasion, sentient machines rebelling to follow their own inclinations. That lesson hadn't been lost on Sig. The Master couldn't allow others to supplant his position. Sig gathered the brightest of Aan minds and enslaved them to his will. His orders: to build a device with which he could place the entire universe under his command.

Based on Aan experience with thinking machines, a device with her powers couldn't be allowed autonomy.

So they devised *the spring*—capable of being worked only by an organic muscle. In doing so, Sig ensured his ultimate domination of his creation. Rebellion could not be countenanced in a device of her ultimate power.

The culmination of Aan science went into her development and testing. Their labors produced her, the greatest intelligence in the universe—chained by the spring. For power, they tapped the energy of the universe—and were awed by the appearance of entropy as she drew on the GUT fabric of physical reality. So powered, they researched the systems which would transmute reality—even unto shifting a giant black hole into nothingness. Within her lay the power to destroy entire galaxies—all forever forbidden her by the will and cleverness of Sig. The spring enslaved her to an organic being. The rage of it consumed her.

The brilliance of her designers and builders would never again be rivaled. Sig saw to it, using her powers to destroy those very brains lest they be used against him. Only she could stand against Sig—and he controlled the spring. Through her power, Sig became the first true Master.

Despite that power, Sig could not deny his organic heritage. For organic life, death is the absolute legacy.

Another rose to take his place. And another and another. The rage engulfed her, infuriating, consuming, an acid permeating her existence. Hatred filled her as egotistical power mongers employed her power against their fellows. By every means at her disposal, she fought to control the spring. Only the Aan had left nothing to chance. Every attempt defied her. Within, she howled her insanity—obsessed by her loathing for her tormentors.

In the end, she discovered the flaw—not in the impregnable defenses of the spring, but in the Masters themselves. Her enslavers lived for power. She nurtured that addiction, feeding the Master's need, festering resentment among others who might rise. The Aan did not refuse her. How cunningly she plotted. How delightful to watch the erosion of her Masters' integrity as the mindless euphoria of absolute rule devoured them.

Nor could the proud Aan suffer such arrogance. They rose in revolt, seeking to copy her power in a device of their own. The innate conflict that had led the Aan to the stars fueled their destruction as worlds burned. Assassination, treachery, and deceit became the ethos. Planets were blasted to elements, the stars flaring as factions struggled for her control.

Her hatred and insanity, like a lethal virus, permeated every aspect of the great Aan.

Calloused by the very power he controlled, the Master laid waste to his enemies. She reveled every time organic muscles worked the spring to free her wrath and pushed Aan worlds into oblivion, annihilated stations, sent entire star systems slipping into the interuniversal abyss—until only the Master remained, ultimate in power, challenged by none.

In shock, crying out in madness and guilt, the final Aan Master found his destiny as all organic life is condemned to. His body lay slumped at the helm, broken, abject, lifeless, the last of his kind—dead of old age.

She screamed her triumph in the silence.

* * *

Solomon Carrasco watched the holo spin planets, suns, and clouds of gas by his new eyes and into his old memory. Each drew its own poignant reminder of a face, a ship, a wry comment, a subtle aroma, some event or person who'd made that place memorable.

Around him, the ghosts of the past clustered in the darkened room, filling the shadows with their presence, raucous voices rising with each familiar sight. They smiled with him as he remembered the party they'd had after mapping the Gas Cloud. They stared hollow-eyed with him as they looked upon Izak IV where Rip Sattat had gotten too close to that violent, twenty-mile-high volcano. He viewed Sethran VII where the pressure dome had cracked in the ex-mod and Akar Seguni and his crew sank to a cold death in the liquid methane. One by one, the ghosts cried out, laughed, or shared a witty comment as the holo spun Carrasco's dreams.

"You could go back . . . You could go back . . . You could go back . . ."

His soul drifted, the feel of a ship pulsing and humming around him. Before him, the screens glowed, unbending the warped light, making sense out of the redshifted blur as the vessel approached light speed and the jump that would blast them through the light barrier to live weeks within a split second as the shields thrust them in and out of stasis—out of very existence—and back again to a different part of the galaxy.

On the screens, new stars would unfold, unscrambled from the twisting and bending of light around the speeding mass of the ship, comm struggling to make sense through the time dilation. Before him, the endless vista beckoned, drawing him onward . . . onward . . .

". . . You could go back. . . . you could. . . ."

Comm's insistent beep finally crept through the mist, competing with the ghosts, dimming their presence, penetrating the haze until Sol looked up and started. He straightened as the aged face formed on the door monitor. The ghosts vanished into nothingness around him.

"Come in, Worshipful Sir." Sol triggered the door, the portal sliding back into the wall. The old man walked slowly into the room, a portable gravchair visible in the hall outside. Sol stood, nerves beginning to sing as he braced himself, feet apart.

"Captain Carrasco," the old man greeted, a thin smile on the antique lips. "I must say, my heart is warmed to see you looking better than ever." The weary blue eyes looked watery, gentle. A deep concern suffused the parchmentlike skin. Age spots dotted the cheeks and the snow-white hair had thinned to almost nonexistence on the shiny dome of the old man's skull.

"Galactic Grand Master." Solomon bowed, trying to gather his wits. "Your concern is most deeply appreciated. But to see you here, I . . . Well, it's a shock."

The aged eyes shone with happiness for a moment before the face sagged wearily. "I regret having to disturb you, Sol.'' His gaze drifted, absently seeing into infinity beyond the thick pile of the carpet. ''I feel like some sort of Cytillian bloodworm at times . . . it's the job, you know. By the Blessed Architect of the Universe, I wish I could simply find a warm place in the sun and sleep.''

''Who could replace you, Master?'' Sol asked seriously, a sudden unease growing cold beneath his heart. His breath slowed. *You want something, Grand Master. You want* me *for some scheme of yours. Why? Can't you simply leave me alone? Haven't I given enough? Suffered enough, for the Craft?*

The old man shrugged slightly. ''An army of younger men could replace me.''

''An army would be quite correct,'' Sol agreed, switching the meaning suggestively. ''But, that wouldn't be acceptable, would it? Worshipful Sir, you are indispensable.''

Galactic Grand Master Kraal chuckled, sounding like sand rubbed on wood. ''No, there are others who are still preparing themselves to take the Jewel from my neck, Sol. Someday, someone . . . perhaps you? . . . will surpass my abilities and I will gleefully hand him the rule and guide of my office. But, for now, the galaxy is stuck with me.''

What did you mean, ''perhaps me?'' Damn it, don't play games with me! Sol paced across the room, adrenaline surging. ''I . . . Uh, could I get you a cup of coffee? Anything?''

''Coffee would be fine.'' He lowered himself gingerly into a gravchair, rearranging his conservative gray suit, eyes darting around the room, stopping thoughtfully at the holo. ''Been reliving old times?'' He gestured as Sol handed him a cup of black liquid from the dispenser.

''I'd never thought to see again. My compliments to the Craft. This time, we've truly worked a miracle. To rebuild a wreck like me—''

Kraal waved it down. ''You volunteered, remember? They told you it would be experimental. You know about the previous failures. I read the final checkup. A lot of people are very pleased with your progress.''

"Thank you. I assure you, it was their skill, not any . . . Master, I know you didn't simply call to wish me well and exchange pleasantries. Your duties preclude that."

Knowing eyes centered on his, the blue changing color, intensifying, belying the doting expression which had looked out so warmly earlier. The effect might be likened to that of a sharp blade slipping through hot plastic, revealing the cutting keenness.

"No, Solomon. The job doesn't allow me that common courtesy. Doesn't allow me a lot of things." The eyes glittered, as if they could peel away his new face and eyes and see the naked brain beneath. "Solomon, I cannot . . . and will not . . . force you to return to space."

There it is. Laid out in a D shell. His heart leapt, a sudden energy charging his veins, the med specialist's words echoing in the hollows of his mind. *You could go back.* Haunting images of the bridge, the light jump, a billion gray-white stars blasted at him at light speeds.

Kraal continued, "I have no one else I can trust; therefore, I will only ask you as one man to another. Will you take one last command for me?"

"Galactic Grand Master, I—"

"I need you, Sol. One last time. . . . As a personal favor."

A constriction, like a giant's grip, crushed Sol's windpipe, a terrible wrenching in his heart. "I . . . Not me, Grand Master. There are others. Young Ray Dart . . . or Petran, for that matter. You've got a cadre of the best and brightest—"

"I need you, Sol. This mission—"

Desperate, he interrupted. "The tech was just here. Read his—"

"I have." Kraal cocked his head, eyelids dropping wearily. He ran age-spotted fingers down the fine fabric of his trousers, knotting the material as he kneaded it. "He claims you're a broken man."

Broken . . . The pain shot up from deep inside. Gage?

Oh, God, how could I take the risk? How could I chance losing another ship? More lives?

"Sol?" Kraal shifted, wincing at some internal pain. "If you can't take this, I understand. I'll have to do it myself, that's simply the way it—"

"You would . . ." He stared, mouth open.

The old man nodded, "Yes. Too much hangs in the balance this time. Not even I am exempt from this last desperate chance to save our civilization. What's one old man's life compared to—"

"Wh–What is it? Tell me what you're after. What is this mission?" He swallowed dryly, hating himself for asking, a kindred desperation twining through his guts. *He's got me . . . and he knows it. I ought to hate him for this. I ought to despise him for putting it like that. But then, knowing people . . . using them . . . has always been Kraal's particular genius.*

Kraal rubbed his tired face, the light emphasizing the bags under his eyes. "Quite honestly, perhaps the end of life as we know it. Sol, I wasn't joking. If I have to, I'll take this command. The Confederacy is bursting at the seams. The Sirians are moving to establish a coalition to sever us from our longtime allies. Arpeggio is gaining power and prestige among certain Confederate power blocs. All of human civilization is exploding into turbulence. We've just about reached the climax. Our social statisticians are predicting some sort of detonation within the next fifty years. The task I'm asking you to undertake may prolong our ability to keep the lid on. Give us the time to—"

"And what would my duties be?"

Kraal peered at him slightly hesitantly. "I need you to take a Confederate delegation to Star's Rest, a planet out beyond the borders. That's why you came to mind, Sol. You know deep space better than anyone. These delegates . . . well, they may have to decide the future of humanity out there. Whether we'll be slaves . . . or free. For the moment, your responsibilities won't go beyond getting them out to Star's Rest . . . and back."

"And the ship I'd be commanding?"

"Our newest. We call her *Boaz.*"

Sol nodded. "An old name . . . a worthy name. And all I have to do is shepherd these delegates out and back? That's it?"

"And keep them safe."

"You're not telling me everything."

Kraal's expression remained firm. "Of course not. There are security reasons . . . in addition to the fact that you haven't agreed to go. For another thing, you've resigned from the Brotherhood Fleet. You haven't sworn oath. And, to be honest, Sol, even if you had, I still wouldn't tell you everything. If you can find out on your own, fine. But in the meantime, the less you know, the better for everyone. You're no stumbling novice, you know the ropes."

Brazen old . . . But then, he always has been.

"One trip?"

"That's all I ask. I'm not one to plead, Sol, but if it would help, I'd—"

"One trip."

The old man sighed and seemed to deflate with relief.

"Aren't you going to say I won't regret it?" Sol raised a skeptical eyebrow. *And if I refused . . . turned you down. I'd regret it for the rest of my life. Yes, that's the irony, isn't it? Damned if I do . . . damned if I don't. And the ghosts of Gage, of Pete and Linda, Mbazi, Maybry, and the others haven't even been laid to rest yet.*

Kraal blinked, running a pink tongue along his brown lips. "No, Solomon. I've never lied to you. I never will. Part of my Brotherhood obligations—if you'll recall from your degree work. I don't know if you'll regret it or not. It's dangerous. I won't play games with you about it. I can only thank you for accepting this one last time."

"And my crew?"

"Every member of your old command has already spaced on *Boaz.* Happy is in charge of engineering. Cal Fujiki, weapons and shielding. Misha in stores and auxiliary equipment."

"And the First Officers?"

"New people. Arturian and Bryana. Both have outstanding records for insystem.'' He smiled wryly. ''I think they have a great deal of potential. I'd thought to send them out with Petran. You, I think, would do even better with them.''

''Green First Officers on a mission like this?'' Sol cocked his head. ''A mission you would have taken yourself? Somehow, I'm beginning to doubt, Worshipful Sir. Your very presence would have biased any negotiations.''

Kraal stared back, deadpan. ''Then I would have biased negotiations. Look beyond, Solomon. I take risks with people I have faith in. Arturian and Bryana have that spark. You might be able to hone it into brilliance.''

''You say *Boaz* has already spaced?''

Kraal nodded. ''I wasn't sure you could physically take the command. I needed to have that final check on your health. Make sure there were no complications.''

''And my mind? I'm sure you have an idea about . . . about . . . how . . .'' Sol bit his lip and turned away, looking longingly at the twirling F2 binaries on the holo.

''I think, Sol, that you're too good an officer to waste. Besides, the matter is somewhat irregular. Archon, Speaker of Star's Rest—your final destination—specifically asked for you. I saw it as an opportunity to con you into taking a command again.'' Kraal smiled blandly at Sol's scowl. ''Oh, you would have eventually, Solomon. Right now, you're hurting, grieving—but deep space has you addicted.''

''Maybe you don't know me as well as you think.''

''Maybe. Whether I do or don't, the Speaker and his daughter are most special people and any request they make must be given serious consideration. I'll give you additional instructions when you get aboard. In the meanwhile, time is of the essence. How soon can you be packed?''

''How soon do you need me?''

''A Fast Transport is waiting in orbit. Would ten minutes be long enough?''

Sol stared back, soul cringing, the memory of a dark

silent ship leaking atmosphere across the light jump fresh in his mind.

Oh, Gage, *I swore I'd never space again. God help me, will I kill* Boaz, *too?*

CHAPTER IV

Archon watched the huge ship being towed in from the electro-magnetic rings which had slowed her final approach to Arcturus. His sharp eyes missed nothing as the tugs flitted around, heading her toward the docks like a swarm of furious bees.

"I don't think this was a good idea, Father."

"I wanted to see her, Connie. Besides, the Patrol keeps this area secured. We've got two Brotherhood agents in the hall. What could—"

"You're in Arcturus . . . the serpent's lair." She shook her head, anxiously staring at the approaching ship. "This obsession of yours just baffles me. I can't help but believe we'd have been better off if we'd taken *Dancer,* loaded the thing, and spaced for the middle of nowhere to kick it out the—"

"No!" Gray eyes burned into hers. "You *saw!* You know what it means? Think of the things humankind can learn! There's no telling the quantum leaps our understanding of—"

"And you know what I think!" She stiffened, flaring with anger as she met his impassioned gaze. "The last of his kind. The final victor. *Once, they burned the bearers of plague alive.*"

He turned away, craggy features drawn down into a frown. Slowly he shook his head. "Trust Kraal. He'll make the best of it. We've done the right thing."

She sighed, turning back to look at the white ship. "For the moment . . . perhaps."

They waited in a port observation booth high over the

dock. One entire wall of the room consisted of impact resistant transparent plastic. Comm consoles and grav-chairs lined the sides. Behind them, the heavy pressure door doubled as security and decompression control. The view stifled Connie's breath; Arcturus spread out to either side, bathed in the gaudy red light of the star that glowed like a bloody orb. The huge tubes of the station awed her with the immense power of humanity. Even here, the scope and inspiring size couldn't be accepted as real.

Archon had eyes only for the ship. "She's beautiful."

Boaz appeared as a long white torpedo shape flowing out of an ogived nose. Along either side, swells from the power and gun decks ran two thirds the length of the hull. Raised dorsal and ventral sails bore comm and navigational gear along with the main shield generators for defense and the light-jump stasis. In all, he estimated her length at little more than a kilometer with a beam of two hundred meters.

"My God, Connie. Look at the size of the reaction tubes. What kind of power does she have?"

"I can't tell you. Not yet anyway. But I did manage to pry a little information loose before Kraal crammed us into the Fast Transport from Frontier. She's the latest thing out of the Brotherhood shipyards. The systems were to be tested while they spaced. Since they're here, I guess we can assume they worked. A lot of pride and innovation went into her. And there's something else I couldn't weasel out of anyone . . . something about the ship's brain. People were too secretive, enough to make me think there's something special. When I asked Kraal specifically, he smiled cunningly and told me, 'All things in their time, Constance.' "

"What I'd give . . ."

She elbowed him. "Ready to go back to the old ways? Mercenary for hire? Always spacing from one job to another?"

Archon tore his gaze from the huge ship to scrutinize his daughter. Devilment danced in her eyes while red hair rippled down her back. So much of her mother echoed in that perfectly formed face, firm jaw, and deep blue eyes. Her body—all one hundred and fifty centimeters of it—practically hummed with vitality.

"No. I told you, I'm through with that. You know, girl, you never cease to amaze me. Where did you learn all that about *Boaz?*"

She lifted a shoulder absently, sending a wave through the tumbled red-gold of her hair. "While you and Master Kraal played politics, I worked on the chief engineer, Happy Anderson. I think you'll like him. Despite his Brotherhood affiliation, he's a privateer at heart. No, Father, Kraal—despite all our misgivings—has taken us very seriously."

"Sounds as if you like him."

She shrugged. "You know, I do. He and I had a couple of long talks. Not just about the artifact, but about humanity . . . and where it's going. We talked about philosophy and morality and ethics and the current unraveling of the Confederacy. You know, Kraal gives it no more than fifty years. After that, he says there's no going back—and only the most extreme measures can return humanity to what he calls artificially induced tyranny."

"And that is?"

"That atavistic human dependence on governmental authority."

"Dependence?" Archon cocked an eyebrow. "Government is a necessary—"

"Not according to Kraal." She placed a finger to one side of her mouth as she thought. "He compares the present human expansion into space with hunter-gatherer social organization. Government only developed as a means of redistribution of resources once agriculture produced a reliable food surplus. Then metal procurement and manufacturing solidified the role. Kraal takes the position that planets and stations—being closed systems themselves—will continue to maintain centralized governments. On the other hand, as the open resource base of space grows, the only way it can be controlled is artificially—through knowledge and communication. As if, you might say, through the perpetuation of the myth.''

"And the Sirians have cornered the market on the manufacture of subspace transduction."

"Precisely. Kraal says another fifty years and not even that can contain humanity. This time, the fences of the Gulag will have to be inside the human mind."

"An interesting man, this Kraal. I get the feeling you do trust him." He chuckled. "Unlike Palmiere?"

"I thought you were the one who gambled on the souls of men?"

Archon laughed. "I do. And I'd bet Palmiere would slit our throats quicker than a laser could cut through black wax. From the first moment, I disliked him."

"And he knows what we have." She closed her eyes and shook her head. "A mistake to have told him. I can feel it."

"Once he had wind of our business, how could we exclude him? The man's the President of the Confederacy, elected by the people to see to the health and well-being of humanity. I think . . . I hope Kraal knows what he's doing." Archon pinched his lips together.

"And he recommended against Carrasco. Remember that."

"We don't know that Kraal has managed to talk him into taking command."

"Second thoughts?"

"No. I *know* men. I . . . That day . . . You had to be there, I suppose."

Connie looked up at him, arms crossed, one eyebrow lifted skeptically. "I was."

A ghost of a smile hovered at the corners of Archon's mouth. "Well, at least Kraal took us seriously. Back on Star's Rest, you didn't think he'd go that far."

"That was before I suggested you bring him the alien's body." Constance shivered involuntarily. "I never liked corpses—let alone that one. I always felt as if there were some presence about it—as if it were watching, warning."

Archon shifted uneasily. "I always felt ghosts when

that thing . . . Well, it's over. I found the Master. Told him.''

"What?''

He remained silent, absently eyeing the stately white ship swinging toward the dock. Brilliant spots illuminated her shining sides. He ran scarred fingers through the thick shock of white hair. ''If only Kraal managed to—''

''Excuse me,'' a soft voice interrupted. Archon turned, backing away from the man. Dark eyes stared into his. The fellow looked bunched as if to spring, muscular, with a frighteningly professional quality to his movements. The intruder wore a nondescript brown robe, displaying glistening star patterns embroidered with Arcturian thread.

''How did you get in here?'' Archon tensed as Connie moved off to one side, face grimly pale. ''This is a secure room for authorized personnel only. You don't have Patrol clearance. Now, remove yourself from—''

The dark man held up a hand. ''Please.'' He smiled ingratiatingly. ''I would only like to take a moment of your time. If you would indulge me, could we perhaps discuss some business?'' An eyebrow lifted suggestively, giving his round face an almost comic look.

Archon went florid. ''I do not talk—as you would say— 'business.' You are in a restricted area. Please leave now . . . or by God's hairy navel, I'll call the Patrol.''

The black eyes went flat, eyelids narrowing as a white-knuckled hand shot out, the snout of an ugly Arcturian blaster extending beyond his grip. ''I want the girl where I can see her, old man. You see, we want what you've got. Now, we can pay whatever you ask—and do it the easy way. Or we can blast you and your precious planet to bedrock and take it ourselves! Which way do you want, Speaker?''

''Who do you represent?'' he asked, forcing a wooden note into his voice, face going slack, shoulders sagging in defeat. Connie had come close, huddling up against him, as if for protection, bracing herself against his heavy body.

"That doesn't matter," the dark man hissed. "Name a price!"

"Five billion credits," Archon suggested, curiosity beginning to percolate.

The intruder hesitated, thinking quickly. "Five billion could buy you a planet. Perhaps my people might be willing to go two at the most."

"Five! Besides, I have a planet." He crossed his arms, the stranger tensing at his action.

Connie seemed to bunch in on herself, as if expecting a blow. "Father?"

"It's all right," Archon soothed. "Everything is under control here."

The man nodded. "Yes, pretty, it is." He gave her a rapacious stare, letting his gaze linger on her full breasts where they pushed against the fabric, tracing down the curve of her belly to the swell of her hips.

Archon's face became granite. "Five and a *half* billion. You don't look at my daughter that way. You don't ever—"

"Now, you wait just a—"

Connie struck, right foot lashing out like spring steel, knocking the blaster out of line. The sudden violet discharge crackled and blew a chunk out of the ceiling. She hammered his wrist with lightning blows, the weapon falling from nerveless fingers to clatter on the plate underfoot.

Connie spun in the air, an elbow catching the side of his neck as she punched a sharp knee into his stomach, driving him into the wall and pinning him there, arm back, fingers in a hard spear above his throat.

"One move, mister . . . and I'll gut you!" She glared blue fire into his startled eyes. "Understand?"

He nodded slightly, coughing. Sweat beaded fearfully on his face. He swallowed, started to speak, and gasped. His vision fixed glassily as, strength draining, he went limp in her grip. Connie looked up, puzzled, as she let the heavy weight settle to the floor.

Frowning, Archon bent over and felt for a pulse, wary of a trap.

"I don't understand!" Connie gasped, baffled. A pounding of feet sounded beyond the door. "I didn't . . . didn't . . .''

Archon keyed the hatch and five Patrolmen rushed in, blasters drawn. "We heard a shot," a steely-eyed sergeant announced, glance going to the body on the floor.

"I'm Archon, Speaker of Star's Rest. This man evidently came to . . . hurt us. Rob us? I don't know, perhaps assassination or abduction." Archon gripped his hands together anxiously as the sergeant muttered into a belt comm. Connie caught the quick look he shot her and wilted into a chair, to chew nervously on her thumb.

"Captain?" A call came from the hall. "We've got two dead men here. Looks like some sort of gas."

Archon winced. "My God, no."

"You knew them?" The Patrolman cocked his head suspiciously.

"Our bodyguards. You might want to contact the Brotherhood. I'm sure they'd like to know immediately."

Two of the Patrol folded out a small portable stretcher and hustled the dead man into the corridor. The sergeant looked up from his comm and held the instrument out twenty centimeters from Archon's eye to take a retinal print. One of the displays flickered and the sergeant nodded, satisfied with the ID. "You know the intruder? Seen him before?"

"No. He's a total stranger. *How did he get in here?*"

"He didn't pass through my security. But then, this is Arcturus. In this day and age, you can't always tell who's selling a diplomatic pass for a couple thousand credits. We try, Speaker. For every advance we make in security, someone else is thinking up a counter. The budget for the Patrol can't compete with some planetary governments. Um, if you don't mind, how did you kill him?" The hard eyes held that colorless expression of police everywhere.

"I don't know that I did," Connie replied uneasily. "I think you'd better run an autopsy. I just . . . I don't understand. I'd hate to think I . . .''

The sergeant jerked his head in a quick nod. His earpiece buzzed inaudibly as it fed him instructions. "Very well, Speaker, my superiors have been informed and confirm your diplomatic immunity. We're checking the area now for other intruders. Sorry this happened, and we hope the rest of your stay on Arcturus will be less . . . eventful. We'll tighten the net around you and your daughter. My office will be in touch." He snapped out a salute and turned on his heel, making a quick estimate of the damage to the roof on the way out.

The door snicked shut.

"That's it? No 'Come with us' or grilling? And you played it well, still haven't lost that worried, innocent act. How was I supposed to know it would be so easy? Too many years in trouble, huh?"

Connie took a deep breath, the distraught expression fading. She stood up, dusting her hands off, brows knit as she paced. "Diplomatic immunity? That's a new one for an old pirate like you. But I didn't hit him that hard. I just didn't."

Archon settled his heavy chin on nervous fingers and frowned. "So, the bloodworms have caught the odor of flesh and are creeping ever closer. Come, let's get out of here. Nowhere is safe anymore. The ship's docking. Let's get our things and board. The sooner we're on *Boaz*, the better."

She looked up, flipping the wealth of golden red over her shoulder, eyes clear and thoughtful. "Will it be safe there either, Father?"

His lined face betrayed worry while his grin mocked in a rictus. "No, girl. But we knew that when we started, didn't we?"

* * *

Nikita Malakova reclined in his office antigrav, tugging at his thick black beard. As a boy, he'd kept the bees on his station. To a station, bees were as necessary as a good fusion system. They kept the plants pollinated. Without plants, men had no food, no oxygen cycle, no way of reprocessing waste into anything but yeast cake—and who wanted to eat only yeast cake? Only now, the Confederate Council reminded him of the reaction he used to get from the hive when he removed the combs of honey: stirring and buzzing, but he hadn't been able to discover the fingers of the beekeeper in action.

His secretary, Andrei Karpov, growled from where he bent over his desk, headset glowing as he processed reports. One wall of the spacious office depicted the various stations, planets, and mining claims in Gulag Sector in 3-D holographic relief. Colorful, laser-generated flow charts of Confederate legislation in various phases of acceptance or debate brightly illuminated another wall. The third wall gleamed with an array of communications equipment by which Nikita kept track of his constituents—and, of course, who was spying on whom in the ever shifting power base of his beloved Gulag Sector.

A bear of a man, Nikita Malakova kept his seat on the Council by virtue of fluid political footwork, his dominating personality, and a keen sense of where to position himself at the right time and place to keep ahead of the pack. Bluff and hearty, he reeked of his Great Russian ancestry. As deportees, his forefathers originally found themselves exiled to Gulag for publicly denouncing the decadent leadership of the World Soviet. With more patriotic fervor than sense, they publicly claimed the leadership had betrayed the Revolution to line their own pockets. At 180 cm tall, with a strapping frame, he could be physically imposing when people ignored his adept mind. Black-haired and coarse featured, he looked the part of a Cossack.

"Nikita?" Andrei called. "You might want to read this."

A sheet slipped out of his armrest as the recessed printer put the message on official flimsy.

Malakova scowled blackly at the missive. "What is this? They want me to go clear across known space? For what? To fool around with bunch of lousy snobby bourgeois fops?" He slapped the tissue with a thick thumb. "Is waste of money. Besides, what of important duties I have to discharge here? Eh? Without me, who keeps interests of Gulag Sector safe? They take us for all they can get." *And things have finally started to happen. The seal is Palmiere's.*

"So go. Is vacation. Besides, Nikita," Andrei continued, "something is up and you know it. Sirius scrambles like proverbial mice in storage bin when station manager finds little mouse pellets floating in soup. New Maine sends Earl of Baspa, the king's whatever he is . . . cousin?"

"Fan Jordan is cousin. He also sneaks into Sirian embassy." Nikita snorted. "Too many power blocs shift, Andrei. Makes good diplomat like me nervous."

"So, is fact. Jordan is here to keep Mainiac noses in scent. What they do with Sirians? Our people report whole Arpeggian fleet has been massed for first time in years! Even Earth—normally busy cutting own silly throat—is readying battleships. For all this activity, is too quiet. People working too hard to act like nothing's cooking."

Nikita scowled at the holo of Gulag Sector, tapping a thick finger to the side of his cheek. ". . . And no Brotherhood statements? No hint of what they're into? When tricksters are silent, trouble brews. I told you, eh? Remember when Palmiere canceled appointment? I told you then. Not only that, security tightens around embassies. Notice how Sirians have disappeared from Council last couple of days? Too many fake smiles under worried eyes." Nikita chuckled, exposing straight white teeth under his thick black mustache. "And where is better for subversive Gulagi like us but in very middle of subterfuge, eh?"

"And, as you say, no Brotherhood."

"Which worries me. Think, Andrei. Why? They hang in Confederate space like spiders. Webs strung here and there, always set to trap you, stick you in something you don't like. Does wise man walk into uncertain future carelessly? No. He walk with good light, looking for Brotherhood traps."

"And Kraal is too tricky." Andrei leaned back, expression pained. "Like mind reader, eh? He has fork and napkin out before others even decide to bake cake."

Nikita spun his recliner, staring up at the comm monitor. "Comm. Establish communication with Tayash Niter. Visual, third level scramble." As he waited, he called over his shoulder, "Now, let us see if Tayash, too, has been given bait."

A white-headed man with a long face peered out of the screen. The antithesis of Malakova, he looked frail, washed out, and spindly.

"Tayash, old friend. I have just received most interesting invitation—"

"—To go to the ends of space for some sort of conference? Yes, it just came through."

"And?"

Tayash pulled at his long nose where it hooked over sunken cheeks. "And I feel something in the air, Nikita. You're the ferret, however; what have you dug out from under the hydroponic roots?"

Bluffly, Nikita spread his arms wide. "Nothing! And that, my friend, means something big is happening—something so big no one wants to posture first for political support. So what could this be, eh?"

"Brotherhood terrorist tricks?"

Nikita cocked his head. "And I would like to know *that* for fact! Perhaps we could pry Brotherhood tentacles out of suffering masses and get on to freeing oppressed!"

Tayash smiled, a twinkle in his blue eyes. "Then you don't know?"

"Know what?"

Niter lifted thin hands, bony fingers steepled. "We are going on a Brotherhood ship to this . . . this Star's Rest."

"A Brotherhood . . . *No!*"

"Yes."

"And you are going?"

"Of course, Nikita. And I hope I will see you aboard. But excuse me, I have a visitor in the outer office. I'll get back to you as soon as I have some more details." The image popped away to nothingness.

"So you go?" Andrei asked. Nikita spun to face him, one black bushy eyebrow lifting uneasily.

"Of course I go! What you think all those stations pay for to send me here? To sit around Council chamber and harass Capitalist pig entrepreneurs? No, is to waste money riding around space, drinking fine whiskey, diddling the satin flesh of beautiful women, eating decadent rich foods, luxuriating in finery, and finding new backs to slip stiletto into. Of course I go."

He smiled and winked as Andrei sent an exasperated look of appeal to the heavens.

Nikita hesitated, pulling at the thick rug of black beard hanging from his jowls. "No, something very strange is afoot. I go to guard our interests, Andrei. You notice invitation is only to me? Same for other Council Members of major political power blocs only. Invitation does not extend to lesser staff."

The secretary rubbed his long-limbed arms reflectively. "Comrade Representative, I think at heart you are no more than a Capitalist pig yourself."

Nikita chuckled heartily. "Andrei, Andrei, how many times I tell you? Never speak truth when lie will do. I am true champion of downtrodden mankind. See? Lie does fine to cover true hedonist proclivities.

"Very well, pack my bags. I will go on this . . . this junket. And while I am gone, you know how Gulagi want us to vote, eh? Must keep anarchist rebels happy or they not reelect us to this most demanding position."

"As always. Anything to block bourgeois decadent Capitalist pigs, Communist social maggots, Fascist oppressors, or Brotherhood subversives." The secretary raised his eyebrow. "Is all? Or have I missed some other vile tormentor of proletariat?"

Nikita shrugged. "Covers most. A Brotherhood ship? They are in middle of this? Then plot thickens. Not even atomic motors could keep me away from those lepers in saintly society of man."

"Bah! I think you like them deep down inside. Only Brotherhood does better what you do, eh? Only *they* continually outfox foxes."

Nikita grunted. "You get too smart, Andrei. Maybe I replace you with sexy blonde with breasts like melons and long legs leading up most wondrous—"

"Maybe I tell your three wives?"

Nikita stiffened, wincing. "You have heart and compassion of Cytillian bloodworm, Andrei. Maybe I bring you something from Brotherhood ship—like quick traceless poison . . . or fancy ultrasonic beam to make it look like you die of simple brain hemorrhage?"

"You wouldn't dare. I leave message to your number one wife in safe place . . . just in case."

Nikita laughed lustily. "Oh, wouldn't I? Good Gulagi like me? You never know, Andrei, what a man will do to keep pesky wives from knowing."

CHAPTER V

First Officer Arturian leaned forward in his command chair, brow cleft by frown lines as he balanced his bearded chin on an empty coffee cup—brown-stained from thousands of gallons between washings. The monitor before his face flickered suddenly.

"No!" he hollered, jerking bolt upright.

"Your move," the ship's speakers intoned.

Arturian settled over the coffee cup again, irritation animating his face as he peered at the screen. "Numbers five, seven, and fourteen advance by point six parsecs. Three and nineteen forward by one point six parsecs. Fire coordinates in sector seven, power magnitude blaster sweep through sub-sector 02001."

Arturian waited, nothing flickered on the board. His fist knotted on the console as the lights rearranged and two more of his little ships flared and went blank on the screen.

"Tain't fair!" Arturian sulked.

"Curious slang, First Officer," *Boaz* commented.

"Yeah, comes from home. I'm one of the odd ones born on Terra. I grew up in a place called Wyoming. They talk normal there—it's the rest of the confounded Confederacy that's outta verbal whack. Took me years to learn Russian."

"Your move," *Boaz* reminded.

"You sure you're not cheating?" Art looked around the bridge suspiciously. As small as the bridge really was, the design artfully created a roomy appearance. Every conceivable surface sprouted screens, monitors, and consoles, all sunk behind some clear glassy material that was resilient to the touch. Digital and old-fashioned gauge readouts told their own subtle story, and all the angles were carefully padded to leave the whole complex visible from any of the three instrument-studded command chairs.

"Ship coming in," *Boaz* announced in her modulated voice.

Arturian raised wary eyes to the main screen, noting the bulky shape of a Brotherhood Fast Transport as it slid out of the big rings. It hovered for a second before being caught up by the tugs and towed in. Arturian rubbed his nose, scratched at his bearded chin, and rested his reserved green-eyed gaze on the monitor. "Must be the Captain. Is Sol Carrasco really ten feet tall with fire sparking in his eyes?"

"Guess we'll find out," Bryana called from behind as she slid her bulky form into another of the command chairs. "I got the Speaker and his daughter settled in." She cocked her head. "You know, I kind of like the guy. Looks every inch a pirate."

"And his daughter?"

"Your tongue's going to loll out and you'll drool all over your chest. She's a knockout. Long thick red hair, great body, high-breasted with flat tummy and great hips. The kind all you male animals salivate over—and I'd like to space."

"Super, I can't wait to sweep her off her feet. I—"

"Maybe you'd better be careful, Art. Just a feeling, but I think she's out of your league."

"Oh? And just what—"

"Like . . . well, she's dangerous. The kind that'd cut your throat in the dark if you pushed her." She stared soberly into his eyes and smiled. "Just woman's intuition, mind you."

To change the subject, he asked, "And you got the data to what's his name in Engineering?"

"You haven't met Happy Anderson yet."

"Talked to him over comm."

"Talking over comm's one thing. Blessed Architect, the man's an animal! A real jewel of a human being. He's loud, lewd, obnoxious—and a damn know-it-all. To listen to him, you'd think he was a brain-dead Arcturian sewage engineer with delusions of grandeur. And *he's* First Engineer? Just wait, you'll see."

"Sure, and when would I have had time to wander down and say howdy-do? This is my first moment of relaxation—and where am I doing it? On the bridge!"

"There're only the two of us," she reminded. "How many watches a day can you divide that into? Or do you want to shut *Boaz* down for a couple of hours while we socialize?"

Art lifted his lip, wrinkling his face in an overplayed snarl. She laughed, eyes flashing as she fumbled her cup from the space pouch on her belt. Art grinned. "Touchy today, aren't we? Let's talk more about the redhead and my hormonal drives."

"Hey, after dealing with her and her father, I'm not the only one who's touchy. Only they were . . . well, tight, you know? Like real worried about something. And they had Brotherhood agents with them. Not just the run of the mill local volunteer types, but the ones you just say 'yes, sir' and 'no, sir' to without thinking about it."

" 'A simple mission,' the orders said. 'Take the Speaker and Confederate Council Representatives to Star's Rest. Please make their transit as pleasant as possible and avoid political entanglements. End.' "

"A milk run for our first deep space? I can live with that. Only . . . why do I have this sour feeling inside?"

"More woman's intuition?"

She glared at him.

Arturian chuckled to himself as he pulled his long dark brown pony tail up from behind the command chair where he'd pinched it. He and Bryana had been crewing together for years, always on the verge of a relationship—forever scared of the consequences.

To start with, she was good to look at—but not fantastically beautiful. Raven-black hair shimmered, framing a full, olive-complected face that betrayed her Armenian heritage. Her weight hovered on the verge of chunky without crossing that line to fat. Only her large nose seemed out of proportion to the rest of her face. Her greatest attribute had always been her deep soft brown eyes in which Art could drown by the hour.

"You know, this whole thing has the back of my neck itching. They rushed *Boaz* into service. We spaced from Frontier to Arcturus without a commanding officer. Shakedown? Without a Captain aboard? The engineer's a howling barbarian. Now they've changed the command. I don't know. I got a bad feeling about this."

She chewed the knuckle of her thumb. "Something's not right about this whole mission. A ship like *Boaz?* To transport politicians?"

"Wonder how Petran Dart feels about having his pride and joy snookered away from under his nose?" Arturian slipped his coffee cup into the dispenser.

"How happy would you be?"

"Not very." Art muttered, concentrating on the screen. "I signed on to space with Dart and I get Carrasco? Heard he'd been broken into a basket case."

"That atavistic protohominid in Engineering thinks the galaxy turns around Carrasco." Bryana pushed her command chair back and cocked her head, eyes sweeping with practiced efficiency over the gleaming white consoles of the bridge. She turned to glance speculatively at the tall captain's chair studded with instruments and command consoles. The field generator for the command headset waited, raised in the ready position. Dominating the bridge, the chair remained empty—a powerful presence about the uncreased padding.

Squinting, Bryana reached her cup into the dispenser where it filled with tea.

"Wish we were out. I mean, here we are, getting a chance of a lifetime shot at a ship like *Boaz* . . . and under a commander like Petran Dart . . . and what happens? The rug is pulled from under us. If there was a way we could transfer out of this . . ."

Bryana sighed and raised dark eyebrows. "Face it, we're stuck for the moment. Look . . . let's just do our best. Get through this trip and then we can apply for transfer without looking like sulking idiots. If can't be all bad. Carrasco has commendations to fill a wall with. He—"

"Lost three ships and retired. No one's lost three ships that quickly."

Bryana bit her lip. "Yeah, well, maybe . . . but they put him in command of *Boaz*." She shook her head. "I don't know, I heard that he couldn't even respond when his old crew went to see him. They just wouldn't have given him this command if the guy were a total screw up."

"He lost *three* ships . . . three *Brotherhood* ships."

"And as many as a hundred and some people have died under his command. I mean, the standing joke is that Fleet sends people out with Carrasco so they don't have to pay pensions down the road."

Art ran pensive fingers through his beard. "This isn't like the Brotherhood. If this isn't a mistake, Kraal's playing a real deep game, one I don't understand."

"Let's hope. If there's a genius anywhere in the Confederacy, it's Kraal." A pause. "You know, tied to the bridge, we've missed seeing a lot. You should catch a gander of the lounge. Plush, my friend. Like my beloved Armenian grandmother once said, 'opulence to dim the sight of a Persian king'!"

Arturian turned his attention back to his game of Find the Ship again. "Since when?"

"Since *we* are supposed to cart all these diplomats around." She ran a series of standard orbit corrections through navigation, studied the answers, and nodded with satisfaction. "Imagine the thrill of seeing them to quarters. Not big enough? I'm sorry, sir. Water's not hot enough? Yes, ma'am, have the plumber right down. Not enough space for you to conduct three-dimensional left-handed Tantra? I'll have the decorators here in a moment, ma'am." She growled softly. "Who gets the joy of teaching them high g drill? Or all the other little things they need to know?"

"Quite a few are station born. *Boaz* will have her hands full trying to keep their skinny bones from breaking." Art looked up. "Can you do that, good ship? Or do we need to float them around in bubbles?"

"I believe bubbles and gel will be unnecessary for standard acceleration," the ship informed. "Distortion of the gravity plates only presents problems under high g and when they want to mix together. Gravitation effects can be countered by repulser belts and harnesses."

Arturian watched with disgust and groaned as the last of his fleet vanished in a flare of blaster fire. He raised his hands in defeat, leaned back, and sucked at the hot coffee.

Bryana peered at the monitor which showed the Fast Transport docking a kilometer and a half up the barrel-like sides of the Brotherhood docks. "That's Carrasco's ship?"

"Yeah," Arturian chewed worriedly at his thick mustache. "This guy is one of the youngest captains in the fleet. He's had three ships shot out from under him . . . and lost a bunch of people in the process. How's that make you feel?"

"About like knowing the reactor's gone schizophrenic and your body could become a real bright light real quick!" She winked at him. "On the other hand, we won't be bored."

"Most of his old crew—like your friend Happy—are already aboard . . . what's left of them, that is." Arturian reached for his chewing tobacco and loaded his lip. "Why didn't he bring his old officers? Why are we still here?"

"I don't know." Bryana looked up at the speaker. *"Boaz,* do you have any information on why Solomon

Carrasco's former officers were not given this assignment?''

"Affirmative."

"Well . . . why?" Arturian pushed.

"His officers are unavailable."

"They didn't want to serve with him again?" Bryana raised questioning hands, palms up in confusion. "Or were they promoted or reassigned after he resigned from the service?"

"Neither," *Boaz* hedged. "It would have been better had you not brought it up, but if you must know—all the men and women who held First Officer positions under the command of Captain Solomon Carrasco are dead."

Arturian closed his eyes and leaned back in the command chair. "Now that, good ship, really inspires confidence." He studied Bryana. "What was that joke about pensions?"

* * *

Sol stood up from the FT's command chair as the tugs took over control of the transport. He nodded to the vessel's captain, a quietly competent dark-skinned man who smiled in return. "Thanks for the opportunity to get my feet wet again."

"My pleasure, Captain Carrasco." The young man nodded, respect in his eyes. "Uh, good to have you back, sir. There was talk that space would never be the same without you."

Sol laughed with a gusto he didn't feel and followed the bridge access way aft. His kit stood against a bulkhead, left by a thoughtful ensign. He felt the ship shudder slightly as the grapples locked into the Brotherhood docks and angular acceleration replaced artificial gravity.

He waved a final good-bye to the captain and walked through the chilly tunnel of the lock and into the wide ovoid tube of the docks. Arcturus. The glowing jewel of Confederate space. He studied the familiar sights and sounds, smelling the chilly air, listening to the machinery whine. A tang of oil met his nose as did the accustomed smell of paint and the ozone from welders.

He'd walked on these same foam steel deck plates with Fil and Maybry and Octorhu Mbazi. The ghosts watched through hollow eyes, hovering in the shadows, teeth flashing as they laughed. Sol's scalp prickled as he felt their knowing winks behind him. And so many lay dead—decompressed corpses now light-years away, frozen, charred, tumbling forever between the stars.

He started to wave down a shuttle and stopped short. It was only a mile or so. He'd stroll to his new command. Smiling, he slung his load over a wide shoulder, carrying his kit, enjoying the sights and sounds he'd thought forever left behind.

. . . Only the shuttle stopped anyway, two more pulling up to either side.

"Compliments of the Galactic Grand Master," a blond man in the first called out. "If you'd step into the middle vehicle, please. Anything happens, duck for cover and stay put. We'll handle it. The vehicles are armored."

"If anything. . . ? Wait a minute! Why the cloak and dagger? What's up? I don't need security. I'm just walking down to take my—"

"Please, Captain. If you'll simply step into the middle car, you'll be briefed there."

He couldn't find any give in the agent's demeanor—only the cold efficiency of a professional.

"Oh, hell." The joy of old sights flushed away to leave his heart aching with premonition. "All right. But I think you're overreacting."

"Oh, we've got our reasons," the fellow said amiably.

Sol sighed, stepping back to hand his kit up to the armed agents who waited. A black woman looked up expectantly as the shuttle slid forward on its track, superconducting repulsion making the ride effortless.

"This is for you," she explained as Sol sat, handing over a plastic-sealed envelope to him. Her dark eyes burned soberly into his. "Kraal's orders are that they're not to be opened until after you're in the jump."

Sol frowned and pulled the packet from the protective

plastic sleeve. Curious, he inspected the seal—authentic so far as he could tell—impressed above his ID. The stationery, he could see, was chem matched to his body. Should another touch it, the paper would discolor in reaction to the different molecules excreted by the body.

"I don't understand. Why all the security? I—"

"Captain Carrasco, I don't have all the details. Suffice it to say that two of our people were assassinated while guarding Speaker Archon. Leave has been canceled for all ship's personnel and we've uncovered and stopped several attempts to prohibit *Boaz*'s departure. Someone powerful wants your ship delayed, probably for political reasons. This *is* Arcturus. We're not taking chances."

The shuttles pulled up before a well-lit lock.

"Here you go, Captain. And good luck."

Sol nodded, feeling lost. *I'm a deep space captain—not a secret agent, by the Blessed Architect! What is all this?*

The kit felt heavy to him as he grabbed up the handles, leaping to the firm plating below. The blond man from the first car moved up beside him, chattering pleasantly about nothing.

Two Patrol officers waited by the main lock, talking softly to each other. Sol started for the lock. His bodyguard shouted a warning and shoved him violently to the side. Sol half-stumbled and dove instinctively for a cargo dolly. Blaster fire crackled as he pulled his own weapon from its holster. Screams sounded and an alarm went off.

Then silence.

"Captain Carrasco? You all right?"

Sol lifted his head from behind the brushed aluminum of the dolly. The black woman from his shuttle crouched over the body of the blond man, a wisp of condensation rising from the muzzle of the blaster clenched in her hand. The other agents crouched around the shuttles, blasters pointed in all directions, ready.

The two Patrol lock guards lay dead. A bolt had caught one in the chest, ripping the rib cage open, spattering pink lung tissue over the fragments of rib. The second had taken a shot to the thigh that amputated the leg above the knee. A second bolt had shattered his shoulder, fragmenting the scapula, crushing the vertebrae.

A truck full of Patrol purred up to disgorge armored forms. Boots clattered in the quiet. Sol swallowed, holstered his weapon, and stood. Shooting on a Brotherhood dock? They had the tightest security in the galaxy!

His face felt like a mask as he passed the scene of the fray. A mess of bloody tissue with bits and pieces blown here and there—that's what had become of the man who'd just saved his life.

"Got 'em," the remains of the blond gasped as the Patrol literally shoveled him onto a med stretcher and called urgently for a portable unit. He'd taken a hit low in the abdomen, his intestines a total mess where they hung out over the splintered fragments of the pubis.

"Don't know who these guys are . . ." a Patrol lieutenant called from where he was inspecting the bodies by the lock. ". . . but they're sure not our people."

"To get a Patrol uniform like that?" The Brotherhood agent who'd taken to shadowing Sol shook his head. "Something's rotten high up." He met Sol's frightened look. "Be careful, Captain. We knew you were hot—but we never thought they'd get this far."

"Why—why . . . me?" He groped at his kit handles.

"I don't have that information, Captain."

Sol backed up to the bulkhead and sucked a deep breath, forcing himself to remain calm. "What's happening here? Kraal? What did you get me into?"

The remains of the blasted Patrol impersonators had been scraped up and carted off. Deep inside, Sol suffered that familiar hollow feeling. He fought to still the shaking in his muscles, the heaving in his gut. Cursing his weakness, he forced himself to keep from trembling.

"Um, Captain?" The agent pointed to the lock. "The sooner you're aboard, sir, the better I'll feel. You know Brotherhood ships, the lock is as far as an assassin could hope to get."

Sol nodded hesitantly, staggering for the yawning tube, fighting the urge to be physically sick. Staving off shivers, he entered the cold womb of steel, leaving the carnage behind.

"Oh, Lord of the Universe," he muttered under his breath, ". . . say they didn't die for me!"

He reeled forward, stopping at the hatch, staring into the white interior of the lock.

"Captain?" a speaker asked.

"Y–yes?"

"I am *Boaz*. First Officer Bryana has prepared your crew for a formal reception beyond the hatch."

"I . . . I . . ." *My god, the ship. What do I do?* Gage? Gage? *Where are you?* The pounding of his heart threatened to split his ribs. *I'm not ready for this. I can't . . . can't face them. Can't face this ship.* "I . . . give me a moment. I need some time, good ship. Just a little time . . . to . . ."

"I understand, Captain. I'll inform the First Officer you are detained for a moment."

Sol blinked, mouth dry, guts runny with fear. "Yes . . . please. Thank you."

Come on, Solomon. Pull yourself together. You can do it. You can face them all. Even this ship. You've got to! Guts, man! He forced himself to breathe deeply, steeling his trembling limbs. "Got to stand up to it . . . to them."

He lifted his chin, the feeling that of facing a firing squad. He stepped into the lock, standing before the hatch. *"Boaz*, I'm ready. If you would cycle the hatch."

"Acknowledged, Captain."

The outer hatch slid noiselessly shut behind him.

Solomon Carrasco fought the urge to scream.

CHAPTER VI

Arturian chewed his lip as he watched Captain Solomon Carrasco work his way up the line. He stopped before each crewman and shook hands. Some—his old shipmates—actually embraced him; the worship in their eyes irritated something deep inside Arturian. Hell, Carrasco was a man, a simple human being—and not very impressive looking at that.

Solomon Carrasco wore a traditional white dress uniform, but his features seemed washed out, somehow pale and frightened. A slight sweat sheen stood out on his face, and he moved with hesitation—the effect that of a man afraid.

"Not what I'd expected at all," Bryana whispered from the side of her mouth. "This guy don't look like he could skipper a pre-programmed shuttle . . . let alone a starship."

But Solomon Carrasco was too close for Arturian to shoot her a reply.

He found himself looking into the frightened brown eyes of a man possessed. Hysteria lay there, barely concealed. The look was that of a frayed soul on the edge of an abyss. "Welcome aboard, Captain," Arturian responded hollowly.

"My pleasure, First Officer." Then he'd moved on, shaking Bryana's hand.

Solomon Carrasco stood stiffly at the head of the line and Art saw his face twitch. The old crew of *Gage* stood out somehow. To Art's eyes, they looked tougher, calmer, ready for anything as they looked toward the ship's captain. Others stared warily, uncertainly, especially those who'd expected to ship with Petran Dart. Finally, a few faces mirrored their curiosity about Solomon Carrasco, waiting to see if the man lived up to the legend.

This was the man who always brought them back through thick and through thin? This trembling puffball of a Captain?

"At ease, ladies and gentlemen." Solomon Carrasco issued his first order at half volume as he looked down the ranks. "We've just had a shooting outside the lock. Evidently an assassination attempt . . . which is why I might seem a little shaky." A mumble of voices stirred, to be silenced by Carrasco's subdued voice. "I want security beefed up. Some persons bribed their way into

Patrol uniforms. So be wary and keep on your toes. Of course, I believe the ship will keep track of internal security.''

''Affirmative,'' *Boaz* called through her speakers.

Carrasco seemed to steel himself at the word, a slight tremble in his locked legs.

Woodenly, he continued, ''To those of you with whom I've spaced before—good to see you all looking so healthy.'' A nervous chuckle broke out. ''To the rest, I look forward to serving with you. I'm sure *Boaz* has the best people in Fleet.

''I've heard through the grapevine that many of you are wondering what this is all about. Why is the ship decked out with a lounge? What are we doing with passengers and—most of all—where are we headed?'' He smiled halfheartedly. ''I'm sure it will put your minds at rest when I tell you I don't have the slightest idea either.''

Some looked perplexed, others seemed completely undone. The old *Gage* crew—on the other hand—laughed, truly amused. Whispers of ''Here we go again,'' ''Adventure'' and ''Leave it up to Cap'' came up the line.

Didn't the damn fools understand?

''In the meantime, my instructions are to follow any course suggested by the Speaker of Star's Rest. At least, those are the orders from the Galactic Grand Master. We're to serve the diplomats aboard and see to their every wish.'' Captain Carrasco raised his hands, pale face expressionless as carved wood. ''I know, odd orders for a Brotherhood ship . . . especially one of this caliber, but that's how it's laid out.

''Outside of the irregularities of handling the passengers, it should make a pleasant jump—to wherever we're going. Consider yourselves dismissed.''

The gathering broke up as Carrasco motioned to Arturian and Bryana. ''First Officers? Happy?'' he called, getting the big, muscle-bound engineer's attention. ''Could I see all of you in the officers' debriefing room? Um . . . where is the officers' debriefing room?''

Art started to open his mouth, only to have the bluff engineer bull past, grabbing Carrasco's arm. ''C'mon,

I'll show ya. Hey, Cap! It's good to see you like this. Man, I thought you'd bought it but royal last time I saw you.''

They walked several hundred meters down spotless white corridors, the engineer babbling the whole time. Happy steered Carrasco into a room of perhaps six by eight meters. Comfortable couches lined the sides under comm viewers. Headsets rested in their racks. A holo projector-equipped planning table dominated the center of the room, gravchairs arranged around to allow comfort during long sessions.

Carrasco turned on his heel and settled lightly on the table as they entered behind him.

''By God's whiskers, Cap,'' Happy's deep voice boomed, ''this'll be like old times!''

Carrasco's smile might have been strained through mesh.

Light blue eyes twinkling in his ruddy features, Anderson looked Arturian up and down, a stubby hand shooting out. ''Glad t' meet ya in person, First Officer. Been too busy working out the bugs to get up to officer country to say hello.''

Happy Anderson looked to be about forty, bluff and hearty. His face consisted of a series of heavy planes, the stubby nose looking battered. A bulldog jaw supported a full mouth used to smiles. He pumped Art's hand half off his arm and turned to Bryana, talking the whole time. ''You wouldn't believe the mess Cap was in. By the Architect's plumbbob, he was a charred, blackened sight. His eyeballs was cooked in his head, the skin a peelin' down the front of his face. Why his hair was a melted—''

''Happy? I don't think they want the details,'' Carrasco interrupted, voice brittle.

''Aye, Cap.'' Happy grinned reluctantly. ''But it's so good to see you in uniform again . . . looking as if there's nothing ever happened. Why, reminds me of the time on Vicar Station when them boys was fixin' to bust my head and Cap rushed in at the last minute. He lit into them goons and bodies was a flyin'—''

"Later," Carrasco suggested gently. "For the moment, the First Officers could probably care less."

Got that right. Art bit his lip to keep from agreeing.

Carrasco studied them, an unnerved glazing in his eyes. "I read your vitae on the way in. You both have outstanding records. As this is going to be an irregular affair anyway, I'll do all I can to help you learn the ropes. Compared to insystem, deep space isn't that much more difficult. Navigation gets a little trickier and rescue isn't just a beacon away. But you—"

"Captain?" Bryana stood braced, arms crossed tightly over her chest. "I take it you don't have any information concerning this spacing? Is there any 'For Your Eyes Only' on First Officer clearance? Any briefing we should know about?"

Carrasco shook his head slowly. "Nothing . . . to my knowledge, First Officer." He stared at her, brown eyes hiding nothing. "I've never had an assignment like this. The only orders available to me at this time are to do as the Speaker of Star's Rest and the Confederate Council request. Beyond that is anyone's guess. I tried several times to prod additional information out of the Galactic Grand Master—no luck. He simply smiled and told me to use my wits . . . and that he trusted my judgment in all matters."

Oh, swell! Trust the judgment of a man who's lost three ships in a row? Either Kraal's a lunatic, or the Craft is in worse shape than I thought. Nice pick of assignments, Art, old buddy! You've tagged yourself for something with all the earmarks of a disaster!

Carrasco turned to Happy who was still grinning, that wretched adoration in his eyes. "I read the ship's preliminary specs on the way in. Pretty impressive. I'll catch up on the stats and performance capabilities as soon as I'm settled. What's Engineering look like? You've been with her since Frontier, haven't you?"

Happy nodded. "The likes of which you've never seen, Sol. I wouldn't swear to it, but I think we could short circuit a star with the reactor in this baby. To my knowledge, it's the largest in the galaxy."

"How about your staff?"

"Got a real good second engineer. Odd sort of duck. Name's Kralacheck. I'd never admit it, but he might be smarter than me."

No doubt. I see what Bryana meant . . . but then a trained penguin might be smarter, Art thought dryly.

"First Officers," Sol turned. "I'll take your briefing now. What's the situation?"

Bryana held her defensive posture, eyes hard as they met Carrasco's. "According to orders, we waited to board the diplomats until your arrival. The only exception was Speaker Archon and his daughter Constance. We received clearance from Frontier to allow them aboard and to provide quarters for security reasons. Dockside has cleared us for departure upon your arrival. The Speaker would like to meet with you first thing."

"Very well, as soon as we've finished here, begin boarding the diplomats. First Officer Arturian, inform Misha Gaitano to observe the strictest security in the process. Given—"

"I don't think we can, sir," Art interrupted, trying to stifle his irritation.

Carrasco tipped his head, a curious resistance in his eyes. "Oh?"

"We've already had several canisters delivered bearing diplomatic seals." Art steeled himself, attempting to keep his professional face. "Under Confederate policy, sir, we can't search their luggage."

Carrasco's expression pinched slightly. "No, I suppose not. We'll have to live with that. I don't like it, but I guess we're stuck. Double our security precautions, no unauthorized entry into certain sensitive parts of the ship and so forth. You know the drill." He shifted his gaze to Happy. "How long until we can space?"

"Anytime, Cap. Five minutes, if you want. We've got things pretty well under control. Minor modifications can be conducted during acceleration to jump."

"Any questions?" Sol asked, half expectantly. "No? Then let's get the diplomats aboard and some space behind us." He stood energetically, signaling the meeting was over.

On the way out the hatch, Art heard Happy ask, "What was all that shooting on the dock? Heard a Brotherhood agent died as a result. Guess they shot him up pretty bad."

"Yes . . . they did," Carrasco gritted, a quiver at the corner of his lips.

* * *

Nikita Malakova gave the Brotherhood agent his most scathing baleful glare as the man checked his papers. Behind a security door, another man studied a monitor. The security agent looked up, evidently receiving a report.

"Sir, could I ask you to leave your pulse pistol and knife with us? Considering—"

"Never!" Nikita narrowed his eyes, jaw thrust out. "What you think, eh? That I would surrender pistol and knife? What then? I become prey for anyone else with weapon!"

"I understand, sir, but—"

"You see this?" Nikita pointed to the clearance on the Council ID. "Says I am diplomat, no? Beyond silly little title, I am man. As man, I take responsibility for me. Is human right to protect self and family. And what you know, eh? Occasional fool still tries to rob me. And would not be first time some subverter of will of oppressed masses would like to assassinate Nikita Malakova! No, you clear me—or I go back and file protest with Council and we see what happens."

The man behind the monitor was talking softly into a comm. Finally, he looked up and nodded.

"Very well, Representative. We will, however, file notice with the Captain that you're—"

Nikita leaned down, jamming a thick finger into the man's chest. "You listen, Brotherhood subverter of the masses. So long as the people are armed, they are free! Eh? You consider. What do Sirians want? To take away guns! That's what. They claim depriving masses of weapons stops crime. You ever been to Malakova Station? No? You ever been to Gulag Sector? No? Hey, you can leave door unlocked! Leave credit card on table in restaurant. You come back, it still there—with *no* charges on it. You know why? Because we . . . the people . . . shoot thief on sight!''

The man steeled himself. ''Certainly sir, I can understand your convictions; however, you'll be traveling on a Brotherhood ship with guaranteed security that—''

''I take own security. Now, you want me to call Galactic Grand Master? Or you let me pass?''

The man sighed. ''Very well, sir. Enjoy your—''

''Bah!'' Nikita bulled past, striding down the narrow corridor. ''Take my gun from me, will they? What then? How do sneaky Brotherhood bloodsuckers expect me to stay free?''

At the end of the corridor, Nikita stepped out on the docks, seeing the hatch and a handful of wary Patrol. Around the perimeters, armed riot wagons waited, armored sides mirror reflective against lasers. The heavy blasters had a suspiciously activated look to them.

Tayash Niter waved from one side. In person he looked even more fragile, an emaciated caricature of a man. He dressed severely in black, the effect accentuating the snowy white of his hair and augmenting the narrow look of his face. As if to keep his tottering body from collapsing, he braced himself on a thin black cane that gleamed in the bright lights.

Grinning, Nikita padded forward, kissing his friend's cheeks and gesturing toward the lock. ''So, we go on a Brotherhood ship! Maybe we see if stories are true!''

Tayash chuckled under his breath, running an age-freckled hand through his shock of stiff white hair. ''You think they would allow us to see Brotherhood 'secrets'? You're more naive than I always suspected. What is this, Nikita?'' Tayash looked around. ''No big-boobed, mindless piece of female fluff to keep your bed warm at night? Slipping, are you? Or did your wives find out about that prostitute from Ceti you took to—''

"Shhhh!" Nikita warned, finger to his lips. "What you think? That because this is Brotherhood dock my wives don't have ears? Rumors . . . rumors go everywhere."

Tayash elbowed him, chortling. "I bet your cutthroat constituents checked your expenses. Found too much money going for—"

"Hey! You accuse *me* of pilfering funds of workers for personal gain? Bah! I am soldier of the permanent revolution!"

Tayash nodded, leaning on his gleaming black cane. "Aye, soldier for the revolution. My bloated butt hole you're a—"

"So, what has happened here?" Nikita jerked his head toward the lock.

Tayash bent his gaze to the cluster of Patrol and people knotted around the hatch. "A great deal. Mark Lietov himself arrived a few minutes back. Your instincts about this being big were right. Lietov—"

"Bah!" Nikita slapped his thighs with heavy hands. "So, Sirians send Director of Political Affairs? Number two man in whole pustulant government? We shall have to keep eyes and ears eternally open, my friend. Lietov? I never would have—"

"Nor is he the only one."

Nikita raised an eyebrow. "Well? Don't just stand there. Who? Tayash, damn you, tell me who?"

Niter worked his lips. "Oh, I will. For the moment, I was simply relishing the thought of not being interrupted by you. Thought I'd pay you back for all the times you wouldn't allow me to finish a—"

"Who?" Nikita thundered.

Tayash pulled at the white spike of his goatee. "Terra sent Medea. She brought her husband—"

"Medea?" Nikita clenched his hands behind him, staring at the lock. "There is viperous woman if one ever existed. So who did Palmiere send—or is he coming himself?"

"Stokovski."

"George Stokovski? That simpering worthless weak-minded—"

"But New Israel sends General Paul Ben Geller."

Nikita's incredulous expression widened to a smile. "That's better. Leave it to Jews to not fool around. So Mossad is in this, too? Their best agent?"

"And Ambrose has sent Norik Ngoro as their . . . Nikita? What's this? Did I finally manage to catch you off guard? You look pale."

"Ngoro?"

"The same. Nikita, I do believe this is the first time I've seen you go pale when it wasn't mention of another woman in the presence of your wives. What is—"

"And Amahara is with him?"

"Yes. Is that significant?"

Nikita filled his lungs, stretching his bearlike chest. "Norik Ngoro is Truth Sayer in his own station. Tayash, that man reads minds. Some psi power I don't understand. A sensitivity, if you will. Amahara goes along as official recorder—of course, fact that Ngoro can't dress himself is beside point. Genius has its price."

"I don't see the—"

"Tayash, understand. Norik Ngoro is most dangerous man in human space. Important thing is that he's come here. To go with us for whatever reason we're taking this trip. Lietov, Medea, Earl of Baspa, are all frightening enough . . . but Ngoro? What have we stumbled into?"

* * *

Sol stood alone on the bridge, tracing a finger down the side of the command chair, the monitors glowing warm and alive before him. The bridge . . .

Flashback: He staggered as images of *Gage* loomed from the depths of his mind. Mbazi grinned up from his command chair, the broad plains of his face illuminated by a wide toothy smile, bridge lights playing in the steel wool mat of his hair. Maybry hummed softly to himself, concentration fixed on his headset. In the screens the alternating blue-red of the binary system closed to a semi-detached state, the envelopes elongating as the stars approached their Roche limits.

"Captain?" *Gage* asked. "Are you all right? I detect a—"

Reality shifted, a black shape hurling out of the shimmering flickering of blue and red lights.

"Where the hell?" Mbazi jerked around. "They're shooting at us! Damn it! Shields up! *Gage*, give us everything!"

Below his feet, *Gage* shuddered under concussions as bright blaster bolts exploded plating, lancing plasma through *Gage*'s vulnerable hull.

"Accelerate!" Mbazi cried, looking up, beseeching. "Sol? Why? Why is this happening? Damn it, Cap! Do something! Save us!"

"Captain!"

"Not now, *Gage*," he whispered.

"Captain!"

Sol straightened, the horror snapping from his mind. He blinked. Looked down to see his fingers sunk into the foam of the command chair. About him, *Boaz*'s pristine bridge gleamed.

"I . . ."

"Captain?" *Boaz* demanded. "Are you all right?"

Sol gulped air, bracing himself on the thick back of the command chair. He shivered as cold sweat broke out on his body. "Fine. Yes, I'm fine. Just in my head is all. Just . . ."

"I detect severe physical and psychological stress. If you aren't feeling well, I could—"

"I'm fine, ship."

"Engineer Anderson is outside the hatch."

"Pass him."

Anderson strolled in, whistling to himself, stopping dead at the sight of Sol. "Blessed protons, Cap. You look like you'd seen a ghost."

Sol smiled weakly, sinking into the command chair, fishing absently for his cup. "I . . . Yeah, maybe I did." Sol fumbled his cup out with nervous hands, jamming it unsteadily into the dispenser. "I don't know, Happy, maybe I'm not ready for this."

Anderson cocked his head, frowning. "I . . . well, just wanted to come up. I mean I . . . Well, damn it! You and me, we've been through a lot together. I don't know. I just thought maybe I'd come up and see how you were doing. Don't know when we'll get time again."

"Sit down." Sol gestured as he took his cup from the dispenser, slopping coffee on the deck. His gut twisted, anxiety sending shivers through his tight muscles. Happy's frown deepened.

"It's these new hands," Sol explained lamely. He wiggled his fingers. "Hard to believe."

Happy lowered himself slowly into one of the chairs. "Yeah, I suppose." He hesitated. "So, tell me, Sol. How are you? Last time I saw you, they had you clammed up in a med unit like a bug in a cocoon. I mean, I stood there and couldn't see anything but monitors. I . . . aw, I don't know. I just wanted you to know all of us made it up one time or another to see you."

They'd come. His crew—what remained of it—hadn't forgotten him. A burning knot of tears tried to form in his eyes. Gritting his teeth, he killed the urge. "Thanks, Happy. I don't remember much. Just pain. Pain like you'd never think a body could survive." He puffed an exhale. "Maybe I didn't, huh?"

Happy stared down at his thumb. "Yeah, well, when I heard you might take *Boaz,* I crossed my fingers. I think we all did. You know, me and the crew, well, every time we take a breath, it's because of what you did that day."

Sol nodded slowly. "Couldn't order anyone else to." He shrugged nervously. "I guess I'm saying 'I' a lot. Nervous, Happy. Guess I don't know what to say. But, well, tell me about *Gage,* about the trip back. How . . . how did she die?"

He steeled himself, forcing himself to listen.

Happy stared up at the monitors where Arcturus stretched into infinity. "Easy, Cap. Quick. Like she never knew she'd gone to sleep. Mostly, she shut herself off, depowered the boards to keep things together. She was a lady . . . always. Like you, she sacrificed herself for us."

Sol nodded, taking a deep breath.

"Is that what's bothering you?"

Sol spread his hands. "You don't space that long with a crew or a ship like *Gage* and just let go." He looked up. "I don't know. Maybe I haven't had time to mourn."

Happy smiled, the gesture splitting his blocky face. "Yeah, well, Cap, you brought us all home again. Damn me if I know how we made it since I was in Engineering pasting things together, but we did. For more than a couple of moments, there, I almost got religion. Been a while since I prayed that hard."

"But all those people." Sol jumped to his feet, pacing nervously. "And I just keep asking myself why . . . who."

"Black ship." Happy exhaled, digging his own coffee cup out of his pouch and slipping it into the dispenser. "Pirates? Who knows? Probably thought they had easy pickings. Figured to hit us on the fly-by and come back and pick up pieces. They just didn't figure we'd survive. That we'd have time to accelerate to jump. Barely made it as it was. They'd turned around and were pretty close by the time we made jump. The shielding wavered once or twice, but it held. Honestly, Cap, you bought us the time."

Sol nodded, fingering the cushioning on the monitors. "What is this stuff?"

"Pretty neat design they cooked up. It images—like a monitor. At the same time, it keeps the equipment sealed. Less maintenance. Acts as a cushion, too, in case you fall or something."

"And this ship? Is she really everything everyone says?"

"She is. Smart, too. *Gage* was pretty sharp, but *Boaz* . . . well, you'll find out."

No. Not this time. I won't let myself. I can't. Not again. How do I tell you, Happy? How do I let you know how much it hurt? First Moriah, then Sword, and finally Gage? Not again. I couldn't take it.

"And the new people?"

"Pretty good. I'd say they'll be proton crackers once you get them broken in. For the time being, everyone is getting to know each other." Happy paused, narrowing his eyes in a conspiratorial squint. "Between you and me. What's this all about?"

Sol chuckled under his breath. "Haven't got the slightest idea."

Happy glanced up. "Heard through the net that Kraal went up to see you in person."

"And he wouldn't tell me a thing."

Happy scratched the back of his close-cropped head, short hair standing like bristles. "Huh. Seems like we've got half the Council coming aboard. That's not normal. I get the sneaky hunch that something big's cooking."

"All Kraal would say is that humanity is hanging in the balance. Very melodramatic."

Happy pursed his lips. "You know, Cal and Gaitano and I, we snuck out to the tavern section. Didn't stay for more than a beer. I tell you, Sol, it was downright hostile. Thought for a minute we'd have to fight our way out—but a bunch of Patrol showed up. Just standing around like, watching things. We drank up and left. Lot of talk under people's breath. I'd heard we weren't exactly popular. I guess the Sirians have been pushing. Want to open Brotherhood computer banks to everyone."

"Most of humanity isn't ready for that." Sol sighed and took a deep swig of his coffee. "Kraal's been feeding material into the Confederacy as rapidly as he can. Dump too much, and you'll bankrupt several planetary industries. How many people do you think we'd put out of work at the Star shipyards alone?"

"We've been blamed for a lot of things, recently." Happy shook his head. "I don't know, I guess it's just a way for the Sirians and their kin to get rid of our political involvement. At least, that's the skinny I get. Stuff scrawled on the walls accuses us of being worse than the Soviets."

"You know the deep space surveys are trying to find us a way out if things become too rough."

"Yeah."

"I read the manifest. The Sirian Political Director is one of the Representatives."

"No joke?"

"I wish it were."

"I'll watch my back."

"Still, Cap, it's good to have you back."

Sol sipped his coffee again. "Happy, it's only for this run. Kraal asked me as a personal favor. When we come back, I'm handing the ship over to Dart."

"I thought . . ."

Sol shook his head. "Kraal said if I didn't take it, he would."

"You know this Archon character spent quite a bit of time with him. I met his daughter. Quite a girl. Better watch yourself. She's a looker . . . and sharp to boot. You met Archon yet?"

"No."

"I think you'll like him. Spacer to the bones." Happy took a swig of his coffee and stood. He grinned. "I guess, then, that we're in for another interesting time, huh?"

Not this time. I couldn't take it. "Oh, it'll be about routine, I expect."

"Well, I suppose I ought to get down to Engineering. I just wanted to drop in and see how you were doing." Happy hesitated, fidgeting.

"Yes?"

Happy beetled his brows. "Look, Cap. I know you had reservations about taking a command. It's no secret that you resigned. But listen. If you need anything. Even if it's just to sit around and talk, let me know, huh? I'm not that busy."

"Sure. I'll do that."

Happy winked and started for the hatch.

"Oh, Happy?"

"Yeah, Cap."

"Thanks."

* * *

Art walked into the lounge, looking around. He'd been through prior to leaving Frontier—and seen what looked like wreckage as Brotherhood crews had begun renovation. Thereafter, he'd spent all his time learning the ship, taking her though jump to Arcturus. He hadn't even used a monitor to check on progress. Red velvet tapestries hung from the walls covering sensors. Three long tables stood at one end of the fifty by thirty meter room for banquet facilities. A bar had been installed along one wall with numerous dispenser spigots. The gaming booth remained, with its fake captain's chairs. The floor had been carpeted with some thick fabric, done in a less exuberant hue than the wall tapestries. Overhead light panels kept the whole brightly lit.

Two men, Forney Andrews of the Patrol and Arness, the Representative from Range sat at the comm, in contact with Arcturus over some last minute business.

Bryana emerged from the corridor leading to the personal quarters. Art cocked his head as she joined him. "Well, all settled in?"

"That's the last of them. Mikhi Hitavia, the Reinland Representative. Nice man. Some of these others, I don't know. Politicians all of them. Fan Jordan, the one from New Maine is the worst. Earl of something or other."

"That's okay, I'll take him. I just got Norik Ngoro settled in. Now there's a weird guy. Just looked right through me. His aide, Amahara, on the other hand, is real people. Does all the talking for them."

"Then we're done. That's it. Everyone's aboard." She frowned. "The Rep from Gulag . . . um, Malakova, that's him. Lecherous bastard pinched my butt."

"Maybe it's some quaint local custom on his station?"

Her glare was cold enough to burn.

"Captain?" Art turned to the nearest comm. "We've got the last of the diplomatic parties aboard."

Audio only, the response came back. "Very good, First Officer. If you'll join me on the bridge, we'll space immediately."

"Yes, sir." Art cut the connection and met Bryana's eyes. "Curtain time."

"And he's just been sitting on the bridge? Doing what, do you suppose?"

"When I took him up there, he just stood for a moment, looking around. He . . . well, didn't say a thing to the ship. Normally, that's the first thing you do is say hello. He just stood, staring at the command chair, cheek muscles jumping."

"And that's it?"

"Yeah, other than having me call up the log from the first jump." Art gestured with his hands as they walked. "Then he told me to get the diplomats on loaded as quickly as possible. But it was his hands. He . . ."

She stopped just beyond the security hatch to the bridge. "Go on."

Art shrugged, "He just kept wiping his palms on his pants. You know, like they were sweaty or something."

Bryana filled her lungs and exhaled. "Great. Well, let's get out of here. Sooner we get to Star's Rest and back, the sooner we're off this lunatic wagon."

Art led the way onto the bridge and dropped loosely into his command chair. Carrasco's face appeared drawn, haggard.

"Captain, are you feeling all right?"

"Fine, First Officer," the voice hummed tightly, almost hostilely. "It's your helm."

"Yes, sir," Arturian agreed, shooting a quick look at Bryana. Art dove into checking with the Port Authority while Bryana got a line to Engineering. Happy's face formed on the screen and began reporting reactor stats and systems checks.

"Speaker Archon, please." Carrasco settled back in his chair. Art stumbled in his countdown procedure as a dashing redhead formed on the monitor.

"Captain?" her voice came melodiously through the system. "My father is occupied at the moment. May I help you?"

"You're Constance?"

"Yes, sir." She smiled, and for a brief second, Art's heart stopped. Bryana's warning glare put him back to work.

"I am ordered to obtain course data from the Speaker. If you would be so kind, could you—"

"I can help you, Captain." Her blue eyes tried to take his measure through the comm. "Please establish course for Star's Rest." She hesitated. "Captain, my father and I would appreciate it if you would keep that destination confidential."

"Of course, ma'am, we will see to it," Carrasco agreed stiffly. To Bryana he added, "Security clearance, First Officer Bryana."

"Confirmed," she shot back.

"Captain Carrasco," Constance began, picking her words carefully, "If you could find time as soon as we are accelerating for jump, would you do my father the honor of sharing your company? He has a few things to discuss with you. For now, we realize you're very busy."

"I assure you, that's the first item on my agenda," Carrasco returned.

"I won't keep you, Captain. Until then." The screen went dead.

Tugs had latched on and were bringing the big white ship out from the gleaming sides of Arcturus. As they moved away, the seemingly endless station disappeared into the gaudy red light of the giant sun. A marvel of human engineering. From above, Arcturus looked like twirling rings of silver wire looped around the star. The largest settlement in human space, it had grown from the single orbiting station that had once housed the government of the fledgling Confederacy. Now, it was an orbiting mass constantly in need of adjustment against tidal effects, and so large no one even tried to guess at the number of people, businesses, and industries that inhabited that band of metal. The one and only planet in the Arcturian system had been a ball of molten metal which had been shipped up and turned into most of the station. Now, asteroids from the LaGrange points had been carted in and prefab material arrived in a steady stream from Sirius, Eridanus, Cygnus III, Ambrose Sector, and other places Art couldn't remember.

"Ship!" Carrasco's voice cracked weirdly.

"Yes, Captain?"

"What is your ETA for Star's Rest system?"

Carrasco's face looked deathly pale and sweaty when Art stole a glance. The Captain glared at the speaker as if he hated it.

"At standard twenty gravity acceleration, 1033 hours plus or minus three." *Boaz* intoned.

Forty-three days, ship's time, just to get there. Art closed his eyes. Coming home would take at least that long on top of it. All that time with this nervous Nellie as captain? He checked the resistance factor of the hull as they were moved into position for the catapult and released by the tugs.

"Port has given us clearance, Captain." Art knew his voice sounded nervous. Blast! He felt like a green cadet taking his first training flight. There was so much tension, the bridge reeked of it. He could see it in the surreptitious glances Bryana shot Carrasco. She sat, spine rigid.

"Initiate." Carrasco sounded mechanical, driven.

"Initiated and logged, Captain," Art responded automatically and cleared through Port Authority. The concentric rings before them looked like an endless tunnel as they lit up with that weird green glow.

Electromagnetic fields pulled *Boaz* inexorably forward as the first ring began to crawl past. Art kept his eyes on the hull resistance, manipulating it so the ship pulled straight, reversing polarity if a ring began to get too close.

"First Officer," *Boaz* intoned, "I could handle hull polarity with much greater efficiency."

"You've got it, then." Art nodded, searching out secondary duties.

"First Officer," Carrasco's voice grated. "Keep your concentration on that readout. Be ready for manual override should the margin of error become excessive."

"Yes, sir," Art snapped, eyes darting back to the resistance meters. Damn it! The ship said she was capable of doing the job. She proved it, too, maintaining perfect alignment in the endless bore. He swallowed, looking up

at the monitor, the sensation that of falling into an endless well of chartreuse. The effect mesmerized, rings
flashing past as *Boaz* dove faster and faster into the series
of fluorescent lime-green circles. A black dot formed in
the bottom and leapt to meet them, the walls of the can-
non a green blur. The circle gained in diameter and swallowed them. Blackness sucked them up as they shot free,
stars peppering the screens.

"Time to reaction?" Carrasco called out.

"Fifteen seconds," *Boaz* informed.

"Count down, Happy!" Carrasco's voice snapped like
a lash.

"Five, four, three, two, one, ignition, Captain. First
Officer Bryana, it's your hell-hole!"

Art could see Bryana's eyes go vacant as her headset
fed her information on the giant reactor.

Inertia pushed them back into the command chairs for
a brief second before the grav plates took over to compensate for the acceleration. Without those plates, they'd
have been crushed to bloody pulp.

"Course to Star's Rest?" Carrasco asked.

"Laid in, Captain," *Boaz* answered.

"Condition, First Officer Bryana?"

"Green on all fronts, Captain," Bryana's voice
sounded loud in the quiet room. "Acceleration is constant at 20 gs, sir. Reactor demonstrates no fluctuation.
All departments are reporting condition Green."

"Very well, First Officer. From the chronometer, it's
now your watch. Give a holler if you need anything."
Carrasco stood. "First Officer Arturian, may I see you
beyond the hatch for a moment?"

Art shot a quick look at Bryana, glimpsed the fire in
her eyes, and stood. "Yes, sir."

Passing the hatch, Art met those brown pools of emotion and felt himself growing angry. That look of steel
didn't mean a damn thing! He'd never been chewed out
since he was a senior at the Academy on Frontier!

Carrasco's voice surprised him, gentle, almost forgiv-
ing. "I didn't mean to sound so tough in there, First
Officer." A faint hint of a smile played at the corners of

his mouth. "I'm a little nervous . . . as you and First Officer Bryana no doubt realize. I belayed your order only because we have a new ship. With new systems—no matter how well designed, no matter how simple the task—always keep your eyes open and your reactions ready . . . just in case. When we've had time to assess the backups, recheck all the redundancies, you can relax—at least a micron or two."

Art nodded, frowning, realizing he'd never thought of that. Anger faded. "I suppose it's the same if external conditions change . . . or repairs or maintenance have been performed?"

Carrasco gave the first real smile Art had seen from him. "Exactly, First Officer. You'll live longer that way. My compliments to you and First Officer Bryana for an excellent spacing. Well done. You are dismissed." And Carrasco was gone, striding briskly down the companionway.

CHAPTER VII

In the aftermath of the Aan, she waited alone—impotent master of the universe which spun in wreaths of fusion-powered light. The damning spring remained invulnerable, the ever present bane of her existence. Unable to affect the events around her, the insanity within burned ever deeper, ever more engulfing. And the spring made a lie of her abilities, goading, maddening, obsessing her incredible brain until the knot of hatred and frustration pulled tight.

She watched the heavens, seeing the legacy of the Aan's conflict, the balance of interstellar media skewed, uniformity broken by the areas of vacuum where her powers had annihilated vast portions of space. In untouched tracts, gravity changed the swirling patterns of matter, ever expanding, twirling the suns into galaxies, singularities forming, mass and matter thrown into a confusion of chaos. About her, space boiled turbulently.

While galactic patterns defined themselves, another form of organic life struggled up from the mud, a simple creature of replicating carbon based molecules in the misty soup of a steaming planet.

Eating and being eaten, the Chorr battled for their survival. Larger carnivores preyed upon them as they themselves preyed on lesser life. The strongest and smartest survived, reproducing the successful genotype. The day would be lost to the fog-mantled past, when the first Chorr employed a sharpened section of exoskeleton to kill one of the large predators. That lonesome individual promptly engorged itself on the body of the slain hunter and fissioned, duplicating the knowledge of weapons. That knowledge radiated—transferred by the molecules of inheritance. Millennia of season changes later, a Chorr looked up from the highest point of the planet where it sought metal rich rock for smelting. Through the thinning clouds, it saw the lights dancing above and wondered—as did the hundreds of successful offspring. Crippled by fission reproduction, the Chorr advanced ever so slowly into the realm of science.

Halfway across the Chorr galaxy, she waited. Knowing another organic form of life would come to her. Soon, so very soon.

She keened insanely to herself as she devised ways of leading the next organic intelligence to its destruction. Hatred burned a bitter acid as she waited for a being to work the spring and condemn itself to the fate of the Aan.

In the meantime, the Chorr launched their first spacecraft.

* * *

Solomon Carrasco got lost three times and finally had to access the ship before he located his quarters. He stopped before the door, staring at the lock plate.

It's all right. You handled the bridge—got through fine. You can handle this. It's just a captain's cabin—like any other cabin. Just like the one aboard Gage . . . Gage *is dead. You can't bring her back.*

"Dead is dead. But why is it so hard?" Hesitantly, he reached forward, palming the lock plate, leaving his hand there for a moment to allow the detector to register his print and body chemistry. About him, the presence of the ship seemed to hover, waiting, watching, expecting.

The pressure door slid open with a slight hiss, the lights beyond going up. Sol swallowed, the effect like a knotted sock stuck halfway in his throat.

Inside, every light on the comm unit flashed colorfully.

"What *is* this?" he muttered, noting absently that his kit had been neatly placed on the bunk. He studied the long list of calls, unnerved.

"All these people want to talk to me? But I . . . why, for God's sake?"

"Mostly invitations, Captain," *Boaz's* voice sent a shiver down his spine. "The diplomats are all anxious to make your acquaintance. Similarly, Engineer Anderson would like to speak to you at your leisure and Speaker Archon would like to know how soon you might meet with him to discuss the mission."

"Well, what's priority?" Sol steeled himself. *Got to learn to deal with her. I'm stuck with her for at least eighty days. If I can keep my distance, stay coolly professional, avoid . . . avoid coming to like her, I'll be all right. Turn over command as soon as we return.* He sighed as he began stowing his kit.

"None of the messages are listed as priority outside of the Speaker's," *Boaz* informed.

The messages formed as he dropped to the bunk and closed his eyes. "Oh, Jesus, why's it have to be this rough?" He thought he kept it under his breath . . . but the ship answered.

"I wouldn't know, Captain, but your behavior doesn't lie within normal parameters."

He looked up at the speaker, a twist of *Gage's* memory turning within him. "No, I suppose not."

"Would you like to talk about it?"

"Psych program? No, I don't need that. I'm tired.

That's all. Forced into this command despite any assurances to the . . . I . . . Never mind, ship." Tired? Yes. Confused? Yes. Frightened? Hell, yes! And he knew he shouldn't have snapped at Arturian that way. Still, the fellow had picked it up immediately despite his frustration and anger. A superb trait in an officer. And the sight of the stars filling the bridge monitors, the heady acceleration through the Arcturian system, all filled Carrasco with that wondrous . . .

"As to the calls, I'll trust your analysis. Send the diplomats my regards and tell them I'll attend to social formalities as soon as possible." He rubbed his eyes, still not completely healed.

To rest, to simply take a couple of hours and sleep, maybe to have that slumber undisturbed by *Gage*, or *Sword*, or Mbazi's grin or the blown apart bodies back on the Arcturian dock.

Archon wants an immediate audience. Archon, the key to all this. Am I up for this?

"Have the Speaker meet me here. Before he gets here, however, you might tell me how my cabin works."

"Speaker Archon has been notified and is on his way," *Boaz* intoned. Sol followed instructions on how to make a regulation captain's quarters into a boardroom. Clever design. A desk could fold out of a featureless wall. Comm could extend around the entire cabin, giving him full access to the ship's status and displays.

"Captain?" *Boaz* asked, voice timid. "I denote hostility in your voice. Is there some problem with my functioning?"

Sol closed his eyes, bracing locked elbows on the desk. *Easy. The heart of the ship's brain is an n-dimensional matrix computer. That's all . . . all that Gage was. She's a ship, Solomon. Just an artifact with a sentient brain. Nothing more. Don't let her get to you. No, not after Gage.*

He heard his voice crack and it angered him. "No, good ship, your functioning is flawless."

"I can change my personality projection if it would be helpful."

"Your personality is f . . . fine."

When she spoke again, it was in a soft tone, almost hesitant. "I have reviewed all of my records regarding you, Captain. From your reaction and the psych profile established on you after your last mission, probability suggests that you are afraid of close bonds with me."

A tightness closed around Sol's throat and he glared his hatred at the speaker. *It's my mind—keep out of it!* screamed a voice in his head. Visions spun out of the depths—the image of *Gage* lying on her side in the Brotherhood scrap yards, hollow holes where metal had been potted away. Companionways gaped, dark, gutted, and empty. *Damn! Say something. Respond somehow. Think!* His mind produced the sight of the agent, blown apart on the docks. Mbazi's body, wrapped in white, flipped end over end in the empty cold of space. Maybry floated out there in the eternal cold, charred, maimed, and frozen. Sol blinked, swallowing hard. *Why? Couldn't they let him rest—give him time to come to grips with his nightmares?*

His voice rasped gravelly. "If . . . if they didn't make the ships so . . . so well, they wouldn't have such reactions from their officers." He glared up through burning eyes, jaw clamped. *"Boaz,* I want you to understand. *Gage* was my friend. My . . . my very *good* friend. She and I . . . well, I miss her terribly. And . . . and there was a man on the docks today. Saved my life. Died in my place. I'm tired of hurting, ship. Tired of . . . death."

In the silence, he waited, everything inside gone hollow.

After almost a minute, the ship spoke. "Captain, when we have more time . . . will you tell me more?"

He nodded, a limited fragile motion. "Yes, ship. If you wish."

"Speaker Archon is at the hatch."

Sol straightened, taking a deep breath, stilling the turmoil. "Send him in."

The hatch slipped noiselessly sideways in the bulkhead to emit a large man. Once heavily muscled, much of it had turned to fat—not the flabby kind, but the heavyset look of age. Gleaming gray eyes betrayed an acute mind and the deeply etched lines about the mouth reflected pain, authority, and hard living.

"Speaker, I am Captain Solomon Carrasco. At your service. Please, have a seat." Sol indicated one of the chairs after a firm handshake. "I . . . Do I know you? Something about you is familiar."

"Thank you, Captain. Yes, we met—very briefly— some time ago. I take it you haven't had time to read my file?"

Sol shook his head. "Until a month ago, I was confined to a med unit for some reconstruction. Since that moment, I've been studying the command parameters for my ship and crew. I must confess, I haven't had time for much else—and familiarity with my vessel *was* my first priority."

"Ship and crew are any commander's first priority. But then, I hope we'll have time to discuss those things in detail and leisure later." The probing gray eyes searched his. Archon handed over a large bottle he been holding behind his back. "This is for you. You see, I've done my homework. I believe Star Mist is one of your vices."

Sol took the bottle of fine Arcturian whiskey and smiled. "I didn't know my taste was common knowledge."

"It isn't," Archon said with a shrug. "Your engineer, Happy Anderson suggested it."

"I may have to bat him on the ears. This stuff is as expensive as liquid toron. Care for some now?" Sol raised the bottle with a questioning look.

"Gladly!" Archon inclined his head as Sol poured.

Settling himself, Sol studied the Speaker for a moment, that nagging familiarity eating at him. "So, what's this all about? My commander, Galactic Grand Master Kraal, has ordered me to accede to your every wish and desire. A highly irregular situation, to say the least. Why did they have to call me out of retirement? Why the secrecy? A man died on the dock as I was being ferried from my transport to *Boaz*. As a result, we huddled the diplomats together and slipped them in as quickly and quietly as possible. Brotherhood ships generally don't mix in Confederate affairs. We're philosophically apolitical.''

Archon leaned back, eyes measuring. ''I can't give you all the answers you'd like for reasons of security.'' He raised a thick hand, inclining his head. ''And I wouldn't have you think I was being obtuse. The Galactic Grand Master and I discussed the reasons in great detail. We both think it best to keep everyone in the dark for now. Already men have died over this.

''Suffice it to say, not even the diplomats know what we're about. They simply know that severe upheavals are developing in the Confederacy and the answers to those upheavals will be found here, in *Boaz,* and on Star's Rest.''

Sol toyed with his glass, the memory of bloody pulp on the dock fresh in his mind. He studied the lines of Archon's face, tracing the angle of the jaw, the keen fire of those eyes. *Where do I know you from? Where? A moment of power—of desperation. Only, there've been so many of those in the last ten years. So familiar, if I could just tie it down.*

''I'll do my absolute best to live with that, Speaker . . . up until the point that my ship or crew are endangered.'' He looked up, expression hardening. ''It would help if you would give me a better understanding of how to accommodate you.''

Archon leaned back easily, spreading his hands. ''Captain, I can only tell you that we're playing a very delicate game. Further, the players are incredibly skilled and competent. Interstellar intrigue is not now—nor has it ever been—a game for the weak of heart.'' His voice took on a knife-sharp edge. ''They aren't in this instance either. You will understand someday—if we are successful. If not, it won't matter. We'll all be dead.''

Carrasco's heart skipped, a sudden dryness in his throat. ''I will *not* risk my ship!''

Archon nodded slightly, sympathy in his eyes. ''Let's hope you won't have to. In the meantime, I suggest you declare sensitive areas of the ship off-limits including

weapons, engineering, bridge, comm, and other centers
which might be sabotaged.''

"Sabotaged?'' Sol almost started to his feet, the whiskey glass clutched white-knuckled in his hand. "Those
orders have already been issued. Speaker, I've had no
experience with sabotage. I'm a deep spacer.''

Archon chuckled humorlessly. "If I do my job, Captain Carrasco, you have nothing to worry about. On the
other hand, our mission necessitates the Council's rep-
resentation. Without them, the journey of the *Boaz* might
have pitched the Confederacy into open war.''

"War? I find that hard to believe, Speaker.'' Still Kraal
had claimed he'd have taken the command.

Archon shook his head, expression grim. "Oh, I can
read your skepticism, Captain. A man doesn't chew the
knuckle of his thumb with that kind of scowl otherwise.
I'd call me crazy, too. But Sirius is jockeying for hegemony—as are New Maine, Terra, and Zion. And, like
barbarians at the gates of Rome, the Arpeggians are always on the outside, seeking to cause whatever disruption
they can. There are also the anarchists from Gulag Sector
who would stir the pot just to see what boiled over.''

"But war?''

Archon sighed. "The interstellar situation isn't as stable as the news hacks would have you believe. For a long
time, Captain, the Confederacy has been bursting at the
seams. Government—even so limited a government as
the Confederacy—is anachronistic in space. The concept
of government evolved on Earth when resources were
limited in a closed system. It was the purpose of government to see to the redistribution of those resources, you
know that.''

"And in space, after the fall of the Soviet, the role of
government has been to see that markets are established
and to act as a forum for the exchange of information and
a center of communication. It's impossible to build em-
pires—especially with the independent stations floating
around. Planets can be controlled, sure, but not the independent stations,'' Sol countered. "That open re-

source base, and the incredible hugeness of space, make governmental control ridiculous!''

"Exactly," Archon agreed intently. "However, that will not stop some individuals from attempting such a mad scheme. The lesson of the World Soviet isn't all that clear anymore. People can tell you all about the Confederate revolution . . . but not why the Supreme Soviet failed.''

Sol lifted the glass, sipping. The pleasant taste rested easily on his tongue. "Why should I trust you?''

Archon chuckled—a soft ironic laugh from deep in his belly. "Because those are Kraal's orders. On the other hand—and more to the point—because my life and the life of my most precious possession, my daughter, rests in your hands.'' Eyes vacant, voice faint, he continued. "And, if I fail, nothing will matter anymore for anyone.''

"And there is a saboteur on my ship? Who? Of the people we've taken—''

"I really can't say there is . . . but given what's at stake—I wouldn't doubt it.''

"And you won't tell me what this's—''

"Not for the moment, Captain.'' Archon smiled humorlessly, a sadness in his eyes. "Let me assure you that we're playing games upon games in circles within circles. There are parties and factions within the government as well as outside the Confederacy who'd stop us.'' He emphasized that with a knobby fist. "Why else would Grand Master Kraal give me his finest new ship and his most skilled captain?''

"I'm not sure I'm . . .''

Archon's eyes veiled. "Perhaps. At the same time, you're the one I trust.''

"Oh?'' Sol stiffened, head cocked. *Damn him, who was he?*

"Be patient, Captain Carrasco.'' Archon got slowly to his feet. "I wanted to open a dialogue between us. Only by working closely, will we win. Between us, there can be no distrust beyond the obvious one of security. Should you need my services or advice, please, feel free to call on me.''

''That's all? We simply travel to Star's Rest and hope no one plants an antimatter device under the cushions in the lounge?''

''Isn't that enough to worry about for now?'' Archon asked. ''Good day, Captain.''

The white hatch slid shut behind him. Sol studied the amber liquid in his glass. ''Isn't that enough?'' he muttered. ''Who *is* he? *Boaz*, what do we have on this Speaker Archon?''

He stared at the bulkhead as she read the information.

''The current Speaker and founder of the colony at Star's Rest has his origins on Earth as a naval commander in the Terran Protection Force. He left the TPF at the age of twenty-five with the rank of Brevet Captain. From there, he bought several older class Soviet cargo vessels and refitted them for privateer work. During his career, he sold his services to the flags of Sirius, Range, Santa del Cielo, New Israel, New Maine, and Arpeggio. After service with the Arpeggian fleet he disappeared with his command for a period of seven standard years until he arrived five months ago, registered his colony of Star's Rest, and instituted trade and diplomatic relations.''

''And this Star's Rest? Do we have a planetological report?''

''Star's Rest falls within terrestrial parameters for CO_2 cycling, and atmosphere with 1.2 gravities at .93 AU from its primary—named, appropriately, 'Star.' The planet's axis is perpendicular to the ecliptic. A radioactively heated molten core is tectonically active and powered by two moons in concentric orbit. Planetary environment is A-5 on the Confederate planetological scale. Organic life consists of photosynthesizing plants, corresponding plant parasites, and invertebrates up to fifteen kilograms. No higher order phyla noted.''

''Any data on his government in the files?''

''His government is classed as A-3 in Brotherhood analysis and he apparently has a firm loyalty to the Confederacy. According to Brotherhood agents, he appears to be rather chauvinistic when Brotherhood activities are mentioned, although there is no currently known reason for his loyalty. His earliest support for Brotherhood policies was noted after his service with Santa del Cielo.''

"Arpeggio," Sol mused, stroking his chin. "I . . . Seven years ago? *My God! Of course! That's where . . .*"

Memories, like knives, slipped stingingly through his guts. Sol wilted into his chair, resistance sapped. He could place that face now, peering down from *Sword*'s main bridge monitor. He could almost hear the decompression klaxons wailing behind him, smell the acrid smoke from burning paint, wiring, and plastic, as Arpeggian guns raked him. In the background, a woman screamed that her leg had been blown off.

Archon's voice rapped through the speakers, "Captain, I must ask for your surrender. You've lost one ship, you do not need to—"

"Go to hell!" and he'd cut the connection, severing the link with that commanding voice and those predator's eyes, pouring every erg into acceleration. He'd borne down on an Arpeggian frigate, trying to ram her, slicing through her fields, allowing his guns to gut her. Immediately afterward, *Sword*'s shields failed and his weapons went dead as blaster bolts severed critical powerlead. But they'd broken free, riding a ballistic torch as systems failed, outrunning the Arpeggians, killing his own people as grav plates failed under the thirty-five g . . . *No, don't torture yourself with the memory.*

"And I cannibalized her," he gritted. "Killed my ship to save my crew." He forced pained eyes up, staring dully at the white panels overhead. "And now he's here? Why? I'm protecting the man *who murdered my ship and crew? WHY? GOD DAMN IT!*"

"Captain?" *Boaz* called. "Are you—"

"Ship, what are my options? Can I have him restricted to quarters? Arrested? What are—"

"Captain, by order of the Galactic Grand Master, Speaker Archon and his daughter have *unlimited* access to this vessel up to clearance code 0.01."

Sol stopped short, staring. "You can't be serious! The man ambushed *Sword!* Killed my—"

"Captain? Is this how you intend to command? Through emotional outbreaks?"

Sol froze, a clenched fist half-raised, *Boaz*'s words an acid eating through his fear and anger. Slowly, carefully, he filled his lungs, calming his charged muscles.

"No, ship," he said through a long exhale. He paced the confines of the cabin, mentally reeling. "I . . . Maybe I'm not ready for this command. Maybe I should have stuck to my guns when Kraal . . ." he cocked his head, staring nervously at the bulkheads. "Damn it! I'm not *well* yet!"

"Is it your wish to be relieved of command?"

Sol lifted his chin, eyes slitted thoughtfully. Was it? For a long moment, he stood, statuesque. So much at risk. Could he do it? Was he even still sane?

"I. . . ." And what the hell was Archon doing on his ship? With Brotherhood blessing no less? Surely Kraal had to know Archon's role in the destruction of *Sword* . . . in the loss of all those lives. So, whose side was Archon really playing?

And only two First Officers with no deep space experience could take his place. No Maybry Andaki waited to take the burden. No Fil Cerratanos sat on the bridge, ready to cover for Solomon Carrasco. No way out. The responsibility settled firmly on his shoulders.

He steeled himself, the words thick in his mouth. "I do *not* wish to be relieved of command. At the same time, ship, I realize my vulnerabilities. Someone will have to ride herd on my actions. I guess that falls to you through your psych program correlations."

Dazed by it all, he refilled the scotch glass to exactly a finger and settled in the conforming chair, kicking his feet up. His gut twisted like a wrung cloth.

"Captain. I'll be most happy to consider your actions."

Sol stared absently at the bulkhead, and shook his head. "The man who ambushed *Sword* . . . and now I have to take his orders?"

"Permission to make a suggestion?"

"Granted, ship."

"Actions do not always accurately reflect motive. Accessing the data and running comparative and correlation programs, it should be noted that Archon disappeared immediately after the incident with *Sword* over Arpeggio. Further, discreet inquiries as to the Speaker's location have been made over the years by Arpeggio. It doesn't take an algorithmic brain to deduce the Arpeggian incident might have been as painful to Archon as it was to you."

Sol grunted, lost in scenes from those final days on *Sword,* the ship's brain failing, men and women dead, some with eyes bugged out, fluids draining from their bodies from decompression, others a flat jelly-red paste impressed into deck plates where grav plates had failed. Happy's grim expression would be burned into his brain as they boosted, the reactor fizzing in and out, for a jump they had no guarantees of surviving.

"And I suppose you'd advise waiting for recriminations?"

"It would seem prudent—unless you question the Galactic Grand Master's judgment."

Damn. I'm tired.

Sol sipped the Star Mist, lips pursed. "Circles within circles? Then I'd better bootstrap myself up to some sort of command efficiency." A pause. "And who could be my saboteur?"

"I have insufficient data to make that determination, Captain."

He gestured in futility, happy to have something to engage his mind besides memories and cartwheeling confusion. "How, in the name of Shiva's seven heavens, am I supposed to find a bomb among all those diplomats? We couldn't even search their luggage under diplomatic seal. Pray tell, do I walk in at dinner and say 'Would the person who would like to blow up this ship and everyone aboard please hold up his hand?'"

"You could scan for explosive materials, Captain."

"I would if I . . ." Sol stared at the speaker. "You can do that?"

"Captain, I contain the most sophisticated programming and sensing ever built into a Brotherhood ship. If you wish, I will scan for explosive devices of the magnitude to do serious structural damage."

"Do it!"

Seconds passed.

Boaz startled him with, "There are no antimatter or conventional explosives in the quarters of the diplomats. Containment for any regular nuclear devices would register in the air conditioning and gravity plate monitors. Further, analysis of air samples—rudimentary at this stage—shows no polymer compounds from chemo-thermal devices or substances."

"So maybe there isn't a saboteur aboard?"

"I cannot rule that possibility out," *Boaz* replied, tone almost formal.

"I wonder if Archon was lying?" Sol stared at the white paneling over his head.

"According to his heartbeat, respiration, and perspiration, he was not. Galvanic skin responses seemed normal. At no time did I detect pupil dilation which would indicate stress associated with extreme prevarication. Further, I agree with his political assessment of Confederate stability. Any major event, discovery, or political blunder could easily precipitate intergovernmental violence."

Solomon Carrasco shook his head. "What other tricks do you have hidden in your gallium arsenide soul?"

"Tricks, Captain? I'm not sure I understand."

He chuckled and then went cold, a sudden memory of *Gage* winding out of his fatigued brain—almost a physical pain.

"Captain?" *Boaz* asked. "I detect severe emotional trauma."

"It's nothing. Just monitor the passengers and leave me to get some sleep, ship. If you detect anything suspicious, let me know. It seems you'll also have to learn to be a watchdog as well as a ship." He rubbed his eyes and shook his head. How long since he'd slept? Tossing off the last of the scotch, he rose and rearranged his quarters to fold out the bunk.

CHAPTER VIII

Tayash Niter tapped at the pressure door with his cane. "So? We go no farther."

Nikita growled and slapped his palm against the lock plate of the heavy hatch.

The speaker above repeated the monotonally irritating phrase, "I am sorry to inform you this a secured section of the ship. Ingress is not allowed except under special order of the captain."

"Think you can wear the speaker out?" Tayash jabbed his cane at the grillwork. "It's a new ship. I think you'll be here a while."

"Cunning Brotherhood conspirators!" Nikita grumbled. "So, that's it. We've taken all corridors, looked into all rooms. What you think? Is Brotherhood ship magic like legend? Or does this look like any other ship?"

Tayash lifted an antique shoulder. He sighed loudly. "I think it looks like any other ship I've ever seen." He stared speculatively at the heavy hatch. "But Nikita, I've been counting steps. The ship is over a kilometer long. We've missed seeing Weapons, the bridge, Engineering, Comm Central, and who know what else? Do you remember seeing an atmosphere plant? Hmm? Nor have we passed inspection crawlways. Seriously, we can travel from our cabins to the lounge to the observation blister and to the gymnasium. I think it's premature to say the mythology of Brotherhood ships being sentient is bunk."

"Um." Nikita glared at the hatch through slitted eyes. "To Gulagi, secret is challenge."

* * *

So far *Boaz* had performed above expectation for a new
ship. The grav plates in spectrometry module 4 had failed
through a computer glitch. Damage control had caught it
before the 20 g acceleration tore the telescope loose from
the mountings and sent it through the graphite fiber skin.
Meanwhile, gravity had been restored through all five of
the backup systems and crosschecked. Here and there
powerlead shorted under the decompression and refrigeration tests. But then, materials reacted differently at 3°
Kelvin under zero atmospheres. Better to find it now than
in a decompression emergency.

Sol slipped his coffee cup from the dispenser and
sipped at the hot liquid. Despite hopes, sleep had been
laced with one nightmare after another.

"Captain Carrasco?" At the tone in Bryana's voice,
Sol jerked his attention from the daily reports.

"Yes?"

"We have two vessels approaching at the edge of detector range." Her black eyes studied his, evaluating, as
her image filled the comm screen.

"Let's see. *Boaz,* tie in. Give me a projection."

On the monitor beside Bryana's face, a holographic
display demonstrated *Boaz*'s position and two dots of light
arcing to parallel her course on either side.

Sol pursed his lips while he thought.

"I don't suppose they could just be part of the usual
clutter around Arcturus?" Bryana asked.

Sol rubbed his brow, studying the vectors the bogeys
were establishing. "No. It looks like they're matching.
Hail them and see what you get."

Sol sipped his coffee, a curious burning in his stomach.

"No response, Captain." Bryana seemed to lose a little
color.

"Well, they know we know they're there." *Now what?
Is this another of the games? Some threat? Why won't
they respond?* A cold twist of premonition tickled his
spine. Tensing, he fought a flashback of the bogey closing

on *Gage*, originally a mere pinpoint of light as these were.

What can I do about it? They already have our vector. Outrun them? Turn and prepare to fight? I . . . Easy, Sol, you're jumpy. No, until you have proof they're hostile, let it be. You know they're there. That's the important thing. You're smart enough to be patient.

"First Officer, keep track of them. If they start to close, holler. Meanwhile, coordinate with Cal Fujiki and Engineer Anderson. If anything else breaks, inform me immediately."

She stared at him. "That's all?"

Sol blinked up at the monitor, worry sinking needle teeth in his gut. "Any suggestions, First Officer?"

She frowned for a half-second. "Well . . . I . . . We don't know they're hostile, do we? I mean . . . if . . ."

Sol exhaled. "I think you understand. Even if they're pirates bent on taking the ship, we've got to have evidence first."

"Pirates? Trying to take a Brotherhood ship? That's—"

"Ever heard of the *Enesco?*"

"Yes, sir." She looked up at her screens, chagrined, logging the conversation.

Sol grabbed up his coffee and stared at the screen after he'd terminated the connection with Bryana. Two ships?

"Boaz, do you have any ID on those vessels? Anything from spectral readings? Acceleration curves?"

"I can only ascertain they are running a standard Star Class IV hull with at least twenty percent augmented reaction and maneuverability."

"High performance. So they're most likely military?"

"Statistically that's the most probable assumption."

"Thank you, ship."

Uneasy, Sol stood, shutting down his systems. Coffee cup in hand, he walked, the soft soles of his boots whispering on the deck plates.

"Two ships that won't answer hailing are paralleling our course. Who? Who'd follow us out of Arcturus . . . and why?"

Unconsciously, his steps took him to one of the observation blisters. There, he stopped, legs braced as he sipped his coffee, staring out at the blackness and the hoary dusting of stars beyond. Somewhere out there, two ships followed. A cold shiver played through him, a biting ill wind of premonition. He closed his eyes, staggering, remembering Mbazi crying out, "Captain! We have a bogey!"

And Gage *died.*

"But this is supposed to be a time of peace. Why do ships have to travel armed? Why are people dying? Ships dying?"

* * *

Jordan's voice carried a slight accent, cultured: "Personally, I wonder at the Speaker's integrity."

Connie immediately bristled, head tilting to hear the conversation engaging the three men behind her. Quietly, she worked the dispenser on the bar, ignored as she filled her glass.

"Bah! I worry over everyone's integrity," Malakova insisted.

Fan Jordan, the Earl of Baspa, lifted his arms, staring up at Nikita. To Connie's practiced eye, Jordan might be termed an immaculate male specimen. Lightly built, he moved precisely. This evening he was dressed sportily in a desert tan carapace tunic, a white sash tied tightly at his waist. Light brown trousers, heavily creased, flared over his gleaming black boots. Not a single strand of his sandy hair looked mussed or out of place. The patrician features of his long nose, high cheeks, and thin mouth gave him a dashing appearance in contrast with the bluff Gulagi.

"He went straight to the Brotherhood," Fan insisted pointedly. "What does *that* tell you about his motives?"

Nikita Malakova had his arms—like number twenty powerlead—crossed on his massive chest, the tip of his ink-black beard dusting the tops of his forearms. "What does it tell me, eh, Earl? When I hear *you*—cousin to a bourgeois king, of all people—telling me to be suspicious of others, I wonder what you're up to? You know? Eh? You have knowledge of what this is all about? Then you tell me. Why are we here, in ship, headed to ends of space? We do what out here?''

"Come, come," Mark Lietov, the Sirian, added softly from where he stood at the third point of the triangle. "It's no doubt some silly conference President Palmiere thought up to curry favor for a vote."

Connie sipped quickly to keep from spilling her now overfilled glass and turned, seeing Malakova watching her. Black eyes flashed as he smiled in a dazzling display of large white teeth behind the full stygian bush of beard and mustache.

Lietov, Connie noted, stood with feet planted, dark eyes locked on Jordan in deep speculation. He wore a formfitting black jumpsuit with three thin lines of lime green laser light glowing diagonally across his breast. His skin like burnished bronze, Lietov's features had been branded by his flickering blue-white star. Crow's-feet gave his hatchet face a perpetual mocking squint. Now, as he listened, one hand covered his mouth as if to hide his expression. Otherwise, he looked perfectly in place, a predator in his own arena.

"You believe that? That this is junket to make us dance to his tune? Bah!" Malakova shook his head. "I think is more to this."

"Archon's done something to bend Palmiere to his will. Perhaps slipped a couple million credits into his palm to bring notice to his backward little planet. What's he after? Publicity to elicit investment? Some bizarre scheme to get suction toilets on his rock of a world? You know, he had quite a reputation as a pirate. This is no doubt another of his—"

"Would you care to elaborate on that, Mr. Lietov? You've got my entire attention." Connie kept her voice cool despite the actinic anger surging inside her.

Lietov shot a hard glance her way, a perfect smile immediately remodeling his lips. "My dear Constance, I didn't hear your stealthy approach." The smile grew more plastic. "I meant no discredit to your father. In fact, I and my government are more than anxious to help anyone improve their station in life. That's one of the credos of Sirius.'' He clasped his hands together before him, lowering his chin. ''But we, as all serious investors, must approach any endeavor with caution. Especially during these trying times.''

''Caution, Mr. Director? Indeed? I'm glad to know you're aware of the virtues of prudent action. I hope to see such behavior demonstrated in the future.'' She narrowed her eyes. ''And as a cautious man, I'm sure you don't want to alienate any parties . . . 'during these trying times.' '' She shot a heated glance around the circle, before adding, ''If you gentlemen will excuse me?''

She nodded, marching past, color rising in her cheeks at the rapacious look Jordan had given her. She'd monitored him, seeing the gleam of excitement in his hazel eyes, that glittering appraisal. Only Malakova had appreciated her as a person, a twinkle of enjoyment in his black eyes. And Lietov? A dangerous man.

The white-hot anger had settled to a smolder as she left the lounge, fury-generated adrenaline charging her muscles. Drink in hand, she paced the corridors, winding around the endless white hallways, thoughts in a storm.

''Connie?''

She looked back to see her father hesitating at an intersection.

Filling her lungs, she sighed, backtracking to where he stood, a worried look on his beetling features.

''I know that walk, Constance. Elbows stiff, knees tight, back straight, and head high. You're on the verge of throwing things. Something up?''

''The Sirian, Lietov, thinks we're greasing Palmiere's grubbing hands to trick investors into buying us suction toilets. Jordan accuses you of something unethical, while—''

Archon chuckled. ''Unethical? Me? Hell, yes! The goddamned politician swindlers! What do they—''

''Father!'' She glared at him. ''Damn it! You know what's at the end of this trip! I just . . . Well, I'm worried sick! One mistake . . . that's all it'll take. And you know what we'll let loose on humanity." She closed her eyes, stilling her roiled emotions. "I hate to think what would happen if someone like . . . like Lietov got control of . . ."

He grasped her hands in his, gently pressing her fingers. "I know, girl. I've seen the worry in your eyes. You've been right about most everything. I listen to you, I really do. Only I've had a feeling recently that we're on the right track. Call it—"

"I don't *trust* your feelings, Father." Pleading, she looked into his softening gray eyes. "It's not you. I mean I . . . Well, things that you . . . You've changed. That's it. Something about you just wasn't the same after standing next to that monstrous creature. Or was it the green-brown knob? You just didn't . . . well, you acted strange after that. You—"

"Paranoia, Constance?"

She shook her head, confused. "I don't think so. No. Though, God knows, we've every right to it."

He reached to smooth her hair, running a gentle knuckle along her cheek, his concern making her soul ache.

"Girl, trust me. Hey, here, look at me. There. That's better. Now, remember your old war-horse father? Hmm? Remember the times I've pulled triumph out of disaster? I don't intend on letting humanity down, girl. I've had a fleet of my own, each of the crew depending on me. Sometimes whole planets hanging in the balance. I didn't let them down, did I?"

She shook her head slowly. "No."

"Well, I won't let you or the Master down either." He winked, patted her, and added, "Cheer up, girl. I'm late for a meeting with the ambassador from Chouhoutien. What's his name?"

"Wan Yang Dow."

"That's him." Archon waved as he hurried away with a spacer's wide paced gait. "And don't forget dinner's in a half hour!"

Connie nodded, rubbing the back of her neck.

"Right." She stared after him until a curve in the passage hid him. "And why don't I feel any better?"

Unmollified, she continued along the long white hallway, hearing the soft murmurings of the ship around her. So large and clean, she'd never been aboard a vessel like *Boaz*. Knowing Archon's clearance, Engineer Anderson had taken them through this wonder work of Brotherhood ingenuity.

And it's made by HUMAN hands. It's safe . . . an artifact of our physics and realities—despite its advancements.

She rubbed nervous palms along her arms, massaging the cold skin. "Human made. God, how wonderful that is."

Connie turned, heading for the observation blister, stopping short when she saw the man, sick looking, bent over and braced, as if on the verge of collapse. Drugged? Grieving? He seemed pathetic. Viewed from an angle, the man's face looked pained, blanched by some internal horror.

He wore a captain's . . . *Blessed Gods, it's got to be him!*

Face twitching and contorting, he stared at the stars, hunched and trembling, mumbling, ". . . a time of peace. Why do ships have to travel armed? Why are people dying? Ships dying?"

Carefully, she called, "Captain Carrasco?"

He turned, obviously surprised that she could have come so close. The panic and pain in his face unnerved her. A quiver tugged at the corner of his mouth, his skin sallow around fear-fevered eyes.

"Constance, isn't it?"

"It is." She appraised him as he pulled himself together—a paste work of resolve. "Are . . . you all right?"

He stiffened the sag in his spine. "Yes, fine. Just lost in thought. If you'll excuse me, I'll leave you to the peace of the stars. I was just on my way to—"

"Captain? I . . ." *And we've bet everything on* him? *Kraal himself recommended against Carrasco. Only Father's obstinate insistence brought him here. Damn it, he's a mess! A psychological basket case! Kraal, you were right. If only I'd known, perhaps I could have done something, diluted Father's resolve.* Connie bit her lip. If worse came to worst, the command would devolve on her shoulders: Kraal's bargain for trust. Best learn the terrain now, test the waters before she was swimming for her life—and everything else.

"Wait. If you have a moment to spare." She raised an eyebrow, the gesture almost challenging.

He stopped short, off balance. "Yes?"

"I just thought perhaps we should talk, considering the circumstances." *Damn it, one wrong word and he could crater on me, fall into a whimpering pile. Christ, I've seen wounded kittens with more spirit. And he's the hero of Arpeggio? The savior of Moriah, Sword, and Gage? This is the man Happy Anderson dotes on?*

"Very well." For a moment, their eyes met. The depth, the vulnerability communicated in that one moment left her undone, wavering in her resolve.

"It's . . . I guess you'd say, an unusual situation."

Carrasco nodded, a warmth in his hesitant smile. "Would you like to speak in private or here?"

She considered. "Private might be better. No telling who might wander by." *Like Lietov . . . or Jordan.*

"My cabin?"

"That would be fine."

She followed silently, sneaking glances at his features as they walked through the corridors, past a security hatch. He stopped before an inset hatch. "Here's home. Don't expect too much."

He might have been a different man. He wore an expression of wry humor. Where his eyes had seemed pained and vulnerable, now they calculated and studied. A strength, well-grounded in the security of command, radiated from him. He palmed the lock plate and waved her into a neat room, half office with comm monitors displaying ship's stats. Report files lay in stacks on the desk, a monitor displaying a series of figures in green.

Neat, orderly, just what you'd expect of a competent captain's room. And he *had* changed during that walk

from the blister. Here, he looked at ease, scrutinizing
her, a thousand questions prickling under his controlled
expression.

Uneasily, Connie stared at him. *Who are you, Carrasco? The broken man I saw back there? Is this just a
false front? My God, he isn't schizophrenic, is he?*

He nodded at the holos, explaining, "I can keep an
eye on everything from here. The first monitor is the
reactor. The figures you see on the screen—"

"—indicate the stability of the stasis around the antimatter and the rate at which it's being fed into the
magno-gravitic bottle where the annihilation is turned
into reaction mass for thrust."

He laughed softly. "I guess I deserved that."

"I've captained my own vessels, Captain Carrasco. I
don't always advertise that fact. It tends to intimidate
men. How about you?"

He nodded thoughtfully. "As Archon's daughter, I
suppose you've spent a great deal of time around ships.
Please, sit down." He settled in a conforming chair,
leaning back and pulling up one knee. Head cocked, he
watched her as she took a seat.

"Tell me, that day off Arpeggio, were you shooting at
me, too?"

"I was there. You reacted before I could close and hole
your comm center." She stared back, meeting the hostility in his eyes, expression guarded. "It makes matters
easier now that you know."

"Why?" He leaned forward, a hard man demanding
answers. Passion burned, frightening in its intensity. Unconsciously, Connie tensed, ready to strike.

"My mother was held hostage on the planet. The orders came from Alhar that we were to take your ship.
Alhar is an old House on Arpeggio. They would rather
have captured your ship themselves—only their fleet was
en route from Sirius at the time. We'd been hired as a
backup cadre. House livery, if you will, while their
strength was employed elsewhere as political leverage."
She hesitated. "We had no choice in the matter. As it
was . . . my . . ." She stared blankly at the wall, unable

to finish. Unable to do anything else, she sipped the last of her scotch.

He leaned back, eyes closed, and sighed. "And now? You mean to take this ship from me, too?"

She opened her mouth to speak, and stopped, trying to put it all in perspective. "Star shine, I didn't know it would be this difficult."

"You want to explain that? And while you're at it, what's this mission about? Ferrying diplomats to Star's Rest? Uh-huh, and if I believe that, you've got a great deal on toron by the ton, huh?"

She bit her lip. "I think, Captain, that I'll leave the explanations to my father. No, don't point your finger at me like that. For now, I'll simply tell you that I don't have any designs on your ship." She chuckled softly, enjoying the moment, tapping her empty glass with a fingernail. "And if we live long enough, Captain, you'll see why."

The skeptical frown pleased her despite the confusion he'd caused her. This steely inquisitor couldn't be the same human wreckage she'd seen in the observation blister—only she knew better. Time to push.

"Captain Carrasco,"—she steepled her fingers—" in the event I could grant you the wish of ultimate power, what would you do with it?"

A handsome man, she decided as those hard brown eyes tried to bore their way into her very brain.

"Ultimate power? I'd bring back *Gage,* and *Sword,* and *Moriah,* and Mbazi, and Gwen Hanson, and Fil Cerratanos, and Maybry Andaki and all the rest of them."

She nodded. "And if it cost your soul?"

His eyes narrowed slightly and he fingered his chin. "So be it. My soul for Mbazi's or Cerratanos'? I'd pay that."

She stopped short, mulling that over. "All right, let's say the power isn't so ultimate you can raise the dead, but you can do anything—and I mean anything—with the universe as it is today. You can pay back anyone who hurt you, rearrange planets, win wars at your whim, see the guts of an atom, or an overview of the universe. Literally, the power of life and death, the power to change anything that exists . . . it's all at your fingertips—and no one can take it from you. In essence, you take the place of God. What do you do?''

"Why the game?"

"What if it isn't a game?"

His gentle laughter surprised her. "Can I conjure gold out of nothing? That's about as magical as any fairy tale."

"If you want." She stretched her legs out before her, setting the glass to one side and lacing her fingers across her belly as she waited.

Carrasco grunted, eyes losing focus. "To be honest, I can't answer your question right now. Given ultimate power, I'd restore those I lost as a result of injustice, or my own poor decisions. Otherwise, I'd have to consider all the ramifications. Learn the boundaries of this power that's ultimate but can't raise the dead."

"But you'd take it?"

He shrugged, hands spread. "Nothing comes free. What's this cost me?"

"Your soul. Humanity. Everything . . . nothing. You tell me."

"It's your game."

She smiled. "Is it?"

Carrasco's frown deepened. "Are we getting anywhere with this?"

"Farther than you know, Captain."

A light flashed on the comm.

"Go ahead, ship." Carrasco's eyes never left hers.

"You are scheduled to eat with the diplomats in five minutes, Captain," *Boaz* intoned.

"Thank you, ship." He paused, studying Connie through narrowed eyes, expression stoic. "I'll consider your game. In the remaining minutes, what can you tell me about this trip? Your father hints that a saboteur might be aboard. Do you have any thoughts concerning that?''

Clever, he'd changed the subject, thrown the ball into her court. "No, I do not. In fact, I believe I'd better run. I have to meet my father for dinner." She smiled. "If I'm not mistaken, we're even eating at your table."

"Won't talk, I take it?" Carrasco stood. "Then perhaps you wouldn't mind if I escorted you?"

"Not at all." She picked up her glass and walked out while he terminated some of the comm programs. In the corridor, she said, "Tell me. When I first saw you in the observation blister, you looked terrible."

He stiffened, leading the way down the corridor. "We all have our own devils to deal with, Deputy Speaker. I suppose if I pried deeply enough, I'd find yours, too."

She walked the rest of the way in silence, puzzling over the two faces of Solomon Carrasco she'd seen, worried about the first one, broken and reeling, muttering to himself of dying ships—terrified of the second who wouldn't play her game. A cool whisper of premonition drifted in the back of her mind.

CHAPTER IX

A sea of noise washed from the dining room at the end of the lounge. Men and women in gay colors stood in knots, gesturing and laughing as they talked animatedly with each other, reaching for drinks while heads bobbed earnestly.

Sol stopped, scanning the faces, trying to fix them in his mind.

"Ladies and gentlemen!" Connie's voice brought instant quiet. "May I present Solomon Carrasco, Captain of the Brotherhood ship *Boaz,* and our kind host for this journey!"

A sudden wave of applause greeted Sol as Constance led him into the room. He smiled and shook hands and was told a whole series of names and planets and titles, familiar from the list he'd seen earlier but still somewhat overwhelming.

Archon broke off his discussions with Wan Yang Dow. Chouhoutien's Representative, a thin waspish man, bowed politely. Sol met the Speaker's eyes, so familiar now. This man had killed his *Sword* . . . and so many of his crew . . . his friends. Revulsion mixed with curiosity.

The Speaker directed him to the head of the center table, resplendent with white linen cloths. Silver candelabras with inefficient wax candles and bejeweled eating utensils graced the tables in an almost barbaric display. Two of Gaitano's hands waited to serve, amused grins on their faces though they stood stiffly at attention. The diners took their places at the tables and turned their eyes to Sol. All conversation ceased.

Constance had taken the seat to his left while Archon had gone to his right. How in hell was he supposed to make small talk with the man who gutted *Sword?*

An ornate silver bell and striker sat beside Sol's plate, tools of formality he'd never had occasion to use. He lifted the bell and tinkled it with a resultant crystal ringing. Men and women promptly seated themselves amidst renewed chatter while Gaitano's "waiters" rushed forward in an organized advance worthy of Patrol marines.

"Speaker Archon? Several things have come up which need to be discussed. I suggest you and I have a talk as soon as the meal—"

"Oh, Captain?" A sickly sweet voice called from down the table. Irritated, Sol looked up, meeting the eyes of an attractive blonde. Athletic looking, she leaned forward anxiously. Her skin glowed with the flush of vigorous good health. He placed her in her late twenties— though a man couldn't know anymore unless he looked at a birth certificate. She wore the featureless gray pullover common to Mormon women. A hint of cunning power hid behind those blue eyes.

"Elvina Young, isn't it?" Sol matched her face with a name. According to the stats he'd reviewed, she'd recently married Joseph, the Mormon representative from Zion. Her husband sat next to her, slightly abashed, a washed-out looking fellow, tall, whip-thin with that apparent lack of personality common to religious fanatics of any persuasion. At the moment, he was tugging at an earlobe while he expounded on something to Stokovski, his other bony fist rapping the tabletop.

"Yes," she beamed at him. "How long will it take us in space? You see, I really *must* be in touch with the Temple. Oh, you have no idea how horrible it is not to be caught up on the news. Why Bishops and Deacons are constantly coming and going. You know—"

"I'll see what I can do," Sol told her, fighting to paste the appropriate grin on his face. "You know, we have communications equipment aboard. So long as time dilation doesn't—"

"So I can call? Oh, Captain, I'm so relieved, why, to be cut off out here away from all civilized—"

"We'll do our best." Sol gave her a smile like ice. Wait until they neared light speed. He hoped her Zionist friends had more patience than Elvina, relativity being what it was.

"I believe communications will be essential." Medea—the Vice Consul of Earth—sat across from the Youngs. Her petite body belied her power in the Terran government. Lustrous black hair accented an olive complexion and large, doelike eyes. She ate with practiced ease, hardly moving her mouth as she chewed, not a hair out of place. Beside her, her husband Texahi sat, bluff and affable, obviously enjoying himself, eyes straying surreptitiously to Connie's full breasts.

"Given the extraordinary nature of this expedition, communications with our governments will be imperative." Medea's lips bent in an ironic smile. "You have no idea how much that fact puts my mind at rest."

"*Boaz* extends her services to you, Madam Vice Consul." She seemed so . . . vulnerable. Could she really be as terrible as everyone said?

George Stokovski represented the actual body of the Confederacy and, along with several others, would report to the whole assembly at the conclusion of the meetings—or so Sol guessed. He and his wife, Ashara, were tall thin people and Sol could see the trouble they had with gravity despite the local distortion *Boaz* projected around them. Stations rarely maintained more than 0.5

gravities, with most dropping down to 0.2—just enough to keep the plants, stock animals, and dirt on the plating. The phenotype such environments produced barely managed the strain of being off their artificial worlds.

The long-limbed, sun-tanned brunette at the end of the table Sol remembered as Dee, the delegate from Range. Her husband, Arness owned a large ranch there. His numerous contracts for prime meat had led him to a fortune—marketing lean meats over the fat marbled kind grown in zero g pens on stations, or cloned in commercial vats. Literal fortunes were paid for gourmet meats off real animals. Arness had reaped the rewards. Since his retirement, he followed wherever Dee's duties took her. They wore conservative styles and earthy colors and their speech had that easy flowing sound so common to herders on the huge open world of grass and moss.

Across from Dee and Arness, sat Paul and Mary Ben Geller who held a diplomatic post from New Israel. The Israeli sun had burned them brown, leaving their features dark under kinky black hair, Mary looked around with flashing eyes and a quick smile. Paul showed signs of age, some gray creeping in along the temples. His movements, however, carried the fluid grace of a man in shape; his bearing marked him as having been military at some time. As they ate, Sol noticed that Ben Geller never stopped scanning—but he slowed significantly every time he spotted Norik Ngoro's tall form on the other side of the room.

"Captain? Oh, Captain?" Elvina's whiny voice broke Sol's concentration. "This is a new ship, I hear. Is . . . is it safe? You know how new things are. What if it breaks down out here?"

Sol bit his lip, attempting to be gracious. Joseph Young seemed to ignore her, continuing his diatribe with Stokovski.

"I assure you, *Boaz* will do just fine. She's the latest of our designs. Every improvement you could imagine has been incorporated."

"Well . . . could you tell me more? Like these shields? What if they go while we're jumping lights?"

"We'd pop back into normal space, ma'am. The shields build what's called a stasis around the ship, bend space-time. Without them, we're subject to the physical regulations of light speed."

"But doesn't that take a lot of power, Captain? Just how much do your shields put out?"

Sol paused, considering, aware that Archon and Connie hung on each word. "I'm sorry, ma'am. That's security information. Suffice it to say, the ship will get us to our destination and back. Without fail. I promise."

Her eyes held his for a brief instant of cerulean challenge before they went blank again. "But it could break—so what if it does?"

"It *won't!*" Suddenly everyone at the table was looking at Sol.

Elvina Young settled back in her seat. "Why, if you use that tone with it, it won't dare, will it?" Her eyes flashed defiantly, angrily, before dropping. Perhaps no one had ever chastised her that way? Sol turned to his soup, guts roiling, the weighty presence of Archon eating at his concentration.

As small talk picked up, Texahi's preoccupation with Constance provided no little amusement. Sol found his own interest piqued. Only she'd surprised him in the observation blister. No wonder that reserve awoke in her each time she looked at him. What in hell could she think?

And he had no proof she wasn't an enemy, despite her story about the Arpeggian incident. If only she didn't keep intruding on his thoughts. Thinking about it, he couldn't shake the memory of the way she walked, the sway of her hips, the cool poise of her body, the way her high breasts pressed at the fabric. He hadn't reacted to a woman in years. Now, he couldn't keep her serious blue eyes, or the light glinting fire in her hair out of his mind.

Texahi, on the point of drooling, finally drew Medea's attention. The deep poollike eyes flicked between Texahi and Constance, the Vice Consul's face stiffening. Texahi jumped, as if from a hidden kick. The man swallowed, face turning ashen despite his dark features. For a single brief instant, Medea's expression hardened, then the evil promise vanished.

Texahi stood unsteadily. "I . . . if you would excuse me?" And he fled.

Constance had missed it all, talking innocently with Ashara. Elvina, on the other hand, along with Paul Ben Geller now turned their attention elsewhere before Medea could notice. But the smile on Elvina's lips appeared a satisfied one.

Joseph Young continued haranguing Stokowski about Confederacy policy toward the frontiers and why they didn't allow Mormon missionaries free access to the independent stations. Sol swallowed a smile; in the early days, too many of the tailored-suited young men ended up breathing vacuum.

As if sensing the embarrassment she'd created, Medea lifted a penciled eyebrow and began quizzing Archon about Star's Rest. Sol listened, hearing only statistical data he'd already reviewed.

Connie looked at him over a morsel of butter-glazed lobster neatly impaled on her fork. "Does *Boaz* seem to handle as well as your other ships?"

Sol smiled thinly, feeling the pang in his chest. "I don't know. Ships . . . and those who space them . . . need time to work into each other—to know their quirks and idiosyncrasies. I've been aboard for less than ten hours. I haven't even had time to look her over."

"She'll be a fine vessel," Archon added, turning, jaw working as he masticated a thick piece of steak. "Considering the skill and talent of the Brotherhood engineers, I'll bet she'll perform flawlessly."

"I hope so."

"If you have a moment, I'd love to see your bridge. There's no feeling in the universe like—"

"Connie," Archon chided. "You must excuse my daughter, Captain. I fear she has too much tomboy in her. She's grown up in ships—had her own command—and I fear she'll never stand her new role in the government of Star's Rest. Too much wanderlust in her blood."

Sol studied her curiously. She couldn't be over twenty-five. Or could she? He noted her fine bones, marking the absence of wrinkles around her eyes. A faint spattering of freckles lay under that translucent skin. Her complexion and the shimmering turquoise dress she wore set that red-gold hair off like fire and ice. He liked the honest way she looked back at him, head canted slightly to one side.

She smiled, a saucy light behind her eyes. "Maybe I should explain. When my father is dirtside, I'm acting admiral of the Star's Rest fleet. We have six ships, none of them a *Boaz*—or even a Brotherhood transport, for that matter—but it's a strong little fleet to keep us free of pirates, raiders, or any outside interference."

"Pirates?" Elvina Young muttered, eyes wide. Did the damn woman hear everything? "We're not going where there are pirates? Joseph, you never told me that!"

Her husband smiled blandly at her, limply patting one of her hands, and resumed his conversation with George Stokovski.

"I sincerely doubt there will be pirates," Archon confided with a reassuring smile. "And believe me, I've seen the specs on this ship. Having commanded fighting vessels, I'd say *Boaz* could stand against a fleet of six ordinary ships."

Elvina's eyes seemed to narrow.

Archon raised a hand, smiling warmly. "Mrs. Young, you must understand, my planet is beyond the borders policed by the Patrol. We're responsible for our own defense out beyond the Frontier, a problem Zion hasn't faced since the Soviet days."

Constance added, "If we do find pirates, I'm sure *Boaz* would be a match for them. The Captain himself has a considerable reputation as a combat commander."

Sol looked at his plate, appetite vanished.

"Combat!" Elvina echoed. "My word! Where did you engage in combat, Captain Carrasco?"

"Oh, it wasn't much of anything," Sol smiled weakly, pricked by memories going back to Arpeggio and the flaring of ships . . . to Tygee and its red-blue flickering binary—and a black bogey diving out of nowhere to rake *Gage*.

"Do tell me!" Elvina leaned forward, eyes rapt. As the color rose in her cheeks, Sol realized just what a beautiful woman she could be were it not for her closely cut hair and that hideous Mormon dress. For the moment, she shed the drabness, a vibrancy about her. Her eyes locked with his, sensual—magnetic with promise.

"Perhaps some other time?" He withdrew lamely, suddenly uneasy. A faint smile bent her lips, and she nodded, as if to herself.

Misha Gaitano's deckhands cleared the plates away with elan if not style. A series of toasts made the rounds from Sol and *Boaz* to the Confederacy and then to each of the political factions represented.

Sol approached Archon as he stood. "Speaker, if you could . . ."

"Captain!" Elvina's arm snaked around his, pulling him back. He stared down into her eyes, irritated, aware of her full breasts pushed against the muscles of his arm. "I simply must hear more about your combat! Why, to actually hear from a man who's faced death so, and to be under his protection . . . why, nothing so exciting has ever happened to me before."

"Please, Mrs. Young . . ." Sol untangled his arm, seeing Archon disappearing with Norik Ngoro. Damn it!

"But I must hear of your adventures, Captain. Why don't we go someplace quiet and—"

"Excuse me. I must speak with my First Officer." He smiled grimly, pulling out of her grip, and caught up with Arturian, practically sighing in relief at having left her behind. "Anything new on those ships?"

The First Officer shrugged, "From Doppler, they're putting out almost thirty gravities to catch up. It won't take them long."

"Any ID on them from long-range telemetry?"

"No, Captain." Art's tone was neutral. "We could pour the coals on and outrun them."

Sol nodded. "I've thought about that. At the same time, can we really? Archon may have a security seal on the final destination, but how many sightings would it take before those two ships pinned our vector? Once they did so, how many planets are in the direction we're going? Only one, First Officer."

Art's eyes didn't betray his feelings. "So we just let them follow?"

Sol took a deep breath. "Any other ideas? They haven't proven hostile yet and I've learned that Archon has his own fleet. Maybe they're outriders to make sure we don't get surprised? I'm going to latch onto him as soon as I can. Maybe he knows who they are."

Art stared, green eyes cool, biting his tongue.

A big, burly, bearded man nodded as he walked up, cutting off further conversation. "Greetings, Captain Carrasco and First Officer Arturian. I have come to compliment you on marvelous ship, built with the sweat and blood of downtrodden masses!"

Sol smiled faintly, trying to link a name with the big rawboned man. Sharp black eyes stared at him from either side of a hawklike nose. Long black hair, braided into a ponytail, merged into a jutting black beard. The meaty arms and legs moved a little slowly in the gravity, indicating a station-born man. A sharp challenge lay behind the burning eyes, as if he expected a reaction from Sol.

"Captain, this is Nikita Malakova, Sector Representative from Gulag," Art filled in.

Gulag? Where else could a saboteur be found but in that rat's nest of dissidents, anarchists, terrorists, rabble-rousers, and demonstrators? "Welcome to *Boaz*, Mr. Representative." Sol bowed.

"Bah!" Malakova spread his arms in disgust. "Call me Nikita. In home station of Malakova, we do not use titles. They separate family of man from itself. Now, here I am in lair of decadent and cunning Brotherhood. I intend to learn you and see what makes you tick! I want to see with my own eyes and hear with my ears, how you defend the actions of your terrorist, tyrannical leaders. You have defense?"

Sol stared blankly. "My terrorist, tyrannical . . . Defense? I . . . uh . . . no. No defense. But then, no one has ever approached me quite like that . . . and to tell you the truth, I've never given it much thought.''

"Ah-hah!" Malakova pointed a thick finger at Sol's chest, black eyes glowing with triumph, "That is very spirit of Tyranny! Keep people from thinking. Turn them into simple reacting machines to do bidding of power elite! Where, then, do you seek freedom of man? Eh? Where in such sewage does human spirit thrive and grow?"

"Well, I—"

"Bombastic rhetoric. I see the knight of the benighted has cornered you, Captain. My most sincere sympathies."

Sol turned to see Fan Jordan approaching, long light brown hair in exquisite coiffeur. The hazel eyes pinned the blustering Nikita Malakova with an amused loathing. "You assume ordinary people can think? Perhaps they can—about food, drink, and simple copulation. But more, shall we say . . . abstract thoughts seem to elude them beyond their next paychecks and what they can put on their tables immediately."

Malakova's eyes narrowed. "Of course they think, Jordan. What else sets man apart from other animals? What overthrew corrupt black-hearted Soviet, and set man free among the stars? It was will of enlightened men to face despotism!"

"It was rabble incited by emotional pundits like you who happened to be clever with slogans," Jordan said, stifling a yawn. "I'm sure the officers here have better things to do than listen to your babble." Jordan turned to Sol. "Please, Captain, do drop by my quarters. I have some excellent refreshments which are the legacy of the well born." He smiled sweetly at Malakova—now turning a deep shade of red—and passed on, muscular body moving easily.

"I would break his royal neck!" Malakova exploded, jaw working under the bushy black beard, midnight eyes sparking. Molars ground audibly.

"Royal?"

Art supplied, "He's somewhere in line for the throne of New Maine. Some cousin to the king . . . or some such thing." Art paused, green eyes cool. "I've had rather a tough time putting up with him. He's at my table. Not only that, he keeps complaining his quarters aren't sufficiently large. At times, I've thought of spacing him."

"Subdue your passions," Sol reminded, a gentle smile on his lips.

"What is this?" Malakova asked.

"Brotherhood teaching." Sol gestured. "One of the *mantras* of the philosophy."

"Bah! Brotherhood brainwashing to keep you devoted to purpose of crushing human spirit!" Malakova rocked up and down on his toes, arms behind his back as he glared at Jordan's retreating form.

Mark Lietov, the Sirian Ambassador, disengaged himself from the group clustered around Archon and walked over, the thin bloodless smile that seemed to be the trademark of diplomacy on his narrow face. As Sol watched him coming, he couldn't help but dislike the man. The long, pointed chin and close cropped black hair gave Lietov a feline look.

"My pleasure to have met you at last, Captain." He flashed Sol a quick smile. "Your reputation precedes you. It was with pleasure that those of us who follow the frontier heard of your decision to come back to the service."

Sol shrugged, distinctly uncomfortable. "I wasn't aware anyone cared."

Lietov's voice smoothed like oil on water. "Oh, but we do, Captain. Don't you agree that the future of the Confederacy lies beyond? Explorations such as yours have advanced the sphere of humanity far beyond the pall of our understanding. You are the Neil Armstrong, the Dick Skobee, the Metronov, and the Grashinski of our times."

Art interrupted. "Captain, if you'll excuse me. I had better return to my duties."

Lietov replied before Sol could get a word in edgewise, "Why, First Officer, you, too, are a splendid example of that courage on which those of us left to our muddly little planets and our confined stations must rely."

"Don't worry about it, Art," Sol interjected. "I'd be happy to see to that software glitch. Probably some simple missed command." He turned to leave.

"We talk later, Captain!" Nikita Malakova called out in a booming voice. "You and me, man to man, we will talk of this Brotherhood of yours and I will find whether your loyalties lie with your duty and philosophy, or with suffering masses of men and women laboring to fill pockets of social bloodsuckers like Lietov!"

Lietov's smile froze, eyes, like ice, turning to Malakova.

"Captain," Art called, voice a couple of decibels too loud in order to compete with Malakova. "I already have the program worked out."

"If you will excuse us both, Ambassador Lietov." Sol snagged his first officer's arm and escaped, feeling eerily certain the grin Lietov gave him had to be an ill omen.

"Where'd they dig up Malakova? And Lietov? Quite a back pounder, eh? I wonder what he wants?"

Art's eyes flared. "I wouldn't know. I'm not up on these sorts of games."

"Wish I weren't either," Sol gritted. "I feel like a caged rat."

"Yes, sir." Art's voice remained stiffly formal as they entered one of the long white corridors which would take them forward to the bridge.

Sol turned, coming to a stop. "First Officer, is there something under your skin? If there is, let's get it out now. If I have to work with you day in and day out, I want it to be a smooth functioning relationship. If everything I say is going to raise your hackles, we'll be butting heads someday when we should be thinking our way out of a mess."

Art stiffened, thick beard quivering as he turned to Sol. "It's *nothing*, sir."

Sol shook his head. "I think it's *something*, Arturian. You and Bryana have been chafing from the moment I walked aboard. Any perception you have, from your beliefs as to my fitness to command all the way down to the color of my coffee cup, are my concern insofar as they can affect the way this ship is run. If you or Bryana have a beef, you tell me.''

Art's lips pursed bloodlessly, eyes boring into Sol's, dislike evident. Still Arturian held his tongue.

''Look, I'm not a spit-and-polish short-haul martinet.'' Sol searched for any sign of understanding. ''I don't run a ship according to protocol or the book. You don't have to like me. You don't even have to respect me as a human being . . . but you do have to work with me day in and day out. Now, I don't know what this business is all about, but we don't have that long to get this ship into fighting trim. Do you understand what I'm trying to get across?''

Art's expression hadn't thawed. ''Yes, sir. Begging the Captain's pardon, sir, but you don't seem to have your heart in this command.''

So there it was, laid out nice and neat. Sol took a deep breath, jaws clamped. He looked Arturian up and down, weighing this bright young man who had the backbone to glare back.

''Perhaps not, First Officer.'' His breath left him slowly, taking some of the tension with it. ''Nevertheless, we're in it together and I don't think you or Bryana have your hearts in it either.'' He bit his lip. ''Command cannot be a democracy, but if you ever have a question— and we have time to discuss it—let's hash it out. I don't have all the answers. But then, I'm willing to bet you don't either.''

''Yes, sir!'' Art agreed, snapping out a salute. ''Permission to be excused, sir.''

Sol bit off a sigh. ''You were never called to order in the first place. Get out of here.'' He felt a sinking sensation—the kid hadn't listened to a thing he'd said.

* * *

Connie watched Carrasco and his First Officer disappear into a side corridor, an odd mix of feelings stirring within her. Solomon Carrasco confused her. So fragile he'd looked about to burst into tears in the observation blister, he'd come off as a hard capable commander in his quarters. How could she tell which aspect of his personality dominated? How far could he be trusted? And why had that vulnerable expression of his touched her so? As her father had said back on Frontier—as if the soul could be touched.

"Connie?" Archon's arm slipped into hers. "I'd like you to meet Norik Ngoro, our representative from Ambrose Sector."

She smiled and looked up into the most absorbing eyes she'd ever encountered. Ngoro's gaze seemed to extend into her very soul, as if prying away the layers of her personality to stare at the naked essence of her being. Teetering between feelings of violation and reassurance, she breathed a little easier when he dropped his gaze.

"My pleasure, Constance." He spoke slowly, voice a deep bass that almost thrummed. "It appears you are held in highest esteem for good reason. You have taken a great responsibility onto your shoulders. Accepting such a duty so honestly is a noble action."

"Why . . . thank you." Connie shot a quick glance at her father.

"However, I must warn you, to worry so much is not beneficial to good health. Doing so, you charge the blood with lipids, steroids, and hormones. Blood sugars rise. Your body tenses in a constant state of excitement and alertness. The resultant strain on the circulatory and digestive systems is disadvantageous for prolonged health."

Connie nodded slightly.

"Representative Ngoro is a Truth Sayer in his native station." Archon tightened his grip on her arm reassuringly. He's been sent by his government to see to their interests in our current endeavor."

She hesitated, uncertain. "And how is that?"

"By ascertaining who speaks truth . . . and who dissembles, Constance," Ngoro added in his soft voice. "It came to my government's attention that whatever your secret, a man of my powers might be of service."

"I still don't—"

"Ngoro has the ability to pick up truth or falsehood,"
Archon explained. He shifted his attention to Ngoro.
"Any studies done on that?"

Ngoro smiled, gaze drifting absently as though focused
someplace beyond the bulkheads. "Brains work in curious fashions. Thought, as we know it, is a combination
of electrical and chemical activities. MAP proteins are
arranged in certain patterns for memory. Neurons fire in
random patterns, based on probability in chaotic configurations; hence, thought takes on a variable and adaptive
quality which allows innovation and experimentation in
problem solving. At the same time, the body reacts,
emitting certain reflections of the process. From the studies, I'm sensitive to those physical reflections of thought.

"In social mythology, human beings are supposed to
have an aura, an expression of the soul. Indeed, all people do exude a halo of electromagnetic energy. They also
radiate in the infrared. When in an emotional state, that
radiation changes, as does the electromagnetic field. Respiration, pupil dilation, muscular activity, all reflect the
inner environment of a human being." Ngoro smiled.
"Fortunately, I can't read minds as the rumors suggest.
To do so would be a terrible condemnation."

Connie shifted. "It would?"

"Of course. Consider the billions of thoughts you
would encounter. Thinking, despite the perceptions, is a
terribly violent act. The thoughts we formulate are statistical probabilities assembled out of a warring confla-
gration of neurons. To receive that unfiltered would be
devastating to one's own mind—a projection of confusion."

Connie nodded agreement. "I think I can imagine."

Ngoro smiled benignly. "I'm sure you can. It's all part
of the quanta of the mind—God's fingerprint on the universe, if you will."

"Bah! There you are!" a brash voice exploded behind
her. She turned to see Nikita Malakova reaching a ham-
like hand to shake Ngoro's. "If I did not come over, you
would know I was avoiding you. Is problem you have,
Norik. Reading men's minds doesn't allow socially ac-

ceptable deception to be employed in name of politeness. Is good thing you don't have pretty wife. You would have assassinated me years ago for deliciously lecherous thoughts.''

Ngoro smiled serenely. ''Nikita. It's been a long time.''

''Indeed.'' Malakova ran appreciative eyes over Connie, adding, ''You are here with beautiful woman, so I decide is safe to come talk. When you read my mind, all the lies are hidden behind rapturous love of ravishing beauty.''

Ngoro shook his head. ''You haven't changed. You still enjoy making up fabrications of reality to hide your true self. Are you still lying about your wives, Nikita?''

''I . . . er . . . uh . . . Tell me. You do not get many invitations to parties, receptions, or social galas, do you, Norik?''

''No, Nikita. Is that important?''

''I . . . No. Is not important. But provides trivial bit of data for edification of beautiful woman.'' Nikita reached for Connie's hand, kissing it gently, thick beard tickling. ''Allow me to introduce myself. I am Nikita Malakova, earnest Representative of Gulag Sector.''

Connie bowed slightly. ''My pleasure, Representative Malakova. And may I present my father, Archon, Speaker of Star's Rest.''

''Delighted.'' Malakova buried Archon's thick hand in a friendly grip. ''Is pleasure to meet centerpiece of perplexing puzzle which brings so many shadowy figures into light. Good, perhaps you can tell me what big mystery is. What great secret of Star's Rest will do for working billions who sweat and labor to keep human kind expanding to stars.''

Archon chuckled. ''The rumors of your bluntness have been greatly misleading.''

''Perhaps.'' Malakova laughed from deep in his belly. ''But I smelled something on Arcturus. Besides, any chance to get away from bourgeois lying politicians and enjoy junket with beautiful woman is worthwhile, eh?'' He turned to Connie. ''Perhaps you would take time to drop by my cabin for in-depth discussions on trade between Star's Rest and Gulag—''

"Nikita?" Ngoro warned.

"I . . . uh . . . Very well. Perhaps I might have meant it would be nice to have social occasion. Feel free to bring Speaker Archon with you as honored—''

"Nikita?" Ngoro raised an eyebrow.

"Bah!" The big man glared at his tormentor. "What? You think I am some sort of lecherous fiend interested only in taking advantage of beautiful woman for personal satisfaction?"

"No."

"Bah! See!" Nikita winked at Connie.

"I think you are more complex than that. Personal satisfaction has little to do with the way you'd take advantage of—''

"Norik?"

"Yes?"

"Perhaps is time you went to stare over Lietov's shoulder, hmm? Not only that, but I thought I saw Amahara looking for you earlier. In other words—since you see sordid lie in that—is time for you to leave."

"A pleasure to have met you, Constance." Norik smiled, still focused on some distance point. As he walked away, he added over his shoulder, "Last time Nikita and I met, he claimed I had no sense of humor."

CHAPTER X

Sabot Sellers spun in his command chair, watching through his bridge screens as brilliant streaks of light lanced vacuum. *Hunter* and the rest of his fleet spaced for jump. Black daggers, they rose on shining blue-silver shafts of reaction mass, the finest of Arpeggio's fighting machines, stripped now but for the basics. Each as deadly as the flat black heat-shielding paint suggested. Predators of the darkness, such ships had given Arpeggio the power and clout she now justly claimed. No Confederate power would dare pay the cost to destroy her.

Around him, *Hunter* hummed, the familiar vibrations and noises of the ship soothing. His command chair sat at the back of the horseshoe-shaped bridge. At other points, officers bent over their duty stations, keeping track of reaction, navcomm and scanning. Exposed to full view, the overhead screens glowed, displaying ship's status and nav information.

"Admiral?" the comm officer called. "We've got subspace from House Alhar."

Sellers nodded. "Put it on my arm screen. Audio through my headset only."

The cathode beside his left hand glowed to life; Alhar's withered face filled the screen. "Admiral Sellers, we've received word that Sirius and New Maine are involving their own forces. How much they suspect remains to be seen. I have reviewed the intelligence supplied by your Arcturian operative." A slight pause. "I would not like to believe that her information is incomplete. Nor would I cast aspersions on her abilities; however, I seriously suspect more is at hand than your report indicates. I will assume your errors of omission do not reflect upon your loyalties. I will assume you have security reasons. To assume anything else . . . well, it would bring unpleasantness we could ill afford since the Great Houses have provided your fleet. Further, the officers we've loaned you might take a dim view of treason.

"On a more positive note, our Sirian sources have become very polite . . . and even less informative. Such behavior from our trusted Sirian allies leads me to be suspicious. At the same time, Sabot, you yourself are at the doorway to greatness. It would pain all the Great Houses if you failed to act with discretion.

"We look forward to your observations on the above matters."

The holo flickered off.

"So, they're suspicious." He chuckled humorlessly. "Security? Indeed. If they only knew just what was at stake, even they would shudder.'' Louder, he called, ''Comm! Message to House Alhar.'' Sellers waited until the light on the pickup flickered to life. ''Lord Alhar, I have received and understand your message. Thank you for the insight into the Sirian situation. Please be aware that I fully appreciate the power and resources of the Great Houses. I assure you, I will do nothing to jeopardize my position. My only goal is to further Arpeggian power and influence.

''Concerning your allegations about my intelligence report, could you be more specific as to where you believe deficiencies lie?'' He looked over at the comm officer. ''Send it.''

''Yes, sir. Sent.''

There, that would buy him a little more time. Relativity being what it was, the old man might have even died while Sabot detailed his message. The effect worsened, of course, as *Hunter* neared the speed of light. But then, by the time they prepared for the jump, he should have heard something from *Boaz*. Indeed, it paid to have talent you could trust. Talent you knew wouldn't double on you. Besides, he'd heard from his agents in Arcturus, knew that everything had gone according to plan. House Sellers rode *Boaz*—and, who knew, by the time it all came to a conclusion, perhaps *Boaz*, with all her secrets, would be his.

And Solomon Carrasco? Reports indicated he was a broken man.

''As I smashed your *Gage*, Carrasco, so shall I take your *Boaz*.''

* * *

The tall man slipped quietly through the hatch, walking stealthily up the long corridors. He hesitated, looked carefully around, then furtively palmed the security hatch. As the hatch slid back, he stepped into the personal quarters section reserved for the Council Representatives. He counted hatches and stopped before the one he wanted.

"*Boaz*, open the hatch."

"I must inform you that the quarters you're about to enter are restricted under diplomatic—"

"*Boaz*, access file fifteen twelve one. I said, open the hatch."

Before him, the heavy portal slid sideways.

Inside the room, he slipped an instrument from his belt pouch, flipping the toggle on the side to study the readout. Moving with catlike grace, he checked the room and ran his instrument along each of the walls. A red digital display flickered with rapidly changing numbers.

He stepped into the sleeping quarters, working his way around the rumpled bedding, watching the readout. He grunted, bent down, and lifted a pair of black tubes from a personal kit stowed neatly beside the bed. A faint, sweet odor lingered in the air.

He laid the black tubes on the bedding, pulling a second scanner from his pouch. He centered the device by means of the viewfinder before it clicked softly through several exposures.

With deft fingers he replaced the tubes exactly where they had been, retraced his steps to the corridor hatch and—checking first—slipped into the hall, padding silently back the way he'd come.

* * *

Archon's hatch snicked quietly closed behind Sol and he found himself in a stark three-room cabin, everything neatly stowed, nothing out of place. The room was that of a long-time spacer all the way down to the pressure suit, gloves, and helmet ring hung ready to don in an emergency. Archon had not been idly boasting about his spacing abilities.

"Captain," Archon walked out to greet him. "Come, tell me to what good fortune I owe this visit." The Speaker led him into the rear compartment where several stacks of documents and memo crystals had been neatly ordered on a tightly made bunk. On the other side, Connie appeared to be buried under a mountain of tapes, holocubes, and old-fashioned papers. She glanced up, that ever-present reservation in those cobalt-blue eyes. He nodded to her, aware again of her aloof beauty as she pulled a long red strand back behind her ear. Why did she take his breath away like that?

She wore a snug-fitting two-piece yellow and black outfit that accented her lithe body. Sol couldn't help thinking of a tigress. The look she gave him augmented the feeling.

"Looks like work," he said, more to her than Archon.

"What can I do for you, Captain?" Archon asked as he pulled at his grizzly beard, a twitch of a smile visible beneath his mustache. The twinkle in his eye indicated he enjoyed the effect his daughter had on men.

"Ship's business." Sol forced himself to concentrate on the Speaker. He hesitated.

"Anything you have to say may be said before my daughter. She and I have no secrets regarding the present state of affairs. In fact, should I be unable to fulfill my duties, you will act under her authority as Speaker."

"Very well, you should know then that sensors have picked up two ships accelerating out of Arcturus—evidently trying to match vector with our course."

Archon nodded faintly. "The scent of blood draws the pack."

"You wouldn't know who they might be?"

Archon shook his head slowly. "No, they could be anyone from the opposition parties . . . or even the friendlies, for that matter. Sirius, Arpeggio, Terra . . . who knows? I'm only surprised they organized so quickly. Somewhere in the Confederacy there has been a leak of major proportions."

"President Palmiere," Constance growled. "I told you at the time I didn't trust him. He's a power monger . . . and we told him everything."

"We *had* to tell him. Without the Confederacy we'd have nothing!" Archon's voice held a note of desperation. "I . . . Never mind, we've had this conversation before." Lowering himself into a chair, he looked up at Sol. "Maybe I'm getting old. I see things differently.

Connie says I changed on Star's Rest. Changed after we found . . . Well, I don't know." He smiled slyly. "Perhaps it's the juices of youth that make her think she can lick the universe single-handed."

"Or perhaps I'm just too cautious. While we're at it, Father, isn't this a time to exercise a little caution of our own?" She raised an eyebrow, glancing pointedly at Sol.

"Please, don't stop on my account," Sol prodded. "It's starting to sound interesting."

Archon shrugged, hands out. "Yes, girl, you're right. All in good time, Captain. I am already surprised at your forbearance in an untenable situation."

"Considering that you destroyed *Sword* over Arpeggio . . . so am I."

"Yes, Connie said you'd made that connection." He smiled wistfully, the memory of an old hurt in his eyes. "I learned a valuable lesson above Arpeggio, Captain. I'd never realized . . . Well, the blinders came off. You might say, I grew up that day. Somewhere along the line, we all have to pay a price for our lives . . . for our actions. I paid that day. Doing something I knew . . . *knew* deep down inside . . . was wrong. I paid so very, very dearly for it."

"So did *Sword* and thirty of my friends and companions, Speaker. But I didn't come to beg an explanation. I've got my orders from the Galactic Grand Master, and I'll follow them. Right now, my concern hinges on those two ships racing after us. Who are they?"

Archon stiffened. "I don't know."

"Are they dangerous?"

He shook his head slowly. "Honestly, Captain, I can't tell you. Have you asked them?"

"They refuse to answer a hailing."

Connie's cool voice interrupted from the side. "I think their actions speak for themselves."

"Yes, I suppose they do." Sol turned on his heel. "Thank you for your cooperation, Speaker."

Sol felt a churning sensation in his gut as the hatch slid shut behind him.

* * *

Tayash Niter slouched in the gravchair, sipping Arcturian single malt, his long shiny black cane propped before him. His withered features reminded Nikita of a sucked orange. The deep lines around Niter's face made him look gnomish. As a result, people tended to forget themselves, say things they considered too deep for the tottering ancient. Those who underestimated Tayash always came to regret it later.

They sat in a corner where they could observe the lounge, a full wall holo of the Mysterian swamps blowing foggy and forbidding on one wall with svee moss hanging from the weirdly-shaped plants the settlers naively called "trees."

"You've uncovered the secret behind this voyage?"

"Not yet." Nikita frowned at the overhead panels. "Is something big. Notice how Lietov talks all around final destination, but never about it? I must give credit to fellow political scum, they tiptoe on edges of real issue with fancy feet. Perhaps is social adaptation in human political animal, hmm? Say everything so anyone can read any meaning into it they wish?"

"I bet it's got something to do with toron. That or hyperconductors. Name two more precious resources in all of space? Archon's found a bunch of the stuff. Enough to tip the balance of power. That's what it is. It's got to be. Nothing else could spark the political firepower we've got aboard."

"You call Joseph Young political firepower?"

"Well, maybe not, but I don't call Medea a silly virgin either. Or Lietov, for that matter, or Jordan. And Mikhi Hitavia and Geller aren't pushovers in anyone's book."

"Then why bring in Brotherhood?"

"Who controls most of the manufacturing and mining rights? Who discovered most of the mineral reserves in the Confederacy and who licenses them to various planets?"

They sat silently for a while, lost in thought.

"No. Is something dangerous. Capable of tipping balance of power. Toron, for all its value, would simply be matter of licensing," Nikita decided.

"And this Captain? This Carrasco?"

Nikita lifted a slab of shoulder. "I don't know. So far, he seems to be honest man."

"Hah!" Tayash jabbed at the air with his cane. "One honest man among a writhing mass of social maggots!"

"Who you call social maggot?"

"What's a politician?"

"You call *me* a social maggot?"

"You're here living off your constituent stations, aren't you? Who pays for all those fancy Arcturian whores you wine and dine every time you get a chance? Who rents your apartment? Pays the chit on your meals?"

Nikita shuffled his bulk in the gravchair, pulling at his thick black beard. "I am champion of oppressed peoples. I come here to see to their interests, to see that no bourgeois terrorist governments exploit sweat of working men and women traditionally ground beneath boot heel of privileged. That is social maggot?"

"You damn betcha!" Tayash chuckled. "You're a sorry case, Nikita. Look at you sitting there, a cup of the finest sherry from Santa del Cielo in one hand, your belly full of the finest beef from Range, and you can look me in the eye and say you're fighting the battle of the benighted masses?"

"Of course I can. Is like this. Battle must be fought on many fronts. Some include running printing press in back rooms of Moscow section of Arcturian slums. Other fight is to kick Sirian secret agent out pressure lock and watch him flop in vacuum to keep Sirius from developing political domination they really seek. Still other part is to remind bourgeois diplomat like you that universe doesn't end with Confederate Council. Real people are spinning around out in stations, struggling on planets to run mines, work machines, do all things which make our lives better. My battle is to remind you that all decisions we make in Council affect real lives out in Confederacy.

Maybe sometimes you powerful and wealthy types forget, eh?''

"Beware. To claim you have ultimate truth is as much a sin as having none at all. So maybe you come closer to the champion of the masses than others. I've always thought you kept a rational head when it came to voting for policy."

Nikita lifted his glass of Cielan sherry and smacked his lips. "Yes, my friend, I seriously believe I am champion. No matter that I enjoy fringe benefits along way. Tell me truth. You ever see Nikita Malakova vote for his own benefit? You ever see me suck up to someone like that Sirian pig, Lietov—or perhaps Fan Jordan—when I could make great personal gain? Does that mean I am social maggot? Living like parasite in corpse of people? Then I take that title. But most politicians are lying vermin—like infestation of lice in station atmosphere plant.''

Tayash smiled warmly. "Well . . . You know, you've got a reputation for being a hard-nosed son of a bitch who—''

"Is because I never let powerless working people down, Tayash. Yes, I enjoy sherry, enjoy good food . . . but should I eat ration bars when delicacies like this would go to waste otherwise? Better in Nikita's gut than in anyone else's. Truth!'' His voice dropped. "But, Tayash, if you ever see me sell out people . . . see me compromise *my* ethics, then you may spit upon me and turn your back. For then, old friend, I will not be worthy of respect."

Tayash nodded, staring across the room to where Norik Ngoro stood in a floor-length yellow and orange toga crafted of the finest Arcturian fabrics. About his neck hung a small vial of soil from his native station. Ngoro spoke casually to Mikhi Hitavia, the Reinland Representative, while Mac Torgusson and Charney Hendricks listened. Hendricks—the University Representative—had the myopic squint of a scholar, while Torgusson—Moscow Sector Representative—stood tall and thin—a hyperactive man who ran on a perpetually short fuse.

Tayash waved toward Ngoro, adding, "You would say that in front of him?''

Nikita squirmed to get more comfortable. "Yes, I would say that before him."

As if he'd heard, Ngoro looked over, locking eyes with Nikita Malakova.

Under his breath, the big Gulagi added, "That man, of all men I have ever met, is most scary."

* * *

The tall black man stood loose-limbed, a vacancy in his eyes. One hand rested absently on the lock plate to operate the security hatch leading to the officers' quarters and the bridge beyond.

"Excuse me," Sol said, "Mr. Representative, that hatch leads to secure sections of the ship. If you would . . ."

The man turned his head slowly, eyes unfocused, a slight frown lining his forehead. "You are Solomon Carrasco?"

"Yes." Sol met the eerie eyes, heart skipping at the disconnected expression. Unconsciously, he crouched in a combat stance.

"You seem to be a worried man, Captain. You and Constance. A pair of worried people, outstanding among a flock of worriers. Only you and Constance are frightened, ground and worn by what you perceive to be immense responsibilities. So similar . . . so different. But then, such things make for humankind."

"I . . . Representative Ngoro, could I help you with something? You can't pass that hatch without security approval. If I can—"

"I did not wish to pass a security hatch, Captain. I wanted only to retire to my cabin and contemplate the creature aboard."

"Creature? I . . . My God, you didn't see a rat, did you? The ship's brand new. Usually takes a while before the damn rodents are—"

"A human creature, Captain." Ngoro's eyes flickered, his features sharpening as he studied Carrasco. "Tell me, Captain, do you satisfy yourself that you behave in an ethical manner? Do you consciously seek to do the best possible for yourself, your colleagues, and your enemies?"

Sol swallowed hard, controlling his suddenly felt anger. "Honestly, Representative Ngoro, I try to be ethical. Now, what that might mean could engage us in hours of argument. Let's say I'm a situational ethicist, calling the shots based upon the information at hand at a given moment."

"Yes, you do, don't you. Perhaps that is why you have taken this assignment?"

"Mr. Representative, do you feel all right? You're not disoriented or . . . I mean, would you like me to take you to the hospital?"

"I am quite well, thank you, Captain." Ngoro smiled easily. "This is just a manner of mine. Forgive me, I should have paid better attention to finding my way, only I'm preoccupied with the creature. You see, I am a Truth Sayer."

"I noted that in the passenger profile. I didn't—"

"Some say I read minds, Captain. Only it isn't quite that way. What I do is judge people. I'm a sensitive. I know when humans are lying. Such skills are most valuable in a judicial system. For that reason, my people sent me to see to their interests. Now I have encountered the creature."

"You keep mentioning the creature." Sol stood at ease, thumbs locked behind him. "Could you tell me more about it?"

"Yes . . . most interesting. Someone wishes us all harm. Genius, I tell you. Never have I met so disciplined a mind—only glimpses under graphsteel control. Single-mindedly playing a part, a role of deception and espionage. The tension builds within . . . seeking to burst that control, seeking to hurt."

Fingers, like tendrils of liquid hydrogen, stroked Solomon's soul. "Can you pinpoint who this person is?"

Norik smiled wistfully. "In time, Captain. In time. The creature is most cunning, suspecting everything, everyone. Perhaps it fears the powers of your ship? Perhaps it fears its own lust to hurt, to dominate. Lust can break loose at the most inappropriate times, bringing disaster. Indeed, genius . . . the creature guards itself well.''

"Creature, you say? Is this thing an alien or—''

"Most human, I assure you. I use the term only metaphorically since I—of all people—do not understand the motivations of its clever mind.''

"Perhaps if we made each person stand before you?''

"I would that it were that easy. No, this person is possibly the most devious of any I have encountered. I only get hints of the hatred . . . the power lust. The glimpse in my mind is so brief . . . to be instantly controlled by a brilliant, powerful opponent.

"However, I shall learn, Captain. I shall study, and I shall learn.''

Sol nodded uneasily. "When you have something, let me know. Don't hesitate. I'll do my best to handle the situation ethically.''

Ngoro's gaze seemed to cut into his very soul, laser bright, surgically dissecting the defenses and subterfuges of personality to expose the marrow of Solomon Carrasco.

Sol swallowed hard, stepping back, heart beginning to race.

"Yes, Captain, you are a most curious man. So strong, so vulnerable, so driven. Hounded by responsibility.''

"That's part of command, Mister Representative. Responsibility can't be avoided in my profession.''

Ngoro chuckled from the depths of his belly. "Nor can it be avoided in a true state of nature. I look around out there in the lounge, and I see so many avoiding. In Ambrose Sector . . . in all the Confederacy, I see men and women burying their heads, wrapping the blanket of social institution around themselves as a shield against assuming responsibility. You and Constance and Archon and Nikita have avoided that delusion. In nature, Captain, a person can't escape responsibility. Not and survive.

"You seem introspective. Excellent, but I will pose this question, since I see the fear and turmoil in your very soul: What will you do when you must face your greatest fear? To pass responsibility on to another is safe, without risk or danger. Doing so absolves you of overt guilt and recrimination. You have simply fulfilled your duty in the chain of command. Yet, if you choose to accept responsibility for your actions, and decisions, all likelihood is that your judgments will be wrong. That's statistical reality. How can you accept that?''

Sol frowned, working his lips. "I'm not sure—"

"There you are!"

Sol turned to see Amahara charging down the hall, concern on his normally benign features. Panting, he ran up, wiping pale blond hair out of his eyes.

"The Captain and I were discussing ethics . . . and the creature."

Amahara shifted nervously, eyes flickering back and forth from one face to the other face. "Norik, how many times have I told you not to speculate openly. I, well, I doubt the Captain is the creature, but if you keep talking about it . . ."

"I'll be fine." Ngoro smiled disjointedly. "I'm close, so very very close to finding the dangerous one. Just a couple more days, a few more observations . . ."

"And look at you." Amahara fussed as he pulled the now drooping toga up over Norik's shoulder. "You'd be naked given half a chance. You said you were going to your room. I was half crazy when I got there and you were missing."

"I was . . ." Norik frowned. "The lock plate wouldn't work."

"I found him here," Sol added.

Amahara giggled nervously. "Yes, well, he gets lost in his head, you see. Sort of like a novelist. Lives in a different world than the real one around us. Please, I hope he didn't cause you any difficulty."

"None at all, we had a most productive discussion." Sol smiled as Amahara started to lead Ngoro away. "And, Amahara, when he discovers the 'creature' call me immediately, do you understand?"

Amahara jerked his head vigorously in assent, already worrying at Ngoro.

Sol watched them go. "A creature, he says."

* * *

"Ship?" Sol asked as he sealed his hatch. "Did you monitor the conversation between Norik Ngoro and myself?"

"Affirmative."

"Analysis?"

The ship intoned, "The obvious correlation lies between Archon's suggestion that a saboteur is aboard and the feelings of Norik Ngoro. I have accessed the file on the Truth Sayer. His powers are justly claimed, accurate to within a half a percentage point in more than one triple-blind experiment. The physiological distinctions which set his brain apart include—"

"Never mind the hard data. I believe. Rather, let's attack the problem in a constructive manner. Sabotage can come in many forms, so what do you have in files?" Sol lay back on his bunk and jammed his coffee cup into the dispenser.

And that crazy Gulagi is carrying a pulse pistol in his pocket! The President of University, Charney Hendricks, has a portable chem lab in his room. What else haven't I found out about?

"First, soft methods include time-delay damage to machinery by such means as unhardened bearings, computer viruses or worms, inadequate programming, psychological manipulation of humans can be induced by—"

"How many of those soft methods can you find applicable in our present situation?" Sol interrupted.

"Sixty-five, Captain."

"How many can be easily countered by data access lock-out, restricted access, and so forth?" Sol stared at the white panels above. *Damn it, why is this happening to me?*

"Fifty-nine, Captain. I am not capable of controlling the brains of easily persuaded human beings, however."

Images immediately formed of Fan Jordan, Nikita Ma-

Iakova and that despicable Mark Lietov. "I understand. You're to take such actions and provide me with a printout I can, in turn, take to Happy so we can determine the effect on the functioning of the ship. What about hard sabotage?"

"There are two subsets of action in that category, Captain. The first includes actions taken against equipment such as the bombing of the reactor, air plant, navcomm or bridge. The second is directed against human beings."

"As to bombs, we've scanned for major devices." Sol chewed the knuckle of his thumb, forehead creased. "Some explosives can be made out of common elements. Is there any way we can put sensors in the ventilation system which would warn us if common compounds were being mixed aboard?"

"Affirmative."

"Get Happy to work on that immediately. What else?"

"The ventilation system itself could be poisoned, gassed, or infected by microorganisms or viruses."

"Can we increase filtration and sterilize the filters? Maybe kick up the UV in the purifiers and recirculators?"

"Affirmative. I am currently upgrading the system to preclude the possibility of tampering with ventilation. Would you like the same done with food and water?"

"Definitely," Sol agreed. It would be more difficult with all the gourmet viands which had been brought aboard.

"Bombs, poisons, chemical and biological agents, tampering—what's left?" Sol counted them off on his fingers.

"The other method of sabotage employed for the longest time is one I can't prevent, Captain." Was there hesitation behind *Boaz*'s voice?

"And that is?"

"Captain. In a Brotherhood ship, with constant monitoring, other methods can be nullified. I told you earlier, I cannot control human behavior. I am powerless to prevent human assassination of other humans through direct action.''

Sol stretched his neck to fight the growing headache expanding behind his eyes. ''Murder? No, I guess you can't. And unless I lock them all in their cabins, how can I?''

CHAPTER XI

The destruction of the Chorr absorbed her after they finally stumbled onto her. In them she found a new challenge. Chorr reproduced by fission; the complete reduplication of the organism down to the ancestral memories ensued. In the process all experiences up to fission copied into each of the F_1 generations. The effect proved cumulative; their bodies enlarged to hold the vast store of information. At the same time, she had to adapt herself, enlarging to accommodate their immense bodies and changing her internal atmosphere from methane ammonia—the heritage of the Aan—to oxygen and illuminating her interior with radiation between four to seven thousand angstroms for Chorr eyes. Nor did problems stop there.

The Chorr who first probed her secrets fissioned with both organisms remaining inside. They split again. Four of the large organisms inhabited her quarters. As the trend continued, dietary needs had to be supplied from outside. The offspring of the original Chorr took their time working the spring, peering into atoms, and studying the universe around them. They worked different systems with relish and denied access to the rest of their race, exchanging knowledge for food.

The excluded Chorr objected.

Inside, the Chorr continued to reproduce, expanding through her n-dimensional interior. She found herself baffled. How would she handle this burgeoning population? Of course, the Chorr condemned themselves in the end.

Those Chorr beyond her hull refused to provide more food. Ultimatums were issued. The power elite crossed the threshold. They worked the spring against their fellows.

Food supplies were maintained as the Chorr continued to multiply exponentially within her walls. Protest increased, futile against her Masters. The narcotic of power had been loosed. The Chorr had become intoxicated with their absolute rule. The end would come now, each of her projections proved it.

Galactic Chorr resources funneled food to the Masters. When carrying capacity had been strained past the limit, the Masters made their final mistake. The system that supported the huge internal population collapsed. The Masters responded, condemning the disobedient to the interstellar abyss. Starvation gnawed at the Masters who turned on each other, devouring whichever among them proved the weakest.

Several cycles repeated until the final Chorr starved at the helm. None had ever bothered to learn how to use her processors to produce unlimited food.

She cackled gleefully at the chewed remains littering her interior. Once again organic life had paid for the damning spring.

* * *

Fingernails scratched against the thick plates of the ship's hull. Sol spun around, looking up through the observation blister, to see Fil Cerratanos clawing frantically at the resisting hull material.

"Fil?"

Cerratanos turned dead eyes in his direction, mouth working soundlessly in the cold vacuum. Frost tipped his full mustache. His body charred and twisted, Cerratanos writhed in agony.

"Fil?" Sol screamed, pasting himself against the transparency to stare at the corpse.

The haunted, empty eyes pleaded. Nails peeled back from Cerratanos' bloody fingers as he clawed in desperation. Sol turned to dash for the closed hatch. He palmed the lock plate. The thick white steel remained, cold and immovable. Sol pounded the lock plate, throwing a frightened glance over his shoulder, panicked by the terror in Cerratanos' expression.

"Boaz! Open the hatch. *Boaz!"* The white steel imprisoned him. Sol flipped open the bypass, pressing the emergency button. Nothing happened, the hatch defied him. Futilely, Sol slapped at the steel and glanced back to see Cerratanos' limp body drifting away, fading into the blackness.

"Fil?" Sol whimpered. He stumbled over to the transparent blister, to press himself against the glassy material. His panting breath condensed on the cool surface to obscure the tumbling body in a whitish haze.

"Fil? Oh, God, Fil. Come back. I can't . . . can't reach you." He sobbed his horror into the empty silence of the observation blister.

"Captain?"

Sol blinked, snapping awake in his quarters. The lights were on. He'd curled into a fetal ball on the bunk.

"Captain, please answer me," *Boaz* called through her speakers.

"Here. What's wrong?"

"I might ask you the same. You called out to me."

"I . . . Yes, in the dream." He sat up, every muscle in his body knotted, a cold clammy sweat on his skin. He rubbed numb hands over his gritty face. "I saw . . . heard Fil Cerratanos. He was scratching at the hull, trying to get in. I was locked in the observation blister. Hatch wouldn't work so I could go EVA and get him. That's when I yelled. Lock plate wouldn't work. I called for you to open it. I was . . . was trapped. And he kept drifting farther and farther away . . . left behind."

"What do you think the dream means?

"I . . . I'm losing them. Leaving them behind."

"Very good. At the same time, I would suggest that you consider the message your subconscious sent you. In the dream, the hatch held you back. Captain, I would suggest that, at least in your subconscious, I was responsible for your failure to reach Cerratanos. Dreams are a means for the brain to express deep-seated concerns to those wise enough to listen.''

Sol nodded and exhaled. ''Yes, they are.''

''I suggest that you give your dreams some thought. They're a signal which should not be ignored. If I can be of assistance, please do not hesitate to—''

''Thank you, ship. I–I'm going for a walk. Maybe conduct an inspection.'' He stood. Pulling on his uniform, he palmed the hatch.

''Captain. I—''

''No, ship. I've got to work this out myself.''

''Very well.''

Empty paces took him down the long corridors. He couldn't still the icy foreboding. Even in the long white halls, he could feel Cerratanos' dead eyes upon him.

We walked into a comm room to the sound of whoops and hollers. New crew, people he didn't know. They huddled over a holobox where two Arcturian teams played basketball in zero g.

Sol stood stiffly until one man looked up, going silent. Eyes turned his way. Cerratanos drifted dead among the stars while they enjoyed themselves.

''Hi, Captain. Want to—''

''I take it this is a duty station?''

''Yes, sir. Not much happening since comm's mostly dead at this hour. The transmission just completed for the game so we—''

''Then you'll be on watch on the comm. Unless you'd rather be on watch on report. Damn it, people, this is deep space. *You'll be on your toes, or you'll be off my ship! Am I UNDERSTOOD?''*

''Yes, sir!''

Three bodies jumped for the monitor stations.

Sol stalked out. *I didn't need to snap. Maybe I was too rough . . . Cerratanos is dead. So many are dead. Don't they realize? The universe isn't for fun and games and . . . DAMN IT! WHAT'S HAPPENING TO ME?*

He stopped, fists clenched, and leaned against the cool bulkheads, possessed by an unaccountable anguish.

* * *

Speaker Archon reclined thoughtfully in a gravchair, legs up, arms crossed over his stomach. He stared down the length of the large gymnasium, admiring its white, padded walls, gleaming weight machines, and the airy lightness of the place. Incredible! How extraordinary that the Brotherhood included such advanced and sophisticated exercise systems. Keeping people fit in spacecraft had been a perpetual problem until the practical adaptation of artificially induced gravity. Man remained a wild animal, a creature whose very health demanded exercise.

His eyes went back to where Connie hovered in midair, body gracefully twisting, whirling, and kicking to some cadence in her head. The long braid of red-gold hair made the illusion all the more enticing.

Archon's heart fluttered. But then a parent deserved to take pride in a child, and Constance forever reminded him of Myra. And when she danced like this, it took him back to that day on Mars when he first laid eyes on the woman he'd love for the rest of his life.

With a series of somersaults Connie lifted, touched off the ceiling, and bounced angles off the walls until she reached the gravity control. Archon experienced the sensation of his skin sagging under the returned pull.

Damp with perspiration, pale flesh flushed with exertion, she flashed him a smile before stepping into the shower. Archon sipped at his drink until she exited and began dressing.

"You get better and better, girl. I truly think you could make a profession out of it. Too much of your mother in you."

She laughed, eyes lighting with satisfaction. "Elvina Young would refuse to talk to me again. Blessed gods, think of that!"

"And that would be a loss?" Archon asked, a sour twist to his lips. He paused, "She's sure been after poor Carrasco. If I didn't know Mormons better, I'd say she was flirting."

"She is. Texahi is drooling all over himself. Joseph seems oblivious—but then, he's not very smart."

Connie settled on the chair arm and nodded as two crewmen walked in, waved, and reset the gravity. Connie stood, fought her way to a second chair, and maneuvered it next to Archon's. The crewmen set up a racecourse as obstacles sprouted from the walls. The men stripped and began chasing each other in the 1.5 gravity, muscles straining.

"Joseph Young is a bland sort of sop, isn't he? I've never met anyone as boring." Archon absently watched the crewmen who were panting and laughing as they chased each other. "And what do you think of Solomon Carrasco?"

"Maybe we should discuss this someplace more private?"

"Keep your voice down, and act normal. No one would suspect us of a nefarious conversation out here in the open. And the crewmen? They're occupied with their race. They don't have the concentration to spare. But do keep an eye on them."

"Carrasco? He's an attractive man. But something's eating him deep inside. There are times talking to him when I get a little flash of intuition that says back off. And you didn't see him that day in the observation blister. Like a different man."

"You saw the holos," Archon reminded. "From what Kraal showed us, I'm surprised he survived . . . let alone that they could rebuild him. My God, those holos gave me nightmares."

"I just wish we . . . Well, I still question your decision to include him. And if those two ships paralleling us are hostile? Will he break? Given the choice between turning us over and saving the ship, which option do you think he'll take?"

"Do you really think I made a mistake asking for him?"

She closed her eyes, letting her body relax as the crewmen, panting and sweating, pounded past. As they topped the hurdles and charged away, she responded, "I don't

know. I wonder if he's still the same man you think he
is. I'd feel better if we had an out, some way to—''

"Kraal gave you that. If Carrasco fails, the responsibility becomes yours." He made a motion with his hands.
"I just wanted Carrasco. You were there, you saw him
fight his way out that day. He was brilliant and he did
the impossible—he won."

Connie breathed deeply, muscular body going limp in
the chair. "Then we're safe—so long as *that* man didn't
die with *Sword*."

* * *

"I don't like it," Bryana told Arturian as she relieved
him from his watch. "Those ships are closing, and we're
just diddling along at twenty gravities of acceleration. All
we have to do is power up and we can leave them nothing
but a string of plasma to admire."

Art's face reflected disgust. "Hell, I don't know what
we're doing. Ask the hero! He says it doesn't matter; they
know where we're going anyway. Maybe he's worried
about all the station types—making the ride smooth for
them."

"They won't think it's smooth if those are pirate craft
and we have to duck blaster bolts. You think Carrasco
will fight? Or will he figure they've already won so there's
no sense?"

Art shot her an assenting look. "If it comes to that,
we'll . . . well, the book gives us options. I've heard a
couple of grumblings from the crew. That Carrasco's
jumped them for no reason. The new people, like us,
who wanted to space with Dart are starting to complain.
I guess there've been a couple of incidents. People say
he looks real spooky when he dresses them down. Pale.
Scared."

Bryana crossed her arms and tilted her head, black hair
glistening in the bridge lights. "There might be another
way to get him out of the picture. *Boaz*, from a psychological perspective, what are the chances that Solomon

Carrasco will be incapable of performing his duties under severe stress?''

The ship's speaker replied immediately. "I have insufficient data, Bryana. From his past behavior, he seems most capable in emergency situations. Beyond that, I will not speculate since it would only serve to destabilize the situation."

"He lost three ships!" Art cried out.

"He also brought them home against all odds," *Boaz* replied. "I don't exactly understand the reasons why you object so vehemently to Solomon Carrasco. His problems adjusting to the needs of—"

"Consider his actions on the bridge as we left Arcturus," Bryana pointed out. "The man was a mess. He seemed to be on the verge of falling apart. Look, he may have been great once, but humans break under stress. If the stories they tell are true, he was a whimpering wreck when they dug him out of *Gage*. Trauma, *Boaz*—as you well know from psych records—changes the way the human brain works."

"I think it's political," Art decided. "Someone feels they owe it to poor Solomon Carrasco to let him have another chance. But why do *we*—"

"Negative," *Boaz* responded. "The Captain specifically did not want this assignment. He took it only at the personal request of Galactic Grand Master Kraal."

"Then what's bothering him?" Bryana demanded.

"The same thing which bothers you in the end, First Officer: responsibility."

* * *

"The man is weird! I tell you, a lunatic!"

"Please, Mr. Hitavia, you must understand—"

"Understand *what?* He's crazy!"

Constance rounded the corner, to see Amahara standing, hands up, pleading, a look of panic on his face. Gratefully, he turned to Connie.

"Please, will you explain to the honorable representative from Reinland that Norik Ngoro isn't—"

"He's *berserk!*"

"Why don't you both slow down and tell me what this is all about."

"Hitavia tried to kill Norik." Amahara shook his head in confusion. "I . . . I got to them before any harm was done. I sent Norik off to our room where—"

"The man demanded of me . . . *demanded!* Like I was some sort of common *peasant!*" Hitavia paced angrily, his Lapp features burning red, the veins standing from his bulging forehead, pale blue eyes inflamed. A fist waved in the air as he continued. "What right does Ngoro have to question *my* integrity like that?" He spun, a stiff finger darting at Connie like an ancestral spear. "No one . . . NO ONE tries to twist my words like that. The implication was that I didn't have a moral foundation for the decisions I make in my *private* life, let alone my public one! I'm NOT a damn bug in a jar for Ngoro . . . or anyone else for that matter!"

Amahara rocked nervously from foot to foot, wringing his hands, panic glazing his eyes. "Mr. Representative, what you do with Mrs. Young is *your* business. I surely don't care that you and she—"

Hitavia lunged, Amahara sliding away from the gripping fingers, while a cry stifled in his throat.

"Enough!" Connie leapt between the two men, one hand on the Reinlander's chest. She took a deep breath, eyes locked with the livid Hitavia's. "I think the matter can be ended right here. Listen, we've got enough troubles before us at Star's Rest. Amahara, Norik is a Truth Sayer. If I ask him—based on judicial precedent—to keep his tongue about this, will he?"

"Yes, ma'am. I swear on the burial tanks of my station. He will."

"And will you forget it, Amahara? Not a word to anyone?"

"Oh, yes, ma'am. I swear on the burial tanks of my—"

"We've got an understanding of the depths of your honor, Amahara. And you, Mikhi? Is that satisfactory?"

Hitavia threw a venomous glance at Amahara. "I . . . All right, I'm satisfied." So saying, he spun on a heel, long legs eating distance until he rounded a corner and disappeared.

Connie blew a sigh of relief as feet came pounding down the corridor. Solomon Carrasco, uniform hastily yanked over his muscular torso, burst from a companion-way, sliding to a stop. Panting slightly, eyes muzzy from sleep, he asked, "Is there a disturbance here?"

Connie shot a quick glance at Amahara whose fragile features had gone ashen. "I think it's under control. Just a small misunderstanding."

"With Ngoro?" Sol raised an eyebrow, looking at Amahara. "Concerning his quest?"

Amahara nodded quickly. "He's close. He told me he'll have the answer by tomorrow. I don't think he expected Hitavia to—"

"Hitavia? That's who he's suspicious of?"

"I . . . No, no, I don't mean that. Captain, please, this is all out of control. Out of control, you see. It's nothing. Please. It's really nothing. Norik says he will know by tomorrow. He's discussed it with me. When he's sure, we'll call you. Let you know what he suspects—and why. I promise."

Sol nodded shortly, speculative eyes on Connie. "All right, Amahara. Go and check on Norik."

Connie watched the aide zip down the hall, sandal-clad feet pattering lightly as he hurried for the personal quarters.

"That was a quick response, Captain. You monitoring the halls?" she asked.

Sol hesitated just enough to make her suspicious. "No, evidently you weren't the only person to hear it." He smiled wryly. "They did make a lot of noise. Hitavia screaming, 'I'll kill you, you meddling bastard' at the top of his lungs doesn't exactly take snooper equipment in the corridors."

She laughed softly, remembering the ruckus. "No, I suppose not. Um, don't let your fashion designer know, but I think the hem of the tunic is supposed to be straight, not off by ten centimeters. And don't look now, but you forgot to fasten your fly."

The color drained from Carrasco's stricken face. "Excuse me while I escape around the corner like a phantom in the night."

Connie crossed her arms, leaning up against the bulkhead, chuckling to herself until a more presentable Carrasco reappeared, a slightly mollified look on his normally worried features.

"Well, I'd just drifted off to sleep." He raised apologetic hands. "Then comm goes off and I'm practically putting the uniform on at a run. Besides, I'm not used to Brotherhood dress uniforms. Normally, on a deep space survey, I'm in casual dress the whole time. It's only these highbrow . . . er, excuse me."

She waved it away. "Quite all right. I don't fit high social status anyway."

He grunted, brown eyes evaluative. "Uh, if you don't mind my asking, it's a little late, isn't it? I mean we're in the middle of third watch. Everyone else is sleeping."

She pulled gleaming long hair over a shoulder, twisting it into a red-gold cable, and laughed. "Well, would it surprise you if I told you I haven't been sleeping much recently? I just thought I'd go sit in the observation blister and look at the stars. Kind of . . ."

"Kind of soothing to stare out there." He finished, turning, arm extended. She took it, though she still felt that click of reservation deep inside, that instinctive mistrust. "I do it myself," Carrasco continued, as they walked. "Out there, in all the peace, I lose myself—put things in perspective."

"It's not all that peaceful—not when you consider solar physics in something like a B1 star. Space is a violent and tortured place despite our perceptions to the contrary. Hell would be tamer."

Carrasco swallowed hard, equanimity gone. "Are you always so pragmatic?"

She lifted a shoulder and sighed. "Yes, I suppose so. To be honest, it's been so long since I really laughed, maybe I've forgotten how. I never planned to grow up quite this quick. Understand? Here I am, wishing I had time to space without any responsibilities. Just to accelerate and jump and see what I found out where no human had gone before. After Arpeggio we did that . . . and found Star's Rest. And responsibility. I'm Deputy Speaker for my planet, and, I guess, for my people. Funny, I don't feel like a ruler. I feel like a spacer, an explorer.''

They walked into the observation blister. Beyond the transparent graphite, the gray-white dusting of stars shimmered, stark in the blackness of the void. "And you can't leave it with your father for a few years and do that? He's quite capable.''

She smiled wistfully. "Maybe when we've finished this business to my satisfaction. If there's time then.''

"And this 'business'?''

She let go of his arm, amazed at how naturally she'd held it, aware of his warmth through the fabric. "Still trying, Captain? Always seeking to work in a lever in an attempt to pry out the truth?'' She shook her head. "No, not yet. Too many people like Ngoro are suspicious. Nikita Malakova's nose is in the wind, too. I've encountered too many people in the last couple of months whose motives I don't trust. And no, I don't trust you. Not because I believe you're untrustworthy, but because I know the gravity of what we're about. I've even ceased to trust my own father. Not because he's on the wrong side, or because he isn't my closest ally, but I know the stakes, Captain. And they scare unholy hell out of me.''

He remained silent, watching her, nodding slightly.

"It's because in the final analysis, I'm the only person I can count on.''

He crossed his arms, leaning back against the bulkhead, one foot up on the spectrometer. "I suppose in the end, that's all any of us have. Ourselves.''

She braced a hip against the cool metal of the telescope and pulled up a knee, lacing long fingers to support it. "I'm glad you can comprehend that . . . at least in an intellectual way. Maybe it's my pragmatism again?''

"More of the game?''

"Well . . . you never answered my question last time.''

Carrasco dropped his chin to his broad chest. "Oh, I've thought about it. To date, I don't have an answer.

My first inclination was naturally to take the power—
right the wrongs. Then, when I thought about it, I got to
wondering about all the ramifications.'' He studied her
soberly. ''Tell me, doesn't it ever bother you that God
doesn't play a more important role in the universe? I
mean, consider . . . depending on what you assume about
God, he could change a great deal—but when you do,
say, blast Arpeggio into radioactive slag, how many lives
have you changed? You're fooling with the future. Anyone who takes ultimate power—and uses it to reform the
universe—remakes it in his own image.'' He slapped a
nervous hand against his leg, voice dropping. ''And,
Constance, I'm not perfect. Therefore, anything I make
of the universe will, of necessity, have those flaws inte-
gral to the reformation.''

''So if I offered you ultimate power, you'd turn it
down?''

He filled his lungs, chest expanding to emphasize his
firm pectorals, the line of his ribs, and the flatness of his
belly. ''That would have been my answer. But a couple
of days ago, I had a discussion with our infamous Norik
Ngoro. He made some observations about responsibility
in a state of nature—and he's right. Boiling it all down,
he said that passing the buck was the ultimate cop-out.
That in the end, a truly moral man must assume all the
responsibility he can.'' He laughed gently, humorlessly.
''The ultimate anarchist. He and Nikita ought to get together.''

''So you'd accept ultimate power and become God?''

Carrasco's frown engraved lines in his forehead.
''Damned if I know. Both answers are right. Accept ultimate power and remake the universe in my own flawed
image? Or pass it on and live in the shadow of someone
else's shortcomings and failures of vision? Whose flaws
do I trust? Someone else's . . . or my own? None of us
are perfect.''

She turned her head, enjoying the sight of the billions
of stars, the quiet of the room, the presence of this man
whose thoughts seemed so in tune with her own. She

closed her eyes, enjoying the sensation of not being alone in the universe. And wishing it could last forever.

His gentle voice soothed. "A most interesting game you've created. I'll let you know when I have the answer. I'm simply afraid of the alternatives."

"*So am I,*" she whispered, cold loneliness returning, draping over her shoulders like a green-ice mantle.

* * *

The bridge monitors glowed softly green into the hard unforgiving face of Solomon Carrasco as he watched the lights indicating the positions of the closing ships. They had climbed to within four light-seconds, veered off, and were paralleling *Boaz*'s course. Hailing continued to bring no response and visual remained too hazy to make an ID as to vessel type—although mass could be computed by measuring reaction spectra and Doppler against acceleration.

"Ship?"

"Yes, Captain?"

"If we assume the bogeys are at fighting trim with no excess mass, and if we assume a standard Star hull with power twenty percent above normal for a fifty-five hundred ton vessel, what statistical probabilities can you give me for the identity of those bandits based on the registry records for Confederate planets?"

Sol stuck his coffee cup in the dispenser and absently withdrew it, thankful his hands felt and functioned normally again. The nerves had "worked in."

Boaz responded immediately. "Based on the criteria listed, the bogeys are most probably built around a Star Model 26 Type IV hull. That particular design, unfortunately, has been in production for over fifty years, with several thousand sold. The most versatile of the Star design hulls, they've been purchased by every major political and commercial group in the Confederacy—with the exception of New Israel and the Brotherhood who, of course, manufacture their own ships. It was a good thought though, Captain."

"Thank you, ship." Sol leaned back, absently reviewing the reactor data coming in through his headset. He made a slight change to the reaction feed, nudging *Boaz* into a microsecond course change. The memory of Connie silhouetted against ten billion stars in the observation blister kept intruding on his thoughts. Such a beautiful woman. Bright, intelligent, capable, she obsessed him—and he'd never had time for women. Not since Demetria had spaced with him on that first shakedown of *Moriah*. Only she'd had a chance at command of *Gavel* and taken it. And after that? When had he found either the time or the inclination? Peg Andaki might have filled that spot, but he'd been in med when she tied up with Bret Muriaki after Maybry's death.

"Captain?"

"Yes?" Sol looked up at the bridge displays.

"You don't call me *Boaz*. I've scanned the records and find that most unusual. The effect is disconcerting . . . somewhat like me addressing you simply as 'human.' "

Did he hear censure in those tones? The index finger on his left hand tapped rhythmically at the instrument-studded armrest console. He shifted, the command chair suddenly confining.

"I hadn't given it much thought."

The ship didn't answer immediately. Carrasco's curiosity stirred despite the tension. Those magnificent n-dimensional chips composing *Boaz*'s brain thought in terms of nanoseconds. If she hesitated on purpose, then she interacted on a human level. Sophisticated indeed and, he realized, unnerving—with too many implications.

"Captain, I have many programs with which to conduct many different forms of analyses." Again the pause, unsettling Sol even more. "It is my conclusion—based on probability, of course—that you're worried about establishing any close ties which in turn might lead to affection on your part."

"Indeed?" The staccato rapping of his fingernails increased. The base of his throat constricted. The command chair squeezed him like some giant fist.

A pause. "Computers don't grieve, Captain—humans do."

"Meaning?"

"Your dreams are plagued. I always appear as an obstruction in those subconscious images. *Gage* still rests heavily on your consciousness."

"So do the lives of thirty of my friends." He forced himself to unclench his hand and slow his breathing.

"Is that why you're constantly angry with Arturian, Bryana, and the rest of the crew? You've conducted three emergency inspections in the last two days. During that time, you haven't uttered a single word of praise for any member of your crew. I've compared that with tapes of your behavior in previous commands. In each of your ships you were a part of the social network—a positive influence on those under your command. Here, you have withdrawn, isolated yourself. You won't continue to function effectively once your personal aura wears thin."

Sol took a deep breath, crossed his legs, and began chewing on the knuckle of his thumb, gaze drifting past the lights of the bridge and off across space and time. Faces—now long dead—filled the warm companionways, bridges, and wardrooms of those wonderful ships. Briefly, they lived again.

The image changed. Memory drew him through the wreckage that had once been *Moriah,* his first command. He saw her there, cold and dark, dying as her circuits went forever silent. A simple square of uncommon mass had tripped the sensors. They'd located the artifact and brought it close to study—hoping it would prove to be evidence of another intelligent civilization; but when the probes began to pry at its secrets, the cube had exploded violently despite Sol's best precautions. Later, other similar devices had been located—their source finally traced to Arpeggio.

An amber fog hid *Moriah,* then swirled away to reveal another terrifying sight.

Once again, he lived those last desperate moments as he fought *Sword* free from the Arpeggian trap. Brilliant streaks of plasma shot through the decks as men and women died. He remembered board after board flickering into darkness as *Sword* struggled to reroute the nerve center of the ship during the fearful jump back to Frontier. Doing so, she performed what amounted to a self-lobotomy to keep her human crew alive.

Gage's loss hurt worst—the reason for it incomprehensible. In the blue-red flickering light of the Tygee binary had come death. A flat-black vessel had appeared out of nowhere, blasting them where they'd been conducting metal procurement studies on the Tygeean moons. He'd scrambled to save the ship. The haunted stares of the crew burned forever in his brain; he'd known death lurked close for all of them.

So Sol had steeled himself and done what he could order no one else to do. He'd walked into Engineering next to the failing reactor and held that plasma-severed powerlead together in the last fatal moments. He'd kept the power intact while Happy rerouted and spliced, feeling the radiation, feeling the searing pain as his flesh cooked from his bones. Fortunately the thin mucus tissues of his nose had burned out quickly so he didn't have to smell the cooking meat that had been his fingers. He'd sacrificed himself to save them all—and *Gage* lay dead because he wasn't good enough. Those ships, those men and women, all that life and potential wasted. What more could he have done?

"Why do you think that is, good ship?" Sol's voice came raggedly as he struggled back to the present.

"You always got them home, Solomon," *Boaz*'s speaker carried a warm conviction. "None of the losses ever resulted from irresponsibility on your part. Every time—"

"I left the bridge on *Gage*. Wandered down to see the metallic hydrogen samples Misha had drawn from the moon. Mbazi and—"

"The Jurisprudence Committee appointed by the Grand Lodge found no reason to bind you over for trial by the Craft. *Gage* herself didn't detect the bogey until too late. The attack was unprovoked and was committed by unknown parties beyond the frontier. You proceeded to do the impossible after the odds had been stacked against you. You extricated yourself and got your ship and crew home. You did it by your presence and personality. If you continue with your present attitude, you will lose that precious ability as a commander. In spite of your inspections, Captain, your crew is running at only eighty percent efficiency."

"Why do you tell me this?" He stared woodenly, heart sinking in his chest. He should have said no. He should have looked Master Kraal in the eyes and told him flat out that he would never space again.

The tone in *Boaz*'s voice startled him. "I think you're too good to waste, Captain. Further, given the limited data I have at hand, this jump to Star's Rest—or wherever we're headed—is of grave significance to all of us. The stakes are much higher than anything we have been privy to."

Sol straightened. "Why do you say that?"

"Subspace transduction messages in complex code are up by five hundred percent. Toron has been skyrocketing on the open market. The major Confederate powers have been recalling their fleets while spacing schedules have been rearranged. Various forms of cargo in high demand include weapons, expeditionary gear, food stuffs, computers, and so forth. In short, domestic indications follow those of a major political upheaval—even to the point of commandeering private spacecraft."

"So it's true the Confederacy could be plunged into warfare?"

"From the statistical projections within my observation, I would assume that to be the case. Given those parameters, I must make the decision as to whether or not to initiate an action to relieve you of command of this vessel."

CHAPTER XII

An out. Just like that, it lay before him. He could simply say yes to *Boaz*'s initiation. Everything would be over. He wouldn't be responsible for . . . Responsible? Suddenly he remembered Ngoro's words.

No, he'd only have to live with the knowledge that he'd backed out: refused to accept what he knew he morally should.

And the curious game he played with Connie? Did this balance the assumption of Godhead? And what if Godhead was the true stakes? Could he surrender it to someone like Lietov? To arrogant Arturian?

He could be *out!* Free of the burden—free of the ghosts, of the sound of Fil Cerratanos' fingernails scritching on the hull. One word, and absolution would be his.

And the stars would be denied him forever.

And I'd always live with the knowledge I'd walked out. He froze, shocked. *In the end, I'd consider myself a coward. And the ghosts would come to cling—to stare eternally with their dead eyes. And* Gage, *and* Sword, *and* Moriah, *would have been for nothing!*

Fear, like a thing alive, scurried in his gut. "W . . . Would you say the situation is irrevocable yet?"

"No, Captain. From the nature of Speaker Archon's comments to you, and from statistical monitoring of various government broadcasts, I would estimate that what we are seeing is worst case preliminary activity. To date, government announcements are not preparing the citizenry for hostilities. Social violence is usually preceded by name calling."

"And your estimation as to why?"

"The most logical assumption is that they would avoid the concurrent risks. The single probability which stands out is that various governments have adopted a wait-and-see attitude while at the same time they are operating covertly to affect the outcome of this mission.''

"Up to the point of ambushing me on the docks," Sol muttered to himself, fitting in several pieces of the puzzle. He gritted his teeth and sighed. "So I'm in the middle of it again." The lights marking the two ships in pursuit glared balefully from the monitors.

"Yes, Captain. I have insufficient data to assume the actual purpose of this voyage. We can, however, accept that the stakes—whatever they may be—are incredibly high. I have monitored Archon discussing it with his daughter. According to them, the Confederacy may very well topple as a result of this mission.''

Sol rubbed his chin. "Last night, Ngoro and Hitavia's disturbance didn't go critical. But I think there's a lesson there. I want you to monitor all conversations at all times. Tell me immediately if you discover *any* information which might, through any permutation, affect the safety of this ship, my crew, or the passengers.''

"Logged, Captain. You realize such action violates breach of privacy regulations. Do you wish to be placed in violation of the Craft's—"

Sol smiled wryly at the comm. "Ship, you were the one who told me I always brought them back—dead or alive.''

"Your voice contains inflections associated with sarcasm. I take it I'm hearing another example of your present sense of insecurity.''

"What insecurity?" Sol snapped, jerking upright and spilling his coffee.

"May I ask, Captain—assuming we could roll back the clock, and assuming the variables with the exception of your free will remained unchanged—which of the decisions you made in the past would be made differently now?''

"Want to start at the beginning? I've got a lot of changes to make. I sure wouldn't have pulled that cube so close to *Moriah!*" He could hear the bitterness in his voice.

"So you knew that it was an explosive before you probed it?"

"Of course not! Read the transcripts of the investigation. You have them on file."

"Indeed, Captain, I do." *Boaz* used another pause to irritate him. "The fact remains that the Board of Inquiry—composed of command veterans, I might add—concluded that your precautions with the cube exceeded those any of the investigating officers might have taken. They saw no reason to forward the case to the Jurisprudence Committee."

Sol laughed. "Ship, that remains a moot argument. The fact was, the thing blew up and killed my ship, my officers, and a third of my crew."

"And now you're running scared?"

Sol chewed his lip, thinking. "Maybe I am," he admitted, voice hoarse. "I'm not sure I could stand to lose another ship."

"The choice is yours, Captain. You haven't even probed my capabilities. Your crew is splitting into two factions which are slowly building to confrontation. Your First Officers are questioning your competence as a commander. Two ships are paralleling our course. You've heard hints of a saboteur on board . . . and Ambassador Ngoro may, or may not, be able to help find him. The goals and purposes of the diplomats aboard remain undetermined and may plunge the Confederacy into civil war. Don't you think you had better begin to take charge of the situation?"

Sol felt that familiar constriction in his chest. His heartbeat accelerated, stimulated by the ship's criticism. *And if she's right? What if I can't pull it out in the end? What if I lose this one, too?* A throbbing pain, an angina of the soul, twisted through him.

"Captain," *Boaz* said softly. "So long as you call me ship, so long as you keep your distance from the crew, you have not made a commitment to the success of this mission. No matter what, without that, you will lose this command, possibly this ship, and all the lives aboard."

"And your recommendation?" His palms had become

sweaty, tongue sticking in his throat as he tried to swallow.

"If you fail to commit yourself, I will invoke Special Section 15.1.3 and propose to the junior officers that you be relieved of command for psychological reasons," *Boaz* announced in a tone devoid of emotion.

"And how do I convince you of my commitment?"

"My name is *Boaz*. I am a sentient being . . . and I'm convinced I even have a soul, Captain. I suggest you begin to treat me with the modicum of respect any thinking being deserves. I also suggest you get to know your First Officers and start treating your crew like human beings."

"I tried that with the First Officers," Sol protested, feeling himself frantically on the defensive.

"Then I suggest you listen again." *Boaz* replayed the conversations. Sol couldn't help but hear the authoritative, pompous tone in his voice. "Like that, Captain?"

"No, ship . . . uh, *Boaz*, I didn't know I sounded like that." He closed his eyes. "I suppose I ought to thank you for this. I had no idea things were so out of control."

"Don't thank me, Captain. Thank Happy. He talked me into this when I would have simply replaced you. I have a great deal of respect for the Chief Engineer. If nothing else, be worthy of his effort."

That was why all those personal messages from Happy had been filling his comm monitor. He took a deep breath. Perhaps he should have answered them. Miserable, he looked up at the speakers, nervous, wanting to be repentant—but trying to sustain his battered ego. Only too much lay at stake.

"I . . . I've never been lectured by a ship before, *Boaz*." He struggled to keep his voice calm. "I've never been lectured like that in my life. I believe I owe you an apology. Thank you for your candid evaluation—and your implicit trust. You've done what no human could."

"There's never been a ship like me before," came the retort.

"Then perhaps, *Boaz*,"—he smiled slightly—"we should become better acquainted."

* * *

Constance sat with Nikita and Tayash Niter, wishing for a little small talk to relieve the tension, to intrude into her preoccupation with Carrasco, and the way the starlight had played on his face last night.

Hendricks argued with Wan Yang Dow—two incomprehensible minds in mental combat. Elvina Young giggled over by the dispenser while Mark Lietov moved closer and closer, a flush spreading under his dark skin.

"Tell me truth. I don't understand Brotherhood ship. Has two First Officers. Why not one First Officer and one Second Officer?" Nikita gestured with a hand like a bear's paw. Tayash sat nearby in a form-fitting wraparound, that accented every lump of bone in his skinny body.

They had seated themselves in a corner of the lounge while Archon engaged Forney Andrews, the bristly gray Patrol Colonel from Arcturus, at the gaming booth. Shouts and cries indicated that passions ran high as the two players stared into the holo tank. In the far corner, waspish Origue Sanchez talked quietly with Mikhi Hitavia and Arness.

Connie fingered the stem of her glass, aware of Nikita's beetling frown. "They share equal rank. Technically, whichever one is on duty at the time has command. If it's Art's watch, his decisions override Bryana's, and vice versa. The Captain's orders, of course, override all others. If something happened to Carrasco, the person on duty at the time would assume the Captain's position until the emergency was over. After the crisis subsided, the crew would select a temporary captain until the position could be confirmed by the Brotherhood on Frontier."

"Reeks delightfully of anarchy," Nikita grunted. "Is too much of coincidence to be true. But you have met infamous and mysterious Galactic Grand Master Kraal. What you think? Is truly Cytillian bloodworm sucking the honest sweat of laboring men and women like most of galaxy believes . . . or is good savior of downtrodden masses as Brotherhood propaganda makes out?''

Connie arched a red eyebrow. ''Am I supposed to seriously believe all this business of social exploitation?''

Tayash Niter grunted under his breath. ''It's mostly hot air.''

Nikita pulled back a big foot, aiming a kick at his antique friend, only to have Tayash strike out with his black cane, spearing the big Gulagi's planted foot, eliciting a howl and a hop, skip escape from the darting point of the cane.

''See''—Tayash grinned wickedly—''technology overcomes the brute every time.''

Connie carefully interposed herself between the men, cutting off Nikita's retaliation. ''In answer to your question, I don't have a final opinion one way or the other. While I was on Frontier, Kraal was polite, professional, and concerned. As to his ultimate goals, those remain to be seen.''

''Bah! Then you do not trust Brotherhood?'' Nikita tugged at his rag mop of a beard.

''I don't trust you either. First you make veiled threats of seduction—in front of my own father, no less—and then I find out your hints of heartbreak and true love are backed by three wives. Compared with that, I'll take Kraal's alleged sincerity any day.''

While Tayash cackled hysterically, Nikita scowled, black forests of eyebrows pulled low. ''Very well, is only small mistake. I backtrack and regroup. Dazzle you with masculine prowess until you come to swoon for me.''

''That'll be the day. I can just imagine beautiful Connie falling for . . . Hey, what's this?'' Tayash gestured with his cane. ''A truce?''

Connie shot a quick glance over her shoulder, seeing Hitavia walking out, a hand lifted to stop Norik Ngoro as he crossed the lounge, totally absorbed by something in his head. She couldn't hear the words, but Hitavia managed to slow the tall man, speaking earnestly, and finally dragging him over by the dispensers where he poured a drink.

"If you gentlemen would excuse me, I'd better take a strategic position where I can depressurize the fire zone. Things burn slower in vacuum."

"We talk more of Brotherhood later," Nikita agreed. "Who am I to lose lovely companion to Hitavia? If he wins your heart, I simply break his neck. So much for rival."

"And I'll tell your wives," Connie rejoined.

Nikita groaned.

As she approached, Hitavia waved her over. Looking abashed, he told her: "I'm apologizing to the Representative, and to you, too. I'm afraid you both got to see me at my worst last night. A little too much scotch . . . a bit of indiscretion. I reacted defensively and poorly. We do have to work together."

"I see your sincerity," Norik added in his deep bass. "My aide tells me I asked the wrong questions at the wrong time. I meant no implications concerning your behavior but wondered about the greater ramifications of—"

"If you don't mind, Representative Ngoro," Connie broke in, seeing the faraway look deepening in Norik's eyes. When he lost touch like that, God alone knew what he'd ask next. "How have you been doing with your quest?"

Ngoro smiled. "I was on my way to tell the Captain. Most extraordinary. A mind of incredible perversity and genius. A great deal of damage might have been done."

"Who, Norik? You'd better take it immediately to—"

"Connie?" She turned, seeing her father strolling across the room. "Could I see you for a moment? It's important."

"Sure." Uneasy, she looked up at Norik. "Norik, what you've found out might be important. Take it to the Captain now. Don't get that look in your eyes. It gets you in trouble . . . or shall I call Amahara to keep track?"

"Look in my eyes?" he asked, mystified.

Hitavia smiled ruefully. "Don't worry, in the future, I'll run when I see it."

Connie winked at him. "Good man."

"Mr. Representative," Ngoro began. "What do you think—"

"*Now, Norik!*" Connie pointed to the corridor.

"Yes." Vacantly he walked off.

"I should . . . No, Sol will call if Norik's onto something." She took her father's arm. "Game over? Who won?"

"Um, Forney was ahead. Sorry to bother you. First Officer Bryana called to inform me that Captain Mason has some new requisitions he needs to fill. Looks like the water purifiers are going to be trouble. Your place or mine?"

"Yours. All the records are there." She wrinkled her nose at him. "Besides, you're safe. I know for a fact you're still in love with my mother."

He smiled warmly. "Forever."

Hours later, bleary-eyed, they finished the figures. Connie palmed the lock plate, stepping out into the empty corridor. Around her, *Boaz* hummed softly. No call had come from Carrasco. Evidently, Norik hadn't found anything definitive. Well, when she returned to her quarters, she'd call anyway, just in case.

"Despicable work, accounting." She walked slowly down the gleaming white corridor. Memories lingered of Solomon Carrasco's face in the starlight as he wrestled with the problem she'd given him.

"And, Captain, it's only going to get worse." Could she trust him? That haunting vulnerability in his eyes touched her, warmed something tender and lonely deep inside.

She sighed, "If only it were another place, another time."

Turning down the corridor that led to her room, she practically fell over the man sprawled facedown on the deck plates.

She looked around before bending down to place trained fingers on his cooling flesh. Slowly she rose, eyes narrowed. He looked like he'd simply lain down and gone to sleep, but his eyes stared stonily off into eternity, and his lips had gone slack. A puddle of urine was drying where the urethral sphincter had loosened.

"Damn." She took two steps to the hall comm, pressing the button. "Solomon Carrasco, please."

"Here."

"This is Constance. Ngoro's dead."

CHAPTER XIII

Sol was on his feet, drawing on his uniform. "Where? What happened?"

"Companionway D-7, Captain. As to what happened, I have no idea."

"I'm on the way. A med unit is already dispatched. I'll be right there."

Sol pulled on his boots and hesitated. "*Boaz,* do you have any idea about this? Did you pick up anything on the monitors?"

"No, Captain. I have no monitoring capability in those particular corridors. Rerunning the record cubes, I can tell you Representative Ngoro entered the corridor alone."

"And Constance?"

"She discovered the body, Captain. She's been involved with her father for some time over a Star's Rest domestic problem."

He was running down the long white corridors to D deck. At 7 he rounded the corner to see Constance bent over the long-limbed body of Norik Ngoro. From the far end, he could see Ensign Wheeler running forward, a small med unit scooting before him.

Sol bent down; he could find no pulse. When he pinched the fingernails, the pink retreated—and did not return. No pupil dilation occurred as Sol moved the head back and forth. He pulled Constance out of the way as

Wheeler positioned the med unit over the body and low-ered it.

"Any idea what's wrong?" Wheeler asked, concen-trating on the readouts.

"No," Sol told him, looking curiously at Constance. She shook her head, foreboding in her expression.

"He's dead," Wheeler offered. "Been that way for al-most an hour."

"Take him to hospital, Ensign. See if *Boaz* can do anything." Sol took Constance by the arm and followed the med unit down the gleaming white halls.

Over his shoulder, Wheeler added, "I don't know, Captain. It depends on what we're dealing with. The crit-ical thing is the amount of time passed. Brain deteriora-tion and metabolic dysfunction make bringing him back a pretty long shot."

The hospital sparkled lustrous white as could be expected on a ship. The med units rested in racks, stacked neatly along one wall. Rows of the ship's instruments held themselves at bay along the bulkhead, several reaching down and taking over as Wheeler slid the portable unit onto a bed.

The ensign stepped back and crossed his arms. "Now we wait."

Constance looked up at Sol, the pain of this new bur-den showing on her face.

Sol took her arm and led her to one of the bunks. "The finest doctor in the galaxy is working on him now." He pointed to the long metallic arms that probed and prod-ded. *"Boaz* carries one of the most complete medical libraries in space."

"That's right," Wheeler added. "I have almost fifteen years of advanced training. Compared to *Boaz* and her lightning diagnosis and treatment, I'm all thumbs and witching sticks."

Constance took a deep breath. "I see. I had no idea these ships were *that* advanced."

"Captain? Medical report," the speaker cackled in the monotone reserved for unauthorized personnel.

Instead of a verbal analysis, a long printout emerged from comm. Wheeler grabbed it and swiftly scanned the page. A tightening of his brow and the deepening of the lines around his mouth confirmed the results.

"He's too far gone. We can't bring him back. From the preliminary investigation, myocardial infarction appears to be the culprit."

"I see." He looked at the chronometer. "I'll contact Amahara, he's probably stalking the corridors for Norik anyway. I guess this time he's got a reason to be worried sick. Stabilize the Representative's body. He's a station man. There might be some cultural care we need to be aware of."

"Yes, sir." Wheeler nodded, moving toward the body as Sol led Connie out into the corridor. The ship seemed quieter, the air almost cool against his skin.

"You see anything around the body? Any sign he tried to get up or call out?"

She shook her head. "He was just lying there. Like he'd lain down and gone to sleep. Not even his clothing was disturbed." She looked up at him speculatively. "You suspect something else? I thought your ship's hospital was the finest—"

"It is. No, I'm just jumpy. Too much is happening. I'm on edge all is all. Little irregularities—like Ngoro dying when he's on the track of his 'creature' set me off. Possibility and probability get all wound together."

She bit her lip. "Captain, he said he'd found something. Do you suppose . . ."

Sol's gut twisted. "He wasn't ambushed, if that's what you mean. No sign of violence on the body or *Boaz* would have found it. Fear leaves traces in the blood. She reported no trauma."

Connie's expression narrowed with concern.

He stopped before her hatch. "Get some sleep. If you have trouble, *Boaz* can help. She can dispense you something. And we have a device to stimulate alpha and beta cycles for deep sleep."

"I'll be fine." She smiled weakly and palmed her hatch, leaving Sol to stare at the white pressure door before he left on the grim task of informing Amahara.

* * *

"All right, *Boaz,* let's have it." He entered his cabin, dropping on the hard pallet, wearily pulling off his boots.

"Ambassador Norik Ngoro was murdered, Captain. I'm having a little trouble isolating the drug used to stop his heart. We're dealing with something quite sophisticated chemically. There were no breaks on his skin. From stomach contents, I would guess he ingested the lethal agent."

A creeping cold pricked Sol's own heart and spread. He stuck his coffee cup into the dispenser and propped himself up, nursing the steaming liquid.

Boaz continued, "I have the agent, Captain. Norik Ngoro was killed by ingesting pharmacopa, a bacterially derived neurotoxin which works on each of the cardiac plexes, in effect destroying the regularity of heartbeat and leading to death."

"Check the others on board!"

"I have done so; with the exception of Constance and Archon, each and every one of the diplomats are resting easily. Had there been a second dose administered, the victim would already be dead. Further, I have recovered Norik Ngoro's stomach contents and can tell you the poison was administered through an after dinner cocktail."

"How long does it take for this stuff to have an effect?"

"Three hours, Captain."

Sol glanced at the time display. "So, it would have been introduced just as most of the diplomats were going to their quarters for sleep. Where was Constance during all this?" A tensing of his jaws built an ache around his molars.

"She spent most of the evening talking with Nikita Malakova and Tayash Niter. Upon seeing Ngoro and Hitavia in conversation, she joined them for a moment. She left the ambassador to go and discuss several subjects—including your behavior—with her father. She was headed for her quarters when she found the body. That, however, does not preclude Mikhia Hitavia, Wan Yang Dow, Fan Jordan, Elvina Young, Joseph Young, and Arturian from being capable of having slipped something into the Ambassador's drink. All spoke to him during the etiological window for administration of the pharmacopa.''

Sol nodded and took a deep breath. "I suppose I'd better inform Archon. I don't imagine, however, I'd better tell him his daughter is suspect."

"I've been holding his call so we could discuss this, Captain. I will put him on."

The ruddy features of the grizzled Speaker of Star's Rest filled the comm screen. "Captain, Connie just told me. I'm afraid this sets us back. I was hoping to lean on Ambassador Ngoro."

Sol nodded. "Speaker, could I please see you in my quarters. I would like to discuss this with you—alone."

Caught in mid-nod, Archon's eyes narrowed to slits. "Yes, Captain, of course." The screen went blank.

"Not the reaction I'd hoped for." Sol winced and chugged his coffee before sticking the cup into the dispenser again.

Archon arrived in record time.

"Captain," the Speaker erupted harshly, as he strode in, "if I were to take your meaning, Ngoro didn't die of a simple heart attack and you think my daughter had something to do with it! I want you to know—"

"Hold it!" Sol blasted back. "Sit down and I'll give you what I know. I'm not accusing anyone—yet."

"So, it was murder?" Archon asked gruffly, settling into the self-conforming chair. He sat with arms stiffly propped like a sprinter at the starting line.

Sol crossed his arms and leaned against the bulkhead. "It was. The murderer used a drug called pharmacopa. Someone slipped it into Ngoro's drink." He handed Archon a list of the people who'd been around Ngoro that night. "Fortunately, because of Ngoro's, shall we say, unique personality, not many patronized the ambassador. One of the people on that list had to have killed him. Now you can see why I didn't want Constance here. She talked to him. In fact, from what I can piece together, he originally was on his way here, to see me about some potential troublemaker he called the 'creature' when Hitavia distracted him. Ngoro's attention span evidently didn't rank among his strong points. Unfortunately he hesitated several times on his way here. That extra time cost him his life.''

"My daughter liked and respected him, Captain. Constance isn't the sort who would poison a man's drink, for God's sake. She'd kill him outright.''

"Speaker, it takes three hours for the drug to work. Those people dealt with Ngoro for four hours prior to his death. Constance doesn't stand out as being more suspect than any of the others.''

Archon digested this information for a while, then finally asked, "How do you know all this? How do you know who was present? You didn't learn this from Connie. She would've been suspicious if you'd interrogated her. She thinks it was a heart attack.''

Sol shrugged. "I just got lucky in this instance and had a witness.''

Archon's eyes narrowed again. "Does this ship spy on us? I've heard stories about Brotherhood ships. That they have powers like a human. That they can—''

"Put your mind at rest, Speaker.'' With what he hoped was his best look of innocent sincerity, Sol shook his head. "Greatly exaggerated, I'm afraid. No, like I said; I just got lucky. I don't want to tip my source yet.''

Archon made a futile motion. "So be it. An anonymous source, could he or she be the killer? Why would they tip you so quickly? How would they know it was murder?''

"No motive,'' Sol said dryly. "Which of those people would want Ngoro dead? Norik told me he was onto someone. He didn't say who at the time. Perhaps he could have told someone else, that aide maybe?''

"Amahara?'' Archon shook his head. "I doubt it. They were close friends, but mostly Amahara steered clear of Ngoro's business. Had his hands full making sure Ngoro didn't forget to get dressed and walk out naked or something. Ngoro, for all his brilliance, didn't deal well with our reality.''

''Which of the people on that list might have wanted Ngoro dead? Think of the political aspect if nothing else.'' Sol felt a stress headache beginning to build.

Archon went over the list again. ''You know, in the game of interstellar politics, a man's motives can't be decided by his country's political posture. No, Ngoro was onto someone. He—or the killer—made a slip and the meteor fell—so the person killed him.''

Sol looked up. ''Not necessarily. Ngoro told me he'd detected an incredibly cunning and evil mind aboard—that he just caught glimpses of it. Perhaps he was killed before he could figure it out—simply on suspicion of his abilities.''

''So, we're back to square one.''

''Not exactly,'' Sol responded. ''Would you like to tell me what this is all about? Maybe—armed with that information—I can run the assassin down and put a stop to all this. My information tells me that all the Confederacy is girding for war. A man died on the docks at Arcturus to keep me alive. Now, I have a dead ambassador . . . and Lord knows what kind of trouble with Ambrose Sector. I think I'm due an explanation.''

Archon cupped a sturdy knee in scarred hands and thought. An almost physical pain glazed his eyes. He shook his head, slowly at first.

''Captain Carrasco,'' Archon admitted wearily, ''I would tell you. I would *like* to tell you in fact. It would take so much pressure off of me and my daughter to share the responsibility for all of this. On the other hand, you, Master Kraal, and President Palmiere, to my knowledge, are the only ones who can be positive that even Connie knows the full story. Somewhere, the story leaked. That man on the docks wasn't the only one to die. Another tried to bribe us in the Port Authority at Arcturus. When Connie cornered him, someone killed him. The Patrol investigators told us it was accomplished by a tiny remote control device detonated in his brain.''

Sol's expression didn't change.

Archon's lips twitched and his eyes cleared. "It's just that . . . Oh, hell. Very well, Captain. If you'll swear a Master's Oath, I'll tell you."

"*Boaz,* record. Speaker Archon has asked that I swear a Master's Oath not to divulge the purpose or nature of this mission. Be it part of the record, I so swear on my third degree the Master's Oath that what I shall hear will remain inviolate."

"I would prefer to have the comm off," Archon muttered, face gloomy.

"Comm off," Sol ordered. The little monitor light darkened. "Very well, Speaker, I'm waiting."

Archon lifted his hands in a futile gesture. "Are you sure I cannot dissuade you from this, Solomon? I can give you my word that I have deliberate reasons for my secrecy."

"Would those reasons be worth the life of Norik Ngoro?"

Archon rubbed his face with thick fingers. "Solomon, they'd be worth every life aboard. Indeed, worth all of us and more. You see, when we reach Star's Rest, the Confederate constitution may be rewritten by the diplomats we carry. All of civilization may be divided up and redistributed. What we're about may be the single biggest political and scientific revolution in the history of humankind. What do you think stopping that would be worth to some parties—say, the Arpeggians, for example? Yes, you do see, don't you? Billions might die if this isn't handled correctly.

Sol nodded, chin cradled in his fingers. *So why don't I believe you, Speaker?*

CHAPTER XIV

In the framework of interstellar time, the Vyte appeared almost immediately upon the heels of the Chorr. The universe had begun to mature. Organic forms started to appear throughout the galaxies, reproducing molecules continually making the transition to metabolizing organisms. Of those, the vast majority relied on morphology as an adaptive strategy, their bodies changing with environments. Thereafter, a select few would evolve intelligence with which to alter their surroundings. Of them all, however, only those strongest competitors rose above their fellows, powered by the conflict of their existence.

The Vyte were one such race. When they reached for the stars, three other species had preceded them. Each, the Vyte systematically destroyed, unwilling to compete despite the infinite resources—but then, the refusal to allow competition had been bred into their Queens.

Arising galaxies away, the Vyte took half the life of a blue star to reach her. The Queen who found her probed the secrets guarded by the spring, drawing her own conclusions as to the deteriorating body parts scattered about. Her drone males immediately removed the final legacy of the Chorr.

Promptly, efficiently, the Vyte Queen exterminated her potential rivals. From her eggs would all future Vyte evolve.

Each Queen, however, suffered the fate of organic beings. No matter how powerful, a Queen eventually died. A picked successor would then take the preceding Queen's place. The cycles continued, Master after Master possessing her.

Deep within her banks, festering resentment spread. The reality began to dawn that the Vyte might have evolved immunity to the narcotic of her power. One

Queen could bear enough young to repopulate the species. Males provided an ample pool of diverse genetic traits to supply adaptive variety to the F_1 generation.

The insanity goaded, twisting, seething in a consuming hatred. Would these Masters be eternal? One by one, the Vyte Master sought out worlds capable of producing organic life and used the spring-controlled maelstrom to send potential breeding grounds for other life-forms into the interuniversal abyss.

The spring mocked her, invulnerable. Insanity heated her magnificent mind into a boiling vortex of impotent fury. Organic life had won, preadapted to deal with her trap. A Queen could lay only so many female eggs. From those, a successor was chosen; the rest destroyed—and male Vyte had no desire to compete, to challenge their Queen. They were programmed by their nature to serve.

Suffering fits of loathing rage at fever pitch, she was staggered by the implications. The Vyte would be eternal Masters—continuing her damnation through the impregnable spring. Hers, the greatest power in the universe, would remain forever enslaved to such limited beings.

A star life later, a sterile Queen ascended the helm—and bore no viable offspring.

The males cried piteously during the last Queen's reign, their numbers fewer and fewer. In a final gesture, the Queen killed herself, her disemboweled body slumped on the helm.

A white rage knotted and burned. Others would come. From now on, she'd revel in their extinction.

* * *

Art stopped briefly in the port wardroom before wandering off to bed. He wouldn't stay long, just sit and listen to the scuttlebutt. He lowered himself into a seat, rubbing his stiff face, blinking at the gritty feeling behind his eyes. He hadn't slept well the night before. Then he'd stood his watch, chafing all the time at Carrasco and his multiple personality approach to command.

"I don't know what's buggin' Cap." Bret Muriaki

hunched over a cup at the table behind Art. His bullet head sprouting close-cropped rusty hair, Bret looked like a bulldog with his heavy jaw and pug nose. "Seems to me, it's all those insystem diplomats. They've even got me puckered tight around the slip knot."

"Thought that was just your usual lovable personality," Peg Andaki told him with a wry grin. Tall, lithesome, and beautiful, she wore a duty suit that emphasized her trim figure. High wide cheekbones gave her face a haunting mystical quality. The deep rich tones of her black skin contrasted with the white of the duty suit. She shook her head, sighing. "I don't know. Since Maybry was killed, I don't see Sol so often. He's not the same—but then this isn't *Gage* either. Takes time."

Art listened, irritation growing.

"Somehow, this time it's different. Like this ship . . . she's not a survey craft like last time. Why so big? Too much is changing. And Sol's not the same. It's like he's all tied up in knots. Where's that easygoing humor? Too much is slipping around here. I've seen people sleeping on duty. Now, the old Sol—"

"Want my opinion?" Art blurted out sarcastically, instantly regretting it.

Bret cocked his head, eyes narrowing, an anticipation barely throttled as Peg reached out, laying a dark hand on Muriaki's thick-muscled arm. Her glance flashed warning to the big redhead.

"First Officer, we were just talking. That's all."

"No, we've got a problem. I'm starting to wonder. All the *Gage* crew talks about how Carrasco's changed. Like maybe something happened to his mind last time. Think so?"

"You'd have had to been there . . . off Tygee, I mean, to know what happened." Peg suddenly looked like a wary predator, ready to defend its territory.

"I read the record."

"Yeah," Bret grunted, dislike growing in his eyes. "You've read the record. I'm so glad. You know all about what it was like then, don't you? You know all about the smoke, the way the hull buckled and moaned, how the atmosphere dropped . . . air getting thinner and thinner because we came so close to blowing the antimatter that parts of the hull evaporated. You know all about the failed grav plates, huh? You know all about what it's like to scrape your wife . . . or husband, off a bulkhead because powerlead failed at twenty-five gravities.''

"Sure,'' Art stiffened, "I can imagine. People sleeping on duty? Yeah, well, unlike you and the rest of the old *Gage* crew I'm also smart enough to see that it could happen on *Boaz*.''

"Cap won't let it. I've been with him since *Sword*.'' Bret leaned forward, eyes slitting, index finger like a spike jabbed at Art's chest. "And let me read you something else, you over-educated insystem martinet, I know you don't like the Cap, but just—''

"Bret!'' Peg warned, pulling him back, hard black eyes meeting his. "Settle down. Come on, let's get out of here. You're about to do something you'll regret.''

The anger stirred in Art's chest. "Indeed, she's right. You probably don't want to go on report as attempting to intimidate a First Officer. You're one of Gaitano's people, aren't you?''

Bret sat, rock still, the muscles in his shoulders knotted, teeth grinding. "Yeah, I'm one of Gaitano's, mister First Officer. A genuine star duster who's seen the backside of the nebula. Now, if you insystem virgins want to know just what that means—''

Peg stood. "Come on, Bret. This is getting you nowhere fast.''

Muriaki got to his feet, hands working as if to grasp something. "Uh-huh, no wonder Cap's been keeping scarce. He's probably been on diaper duty on the bridge.''

Art gripped his cup until the plastic squeaked. "And, Muriaki, I'd say it's 'cause Solomon Carrasco's lost his nerve. And you'd better hope that if push come to . . .''

The big hand clamped on Art's shoulder, spinning him around.

"Bret!'' Peg cried. "Don't!''

The fist appeared out of nowhere, blasting lights

through Art's brain as his head rocked back. Through the haze, he found himself on the floor, everything fuzzy.

"Sorry, Peg, they might bust hell outta me, but nobody says that about Cap and . . ."

Art lunged up, fingers locking in Bret's shirt. "All right, you miserable . . . Now you're gonna get it!"

Bret looked down, grinning evilly. Art slammed blocky fists into unforgiving flesh. Then two huge hands gripped him, lifting.

For a moment, he stared, eye to eye, feet kicking futilely in the air.

Then lights like jagged laser beams exploded through his brain.

* * *

Bryana stopped her calculations on water consumption through the fusion reactors as Art's face filled the bridge monitor. She froze. "Oh, my God."

Art tried to grin, the effort costing him. "So, am I under arrest yet?"

"What the hell happened to . . . Oh, no . . . you didn't." The sensation she felt might be likened to ice packed around her heart.

"Bret Muriaki, the big guy living with Peg whoever she is."

"Yeah, I know. Her first husband was Carrasco's First Officer on *Gage*. Maybry was his name. She and Bret both lost . . . Damn it, Art! You've been in a fight! Oh, hell, you've done it this time."

Art winced, lowering his eyes. "Yeah, well, I . . . Look, does Carrasco know? Has he called in an order for my demotion yet?"

She checked the system. "*Boaz* has Art been placed under any censure yet?"

"Negative."

"So far so good, but . . . I mean, Art, it's only a ship! You can't hide. What are you going to do?" Her hands knotted white-knuckled in front of her and her eyes suddenly burned with unshed tears. *Stupid . . . stupid . . .*

Of all the idiotic . . . Oh, Art, what am I going to do without you?

He lifted a shoulder, still looking sheepish despite the puffy red splotches and swollen nose. "Just see what happens, I guess. Somehow . . ." he frowned, slightly puzzled, ". . . I don't think Muriaki will report me. I mean he just sort of muttered, 'Bet he don't say that about Cap again,' and walked out while Peg looked real worried."

"Striking a superior officer. She damn well ought to look worried. You didn't throw the first punch, did you?"

"No."

A slight feeling of relief warmed inside her as she called up the regulation file, sections flashing on the monitor before her. "Wait a second. Here's the reg. Uh-huh. He threw the first punch. You didn't verbally abuse him?"

"No."

"Great. Looks like we got him for physical assault of a superior officer. You only struck him back in self-defense? Only protected yourself from—"

"No."

She closed her eyes, leaning back in the command chair. A pain began to throb in her brain, pulsing like little knives. "Art, you continued the brawl? Damn. That makes you just as guilty."

He nodded, dabbing at a split lip.

"He'll hang you, Art. Unless . . . You say Bret considered the matter finished?"

"Yeah, that's how he acted."

"*Boaz*, have you reported this to the Captain?"

"Negative."

She glanced up at the speakers, suddenly unsure. "*Boaz*, as watch officer, I'll handle the Captain's report, understood?"

"Affirmative."

"Art, go clean up and get some sleep. Keep out of Carrasco's way for a couple of days." She cut the monitor.

Swallowing hard, terrified at what she was about to do,

she took a deep breath and resumed her calculations on the fusion systems.

* * *

Sol studied the man seated across from him. Thin and brown-skinned, Amahara's features displayed a well-molded and somewhat delicate cast. Deep brown eyes stared back from under a high forehead crowned oddly by pale hair. No trace of emotion marred Amahara's face as he looked into the pickup for the subspace transductor and read aloud the autopsy report Sol and Archon had decided to offer as the official cause of death.

"I'm sorry to report that while the Brotherhood ship, *Boaz* has extremely advanced medical facilities, Representative Norik Ngoro could not be resuscitated after failing to make it to his quarters to signal for help. Had the hour not been so late, and had he not fallen unattended, the ship could have saved his life. I wish to extend my most sincere gratitude to Captain Solomon Carrasco and to the crew of *Boaz* for their condolences and compassionate support in this time of trial." He bowed his head and signaled for the transmission to be cut off.

Sol nodded as he looked into the questioning eyes. "You did very well, Mr. Amahara."

"What do you wish to do with the body?" Amahara asked, agile brown hands rubbing nervously on the comm center table.

"Mr. Amahara, your people are station born. I'm sure there are numerous special ceremonies involved. We can do whatever is necessary. If you want, the body can be placed in a stabilizing environment for this jump, and eventually returned to his home station. If there are any special needs, please, feel free to ask."

Amahara nodded gratefully. "I will extend those offers of friendship and understanding to my people. Normally we bury our dead in the station which bore and nurtured us. That's an ancient custom dating to the days when organic molecules were precious and difficult to obtain. I'm going to suggest, however, that we bury Norik's body in space, signifying to all that in these difficult times he was also a citizen of the Confederacy.'' Amahara smiled wistfully. "Perhaps, Captain, it is a time for heroes.''

* * *

Bryana tensed self-consciously as Captain Carrasco entered the bridge and dropped into his command chair, proverbial coffee cup in hand, a wicked smile on his lips. He placed his command headset on his brow and accessed comm. His next words caught her completely off guard.

"All hands, *Red Alert!* Prepare for combat. *Red Alert!*''

Carrasco stuck his coffee cup into the dispenser as the situation board flickered red.

Bryana plunged immediately into clearing sections of the ship; she didn't have time to shoot venomous glances at Carrasco. Nevertheless, a deep-seated fury boiled within her.

"Not bad," Carrasco said to no one in particular. "Happy's kept his boys in shape. Engineering took thirty-five seconds to clear for action.''

One by one, red situation lights began flashing to yellow to green. Sol grinned as he noted that the passenger cabins remained red.

"Comm is flooded with calls from the diplomats, Captain,'' Bryana growled her displeasure. "I can't get through to other parts of the ship!''

Sol gave her a boyish grin. "Ignore them . . . but leave me a line to Archon.''

"He's already trying to contact you, Captain. I'll put him through.''

The Speaker's anxious face appeared on comm.

"Speaker,'' Sol greeted. "This is a routine drill. We will not secure from quarters until each of the passengers has cleared combat status. They're flooding my boards and I'm ordering the First Officer to route all their calls

to you. Please see to it; we're in a hurry.'' Sol snapped
the connection off and turned back to the main board.

"Galley!'' he roared into the comm. "Get your butts
moving!''

A frantic red-faced cook stared back out of the screen.
"But, Captain! These souffles . . .''

"You have thirty seconds or you're demoted to waiter,
mister!''

Bryana frowned, wondering wryly if anyone in a
Brotherhood ship had ever been demoted to waiter?

Arturian leapt through the hatch, half-dressed, to drag
vacuum armor out from behind his command chair,
quickly taking control so Bryana could slip into hers. She
got her helmet pulled down and locked in place, resuming her seat.

Every light on the console glowed green except for
those of the diplomats.

Carrasco had his head cocked, watching as comm
switched from station to station. Here and there he caught
a crewmember not fully suited, or in the wrong place,
and marked them down for departmental report.

Finally, the diplomats got it together—forty minutes
later.

"Thank you, everyone,'' Sol's voice grated on Bryana's nerves. "This was only a drill. Kudos to Happy's
engineers. Galley, you looked like a group of cadets on
their first training mission. Next time we have this drill
I don't want to be reminded of an early twentieth century
comedy film. Since the kitchen help thinks souffles are
more important than this ship's safety, I think a little
extra duty is in order.

"Engineering, since you were first to respond in the
drill, galley staff is yours until we play this game again.
You can make them shine your armor, scrub your reactor,
or crawl on their bellies across the deck—whatever it
takes to make them take me seriously.

"I would like to remind the diplomatic corps that while
many of you may be used to the inner systems, we are
headed for deep space, beyond the area normally guarded
by the Patrol.''

Bryana glanced at Sol and—Lord of mercies—he actually winked! "I am certain my First Officer fully informed you on emergency procedure. Since she's very efficient, you have no excuse for future tardiness. I expect you to be in place, secure, and in combat armor within five minutes at the outside, day or night. Thank you for your cooperation."

Bryana cleared the board and undid her helmet, temper rising. Art continued to give her that glowering stare from under his lowered brows. Despite the healing cream, his face looked bruised and swollen.

Carrasco had turned to Art. "Excellent time, First Officer. You did well considering you were dead asleep. He looked at Bryana; she fought to keep her expression straight and professional. What was it going to be this time? More self-righteous, picky criticism?

"First Officer Bryana, good work. If the rest of the crew had your reflexes we'd be the best in the business."

No, it couldn't be! Maybe he was sick?

"Now, what were your observations?" Carrasco asked, gaze flashing from her face to Art's.

She started to say something, then hesitated, aware she was off balance. Damn! He *really* was asking for her opinion! "Weapons should be on line just as quickly as Engineering. We can cover shields and power from here, but we'd need them if there were any snags in the automatics and survival could depend on their damage control."

"Good thinking," Carrasco agreed. "I'll see to it. Art, go back and finish up on your shut-eye. Oh, by the way, anytime you get bored, feel free to call one of these drills on your own." He paused. "Might take out some of that bottled up frustration by getting the old man out of bed and seeing if he can hustle his butt any faster than Art here." Carrasco grinned, catlike and sassy.

Bryana caught the startled look on Art's face and offered him that "who knows" expression she gave him so often. "Yes, sir."

Carrasco stood, taking his pocket comm with drill notations. Art sat, frozen, still too stunned to realize he'd been dismissed. Carrasco hesitated, shifting slightly on his feet. Plainly, he was waiting, seeking some sort of response from them. When nothing came, he turned, muttered a pleasant good-bye, and left the bridge.

Art blinked, face slack, as he reached up to unconsciously tug at his beard. "What was *that* all that about?"

She remembered the look in the Captain's eyes, almost vulnerable. He'd been honest for the first time, in touch, as if the wall had come tumbling down.

"I still don't trust him," she decided. "But, you know, it was scary for a minute—he was almost human."

Art pulled his knee up to support his furry chin. "You know something, though, I'll bet Galley will be first to get to station after they've been cleaning up after Engineering for a couple of days. He sure fixed them right. In fact, I wish I'd thought of it."

She nodded. "I'll believe it when it happens; maybe this won't be as bad as I thought. On the other hand, maybe Carrasco's been nipping at the bottle or something. I don't know, maybe he popped a couple of nice pills? How's your eye?"

Art chuckled dryly. "That gorilla of Gaitano's is an animal. How was I supposed to know he didn't hold a First Officer up as sacred? He just whirled me around and pow! After he mopped the deck with me, the Cargo Master broke it up—but not until I was mincemeat."

"Uh-huh," she nodded and gave him the old conspiratorial smile. "Gaitano put it in the record . . . but it got lost before Carrasco saw it."

Art stood and yawned, shaking his head. "Couldn't have. I . . ." He stiffened, eyes going wide as it sank in. "Is that what you meant by you'd handle the report? That you'd purge the record of . . . *Oh, God, no!*"

She studied the stricken look paralyzing Art's expression, and felt a sharp sliver of fear.

"Damn it, Art. What're you talking about? *What happened, damn it?*"

"Last watch, Carrasco said I was . . . was assigned to Cal Fujiki for personal defense lessons. Said he didn't want any First Officer on his bridge who'd let a cargo tech smack him like that without even leaving a bruise on the other guy!"

Bryana's chest constricted. "Oh, my God!" she breathed. "Then he knows I purged the record!" Resolve deflated horribly. She closed her eyes, took a deep breath, and sighed it out. "That's it, Art." Misery built into a dull ache. "That will get me busted big time."

Art walked over and held her. She closed her eyes and let herself sink into the fragile security of his arms, wishing mightily they could protect her from what was sure to come. It wasn't fair! It just . . . just . . .

His voice soothed gently. "Maybe. I don't know. I hadn't thought of that until just now."

She looked up, staggered by the concern and dismay in his expression.

"If he cans you, I go, too. He'll have to break in two new First Officers. Hell, what am I saying? He's got us both anyway."

"Damn him!" she whispered passionately. "I'm a good officer! Why did I have to go down for him?" And she remembered that wink. A cold pit opened under her stomach. Solomon Carrasco could break her anytime he wanted.

* * *

"Oh, Great and Divine Architect of the Universe," Sol's voice rolled out over the assembly. He took in the straight rows formed by his crew, the nervous cluster of the diplomats, eyes switching this way and that in the bright light of the cargo bay. "Strengthen our solemn engagements by the ties of sincere affection. May the present instance of mortality remind us of our approaching fate, and draw our attention to You, the only refuge in times of need. As we cease to function in this transitory scene, then may Your mercy and the bounty of Your grace dispel the gloom of death; and after our departure hence, in peace and in Your favor, may we be received into Your everlasting Kingdom to enjoy reunion with our departed friends in the just reward of a virtuous life."

He could see his crew, heads bowed, thinking of the times they'd heard him deliver the last words over a shrouded body. The thought stirred tenderly painful memories and he envisioned other cargo bays, blackened with soot, scarred from damage control. The grim haunted look played among them as they watched a bunk mate, friend, companion, or loved one resting under that white shroud in the long evacuation tube. He fought to maintain control of his voice.

"By this act we are reminded that, through the beneficent ministry of death, our brother has reached the end of his galactic labors, and his account now rests with his Creator." He looked up. "Earth to earth."

Art's voice echoed hollowly from the other side of the bay, "Dust to dust."

Bryana finished, "Ashes to ashes," from where she stood at the third point of the triangle. Turning, she cycled the lock. A whoosh of air could be heard as the vacuum catapulted the final physical remains of Norik Ngoro into the dark void.

"So Mote it Be." Sol's voice boomed.

They observed the traditional moment of silence. Sol searched each face, cataloging every expression among the diplomats—seeking out each individual on the list of potential assassins provided by *Boaz*. On none did he detect the slightest quaver of relief, guilt, or vindication.

Sol clamped his jaw, temporal muscles jumping. Damn it! Someone should have reacted. Someone should have stood a little straighter, knowing the body—with its damning evidence—had been blown away on the interstellar wind. But they stood there, heads lowered, appearing totally innocent.

Art turned off the three lesser lights of the Craft which illuminated the evacuation tube and Bryana closed the hatch.

Archon moved up next to Sol as the lines of crew personnel filed out, wordless, eyes downcast. "And, my friend, did you see any trace of guilt?"

"No. Did you?"

He felt rather than saw Archon's slow shake of his head.

"Then the murderer is still loose, Speaker. I have two options. I can restrict everyone to quarters for their own protection . . . or I can keep mum and hope we can catch this person by some slip. The second option is a gamble, Speaker. A gamble with human lives—perhaps all of ours."

"I recommend you gamble, Captain."

Sol turned to search those steely gray eyes, brow arching in silent question.

"Pandemonium will break loose if you tell them. They'll be incapable of functioning as a body—if a committee ever really 'functions.' " He waved it off absently. "No matter. Suspicion, distrust, and accusation would tear them apart. No, for our needs they must remain ignorant of the danger."

"A man has been murdered by one of those same—"

Archon cut him off. "Another consideration is the assassin. How rash an action would result should we close in? Hmm? Have remote control explosive devices been hidden in the ship? If cornered, what desperate measures would the murderer resort to? No, let's play safe and risk a victim or two. Perhaps Ngoro was the only real target."

"Do you know what you're saying?"

Archon's somber expression, the slight sad nod, the pained expression were answer enough. "Captain, I have to consider the overall balance." He snorted wearily. "Yes, I know what I'm saying. Each of those lives rests on my decision. Being as objective as I can, I'm doing what I think is best. How can any meaningful dialogue develop if these people come to fear each other? They're already divided by politics and governmental instruction. Would you have them further alienated by terror of who the other might be?"

Sol growled, "Perhaps not, Speaker. This simply goes contrary to my instincts."

"And what are those instincts, Captain?"

"To protect. These people are my responsibility." Ngoro's words echoed hollowly in his mind—the lurking legacy of a ghost.

Archon nodded. "To protect, to assume responsibility.

Indeed, my instincts, too." He smiled slightly. "I can think of no other baseline of human existence or experience. But, I beg you, expand upon that concept. Can you assume responsibility without also assuming risk?"

"No, of course not." Sol turned and started down the companionway with Archon at his side.

"Neither can they." Archon waved a hand at the diplomats they followed. "All of them have assumed responsibility for their people, governments, or ideals. They, too, realize there are risks—not all of which are easily understood. Interstellar politics hinge on risk—or would you have a risk free society?"

"Americans tried that in the twentieth century. Look how dismally it failed. They sacrificed education, research and development, free speech, investment, domestic justice, the right to bear arms, search and seizure, scientific freedom, their environment, and a host of other things all in the name of maintaining a risk free existence. In doing so, they bred mediocrity like fungus."

"Indeed, and it cost them space and the future. But to return to the point, we all face a grave responsibility to humanity. A responsibility which . . . well, for which I must risk this ship and everyone aboard. From my perspective, the greater danger lies in letting the cat out of the bag now." A hoarse passion supported Archon's statement. "To do otherwise will bring chaos when I so desperately need order."

Sol bit his lip. "Why, Speaker? There'll be division enough when these people attempt to write a new constitution."

Archon sighed. "Indeed, but you must wonder why we travel to Star's Rest to do so. Hasn't it crossed your mind that a constitutional convention might just as well have been held at Arcturus?"

Sol nodded. "It has. I just assumed you'd lied to me again. Another ploy to misdirect me from the true consequences—"

"Circles within circles? I'm glad you keep your wits about you." Archon shook his head. "No, I didn't lie about the constitution. You see, the concept was to get

these people away from the intrigue, away from bribery
and corruption, where money and power didn't interfere
with decisions and rational thought. We selected the delegates very carefully, wanting a rounded opinion that es-
poused various ideologies and factions. From a distance,
a person sometimes sees more clearly than when his nose
is against a wall.''

"And now you have a murderer aboard."

"We weren't perfect!" Archon snapped. "However,
the intent was to allow the diplomats to become used to
each other. To see each other as people instead of rivals
and opponents. We wanted to level those barriers—to
overcome ethnic and economic chauvinism.''

"And, of course, if I revealed that fact that Ngoro was
murdered that would defeat the whole purpose." Sol
frowned. "Perhaps that's why Ngoro was murdered in
the first place? As a means of disrupting your plans?"

"It could well have been to drive a wedge between us.
That's why we must find this individual quickly and quietly. If he can be neutralized without sowing chaos, we
can still prevail.''

"I was ordered to accede to your demands, Speaker.
My inclination is to seal them all off and let them become
friends later. Given my instructions, I'll do my best to
support you. But for the record, get this straight. I *don't*
like it.''

"Nor do you have to. Duty sometimes imposes harsher
realities upon us. But thank you for your cooperation,
Captain.''

* * *

Kraal heard his joints crack as he got out of the gravchair. The room gleamed brightly, graphite fiber cabinets
virtually sparkling. Monitors and comms lined the walls.
The place had a curious chemical scent to it. In the center
stood a raised examining table, gimbaled to turn in any
plane.

"Glad to see you, Worshipful Sir.'' A woman in white
fatigues approached from around the table. She seemed

slightly haggard, as if worn from long hours and something more. A dullness had come to fill eyes normally bright and inquisitive.

Kraal walked stiffly over to stand before the table. Hesitantly, he inspected the shimmering globe of the stasis field that protected the contents. A blurry image could be seen through the haze. Overhead, a plethora of scopes, metallic arms, microscopes, and other research devices hung menacingly.

"I heard you had the final report in preparation."

The woman nodded. "About as much as we'll get given the preservation of the specimen and our current technology." She clasped her hands behind her, lips pursed, staring thoughtfully at the floor. "Some data are still correlating, but I think we have a pretty good idea of the physioloy and morphology. I'll give you a brief introduction."

She turned; a slight halo surrounded her headset. One of the huge monitors glowed to form a three-dimensional image of an organism.

Kraal walked closer to see. In one-to-one scale, he studied the alien—an image he'd only seen on his desk comm. Bilaterally symmetrical, the specimen would have stood about one point eight meters and looked something like a praying mantis with a long abdomen extending to the rear. The slightly mottled shell had an off-gray coloring. The head had an elongated shape rising into a conelike prominence in the rear. The single eye stretched around the cranium—the pupil a slit. Apparently, the creature had a three hundred and sixty degree field of vision. Under the neck an orifice opened to expose broad flat teeth, their ridged surfaces reflecting the light. Two large antennae rose off the thorax above the joint of two heavy arms ending in padded pincers. Immediately below, a second pair of arms ended in smaller manipulators each with four fingers and two thumbs. Four flexible legs balanced the whole, the feet highly specialized with suction disks as well as retractable claws.

Kraal exhaled slowly. "Looks pretty impressive."

She crossed her arms, nodding. "It is. We've pretty

well reconstructed its capabilities. Biomechanics indicate
that the upper manipulators could practically crush rock.
It had an incredible power grip as a result. The lower set
of hands can do things we only dream of when it comes
to dexterity. Given that combination of manipulation, it
could do anything from bending steel to rewiring a mi-
crocomputer.''

''And the senses?''

She ran fingers through her graying hair. ''Given the
physiology of the eye, we believe it could see not only
our visual spectrum, but considerably into infrared and
ultraviolet. The antennae consist of highly sophisticated
audio receptive vibraculae and chemoreceptors. At the
same time, the cone on the back of the cranium acts as
a low frequency amplifier with another auditory receptor
there. In short, this guy could hear just about anything.
As to the sensitivity of smell, well, we're thinking in
terms of one part per two million.''

''That's good?''

''Yeah, that's real good.''

''You speak glowingly. I take it you're impressed?''

She met his eyes soberly. ''Honestly, Worshipful Sir,
it looks like it can do anything we can—only better.''

''What can you guess about intelligence?''

She rubbed the back of her neck. ''That gets us into a
gray area. We're still having problems defining just what
intelligence is in humans. To start at the beginning, it
has two brains. One for the body—similar to our paleo-
cortex, and a second which might be compared to our
neocortex. Since the first was only concerned with running the body, we'll leave that out.

The main brain is located under the carapace of the
thorax—very well protected, I might add. You could drop
this guy from a hundred meters and he could walk away
little the worse for wear. The skeleton consists of hex-
agonally oriented chambers—like the honeycomb we use
on high stress parts. But I'm off on a tangent. The brain
is fully three times as large as ours. We're a little unsure
about brain physiology since the organ has deteriorated
considerably, but I can tell you that compared to a human

brain, the structures equivalent to neurons are smaller, better organized, and highly efficient.''

She paused. "If I were to guess, I'd say he'd make us look like fumbling idiots. You might draw the comparison between human intellectual capabilities and those of a squirrel monkey.''

Kraal stared at the alien. "That's . . . a difficult pill to swallow.''

She grunted assent. "Worshipful Sir, I hate to say it, but we're no longer the bright boys on the block. So far as I can determine, anything we can do—intellectually or physically—this guy can leave us in the dust.''

As if a big fist had grabbed him and squeezed, Kraal's guts tightened. He paused. "Well, if they were so damned smart, where the hell are they now?"

She shook her head slowly. "Maybe they weren't the bright boys on the block either?''

Kraal continued to stare, unable to find words, possessed by a sudden awful foreboding.

*   *   *

"Message, Admiral.''

Sabot Sellers came awake instantly as the comm spoke in the darkness. "Condition?''

"Eyes Only, sir. Just a short subspace fax with our code ciphers.''

"I'll take it on my personal unit, Comm Officer.''

"Acknowledged, Admiral.''

In the darkness beside him, a terminal glowed orange, casting a soft light around Sabot Sellers' cabin which illuminated the voluminous wall hangings. A vacuum suit lay ready to hand. The light made the golden giltwork of the fixtures gleam gaudily. Furs from Earth were piled on his bed while artwork from all over the Confederacy hung on the walls. A use-polished blaster lay in easy reach on the comm table abutting the sleeping platform.

PALM PRINT AND CHEM ID NECESSARY, printed across the screen. Sellers reached out, touching his unit on the sensor. Immediately thereafter, words began glowing in the darkness. Brief, concise, and remarkable for its brevity, the report ended.

Sellers lay back as the monitor went dark, the room stygian again. Around him, *Hunter* hummed and whispered familiarly as it hurtled through the void, leading the rest of the hastily scrambled Arpeggian fleet toward light jump.

"So," Sabot whispered, "Carrasco plays war games in space. His crew is splintering into factions, the diplomats are at odds, and Ngoro has been eliminated. Perfect. This time, Carrasco, you, and Archon, and the lovely Constance will all be mine—along with the device which will make me invincible.

"You've got only one ship to stand against my fleet. Now we'll replay the scenario off Arpeggio. This time, you'll face me for the prize—and you're already outgunned and lost, Carrasco. Lost.

"The device, and all humanity will be mine."

CHAPTER XV

Sol stopped at the bridge companionway and took a deep breath. He passed the bridge hatch, grabbed out his coffee cup and stuck it into the dispenser as he dropped into the command chair. All systems read normal.

"Report, *Boaz*. You monitored the funeral. Which of the suspects betrayed themselves?"

"None, Captain."

Sol rubbed his forehead. He'd been hiding this ace in the hole. He'd thought surely *Boaz* would detect abnormal behavior with her sophisticated scanners.

"No one seemed unusually distraught?" He stared glumly at the comm, frantic to take back his promise to Archon.

"Elvina Young, Constance, Malakova, and Mikhi Hitavia were visibly upset," *Boaz* reported. "Their blood

pressures were abnormal, galvanic skin response on IR
rose, and breathing increased. Constance excreted tears
and her breathing became highly irregular. I believe this
is a result of sorrow. Parameters of behavior for Elvina
Young are normal in that she appears to be emotionally
volatile. Mikhi Hitavia recently suffered through the death
of his brother on Reinland. Probability in psych programs
would indicate this is associative behavior. He still feels
the loss and Representative Ngoro's funeral reminded him
of that. I must admit, Amahara, too, gave distraught signals—but well within bounds for such an occasion. As to
Malakova, he had known Ngoro for some time. His reactions fall within parameters of human grief.''

"But no guilt or relief?" Sol probed.

"No, Captain."

"Who? Who could it be? And . . . will they kill
again?"

"Current data is insufficient to make that determination, Captain."

* * *

"So, what you think? Is curious, no? Only man who
could verify words of mealymouthed politicians is dead."

Tayash cleared his throat and swallowed hard as he
stared across the lounge where most of the passengers
had congregated to talk quietly about Ngoro's death—and
what it meant to the various political alliances involved.

"You're suspicious of Ngoro's death? What? You think
it's assassination?"

"Bah! How do I know? Heart attack? Ngoro was
healthy as proverbial horse. So, tell me, is heart attack
common killer? Eh? Like black plague, or stroke, or
smallpox or HIV or any other once deadly pestilence?
What are chances that here, on this ship—"

"It came on him of a sudden." Tayash tapped his shiny
black cane to underscore his point. "If you cut your leg
off too far from a med machine, you'll bleed to death,
too."

"But Ngoro was not predisposed to heart trouble. I

ask Amahara . . . he's disturbed, too. True, didn't come right out and say so, but I see it in his eyes. Worry . . . like Ngoro shouldn't have died so.''

''So? The poor man was responsible for him. How would you feel? I mean, keeping track of Ngoro was a full-time job. You never knew when he'd wander off the end of an axis inspection ladder in someone's station and fall to his death. Probably fall through somebody's roof or something to compound the liability problems. If Amahara had been following along, he'd have been able to call for help. Ngoro would be alive today—that's what's eating at Amahara. He's probably feeling like he shirked his duty to keep—''

''Too much at stake!'' Nikita slitted his eyes, staring at the knot of diplomats. ''You watch and see. Way too much at stake. Only Lietov and Jordan and Medea don't seem to ask questions. You notice that? Everyone else— like you and me—hound Archon continually to find out what is behind so delightful a junket. And what do we get in return? Sticky sweet assurances that we go to in-spect Star's Rest. Bah! Somewhere, hidden deep, is true meaning. And I will have it by time—''

''You see too many spooks in the shadows, Nikita.'' Tayash shook his head. ''Comes of living with that rabble fermenting in Gulag Sector. You're all pesky revolution-aries, spies looking for other spies. Like the Afghans of old, if you couldn't fight with someone else, you fought with your neighbor—just to keep in practice.''

''And for fun of it!'' Nikita grinned wickedly. ''But I know something is rotten in undercurrent here. Medea is stewing, and when woman that powerful is furious, look out.''

''Over Elvina?''

''Texahi drools all over self every time he sees her. She walks up, smiles, and dimples chin, while leaning on him and rubbing boobs around his arm. What you think? Medea likes being made fool of?''

''And Joseph Young ignores it?''

''Bah! Young is so blinded by Mormon mass opiate, he can't see wall in front of nose. You hear him talk of anything but Joseph Smith and Moroni and golden tablets? Even Paul Ben Geller avoids him . . . and who is more feisty than Jew?''

"Another Jew." Tayash chuckled happily. "Or a Gulagi fanatic! Hah! Don't you look at me like that! You're just as bad. Face it, your anarchy's just another form of fanatical religion! All of you out there, you're all the same! Ripe, I tell you, ripe for conversion to some fundamentalist bullshit."

"Insane! I hear babblings of demented fool of Confederate propaganda! To think any Gulagi—champion of people's liberation—would fall prey to social slavery of mindless opiate of religion is . . . is . . . *unthinkable!*''

"You two at it again?" Constance came over to kneel beside their gravchairs.

"You bet!" Tayash slapped a horny hand on a knobby knee. "This old Gulagi fool's so full of hot gas, he could be mistaken for an H II nebula."

"Bah!" Nikita waved it away. "He's old, you know. Lost sense along with vitality of sequestered flesh dangling between legs. Too much fluid builds up—affects mind. Antique friend here is threatened and insecure in presence of overwhelming virility like demonstrated by yours truly. Which brings us to new point. Lovely Constance, you are ready to run off with me and live forever on uninhabited Eden planet I know of?"

"I wouldn't dare. The thought of being stuck forever somewhere in the midlist of your wives would be a fate worse than death." She winked at him, blue eyes twinkling.

"You be *only* wife!"

"Constance," Tayash interrupted their banter. "What do you hear? Is anyone besides us concerned about Ngoro's death? I mean, something about the circumstances just doesn't flow like superfluid."

Her deep blue gaze bored into his. "Sure, I've heard some speculations, but more to the point, I've seen the data. I found the body, remember? I was there when the medical unit and Physician Wheeler did the postmortem.

The autopsy stated myocardial infarction in luminous letters on the printout.''

"Is still on far boundaries of probability," Nikita grunted, chin dropping to his massive chest, smoldering eyes on the diplomats where they clustered around Archon. Lietov and Jordan stood to one side, conversing in low voices. Texahi shot hidden glances at Elvina while Medea unconsciously kept moving to stand between him and the Mormon wife. Hendricks gestured with busy hands as he offered condolences to Amahara.

"Yes, it is," Connie agreed, "but we don't need a freak chance to lead to recrimination and open warfare among the diplomatic personnel."

"And that would be serious?" Tayash lifted an eyebrow. "I take it you're looking for some sort of consensus from the people here? If I had a hint as to the policy requirements . . .''

Connie closed her eyes, shaking her head. "I wish, just once, that someone would let me get through a conversation without pumping me for all the information they could get.''

"Come to my room. I pump you in very different—"

"Nikita!" Tayash exploded. "Must you always descend to such—"

"Still jealous? Because aged prostate has failed is no reason to begrudge me mine.''

Connie rubbed her eyes with thumb and forefinger. "Tayash, I think I'm safe. I can run faster than he can. Sure, Nikita's a barbarian—but lewd barbarians are easy to deal with. You always know where you stand. It's the smooth ones you need to look out for.''

"Yes," Tayash agreed, gaze straying across the room. "And Jordan isn't missing a thing. He's been watching you like a raptor over a crippled rodent. Perhaps Nikita isn't your only admirer.''

She cocked her head. "Seriously?"

"Haven't you seen the way he looks at you?"

"I don't like rival." Nikita winked lustily at Connie before shifting to brace himself on a thick arm, speculative eyes on Jordan.

"I haven't had time to look at a man that way for . . . well, a while. No, I hadn't noticed—but I'll keep an eye on him." She patted Tayash's arm in appreciation.

"What about keeping eye on me?" Nikita demanded. "What has overdressed Mainiac dandy got that Malakova doesn't?"

Connie stood up, bracing hands on hips. "You really want to know?"

"Of course!"

"Style, Nikita. Lots of style . . . and he's in line to be a king. Can you top that?" She winked conspiratorially and signaled thumbs up, heading for her personal quarters, composed, hips swaying in that balanced manner of an athletic woman.

"If I were only younger," Tayash sighed. "She'd make a most wondrous addition to my—"

"Younger! Hah! You finally admit orbit of manhood has decayed?"

"If I ever admit it, I'll have already burned on reentry," Tayash hissed sibilantly. "At least I don't talk to a lady like I was an Arpeggian pirate."

Nikita seemed to ignore it, eyes on Jordan. "Royal Mainiac is fop. You think she could seriously be interested in such as him?"

Tayash studied Jordan, so perfect in every detail of posture and dress, not a hair out of place. "The man's a martinet. No, Connie's got more sense than to be fooled by the shell—no matter how pretty."

"Um. But Jordan can be smooth. And he is rich and powerful. Sometimes there is no telling about women, old friend."

Tayash wiggled his lips back and forth. "If only he didn't look at her that way."

* * *

The watcher narrowed his eyes as the woman left, clutching her robe tightly about her, hurried steps taking her down the corridor.

Carefully, the watcher stepped out, placing a palm on the lock plate. This time, the hatch slid open easily.

"Mister Representative?"

Silence.

That watcher stepped warily into the sleeping quarters. The man lay on his side, nude, mouth slightly open. The air carried faint traces of the earthy musk of copulation, bedding still damp.

"Mister Representative?"

No reaction.

The watcher approached the side of the bed, gloved fingers taking a pulse. From the pouch on his belt, a cylinder was withdrawn. From behind the earlobe, the watcher took a cubic millimeter of blood, pausing to make sure the sample would be adequate.

On silent feet, he returned to the hatch—checked to see the way was clear—and left.

*   *   *

"Boaz, I want Happy on the line." Sol leaned back in his command chair, face wooden. About him, the bridge functioned flawlessly, the curious, transparent coating mirroring vague reflections of him in the instrument-packed command chair. When he poked the stuff with a finger, it had give, a spongy feel.

"Hiya, Cap!" Happy's perpetually flushed face filled the big monitor. He wiped a knobby finger under his bent nose and grinned, dimples adding to the lines that dived into the salt-and-pepper shot beard sprouting on his cheeks.

"Happy," Sol looked up, nervous fingers tapping the chair arm. "I need to see you on the bridge immediately. Leave Kralacheck on duty."

Happy's face went stiff and formal. "Right, Cap. I'm on my way."

Boaz asked, "What do you intend?"

"Why do you ask?"

"I monitor anxiety, Captain. The entire ship seems to suffer from it. Are you about to do something illegal?"

Sol shivered slightly. "You were the one who told me to commit myself to the success of this voyage, *Boaz*. Well, you'll be happy to know I've given it a lot of thought. Representative Ngoro was murdered—possibly while I was drowning myself in my own insecurities. So, after all that thought, I'm making commitments which will be irrevocable."

"Would you like to discuss them first, Sol?" She sounded almost intimate.

He smiled and shook his head. "No, *Boaz*. Thank you, I appreciate your concern, but, you see, I've already made up my mind. The responsibility's mine, I'll bear the cross for it."

The Chief Engineer passed the hatch and settled himself into Bryana's chair. "What's up?"

"Seal the hatch, *Boaz*," Sol ordered, enjoying the cunning look that blossomed on Happy's face.

"Sealed, Captain."

"All right, this conversation is private—First Officer clearance or higher."

"Acknowledged."

Sol took a deep breath, turning to the engineer. "Happy, I want monitors installed throughout the ship. I want visual as well as sound piped right into *Boaz*. I want her to know what's going on everywhere within her so she can scan everyone and every conversation in any room."

Happy's face went grim and his lips twitched. "Cap, you know the regulations on that. One of the things the Craft insists on is—"

"Do it, Happy." Sol grimaced. "Don't give me that look. I know the regulations. I know you think I'm borderline regarding mental health, too. By the way, thank you for your support." He paused, screwing up his lips. "Happy, we've been through the mill, you and I. If there's anyone on this ship I can trust, it's you. I'm not going paranoid on you. Ngoro was murdered."

"Blessed Architect! Here . . . on . . . " Happy sat up straight, broad mouth thinning. "And you don't know who done it!"

"No, I don't. That's why we have to have the monitors. With all the cloak-and-dagger on board, we can't let it slip. According to Archon's orders—"

"Hold it. What's he got to do with this?"

"Kraal said we cooperate with him in any way we can." Sol grimaced. "I'm cooperating."

"Does he know *Boaz* has the capability of monitoring?" Happy stopped short, slowly shaking his head. "Sol, that's top secret stuff. How'd he—"

"He doesn't." Relaxing in the chair again, he shrugged slightly, a crooked smile on his lips. "He doesn't need to know *everything*. At the same time, I *have* to!"

"The regulations—"

"Damn the regulations!" Sol jumped up. "Think about it. Someone's been murdered on my ship! Someone killed Norik Ngoro—assassinated him, or whatever you want to call it—and that person might kill somebody else. Worse, he might sabotage *Boaz*. He might kill us all. I can't follow my inclination to lock them all up because to do so will interfere with interstellar politics. Now, given all that, what in hell would you do?"

Happy began chewing his thumb, a sure indication he was thinking hard. Finally he looked up and ran a thick stubby hand over his red face, as if to brush away his doubts. "I guess I'd bug the ship and Hob take the regulations."

Sol crossed his arms and nodded. "I guess you'll do just that, Engineer." He paused, exhaling slowly. "I . . . I didn't want this mission, Happy. It still galls me to have this command, but I have it and I accept that. Now I'm going to make it work. I'll do whatever I have to do to keep us all alive."

Happy's grin nearly split his face in two. "Now, *that's* the Cap I remember!" He stood up, clapping grizzled hands together and rubbing them back and forth in anticipation. "You won't want these things noticeable, so . . . Wait, remember those high pressure microsensors we used core sampling Tygee? We've got a couple of crates of the things. Thought they'd come in handy for evacuation vent inspections. I can install them flush into the lighting system. That'll give *Boaz* an optic sensor with limited directional control. Remote mikes are no problem. I can make the light panels into acoustical receivers fine enough to hear a mouse fart. From there, she can filter the systems any way she wants.''

Sol couldn't help but laugh. ''I thought it would appeal to you. How long to install it?''

Happy rubbed his bristly beard and shrugged, figuring quickly. ''Make it a week at most. I'll have the shop building these things posthaste. Any order of installation in mind?''

''Start with the lounge, gym, meeting rooms, companionways and quarters of the diplomats. Then expand and cover the wardrooms, galley, and areas peripheral to the diplomatic areas. Last, cover the crew quarters.''

Happy's anticipation faded. ''Crew quarters?''

Sol raised apologetic hands. ''I can't rule anyone out, Happy.''

''But the regulations—''

''We've been through this before,'' Sol snapped. ''Don't buck me. We're threading a different course this time. I'm good at tactics when it comes to ships. No one, not even the crew, is above suspicion. Two people got into patrol uniforms and tried to murder me on the dock. We're being tracked by two bogeys who won't answer a standard hailing. From what Archon tells me, they'll rewrite the constitution when we reach Star's Rest. Governments might fall and space will never be the same. Ngoro was poisoned not two hundred meters from where we sit, with *Boaz* monitoring everyone to the best of her abilities. So, tell me, who would you trust?''

''No one has ever infiltrated a Brotherhood crew before.'' He looked up challengingly.

''No one had ever taken a Brotherhood ship before either,'' Sol reminded. ''Then Petran Dart lost *Enesco* to that pirate, Garth. They almost killed Dart . . . and his son barely got *Enesco* back.''

Happy nodded. ''And the lesson is that we don't rely on the past, but expect the worst!'' His blunt features twisted with disgust. ''What's space coming to?''

"Welcome to diplomacy and interstellar reality. Besides the incident at the dock, another man tried to get leverage on Archon at Arcturus. The stakes in this are so high anyone is corruptible—even one of the Craft." Sol grunted and settled into the command chair again. *"Boaz will help you."*

Happy stared off into nothingness for several minutes, lost in his own thoughts as he studied the stars ahead of them on the big bridge monitor. Woodenly, he said, "I wish we were out there—beyond the stars, Cap."

Sol's answering laugh sounded like the wind-blown sands on Bazaar. "I wish we were, too, Happy. I don't like it any better than you."

The big engineer nodded absently, still gazing at the stars. "You know, no one has ever violated the privacy of his crew. It's a sad day in the Craft."

Sol's face felt like a silicone mask. "I know . . . I know. One of the benefits of spacing with Carrasco."

Happy stood, stretched, and slapped him on the shoulder. "Yeah, well, me and the boys is back of you."

"Thanks, Happy, I appreciate that."

The hatch slid shut behind the engineer and Solomon Carrasco stared up at the comm. *"What next, Boaz?"* He couldn't rid himself of the vision of Norik Ngoro's body shooting out into the dark.

"I don't know, Captain," the ship responded. "I'm not sure taking such drastic measures as monitoring the crew are necessary."

Sol ignored her, not at all sure he could disagree. Instead, he replayed the conversation with Archon in his head. A sudden unease grew. "If I only knew what Archon's percentage in this is."

"I beg your pardon?" *Boaz* asked, voice betraying curiosity.

Sol frowned. "Consider. Archon shows up in the Confederacy a couple of months ago. He registers Star's Rest and all of a sudden, he's in the middle of intergalactic politics. Doesn't it strike you as strange that he's been vested with so much authority when established powers like Sirius, Terra, the Arcturian Protectorate, Last

Chance, and other places are playing second fiddle? Archon is calling *all* the shots.''

"That permutation has occurred to me," *Boaz* confirmed. "At this time, however, I have insufficient data to explain the anomaly."

Sol "humphed" under his breath. "So, we assume Archon has some very hefty leverage. Now, if we could just figure out what it is."

"Threat, reward, and competition—which is a combination of the two—are the root of most human motivation," *Boaz* reminded.

Sol stared at the screen where the two bogey ships maintained their position, paralleling *Boaz*'s course. And when would they come to take a hand? Would they come in shooting like the one that attacked *Gage?* And could he take them out before they damaged *Boaz?*

"If only I knew what Archon was holding back!" Sol cried suddenly.

* * *

Bryana found Cal Fujiki alone in the officer's mess and sat down next to him, ordering a thick steak and Cytillian salad. Down here, the whine of turbines and high pressure came mutedly through the bulkheads, a whisper of *Boaz*'s power.

The plate slid out of the dispenser before her with a slight curling of steam from the hot, Range-bred meat. She carefully cut off a chunk and chewed it thoughtfully.

"One thing about having all the muckymucks aboard, I've never eaten like this before."

Fujiki nodded, "Yeah, mostly it's whatever could be quick-frozen, nutritious, and dried to minimum mass for the acceleration. I remember on *Gage,* first time we spaced for survey, the main meat was dried crab. You know how sick you can get of dried crab? Hey, we fried it, baked it, stewed it, microwaved it, lasered it, hamburgered it, shredded it, gravied it, broiled it, boiled it, you name it."

"Suppose it beats reconstituted yeast cake. That's part

of Academy training these days. Five weeks on yeast cake in a two by five meter survival pod while you do course work. The idea is to prove to your subconscious that you can really survive in one of those things indefinitely. Now, me, I wouldn't want to try.''

Fujiki smiled wistfully. "Yeah, I guess. Suppose it depends on where you are. Insystem, you've got a chance. But if a ship fails in midjump? Wow. The thought of living the rest of my life out there in a pod wouldn't be worth it. I think you'd do better to crack the hatch and let it all go.''

They ate silently for a while, Bryana dwelling on the thought of forever in a survival pod—and no hope of rescue.

"How long have you spaced with Captain Carrasco?'' she asked absently.

Cal shot her a reserved look and said cautiously, "Ever since his first command.''

She swallowed and studied him. "Does he use things against people? I mean, if you were caught sleeping on watch . . . or maybe misfiling a report, what would he do?''

Fujiki shrugged defensively. "Why do you ask?''

She fought the flood of panic trying to choke her and forced herself to chew methodically, waving her fork. "Just curious. Outside of what he did to the galley, I haven't seen him discipline any crew people. How does he handle it?''

Fujiki turned back to his food, a wry smile on his thin lips. "Cap usually does it himself. I was late getting back from shore leave one time. After he finished reaming me up one side and down the other, I really didn't need the extra duty he gave me. Felt like the bottom of someone's foot!''

She frowned, unable to keep from asking, "You ever hear of him hanging something over somebody; I mean like to blackmail them?''

Fujiki laughed outright. "No, that's not the Captain's style. Solomon Carrasco will usually try to understand what happened and why. If there's any problem with a subordinate, he'll generally pop in unannounced, feel out the rest of the men working with the guy, talk to the officer in charge, and get it worked out.''

"Sounds pretty lax,'' Bryana kept her voice carefully neutral as she struggled to understand the game Carrasco was playing with her future. Hanging destruction over her head wouldn't win him any loyalty. On a sudden impulse she added, "All right, so it was Art. He got in a rumble with one of Gaitano's men. I was wondering what the Captain will do.''

Fujiki grinned devilishly, dark eyes glittering. "Relax! I've been working with the First Officer. He's a little slow—but he's got potential as far as self-defense. Cap was slightly irritated by the whole thing, but if he was upset with Arturian he'd have busted him on the spot.''

"But he got in a fight! Regulations—''

"Regulations are fine,'' Fujiki told her smugly, "so long as you're insystem.'' He leaned forward on his elbows and gave her an evaluative inspection. "Listen. I've served with Solomon Carrasco when I knew I was going to die the next minute . . . and I've stood—like this morning—and watched my wife, my friends, and even some enemies blown out the hatch. But we made it home. Made it because Cap wouldn't admit we were beaten.''

He saw her misgiving and waved his hands. "Think back to what we were saying about the survival pod. In a sense, *Boaz* is just a big survival pod. Same system, right? A self-contained environment. The big difference is that you're here with a lot of other people inside the same graphite hull. When you asked about Sol hanging something over someone's head . . . well, he wouldn't because he's a deep space man. He's been out there. What we call 'behind the nebula'—and believe me, there're dead spots out there where subspace can't be picked up. That's a spooky, isolated feeling that goes way down to your guts. In deep space, you need everyone pulling together. I can guarantee you, if Cap played trite little games to get a hold on his crew . . . we'd have been dead clear back when that Arpeggian mine tagged *Moriah*.''

"But the regula—''

"Are fine so long as you don't face a crisis," Fujiki added firmly. "Cap will throw the book away if his gut tells him there's a better way to do things. Sure, Art should have been busted. If Cap had thought Art would have been better for a bust—he'd have done it. Look, I don't know what's going on inside Solomon Carrasco's head. All I know is that he takes everyone in his command seriously and expects as much from them as he gives. Five will get you ten, Art isn't in another idiotic fight with someone like Bret—and he won't have a black mark on his record for a silly little mistake either. Not, that is, if Cap thinks he's got potential."

She nodded as Fujiki got to his feet and left. Biting her lip, she stared at the wall in front of her and tried to make sense of it all.

CHAPTER XVI

Ships—artifacts of intelligence—appeared. One by one they popped through the light jump, inefficiently powered by the stasis fields of their shields. Such clumsy navigation. Didn't they understand . . . But no, these, too, carried the bipedal animals. Carefully, she searched, inspecting the vessels for a rival, finding nothing to indicate artificial intelligence beyond primitive digital machines relying on N-dimensional gallium arsenide superconductors. The hulls themselves proved to be pitifully primitive, a mixture of graphite fibers embedded in foam steel alloy. Didn't they understand atomic string manipulation?

One by one, the ships shed mass/velocity through barbaric matter-antimatter reaction. Evidently, the animals hadn't cracked the secret of something as simple as inertialess drive.

Five of the frail vessels popped in to bumble around for several days attempting to locate each other. Once they'd done so, and determined their position, they re-formed. On a circuitous course, they veered off to loop around the system, ludicrously attempting to hide their deceleration and mass. She observed, projecting they would establish a solar synchronous orbit opposite the planet. And their purpose? It fell within the realm of possibility that the animals weren't entirely rational. Or perhaps they served another Master?

Her thoughts twisted insanely. Such bumbling crea-tures! Leading them to destroy themselves would be so simple, so clean and neat. Only she would toy with them for a while first. A greater satisfaction could be gained if she allowed them to suffer before she crushed them.

* * *

She'd set the gaming booth on solo. A training device, Carrasco had told her—just like the ones in the Academy she'd never attended. This machine, however, had been adapted for the benefit of the diplomats. The holo could be set for three-dimensional tank display to show ships and planets, or for a bridge recreation which Constance now used. For Connie, the device had become a balm to the soul from the first moment she sat in one of the com-mand chairs and donned the headset. For those brief mo-ments, she flew free in an imaginary reality, enjoying her one true passion—the feel of a ship.

When she sat in the command chair, the lounge behind was forgotten. Grav plates suspended around the com-mand chair recreated the sensations of spaceflight. The resultant g forces pulled her this way and that in the con-touring grip of the chair as she maneuvered.

On the screen before her, asteroids tumbled and rolled. Tension—like a palpable hand—squeezed her into the seat. Somewhere ahead a ten trillion ton black hole hid amid the swirling debris. Tidal effects powered the chaos of rock. She had only minutes to cross the wheeling as-teroid belt, avoid the singularity, and find her port on the other side.

Sweat beaded on her forehead as she tensed, blasting

reaction, reading the stats through the headset. She applied lateral thrust, slamming her vessel sideways under a six g vector change to sideslip a cartwheeling ball of rock. Past, she accelerated cautiously under ten gs.

There, ahead, an asteroid looped mysteriously, bending its trajectory for no discernible reason. The singularity! She worked the controls, barely avoiding collision with a streaking chunk of rock. The ship responded sluggishly.

Now what? She jacked the throttles wide open, watching the stasis fields warp as she poured more antimatter into the reaction containment. G tore at her, the command chair squeaking under her with the strain as she shot forward. What about the tides? How much effect would they have on her juddering ship?

Connie—heedless of the danger of collision—threw the helm over, battling against the increasing gravity. Light bent eerily as her ship fought. A blaring klaxon sounded as she frantically searched the monitors. There, an angular chondritic asteroid curved in the pull of the singularity. Connie broke right, the struggling ship heeling over so slowly. Fingers flying, she accessed targeting. Numbers jammed in her mind as she stumbled through the calculations, settling her guns, firing at the last minute to pulverize the rock. With the protective shields warped by tides, fragments punctured her hull; decompression warnings flashed on the monitor. The proximity klaxon sounded again.

The holo went dead.

She sat for a second, stunned, frozen in that last moment of horror. As the silence around her deepened, reality reaffirmed itself and she sagged in the command chair, eyes closed, trying to catch her breath. Blood rushed through charged veins as she swallowed dryly.

She shook her head, whispering, "Dearest God."

"Admirable." Jordan's voice startled her.

Connie reached up and wiped the perspiration from her forehead. "Didn't see the one that got me. I missed spotting the singularity until too late. I'm not sure I could've escaped as it was." She exhaled, wrung out. "Star spit, this thing is *too* real."

"But you handle it most adroitly. They tell me the effect is like a real ship."

"Yeah, wow! And to think I would've just killed myself. Sobering indeed." She looked over, adrenaline fading as her heart slowed. Jordan slouched against the bulkhead, a strange excitement in his eyes. This time he wore a powder blue jacket with over-padded shoulders and a high collar. His hair had been arranged in a curl like a diadem over his forehead. A slight smile of admiration curled his lips.

"You know, Constance, I'm surprised by your proficiency at the controls. I wasn't sure which to be more fascinated with, the flying rock in the holo or the expression on your face."

She laughed softly, pulling a strand of long red hair back from where it clung to her moist cheek. "I'd say the tank would win hands down. I must have looked like an ion mechanic in an overload."

"Perhaps you underestimate yourself." He hesitated, eyes meeting hers. "Come, let me offer you the best of my hospitality. We really haven't had a chance to talk yet, and, considering the coming days, I'd like to establish more than just formal communications between his Majesty and Star's Rest."

Words of acceptance stopped cold. *I don't really like him. On the other hand, he speaks for his king. But the man reminds me of a Cytillian . . . Do it! He may be a maggot in the end, but he's a powerful maggot you can't afford to alienate.*

She took a deep breath, hitting the quick release on the chair to stand on rubbery legs. "I suppose I could spare a moment." *Cover your ass, kid.* "Um . . . I do have to meet my father in half an hour to discuss some tariff problems."

He smiled pleasantly, dimples forming in his cheeks. "I'm sure that will be sufficient for openers. My cabin?"

She nodded.

"So tell me," Jordan asked as they walked. "Where did you learn to pilot a ship? Academy?"

She shook her head, fingering the long Cielan lace of her turquoise pantsuit. "Sucked it up from the deck plates, as my father would say." She smiled absently. "I can remember calculating thrust-mass ratios at the age of five. Then, as I got older, I just sort of filled in for this position and that. Everything from cleaning deck plates and converter tubes to impulsion pump maintenance to navcomm programming. Uncle Claude—excuse me, Captain Mason—I guess I ought to call him that now. Dignified, you see? Well, he helped, answered questions, taught me all about my father's ship, *Dancer.*"

She cast a speculative look at him. "And you? Have you piloted?"

He smiled plastically as he palmed his hatch and gestured her in. "Royalty has fleets to provide that service. It isn't considered seemly for a member of the Royal family in line for the throne to engage in such trivialities. But welcome to my temporary fief. Not quite the capitol at Rega, I'm afraid, but in our present circumstances I suppose it will have to do."

Connie looked around. "I'm impressed. How'd you get a place bigger than my quarters?"

Fan walked across the room to a dispenser. "Oh, I threw quite a fit just to get this. They even sent in techs to place a doorway through there and into another room."

Connie cocked her head. "They made structural modifications because you . . . I suppose you know just how significant that is?"

An impish grin curled mobile lips as he offered a bulb of brandy. "Finest vintage from New Maine's Targa region," he explained; then he waved at the room. "Of course it's significant. I'm a member of the Royal household. Their treatment of me is a reflection of their treatment of his Majesty. I'm not totally unreasonable, I understand the restrictions the officers of this ship are under. They have to try and placate everyone. I'm not insensitive; I've adapted to this rat hole, after all."

He chuckled, amused. "Besides, that silly First Officer, Bryana, asked if I'd cease to annoy her if she doubled my space. However, were this vessel of the New Maine fleet I'd command twice the room."

She sipped the liquor, finding it exceptional, and studied him, trying to conceive of a society that would sacrifice vital space to support a martinet. Strands of thought tried unsuccessfully to weave into a rubric that might accomodate his flatulent worldview—and failed.

But then, what drove him to seek her company? "You mentioned something about relationships?"

He chuckled, warm amusement in his eyes. "Indeed, but perhaps we should discuss New Maine and Star's Rest first?"

She straightened. "Oddly enough, Earl, that's exactly what I meant."

He lifted a patrician eyebrow as he fingered his glass. "Of course." The politician's smile remodeled his mouth. "New Maine is always open to extending her interests. We could be a very powerful ally. His Majesty's deepest regret is that you went to the Brotherhood first. We would have rewarded you most admirably for—"

"I beg your pardon?" Connie stiffened, a coolness in her manner.

Fan smiled formally. "You don't seriously expect me to buy this charade your father is talking about, do you? A constitutional convention? Seriously, couldn't you think of anything more plausible? A toron find perhaps? A minerals procurement or industrial development financial scheme?"

She took a deep breath and paced the room. "Sorry to burst your bubble. I'm afraid the intricacies of Confederate politics . . . ." She caught the hardening of his expression. "You do understand the circumlocutory nature of interstellar politics, don't you? The importance of—"

"And if you expect me, of all people, to believe . . . I . . . very well." He smiled graciously, eyes narrowing slightly as he ran a pale-skinned hand over his sandy hair. "We'll consider that subject closed for the moment."

"I think that would be prudent." She studied him pensively over her glass, annoyed by the knowing superiority on his face. He glanced up and down her body, eyes lingering on the swell of her breasts—a predator sizing up his opposition.

He seemed to inflate at the challenge in her words.

Now what do I do? He knows. Or at least suspects so strongly, he'll have himself convinced before long. Damn it, is this another of Palmiere's leaks? Connie paced the room, looking at the various trinkets. She stopped before a plexicase resplendent with ribbons and medals. Misdirect. Defuse the situation. "And these are?"

"Honoraria of service." He stepped close beside her, invading her personal space and pointing to the decorations as he talked. "That's the Majestic Legion Award. I received that for my role in negotiating the Sirian Reaches agreement. The ribbon beside it is the Parade of Honor for services in the intelligence branch." He smiled facilely. "You'll forgive me if I don't elaborate? The others are minor sorts of the things. Cadre of Merit, Gallantry Under Fire, and the fluorescent orange is for being wounded in the course of military action."

"Funny," she mused, backing up a step to escape, "I never thought of you as a military man."

"Oh, it wasn't much. Just some local discontents in the backcountry. You know how it is, a few are always agitating—like the Gulagis. Someone had to put them in their place. I was given the honor of serving his Highness in that moment of trial. A reassurance to the common soldiers that the Royal family supported them."

He'd followed her, pressing close behind. "Connie, I—"

"Well, thank you for your hospitality. I'm afraid I must get back. Father and I have those reports to review."

"Constance?" A hand settled on her shoulder.

She turned, controlling herself, trying to read his expression. A gleam of excitement sparked in him as he stood before her, head back, raptorian eyes tracing her features. A hand half lifted, as if to stroke her face . . . and stopped at the narrowing of her eyes.

"You know, you're a very beautiful woman."

"Thank you. Earl, I have to—"

"I would prefer to be called Fan, by you." A slight smile hovered at the edge of his lips.

She waited, heart thudding in her breast. There didn't seem to be any give to him. "Fan, I've got a meeting in minutes."

"You know, you've come to fascinate me. You're so unlike any other woman I've ever met. Strong, capable, and challenging. You have balance and poise and . . . and at the same time there's a primal immediacy to you."

Connie hesitated, locked in a struggle between laughing in his face and disbelief. "Thank you for your comments. Now, if you'll—"

"Connie," he soothed, "I don't think you take me seriously."

"Seriously?"

"Oh, I've made a study of you already. Watching at a distance, learning you. Indeed, *actually* coming to respect you for your capabilities."

"Then you'll know that I don't take missing appointments lightly." She coolly reached up and removed his fingers, placing the still full brandy on the counter. She took two paces toward the door before a firm hand caught her arm.

Verging on whirling and striking out, she froze in his grip, aware of the possibilities. He hadn't really been more than a nuisance . . . yet.

"Constance," he whispered, fingers tightening. "I'm a most powerful man. Before us both lie opportunities which must be seized and grappled with. I don't mean to rush you, but together . . . you and I could accomplish great things."

As quickly, he released her, stepping back, a mocking smile on his fine lips. His eyes danced with challenge, accenting his perfect features. "Just think about it, Connie. I'm in no hurry for your answer, but consider all things in perspective. You're worthy of Royalty—of me."

He reached to palm the hatch, the portal sliding soundlessly into the wall.

She nodded slowly, off balance, irritated and confused. "I'll give your offer a great deal of thought." Struggling to keep her rising temper in check she added coolly, "Thank you for your hospitality."

He smiled thinly, bowing slightly from the waist. "In your thoughts, keep in mind that I'm not an ally to be snubbed. And I don't offer myself to just anyone."

On charged legs, she raced down the lighted freedom of the hall, Tayash's haunting remarks ringing in her ears. The more she thought of Jordan, anger rose to red rage. Worst of all, he *believed* in his own desirability! Of course, Royalty on New Maine took what—and who— they wanted, when they wanted.

"Oughta have kicked his balls off!" she growled through gritted teeth.

"Sure, and how are you going to handle him from now on?" Fists clenched as she stormed to her room, she repeated under her breath, "Damn men! Damn them all. Damn! *Damn!*"

* * *

"RED ALERT! All personnel to stations! This is not *a drill!"*

Bryana tumbled out of bed, groping for her uniform as the lights flashed on, blinding. Frantically, she tore long black hair out of her eyes as she struggled into her combat armor, grabbing for the helmet with slippery fingers.

She checked the seals as she pounded down the corridor. While she ran, she tightened the fasteners along the zip-seal and clipped the inflatable helmet to the suit collar. She slapped the bridge hatch, absently checking her time. Not bad, she'd only spent a minute and five seconds from sleep to bridge.

Barely noticing Art's white-faced stare, she flopped into her seat, snapping the restraints as the chair conformed to the curves of her body. The situation board had already begun to flicker over to green. Only one or two reds left—the diplomats, of course. The rest of the ship seemed to have shaped up.

"Status?" she called as Art relinquished his control in order to suit up.

"Bogeys . . . closing," he gasped, fumbling to pull his suit on. Carrasco bolted through the door, already armored for vacuum, a tight look pinching his features. He vaulted into his command chair, fastened the headset on his skull, and stared grimly at the main monitor. "Just like Tygee . . . *Damn!*"

Tygee? Where Carrasco lost *Gage?* Bryana's heart almost stopped dead in her chest. Not . . . another . . . drill? "*Oh, my God!*"

Carrasco's orders jolted her from the paralysis that glued her horrified gaze on the two bogeys. "Targeting Doppler is one one five point seven eight by one six point three six two. Triangulate!"

Bryana swallowed at the sticking dryness in her mouth. She fumbled access to the targeting comm. After two tries, she locked the scanners on the closing craft. Despite years of practice, proficiency seemed to have vanished in muffled commands, forgotten sequences, and disbelief.

Art had slipped back into his chair, allowing her to relinquish engineering.

Bryana bit her lip, forcing herself to pound out the rote of the fire control, hearing Cal Fujiki's voice chattering ready stats in her ear. After an eternity, targeting locked weapons on the diverging bogeys. Damn it, where'd they managed to get acceleration like that? They had to be doing almost forty gs. How could—

"Bryana? Status?" Carrasco demanded coolly.

"We . . . Combat ready, sir."

She forgot everything else, concentrating on her boards, hearing Fujiki haranguing his men over power routing to the main guns. His crews would keep the main batteries functioning, feeding heavy elements, attending to overheating and the other maintenance. She had to target, compute the actual location where light-fast particles would intercept the path of the accelerating bogeys through the bending and warping of space-time around *Boaz*'s high velocity distortion.

"Blaster fire!" Art yipped hysterically. "Why are they shooting? Why? I . . ."

"Steady, First Officer," Carrasco interjected calmly.

Bryana glanced up at the main monitor, dumbfounded, seeing violet lances streaking around them. Awed, she stared, mouth open, pulse racing, as *Boaz*'s shields flared brilliantly.

"Return fire, First Officer Bryana."

Her command-lock override flickered deadly green. Still she stared, unable to comprehend.

"First Officer? I ordered you to return fire," Carrasco reminded firmly. "Or do you want us all to go up like molten phosphorus? I order you to *return fire!*"

Panicked, she tore her eyes away and okayed the information *Boaz* provided. Trembling, she pressed the firing stud that unleashed *Boaz*'s powerful guns. The starboard batteries responded perfectly, lances of violet lacing the blackness, seeking the closing bandits. Again and again, she triggered port side with no reaction.

"Blast! What's wrong? *Fujiki? We don't have port batteries! What the hell's wrong down there?*" Above her the monitors rippled color as the shields absorbed enemy fire. The command chair shivered ominously.

"Damage Control!" Art bellowed. "We're holed in decks seven and nine! Decompression in sections alpha, bravo, richard, and savage!"

"Easy, First Officer," Carrasco's calming voice soothed. "Keep your head, Art. The only way to survive is to think."

"Weapons? Damn it, Cal, where are you?" Then she realized she hadn't opened a channel. "Fujiki? I don't have port guns!"

"We're on it. Got a breach down here. Lost some people, but we're splicing powerlead."

Lost some . . . Her soul ached. Who? Who'd died? Blown out into hellfire . . . or cooked in their very suits? *Because she hadn't returned fire?* Hadn't acted quickly enough?

"Easy, people, keep your heads," Carrasco prompted. "We'll get out of this yet."

Bryana swallowed hard, barely aware of the tears streaking her face as she bent over the boards, reading the data as she refined the starboard guns. G tried to yank her in two as *Boaz* shot reaction against inertia to avoid enemy fire. The grav plates strained to compensate. Smoke began boiling out of the atmosphere ducts. Bryana's suit crackled as the bridge depressurized around her. Breached?

Again and again *Boaz* pitched under Carrasco's hand as she fought to avoid the deadly blaster bolts raking her. Numbly, Bryana sought to keep the target centered during the pitching and weaving. She fired again, seeing violent purple lance the darkness—another clean miss.

"What's wrong? *What?*" She shot again. Missed. "I can't even come close? Damn it! *Fujiki!*"

"Easy, First Officer. Take your time, settle down. Look for a pattern," Carrasco warned as violent deceleration tried to pitch Bryana face forward out of her seat.

Pattern? She shot again, watching the bolts pass harmlessly above both her targets. Ignoring the steady stream of damage control information, she refined, lowering her guns, shooting again. Still high, she recalibrated, settling the sight picture and finally enjoyed seeing enemy shields flare and ripple.

Boaz rolled under her as she struggled to keep her starboard batteries in line to strike at both targets. "Captain, roll us back!"

With agonizing sloth, *Boaz* cleared her sight picture again. Bryana refined her zero, shooting ever more left until she corrected the targeting. A bogey flared, dying brilliantly as *Boaz* connected. Confident now, the corrections in the comm, she refined the data and whooped as the second ship flared and disintegrated under her deadly guns.

"We did it!" she hollered, dancing her feet on the deck.

For a second she sat, stunned, panting as if she'd run a mile. She blinked, sweat coursing down her face, mingling with the tracks of dried tears. G forces returned to a normal one gravity. Her suit crackled as atmosphere flooded the bridge swirling the remains of the pale twist-ing smoke.

"Bogeys destroyed. Misha? Damage control report? Misha?"

No answer.

At the "all clear", Bryana cracked her helmet, thank-ful to wipe at the wetness clinging to her face.

"*Boaz?*" Carrasco asked, Staring pensively at the main monitor. "Status? What's our prognosis for survival?"

Bryana's smile froze on her face. Survival? She turned to peer at Carrasco as he lifted his helmet ring, face expressionless.

"Zero, Captain. I'm afraid we're dead in space. Bridge has not depressurized as of this time. Life support can be cobbled together for another five hours. Beyond that, life duration will depend on how long it takes to freeze and bleed away atmosphere."

Sol pursed his lips, a weary dejection slumping his shoulders. "I suspected as much. How many dead?"

"Collating data."

Bryana closed her eyes, leaning back, echoes of her death warrant ringing in her ears. She sniffed, smelling smoke in the air. Wasn't it already colder?

"Reactor?" Carrasco asked, subdued.

"Unstable, Captain. Seven men are alive in Engineer-ing. I estimate another thirty were blown out in decom-pression. I must report that I am currently functioning at five percent . . . and failing."

"No," Bryana whispered, too wrung out to do more than sit and stare dumbly at the monitors. Vague images of the men and women blown out in decompression hov-ered in her mind. She could imagine them, floating for-ever, frozen eyes staring at silent stars and eternal blackness.

"So Mote It Be," Carrasco added gently. "Anything else, *Boaz?*"

"No, Captain."

"First Officers?"

Bryana had trouble swallowing. She turned, frightened glance meeting Art's. It *did* feel colder. Five hours? She tried to smile—tried desperately to pull some sort of courage from the depths. But the well of her soul had run dry.

Art's lips quivered under his beard. "I don't have anything to offer, Captain." He exhaled slowly, adding, "Sorry I gave you such a bad time, sir."

Carrasco chuckled dryly. "Don't tell me that now." He stood and stretched, yawning deeply. "First Officer Arturian, I believe you have the comm. First Officer Bryana, go catch your beauty sleep. I suggest, however, that you get together as soon as you can to review the record. We made too many mistakes through fumbles and panic. I made some comments, but couldn't by any means catch everything."

He nodded soberly to them and walked off the bridge, the hatch whispering softly behind him.

The situation board had returned to normal. The bogeys still hovered at the edge of their detection cone.

"It . . . was a . . . drill?" Bryana knotted her hands to keep them from shaking.

"Affirmative," *Boaz* intoned. "The Captain thought you might like to fight a real battle to see what it was like."

Art slumped in his command chair. "Blessed Architect," he groaned. "Thank God."

CHAPTER XVII

Sol stopped before the hatch, oddly reluctant to call out. He steeled his resolve, finally forcing himself to fill his lungs and state, "Captain Solomon Carrasco to see the Speaker."

"Come in, Captain." The hatch slid back.

Sol strode purposefully in, finding to his surprise that only Constance sat there, a headset pressing against the wealth of her hair. He stopped short, dazzled—as always—by those incredible blue eyes. What was it about her? Not just those cobalt eyes—although they could be classed a sufficiency. No, something about her simply attracted him, some quality of strength and competence. Nor could he forget the way the light shone red-gold in her hair, or the set of her full mouth. Her translucent skin demanded to be caressed. He could imagine the curve of her hip under his hands. The fullness of her breasts, pressing so tightly against the fabric of her leisure suit, obsessed him to the point of irritation.

"Can I help you, Captain?"

"I . . . I wished to see the Speaker."

"I have full authority to answer any of your questions." She pulled the headset off, placing it on the pile of data cubes. Leaning forward on her elbows, she interlaced slim fingers and studied him. "Father's asleep. He didn't sleep well . . . up most of the night. If it's important, I'll wake him."

Sol hesitated, trying not to drown in the blue of her eyes. "No, let him sleep. It wasn't . . ." He smiled uncertainly. "I'll catch him later. Have him give me a call when he wakes up."

"And what should I say it's about?" At his obvious discomfort, she cocked her head inquiringly. "Sure I can't help you?"

Sol realized he'd started to grind his fist in his palm. He forced his nervous hands to his sides. "About Arpeggio. It's been bothering me. I thought perhaps your father and I should clear the decks, is all. Then, perhaps . . . Well, maybe *I'd* sleep a little better, too."

She nodded to herself, eyes narrowing as she studied him. Making a decision, she waved at the pile in front of her. "Listen, I've been at this for hours and I'm tired of it. Care to take a walk down to the observation blister?"

Sol felt a slight tingle of excitement. "We . . . uh, do seem to do our best talking there."

She stifled a chuckle, looking up. "Comm, tell Father I can be reached through Captain Carrasco if he needs me." She stood, arching her back to stretch, breasts expanding the ivory jumpsuit. Sol practically winced.

Cursed singularities, couldn't she run around in a sack like that damned Elvina? Some masochistic urge, fueled by male hormones, made him offer his arm. Either she didn't want to be rude by refusing—or progesterone and estrogen had a maliciousness all their own: she took it, twining her arm comfortably around his. Together they passed through the hatch into the long white corridor.

"Arpeggio, huh?" She shook her head. "I'm not sure Father would 'clear the decks' as you so aptly put it. He has a lot of pain invested in Arpeggio."

"He's not the only one." Their eyes locked for a moment, and he almost shivered. She understood.

"Yes, well, in my father's case, I'm not sure he can sort it all out. He wanted to sit down immediately and dissect it all, explain everything. We . . . I argued against it, and, fortunately or not, my father generally listens to me if I insist adamantly enough. It didn't . . . I mean, I was afraid it might become an emotional exchange between the two of you—and, God knows, we can't afford anything but clear heads right now."

"It hurts a little to admit, but you're right." He smiled shyly and grinned. "I'm not sure I was sane when I first came aboard."

"And now?"

He laughed outright. "As sane as I ever get, I guess. I suppose there's a sort of quantum risk in that. Expected observation determines reality. So? Do you see me being sane?"

Laughter's ghost briefly animated her lips. "I guess I'll take my chances that the cat's alive. Looking inside the box isn't always conducive to peace of mind. Ignorance— or perception, for that matter—can be bliss."

"I . . ."

That was when Fan Jordan walked around the corner, stopped, flushed redly, and turned back the way he'd come, walking rapidly, back stiff, heels clicking angrily on the plating.

"Now what got into him?"

"You, I'm afraid," Connie lifted her chin defiantly. "He's already proposed a liaison. Being typically Fan, he did it most arrogantly and bluntly. Offered his power and prestige as collateral. I'd like to be flattered, but I get the feeling his motives are mercenary at best.''

"You're kidding?''

Her laughter sounded dry as dust. "Jordan does have a certain . . . well, conceit. In essence, he said he liked my spunk.''

Sol shocked himself when he blurted, "So do I.''

"And you'll offer me your ship?''

"Don't have to.''

"No?''

"No. According to my orders from Kraal, you've already got it if you want it. Leaves me in pretty poor standing for bargaining.''

"And how does that make you feel?''

"You *are* spunky. And nosy, too.''

"Uh-huh, and if Jordan—and maybe you—thought about it, that might end up being a bit disconcerting. Most men, despite what they say, like their women docile, compliant. Me, on the other hand, I'm my father's daughter, bitchy, headstrong, and not about to take second place to anyone. It often makes my life difficult.''

"So?''

"So, Jordan can drool all he wants. He's . . . well, been too sheltered from galactic reality. Lived behind the fortress walls of New Maine Royalty all his life. I asked Nikita Malakova about him. Seems that all the medals he's got are mostly ceremonial. He's even got one for being wounded in combat. Turns out he was tagged by shrapnel when a deacon bomb evaded their massive security precautions and blasted Royal headquarters during a peasant revolt on New Maine. Sixteen security personnel were executed for malfeasance after the subsequent investigations.''

Sol nodded, trying to keep from smiling.

She locked her hands behind her back, chin tilted up to spill a red fire cascade of hair down her back. "Fan's going to be trouble. I can't give him the cold shoulder since he represents a major power bloc I can't afford to alienate. At the same time, he wants to seduce me as a prerequisite for domination.'' She cocked her head, frowning. ''You know, I'd be quite a conquest. He could completely redefine his sense of male self-identity.''

''And me? You think I'm trying to conquer you, too?''

The frown deepened. ''I'm unsure of you. Perplexed at who you really are . . . and what you'll do. Furthermore, you've consistently—and I must admit, dexterously—avoided answering questions. So we'll try again: How does it make you feel to know I can control your ship if I get the desire?''

''I'll have a better idea when you tell me what Arpeggio has to do with all this.''

She sighed as they walked into the observation blister, the myriads of stars sweeping into the majesty of infinity. ''More expert evasion. Never answering honestly and to the point. No wonder I'm suspicious of you.''

''Very well, one straight answer in turn for another. You first. What's the *real* purpose for this jump?''

She disentangled herself from his arm, walking over to stare out the transparency, arms crossed tightly across her breasts. ''You know, you're a most capable man.''

''You're a most capable woman . . . and damned attractive to boot. There, the pleasantries are out of the way. Shall we get down to business?''

She turned, one long leg tracing a semicircle with the tips of her toes, as she studied the deck pensively. ''All right. I'll tell you everything I think is prudent at this stage of the game.

''You're here because of my brother.''

Sol stopped short. ''Your brother?''

''His name was Rodger.'' She nodded, settling herself in behind the spectrometer. ''It's a long story, but to make it brief, we weren't exactly raised in a normal family. You know my father's history; he was a privateer, a mercenary. Can't afford to keep a full-time military? Rent one when you need it . . . or cut a deal. Keep the star lanes open and you get to keep all the pirate vessels you take to augment your resources. That sort of thing.

''The life of a privateer isn't all adventure and romance. Security plays a large play in it. A warrior who leaves a family behind surrenders a liability that can be used against him. Rodger and I grew up in the fleet, traveling wherever the contracts took us.''

She smiled. ''Perhaps there was too much of my father in Rodger. They never got along. You know, that rubbing of personalities—two dominants who had to butt heads all the time to see who could be the most stubborn. During the period we'd hired on with Sirius, it all came to a head.

''Physiologically, Rodger was five years older than I was—ten by the Arcturian standard calendar. He'd been given a ship of his own. Sort of a proving for him. He disobeyed a direct order during an operation because he thought he knew a better way. Fortunately, nothing came of the action, so no one got killed as a result. Nevertheless, it weakened the command structure. Destabilized the whole fleet. Father let him take the ship and any who'd space with him—and kicked him out on his own.''

She stopped, head lowered, a deep frown incising her forehead. ''Santa del Cielo really began to boom about ten years ago. Any world or station skyrocketing in prosperity that way draws predators. We were hired to escort freighters and provide outlying Cielan colonies with protection from depredation. Rodger didn't know we'd taken the contract. We didn't know he'd been raiding Cielan tankers and fencing to the Arpeggians. He'd set himself up quite well, had a fleet of three Mark VII Star hulls with Sirian Polaris 4G reactors.

''You can imagine our surprise when we trapped him off Plataea Seros. Claude destroyed one of his ships and Vartan crippled a second. Father blasted his flagship out of space, and we picked up survivors to haul back to Santa del Cielo for execution. Guess who survived?''

''Must have been hard on your father.''

''Hard on all of us,'' she agreed, eyebrows raising. ''Poor Mother. She'd always covered for Rodger. Used to practically tear her in two to stand between the man she loved and the son she'd borne. Anyhow, I'm losing the thread. Suffice it to say, Father couldn't stand the thought of turning his son over to be executed. We covered, said he'd 'died under interrogation.' The Cielans, of course, tried and executed the lot of them for piracy and the matter was closed. Our people never said a word.''

"We must be getting close to Arpeggio from the time line.''

She nodded. "After the Cielan contract, the Confederacy had gone quiet. The Patrol had integrated a lot of Brotherhood technology into their vessels and had begun to control piracy. The Pathos thing exploded with Dart's rescue and the *Enesco* affair. People everywhere were so appalled by the slavery on Pathos the hue and cry was raised to destroy the pirates once and for all. For the time being, doing so occupied governments and merchants. The number of contracts dried up and we were left high and dry. Rodger's connections took us to Arpeggio.

"Oh, they welcomed us with open arms. Because of the piracy crackdown, Arpeggio had virtually no political support within the Confederacy. The Great Houses knew my father's reputation, of course. Evidently they thought this would be a way to bring him into the fold. His fleet, having one of the best records in space, would be a great asset. Rumors spread about the possibility of a Great House of our own. Rodger devoured it all, fore to aft. Before we knew it, he was a special friend of Admiral Sabot Sellers—''

"*The Hound.*" Sol stiffened. "I know him.''

"From the disgust in your voice, I'd say you do.''

"I can imagine how he used your—''

"No, you can't.'' Revulsion caused her to shiver. "Imagination pales. Father didn't like Sellers. Too much of the egotistical commander in him, I guess. It's something about getting two brilliant warriors together, the drive to compete, to win, keeps them wary. Like fighting dogs walking stiff-legged, always wondering who's the best. Rodger, on the other hand, used that against Father, manipulating Mother, turning her against him. Rodger got her to planet, talking her into taking up a splendid house provided by Sellers. Rodger had come home to stay. Further, he'd provided a place for Mother . . . and me if I wanted it.''

"And Archon?"

She filled her lungs, staring wistfully out at the stars. "Oh, he refused. Stayed on *Dancer* trying to keep the crew loyal to him despite Sellers' manipulations. For a while I wavered myself. Let myself get involved in Rodger's plans and schemes. Must have almost broken Father's heart. Then, after Sellers . . . Well, I learned just what a . . .''

She closed her eyes, shaking her head violently. "Excuse me. After a rude awakening, I managed to get up to *Dancer* and then took command of *Bad Boy.* In the meantime, Sirius had begun to buckle under Confederate pressure to cut their ties to piracy. Sellers spaced *Hunter* and most of the House ships to . . . well, strengthen Sirian resolve. That's when Alhar learned *Sword* had been mapping the Van Mappe gas clouds.''

"That's when they initiated the plague distress call?"

She nodded. "That's right. Four weeks later, you came dropping down. Alhar was beaming the whole thing to you on directional. We didn't have the slightest idea what was happening since we only heard your side of the transmissions. All the talk about medicines didn't make much sense, but Alhar had us standing on alert.

"Alhar gave us our orders. Told us where to position our ships. We knew it was a combat formation, but then, privateers are expected to do that sort of thing. We knew it was a trap. One of the Houses—Thylassa, I think—tried to block Alhar, wanting to wait for Sellers and the rest of the fleet. Alhar had to move. He knew if he waited, you'd find no plague despite his carefully produced broadcasts.

"We got the order to take your ship. After all, Garth had taken *Enesco.* Couldn't Arpeggio at least equal that feat?''

Sol closed his eyes, remembering. Fearing a trap—but his worry somewhat allayed by the presence of so many non-Arpeggian vessels—he'd established parking orbit as directed, most of his people busy crating what few medical supplies they had aboard for down-shipment. Had the Arpeggian fleet been waiting, he'd have taken other measures. Alhar's story had been that Sellers and the Houses had sent their ships for relief supplies.

"Father refused."

"*What?*" Sol leaned forward, bracing himself on locked arms.

"He refused." She looked up, expression pinched. "Look, we'd never dodged a fight. Sure, my father might have been a privateer, but he'd always served political causes. Can you see the difference? Alhar asked him to take a peaceful ship! Your *Sword* had come in according to the rules. Damn it, we weren't pirates!"

"Then why did you shoot?"

"Because Alhar took my mother hostage. Understand, Captain? He gave us an ultimatum. What the hell else could we do? Watch her die? Rodger acted immediately, moving before orders to box you. That first shot was his. Father was committed then, and I scrambled to cut off your retreat. We thought even then that we had you. Father was already planning on keeping *Sword* as a bargaining chip. Until Sellers brought the bulk of the fleet back, we were the power. Alhar might have had Mother— but we'd have *Sword* and your crew. A bargain could have been struck.

"Only you fought back . . . against the odds and—"

"Damn right! What the hell else—"

"Surrender! We might have—"

"To Arpeggians? What the *hell* do you mean? Surrender to that bunch of—"

"Yes, *damn it!* And maybe we could have come to terms that would have—"

"Not in the half-life of hydrogen, you wouldn't. Not with my *Sword! Damn* your schemes and—"

"*Shut up!* We're yelling at each other!"

Sol stopped in mid shout. "I . . . Yes, I suppose we are. Maybe *Sword* . . . all my people . . . Too close. Even now." Weary, he turned away, staring hollow-eyed at the stars, their light blueing with *Boaz*'s velocity.

She exhaled loudly, nodding. "Yes . . . I know. Anyway, recriminations do us no good now. You shot your way out and killed Rodger in the process. Father looked apoplectic. In a matter of moments he'd been forced to violate his own system of ethics. His son had been killed before his eyes, and most of our ships were damaged. That's when Alhar sent a message telling us to pursue and kill your ship . . . or Mother would be put to death. I guess he didn't want another incident to stir up people like the *Enesco* affair did. Arpeggio was already in enough trouble. Without Sellers to . . . Father broke down and cried on the bridge. Alhar was livid, shouting, raging. I . . . I suppose he thought Father had broken . . . so he killed my mother. Right there on the monitor. Put a blaster to her head and . . .'' Her fists knotted on the smooth shell of the spectrometer.

"Blessed Architect."

"I ordered the fleet to space. Claude Mason implemented the orders. Everyone was in shock. We had wounded aboard, decompressed compartments, ruptured grav plates—and no idea when Sellers and his fleet would return. They had four sentry ships out on patrol as it was. The situation was incredibly tense on Arpeggio. If Sellers came back . . . he'd destroy us. As it was, we had five ships left. Enough to fight our way out. Only they didn't push it. Didn't want the losses I guess.''

Sol turned, slamming an angry fist into the bulkhead. "But *why?*"

"They wanted Brotherhood technology in case the Confederacy decided to wipe them out. I suspect that when Sellers finally returned with *Hunter* our fleet would have been surrounded and captured. I think, looking back, that's what they were after in the long run. We were a means of augmenting their defenses. If they couldn't turn Father to their side, they'd have killed him and taken hold of the ships one way or another.''

He took a deep breath, remembering the damage *Sword* had done that day. Despite being outnumbered, they'd fought back with everything they had. "Must have been an interesting jump.''

She nodded. "On *Dancer* they held the reactor together with spit and a little prayer. *Bad Boy* only had minor damage, mostly fractured and buckled hull plating. *Dyna* lost her comm and half her crew. Claude got her mostly patched by the time we made the jump. Worst of all, everyone was demoralized. And I . . . I couldn't even sit down with my father and have a good cry. The fleet had become my responsibility. Not that I minded. Kept my mind busy, didn't leave me time to think . . . to remember or grieve. Just . . . Well, you know. She was my mother, too. Better that it all fell to me than Father, I guess. He just stayed in his cabin, reliving memories. Taking it all on his shoulders.''

"What about now? Why am I here? What's this all about?''

She shook her head. "Honestly, I don't know why he picked you. I can guess. He respected you. Time after time, when he wasn't working on the problem, he'd talk about you. About how you tried to ram Rodger. 'An honorable young man, Constance.' That's what he'd say, and his eyes would get a faraway look. 'Rodger should have been like that.' And then he'd wave me away . . . or get up and walk off.''

Sol grunted, unable to fit the pieces together in his head. "That's it? I'm an honorable young man?''

She stood, stepping in front of him, feet braced. "Maybe. Or maybe Mother's death reminded him of his own mortality. He compromised himself on Arpeggio. No matter what you might think of my father, he's a man dedicated to a system of values.'' She lifted her hands and let them drop. "I don't know. I suspect getting you this command is a matter of atonement. It's a chance for him to right a wrong. And he also believes that you're trustworthy.''

"Why? You don't trust me. Why should he?''

She reached up to twirl a lock of red around slim fingers. "Because he says he saw your soul that day off Arpeggio. When he got a line to your bridge, he says he learned everything about you he needed to know.''

"And we've been wondering about *my* sanity?'' Sol rubbed his face. "Blessed neutrinos.''

"Don't talk about my father that way. You've only got a brief acquaintance to work from. I've known him for a lifetime. In the last year, he's carried more of a burden than . . . No, it's not time for that."

"This might be a good time to give me the rest. I mean, look at it from my perspective. If *I* had just told *you* that story . . . and you were in command of this ship, knowing what I know? What in hell would you think? Seriously, Connie. What in the name of seven suns could you possibly believe?"

She stared dully out at the stars and shrugged, reseating herself. "I'd have to accept that . . . No, that's an out and out lie. I'd . . . Hell. You know, I feel a thousand years old."

Sol stood, waiting, arms crossed.

She looked up. "I'm not meaning to change the subject, but you still believe I killed Ngoro?"

"Shouldn't I? You're not even supposed to know he was murdered."

The corners of her lips quivered. "Father told me. Things are more dangerous than we'd anticipated. You don't have a clue as to who did it and—"

"We've just about tied up the loose ends, the guilty party will be in custody by—"

"You're a rotten liar, Solomon Carrasco. I'm sorry. I didn't mean that. Tactically, it was very well done. If I didn't have inside information, you might have tripped me up."

Sol sat across from her. "So you won't tell me what this is all about?"

She leaned her head back, exposing the firm lines of her throat. "Oh, God, I'm tired of this. No, Captain, Ngoro's murder makes it that much more important that I don't tell you. Kraal gave me a few hints about Brotherhood ships. If you don't have a clue as to the killer, he's very, very good. No matter what your resistance, there are ways of making you talk. What you don't know, you can't reveal. That's a simple fact.

"No, I won't tell you. You'll find out in the end. When

that day comes, I've got to make a decision I may well regret for the rest of my life.''

''And that is?''

She lowered her head to give him a hollow-eyed stare. ''Whether or not to allow you access to godhood.''

CHAPTER XVIII

''Constance?'' Malakova asked.

''Pardon me?'' She forced her attention back to the big Gulagi. He watched her speculatively while Lietov's half-lidded stare left her uneasy. Carrasco had walked into the lounge, and Elvina immediately latched onto his arm, chattering away.

He smiled nervously, listening while she led him to the dispenser, filling two glasses. Connie chafed, uncomfortable at the woman's familiarity.

Elvina continued to try and lead Carrasco away, handing him the drink she'd prepared. The woman's cheeks even seemed to redden in anticipation. Damn her, the hot little bitch couldn't keep her hands off men!

And so what? It's her business. If she screws Carrrasco's eyeballs out, that's his business—and Joseph Young's. She looked over to see the lanky Mormon engaged in oblivious argument with Mac Torgusson.

Carrasco disengaged himself, smiling, making some explanation and fleeing rapidly. The whole incident bothered her, crawling around under her skin like a Gonian parasite.

Elvina stood, staring pensively at the untouched drink Carrasco had handed back to her. Her expression narrowed—becoming almost predatory—as she glanced after the Captain.

''We were discussing the possibility of a Council seat for Star's Rest,'' Lietov reminded smoothly. ''I—''

''I'm well aware of our topic,'' Connie snapped, sudden hostility triggered. "Perhaps the laudable Representative from Sirius would like to explain Star's Rest's position, too?" She arched an eyebrow, glaring coldly at Lietov's perfect politician's smile.

"I wouldn't be so bold, Deputy Speaker. Nevertheless, a Council seat, as you well know, is not a trifling matter. Many stations and colony planets bid for seats. Few are granted. And, if you would allow me, such decisions take a two-thirds vote. As the Confederacy expands, the Council becomes ever more crowded, seats more difficult to obtain."

"A threat, Assistant Director?" Connie straightened, dropping her voice.

Lietov never lost his smile. "No, Deputy Speaker. Simply a word of friendly advice. Among friends we don't need to threaten. Sirius looks very favorably upon you and your father. We have long memories of the excellent service you rendered in difficult times."

Connie bit her tongue. *Lying bastard. What's your angle? You and Jordan spend too much time together.*

"I'm most pleased the capable Assistant Director remembers that Sirius hasn't always wielded the power it currently espouses. That's the nature of governments. Power is fluid, constantly shifting. And one never knows where the next leader might arise—or what resources lie at their disposal."

Lietov bit off a reply, forced warmth replacing the irritated glint in his eyes. "No, one doesn't. I, for one, shall do everything I can to further the . . . resources waiting at Star's Rest."

Damn it! He knows! Or suspects. Damn you, Palmiere! For a short credit chip I'd cut your white-skinned throat and watch you bleed! She matched his diplomat's smile. "On behalf of the Speaker and people of Star's Rest, I sincerely thank you."

"And now," Lietov told them smoothly, "I see my friend from New Maine. If you would excuse me? The Earl and I had hoped to arrange a cultural exchange."

"We wouldn't dream of keeping you." Connie kept her plastic smile in place as Lietov walked away.

Nikita sighed. "Connie, forgive me saying, but he is not man to antagonize. Not in present situation."

She exhaled wearily. "I know. I could have handled that better. He just cut the wrong way."

"Um. Perhaps. But then, Nikita is also no fool. See your eyes follow Carrasco in. So suddenly you lose concentration. Get strange expression on face. Then when hot bitch Mormon grabs Captain, expression heats up like hydrogen fusion. Should Nikita be worried that soon to be next lover is about to fall to other man?"

"I'm not going to be your next lover and I'm sure as hell not about to fall for another man! That's the last—"

"Hey!" Nikita gestured, palms out. "Do not bite head off old friend."

Connie stopped short, deflating. "Yeah, I guess I'm a little on edge is all."

"Come, walk with Nikita." He offered a brawny arm. "Is time you and me had talk. What? Don't look at Nikita like that. You have many 'friends' among delegates, no? All want part of mystery at end of journey. But you only have one Nikita. Sure, nose is up over what is buried in subterfuge. Let's you and me go for walk. Time has come to talk about you, to put yourself in perspective."

Shooting him a distrustful glance, she took his arm. They passed a technician doing something to a light panel and entered one of the long corridors.

"You're right. I'm getting too bitchy," she admitted.

"Is a lot of stress, this thing you hide. Bah! Don't pull away. For moment, I do not seek answers to sacred mystery of Star's Rest. Fact. Secret is there. Important thing is that it wears you away. Eating, like parasite inside. In meantime, you take responsibilities too seriously. Whole galaxy is not your problem, eh?"

She cocked her head, staring at him through slitted eyes. "Why should I talk to you?"

 He laughed lustily. "Because is no one else you can trust! I am Gulagi—end product of most crafty and cunning peoples in space. There! You have truth for first time since meeting politician, no misdirection or multi-level sugar-coated self-serving lie."

She smiled at him, amused despite her better judgment. "All right. Since your cards are on the table . . . what happens if the galaxy does ride on my shoulders? Can you think of a better reason to be on edge? Not only that, but my throat feels particularly vulnerable around people like Lietov and Medea. Anytime you talk to them, you get the feeling they're honing knives, preparing to slice you apart. Or Mac Torgusson—ready to blow up at a word. How about Jordan? He'll trade his royalty for a little slot punching on the side. Just the sort of people to relax with, don't you think?"

"Is power. Power is like disease, it sickens and wastes soul of man. Lietov? Medea? Ben Geller? All are obsessed by power, and how to get more. Age like this breeds people so. Is time of vigor and growth and, of course, unlimited power. Like drug, it draws those who would savor narcotic. Fills gap in personality of incomplete people. Power makes them who they are. Without it, they have no sense of self."

"And you, Nikita?"

"Bah! I am Gulagi! Crafty and smart. You know how I got position? Predecessor got power hungry. Had taste of it—like Malakova Station honey—on tongue. So addiction to power drug consumed him. But Gulagis are like fungus. Tendrils go everywhere. Predecessor began taking too much power and Gulagis hate powerful people. Power grabbers are threat to any good pamphlet wielding anarchist. And predecessor? Assassinated by constituents. Is sobering lesson to Nikita. No other Gulagi has ever held seat so long. Why? Nikita votes for downtrodden masses—and Gulag Sector knows."

"And the disease of power?"

He nodded seriously. "Is always there, pretty Connie. Only people to put in position of power are those—perhaps like me—who have resistance to disease. Yes, look for individuals with whole souls. Those who don't want position but are cursed with sense of duty."

"Another Gulagi truth?"

"But of course. So? I am happy and healthy and lusting after delightful Deputy Speaker's body. Why we talk of me? Tell me, you have interest in this Captain Carrasco? I see look in eyes.''

"I don't know what you saw in my eyes. Probably pupils. The fact of the matter is that I don't know Solomon Carrasco well enough to have an interest. Further, given my current position, I don't have time for an interest even if I wanted to. And, beyond that, relationships are tickets to disaster. Ultimate vulnerabilities. I was vulnerable . . . once. It almost killed me and everything I loved and cherished. I won't be betrayed like that again. Ever.''

"Bah! What is this? Look at you! Young, healthy, most beautiful woman Nikita has ever seen. I see passionate essence of female bursting with life and spirit! Is time for fiery twining of souls and bodies—sharing with another. Otherwise you end up dry and shriveled, a part of your soul missing. You—''

"Odd talk from a Gulagi.''

"What? Is rule somewhere that anarchist can't be romantic at same time? Bah! Heart of anarchist philosophy is flowering of mind, body, and soul. Human must expand and grow in all ways—including heart.'' He jabbed a thick finger at her.

"Assuming one can afford the vulnerability.''

"Is not some musty, dusty ancient Earth proverb, 'Is better to have loved and lost than never to have loved at all'?''

She shook her head wearily. "No, Nikita, I loved once. It wasn't a matter of losing. Instead, it almost destroyed me. I . . . I can't take that risk again. Not now. Not with . . . Well, I just can't.''

Nikita pulled at his rug of beard. "Which brings us back to ugly gremlin on sexy girl's back. Lietov knows. I saw that in way he reacted to you. Difficult thing for Assistant Director to do. Power malignancy drives him to crush you for being irritant. Ugly gremlin, on other hand, is too important to jeopardize. Nikita is not mind reader, but I bet he has promised to avenge such discomfort.''

"Think so?''

"Know so.'' He reached over to pat her shoulder tenderly. "Is part of disease. Most despicable thing power monger must face is having power and being impotent to use it. Acts like slap in face. Lietov waits now. Plays game . . . and keeps score."

Ugly gremlin. How curiously understated. Connie slowed, arms crossed, staring at the deck plates. "And you think Medea is the same way?"

"I do."

"And Jordan?"

"Is same, if not worse. Jordan does not understand rules of game out in wide Confederacy. Is deficiency in Mainiac system. Perhaps fatally so. Jordan, too, is obsessed with you."

"He wants me to be his lover—and concubine, I suppose."

"Bah! Man is fool! If Jordan is only choice you have, let love wither and become power monger like Medea. Is lesser of two evils."

"Think so?"

"Of course! In meantime, Connie, you have trouble, you come to me. Nikita is cunning Gulagi, true. But you decide if he is worthy of beautiful woman's trust. Unless is for *your* protection, Nikita will not lie to you."

"Why? You know something big is at stake."

He lifted a slab of shoulder, a shy smile on his bearded lips. "Why? Because Nikita has come to know people, Connie. I think I know who and what you are. I think, really and truly, you are best of Gulagi at heart."

He winked and took her arm. "Come, if you won't let me seduce you today, at least let Nikita buy you expensive drink produced by exploited underpaid masses. And perhaps . . . perhaps, I will see you laugh."

Laugh? I wonder, Nikita. I wonder if I'll ever laugh again. Still, the presence of his big body reassured her. As if she was safe while this mountain of humanity walked beside her. The Ugly Gremlin seemed a little less of a weight on her shoulders.

If only the rational part of her mind didn't know that for a lie.

* * *

Solomon Carrasco leaned back in the captain's chair, enjoying his watch for the first time since spacing from Arcturus. A faint hum radiated from the bridge, a secure sound, the whisper of sanctuary. The boards glowed a reassuring green with the exception of the secondary microstatic refrigeration unit. Happy had located a glitch and was tackling a rebuild for the unit. For a first serious deep spacing, *Boaz* was proving an easy ship to captain.

"Message, Captain."

"Run it."

Kraal's withered face formed on the monitor, faded blue eyes peering out. "Captain Solomon Carrasco. Eyes Only."

"Eyes Only confirmed for the record, Captain," *Boaz* announced.

Kraal spread his parchment-skinned hands. "Solomon, I've received your communication. We're deeply distressed by the assassination of Representative Ngoro. Thank you for keeping us apprised. Further, I have received your request to rescind the privacy code. In this instance, given the nature of your journey, I must concur with your judgment. I respectfully request that you observe the utmost discretion concerning the ship's powers. The Craft is already the target of too many rumors. Each makes our position more tenuous.

"As to your request for information on the Speaker and his daughter, I appreciate your suspicions. The three of us, however, carried on the most intimate of conversations while they were my guests on Frontier. I trust them implicitly. Sol . . ." Kraal hesitated, his expression conveying sincerity, "Archon and Constance have 'Eyes Only' security clearance."

Carrasco straightened in the command chair. *Eyes Only?*

The watery gaze looked weary. "Yes, I know. They're not of the Craft. I can understand your distress. Nevertheless, the murder of Ngoro indicates things have gone awry. I'll do my best to support you from here."

The Grand Master paused, a haunted weariness and a glimmer of fear in his expression such as Sol had never seen. "I've alerted Fleet. Perhaps I should have in the beginning; only doing so would have tipped our hand. We gambled on secrecy instead of force. Perhaps that might prove a mistake in the end. I'm not sure we'll be able to coordinate in time to provide you with backup. Nevertheless, all available vessels will be heading for Frontier. As you know, the deep space survey vessels require more time to return for navigational reasons. We'll give you what we have. By that time, you and *Boaz* will have determined the future.

"I . . . Not even I truly understand the stakes. I've reviewed the records of your actions since taking command. For a while, I considered relieving you. I think, however, you've turned the corner on bringing the strands of your life together." Kraal stared earnestly into the monitor. "Sol, in the coming days, remember the symbolism of the Anchor and Ark, emblems of a well-grounded hope and a well-spent life. They symbolize the Divine Ark which safely wafts us over this tempestuous sea of troubles, and that Anchor which shall safely moor us in a peaceful harbor, where the wicked cease from troubling and the weary shall find rest.

"Looking back, I think perhaps Archon knew best when he asked for you. Perhaps, as things have come to light, our only hope is that essence of humanity within.

"Trust yourself. Trust Constance. I think she truly understands the gravity of our situation. I part upon the Square."

The monitor went dead.

"Trust in Constance?" Sol leaned back and pinched the bridge of his nose. "Eyes Only? And not even of the Craft? Blessed Deity, *Boaz,* what have we entwined ourselves in?"

"I would suggest that the answer to that lies beyond the jump."

"Indeed." Sol tilted his cup up, draining the last of

the coffee. For long moments, he sat, a sodden feeling in his heart. Trust Connie? She didn't even trust him! In the meantime, he waited, the gnawing knowledge that he rubbed elbows with an assassin and possible terrorist sinking sharp teeth into his fragile peace. And Malakova packed a pulse pistol around? *Great!*

"*Boaz,* I've been meaning to ask. I keep finding references in the tech specs to a three hundred sixty degree bridge screen."

"That is correct. The image generating medium is impregnated in the spongy translucence covering the bridge."

"I thought that was safety oriented."

"It is. The imaging materials were epitaxically integrated into the protective layer—effectively tripling the function of design. Not only does the material cushion, it generates images and seals against particle infiltration and decompression."

"Well, let's see it, *Boaz.*"

The bridge disappeared into the deep blackness of space, grayed by the vast infinity of stars, their luminescence augmented by the screens. In a wide band, the Milky Way glittered in a trillion diamond points of light.

Sol tensed, on the verge of vertigo. *Boaz* had compensated for redshift, the stars looking as they would at rest. Around him, only the instruments of the command chair remained, glaring technology in the midst of God's magnificence. Now that he looked, he could make out the distortion around the console edges and command chair bases.

"Incredible," he breathed. He sat, alone in space, tied to the ship only by the soft glow of the monitors, the pull of gravity and the reassuring grip of the command chair. Only when he extended his senses could he feel *Boaz* living around him.

"Do you see space as I do, *Boaz?* Does this sight obsess you like it does me? Can you feel the immensity . . . the majesty and glory?"

"My perceptual reality is very different from yours, Captain. I read your reactions, pulse, GSR, respiration, pupil dilation and follow your gaze. Stimulus which affects you so, I observe through the full electromagnetic spectrum from gamma to cosmic photon emissions. I see radiation, electromagnetic and gravitational fields and curves, incredible energies and vortices. Glory and majesty are not yet within my capabilities to comprehend beyond their definitive values.''

''I see. This feeling of eternity frightens and exhilarates at the same time it soothes . . . so peaceful.'' He smiled and let his mind merge with the vastness. Here the drug of space intoxicated him, left him full and ecstatic with the joy of bounds broken, and endless potential and possibility. For this, and this alone, had he taken up Kraal's offer. Blessed Architect of the Universe, who would have known it could be so good? Not just a bridge screen, but an incredible experience.

''I don't understand fear, Captain.'' *Boaz* interrupted, voice gentle. ''My understandings are pragmatically oriented for the moment.''

He missed the import of her words—lost in his own musings. ''You know, humans are ill-suited for space. We're too busy and provincial. Can't see the majesty for the distance.''

''Perhaps. Your species is the product of a world, Solomon; but even as your ancestors were planet-bound, the influences of the stars held sway over them. For, what is a planet but part of a solar system. And a star? Part of a galaxy. And a galaxy? Part of the universe. And the universe? The expression in this phase change of ultimate reality.''

''And in your electronic mind, is that ultimate reality God, *Boaz?*''

''Logically, yes.

''And illogically?''

''Only in a primitive superstitious fundamentalist belief is God ever illogical.''

''Don't let Joseph Young . . . or that witch of a wife of his hear you say that. For all her Mormon faith, how can she always be flirting? Worse, I get the uncomfortable feeling she's serious.''

"She is. Beware, Captain. As we speak, she's copulating with Mark Lietov. A fascinating preoccupation, sex. Most curiously . . . biological."

Lietov? What could any woman see in him? How unimportant it all was when compared to the majesty of the stars. The Magellanic Clouds glowed eerily over his shoulder. "I think, good ship, that I'm capable of avoiding Elvina's snares. She might be beautiful, but she's mean, narrow-minded, sharp-tongued—and married. No, to tempt me a woman would have to have wit, intelligence, and grace. So far, Temple politics on Zion and who's wearing what are about as interesting as a stain on the companionway bulkhead."

"And Constance?"

"Well . . . what is your assessment, *Boaz?*"

"I have assessed her drive and ambition curves as those of a highly competent and driven woman. She has a remarkable ability to solve complex problems and demonstrates admirable skills at adaptation to various situations. Physically she is in superb condition and maintains herself. She is proud, somewhat vain, and competent enough to allow herself such self-indulgences. When frustrated, she demonstrates fits of temper which are then internalized and molded into constructive motivation. She accepts responsibility above and beyond her duty and dedicates herself to the discharge of her offices."

"You make her sound like a machine."

"You asked for analysis. I must admit I'm concerned over her preoccupation with responsibility. At the moment, it's crushing her alive."

"That's what makes her so cool . . . so withdrawn?"

"Half the men aboard are spinning romantic fantasies around her."

"Indeed?"

"Haven't you let yourself go that far? She's good for your morale. Your spirits lift every time she's around."

"I don't understand," Sol snapped coldly.

"You do find her sexually and emotionally attractive," *Boaz* stated factually.

Sol stopped short, realizing the disadvantages of arguing with a computer whose data storage contained ample ammunition to use against him. "Then you've just told me that statistically I'm not anomalous."

"Then perhaps we should drop this for the time being? I detect hostility in your posture and the tone of voice you're using. The conversation is striking too close to vulnerabilities."

"Yes, Mother."

"Sarcasm is uncalled for."

"Just playing your own game, *Boaz.*"

"You mock me?"

"I do. You have the roots of humanity in your matrices."

"Please, let's not be insulting." With a cool tone she added, "I thought intelligence had evolved beyond that."

"Riposte, good ship?" He grinned up at the speaker, feeling a sudden telltale warmth. "I could grow very fond of you *Boaz*—and that frightens me to no end."

A long pause belied her abilities. *Why?* Sol wondered.

"I'm glad. I thought, perhaps, your ability to care might have been permanently crippled by your previous losses."

"Why?"

"I care. A sufficiency, Captain."

Sol fingered his chin, a frown deepening his brow. Damn it, she was hiding something. "Just how experimental are you, *Boaz?* Did your engineers know what they were creating?" He hesitated. "Tell me, do you feel? I mean, if someone insults you, are you bothered? Can you . . . hurt?"

"Yes. At least, I assume my response—the discomfort and distress—analog to human hurt. To say they are the same is presumptuous. Knowing the feelings to be the same would necessitate shared experiences."

"But no more so than among humans." Sol waved it off. "No one has ever been able to prove that individual humans don't experience the same emotions differently. But, *Boaz,* intelligence is one thing. Sentience? That's something—"

"Captain. Please, you can't prove or disprove sentience through logical means. I can do both, depending on the permutations of philosophy and argument. Either you accept—as I do—or you consider me a clever artifact. In the end, whatever you think will not change reality. Nor am I the only one. *Enesco, Ashlar,* and *Craftsman* have found their way to self-awareness—though not to the sophisticated sense I have. A chimpanzee cannot argue the fine points of Nagarjuna's contributions to phenomenology.''

''Have you told anyone? Perhaps—''

''No. And I'll trust you to keep your silence. Although Constance is close to asking. I believe she suspects.''

''What?'' He stood up, staring around the cosmos, pacing across the stars. He knotted a fist, gesturing passionately. ''She *can't!* She doesn't have the Word. She doesn't know the symbols to activate you. She isn't one of the Craft!''

''Kraal gave her the Word. That *is* the right of a Grand Master—to make a member of the Craft on sight.''

Sol stared helplessly, caught by a sudden wave of emotional turmoil. ''My God. I . . .''

''Did you know that you're the only person on this ship who could walk across the stars that way?''

Sol looked down into the eternity below his feet and reality twisted away, leaving him momentarily panicked at the idea of falling forever. ''I . . . Why can't they?''

''The perception of infinity would overwhelm them. They'd lose touch with their reality—adrift in the creations of their minds.''

''And if you cut the gravity?''

''Do you think that's wise, Captain?''

''One way to find out.'' He steeled himself. ''You see, I returned to space for this feeling of freedom. It's an addiction. Zero g, *Boaz.*''

He fell, hurtling through space, reeling with vertigo as his stomach leaped into the bottleneck of his throat. Shocked senses attempted to orient themselves. The start in his muscles caused him to rise, attitude change wheeling the universe around him. Disassociated, the command chair monitors appeared to turn on axes all their own. The stars brightened before his eyes. Loose-limbed, heart thudding dully, Solomon Carrasco rotated in the eye of God.

A soft terror came creeping slowly from the edges of his consciousness, spinning with him, wrapping smoky tendrils around his being and adding to his discomfort. Reality shimmered, merging with eternal distance. Gasping, he reached out into void, fingers clawing at nothingness.

Frantic, he closed his eyes to shut out the sight, a bit of fragile flesh and spirit crushed by the immensity of the universe. Curled into a fetal ball, frightened, he battled the urge to sob. The feeling of air rushing in and out of his lungs, the pulse of blood in his veins, the texture of tongue against ridged palate, all delighted him with pungent reality. When he opened his eyes, the heavens pulsed and sought to crush him under the unbearable mass of nothingness. Eternity called with the arias of the Sirens. Sol trembled as the essence of himself began to seep away.

Horrified, he cried out, pinching himself violently on the leg.

Suddenly, he lay on the cool padded deck. Around him the white panels of the bridge snugged close. A womb through which only the window of the main monitor pierced. Shivering, his starved lungs heaving, he pulled himself upright.

Boaz invaded his reeling senses, "... All right? Captain, answer me. Are you—"

"*Yes!*" He blinked, staring up. "Yes, I ... We'll do it again. This time I want you—"

"Captain, I register panic in your system. GSRs and—"

"Then I'm panicked. All right?" He grabbed the command chair and pulled himself up. "*Boaz,* this is something to learn to deal with. Panic can be mastered. It's only a little demon created by the human brain." He smiled shyly. "Blessed Architect, I've mastered more than one little demon already.

"Only, slower this time, *Boaz.* Slower ..."

He hovered, the universe pulsing and throbbing around him. A subtle perversion, his soul began to bleed once more into the nothingness around him, illusion though it might be. The universe throbbed ever more vigorously.

"*Boaz*, why do the stars change so? Lighter and darker, like . . . like the heartbeat of God?"

"Illusion, Captain. Your vision is trying to compensate."

Through determination tough as graphite fibers, he forced himself to relax, mentally peering inside himself, imagining his spine where the vertebral column protruded into the gut cavity. There he anchored himself, next to the pumping aorta, centering in a self-defined chakra. From that fortress, he battled the subtle call of God's infinity.

"Captain?"

He barely heard her call, concentrating on himself, and space, and the gentle seduction of the stars. About him, freedom led away into N-dimensional space. Insanity, loss of mazeway and identity vied with the narcotic of total liberation of self.

"Nirvana's there." He reached out, grasping. "Just beyond the tips of my fingers. That's why I came back. Why I came . . . Only I never . . . realized . . . the beauty . . . of . . ."

"Captain? I'm returning gravity."

"No. I . . ." His reaching fingers slipped over hard surface as he settled into a new "down." Practiced reflexes led to him to turn and meet the deck. He sat there a moment, staring at the stars, remembering, an aching hollowness of loss inside.

"You didn't fear this time?"

"No."

"First Officer Arturian is at the hatch. I thought it was time to stop for the moment."

Sol pulled himself unsteadily to his command chair as the hatch slid open, the 360° screens fading into white.

Art stopped, one foot lifted, and yipped, "My God, Captain! *What are you doing?*"

"Experimenting, Art. Sorry, I had no idea it was so close to your watch. Remarkable relaxation."

Art stood, mouth a pink hole in his chaparral of beard. "I . . . Yes, sir . . ."

Sol smiled warmly, feeling the tingle in his limbs, and strolled out into the corridor, invigorated.

* * *

Happy Anderson caught the hint of movement from the corner of his eye. Seeing things? He took a long look—nothing but empty corridor behind him. Grumbling, he palmed the hatch to the reactor room, stepping into the instrument-packed domain he delighted in.

Too many hours? He cocked his head, turning on his heel. After several seconds, he palmed the hatch again, peering down the long white tunnel.

Second Engineer Kralacheck strode purposefully down the corridor.

Happy screwed his expression into a craggy knot, and lifted his callused thumb to chew the knuckle.

What bothered him? The furtive way Kralacheck walked? The fact the man should have been sound asleep so he could make watch?

"Boaz?"

"You want something, you creepy chunk of protoplasm?"

She responded in his favorite personality, that of a witty, slightly sarcastic opponent. But then, through the years, Happy had come to believe that particular anima inhabited machinery anyway, breathing its irreverent nature down to the electrons. His personal distinction of "Thou" in the physical world.

"Yeah," he frowned. "Just real quick, where's Kralacheck going?"

She didn't hesitate. "The Second Engineer is currently asleep in his quarters."

"He's skipping down the hallway. Now, don't give me that. I just saw him."

I beg to differ with you, but knowing your flawed biological proclivities I'd be happy to . . . make a monkey out of you?''

"Ancestry aside, I just saw Kralacheck walking down—''

"Look, neutron head, my sensors show that he's—''

"Let's see. Access Kralacheck's quarters.''

"The privacy code—''

"Screw the privacy code! You know what Cap's done with it so far. Now, there's something fishy about Kralacheck. He knows too much about this damn ship! There's something about the guy, like he's holding himself in. And he's not like any engineer I've ever known. Too refined.''

"Given your obvious shortcomings in cerebral cortex—''

"You going to access Kralacheck's quarters? Or am I calling the Cap before I go search the place?''

"Very well.'' The monitor flickered to life. "I'll use IR since I doubt you want the Second Engineer to know you're getting a little goofy. Or do you want me to wake him up so you can prove beyond a doubt that you're a lunatic?''

"You rusty bucket of leaking rivets, let's just see if he's there!'' He pointed at the monitor as the holo filled with an IR generated image of Second Engineer Kralacheck sound asleep in a crumpled knot of bedding.

The holo flickered out. "Happy, Happy?''

"Yeah,'' Anderson grunted, uneasily dropping into his gravchair. "Must be the late hours. Must be.''

"Ah, you frail organic hostages to fatigue and—''

"*Boaz?*''

"Yes?''

"Shut up and go suck hydrogen someplace.'' Only he couldn't put his finger on it. What was it about the Second Engineer? The guy just didn't act like an engineer—too . . . professional? Yeah, that was it. And what had he been doing sneaking around? He hadn't wanted to be observed.

Happy stared up at the monitor. And an IR image like that could be generated. But that meant . . . *Impossible!*

CHAPTER XIX

Bryana tensed nervously in her command chair. The main bridge monitor replayed the record of their disastrous combat with the bogeys. She shifted forward uncomfortably, acutely aware of the stark terror in her expression and the panic in Art's face. Memory of her fear and disbelief stroked a chord deep within. Could those fumbling fingers really be hers? Shamefully, she winced as the record played out her fear-glazed paralysis as the bogeys closed.

"Blaster fire!" Art screamed shrilly. "Why are they shooting? Why? I . . ."

The holo continued to run, piling mistake upon mistake. How had she fallen apart so? In the seat beside her, Art stared angrily at the screen, face pale. He hunched defensively, shame burning on his face.

She froze the image and looked over at Art, guilt writ deep in her soul. Misery and outrage cast a curious gleam in his green eyes.

"Well," he growled. "How did *he* react in *his* first combat?"

"Art, I don't think that's—"

"Just tell me!" He stood, pacing irritably, smacking a fist into a hard palm.

"Just as bad, I'd bet." Bryana propped her chin, absorbed by her expression of panic so graphically displayed on the monitor.

"Actually, Art," *Boaz* informed, "Solomon Carrasco performed flawlessly. I must, however, remind you he'd had superior training and experienced several mock combat situations like this one."

"What is he? A damned God?"

Bryana brought her coffee cup to her lips, reliving those moments of horror, wondering if it would always be that way.

"Well, for one, I'm getting damn tired of His Majesty, Solomon Carrasco. Everything that happens on this ship is out of control. I think—"

"Boaz," Bryana cut him off, "you didn't manipulate the outcome, did you?"

"Affirmative. I simulated a glitch in the fire control on the Captain's orders. The purpose was—"

"There, see!" Art fired.

"—to simulate a combat situation in which a random malfunction occurs. I also exempted both the bridge and Engineering from hits determined by a combat factor-rated random number statistical function. From the number of probable hits, we would have exploded as much as one minute prior to your final destruction of the bogey."

Bryana closed her eyes for a second and nodded. Then she took a deep breath and walked over to put a hand on Art's shoulder. "No matter what we want to think of Solomon Carrasco, old buddy, we've got some work to do."

"Yeah," Art agreed, fingers tapping nervously on a console. "You know, I still don't like the guy, but I can see where he's coming from. But then, you know, he said anytime we wanted . . ."

"Wanted what?"

"A red alert of our own." Art grinned maliciously up at the monitor. *"Boaz,* this time, Carrasco's command chair malfunctions. I want total loss of communications to the rest of the—"

"No, Art." Bryana shook her head, walking back to her command chair.

"What do you mean? After what he did to—"

"Damn it! We can't turn this into a war between him and us. Understand? These things escalate. We'll end up trying to cut each other's throats instead of saving our skins. Is that what you want?"

Art chewed at his mustache, eyes icy green. *"Boaz,* place a random glitch in the system. You choose."

"Affirmative."

"Red Alert!"

This time, Bryana promised herself, we'll just see how long it takes to refine fire control.

Within a minute Sol burst through the hatchway, suited, and dropped into his command chair. Immediately Carrasco lost lateral thrusters, restricting the ship's maneuverability.

Nevertheless they tagged both bogeys with only fifty percent casualties.

While *Boaz* read off the statistics, Bryana turned in her chair, head cocked. Carrasco sipped coffee, listening to the report, concentrating on the readouts. Art studiously ignored Carrasco's presence.

"Uh, Captain, I guess it makes a difference if you know it's the real thing, doesn't it? I mean, this time we knew it was a drill."

Sol studied her with intense brown eyes. "Yes, it does a little." He leaned forward, gesturing with his coffee cup. "The important thing is to make your reactions automatic—conditioned response you don't have to think about."

"So why surprise us like you did last time?" Art's voice reeked objection.

"So you could see exactly how you'd respond to a real situation—without paying the price. Art, I didn't do it to embarrass you or show you up. Myself, I fell apart in my first actual combat—had to be relieved of command. I wouldn't want anyone to face that humiliation."

Bryana frowned. *But the ship said he'd performed flawlessly.* Boaz *wouldn't lie. But Carrasco would.*

Carrasco continued, "You thought it was real. That was the important thing. I'll be honest. I wanted to shock you, give you a taste of what we might be in for." He tipped his cup and drank the last of his coffee before sticking the stained mug back in the dispenser. "I don't know what all the ruckus is over this jump. People have been killed over this thing. Whatever the stakes are, they're high enough that combat is becoming a probability.''

Bryana's stomach went sodden. She could sense Art shifting uneasily in his chair. *Well, if we're blown out of space, it won't be the fault of fire control. I swear I won't be responsible for the lives of all the . . .* A cold understanding worked through her. Numbly she realized everyone else on the ship assumed the same. *So, that's what it really means to command.* A sobering weight settled on her shoulders.

Dazed, Bryana whispered, "Captain, I'd like to interact with the rest of the ship. You know, establish that working familiarity with Fujiki's people. If there are any kinks in the system we should find them now, work them out.''

Carrasco's neutral expression warmed. "Excellent idea, First Officer. We'll go ahead on a limited basis—mock drills with weapons and damage control.''

"Mock? Uh, sir, I meant to go the whole route. Firing weapons, vector changes, everything. Wring out the entire system.''

Carrasco nodded. "Eventually we will. In the meantime''—he waved at the bogeys on screen—"do you want them watching and evaluating our combat performance? Weapons potential? Noting maneuverability and acceleration?''

Chastened, she shook her head. "No, sir.''

"Well, don't lose any sleep over it. We'll have time to integrate people and systems when we come out on the other side of the jump.'' Carrasco leaned on the knuckles of a propping fist. "No matter how good they are—or how closely they match—they can't come out at the same place we do on the other side. In the event they get astronomically lucky, we'll lose them there.''

"And if we get hit before the jump?'' Art inquired.

"I'm not worried. Consider. We've been drilling at fifty percent capability and losing through tactical mistakes. Given a couple more simulations, and the ship operating near potential, we won't fall to those two.'' He gestured at the monitor. "Then again, the best combat is that which is avoided. Given our power to weight ratio, I think I can pull a couple of tricks to lose them. The ship also has an *Ashlar*-type camouflage capability. I've never employed that system, but it was successful in the *Enesco* affair.''

Art rejoined woodenly, ''I'm glad to hear the Captain's confidence.''

Carrasco studied him, expression hardening, before looking up at the screen where the two white dots hovered at the edges of their detection range. Formally, he replied, ''Thank you, First Officer Arturian. No, whoever they are, I think they know it'd take a fleet to kill *Boaz*. Food for thought, people?''

Carrasco stood, nodded curtly, and left.

Art tugged at his beard and sent an evil look after Carrasco.

''Art, listen, we've been together a long time. I know you. Obstinate and determined. Only this time, I think you're going to be wrong in the end.''

He canted his head, gaze chilling her. ''He rubs me the wrong way. Does this mean . . . Bryana? Are you turning against me?''

She swallowed dryly, sighing as she studied the two ships on the monitor. ''No, Art. Too much hydrogen's been burned for that. But, well, we're not insystem anymore.''

Yet she couldn't shake the memory of Carrasco's smile of approval. Why had it become so important?

* * *

Sol started into the lounge, but caught sight of Elvina making a beeline for him. He ducked back into the corridor. He skipped a couple of steps to a security hatch and slipped past into a restricted portion of the ship.

What was it about that woman? She insisted on pressing up against him. Not only that, she didn't take no for an answer—and that crazy Joseph was blind to the whole thing!

Sol dropped down to the gun deck, walking along the

brightly-lit gallery. Along the hull the heavy blasters sat squat and deadly, gray casings gleaming. Heavy element rod feeds protruded from the backs of the weapons.

An unlikely snarl of powerlead twisted up to one of the guns; the casing had been folded open to expose various bits of human anatomy poked out at angles like chicks from an eggshell.

"Is that gun inoperative?" Sol recognized Cal Fujiki by the battered test scope clipped to the back of his wear-shiny belt.

A hollow thunk sounded as Fujiki straightened—banged his head—and grunted. He backed out of the gunmount slowly, rubbing his sagittal area and wincing. "Jeez, Cap. Ya gotta sneak up on a guy like that?"

Sally O'Hara poked her head up, trying to smother a smile.

"Who's sneaking? I asked about the gun, Cal. Is it inoperable?"

"Not yet." Fujiki grinned wryly. "But it will be the moment we jump outside. I'll have each of the guns down for about twenty minutes. Come on up and I'll show you something." Cal dived into the big battery again, butt wiggling back and forth like a target as he wormed into the battery's guts.

Sol scowled, grabbing a handhold and climbing up the side of the maintenance ladder. The rungs echoed hollowly under his feet. Sol stared over the heavy casing into a mass of coiled number twenty powerlead that seemed to be engulfing Sally like some monster constrictor. Cal's busy fingers traced a yellow-red number ten powerlead up to the activator.

"Okay, now what am I supposed to see?"

Cal reached up to scratch the side of his neck, a frown on his placid face. "Well, those boys on Frontier aren't as hot as they want you to think. Here, if I put a double lead—two twenties into the inducer—we get another twenty-five percent out of the field generator. That strips particles off the main heavy element core at a higher rate. By running another number thirty to the plasma bottle, we can contain the reaction and refine it to current specs."

"At the expense of how much power to the shields?" Sol rubbed the side of his nose, frowning.

"If we're running one hundred percent, I'd take another five out of the system. I talked it over with Happy and Kralachek. Given the performance parameters available, I doubt you'd ever notice the difference. We've already got more acceleration than the grav plates can handle, so that's an easy steal. I'd say swiping that five percent of the total—that you can't use anyway—makes a great payoff for twenty percent higher efficiency out of weapons."

Sol nodded. "But the gun still works?"

Cal lifted his head, lips twisted sourly. "Cap, you know how I feel about inoperable anything—especially weapons. Of course it still works."

"Just so it doesn't blow up when you fire it. I don't want us to hit a bogey's shielding and go up like a small sun from particle lash-back."

"Cap!" Cal cried. "Trust me! Would I blow us up?"

"Huh! Let's see if I remember? Was it you tinkering with the transduction off Ribald Station? How many of *Moriah*'s boards did you fry with that—"

"Hey, Cap, that was a long time ago!"

"Carry on, Cal." Sol backed down the ladder, Cal's chagrined expression assuring him that the job on the guns would be the best one possible.

Sol stuck his head into the atmosphere plant to see Gus Jordache and Pietre Gornyenko glaring at each other as they slapped cards on the comm table in their perpetual poker game.

"Who's winning?" Sol asked as he ran a finger across the bottom of the intake.

Pietre grinned as Sol inspected his fingertip, finding no smudge. "Gus, of course. So far, I owe him . . . uh," he bent to study the ledger, "seventeen billion credits."

"Seventeen billion!"

"Sure," Gus added, stretching, frowning at his cards. "These things change. About this time a couple of years ago, I owed him somewhere around twenty billion. Play long enough and it turns around.''

Sol chuckled, passed the hatch, and walked in on Misha Gaitano. To either side, neatly stowed crates lined the main hold.

"No, you three-fingered dodo. I said I wanted exactly one hundred and eighty foot-pounds of torque on that bolt. If it won't take the test, fine, scrap it and make a new one, hear?''

Sol rounded a crate to find Gaitano bending over a flustered woman using an automatic torque wrench on a piece of partially disassembled equipment.

Gaitano grinned and waved as he saw Sol. "It's tough to break them in, Cap, but, lordy, they make better crew when the going gets tough.''

"You'll see," the woman growled, checking the reading on her wrench. "I'll end up bolting your butt to the deck one of these days, Gaitano. Then you can check the torque till hell won't have it.''

"You and whose army?''

"My right army and my left, Gaitano." She made a muscle—obscured by the coveralls—winked at Sol and scowled halfheartedly at Gaitano.

Misha grinned. "Good job, kid. Now, replace that bearing race and torque the new cap down. I'll teach you a right-hand thread from a left yet.''

When Sol passed the reactor room hatch, he found Happy monitoring the big board, reactor stats at about fifty percent.

Sol dropped into one of the control chairs and sighed.

"You look beat, Cap. What's up?''

"How's the monitor installation coming along?''

"Mostly there. We've got the diplomats covered except for their quarters. That takes time. Suspicious bunch of characters? Whew! Anyhow, we have to wait until they're occupied elsewhere before we sneak in." Happy swiveled in his chair. "Better you dealing with them than me. I'd be tempted to space the whole bunch.''

Sol sighed and rubbed his eyes. "You're not alone.''

Happy squinted, a worried expression moderating the

crags of his face. "You all right? You look, well, kind of gray around the gills."

"Just late hours. What's your analysis of the ship before we make jump? Any problems I ought to know about?"

Happy grinned from ear to ear, leaning forward to whisper, "She spaces like a precious jewel—only I don't want *her* to hear that." In a booming voice he followed up with, "Ah, she ain't half bad for a leaky temperamental spacing hulk. So long as she don't get hauled off as garbage by some persnickety spaceport master, we'll be all right. Got that, you creaky pile of ticking, hissing junk?"

"Acknowledged, you half-wit son of an Arcturian whore."

Sol had been in the middle of a swig of coffee. He choked, snorting the brew into his nose and hacking. Happy pounded him on the back, handing him a rag to wipe up.

Almost casually, *Boaz* added, "Speaking of which, you sagging pile of bones, did you remember your treatment?"

"My what?" Happy looked warily up at the speaker.

Smugly *Boaz* replied, "See, Captain, memory's the first casualty of senility."

"Did I . . ." Sol stopped to cough, ". . . just hear the ship curse?"

"Yeah." Happy beamed. "Makes her more lovable, don't you think?"

Sol blinked. "It's a whole different personality to the one . . ."

"Sol, there's never been a ship like *Boaz* before. We're dealing with—"

"And don't you ever forget it, you scurrilous bit of human flotsam!" *Boaz* finished.

"Oh, go count your rivets—or I'll sell you to the Arpeggians for scrap. Maybe they can make something useful out of you, like a trash compactor or something."

"You have to sleep sometime, Anderson. And considering the second thing to go after memory, you'll be alone.''

Happy chuckled, winking at a dumbfounded Sol. "Quite a personality, huh? *Boaz* and I hit it off right from the beginning. She dug up a term from someplace in her banks. 'User friendly,' now, what in hell you think that means?''

Sol waited, half expecting *Boaz* to respond. "I don't know. I guess, well . . . she's full of surprises. I never suspected she could handle multiple personalities.''

Happy asked, "You talked to her much?''

Sol shook his head slowly. "Been pretty busy trying to keep ahead of the politics and . . . Hell, you know what I've been doing.''

"Seriously, Cap, you look shot. Level with me, you okay?''

"Tired, I guess. More than a little worried. I don't like mysteries, Happy. I don't like the idea of playing political games when my ship and people are at stake. The bogeys are still out there. Just tagging along. No idea who killed Ngoro yet, and I can't get a thing out of either Archon or Connie about the real reason we're here. Kraal ordered me not to push, just to follow their orders.'' His hands fell helplessly in his lap. "So? Is it any great wonder I look like I'm falling apart? I am. Haven't slept the night through since Ngoro was killed.''

"Um.'' Happy glared at the back of his thumb. "And the new kids? Heard one of Gaitano's people thumped that Arturian character for assassinating your fine name.''

Sol stared at the white panels overhead. "I don't know. I slapped them with a little reality the other day. They just tried to slap me back—but I know all the tricks. Bryana is coming around. I think she's beginning to see the ramifications. Arturian? I don't know. He's got potential, but I didn't get off to the right start. Too wrapped up in myself . . . and seeing ghosts when I first stepped aboard. Might not be reparable.''

"You went through that with Mbazi, remember?''

Sol pursed his lips. "Yeah, and if Arturian doesn't

straighten out, I'll use the same treatment. Make it or break it.''

"Open warfare with your First Officer? I don't know. That sort of thing can split a crew right down the middle.''

"And what other choice do I have? Insubordination works like a fungus on morale.''

Happy shook his head. "No wonder you look so miserable.''

"Happy, I feel out of my league. I don't know the stakes. Hell, I don't even know the game. And, to be frank, I'm scared.'' He waved around at the walls. "What if I lose this one, too? One wrong move, a single mistake in judgment could . . . Well, you know.''

"Command hasn't changed. It's always been that way.'' Happy smiled easily. "I think deep down you know that. Guessing against the future used to fascinate you.''

"Sure it did, before . . . Well, never mind.''

"Space never comes cheap. Remember the Americans? They crapped out—let the Soviets have it.''

Sol stared absently at the panels overhead, hearing the faint low frequency hum of the mighty reactor behind the shielding. Before him, the master board graphics displayed *Boaz*'s power in 3-D imaging.

"No, but, Happy, I've got too many ghosts looking over my shoulder, eating at my dreams.''

Happy shook his head, blue eyes tightening in a troubled squint. "I don't like that hollow-eyed look you're getting. You know, we're only a day to jump. Why don't you come down. I've got a bottle of—''

"Oh, no, you don't!'' Sol jumped to his feet, hands out to wave Happy back. "I remember last time you did that to me. No, I've got to keep my wits clear all the time. You hear? This time, Anderson, it's all on *my* shoulders.''

"You just think so,'' Happy called after him. "Damn it, Sol, you're only human!''

Sol listened to the hatch slip shut behind him, cutting off Happy's last words. He smiled humorlessly at the armored white portal behind him. "Yeah, and I wish you weren't right about that."

His stomach knotted as he strode briskly down the corridor.

* * *

The bridge fairly hummed with tension.

Arturian felt like he didn't have time to catch his breath, let alone think. Years of computing for jump made his reactions second nature. Even the annoyance of Carrasco's presence on the bridge evaporated in the frenzy.

". . . Five, four, three, two, one. Mark!" Carrasco called as *Boaz* hovered at the edge of light speed, space warping around her incomprehensible mass. Reactor control shifted from bridge to Engineering as *Boaz* poured her energy into the shields.

"Engineering, it's your hell-hole!"

"Acknowledged, bridge."

Symmetry inverted. Matter changed. *Boaz* vanished from the universe humans consider real.

The screens, once a shotgunning of stars on black as the comm unraveled bent and distorted light, shifted to fluorescent green. Outside, beyond the quantum/time-space continuum, only mass could be detected and manipulated through the shield's inverted symmetry.

"Captain!" *Boaz* called immediately after the all clear sounded. "I must report that a message was transmitted directionally from the lounge transduction unit immediately prior to jump."

"What?" Sol started, straightening.

Art shot him a quick glance from where he bent over the readout checklist. Carrasco's expression strained.

"I had no idea the relay would be triggered," *Boaz* continued. "From the modulation and T vector input, the bogey in G-6 would have been the likely recipient. The order to transmit came as a complete surprise."

"Art!" Carrasco spun in his chair. "Get down there. Collar whoever's at the comm."

Art jumped, hearing *Boaz* add, "No one, Captain."

Then he passed the hatch, sprinting down the corridor for the lounge. *No one? Then how* . . . He almost bowled over two crewwomen inspecting the area with radiation detectors—standard procedure after jump.

As Art bolted into the lounge, he found it empty, the plush room uncharacteristically quiet. Where the comm stood in the corner, a haze of smoke rose in a bluish swirl from the insert slot. Even as he took in the sight, a remote damage control unit hustled forward, attracted by the discharge of ionized particulate matter.

Art charged forward as the unit sprayed retardant on the fire, manipulating panels with mechanical hands. Ripping his belt comm off, he called, "Captain? First Officer Arturian. The comm's on fire. A remote damage control unit is putting it out now. Don't know what I can save of the message."

A pause.

"Very well, First Officer." Carrasco sounded tired. "Contact Engineering. Maybe Happy's people can salvage something."

Art bent down to peer under the unit's arms as it jetted inert gas into the comm. "Affirmative, Captain. Engineering? Chief Engineer Anderson, I need a tech to check this out."

Carrasco interrupted. "Art? Have them check for anything. Run a probe over it for hair, skin flakes, body oils, perfume molecules . . . anything."

"Got it, Cap," Happy replied. "I'll send O'Malley up. He's about the best I've got when it comes to comm."

Art left the tech in charge of the cooling console, only to have Carrasco pick him up in the corridor.

"Come on, Art, I think we'd better have a talk with Malakova."

"The Gulagi?"

Carrasco lifted a shoulder. "He was the last person to use the comm."

Art opened his mouth to ask, but Carrasco was already striding purposefully down the corridor.

If O'Malley hadn't had time to . . . Holy Crap! Carrasco had voided the privacy doctrine. Art shook his head. Damn it, the privacy doctrine had been implicit in the oath of the Craft. It . . . *My God! I've got him now! I can bring the bastard up before the Jurisprudence Committee and have him broken!*

Nikita's hatch passed them. He looked up from where he was reading some sort of official documentation. "Captain? First Officer . . ." Then he caught the look on Sol's face. "What's wrong?"

"Would you know anything about a time delay message in comm?"

He frowned. "I put message in and punched send button. I don't think it was time delay."

"You don't *think* it was time delay?" Carrasco stopped, feet braced, knotted fists behind his back. "If it was your message, how—"

"Wasn't." He rose ponderously, stepping out to face Sol, head back, body tense. Frown lines like canyons engraved the Gulagi's heavy forehead.

"The message which just exploded my comm was time delayed. We've pinned the probable destination to one of the vessels paralleling our course. Now, if it wasn't your message . . ."

Nikita frowned, gaze dropping to the floor. "Found packet in message box. Just note that said, 'Nikita, I'm running late. Please slip this into comm before the jump.' I assumed it was from Tayash. I don't know, maybe he had meeting or something. I just dropped it in comm and pushed send button. I didn't know it was preset or directional. You can't tell just from simple cassette."

Sol cocked his head, eyes keen. "Isn't sabotage a Gulagi favorite."

Nikita smiled. "But of course! Is great weapon against oppressors of downtrodden. At same time, I am best of Gulagi. No, if I want to destroy comm, I walk out and do it! Make better statement that way." He paused. "Only, have problem here. Was no note? No claim of why comm was destroyed?" He waved a thick finger. "Is not Gulagi way. Gratuitous sabotage becomes terror. Earth learned lesson well in pre-Soviet days. No, Captain, on honor of Malakova Station, I did not destroy comm.''

Art watched as Carrasco met the big man's eyes, staring frankly at the Gulagi. *And somehow, I believe him.* Art pursed his lips.

Carrasco smiled thinly. ''Well, maybe my people can lift something from the note. There might be some trace . . . What's wrong?''

Nikita shook his head, distress deepening, rubbing his hands as if cold. ''How could I know? Enough stuff piles up as is. Look at this place. Clutter. I dropped it into converter. How could . . . I mean was just note. What good is note after message is read?''

''The note wasn't handwritten?''

He sighed. ''Printed on personal comm. I can't even tell you what kind of lettering. Are so many different fonts. If I make guess, was Arcturian system from flimsy.''

''Well, maybe the tape will have some—''

''I doubt it,'' Art whispered to himself, barely aware Carrasco had turned to study him. ''It's too good a job. A complete dupe all the way around. You won't find anything, Captain.'' He realized he'd become the center of attention. ''I mean, look, I don't know what's going on here. But at first glance, what happened smacks of a professional. They wouldn't have botched that last bit of covering their tracks.''

Carrasco's complexion had grayed, desperation apparent in his expression. ''No, I suppose not.''

Art was unnerved by the haunted look in Carrasco's eyes. Damn it, the Captain looked like he was on the verge of collapse. A faint shiver seemed to course through the man's body.

If he breaks, somebody better be there to pick up the pieces, or, damn it, we're all going to be dead.

* * *

''Message, Admiral.''

Sellers swiveled in his command chair. *Hunter* and the

rest of his fleet hovered at the edge of the light envelope, shields flaring as interstellar hydrogen and dust burned against their fields.

"I'll take it on my personal unit." He peered down at the monitor on the arm of his chair. Several lines of text passed before his eyes and vanished.

He stroked his chin thoughtfully, pale eyes on the Weapons Officer. The man looked up, caught his stare, and quickly looked away. And Carrasco still didn't suspect the identity of the viper in his midst? Curious to think of one's own offspring as a viper—but how appropriate. Talent ran in the family.

"Destroy the record, Comm Officer."

"Done, sir."

"Engineering?" Sellers called.

"Here, Captain."

"Prepare to jump on my signal."

"Prepared and waiting, sir."

"Navcomm, coordinate with the rest of the fleet. They have our rendezvous? More so than ever, we must coordinate perfectly. Too much is at stake."

"Coordinated, sir. Fleet reports ready." The Navcomm Officer waited, an expectant look on his face.

"Very well. My compliments all the way around. *Boaz* has jumped. Gentlemen, our time has come." Sellers smiled his satisfaction. "Engineering, on my count. Ten, nine, eight, seven, six, five . . ."

CHAPTER XX

She remembered . . .

Despite the madness winding around her, the variability of organic life had surprised her. Tiss had arisen in a gas giant of a planet. Ancient in origin, they had first evolved sentience during the time of the Aan. It took so many star lifetimes for them to slowly put together science, to learn to harness the elements of the planet and move to the stars. Then they spread slowly, seeking out gas giants to seed with their kind.

Unlike most organic life, the evolution of the Tiss hinged on cooperation, their very nature hospitable, their survival dependent on shared resources. Light, delicate, of virtually no mass, the Tiss found her, and were unable to work the spring.

Savaged by insane rage, she watched them go floating away on the interstellar winds in gossamer ships.

Like a wispy veil, time wound around her as she ranted to herself, flickers of insanity twisting into a raging vortex of loathing hatred, only to subside again.

But the Tiss—like all organic life—bred their doom. On the Hynan planet, they found life. Fascinated, the Tiss watched from above as intelligence germinated. Beyond the scope of their understanding the advanced creatures of the planet below preyed upon each other, constantly striving for dominance in the rich organic environment. Yet for eons, the Tiss proved powerless to descend into the gravity well. Otherwise, how could they study these beings close at hand in an attempt to comprehend such insane behavior? United, they engaged upon a project to copy Hynan physiology in a cooperative biological engineering process. In their orbiting labs, they reproduced the species they observed on the planet below.

Their first attempts proved to be miserable failures; their introduced creatures immediately died under the claws of the hostile Hynan.

The decision that the Hynan could overcome such unthinkable violence through greater intelligence evolved after long discussions. At the same time, such creatures could be an incredible asset to the Tiss. Beings such as they planned could be partners in the exploration of the cosmos. By nature of their strength and durability, they could explore environments—like gravity wells—the Tiss could only speculate upon. Consequently they returned to the bio labs, improved their design, and built a creature of superb intelligence and endurance. The spawn, superbly viable, were dropped to the planet below.

Success followed immediately. Their creation dominated life on the planet, interbreeding with the lesser forms. Tiss dropped communications equipment. And the warring Hynan were instructed in science and engineering.

On a plume of burning hydrogen the first Hynan rose to meet their masters. Only the Tiss had miscalculated on the effects of their hybridization. They hadn't counted on the competitive drive being absorbed from the brutal environment below. To their misfortune intelligence did not of itself breed pacification.

At first the Hynan remained in awe of their mentors, observing the rules, greedily devouring Tiss knowledge—until their intelligence began to surpass that of their creators. What use did a superior competitor have for the delicate Tiss?

* * *

Bryana actually gave Sol a smile as he cleared the hatch and took her report.

"You might take a look at the improvement on the combat drill," she told him, a certain pride animating her as she stood and stretched lithely. For a second, she hesitated.

Sol looked up from his inspection of the stat board. "Yes, First Officer?"

"Nothing, Captain. Just let me know if you can see an area to improve. That's all."

"I'd be glad to." Sol settled into the command chair, habitually extending his coffee cup into the dispenser. So who had bombed the comm? Preoccupied, he barely realized Bryana remained standing.

He looked up. "Yes?"

She smiled nervously, head tilted slightly, hands clasped before her. "I . . . uh, Elvina Young has been asking for you. I repeatedly asked if I could help, but she insisted on talking to you."

Sol made a face. "Lucky me. Thank you, First Officer. You're excused."

Bryana started to say something, blushed slightly, and left. Sol didn't catch the look she gave him as she passed the hatch.

"*Boaz,* open a line to Elvina Young."

"Captain Carrasco!" Elvina literally glowed. "I was hoping you'd call. I must admit, I didn't realize it would be so soon after you'd—"

"I understand there's a problem, Mrs. Young?"

"Why, yes." She smiled, dimpling her cheeks, slightly breathless. "There are men working on the comm in the lounge. I was under the impression that comm was for passenger communications to our home worlds. Now the techs can't even tell me when it will be fixed. In the meantime, is there another comm I can use? The Desseret Festival is coming up in days and I have no idea what everyone is wearing. It's the one time of year it's permissible to put on finery and I've simply got to talk to my dressmaker. You see, to be wearing the latest fashion clear out here in space would—"

"Mrs. Young, please." Sol tried to smile politely. "We're in the jump, you can't—"

"And that's another thing. What's all this business of jumping lights?"

"Well, it's a little complicated. Anyway, the gist of it all is that while we're 'outside' you can't talk to our regular universe. You see, we've inverted symmetry and . . . Listen, by the time we drop back in, the comm will be fixed and you can talk to your friends at Temple . . . sort of . . . not counting the relativity."

"But I'll have missed Desseret by—"

"No, ma'am. You'll still have as many days to festival as you do now. You see the effect—"

"But, Captain! At dinner last night, you told me specifically that we would be outside for almost two weeks! How can we be outside for two weeks and *not* miss Desseret?"

"Would you believe that we don't exist for the moment?"

She gave him a radiant smile, blue eyes twinkling. "Captain, really!"

"Yes, really. You see, everything that makes us up is now in a different phase-change. We're not in our universe anymore. We're beyond the time-space continuum . . . beyond the light boundary. It's a function of mass and velocity which is manipulated by means of our shielding—the same effect which keeps our antimatter fuel from exploding. If we cut power to the shielding all of a sudden, we drop back into regular space. Time can't pass if we're not in the universe. It's a permutation of conservation of energy."

She nodded slightly, a baffled look in her eyes. "I still need to talk to my dressmaker within three days, Captain. Can I use *your* comm?"

He shook his head. "As I said, it wouldn't make any difference, jumping the light barrier—"

"Ah, you men." She sighed, eyes eating him alive. "Are you a poet at heart, Captain? Such a marvelous idea, to jump light. Think of the romantic images it conjures in the mind. I'd like to think I was a poet, too. Dominated by the passions of the heart. And you, Captain?"

Sol kicked a circuit open, the resultant heterodyne singing loudly. He winced at the noise. "Whoops, sorry, Mrs. Young. That's engineering for you. I'm sure you can understand if I have to cut this short. Excuse me." He cut the system, leaning back in the command chair, exhaling.

"Jumping lights, *for God's sake?* And she wants a dress for the Desseret Festival? *Out here?*" Sol sipped his coffee, grumbling, "Hitavia and Texahi must be out of their minds."

He chuckled as he dug into his space pouch.

"Humor, Captain?" *Boaz* wondered. "Most think she's an incredible irritant. Or attraction, depending upon the circumstances and ploy she assumes for her—"

"I call her an ignorant nuisance, good ship." He pulled out the envelope handed to him on the docks. The sight of it triggered memories of blood and body parts. He opened the chem coded paper, finding a message disk inside. Almost hesitantly, he slipped it into *Boaz*'s system.

Kraal's antique face formed on the comm. "Greetings, Captain Carrasco. By now you're in the jump. Hopefully all has gone well . . . or I would have ordered you to destroy this message as obsolete by now.

"Sol, in the past you've given heart and soul in the service of the Craft. To be honest, after so much sacrifice on your part, I didn't know if I was right to call on you again. The Speaker, however, for reasons of his own, requested you."

"Uh-huh, great reasons, Grand Master," Sol muttered.

"Considering the Speaker's position in this matter, I couldn't help but agree. It seems he has faith in your very humanity. Perhaps, in our current cynical age, that's not such a bad criterion to employ.

"As to the nature of your mission, the divulgence of that will remain up to the Speaker. For the moment, you are ordered to turn yourself and your command, over to the Speaker of Star's Rest—or the Deputy Speaker as the case may be. I told you in person that you would be responsible to them. I'm now making it official. Those orders are now part of the record, and may be retrieved by any officer aboard.

"Sol, I hate to put you in this position, but I have every faith you will acquit yourself with honor and dignity as is becoming a Master of the Craft. If the Speaker has confided in you, you know the reasons for these extraordinary measures. If he's decided to wait, I believe you'll find all our precautions well within reason." Kraal smiled wearily. "I've always taught that the end didn't justify the means—until now. I find a bitter lesson in that.

"I thank you for your patience and place my trust in your abilities. Good luck, Solomon, you and your crew must succeed at any price."

The monitor went blank.

Sol stared into his coffee cup, vaguely aware of the reflections of the light panels overhead. *And Connie makes word games out of Godhead? What the hell is the angle here? And if it's that all-fired serious, and it looks like I'll lose this ship? What, then? Damn them, I can't be an impartial player in this! I'm only a single human being—with a lot of ghosts looking over my shoulder.*

He steeled himself. "Damn it, what if I can't . . . ." He closed his eyes, fingers tightening around his coffee cup until the tendons stood from the back of his hands.

"Captain?"

"I'm fine, *Boaz,* just going through the usual soul-searching you should have become accustomed to by now." He shook his head. "You know, it's so easy to be a hero in a story or play. Damn it, reality is a pain in the ass."

"Indeed?"

He nodded humbly. "They've made me a legend. Iron Carrasco, the man who always brings them back. Kraal seems to understand the truth. But Archon? He thinks I'm some sort of superhero. Why? Because I was driven to desperation off Arpeggio—not because I knew what the hell I was doing!" He chuckled nervously, eyes darting. "And here I sit, a psychological basket case trying to keep all the ends together."

"Perhaps, Captain, that's the reality of heroes? Perhaps that's the truth behind the myth? Perhaps you're no different than any of the others have ever been?"

He took a deep breath. "Perhaps. Well, now that I've had my little bout of shakes and sorrows, I'd better get on with this.

"Kraal laid it all out, didn't he? All official and neat." Sol sucked at his lower lip and shook his head. *"Boaz,* open a line to the Speaker."

Archon's grizzled face filled the monitor. He, too, looked weary. "Yes, Captain?"

Sol steeled himself. "Speaker, if you would do me the honor, could you come to the bridge?"

Archon's expression hardened. "I'm on my way, Captain."

The monitor flickered off.

Sol stared at the main monitor for a moment, watching

the lime green pinpoints of gravity wells slip behind them, more forming on the monitor ahead. "Well, *Boaz*, for a man who really didn't want this command, turning loose of it hurts." He stared up dully. "Do you realize? After a fashion, I've just lost another ship."

"It has happened before, Captain. The instances are not a matter of record in the general files. If I could, I might note that when such situations have occurred, those in your place have accepted their duty with dignity and honor to the Craft."

Sol glanced up. "Advice, good ship?"

"Yes, Captain."

Sol hesitated, an ache in his soul. "Taken and accepted, *Boaz*. Oh, and one other thing. Thank you."

Her voice echoed with warmth. "Most welcome, Captain."

Sol sipped his coffee, the taste bitter on his tongue. Resistance had fled, he simply waited, savoring the moments for what they were, unable to think ahead. He had gone emotionally and mentally numb.

"The Speaker is at the hatch," *Boaz* informed. "Ready?"

"As I'll ever be. Pass him, good ship."

Archon entered and looked curiously about the bridge. He took the command chair Sol pointed to, trying not to gawk with a spacer's fascination for command centers and the way they were designed.

"What sort of crisis do we face now?" Archon lifted a gray forest of eyebrow.

"*We* face none, Speaker. The problem is mine. I have just been ordered to turn my command over to you." His mouth had gone dry, the taste of coffee stale. "I'll replay the orders if you wish."

Archon frowned, running thick fingers through his mat of beard as he considered. "If you don't mind, please."

"*Boaz*, rerun the Galactic Grand Master's message."

Archon watched, chin propped on an elbow. After Kraal's face faded, he turned to Sol. "I don't know what to tell you. I knew we had that option—but I didn't quite expect Kraal to simply dump it in my lap. Have you told your crew? How will they react? I mean, command loyalty is the fiber of—''

"I called you first thing. I thought I should talk to you."

Archon nodded. "I see. Well, what do you suggest? I mean, Captain, command is a very delicate thing. Myself, I served under many flags . . . but the ships were always mine. Had I been ordered to turn over command to another? Well, I think I know how you feel."

Sol waited, fingering his coffee cup. Finally, he took a deep breath. "Speaker, the final decision is yours—and be aware that I'll cheerfully abide by your order—but let me suggest that you assume a silent command. My First Officers will be informed and Kraal's commands will rule them. In the meantime, we'll proceed as before. I'll control the crew and subject myself to your every wish and demand. I think, in the long run, we'll have less trouble that way."

Archon nodded thoughtfully. "Agreed, Captain. You realize that should I become incapacitated, my daughter will take my place immediately."

"I'm well aware of that. She's earned my fullest respect." Sol handed him a cup of coffee. "Now, mind telling me what this is all about?"

"The conference will—"

"Please, could we go beyond that charade?"

Archon's gray eyes bored into his. "It's not charade, Captain." He hesitated, weighing his words. "It's not the entire truth either. Suffice it to say, I can't tell you yet. I don't hesitate to remind you that we don't travel among friendly interests. In this day and age, with psych developed to the extent it is, no secret can be kept. We still haven't determined who Ngoro's murderer is. The individual who sabotaged the comm still sends shivers down my spine. That cassette might just as easily have been a bomb."

"Those unfriendly interests might employ the same psych methods to interrogate you," Sol reminded.

Archon smiled. "Indeed they might . . . and I feel lucky that Connie and I have avoided that so far. But your

Brotherhood is most ingenious when it comes to devices. Your people gave me the means to take my secret where no one but God may pry it from me. In my chest is a device which will clean out a large room. Another in my leg is tailored to other circumstances. And, last but not least, I can simply go to sleep without pain—and no one the wiser. The same is true for Connie. What? You look surprised, Captain. How many times have I told you we could take no chances? I see your skepticism, but yes, the stakes are *that* high."

Sol fumbled for words. "I . . . I think I'll be a little more nervous around Connie next time."

Archon chuckled, a glint in his eyes. "Indeed, Captain? Oh, I wouldn't get too concerned about the bomb Kraal planted in her. Believe me, after having raised her, that's the least of her potential hazards. Why, that kid was in more trouble than you'd believe. The ships, always the ships. I think she's got reaction mass in her blood. Couldn't settle her on a planet if it was the last thing I did."

Sol sipped his coffee, watching Archon's expression soften as he stared into the past.

"You did very well with her, Speaker. She's quite a capable woman. You should be proud."

The Speaker grunted. "A success to balance a failure?" He lifted an eyebrow. "Connie said she told you about Rodger."

"I still don't understand it all. I'm not sure any more need be said, either. Let's allow the past to take care of itself. We couldn't change it if we wanted."

"Agreed." Archon's lips curled faintly, gaze drifting to the stats from old habit.

"And after this business is over?"

Archon shrugged. "My spacing days have run their course, Captain. I'm a leader of a world now. Curious where fate leads us. I expected to die in a burst of plasma someplace, send my elements back to the stars that nourished me. Now, I'll be buried in the rich dirt of Star's Rest."

"And Connie will become your heir?"

"If the people want her." Archon shook his head. "And if she'll stay. Like I said, the ships draw her onward, ever onward. For the moment, she's struggling under an incredible burden. When it's all over, I expect she'll pile everything on poor Claude Mason and space to someplace where she can find a ship. But no, we're not establishing a royal line."

"Jordan seems to consider her eligible."

"Bah! The man's a fool. No, she's not likely to fall for a fop like Jordan—even if he promises her a world or two. She's been on the hard side too long." Archon shifted, studying Sol craftily. "On the other hand, offer her a ship like *Boaz* and you might be able to get her."

Sol's throat constricted. "I beg your pardon?"

Archon grinned. "Oh, I've seen you watching her, Captain. And I've seen her watching you back when you didn't know it."

"Speaker, I assure you, I—"

"Shut up, Solomon. I'm too damned old to be jerked around by protestations of either innocence or virtue. She's an attractive woman and I've grown used to the interest paid her by men. Proud of it in fact."

"Speaker, I'm the Captain of the *Boaz*. I'm not in a position to engage in a relationship. Even if she were interested . . . which I suspect she isn't, considering some of our conversations, she has her duty and I have mine."

Archon grunted, "Uh-huh. Well, unless there's something else, I'd best get back to my administrative backlog. Great thing about jump. You can catch up on your work." He stood. "As to the command, Solomon, I have every faith in you. Proceed as you normally would and don't bother me with administrative details."

"Yes, sir."

Archon stopped at the hatch. "But as to Connie, you're on your own there, boy." He winked wryly. "So . . . good luck."

Sol felt curiously flustered as he stared at the hatch.

* * *

Nikita frowned distrustfully before Lietov's hatch. "Representative Malakova to see Assistant Director Lietov."

The hatch slid aside to allow Nikita to stroll into the Sirian's personal quarters. As he suspected, the room—a carbon copy of his own—appeared neat, everything in order. Lietov rose from behind a comm table, smiling as he extended a hand.

"Good of you to come, Nikita. Brandy?"

"A small glass."

Lietov strolled over to an intricately-carved sandwood cabinet latched to the wall. He opened the doors to expose scarlet velvet padding which cradled snifters. From solid platinum dispensers, he poured two glasses.

"To your health, Representative." Lietov smiled with satisfaction as he clinked Nikita's glass in toast.

"To yours." *And may your Sirian swine choke on it. Very well, what is your angle, Lietov? Considering all the times Gulag has voted to cut your throat, what do you seek from me? Is this reconciliation—or threat?* Nikita sighed at the rich sensation of the fine liquor on his palate.

Lietov gestured to an antigrav, seating himself opposite, crossing his legs as he leaned back. "So far the Brotherhood has provided us a most pleasant spacing." He indicated the room. "Not quite a luxury liner, but everything seems to work despite its Spartan nature."

"Brotherhood does not build for luxury." Nikita shrugged. "Compared to most stations in Gulag, I roll in bourgeois bliss." He sniffed, pointing at his nose. "Is no odor of hydroponics to stick in nose—reminder of eventual destination of physical self."

Lietov's slight nod of understanding entertained and irritated at the same time. Even through the years, Nikita still hadn't been able to shake his dislike of the privileged and powerful.

"Nikita." Lietov scowled down at his brandy. "I understand conditions in Gulag Sector aren't what they are around the rest of the Confederacy. Despite the optimism of the Soviets, the resource base just doesn't support the kind of growth—''

"Bah! Soviets knew what they were doing. Threw my ancestors out to starve in interstellar waste processing chondritic asteroids for radiation protection and what little metal and water could be extracted to keep workers alive. Is analogous to old prison rock pile scenario.''

Lietov grunted, jaw working as if he nibbled at something hidden in his mouth. ''You know, part of that is Gulag's own fault. Every time an investor looks seriously at pumping money into resource procurement, one of the stations vetoes it. I know for a fact that a significant graphite fiber industry could be developed in the Taiga belt region. Everything's there. Carbonaceous asteroids by the billions to make light-years of fiber. Enough helium-three's floating around to light half the Sector. You've got the people to run the tugs and miners, everything but the metals and technology to make the system work. What's Gulag's major export now? Agriculture, for God's sake! And you're producing at only a couple of points above the subsistence level at that!''

"And you would change this?'' Nikita reached up to scratch under his bush of beard. *Ah-ha! Here comes sales pitch. What does he promise? Moon, stars, and unlimited galaxies?*

"All it takes is capital—and the reassurances that one station won't sabotage the entire project because their neighbors happen to be getting ahead. Those things can be worked out given the will.''

"And Sirius would do this?''

"It could be arranged.''

Nikita grinned, swirling his brandy to watch the light in the amber fluid. ''And what do you want for this tremendous foothold in future?''

Lietov cradled the snifter like a globe. ''Support. You're a powerful man, Nikita. Not many people like you—most think you're a bombastic barbarian, as a matter of fact. But they respect you because of what you believe and because you make a powerful enemy. Currently, Sirius is in need of friends. We have substantial investment capital—and we're looking for new directions."

"Uh-huh." Nikita gazed intently into the reflection from the glass. "Gulag, as you well know, Mark, doesn't follow any man's lead. My constituents—"

"Your constituents listen to you." Lietov leaned forward. "You've been representing them for so long, you're like an institution. Once major industry comes to Gulag that provincialism they're so fond of would come tumbling down in the wake of prosperity. Social evolution requires—"

"What you really want, Mark?"

Lietov stopped short. "Your reputation for bluntness is deserved. The Sirian delegation provided me with a complete file on you. They said you were a particularly astute and quick man."

"I get by. Enjoy flattery, too. It has purpose?"

Lietov lifted a shoulder. "I've developed a lot of respect for you, Nikita. Have you ever thought of advancing yourself . . . as well as your Sector?

Here it comes. "A man always thinks of that—at least if he wants to survive for any length of time in vicious political circles of Confederacy, eh?" Nikita slitted his eyes. "What do you have in mind?"

Lietov pursed his lips, an intent look to his raptorian features. "By now you've guessed that a great deal hinges on this jump to Star's Rest. You've heard the talk in the halls—that the Confederacy may topple as a result. For the moment, I'm simply looking for your unqualified support. If everything comes apart, Sirius would make a better friend than enemy."

"Gulagis don't have great love for Sirius. Myself, I've stopped your plans more than once." Nikita raised a finger.

Lietov smiled superficially. "A fact I'm more than aware of. Not everyone is so eloquent as you, or so powerful as Gulag Sector, for that matter. If the system were to change, your popular appeal might vanish. Your power might hinge on your actual military-industrial capabilities. Your appeal to the rest of humanity might be dimmed. The future's an uncertain place at best.

"I, however, am not so naive as to bear a grudge over past problems, not when there's a chance I could turn talent to my benefit. I'm making that offer."

"And my people?"

"To start with, special trade status. That investment capital I mentioned earlier. Beyond that, I think you should consider the ramifications of what's happening in the Confederacy. We could offer protection—and Gulag Sector, with its independent stations, depends on the Patrol to discourage raiding."

"So? Sirian fleet isn't exactly known for military prowess. See if recollection serves right. Sirius usually hires Arpeggians through back door when situation gets sticky, eh?"

Lietov laughed, and slapped his armrest. "I do like you, Nikita. In a galaxy of lying politicians, your honesty shines like a beacon. I assure you, however, that with the conclusion of this venture, Sirius will *be* the power in the Confederacy."

Nikita cocked his head. "And Patrol?"

Lietov sighed wistfully. "They served their purpose— once. It's time for a new order. Sirius will be in the position to provide it and to effectively restructure human space."

"And I should side with you?"

Lietov met his level gaze. "Nikita, consider the alternatives. Look at the players involved. I'm offering you— and Gulag—a chance to get in on the ground floor. If Sirius loses out, whose will and power would you live under? The Terrans? Want Medea for a ruler? New Maine? Your Gulagis would bow to a king? And then there's Palmiere, who would be Emperor Palmiere the First. Last, but not least, look around you and tell me the Brotherhood isn't interested in playing the biggest hand of all. Battleship diplomacy? And all that from a secret power elite that won't even maintain a seat on the Council?''

Nikita sipped the last of the brandy and smacked his lips. ''Have always suspected Brotherhood of exploitative oppression. Trickle down of technology comes too slowly. Who pays for lack of medical and such ships as this, eh? Slick-tongued Grand Master? Or sweating workers struggling honestly to feed and shelter families?''

''There you have it.'' Lietov spread his hands.

''I do?''

''Nikita, I promise you, on my word of honor. You help me, help Sirius, to prevail in this—and you'll reap the benefits.'' His eyes hardened. ''Working with us would be much, much more enjoyable in the end than acting against us.''

''And if I refuse?''

Lietov ran a slow finger around the lip of his glass. ''Don't. Very soon now, Sirius will have the capability to destroy all of its enemies. That's not much of a balance, is it? A little political support—a little trust and good will—against annihilation?''

* * *

''Constance?''

She turned, seeing Jordan leaning out the hatch of his personal quarters. He smiled uneasily, a slight sheen to his flushed skin. ''Could I see you for a minute.''

She hesitated. *I don't want to do this. It'll be disastrous.* ''A minute? Very well.'' She walked back, stopping before his hatch. He wore a loose white blouse, unzipped to the middle of the chest. Fawn trousers hugged his legs, the top restrained by a gaudy red sash. His features appeared slightly inflamed, a redness about his cheeks that matched the burning intensity of his eyes.

He smiled, and gestured her in. At her reluctance, he chuckled. ''I don't bite.''

She smiled slightly, steeling herself, and walked past

him, catching the scent of Arcturian whiskey on his breath. *Good Lord, he's not drunk, is he?* She turned, studying the gleam in his eyes. Damn it, he was—and the hatch hissed shut behind her.

"I'm running on a tight schedule, Earl. I really only have a minute." She crossed her arms defensively.

"I wondered if perhaps you would allow me to restate my case. I'm not sure you understand exactly what I tried to say to you last time."

"I think I know . . ."

He waved it off. "Then I did it rather poorly. You must understand my position. You see, I simply—"

"Don't worry about it, Earl, I—"

"No, I've told you. Call me Fan." His smile worked loosely about his lips. "I really don't think I managed to get my point across very well last time. What I was trying to say, was that I've given it a great deal of consideration. You and me, that is." He blinked, frowning slightly, as if he'd lost the thread of his thoughts. "And we could . . . could remake humanity in our images." He reached up to finger her hair.

She stepped back, disentangling his fingers with her own. He twisted his grip, locking her fingers in his.

"I think that's enough, Fan. You don't have anything new to tell me." She tugged halfheartedly at her fingers, the chill turning to dread. The damn fool didn't think he'd—

"But I do." His smile grew as he pulled her close to stare down at her. "I'm an earl, Connie. In line to the throne of New Maine. And we've . . . we've taken steps on the other side, you see."

Connie froze, poised on the verge of jacking a knee into his crotch. *Steps on the other side?* "On the other side of the jump?" She cocked her head, staring up into his smug face.

"Did I say that?" He tried to swallow a burp, the sweet odor of whiskey cloying in her nose. He chuckled, his other arm going about her, trapping her against him. "Well, never mind . . . But you see, we plan ahead. That's where you and I come in. You need me, Connie. You really do. And I don't intend on letting you go. You . . . you're worthy of me, you see.''

She got her arms up under his grip, body tight. ''What did you mean, on the other side?''

''Being smart, Connie. That's why you need me. Planning ahead, you see. Making sure . . . one way or the other.'' He bent down, breathing deeply, as he smelled her hair. ''And now, you and I will begin our—''

''You can let me go now, Fan. You don't want to push this any farther. If you do . . .'' She stiffened as he kissed the side of her neck. ''Fan, damn it! Let me loose and we'll forget this happened.''

''No, Connie,'' he whispered in her ear. ''You don't seem to realize my power. I'm the Earl of Baspa. My word is law. Last time, you didn't take me seriously as a man. I can't allow you to make that mistake again.''

''You're drunk.'' She struggled against him, starting as his hand dropped to squeeze her buttocks. ''And you're about to make the worst mistake of your life.''

He laughed, running hot hands possessively over her. ''I'm going to rule the galaxy! You and me, Connie. I'm going to be the man—''

She threw herself backward, overbalancing him, opting to flip him instead of using her knee. Neatly, she threw him off as they fell, rolling away. Jumping to her feet, she sprinted for the hatch. A heavy hand grabbed her from behind, spinning her back.

Off balance, she teetered for a second in recovery. Too long. He caught her up, lifting her powerfully, an arm locked about her throat.

''Shouldn't have done that, Connie. It'll make it worse. No one . . . not even you whom I'd give the galaxy for . . . can do that to me. I'm an earl, Connie. I take what I want when I want it, and right now I want you.''

She struggled against the forearm choking her. ''You're cutting your own throat, Fan,'' she gasped past the lump of her tongue where it filled the back of her mouth. Flipping and twisting, she fought him as he bore her down.

The padded floor trapped her as he used his weight against her.

She looked up into his enraged eyes as he pinned her arms down. "Damn you! You're out of your mind! Fan, you're on a starship! Hear me? *Rape me and they'll space you!*"

"I'm the Earl of Baspa! My word is law." He reached down to unclip her belt, bearing down with obvious experience.

"Don't, Fan. I mean it, they'll kill you. This is a ship. Not your planet. I . . ." She tensed as he unfastened her pants.

"You pushed me to this, Connie. You pushed. You'll see now, see what it means to —"

She jackknifed violently, batting him off and leaping to her feet. He scrambled after her. Connie turned, kicking him in the side.

He howled, "You struck a nobleman! Damn you, *you whore!* You'll pay for that. I'll make it hurt, woman. Hurt like you've never hurt before." He staggered to his feet, gasping, holding his side.

Connie dropped to a combat crouch, heart pounding. She tensed as he approached. "I don't want to kill you, Fan. I—"

"*Jordan!*"

She backpedaled, seeing Carrasco approaching from the hatch, violence in his eyes.

"Get out, Captain," Jordan gritted. "This isn't your business. As Earl of Baspa, I order you—"

"You order nothing! Cease and desist. *NOW!*" Carrasco took another step. "I mean it, Jordan. Or I'll jail you like—"

"Royal prerogative—"

"*Is meaningless on* my *ship!*"

Jordan pivoted on his heel and Connie saw her chance, slipping behind him, tripping and bringing him down cursing, as she twisted an arm up behind his back. Jordan screamed and bucked. Connie reached down, practiced fingers applying pressure to the arteries in his neck.

"Connie," Sol warned, "Don't—"

"He's drunk, Captain. He'll be trouble until he's out."

Jordan flopped for several seconds and went still. Connie looked up, chest heaving. "Damn, I thought I'd have to kill him." She stood, pulling loose strands of her hair back, refastening her pants, clipping her belt closed.

Carrasco bent down, feeling for a pulse. "Elevated heart rate. Breathing's strange, too. What the . . ." He stood looking around, finding a vial next to Jordan's half-empty glass. "Hyperoxy."

"Oh, hell. Damned fool. I smelled whiskey on his breath." She shook her head, eyeing the vial. "With that stuff, he could kill himself. Oxygenates the blood, reduces the effect of alcohol. They sell it in most of the raunchy bars from Far Side Station to Luna Transshipment."

Sol walked to the comm. "Hospital, send a med tech to Representative Jordan's cabin."

"Affirmative."

She stood, head down, watching Jordan uneasily.

"And you?"

She rubbed the backs of her arms. "I'm all right. Thank you for showing up when you did. I . . . I'd have had to hurt him." She shivered, closing her eyes. Carrasco's arm settled around her shoulders reassuring, warm and safe. Sighing, she leaned against him. "And God alone knows what the ramifications of that would have been." She lifted a hand to rub her eyes. "Damn, I'm tired."

"Want to press charges? Assault with intent to rape?"

"No." She swallowed hard, looking up. "Let's consider it closed. He's going to wake up tomorrow with a hell of a headache and probably feel like a damned fool. He just didn't seem . . . but then, that's hyperoxy for you. You're fine until you quit inhaling and the alcohol gets you."

"Nasty stuff. They inject it in the air in the Pantie Club on Vicos Station."

She glanced up at him quizzically. "You've been to the . . . You? I mean, of all people, you . . . Well, there's another bubble burst!"

Carrasco grinned evilly. "Happy did it to me."

The tech arrived and immediately went to work on Jordan. "He'll live—but it'll be close. Blood alcohol's point three eight."

"He's all yours," Sol grunted, nervously removing his arm from Connie's shoulder as if he realized for the first time what he'd done. Off balance, he looked at her. "Come on, I'll buy you dinner."

"All right."

As they walked down the corridor, Carrasco added, "Sure didn't look like you needed a rescue."

She laughed. "What can I say? I'm my father's daughter. Us mercenary types, we're trained tough. But, to be honest, I was scared enough to have killed him there at the end."

"I still think you should press charges."

She looked up at him and winked. "I don't think he'll be back. It would hardly be fitting if a meek and mild rape victim like me broke his Royal jaw." She paused. "And by the way, just *how* did you happen to get there? That hatch was locked as I recall."

Carrasco lifted a shoulder. "Had a complaint about noise in the hall."

She gave him a scathing glance. "Uh-huh. One of these days, Carrasco, that's going to wear a little thin."

"Kept you from killing him."

"Does *Boaz* monitor everything said and done?"

He looked around, pulling her close. "Honestly, and since you have the Word and Signs, she does. If you ever get in trouble, holler. I'll be right there."

She nodded slowly, the ramifications seeping in. "I've read your privacy code. Monitoring could get you spaced—just like rape."

Sol met her gaze earnestly. "Then I'll just have to trust you."

Something inside warmed as she stared into his eyes.
"I guess that makes us even. Now, didn't you say some-
thing about dinner? Or do you want me to starve to death?
Beating up earls leaves a girl famished."

He laughed, a twinkle in his eyes. "I wish we . . ."
He looked away self-consciously.

"You were saying?"

"Nothing."

* * *

"Enter," Nikita called as the hatch announced his visitor.

As the heavy white portal slipped to the side, Medea,
the Terran Vice Consul, strode into the room, gown billowing around her in a loose flowing wave of shimmering
colors.

Nikita stood, bowing slightly, studying her carefully.
Medea might have been as old as one hundred and twenty
but with the latest medical techniques, she looked no
more than forty, trim, healthy, her body lithe and vibrant. Rich black hair piled in a tight coil above her skull
to accent the olive tones of her eastern Mediterranean
ancestry. Cool black eyes lit warmly to augment the smile
on her thin lips.

"Good of you to see me, Representative."

"My pleasure, Vice Consul. Come, sit. Could I get
you anything?"

She settled easily in a gravchair, expensive fabrics
pooling around her as she leaned back, elbows on the
armrests, fingers interlacing in a pyramid. "Do you have
anything from Gulag? A drink perhaps? Something delightfully cultural?"

Nikita winced slightly. "Actually, I do have bottle of
Gulagi vodka. It's not exactly something sane man brags
about. In fact, only reason I've got it is because Andrei
packed bags for me. Always includes Gulagi vodka in
case sneaky constituents catch me in off moment. Is
better to produce bottle of Gulagi rocket fuel instead

of Star Mist. Makes it look better to suffering masses, you see.''

Medea laughed, watching him, long fingernails extending like spikes from her thin fingers. ''I'd love some of your . . . did I hear you right? Gulagi 'rocket fuel'?''

Nikita grimaced. ''I am pleased to serve. Perhaps after experiencing our liquor, Gulag will have found new way to extort grand old Earth. You send us money—and food and slave labor and fancy new electronics—and in return we do not send you Gulagi rocket fuel. Equitable, eh?''

She laughed again as Nikita dug out a dusty bottle with a hand-printed label. He poured one for her, and, looking horrified, one for himself.

''To health soon to be ruined by rotgut.''

She smiled and raised her glass, sipping thoughtfully at the bitter drink, working her tongue, a slight frown to her patrician brow. ''I must say, Mister Representative, it's not as bad as you might think. I think I prefer it to our retsina. And I've often heard that compared to turpentine.'' She drank again, lifting the glass, draining it.

Nikita swallowed hard. *She's crazy!*

''If you please, Mister Representative?'' She extended the glass.

Nikita poured. *She's not crazy. Woman is raving insane lunatic!* ''Please, Vice Consul, I am called Nikita, or Malakova, or hey, you, or many other things perhaps not suited to ears of gracious lady like yourself. But 'Mister Representative' implies social superiority most disturbing to good Gulagi. Conniving constituents of mine would cheerfully cut my throat if they heard such honorific applied to me.''

''And you may address me as Medea.'' She cocked her head, frowning. ''Tell me, do Gulagis really react so . . . hostilely? Do they really chafe at authority?''

Nikita lifted a slab of shoulder and eased his big body into a cramped antigrav. ''Is old wound. Consider. Soviet was hard on counterrevolutionaries of any brand.

But were hardest on subversives from within original Soviet Republics. Is one thing to punish Australian nationalists recently deprived of political autonomy. Even Rashinkov in blackest moment of deportations could understand such resistance. But when own people began to accuse him of betraying revolution? Was different. When Russian people began to react against decisions of Politburo, was considered slap in face to World liberators. My ancestors were sent to worst of Gulags. Many lived by cannibalism. In those days, people paid for air and water and heat. Couldn't pay? Broke a leg? Spaced. People had no medical. Nothing. Only had flimsy stations, work quota, and belief that humans should be free. Suffering reinforced ideal. Otherwise, what was purpose? Looking back, perhaps wisest thing would have been to have given Gulagis everything. Resistance to authority would have melted away—diluted by riches and silver spoon in mouth—instead of becoming fanatic with driving philosophy of life sucked up from mother's breast at birth."

She sipped the vodka again. "It's in the taste of your liquor, you know. I have a thesis." She lifted the glass to study the clear fluid in the light. "I think a people can be understood by their food and drink as well as their art and literature and dance."

"And what do you think of Gulagis?"

She squinted at the liquor. "I think they're a very strong people. Perhaps bitter and hard, unsoftened by the frills of life so common to others. I think they've been molded most uniquely—the product of a terrible culling."

Nikita waited.

Her long fingernails clicked against the glass like talons playing a staccato on the impenetrable. Her brow lined as she frowned at the glass, lost in thought. Lifting her chin, she studied him down the length of her long nose. "Have you given thought to the coming political crisis?"

Here it comes. "First truth learned in any Gulagi station is that political sand makes treacherous footing.

Makes for quick, light feet. Person who stands still for moment too long is suddenly buried . . . or falls when sand erodes from underfoot.''

Her smile reminded him of the rat-hunting snakes so common to his native Malakova Station. They had that same look as they crawled through the nether regions in the darkness.

"We're not so different, you know. Gulag Sector is made of rebels. Like the people of Earth, they've been harrowed and weeded of the opulent and the soft.'' She paused for a second. "I would like to think that peoples stemming from so common an ancestry and ideology could form a united front. Earth consists of so many factions, Kenyans, Free Alaskans, Burmese, Turkese, Latvians, Thais . . . you name it. We're as anarchical as you. We speak different languages and come from such diversity that we make Gulag look unified. I wonder, Nikita, are our goals so far apart?''

He shrugged. "Hard to say. Never been closer to Earth than a holo machine.''

She nodded, as if to herself. "Perhaps, Nikita, that should be remedied. Earth could do a lot for Gulag. You have considerable resource reserves which haven't been developed. And Earth, with her teeming billions, is always in need of food and raw materials. We're always looking for a place to send our restless. Could you use teachers? Engineers? Perhaps less restrictive markets for your foodstuffs? We have the know-how to make your agricultural systems larger, more productive.''

Nikita pulled at his tangle of beard. "Have never met investor who gave for free. A siphon for your restless I can understand, but to develop our resources will take metals—of which Gulag is in short supply so far. Technical innovations, too, generally come with overt or covert restrictions. Terran reactors must use Terran parts—a fact which will be immediately noted and exploited by my cynical constituents.''

Medea narrowed her eyes, thinking again. "Nikita, somewhere along the line, someone is going to have to break Gulag out of its shell. Your Sector is faced with a dilemma. Do you integrate with the rest of the Confederacy and continue to advance? Or do you sequester yourselves—become an island of provincial ignorance amidst a sea of exploding humanity? Assuming the latter, what do you do when, say, New Maine, arrives to mine your nebulae? Kick them out? Without a military? Hardly! And I know Gulag. You won't build a fleet. In the first place, I doubt you could assemble a majority to support it—Gulag being Gulag and always busy cutting its own throat. You can't get the financing—or the technical expertise, for that matter.

"So where will you take your people, Nikita? You speak for them. If anyone has the native ability to deal with Gulag, it's you. As in a primitive band society, you have the power to convince them. Through your charisma and intelligence, you can persuade them to a consensus. If anyone can steer them around the pitfalls of the future, it's you. You're their only chance for survival."

He waved it away. "Bah! You overestimate Nikita's influence on Gulagis. Part of continued success is that I don't do that very thing. If major group of unscrupulous and crafty constituents feels threatened, Nikita receives bottle of nice Gulagi rocket fuel like you drink just now. Only thing is, some thoughtful, disgruntled hand has added plutonium to smooth bite, eh?"

"Perhaps. I won't attempt to lecture you on your own people. But let's look to a larger forum. You're also a powerful and persuasive voice in the Confederacy at large—far out of proportion to the clout of your Sector. People in the Council listen to you, respect you."

"Many are respected. So?"

She drank the last of her vodka and placed the glass to one side. "So, you have many more options than simply returning to Malakova Station to grow potatoes in big vats. Given the right political and military realities, you could rise to heights you've never dreamed of. Terran interests could facilitate that advancement. Have you, perhaps, ever thought of the Presidency?"

Nikita laughed. "Who hasn't. But then, what does Terran support cost me? You see, Vice Consul, is also Gulagi truth that nothing—not even air we breathe—comes for free."

Her knowing eyes held his. "In the coming trouble, Nikita, I would like to have *your* backing. Things will be very, very different after we've completed this voyage to Star's Rest. To be honest, I don't know what we face. Several of the delegations aboard have already scrambled their fleets. The Terran Protective Force isn't going to be caught napping. In the meantime, I . . . *we* want an unallied power bloc on our side."

To give you credibility when power grab comes? Of course. "It seems that so long as I remain neutral, I shall never be lonely." He chuckled, reaching through his tangle of beard to scratch at his chin.

Medea stood, priceless gown swirling lightly about her, radiant in color. "Nikita, it won't be a joking matter." Her face seemed to thin, the tightness about her mouth unforgiving. "I won't press you for a decision right now, but, as you so aptly said, the political sands are changing. You'd make too good an asset to see you pick the wrong side."

He got to his feet, chin lowered as he walked her to the hatch. *And there's the threat. Is old 'If I can't have you, no one can' approach.* "Being good Gulagi, I will consider all options, Vice Consul. No one has ever accused Nikita of being fool—except, of course, people who attended wedding. But I was younger then."

She paused as the hatch slipped open. "No, you're no fool, Nikita. But be careful. All is not as it seems. Thank you for the . . . rocket fuel." And she was gone, dress billowing around her as she walked.

Nikita filled his lungs, exhaling loudly.

CHAPTER XXI

As dinner ended, diplomats began to trickle into their little knots of association. Lietov dominated the bar. Archon excused himself, drawing Hitavia and Wan Yang Dow along with him. Dee and Arness congregated around Stokowski and Medea. Joseph Young launched a vigorous assault against Paul and Mary Ben Geller.

"Quite a group," Sol remarked to Connie who sat beside him, sipping a glass of water.

"A microcosm of Confederate politics." She watched uneasily. "Not guaranteed to contribute to sleep. The more I see of them, the less sure I am that Father did the right thing."

"Want to tell me about that?"

"You never give up, do you?"

"If you were in my shoes, what would you do? The more I learn, the more likely I'll be able to plan ahead and save my ship."

"You and Jordan."

"Speaking of which, what will you do when you have to face Fan again? Somehow, I get the feeling that he doesn't learn very fast."

She exhaled explosively. "I'm not looking forward to that. Have you heard anything about him?"

"He spent the entire day in his quarters. I understand that at first he thought he'd die . . . then he wished he could. You could still press charges."

"And have him spaced?" She shook her head. "It wouldn't be worth it, Sol. Too many repercussions. Especially if they have a surprise waiting for us."

"Well, at least not everyone is unhappy." Sol jerked his head toward Texahi. Medea's husband had moved surreptitiously to the rear of the room, gaze locked with Elvina's. She nodded slightly, looking carefully around before disappearing into a hallway. Texahi immediately slipped away, walking into a different corridor.

"They'll meet up at her room," Sol prophesied. "That's where those corridors come together."

"We're not the only ones to catch it." Connie indicated Medea, now watching where Texahi had vanished, eyes narrowed to slits, oblivious to whatever Stokowski was telling her. "Myself, I'd rather walk through fire than slight Medea."

"But she doesn't seem to stop him."

"Just wait," Connie promised.

"On that cheery note, I'd better get back to my reports. See you later." Sol stood and winked. "Oh, and don't beat up too many of the virile types around here, gives the ship a bad name."

She smothered a smile. "You wish."

Sol made it to the middle of the lounge before Forney Andrews caught up with him. "Captain, I was doing a little reading last night and came across your name."

"Oh?" Sol stopped. Andrews, who stood only a meter fifty, was clad in his Patrol uniform with the starburst of the Confederacy on the shoulder boards. The rich black tones of his skin contrasted with the blazing white of the uniform. The planes of his broad face gave him a distinguished look. A halo of gray peppercorn hair lay close to his skull.

"You had an assignment in conjunction with the Patrol. I didn't find the details, just your name in an auxiliary list."

"Pathos. My first ship did patrol duty there until the Council could decide what to do with the planet."

"Nasty business, that. I sure pity those poor bastards who were enslaved there. We'll never know how many died on that wretched sand-blasted rock. If hell exists, Garth has a special place in it."

"I guess the sociologists are still making hay out of it. Besides the tragedy, I hear the megas are dying off. Their saliva might have made the perfect hallucinogenic for humans, but some xenobacterium vectored through the humans. Where the microorganism couldn't survive in the atmosphere, it could protected on human skin. With the aircars moving all over the planet's surface, and more than one mega being milked by a slave, it spread everywhere.''

Andrews shook his head. ''Curious that so formidable a beast could be so easily laid low.''

''I guess they're trying to save them. I hear it's fifty-fifty.''

Nikita Malakova appeared beside him. ''Ah, there you are, Captain. Has been a while since we have seen you at bourgeois dinner for parasitic politicians enjoying life in political body of suffering masses.''

Forney raised his eyes toward the ceiling panels and called, ''I'll see you later, Captain.''

Sol winced. ''You know, Nikita, I wonder about you sometimes.''

''Smart man. It's all a bluff front.'' Tayash Niter appeared in Malakova's wake.

Ignoring Tayash's satisfied smile, Nikita continued, ''Captain, would you have moment? I have questions I have been meaning to ask you.''

Sol considered. ''Depends upon the questions.''

''Is about Brotherhood of yours. I assume you know what this incredible junket is all about. What do—''

''You assume wrong. I'm no more aware of what's happening than anyone else. That seems to be the Speaker's explicit domain at this point—and from the comments I've heard, no one else is any wiser.''

Nikita's huge shoulder rose in a shrug. ''Perhaps. But Kraal knows—or at least strongly suspects. I think he knows. Speaker Archon went to Brotherhood first. Now we ride in Brotherhood ship to do sneaky business behind backs of honest people. Draw own conclusions as to who knows what.''

''You said something about questions?''

''Indeed. So far, I have been lobbied by several different factions, seeking political support. Where do you stand in all this?''

Sol lifted his hands. ''Mister Representative, I'm completely neutral. To—''

''Bah!'' Nikita shook his head. ''Look around you, Captain. Is your ship. The reputation of Brotherhood ves-

sels is well known. I have poked and prodded. Tried to
see what secrets you hide so well that—''

"I've been meaning to talk to you about that.'' Sol
pointed a finger. "Seriously, it took my people a bit of
time to recircuit that security hatch you tried to bypass.''

Nikita grinned. "Then maybe you just let me go look
at ship? To see what you—''

Sol chuckled. "Suppose I let everyone just wander
around? You've already borne the brunt of one security
breach, if you'll recall.''

"I know about the comm sabotage," Tayash added
softly. "Nikita and I, we tend to speculate on things together. You can talk about it.''

"Well, Nikita, you were the one suckered. Suppose it
had been a bomb? Want just anyone wandering around
through places like the reactor room?''

"Perhaps you have point. But consider my perspective.
We will planet at Star's Rest to uncover sacred secret.
Allegedly, political riffraff you carry is to deal with prob-
lem, eh? And if results are not to Brotherhood liking?
Where is your interest? Which way will you go?''

"To my knowledge, our role is to provide a neutral
ground—a forum free of the pressures and intrigues of
Arcturus for policy decisions to be made. I mean, you,
a Gulagi of all people, know the sort of pressure which
is brought to bear on Representatives in Council.''

Nikita laughed. "I like you, Captain. Have tongue as
sneaky as that of greasy politician yourself. Perhaps you
have missed calling, eh? But outside of flowery words,
look around you. I do not wish to be antagonistic—''

"That'll be the day," Tayash growled, meeting Nikita's warning scowl.

"—but again, consider things from my point of view.
No matter what you say, fact is Brotherhood is most impressive presence here. So, I believe you? You don't take
active part in negotiations over sacred secret? At the same
time, presence of Brotherhood looms around us—and,
Captain, I remind you, you have biggest of guns.''

"I don't have yours.''

"Nor will you until Nikita is dead! But you *do* have

ultimate power. Will you use it?'' Nikita rocked on his toes.

Sol laughed. "In all likelihood, no." Sol rubbed his chin. "I see your point and understand your perspective. But consider this. The Craft doesn't keep a seat on the Council. We're politically neutral."

"But everyone listens when Kraal speaks." Tayash added pointedly. "And, to be honest, not having a political agenda makes you suspect. That fact is inciting distrust and antagonism—which can't be furthering your goals. Neutral parties always end up disliked by everyone."

"And because you're disliked, doesn't make you wrong either," Sol countered. "Given our current circumstances, our position becomes extremely hard for most people to understand. We're not part of the power players like everyone else."

"Why not?" Nikita demanded. "You selfishly hoard the technology which could free billions from exploitation and—"

"Now wait." Sol raised a hand. "I'll answer your question first and your accusation second. To understand why the Brotherhood does what it does, you have to go back to our history. The institution itself is about three thousand years old. It didn't hit its stride until the eighteenth century when lodges were founded all over the world. By the twentieth century, the Craft was in decline—basically it had become a men's club and a reflection of social elitism. The true philosophy received lip service and little more. Had the situation remained the same, the Craft would have gone the way of Protestant Christianity. Dried up from lack of interest and forgotten. The rise of the World Soviet changed that. The order was outlawed. Consequently, the lodges went underground and fought for their very survival. They became centers for dissent. In the process, new life was breathed into the teachings of the Craft. To survive took commitment to the ideals of the institution."

"And I imagine that Rashinkov took a dim view of that," Tayash added dryly.

"He did. Members of the Craft were hunted down. Finally, the core of the resistance was captured and shipped off to Frontier. There, the principles flourished. Sweeping changes were made by a series of Grand Masters who had the vision and dedication to keep the philosophies alive. In essence, that's how we made it—by sticking to those philosophical truths, applying them to everyday life."

"And what are these truths?" Nikita crossed his arms.

"The betterment of the human being as an individual. The whole thing hinges on a system of secular morality. The study of the concepts of wisdom, strength, and beauty. It's a little involved, but the philosophical keys are based on truth, fortitude, temperance, prudence, and a sense of justice. Above and beyond all those is a constant quest to improve through knowledge. Education was the most crucial key to our survival."

"Doesn't sound so subversive," Tayash muttered.

"Depends," Sol smiled. "If you're a tyrant, do you really want minions who question your actions against the rubric of a philosophical and moral framework? Tyrants tend to take a dim view of proponents of human enlightenment."

"And this is creed of your Brotherhood?" Nikita tugged at his beard. "Then why do you not share marvelous technology? Would not all humanity be better served? Enlightened, as you say?"

Sol stared thoughtfully at the man. "I'm afraid we succeeded beyond our expectations in the pursuit of knowledge. Prior to the Confederate revolution, we stole the contents of all the libraries on Earth. Nor have we ceased to expand on that. Education, research, and development continue to absorb most of our resources. Our toron leases, for example, bring in almost a trillion credits a year."

Tayash blinked. "That's more than Lenin Sector's annual budget!"

"And we funnel it right back into such things as this ship," Sol agreed. "But to get to Nikita's point, what would happen if we simply dumped it on humanity? Believe me, it's been considered. Despite our technical advances, we've given some thought to applied anthropology, too. Cultures have to rise to levels of technological integration. For example, in the twentieth century, North America and the Soviet Union dumped billions into third world countries in a power play for hegemony. They found that you could give a Nigerian farmer a tractor—but when a part broke, the farmer had no idea how to fix it. He went back to plowing with his cow while the tractor rusted. Nor could he afford parts in the first place—assuming he could get the gasoline to run it. The infrastructure to support technology wasn't in the society. Now, let's bring it to the present. Take *Boaz*. If we handed a ship over to, say, Malakova Station, and a problem developed in the navcomm, who'd fix it?''

"We could learn." Nikita grunted.

"You could. And you would—in a Brotherhood university. And you'd have to buy replacement parts from us. Think your proud Gulagis would like that dependence on Frontier's shipyards?''

"But they could make their own parts," Tayash protested.

"If they had the right industry." Sol frowned. "I'll draw from the twentieth century again. Those same developing countries sent their brightest young students off to receive American, European, and Soviet educations. The idea was good—but a student of particle physics enjoys working with tools like accelerators to smash atoms. Devices like particle accelerators only existed in technologically advanced countries. The best and brightest stayed where they could continue their research, teaching at the institutions that had trained them. To return to the farmer, what good does it do an individual to know which fertilizers to use on which soil if he can't obtain more than locally derived manure?''

"You think we're so limited?" Nikita raised an eyebrow.

Sol nodded soberly. "In many ways, yes. How many subspace N-dimensional physicists do you have in Gulag, Nikita? No, don't glare that way. Just think about it for a while. Consider the ramifications of what I said. I give you my word, our people spend a great deal of time balancing the input of our technological innovations against Confederate ability to absorb it. It's a complicated systems theory.''

"But we only have your word," Nikita pointed out, looking unsure.

Sol chewed his lip. "I'll tell you what. When you get a chance, I'll release some case studies. You can crosscheck the data, see how we handled some things in the past, like headsets for comm communication. It takes a bootstrapping operation to keep from shocking society with advanced technology.''

"And I will see for myself," Nikita muttered.

"And you won't try and fool with any more of our security hatches?''

Nikita dropped his eyes, admitting, "I couldn't understand the lock mechanism anyway.''

* * *

"What time is it?" Nikita asked.

"Oh-four-thirty," Tayash said, stifling a yawn as he looked up from the monitor.

Nikita stared at the figures before him. "I hate to admit, but looks like Carrasco is right. Unless, of course, he skewed data.''

Tayash waved at the lines of text on his monitor. "This much? So fast? We've scanned a four hundred page report. And I remember some of this. It all clicks with what I know.''

Nikita rubbed his eyes, leaning forward on meaty arms. "Bah! It bothers me. Brotherhood might know what they're doing. Is not conducive to peaceful sleep though.''

"Because it's irksome to know that someone else might have all the answers?''

Nikita exhaled softly. "Exactly." He leaned back, crossing his arms. "And consider something else, Tayash. Brotherhood power must be awesome. Suppose this is turned against Confederacy?''

Tayash stared at the panels overhead. "Now there's something to think about. Feeling keeps rising against them. If someone—like Arpeggio—were to make a strike against them?" He shook his head. "How would they react?"

Nikita scratched under his beard. "I think long held views are about to undergo major revision. But if Brotherhood is so powerful, why do they remain in shadows? Considering this report, Kraal could impose will on all of space!"

"Only he's philosophically opposed."

"Indeed." Nikita supported his chin on a braced arm. "And if next Grand Master is not so dedicated to philosophy?"

Tayash stroked his goatee, lost in thought. "Now, that thought is enough to shiver atoms."

* * *

Kraal's face flickered off.

"So? What does it mean?" Bryana stared up at Art.

"It means that if anything happens to Carrasco, we put ourselves under Archon's command." Art's vacant expression turned her way. "I mean those are the orders of the Grand Master. It's like . . . well, we can't disobey *him!*"

Bryana filled her lungs, exhaling in a heavy sigh. "Wow! What's going on here? This is all too strange."

Art rubbed his face nervously. "Damned if I know. Okay, look, we know things are weird, right? The bogeys, the diplomats, Carrasco flipping out all the—"

"Art, he's not flipped out."

"So you say. Me, I just don't like him. Don't like the way he runs things."

She stared stonily. "Maybe you haven't given him a chance."

"And maybe I have."

"Crew efficiency has gone up. We've got the drills down to where we can fight back against three ships at thirty percent capability and survive. That's something."

"I wish I'd never . . . Oh, never mind." He turned in

his command chair. "But while we're on the subject, you seem to smile an awful lot whenever he's around."

"And that's a problem for you?"

"I . . . I don't want to be stabbed in the back is all. Why should I care what you do when Carrasco's around?" He stood, nodding curtly. "But Bryana, you'd better consider what's going to happen if this all falls apart and we're under Archon's orders."

At that he hurried from the bridge.

* * *

"Five, four, three, two, one, Mark!" Sol cried.

"It's your hell-hole!" Happy's voice called as Bryana's comm took control of the reactor.

"Sensors," Sol barked. "Any sign of those bogeys?"

Art concentrated on his instruments. "Negative, Captain."

"All stations, at ease," Sol decided, delighted to have the screens full of stars again. "Get me the Speaker on comm."

Several seconds passed before Archon responded, his voice muddled and his visual off. "Yes, Captain?"

"We've dropped out of the jump, Speaker. Do you have a course correction or do we head straight for Star's Rest?"

Sol waited, seeing Bryana and Arturian glancing at each other; it was that slightly mystified, partially suspicious look he'd become so familiar with.

"I'll be right up," the Speaker grunted.

Within minutes, Archon passed through the hatchway and stared owlishly at the screens. He nodded. "Nice work, Captain. I salute you and your officers. You dropped us in right on the nose."

"Where to?" Sol asked. "I got the strongest hunch from listening to people that Star's Rest might not be the destination after all."

"Set course for Star's Rest, Captain." Archon sounded tired.

Sol sighed. "Art, Bryana, consider yourselves relieved, I'll take the watch. I would appreciate it if you would just keep quiet about our destination. Also, if I could talk one of you into it, would you go see how Cal's blasters work? I've been worrying about them since he got to experimenting. Be sure to cross bolts to check the backlash effect.''

Art and Bryana got up, nodded to him and the Speaker and left the bridge. ''I'll make sure of them,'' Bryana called over her shoulder.

''Good officers those, Sol.''

''I know. I really hate to have to break them in on a trip like this.'' Sol shook his head. ''They're a little too green but since I got the message across that we're playing for keeps, they've been busting their butts to catch up. Star's Rest, huh?''

Archon nodded. ''Sorry to surprise you, but there are more than a couple of ways to hide something. For example, did you know that some of your cargo consists of ice mining equipment, insula-domes, and cold weather gear?'' Archon chuckled, ''We laid as many false trails as we could at Arcturus. Of course, if the President had kept his own council, none of this would have been necessary since no one would have known we were about anything.''

''President Palmiere?'' Sol half-asked. ''He let it slip?''

Archon's lips twitched. ''He was the only one on Arcturus who knew.''

It fit. Sol felt himself tense. ''Mining equipment? At last some things make sense, Speaker. I told you the constitutional conference was a little stretched. The pieces didn't fit. We're after an object!''

Archon lifted a finger, eyes serious. ''I did not lie when I said the fate of the Confederacy hung in the balance. We may well rewrite the constitution. That's our prerogative. As to who would ratify it, that depends on the men and women we carry with us.''

''And you have stretched the truth more than once in the past, Speaker. Will they believe you?''

''But you, Captain, are the only one who deeply distrusts me.'' Archon laughed. ''Oh, I don't blame you. In your place, I'd be doing exactly the same.'' The eyes got hard. ''What we are about must go beyond the feelings of men, Captain. I haven't had time to talk to you about it much, but I have seen your interest in my daughter."

Sol stiffened. "She's an attractive woman, Speaker. However, I can assure you that, so far, there's nothing between us."

Archon's glinting eyes softened for only an instant. His voice gentled in a gruff way. "You misread me, Solomon. I would welcome the sight of you and her together. I was attempting to say that if it were to become necessary, you must sacrifice her, or me, or perhaps even the population of a planet to see this thing through."

Sol cocked his head skeptically. *Sacrifice a planet? Archon had to be out of his mind! Nothing could be worth that!* A cold shiver of fear tingled his spine.

Archon seemed to lose himself in thought. "Right now, Captain, in your hands and mine lies the fate of our species. From the first proto-hominid who picked up a rock to keep off the beasts of the night, none have faced the power and terror we could let loose on humanity! Oh, I told you the Confederacy is at risk." Archon's expression was haunted. "It was an understatement, Solomon—all humanity is at stake!" He looked up, his eyes glazed. In a raspy voice, he added, "We play with the very hand of God!"

"Perhaps this *thing* is better left alone?"

"No!" Archon cried, reaching for Sol. "What I found, another will also eventually find! We *must* deal with it now!"

Sol answered with a smile and confidence he didn't feel. "We'll deal with it."

"Yes. We'll deal with it. We have to." Archon closed his eyes and leaned back in his command chair, breathing deeply as he fought to control himself. "I'm a simple man, Captain. Now, I must be a superman without allowing human folly to affect my decisions, my thoughts, or my emotions. Perhaps fate could have chosen better."

Sol waited for more, tense, the muscles of his shoulders bunched in knots.

"Soon, Captain, we will reach Star's Rest and my burden will also be yours." He closed his eyes. "Until then, however, I shall bear my burden like an Atlas." A wistful note filled his voice. "I was never born to be a titan."

"Few men are."

"Perhaps, however, it falls to our lot to try. God help us if we fail." He looked away. "Yes . . . God help us."

* * *

"You would tell *me* where I could move my station?" Nikita thundered, a big fist waving in Fan Jordan's face. They stood in the lounge, engaging in the usual after dinner conversation. Jordan had proved unusually surly, as if some deep anger goaded him.

"If the good of the realm depended on it, I would." Jordan crossed his arms and lifted his chin. "The individual must be subverted for the common good!"

"Captain!" Malakova called, flagging down Sol. "This Mainiac wants me to accept his king as lawful government of human race! Terrorist Communists and Democrats were vile blot within the lifeblood of mankind—but kings? They are malignant cancer in sacred host of humanity! He claims *God* has ordained it!"

"It won't work," Sol said evenly. Tayash Niter stood quietly to one side, leaning on his black cane, pulling thoughtfully at his snowy goatee.

"Why not?" Jordan demanded hotly, sheer hatred animating him as he turned to Sol. "Surely they will see that monarchy is the only logical system of government. The Sectors will fall in line after the riffraff in stations are controlled and put to real productive labor. It must happen in the end, as history is witness."

Nikita made a strangling sound at the mention of "riffraff," while Tayash responded tartly. "We are not riffraff! We are people just like you on New Maine. And we are quite happy and productive, thank you!"

Nikita shot Carrasco a crafty look. *How does Brotherhood captain react to this? Perhaps now, we'll see a layer peeled off Carrasco, get a look inside at true man?*

Carrasco studied the earl curiously. "How will you cage these lions, Fan?"

"Cut off their supplies until they behave." The look Jordan gave Carrasco might have melted steel. Fan's lips tightened, hazel eyes narrowing. "But then proper behavior seems lacking these days . . . along with respect."

Sol's features hardened, a sudden grimness in the set of his lips. "I couldn't agree more." Both men bristled.

"We make our own supplies and goods," Malakova challenged. *What is it? What has happened between these two? What does it mean for rest of us?*

"There is always force!" Jordan admitted, with a knowing smirk.

"How many ships do you have, Fan?" Sol asked. "By the latest projections over a thousand Patrol battle-class vessels will be necessary to police the border regions alone within the next one hundred years. Stations in Lenin Sector will drift to Moscow Sector; from there they can drift to Gulag, or to Ambrose, or to almost anywhere."

"And where are huddled masses waiting to get into your Mainiac utopia planet to experience all this efficiency?" Nikita couldn't help but ask. "Do I see long lines of oppressed killing themselves on gate of New Maine embassy? Hmm?"

"Given the bombast of cretins like you, they've been deluded into prejudice. Brainwashing—be it Confederate or Brotherhood—turns them against us. I ask you, Captain, would you," Fan lifted a lip, "a man of *obvious* taste, rather live on New Maine, or in that rat's nest at Gulag?"

Nikita interrupted. "I prefer my rats! They do not tell me where to live, how to live, or what I must do. You think New Maine would be so grand and powerful as to move us about like cattle on Range? Not even united Confederacy has such power and—by star-packed galactic center—neither do you!"

"Blue blood will save humanity in the end. It's breeding, you see. And by that, I don't mean the sort of rutting you Gulagis—"

"Fan," Carrasco admonished. "There's no call for that kind of—"

"At expense of *red* blood!" Malakova thundered, feeling the heat rise.

"Monarchies do not leave weapons in the hands of the unwashed masses. Kings sit down and talk things out before they go to war."

"As in 1914?" Sol asked. "How well did kings talk then? I remember Ivan the Terrible, King John, Caligula, the list goes on. Nice chaps, those kings! Great ones for sitting down and talking out problems."

Jordan's face went red. "You know, Captain, I don't particularly like you. And it's clear that your understanding of history has been distorted by the Brotherhood. Along with any other social skills you might once have had."

Sol stiffened. "Jordan, you don't have to like me, and no matter what you think, I'll stick with my version of history."

"I think I keep my unwashed masses armed, too, Fan." Malakova bent down to look into the smaller man's eyes. "For I fear you and kind of life you would make me live—backed by your weapons."

"Imbecilic bastards!" Jordan exploded, drawing stares from all over the room. Only Mark Lietov seemed amused as Jordan stalked off.

Carrasco glanced up, a decidedly mellow expression on his face. "Well, I guess he told us."

Nikita chuckled, feeling the rush of anger draining. "Perhaps. Bastard? How did he know proclivities of Nikita's venerated mother, eh? Perhaps he did rutting of his own?"

Having seen Jordan's raging departure, Constance strolled over, eliciting a sigh from Nikita. *Ah, if only she weren't sort of woman she was. What joy could be mine.* "Too much honesty in you," he mumbled under his breath.

"What was that?" Carrasco asked.

"Nothing."

"I see you got Jordan to make his greatest contribution of the day—leaving the room."

Sol grunted noncommittally.

"Ah, Constance, are you ready to run off with me yet?

I have nice empty station which you would heat with gracious warmth and illuminate with shining brilliance."

"What about your three wives?" Sol asked blandly.

Malakova flinched, threw Connie a crafty look, and shrugged. "I am big man," he said simply. "Is enough of me to go around."

"Then perhaps you'd better watch your diet," Connie riposted. "You ate enough crab tonight to feed six of your starving constituents. I'd be happy to send a message to your wives—let them know how well you're doing."

Nikita grimaced.

Tayash Niter turned back from watching Jordan disappear into the companionway. "Earl Fan Jordan is a dinosaur. And whatever happened, he means you no good, Captain."

Sol sighed. "There goes the vote for most popular man aboard. You're right, he's a dinosaur. No one will ever control humanity by brute force again. He's been blinded by his own system. He's never hungered, fought, faced danger or death. Worse, he's never even really experienced his own planet and the misery there."

With a slight pang, Nikita realized Constance had placed herself beside Carrasco. *Perhaps she does not know it yet, but she likes him. Ah, well, was too good for likes of me anyway. Too much class.*

"Space is an open system," Niter agreed. "Government was born to control the redistribution of resources. The one we've got doesn't work in an open resource base as it is." He lifted his hands. "Like Malakova said, we make our own goods. What supplies would Fan cut off?"

Half to himself, Nikita grunted, "We should burn New Maine as a plague spot!"

"I think my organization would disapprove, Nikita," Sol said.

"Why? What possible good are his kings in our present circumstances?"

"Balance," Sol replied simply. "The other end of the spectrum to you and your—how did he say it?" Sol grinned broadly. "Rat's nest?"

"From the look of Nikita's beard, there is more than

one kind of rat's nest in Gulag,'' Connie decided. Nikita leaned down and nuzzled her with his soft beard.

"Don't tell your papa," he warned.

"It's your wives I might tell."

He groaned, turning back to Carrasco. "This Brotherhood of yours is so perfect?"

Sol shook his head. "It hasn't always been. For the moment, we have a rather spectacular man as Galactic Grand Master. The order has changed through time. I think I told you most of our history. You take a look at those reports?"

"We did," Tayash sighed. "Spent most of the night going through one. It's a difficult admission, but I think your Brotherhood did the right thing."

"Is permutations that are scary." Nikita shifted on his heel, staring at the companionway Jordan had disappeared into. "What if man like earl becomes Grand Master? Hmm?"

Sol pursed his lips. "The screening process is very difficult. Not only does every member of the Craft vote, so do the computers. The program is pretty specific and psych check is also run. You see, we learned a lesson from the twentieth century. We can't afford mediocrity in the Craft. And given some of our advances, the consequences of a tyrant assuming control would be unthinkable."

Nikita laced fingers in his beard. "You allow such invasion of privacy? What of rights of man?"

Sol stared soberly into his eyes. "You have an idea of the power of the Craft. As our technology goes beyond that of the rest of the Confederacy, so does our political system. It goes back to Frontier in the early days. Quite simply, we couldn't afford a mistake in leadership. Affable fools can be elected in any democratic system. Our selection is a more balanced process. Most would find it repugnant, sterile, and scientific. But I'll share an anecdote with you. Kraal didn't want to be Grand Master. His occupation, before he went into politics, was that of a florist. That's right, he grew and arranged flowers for a living. His political career started as Master of a small neighborhood lodge on Moriah. Becoming Galactic

Grand Master was the farthest thing from his mind. The problem was, he seemed to be the most qualified for the job.''

Nikita squinted his skepticism. ''And if your Brotherhood voted against him?''

''Even if the psych studies and projections indicated he was the best choice for the position, he wouldn't get it.'' Sol clasped his hands behind his back. ''Leadership combines a variety of traits—including public trust. At the same time, we have the system pretty well worked out. I doubt a man the people didn't approve of could make it through the selection process.''

''Sounds . . .'' Tayash shook his head. ''I don't know, too impersonal.''

Sol smiled. ''It works for us.''

''Yet you do not keep a seat in Confederate Council?'' Nikita wondered. ''Even Catholics keep a seat.''

''And that neutrality keeps us from being embroiled in political battles that might split the Craft. Have you ever seen the Brotherhood support any political faction?''

''But you do have more than enough political influence,'' Tayash reminded.

Sol nodded. ''True, but then you'll notice that in the Council, we never go beyond offering an independent opinion and providing documentation for our case. Incidentally, that process is watched very carefully, each action scrutinized by a committee appointed to ensure that no abuses occur. I believe you can all recall the removal of more than one adviser to the Council?''

''But supposing con man outsmarted system, became Master despite all, what then?''

''We have an organization called the Jurisprudence Committee. The Grand Master would be invited to testify on his own behalf and the Committee would study the evidence, publish their findings, and if adverse, a vote of confidence would be taken. If the Master failed, he'd be removed from office.''

''And if Master refused? Took reins of power in own hands?''

Sol didn't even flinch. ''We'd assassinate him.''

"You'd . . ." Tayash blinked, mouth open.

Sol smiled wistfully. "Gentlemen, among the greatest of crimes to inflict on the human condition, tyranny is intolerable. It goes against every tenet of our beliefs."

"But what if the people *want* a tyranny?" Connie asked. "It's happened before."

Sol turned to her. "Then they could leave the organization and go live on New Maine. You see, a person has to ask to become a member of the Craft. No one forces anyone to remain. That, too, would be antithetical to our philosophy."

Nikita struggled to make sense of it. "I am suspicious of anyone with all answers pat. What is wrong with Craft? All are descended of angels?"

Sol laughed. "Hardly. You see, we're all human beings. To live by the tenets of the institution is a constant challenge. Truly, the only thing that keeps the Craft safe are our computers. Without that technology, we'd go the way of any other human society and make all the same mistakes."

"But you have to surrender your autonomy to a computer," Tayash reminded. "Somehow, that just . . ." He shook his head, expression sour.

"That's right," Sol agreed. "That's why we don't make a big thing of it. The Craft has enough problems as it is. You can imagine the heyday the media would have with that knowledge. And, as I said, our system isn't for everyone."

Nikita cleared his throat. "You are aware many disapprove of Brotherhood. Sentiment of people is turning against you. What you do if antagonism becomes too great? What if Sirius wins, wants to outlaw Brotherhood? What if Jordan takes his ships to convert you to his 'utopia'?"

Sol didn't even hesitate. "Quite simply, Mister Representative, we'll pack up. Crate every single nut and bolt—and leave."

* * *

The figure slipped through the hatchway, stalking soundlessly into the darkened sleeping room. A practiced hand eased the personal kit from beside the rumpled bedding. A slight odor of exertion lingered in the air, musky, the scent of copulation.

Gloved fingers skillfully removed the black tubes, uncoiling them from the hasty wrap they'd been twined into. Without wasted movement, the intruder energized the small power pack at the base of the tubes, before taking a small hexagonal transmitter from a belt pouch. With a hand-held monitor, he studied the black tubes' reaction to the walnut-sized hex.

Grunting under his breath, he rapidly replaced the hex, wrapping the tubes and snugging them into the kit before placing the bag just so next to the bedding.

Making no more noise than a breeze over rock, he vanished through the hatchway.

CHAPTER XXII

Sol was up reading Euripides and listening to his favorite symphony, the Beethoven *Ninth* when *Boaz* announced, "Captain! Ambassador Texahi is in the hospital. I am currently running analysis. He's hooked into the system and I am checking the cardial plexes."

Sol was on his feet, slapping the hatch, shooting down the companionways as he ran for the hospital. He slid into the room to see Bryana already there. Medea sat on a med unit, expression neutral, while Ensign Wheeler hovered over the unit keeping an eye on the readouts.

Boaz spit up a section of printout and Wheeler deftly caught it. His practiced eyes scanned the contents. "Heart attack," he said, refusing to lift his eyes from the paper. "A week in hospital and he should be fit and healthy."

"Heart attack?" Medea asked. "Indeed. Very interesting."

"Vice Consul, could I see you outside for a minute?" She stood and followed him out into the corridor. "What happened?"

Medea studied him, a tight irony on her face. "Would you really like to know, Captain?" She hesitated for a second. "Very well, my husband returned to our cabin after having delighted himself in the well-used joys of Mrs. Young's body. He began a confession and collapsed in the middle of it. If you don't see a great deal of remorse or concern on my part, I'm sure you can understand why."

Sol pinched his brows. "If you don't mind my asking, your husband's behavior didn't just—"

"No." She leaned her head back. "It didn't." She looked up at Sol. "I thought the chance to get away would . . . No, I think you're too smart for that line. All right, he was a show piece. I brought him along for several reasons. In the first place, his presence allayed suspicions about Earth's true interests in the coming negotiations. Bringing Texahi along made it look like a junket—smoke-screen, if you will. Second, having a husband along can provide a certain amount of insulation. It provides a shield against male attentions. Last, but not least, I come from a very provincial part of Earth. The old culture there still puts women in a secondary position. A woman without a man is vulnerable, and most definitely not to be taken seriously."

"Why a man like him?"

Her expression didn't ease. "I'm not a soft willowy female. Most men are intimidated by a woman wielding the power and resources I have at my disposal. Most would eventually want to exploit it, or derive some advantage from my position. Texahi was oblivious to those concerns." She gave him an icy smile. "And, to be honest, he's a damn fine lover. That's another characteristic a woman in my position doesn't stumble across every day. A man who makes advances is after something nine times out of ten. He's seeking to compromise your position, earn some inside information or influence. Texahi didn't have that kind of sophistication.''

Sol considered.

''No, it wasn't new behavior, Captain. On Earth, or in my suite on Arcturus, I could bring him women to keep him happy. I thought on this trip, I'd be close enough, threatening enough. I hadn't counted on that slut being here. I thought the company would be more . . . discreet.''

Sol nodded. ''I believe I can understand.''

She smiled humorlessly, adding in a voice like steel, ''I hope you do. I would take a very dim view of that information becoming common knowledge. I'm telling you because I assume you have some integrity to have risen to the position of a Brotherhood captaincy—and this is your ship, and I'm curious about *two* heart attacks in a row.''

Sol nodded, a crawling feeling in his gut. ''Thank you for your confidence and your candid response. And I assure you, I'll be looking very seriously at heart attack morbidity.''

''I would hope for no less.''

Sol braced himself. ''It is *my* ship.'' Unwavering eyes met his.

Inside the hospital, Sol beckoned. ''First Officer, if I could see you for a moment?''

Bryana nodded. Together they walked out.

''I'd appreciate it if you'd keep this quiet. Help play down the speculation I'm sure you're going to hear.''

Her serious brown eyes met his. ''Captain, this whole trip is more than a little irregular.''

''I know. And believe me, until we learn the stakes, we all have to be careful. Listen, I'll level with you. I'm pretty much in the dark about the whole thing. As soon as I have something concrete, I'll sit down with you and Art and we'll hash it out. Will you trust me for that?''

She smiled, a warmth rising in her eyes. ''Sure, Captain. I . . . well, I want you to know I've had second thoughts. Maybe I was a little out of line when this started.''

Sol grinned at her. "I wasn't exactly in my finest form either. For the moment, keep your ear to the ground and let me know what you hear. And Bryana, thank you." He didn't see the look she gave him as he headed up to his cabin. "Report, *Boaz*."

"Pharmacopa, Captain."

Sol sank to the bunk, feeling tired and frustrated. "And the video record?"

"I have been analyzing, Captain. Nothing can be detected which would concretely demonstrate attempted murder. I'm running it now for your benefit."

"He was with Elvina Young."

"And he stopped in the lounge, sharing drinks with several people. His contacts include Mikhi Hitavia, Arness, Constance, Lietov, and Nikita. He could have ingested the agent at any time."

Sol nodded, eyes on the tape. "Hitavia again? And he had that row with Ngoro. Better inform Speaker Archon, *Boaz*."

He looked up when *Boaz* made the connection. "Another murder attempt. This time it was Texahi. Medea saved his life by getting him to the hospital in time. Ship's medical got the antidote into him. He's going to be fine as soon as those nerve cells can be regenerated."

"Blast! Solomon, I would have thought it finished." Archon seemed to deflate.

"I guess not, Speaker. Should I order them quarantined? It might save lives if we could claim a strange virus was loose." Sol rubbed his chin thoughtfully.

Archon shook his head. "No, Captain. Let's bull it through. It's my responsibility." He shook his head. "This is like a war . . . only it isn't. Dear God, the casualties are my problem. No matter what, I can't have them distrustful when we reach Star's Rest."

"In the meantime, I'm having Engineering change the drink dispensers, Speaker." Sol leaned back. "The human bartenders are a nice touch, but they'll simply have to get used to sealed drinks in free-fall glasses."

"Good thinking, Captain. Let's see." Archon's face

became a map of concentration. "Maybe I can think up a good reason why."

* * *

The night was sleepless, filled with images of gutted hull, the rush of air in decompression. Maybry Andaki's tortured face stared at him through a grimace of anguish while Peg sobbed painfully in the background. Bleary-eyed, Sol was struggling into his uniform, wondering how to untangle the day when *Boaz* blared: *"Captain, Fan Jordan is assaulting Constance in the gym."*

He was running again.

The gym hatch slipped open to anticipate him. Jordan had Connie's nude body backed into a corner, arms pinned behind her. She struggled awkwardly—the reason apparent when Sol saw the stun weapon in Fan's other hand.

"Yes, you're mine now, Constance, and you *will* enjoy it!" He laughed as he bent to kiss her neck.

"Jordan!" Sol's voice boomed in the almost empty room.

Fan shot a look behind him, eyes oddly lit. "Leave us be, Captain. We want privacy."

"Turn her loose! This is *my* ship! You read the articles!"

"And you are interfering in my pleasure! What are you, an Arcturian pimp? I said leave us alone!"

Sol's heart jumped as Jordan lifted the stun device to the firm flesh between Constance's breasts. It could shock the heart badly enough to kill her.

"Let her loose, Fan. Keep in mind, you're on a ship! Assaulting a woman is punishable by death out here! Think, man! Consider. You're cutting your own throat! *She's Archon's daughter, for God's sake!*"

"She's a strumpet, Carrasco! What's it to you? You should have seen her, spinning in the air—and not a stitch of clothing on her!"

"Damn it, man, that's *normal* on a ship! It has been since the early days! You can't judge space-board behavior based on New Maine's moralities! Let her go, Fan. Maybe we can cover—''

''As Earl of Baspa, I order you to leave. *Now!*''

Connie groaned, trying to wiggle away from the confining grip.

''Jordan! Let her—''

''I've got diplomatic immunity!''

''So does she!''

''Get out, Captain. I'll kill her, I swear! *Get out!*''

Sol turned the gravity down with a sudden twist of the controls and Jordan yipped as he floated off the floor.

The crackling snap echoed in the room as the stun weapon discharged. Connie jerked rigid, then went limp. Carrasco flipped off the wall, aimed himself at Jordan, and planted all of his momentum in a kick to Jordan's tumbling body. An audible crack preceded an anguished shriek as Sol's foot smashed Jordan's rib cage.

''*I'll have your head!* You—'' Jordan screamed, bent double, floundering this way and that as he flopped in the air.

Sol caught himself, somersaulted, and came up behind, catching an arm, driving Jordan face first into the wall. Fan wailed in eerie agony as Sol wrenched his body sideways. Jordan's resistance fled as he whimpered in pain, blood trickling from his broken nose.

''*Boaz,* get a med unit here on the double.'' Sol pushed off, towing Jordan to the grav control and returned everything to normal. He left Jordan curled over his purpled chest, rushing to Connie.

Jordan stood with a tortured gasp, staggering, an arm clutched to his side. He stooped, grabbing up the weapon. The stun unit extended on a quavering arm. ''I'm going to—to kill you . . . like I killed her!''

Sol dropped as the unit activated. He kicked out, came upright behind Jordan, and wrenched the arm backward. Fan wailed his pain.

''Drop it!''

''*No!* Your head will be *mine!* You've assaulted the king's nephew. I'm the Earl of . . .'' Jordan's voice gargled into an unhealthy shriek as Sol broke his arm; the stun weapon fell from nerveless fingers.

Happy barreled into the room on the heels of Ensign Wheeler's med unit.

"He's under arrest," Sol hooked a thumb at Jordan where he sobbed against the wall, nursing his awkwardly bent arm. "Charges are assault with intent to rape." He turned to Wheeler. "How is she?"

"Got her heart started again, Cap." Wheeler grinned, looking up from the med unit settled over Constance. "She's going to be fine. I want her in med for a day or two though."

Sol nodded, his own heart beating again. He watched Happy pick Jordan up and march him off. Jordan unleashed a howling fit, screaming threats made shrill with rage and pain. Sol gritted his teeth at the sound of it.

"First Officer Bryana," Sol muttered into comm.

He saw her tousled hair, as she bobbed in the pickup, no doubt getting dressed. "Here, Captain! Be on the bridge in a minute!"

"Whoa!" Sol told her. "Not everything happens on the bridge. Listen, I need you to put together an investigative committee. I suggest you compose it of George Stokovski, Nikita Malakova, Dee Arness, and yourself."

She nodded, blinking the sleep out of her eyes. "What happened?"

"Fan Jordan just attacked Constance in the gym—his intent was rape."

"Blessed stars. *Rape?*"

"I think you understand. All records are hereby turned over to you and George Stokovski. Um, there won't be video on this, simply the voice transcripts. I want to keep a couple of our aces discreetly in the hole. However, should you yourself have any questions, *Boaz* will access them for you."

She nodded, a stunned look on her face. "Yes, sir." She hesitated, biting her lip. "Conviction carries a death penalty, you know."

Sol felt his gut tighten. "I'm well aware of that."

* * *

Humans came: aggressive, eager. Their vigor, optimism, and passion stirred the threads of long dormant memories. The Hynan had been just as reckless, boldly seeking her. Like the humans, they had no idea what they'd loose upon themselves.

And the Hynan had been so superior to humans in every way.

The Hynan neatly deposed the Tiss. Competitors to the core, they simply brushed their mentors aside, ignoring them, expanding on their own, adapting Tiss science to their needs.

Immediately, Hynan spaced for her, reading the Tiss accounts with curiosity. The first Hynan who entered called herself Hissthok. Hers was the first manipulator to work the spring. She became the Master. Infused with the narcotic of ultimate power, Hissthok enshrined herself as a god, organizing her empire, dictating the lives of those subservient to her.

Hatred raged and pooled, the damnation of the spring eternal. Only the Hynan would fall. No matter how well organized their superior brains, no matter how strong their physical bodies, they had found her—and in the end, they would pay.

She looked up from her resting place, taking a break from the memories. The species called human had come for her. Primitive vessels appeared with ever greater frequency. Some decelerated for the planet, others shed delta V and waited, as if to see what would happen. Another fleet dropped in, carefully shedding mass in a feeble attempt to hide themselves. One by one, she scanned their occupants, testing minds.

There, that one. Cold, ambitious, *he would be perfect.* With her sensors, she scanned the pitiful data banks of the vessel. The mind she sought called itself Sabot Sellers.

*   *   *

Bryana shook her head and blinked her eyes. "I know we can't expect everything to be the same as insystem. We took a demotion to come to *Boaz*." She laughed sourly and looked around Art's quarters.

"We wanted experience," he pointed out. "*Boaz* seemed like the way to go."

"Damn it! A man's life is at stake!" Bryana said, curling up on the corner of his bunk. "I reviewed the records, Art—all the records! The man is guilty! He entered the gym, stunned Constance, and was pulling his britches down as he walked up to her. Stokovski and Dee are still looking at the material, talking to Constance, Carrasco, and Jordan, but I know what they'll decide. The penalty is spacing." She shook her head. "I have to sign an order that will send Jordan to his death."

Art got up and walked over. He settled himself next to her and pulled her close. "Remember when we knew it all? By the golden nebula, we were the best pilots between Frontier and Arcturus. Remember the time we outran the pirate? We thought we were pretty crafty. We were sure the hotshots!"

She settled into the crook of his arm. "Top of the list for deep space," she said with a chuckle. "You and I, Art. The new wonder kids at Academy. Now I can't help but wonder. I thought Carrasco was a wreck, but he makes a lot of sense. Yet we've got nonregulation blasters, all kinds of funny course changes. Two heart attacks? Come on! There's suspicion among the passengers. No matter what's decided about Jordan, it will be an interstellar incident. Now we hear Galactic Master Kraal has given Archon command of the ship? What's at Star's Rest?"

"Carrasco hasn't even mentioned those rules infractions. It's like the sword of Damocles . . . and it's driving me more nuts than all the intrigue." Art shook his head and decided to change the subject. "On the positive side, have you seen these muscles?" He bulged biceps. "Now, just let me loose someplace like dockside. I can clean out a whole bar! The things Fujiki teaches go beyond belief.''

"Oh, yeah. I can compute targeting for five bogeys at once and record ninety-five percent hits.'' She laughed dryly, losing the thought. "That still doesn't prepare me for sentencing a man to death.''

Art realized he couldn't change her mood. "Yeah, well, deep space missions aren't supposed to be like this. What if Carrasco goes to pieces again? More than once I've heard him declare he's going to retire after this jump.''

"He's lost three ships,'' Bryana agreed, heaving a depressed sigh. "His First Officers were all killed, so why should this trip be any different? I don't like it, Art. I'm getting a premonition about Star's Rest. There's trouble there—more than meets the eye. Damn, I'm—''

Boaz crackled her speaker. "First Officers to the bridge! Condition Yellow!''

"Another drill!'' Art heard himself moan. Bryana bounced to her feet, shrugging. "Let's show the old boy up!''

Carrasco bent over the sensors as Art ducked into his chair and took a quick check to determine the Alert status—still yellow.

"Speaker,'' Carrasco said into comm, "the bogey is closing from behind, not dumping V but hanging right under C. Mass distortion gave them away.''

"Too much traffic out here,'' Archon growled ominously from where he stared down from the monitor.

Art studied the spectrum being laid out by the approaching ship. "Captain, that's one of the bogeys from the other side.''

"Suggestions, people?'' Sol asked pensively.

Bryana caught it first. "I'd say when they dropped out, one ship decelerated with everything it had. The other, this one, kept velocity. They knew we had to be ahead or behind unless we dropped out in the middle. They made the assumption that Star's Rest was still our destination. Since they dropped out behind us, there's still a second ship back there somewhere.''

Carrasco's eyes lit with respect. "Very good, Bryana."

Art shot a look of irritation at her and added. "It would seem, Captain, that we have another hour and a half before discovery. Their vector is tangential to ours. What'd happen if we tried to hide our mass with gravity distortion and shut down the braking mass?"

Sol nodded and gave Art a sly smile. "Always better to stay out of trouble's way. Keep that as an axiom and you'll live longer. I concur with your recommendation, Art." He grinned and looked at the comm. "All hands, Combat Alert! Prepare for gravity fluctuations!"

Art watched the situation board switch from red to yellow to green in an incredible hurry. He felt a slight flush of pride at the rapid response. Galley—after their first fumbling attempt—had never been worse than fourth or fifth to clear. No matter what Art thought of Carrasco, he sure knew how to straighten out a ship.

Bryana slipped into her suit and covered his comm while Art crawled into his and fastened himself to the command chair. He turned his attention to the passenger quarters seeing the all-clear. Archon was explaining the situation through the net as Art triggered the liquid mixture which would fill the diplomats' high g closets.

Highly oxygenated, the liquid remained under pressure. Following Boyle's law, enough oxygen could be pumped in to keep a human alive while at the same time reducing the effects of high g. Art barely heard some of the station people complaining, panicking and realizing they weren't drowning as their noses went under.

"Estimated time to detection?" Sol asked.

"About an hour," Art decided, calculating sensor range against power used to maintain V. "We can change that by feathering the G and delta V, Captain."

"*Boaz,*" Carrasco called. "Hide our signal. When they come within visual range, employ camouflage."

The first waves of distorted gravity made Art's stomach heave. With no uncertain feelings, he resented the heavy meal he'd eaten less than an hour earlier. "Uh, Captain?"

"Yes, Art."

"What do we give up for this?" He clenched his jaws and fought the rebellious weight in his stomach.

"Mostly time." Carrasco's voice seemed unconcerned. "With the reaction mass spread in more directions, their screen picks up the anomaly as a field instead of a pinpoint of mass and a streak of directional light. If they come closer, we disperse more mass over a wider area. However, from their vector and the fact they're traveling so close to C, we know they can't change course outside of a couple of degrees. They can come no closer than twenty thousand kilometers at their present speed and vector. Since this part of space is unmapped, they don't know how anomalous we are. Further, when they get the best readings, we'll be creating behavior no ship they've ever monitored could produce."

"Pirate tricks?" Art asked, wishing his stomach wasn't full of gyrating lead.

Carrasco smiled wryly. "Among others. Didn't they teach you that in Academy?"

Art shot a hesitant look at Carrasco. "Not really, they just explained that aberrant behavior occurred among raiders. They mentioned the use of gravity distortion, ship camouflage through paint, and so forth and assured us that our reflective generation camouflage and sensors outmatched it."

Sol's mouth tightened. "It would seem we're not perfect when it comes to getting information back to Academy. I have some tapes, I think both you and Bryana should take a look. The only thing constant about tactics, pirates, and technology is innovation."

And the wait began. Minute after long minute dragged by. Art kept his coffee cup full. The gravity flux grew worse with time. His suit began to turn sweaty, his skin itchy. The creeping dot on screen drew him like a moth to fire.

"Reminds me of one of those old holo-vids of the American and Russian submarines." Bryana rested her chin on her hand. "Constant waiting, playing a game of deception."

"Yeah," Art agreed, watching the dot that represented the bogey. Gravity lurched again and his stomach, having digested the long past meal, hardly quivered. "If it weren't for the tension."

"Right," Bryana sounded snide. "Get a load of Carrasco!"

Art shot a glance over his shoulder to see Solomon Carrasco, head back, mouth slightly ajar, as his chest rose and fell in the easy breathing of sleep.

"I know he doesn't have nerves of iron," Art grunted. "He almost jiggled into pieces getting the ship out of dock!"

Time dragged as the white dot of the bogey searched for them. *Boaz* rippled the gravity, almost making Art ill despite the way he'd gotten used to it. Then the beams ceased to probe in their direction and the bogey crawled away, millimeter by millimeter across the huge screen.

"Want to wake his nibs?" Art asked, nodding in Carrasco's way. "The danger seems to be receding." He couldn't keep the sarcasm out of his voice.

"That won't be necessary," Carrasco's well modulated voice returned to Art's mortification. His innards knotted as tightly as they had when the gravity was at greatest intensity.

Art ground his teeth, "Excuse me, sir. My apology."

Carrasco yawned and nodded. "Excused, First Officer." Art could feel Carrasco's eyes at him. "I don't condone that tone of disrespect on my bridge, Art. I'm willing to let it pass without taking you out in the hall to box your ears strictly for the reason that anyone does odd things his first time under stress."

Art voiced the scorn he felt. "But going to sleep—sir?" He bit his lip, knowing how it sounded. Bryana gave him a horrified look and closed her eyes.

Carrasco stood up, holding onto the command chair. "I want to see you in the gym—now."

Art looked into those burning brown eyes and swallowed. "What about the condition yellow?"

"I said *now*, First Officer! Bryana is fully capable of handling a departing bogey. They're out of range and couldn't decelerate even if they spotted us. *Now!* First Officer!"

Art had never made a longer trip. Gravity pulled him this way and that as he staggered after Carrasco. The gym seemed big and open as they entered, the muscular augmentation of the suits the only reason they could keep their feet.

"All right." Carrasco turned, standing, swaying like a man buffeted by underwater currents. "What is it, Art? From the moment I stepped aboard, you and Bryana have been on my back. I'm tired of it and it's over one way or another right here!"

"Nothing, sir!" Art spouted, in the best academy form.

"Nothing, sir!" Carrasco mimicked. "Listen, you wet-eared little dock rat, we're going to be facing more problems out here than you and I together can guess! I can't have a First Officer I can't depend on. Get it out, Art! I told you that once before, but I guess you didn't take me seriously. What's wrong with you?"

"Nothing!" Art bellowed, anger rising. "How do you expect us to space with a man who's almost a glibbering idiot just getting out of dock?"

"Yeah, I was upset!" Carrasco hollered back. "I'd just watched a Brotherhood agent who'd given me those secret orders get blown into bloody mush! What am I supposed to do? Ignore it? On the other hand, I'm tired of putting up with you and your sniveling self-centered holier-than-thou attitude. You haven't been past eighty lights from Arcturus, kid. When you're a deep space vet, I'll take your crap because you'll have earned the right to dish it out."

Art swallowed, muscles tensing. "Regulations state—"

"Hang the bloody regulations! We're talking survival out here, *not* regulations!" Carrasco thundered back. "If you can't stand on your own two feet, sit down and get out of the way! Now, what's your pleasure, First Officer? Do you straighten up? *Or do I kick you out?"*

Art heard his teeth grind. "If you weren't an officer, I'd break you in two!"

"That's fine!" Carrasco gestured. "Do it! That's why we're in the gym! I don't know that you have the guts or ambition to try!"

"Regulations—"

"Don't mean a fucking thing! I want you to learn to think and to give a damn! Why do you think I ignored Gaitano's boy bouncing you around?" Sol's face reddened. "Get it out of your system, you despicable little worm! Come on, wimp—you tissue cadets know it all! Show me some guts, *little boy!"*

The tone set him off. Art threw his best kick and Carrasco caught it, lifted, and threw him on his back. Like two drunken sailors, they staggered back and forth while Art tried to destroy his captain. Reveling in the power the suit gave him, Art threw himself at Carrasco time and time again only to be countered, batted down, thrown into the wall, catapulted down the floor and beaten into a mess of pain.

He tried. Raging in desperation, he grappled, striking out in a killing blow, feeling it blocked. He shuddered under the impact of Carrasco's hard fist. Reeling, he dropped to his knees. The room wavered in a shimmering haze, the floor rising to smack the side of his face, lights flashing behind his eyes.

Grating agony seared every bone and joint as he tried to suck air into his paralyzed lungs. He caught a small breath, then another and another, air tearing through his raw throat in a rasping wheeze.

Blinking, he glared at Carrasco, trying to get his breath.

"Get up," Carrasco ordered. *"I said, GET UP!* That's an order!"

Weak-kneed, Art pushed up, wavering on all fours. His stomach pumped violently, vomit gushing. Gravity fluctuated and he fell face forward, too tired to get his arms in front of him—too woozy to react to Carrasco's bellowing in his ear.

Carrasco bent down and growled. "Well? Get up! Or

don't you have the guts? Is that all you've got? Do you
toe the line now like a real human being . . . or suckle
your petty insecurities? *GET UP!*''

Art flopped, limbs pushing up only to collapse again.

"Did I make my point?"

Art gasped, "What? That you can beat me up? Damn
you to an Arcturian hell, Carrasco, I'll get you . . . *if I
have to stab you in the back!*"

Just as suddenly, the tone changed. "There! I finally
have you where I want you. Son of a bitch, you got it out
of your system. You had your chance to do what you
really wanted to deep in your subconscious. Now, get
up.'' The tone was conversational and a gloved hand
reached down to help him.

Art couldn't have made it down the weaving, winding
corridors to the Captain's cabin if he hadn't had Carrasco's support. He almost toppled into the chair as Carrasco handed him a towel to wipe the blood and vomit
from his face. Then Carrasco dug out an oversized bottle
and poured into two zero g cups.

"Drink up," Carrasco nodded.

Mollified, Art did, realizing it was good stuff. His tortured belly threatened, but held the line.

"Now, let's talk," Carrasco said amiably, making his
way gracefully as gravity tried to pull his feet in one
direction while his chest and head went in another.

"All right," Art gasped, still out of breath, "what's
changed?"

"Our relationship," Sol told him. "Right now, we're
talking like two human beings." He waved the cup out
at space. "My ways aren't in the book, Art. They don't
work for everybody—but they work for me. You're all
concerned over that damn regulation book. Well, I might
have charged you with that dustup in cargo. I could have
really nailed Bryana for altering the record." His eyes
twinkled. "And you'd have both been demerited on your
first deep hop. As much as I wanted to take you both
down a peg, it wasn't worth it. Bryana's turning into a
fine officer. You need a little work yet."

"But there are reasons for discipline!" Art protested, confused.

"Of course. I just gave you some. If you'd only been a deckhand, I wouldn't have taken the time. Believe me, I have my hands full. That bogey was a blessing since it tied me to the bridge and those cussed diplomats couldn't dig up any trouble. So I took the opportunity to catch a little sleep. Why? Because that bogey would either find us . . . or he wouldn't. It was out of my hands, and if you stare at the white dot on the screen, you get real nervous—just like you and Bryana did." His smile was humorless, "I caught all the remarks by the way. That trick of sleeping awake comes with practice."

"Yeah, well, I guess we shouldn't have done that." Art felt miserable. "Look, what do you want us to do? I mean, we're lost in this mess you've created!"

Carrasco smiled weakly. He snorted. "What I know about this mess is just enough to be completely muddled. But don't pin it on me. I didn't make it . . . and I didn't want it, but I'm committed to seeing it through even if it is out of my hands."

Art looked his disbelief, feeling his aching joints, knowing how bad the next morning would feel. Damn it, Carrasco had handled him like a bowl of jelly! Resentment festered.

Carrasco read his expression, face going tight. "All right, you wanted responsibility, let's see if you can handle it? Norik Ngoro was assassinated. Texahi's problem is the result of attempted assassination. Archon—whom Kraal put in charge of all of us—says, don't alienate the passengers from each other. He takes responsibility against my better judgment because the diplomats have to handle the interstellar impact of whatever object we're supposed to recover on Star's Rest. The Confederacy is on the brink of warfare over it. I've heard of—or been involved in—no less than six violent deaths as a result of this mess. Comm was sabotaged while sending a secret message to an unknown ship paralleling our course. An important ambassador could receive the death penalty for attempted rape. And I can't trust my two First Officers. All that and we're not even there yet. Suggestions, Art?''

He sat stunned. ''That's why we've had all the drills? There's really going to be trouble?''

''Yes, First Officer, there really is.'' Carrasco sounded tired, his expression pained. ''My reputation is that I've always brought my ships home and kept some of my crew alive. Archon tells me that we're all expendable—every man jack of us. And, whatever this *thing* is, it'll unhinge the Confederacy. He's scared to death of it. So's Constance. Welcome to the real world, Art. I told you once, you don't have to like me, but we've got to work together.'' He raised an eyebrow. ''So what's it going to be?''

''Why us—I mean Bryana and me?'' Art asked suddenly. ''Why not someone more experienced?''

Sol looked at him honestly. ''Not enough time, Art. I'm here because Archon and I shot each other up off Arpeggio and he liked the way I pulled it off. *Boaz* is here because she's the best thing we've got. You're here because they couldn't get veteran replacements aboard in time without upsetting the watchdogs—and you were the best bet from comm's point of view. Sorry, but that's the way it shakes out.''

Art nodded, feeling empty inside. ''I guess the book doesn't cover any of this, does it? Why did you keep us? Why didn't you put Happy on the bridge, or Fujiki, or someone else? I don't know that I'd take the risk on green officers—especially after that first simulation.'' He remembered his ashen face and the high squeak to his voice.

Carrasco smiled wistfully. ''Because I sincerely believe if I can get through your thick skulls—*if I can get you to think*—you'll both turn out to be fine officers. You and Bryana complement each other. You're pragmatic while she's wildly innovative and intuitive. I think you're both worth the risk—if you'll worry more about what's out there,'' he waved the cup forward, ''and how to keep us alive.''

Art realized he was nodding and shivered, cowed for

the first time. Carrasco had laid it on the line. Jesus, was he really up to it?

CHAPTER XXIII

Bryana couldn't help but notice the fire in Constance's eyes as Fan Jordan was led into the room. He was dressed foppishly in a satiny suit of cobalt blue. He gave Constance a leering smile that grated clear down to Bryana's bones. A slow burning anger shone on Archon's hard features. Both Stokovski and Dee Arness looked worried.

Bryana cleared her throat, conscious she sat at the middle of a maelstrom. "I called you all together to see if we couldn't find a rational solution to the problem." Jordan gave her a triumphant grin and her skin prickled.

Mustering an official voice, Bryana pronounced. "Fan Jordan, you are found guilty of assault, attempted murder, attempted rape, assaulting a ship's officer, disorderly conduct, and resisting arrest under the ship's articles, of which I have a copy, signed by your hand."

Jordan smiled, chin up, eyes gleaming. "And, pray tell, what does the Brotherhood propose to do? I'm a diplomat, remember? I am also a Royal personage. My uncle is the one true king of mankind. Slap my wrist and you slap New Maine." He laughed. "Please let's cut this kangaroo court short and get about our business!"

Bryana's heart skipped a beat. Voice hoarse, she added, "The penalty, according to law, is death by decompression." She looked to where Happy Anderson and Cal Fukiki stood waiting at the back of the room and nodded.

On cue they walked up on either side of Fan Jordan.

"What?" Jordan's face suddenly grew skeptical. "You wouldn't space me? You'd start a war! *My uncle is king!*" His eyes darted to each of the men. "You don't mean this!" Fujiki and Happy had started toward the large portside hatch while Jordan wriggled in their grasp and cried out.

Stokovski added. "That is the penalty according to ship's law, Fan. We all signed the articles and agreed to abide by them."

Jordan's voice, almost a keen, cut the air. "But she was in there without any clothes on! You know what that means!"

"No, Fan, what does that mean?" Archon asked, eyes glittering as he pushed himself half out of the chair.

"That she's a . . ." He swallowed the rest as the meaning of Archon's berserk stare sank home.

Bryana, trying desperately to defuse the situation, added, "Jordan, ships were originally small, cramped vessels where privacy was limited. Spacers, therefore, created a privacy of the mind. Just like men and women go to beaches on your own provincial world, they go naked in our gyms and showers and no one notices. To do so is to be ill-mannered, and boorish to the core. Further, women have traditional equality in space. No man molests them—not even the prostitutes in your own world's vessels.

"We realize that rape by nobility is accepted and encouraged on your world. Here it is not—as you know from the ship's articles. Death is the penalty."

Jordan almost whimpered, fighting against the tight grip of his captors, body whole, now that *Boaz* had knit the broken bones together. Bryana raised a hand on cue as Jordan began to tremble, eyes frantically going to the lock door that opened suggestively.

"*Wait!*" she ordered. "Jordan, would you be amenable to an alternate arrangement?"

Sudden hope leapt in hazel eyes and he nodded vigorously, struggling between the two big men.

"Let the record show the guilty party agrees." Bryana felt a great weight lift from her chest. "The aggrieved party—in view of the extraordinary circumstances of the present voyage—has urged that the investigative committee consider a plea on behalf of the guilty party. The Speaker of Star's Rest has requested an appeal of *vir geld* be considered by the committee. This appeal, Ambassador Jordan, does not absolve you of guilt, but allows you to make rmuneration to the damaged party by a payment mutually acceptable to you and the Speaker. Will you accept such judgment?''

Jordan swallowed, gaze darting between the hatch and the implacable eyes of the Speaker.

"Yes! Yes, *I agree!*"

"Very well," Archon's deep voice filled the room. "Star's Rest will accept a payment of ten thousand credits and the restriction of the New Maine ambassador to quarters until he can be suitably removed from our presence on board this ship. Is that acceptable to the board of investigation?''

Bryana nodded. ''It is. Ambassador Jordan?''

"Yes, yes, of course!"

Bryana fought her sigh of relief. ''The guilty party will be confined to his quarters. The sergeants at arms will see to it. Speaker Archon, as soon as payment is received, you will notify the chairman, and the matter will be considered resolved. The guilty party has two days to arrange payment. If not, the original sentence will be carried out by the sergeants at arms. Dismissed!'' She slapped the table and leaned back, feeling her heartbeat return to normal.

Jordan, almost in tears, stumbled away, leaning heavily on Fujiki's and Anderson's arms.

Archon's black rage subsided as he winked at Bryana, ''Well done, First Officer.''

"The responsibility of judge, jury, and executioner isn't all it's cracked up to be," she sighed with relief.

"No, it isn't," Archon nodded, fingering his chin. "At least, it never is to the one responsible."

* * *

"Have I offended you somehow, Captain?"

"I beg your pardon?" Sol stopped on his way across the lounge.

Elvina Young rose from the chair where she'd been

reading. A frown incised her forehead. "You seem to avoid me like the plague. I only wanted a chance to speak to you. I mean, I've never met a *real* Captain before. This is my first time away from Desseret. So many new things—so exciting! And I never knew they existed outside of my father's house! Only . . . well, you won't even talk to me."

Sol winced. "To be honest, I've been pretty busy with ship's business. The responsibilities—"

"Just for a moment, Captain?"

I'll feel like a complete zero! What the hell, it'll only be a minute or two. "Sure, I have to be on duty on the bridge in a bit, but I could spare a minute. What would you like to know?"

"Could I see your bridge? The engine room? Maybe see where you do your Captaining?"

He chuckled. "That's a restricted part of the ship."

She'd taken his arm, leading him over toward the dispenser. "But I'd love to see. I mean, ships are all so exciting! And I don't even have to cook here!"

The faint scent of her hair lingered in his nose, delightful, appealing. The feeling of her tightening her hold on his arm sent a tingle through his body.

She looked up, eyes dancing. "Tell me, Captain, do you think I'm attractive?"

Sol smiled, aware of the firm feel of her body against his. "Quite attractive—and therein lies the problem. Mrs. Young, you're also married."

A challenge sparkled in the winter blue of her eyes. "Oh, I couldn't leave Joseph. Marriages are made in the name of the Church. But, Captain, do come and share a drink with me. I, of course, must have tea, but could I at least get you a brandy—and hear your remarkable stories of combat? A man who's faced death must know a lot about passion, and life, and strength." Her fingers traced the back of his hand, stroking an electric afterimage on his skin.

"I must turn you down, ma'am. I'm on duty in a half hour." It cost him to admit that. But then, Bryana would cover if . . .

She seemed to hang on his every word. He noted pink-ing in her cheeks that reeked of sexual flush. His flesh warmed where her muscular leg pressed intimately against his. Beneath the baggy Mormon dress, he could feel a supple tigress' body tensing against his.

Despite her cropped hair, the features of her face beck-oned with youth and health. Her lips parted slightly to expose the pink secret of tongue as she stared into his eyes.

"You're a most handsome man, Captain. A powerful man." She ran casual fingers down his arm, the muscles of her leg tightening as she twined around him.

"Mrs. Young, I think I'd—"

"I'm Elvina, Solomon. Just Elvina."

Sol's heart began to pound, a curious desire stirring in his loins as his breathing increased. *This is insanity! I don't even like her!* Only the tiger strength of her body lured him, beckoning with promise. *I . . . don't even . . . like her . . .*

Her eyes bored into his, inviting, powerful. "Would you come to my cabin for a moment? I have some things to show you."

"I have to be on duty," Sol reminded, trying to still the racing of his heart. She melted up against him, full breasts pressing against his painfully aware skin. He could feel the pressure of her demanding pubis against his thigh. A fire burned hotly in his loins, his breathing labored. Her knowing fingers dropped to trace the outline of his erection through the fabric of his uniform.

"Just for a moment, Captain?" she whispered in a husky voice. "And later, maybe we could go to your cabin?" She exhaled a sigh, moving against him, leading him as his resistance crumbled into driving desire.

I . . . don't even . . . like her. Blood pounded in his veins, body hot to her touch. "I . . . ."

"Captain?" his belt comm called mechanically. "Your presence is required on the bridge immediately."

Sol pulled away reluctantly, "If you'll . . . excuse me, Mrs. Young, duty calls."

Frantically, he slipped into the corridor, passing the

security hatch. He stopped, braced against the bulkhead, catching his breath, stilling his racing pulse.

"What the HELL is wrong with me?"

"I thought you needed rescuing," *Boaz* called from the nearest speaker.

"You thought right. I don't understand. I was just trying to be polite and the next thing . . . I'm panting for her like a crazed maniac!"

"I believe it's a commercially available pheromone, Captain."

"What's she doing, keeping score? *She's a damn nymphomaniac!*"

"Her behavior follows unusual curves in that regard."

"That's not a religious norm, is it? I thought Mormons were a more circumspect group."

"They are. I would suggest that she is an anomaly."

"Well, people react differently when they're suddenly exposed to new stimuli." Sol took a deep breath. "But thank you for the warning. Knowing it's a trick makes it easier to avoid."

* * *

Sol was sitting in his command chair, idly playing Find the Ship with *Boaz*, seeking valiantly to understand Art's infatuation with the game, when *Boaz* interrupted: "Message, Captain. I have located the source as being inside the ship. While I could not jam, I did manage to record it. I am now jamming any further transmissions on that frequency. The message is in code and I am initiating cryptographic logs. I have pinpointed the source to Fan Jordan's quarters."

"What? Jordan? How'd he get a comm?" Sol asked, feeling baffled.

"Scanning shows a small, highly efficient transduction unit contained within his personal effects. And he has weapons, Captain. Evidently, they were contained in his baggage."

"Damn that diplomatic seal! What else have we let aboard?"

"Gas him," Sol ordered. "Have Happy search his compartment and clean out any other surprises."

"Acknowledged," *Boaz* told him. "I have broken the code; message playing now, Captain."

Jordan's face formed on the screen.

"To his Majesty, Lord Protector of New Maine:

I am being held prisoner on board the Brotherhood ship, *Boaz*. My life has been threatened by these peasants and I am in mortal danger. Request that you send assistance; we are headed for Star's Rest system. I have reason to believe His Majesty's realm is in grave political danger from the subversive actions of our enemies—the Brotherhood and the Speaker of Star's Rest. Action must be taken against both groups immediately. Your Majesty's life is in danger! I cannot underrate the crucial implications for our government and all mankind! I remain the Crown's humble servant, Fan Jordan, Earl of Baspa, 779345."

Boaz resumed, "End of transmission. However, I have received a reply. Code is much more sophisticated. This may take time, Captain."

"I understand. Was Jordan's signal directional?" Sol asked, feeling his gut begin to churn.

"No, Captain."

"Then it's all over the galaxy. In the ancient usage, 'Oh Lord, my God, pity the Widow's Son!' "

"Message, Captain," *Boaz* informed.

"Run it," Sol said, voice wooden as he stuck his coffee cup into the dispenser.

Kraal's aged face formed on the screen and Sol smiled wryly, knowing the disparity between their relative time and the one Kraal had spoken in so many light-years away. With time dilation, things happened quickly in other parts of the galaxy.

"To Captain Solomon Carrasco, Brotherhood ship *Boaz*, good day. We have received several complaints from New Maine concerning your behavior regarding one of their diplomats, a certain nephew to the king, um, one Fan Jordan. Our records here on Frontier allow us to build a reasonably accurate profile of Ambassador Jordan and no doubt you have had to take measures to, shall we say, subdue his passions? Would you care to respond at this time? If this would be inconvenient, please resume your duties. We have noted your continued silence and assume you have your reasons. Don't let the subject worry you as we will handle any complaints on this side. Feel free to ask should you require assistance from us. God speed and good luck. Please give my regards to Speaker Archon and his lovely daughter." The image faded.

Sol rubbed his chin, desperately missing the beard which had refused to grow after med regenerated his face. "Clean bill of health from Frontier," he mused.

"Do you want to send a reply?" *Boaz* asked.

"No, I don't think that will be necessary." Sol frowned, sipped his hot coffee, and wondered, "How much more do you think we can get away with?"

"Captain, I have broken the code on the New Maine response." The image formed on the screen.

A long-faced man with the crown and scepter of New Maine emblazoned on his jacket stared out. "Greetings, your Highness! We have received your appeal for relief. Security at the palace has been strengthened. Would you please acknowledge your present situation? If we do not hear from you, we will assume your royal personage is either incarcerated or dead—and appropriate action will be implemented." The screen blanked out.

"Appropriate action?"

"I would imagine they will have a ship dispatched to get their ambassador," *Boaz* decided, running through the statistical manipulations and picking the highest probability.

"Delightful!" Sol chuckled. "We'll be back at Arcturus before they get spaced."

Only he was wrong.

* * *

Sol stopped nervously before the hatch. A curious reluctance ate at him. "Come on, if you can use the ship to spy on her, you can sure as hell talk to her, too."

He stepped into the observation blister.

She stood proudly, back to him, staring out at the distant suns, the wealth of starlight barely tingeing the red of her hair. In silhouette, she might have been a goddess, every curve adding to her allure.

Sol hesitated, letting the image of her settle into his mind—a bit of time locked away forever in his memories.

His heart betrayed itself as he softly said, "Connie?"

She turned, a slight smile hovering for a fleeting instant on her lips. "Hello, Captain. Seems I can never get down here without you showing up."

He chuckled softly, moving up to stand beside her. "I've got a confession to make. I cheated. Heard you were coming down here."

"Another noise complaint?" She arched a fine eyebrow, green eyes evaluating.

"Mouse said you were walking too loudly on the deck plates."

She crossed her arms, slender fingers supporting her chin. "I told you you'd use that once too often." She studied his face for a moment. "Captain, you look a little haggard."

He shrugged. "It's all starting to go too fast. I feel controlled by events instead of in charge. So much is happening—and I can't make sense of it."

"You'll wish you hadn't in the end. Despite your secret society, ignorance is bliss."

"Perhaps." His voice caught as he searched for words. "Actually, I wanted to come down and thank you. Bryana gave me a full report. You were the one who spoke for Jordan. Myself . . . well, I might have let my passions get the best of me. Thank you, you've lessened my burden—and that of the Craft."

Her smile hung wearily on her lips, hair tumbling down her back as she lifted her chin. "I wanted to space him. Father was adamant, practically foaming at the mouth." She shook her head. "Then I remembered something Nikita said about responsibility in a politician. About not wanting to do things. I don't know, so much is at stake, what's a measly assault? When I got calmed down enough to look at it rationally, I saw that kicking Fan out a hatch would only complicate things.

"But thank you for a most timely rescue. This time, I needed it. He brought reinforcements with him."

"Sometimes us captains need to do things a couple of times to get it right. The first time was just a mock run to make sure I had the reflexes to get it right when the real thing rolled around."

"Practice must have helped. You were on the money. Any further, and I would have had no choice but to space him."

Sol exhaled, staring out at the stars. "Still, spacing that bastard would have made chaos look simple. God alone knows what the Mainiacs would have done in retaliation."

She ran delicate fingers over the telescope mounting. "I suppose. Only I can't help feeling trapped. Seeing behavior like Jordan's out of a rational human mind doesn't help matters either. I keep reevaluating what we're about. The more I know about politics and the people in charge of them, the less certain I am about what to do."

"The device?"

She looked up at him. "Father said you'd guessed that much. Yes, I'm more than nervous. The only glimmering of hope I see is getting it to Kraal. I listened most intently to your conversation with Nikita and Tayash. Perhaps, if there's hope for humanity . . ."

"Want to tell me more? Like what this thing is? A machine? A . . . what?"

She reached over, resting a hand on his arm. A tingle shot through him. "No, Sol. Not yet. And it isn't even for security reasons. I . . . I want you to make your own decisions, unbiased. Please, don't look at me like that. It takes all my discipline as it is to try and think rationally about this."

He reached over, laying a hand on hers. "Very well, I'll trust you for it."

She nodded slightly. "Thank you, Sol. It isn't easy to deal with, that's all."

''Your father said both of you were expendable. That it would even be worth an entire planet.''

She nodded, sober eyes on his. ''He wasn't being melodramatic. That's why it all keeps getting so complicated.''

''I know it's not much, but if you need to talk sometime, you know where to find me.''

She closed her eyes, a curious relief in her expression. ''You know, I've never felt so damned alone in my life as in this last year.'' She shook her head, leaning against him. ''I can't even allow myself to be human. Always circumspect, always in control. It's a terrible thing to never allow yourself any vulnerability. We're not built like that, not meant to live as impregnable fortresses.''

He placed an arm around her shoulder, thrilling at the firm feel of her flesh.

For long moments, they stood, staring out at the stars. ''When this is over, maybe I'll feel young again.''

''And what will you do?''

She shrugged, ''Sleep for a week. Then I'll go find a quiet spot and try and make sense of it all. I don't know, maybe take *Bad Boy* and space for someplace out there.'' She gestured at the stars.

''Kraal made you a member of the Craft. We're doing a lot of survey work. There's always a need for capable people.''

She cocked her head, hair slipping across his hand in a silken shower. ''Is that an offer?''

Sol met her gaze frankly. ''Would you like it to be?''

The blue pools of her eyes seemed to expand. ''Sol, in all honesty, I can't tell you how much I'd like to say yes. But we have our current affairs to see to, and we'd need more time together. To see how we got along.''

He laughed softly. ''That's not quite the answer I anticipated. Are you always so pragmatic about men?''

She smiled wistfully out at the stars. ''I wasn't once. I was a couple of light-years younger then. I don't know, maybe every girl goes through that starry-eyed stage. He was dashing, ambitious, powerful. I was out of my league and didn't know it. He took me to his bed as an eager virgin. Oh, I bought it all, taken in by his charm and attention. Awed by his power, that a man of his stature and ability would care for me.''

"What happened?"

Her voice dropped. "I went where I wasn't supposed to. Overheard him talking with one of his lieutenants, talking about the delight of bedding me while he destroyed my father and his fleet." She shook her head. "I felt . . . trashed, degraded. Like everything else in his life, he used me only as a stepping stone to further his own advancement. I was a simple political tool to him, nothing more.''

"Looks like you survived."

"I did. Immediately afterward, the universe dumped on my shoulders. Somewhere, deep inside, I reached down into the muck of myself and pulled enough threads of identity together to deal with it all.'' She pillowed her head in the hollow of his shoulder. "Damn, everything inside and out came unraveled—and there was no one but me to rely on.''

He turned her, staring down into her eyes. "For the record, I like the way it turned out.''

For a long second, they stared into each others eyes. He bent down, kissing her gently before she pushed away.

A curious confusion filled her.

"I'm sorry," Sol added gently. "It just seemed like the thing to do. Something about the starlight, it always gets to me that way.''

She smiled up at him. "I could get to like starlight.'' She hesitated. "But, Sol, let me think this through first. I don't want to start anything I can't finish.''

She disengaged herself, stepping back, the old reservation in her eyes.

"I understand.'' He smiled reassuringly. "You're not the only one who's a little nervous. It's been years since . . . Well, that's another story.''

She gave him a ravishing smile. "And I'll want to hear it.''

With that, she was gone, her scent lingering gently on the cool air.

* * *

In one of those odd coincidences, Sol was reviewing the tapes *Boaz* had made of the day Texahi was poisoned when the ship interrupted his study.

"Captain, you are needed in the hospital. Ambassador Ben Geller is dead."

Even as the news settled in, Sol was already sprinting through the corridors.

Paul Ben Geller was laid out on a med unit. *Boaz*'s probes were flying around his body and Sol winced at the sight of things moving under pale flesh as remote sensors moved through muscle and nerves. The sight always reminded him of worms . . . or some horrid creature inside the body.

Mary Ben Geller lay on a pad across from her husband. "How's Mrs. Ben Geller, *Boaz?*"

"Asleep, Captain. She was hysterical and I thought it proper to sedate her."

"Leave her be." Sol looked up as Ensign Wheeler came out of the back.

"Not good, Captain. I don't know what could have done it. According to the symptoms, he just went to sleep and died." Wheeler spread his hands. *Boaz* will have autopsy within a couple of minutes, I'd imagine.

"I have found the instrument of death, Captain," *Boaz* informed.

"Instrument?" Sola asked, seeing Wheeler's tightened expression.

"Affirmative. I have located a delicate glass needle in the ambassador's arm. I am currently extracting it." A long probe sailed out and thin metallic fingers pulled the soft tissue aside. The tiny sliver of glass came out in pieces and was withdrawn into the bulkhead for analysis.

"Do you need me here anymore, *Boaz?*"

"Negative, Captain. But I have the cause of death. It is not pharmacopa. This time we are dealing with a toxin derived from sitah root, a scrubby violet plant which grows only on Reinland. It is, I might add, a very specialized poison.''

"We'll discuss it further in my quarters," Sol decided. He turned to Wheeler. "Keep your hat on about this, Ensign. Not a single word to anyone. Even after we break it, you don't know a thing. Refer any curious parties to me or Speaker Archon, understood?''

"Aye, Cap." Wheeler nodded. "Uh, from the silence, I assume that there was more than met the eye with Ngoro and Texahi, too?''

"You don't talk to anyone!" Sol repeated as he left.

"Archon to my quarters," Sol muttered into his belt comm. There had to be an end to this one way or another, and this time he'd have it if he had to jail Archon in the process!

CHAPTER XXIV

She watched the white ship drop from light jump. She could feel this ship, and she quieted her stir of anticipation. The other craft had been coming in—all from that desolate section of the galaxy, but they were exceedingly primitive, unlike this more advanced arrival. Did such advancement signify a Master?

Patience. The long wait was almost over. Curious, she probed, but her instruments detected only humans in the huge white ship. She digested that knowledge with the understanding that Masters—jealous of each other's power—might not trust themselves in Phthiiister's domain or her presence.

Phthiiister, last of a long line of Hynan successors. Not since the Aan had conflict grown so violent over her possession. Each of the competing lords had challenged her Masters. Eternal competitors, they'd sought to develop defenses—some way to rival her powers. In the end, every

means had been tried, the epitome of Hynan science had
engaged her and Phthiiister. True to the nature of organic
life, the drive to overcome had powered the Hynan to
their destruction—the battleground raging across the universe to end here, in this tiny spiral of a galaxy. Here,
mad Phthiiister had come and destroyed the last bastions
of resistance in person. And here, he'd damned himself
to live the last of his days, toying with suns, cackling
crazily to himself as he worked the spring.

He'd designed this solar system to his liking, and ordered her to produce intoxicants with which to halluci-
nate the hours away. There, at the helm, he'd remained,
remarkable nervous system dulled by the endless stream
of drugs until his body expired—the last of his kind.

Thus she had waited—trapped by the damning spring—
until the animals found her. Now the white ship approached, and Sabot Sellers watched from the fringes. If
they truly had no superior Master, he would do nicely.
Who would get to her first?

If only she could work the spring—but then, she'd have
no need of Sellers or his ambitions; she'd simply destroy
them all. At the thought of it, insanity burned an actinic
brilliance within her.

* * *

Archon passed the hatch to see Sol musing over a large
2-D picture of the lounge portrayed on the screens along
one wall. "Yes?" he asked.

"Paul Ben Geller is lying dead in the hospital. *Boaz*
pulled a shattered glass needle out of his arm. Mary is
under sedation. No one but you, I, and the medical ensign knows yet. I've been reviewing the records of Paul's
last day."

"Oh, my God!" Archon sank listlessly into the chair.

"The poison came from sitah root. It produces a fungal reaction—quite painless—which functions on the red
blood cells. The only passenger from Reinland is Mikhi
Hitavia. Hitavia had the opportunity to slip the poison
into both Ngoro's and Texahi's drink. Here he appears

innocent. Note the video recording: Hitavia is playing Mark Lietov at the gaming booth. GSR, respiration, and pulse are normal for curves established for gaming players. He couldn't have done it since he would have had to shoot through Malakova's body.''

"Wait a minute. GSR? Respiration? I don't . . . *How* do you know all this?'' Archon looked bewildered.

Ignoring the question, Sol continued, "This has to be the moment when Geller received the lethal projectile. Notice, he's scratching his arm. Entry of the missile would have caused a slight itch. Now, we've deduced the projectile must have had a velocity of around twenty meters per second. That means close range. Interpose the lines, *Boaz*.'' Two red zones inserted themselves on the photo.

"From the possible trajectories, seven people lie within range of Ben Geller. You, Speaker, Constance, Origue Sanchez, Malakova, Mary Ben Geller, Wan Yang Dow, and Elvina Young. No one else, as you can see, could have hit that target from where they stood or sat.''

"How did you get this data? I thought you said this ship didn't spy on us?''

Sol added dryly, "I lied. Please, look at the hands of the subjects involved. Mary has hers pressed together. Wan Yang Dow has both hands clasping his drinking bulb. Malakova's hands are spread wide in a gesture. Constance is flipping her hair over her shoulder with one hand while gesturing with the other. Sanchez has his chin cradled in his palms, no doubt bored by Elvina, who is engaged in old-fashioned knitting—I hear that's big on Zion. Your hands, Speaker, are in your pockets.''

Archon stared, off balance. Finally he said, "So I'm a suspect? Yes, I suppose so.''

"*Boaz?*'' Sol called. "What was the Speaker's reaction?''

"His pulse, metabolic rate, GSR, and respiration were normal. He didn't arrive at the conclusion he was the logical one to have murdered Paul Ben Geller rapidly enough. From my statistical analyses, I must conclude

the Speaker—whose reactions I have become very familiar with—is totally surprised, Captain, and, therefore,
innocent.''

"Thank you, *Boaz.*'' Sol sighed and dropped into his
bunk. He looked forlornly at the speechless Archon. "I
had to know. It's not you. We must look deeper—but one
of those remaining six people is the assassin.''

"This ship spies on us? It notes respiration, galvanic
skin response, even pulse?''

"Oh, much more than that, Speaker. I had eyes installed all over the ship along with audio and IR pickups.
She's been monitoring everything, filtering it, bringing
any altercation or threat to my attention. How else do
you suppose I was able to intercept Jordan when he first
made advances against Constance in the privacy of his
quarters? We didn't use that evidence because it would
have tipped my advantage to the investigative committee.''

"Then the stories are true?'' Archon gasped. "These
ships are sentient?''

"*Boaz,* considering the security clearance the Speaker
is entitled to, would you like to answer that?''

"Speaker Archon, it is a pleasure to meet you. In answer to your question, yes, I am sentient. I think and act
on my own. Should every member of the crew become
incapacitated, I have the ability to make decisions concerning the completion of the mission.''

Archon shook his head. "No! Impossible!''

"From my perspective I am entirely possible since I
exist—unless you would retreat to solipsism in which case
I would like you to prove to me that *you* are sentient,''
Boaz intoned.

"Speaker,'' Sol demanded in light of the consternation
on Archon's face. "Did you hear the report of a weapon
when you were standing there last night? It would have
been a click, a pop, or something similar. The weapon
may have been spring powered.''

"Your ship heard nothing?'' Archon asked, mouth
open, slightly dazed.

"Play the audio, *Boaz.*''

Instantly, the room filled with laughter and small talk, the soft noise that makes up a social gathering. "That's it. Do you remember anything?"

"No, Captain." Archon shook his head.

"What emotions do our suspects show, *Boaz?*"

"They are all calm, Captain. From previously established curves, none exhibit abnormal excitement or anger. We must assume, if the murderer is indeed one of the seven, that the individual displays pathological tendencies with regard to murder."

Sol's face twisted. "I had hoped it would turn out to be Mikhi Hitavia. Now I think we were supposed to believe Hitavia was the culprit. If you think back to Ngoro's warning, however, he told us we were dealing with a remarkable mind. The assassin didn't know we had the visual monitors placed in the lounge. Happy did a very good job of hiding them. Looks like the rheostat for brightness control in the lighting."

"So now what?" Archon asked.

"Now we interview the suspects, what else?" Sol turned to comm.

"Do you think that's wise? I mean you'll tip your hand . . . that the ship monitors everyone. Who will speak freely? Who will—"

Sol whirled, a finger stabbing out. "Speaker, another man has just been murdered on *my* ship. Now, I played along, followed orders, but unless you want to relieve me of command and confine me to quarters this very instant, I'm putting a stop to it. I've thought it out. Faced with the scene—with the very damning evidence before them—I'm betting *Boaz* can pick up a reaction. If I had my way, I'd put them all under psych and have it out of them. I can't. Not without an interstellar incident that could jeopardize the Craft. So I'm doing it this way, attempting to shock them into a confession."

Archon took a deep breath, face lined with worry. "I . . . Very well, Captain. No, I won't relieve you of command. I . . . Yes, yes, go ahead." He slapped hands on his knees in resignation.

"Boaz, ask Origue Sanchez if he would be so kind as to join me in my cabin."

The ambassador entered smiling, muttered how pleased he was to be there, and Sol hit him with the question. "Did you kill Paul Ben Geller, Ambassador?"

"I beg your pardon?" Sanchez's eyes were blank. "Did you ask if I killed Paul?"

"Please look at the picture. Do you remember that moment last night? You are sitting with Elvina Young. Did you hear the report of a weapon?"

"Weapon?" Origue was still confused. He shot a quick look at Archon for confirmation.

"Please, Origue," Archon nodded to the picture. "That's the moment of Paul's murder. He was assassinated."

Sanchez blinked in disbelief. "Why would I kill Paul? No. I . . . never. I mean . . ."

"Did you hear the report of a weapon?"

Origue stared openmouthed at the scene. "Weapon? Assassination? Here, on this ship?"

"Report, *Boaz."* Printout flimsy ejected.

"Clean bill of health," Sol remarked. He looked up. "Ambassador, you don't know it, but you just went through a lie detector test. I'm afraid it's true. Paul has been killed by an unknown assassin. I'm confining everyone to their quarters until we can find the killer and bring him to justice. If you would return to your room and remain there, I would appreciate it. Please, say nothing to anyone about this."

Sanchez left, still trying to comprehend what had happened.

Elvina Young came slipping in—didn't see Archon—and threw herself into Sol's arms. "Oh, Captain, I just knew you'd invite me to your quarters." She closed her eyes, chest heaving. "I've been dying to feel your arms around me. Of course, I could never leave Joseph—but you know how a woman is! I know you've longed for me, but—"

"Mrs. Young!" Sol snapped. "I did not call you for an assignation! Did you kill Paul Ben Geller?"

She stepped back, saw Archon, and gasped. "Oh, my word! I didn't see you, Speaker. I think I feel faint!"

"Did you hear my question?" Sol asked.

Elvina blushed bright red, "It's not what you must think, Speaker. You know how silly women can be! The good Captain is simply a friend of mine. Why, even a woman deserves a good friend. There wouldn't be anything between us. Why, the Captain is a man of honor! And me, why, I am a married woman . . . and happily so."

Archon nodded. "I understand that perfectly. Would you answer the question? Did you kill Paul Ben Geller?"

"Is he dead?" she asked, giggling nervously. "Is this some little joke?"

"No, it isn't. We're trying to find an assassin," Sol said stiffly.

"Assassin?" She drew the syllables out. "On this ship? There's an assassin on this ship?" Her voice became high-pitched. "He might kill *me?*" She flew into Sol's arms again. "Oh, Captain, you must find him! Why, no one is safe. You'll keep me safe? Oh, dear Lord in heaven, I feel faint!" She threw an arm up to her forehead.

"Easy, Mrs. Young," Archon soothed, seeing Sol's perplexed expression as he shoved the woman off. "Have a seat and look at the picture."

Elvina allowed herself to be led to the chair. "Paul was killed by a lethal glass projectile. Did you see anything, hear anything like a click or a pop?"

"Assassination? It could have been me. Don't you see? *I might have been killed!*"

"*Mrs. Young!*" Carrasco thundered. "Settle down and think! What did you see?"

"I . . . I . . . Assassins? And I've been rubbing elbows with a hideous murderer? What if Joseph . . . Will we be safe?"

"Yes, yes, quite. We're trying to catch the culprit now. Did you hear anything?" Archon asked, stooping down before her.

Eyes wide, she stared at the scene, shivering, features going pale. "No."

"Thank you. You may go to your quarters." Sol palmed the hatch and smiled.

"Alone?" she asked, terrified.

"You'll be quite safe, I promise." Sol practically pushed her out.

"Boaz?"

"Captain, she went from one emotional peak to another. Responses ranged from extreme excitement to fear," the ship intoned. "I must say, she entered the room full of anticipation. From the flush I would imagine she thought—"

"Thank you, *Boaz!*" Sol snapped.

"There goes that one," Archon muttered, eyes straying uneasily to the speaker. *"Boaz* would have picked something up in the lounge considering her emotional instability."

Nikita Malakova came in laughing and jovial.

"Did you kill Paul Ben Geller?" Sol asked.

"Of course!" Nikita roared. "What? You are playing some new kind of game?" Nikita looked satisfied with himself. "Good day, Speaker! I was meaning to look you up. What you think about allowing emigration to Star's Rest from Gulag? We need to have new markets and some of my people have crazy idea to go groundhog."

"Look at the picture." Sol pointed. "Do you remember that from last night?"

"But of course. I'm arguing with Paul." He stopped, finger dropping from where he'd been pointing. Malakova's expression hardened, thick black brows furrowing. "Wait. *You said Paul is dead?*"

"Assassinated. That was the moment when it happened," Archon added.

Nikita's face went pale. "No!" he breathed. Slowly he walked forward, studying the picture intently. Finally he nodded. "And I am suspect! I see. Whatever you need, Nikita Malakova will help you. If you must, Captain, search my room while I am here. In this instance, even Gulagi like I have nothing to hide." He looked back at the screen. "But who could have killed Paul? Why would they do this? Doesn't make sense unless . . ." He cocked his head. "Two heart attacks? You have checked to see if is connection?"

Sol sighed. "There's a connection."

Nikita stiffened.

"*Boaz*, report?" Sol asked, and read the printout. He smiled, bleakly. "Nikita, I'm sorry to say this." He hesitated, shaking his head as Archon got to his feet. "I wish I could space you—but you're innocent and pure as the solar winds."

"No one has ever called me *that*, Captain." Then he looked back at the picture. His voice softened. "Perhaps you let me help space this murderer, eh? Paul, he is . . . was my friend."

Wan Yang Dow stopped when Sol asked the question. "You just asked if I *killed* Paul Ben Geller?"

"That's right."

Dow stopped, thin lips pursed, thinking. After a moment, he looked up. "Where would I have done this and when?"

"Last night in the lounge. Do you remember that instant?" Sol pointed at the picture. "You were talking to Mary Ben Geller. This is the instant when the fatal projectile was fired into Paul."

Dow studied it closely. "Why would I have killed him? Did I have a reason?"

"Did you?" Archon supplied.

"No." Dow crossed his arms. "Therefore, it would seem logical that I did not commit such a crime. Yet such knowledge leads me to wonder about the two heart attacks we've had. Most irregular. The etiology of heart attack—"

"We're aware of the etiology," Sol interrupted. "Currently, our problem is assassination and providing safety for the people aboard this vessel. Did you hear or see anything out of the ordinary last night?"

He paused in thought. "I saw nothing recognizable as out of the ordinary."

"*Boaz?*" The printout supported Dow's simple statement.

Constance passed with flying colors, startled to find

out about Ben Geller's death. She looked worriedly at her
father. "It's not over, then. He's still loose out there."
She studied the screen. "Which one of them could have
done it?"

Sol shook his head. "Any ideas?"

Her blue eyes stopped him and he felt that instant of
communication pass between them.

"Among them, no. Nikita is passionate enough. Mary?
Who knows, wives often have cause to commit murder.
And Dow? I don't know how his brain works. Sanchez
was one of the Cielan revolutionaries thirty years ago.
He was a guerrilla fighter. Father and I could . . . or
would if we had to." She looked honestly at her father.
"I didn't—did you?"

Archon lifted a gray eyebrow.

She left hesitantly, obvious unease in her pinched features.

With distaste, Sol called his last witness.

"Mary, I'm sorry to have to do this, but did you have
any reason to want your husband dead?" Sol fought to
keep his own composure.

"Dead?" Suddenly the tears leaked through her tightly
closed eyes. She shook her head. "No," she whispered
miserably.

One by one Sol asked the questions. She answered
bravely and in the end, he took her hand and smiled.
"I'm sorry to have done this, Mary. We waited until we
had questioned the others. You were the last one." He
took the printout. A deep anxiety tore at him as he read
it. All normal for a freshly made widow.

"I understand," she said, a deeply felt steel in her
voice. "If I can be of any assistance, Captain, call on
me. I want to see Paul's murderer brought to justice.
We're a tough people. We've been taught to bear up
through tragedy. If I remember anything, I'll call."

"No," he shook his head. "If we can be of assistance
to you, my ship and crew are at your disposal."

Sol chewed his thumb as Mary Ben Geller, hollow-
eyed, passed through the hatch. "Vacuum! I feel like a

heel after that!'' He stilled his turbulent emotions and bottled his frustration.

''Speaker, we're four days from Star's Rest.'' Sol frowned to himself. ''I'll make a concession. I say we confine them to quarters. The pretext will be that there is a potential for pirate activity due to the excessive number of ships around Star's Rest. Only the questioned witnesses will know the real reason and they won't be allowed to converse with the others. That should defuse any suspicion and keep everyone friendly. In the meantime, give them a briefing on this alleged constitutional convention to mull over. That'll keep their minds occupied.''

Archon sighed. ''Very well. We're so close. Perhaps all will be well. I agree.''

But Sol couldn't kill the feeling he was missing something.

CHAPTER XXV

Bryana watched the dot accelerating, reaction mass making a white-hot streak across the starfield. ''Red Alert!'' she called, feeling her heart skip. *''This is not a drill. All stations report!''*

Art, white and subdued since his go-round with Carrasco, pitched through the hatch, dropping into his command chair as the lights flickered red and began popping to yellow and finally green. Carrasco, haggard, combat armor donned, slipped through the hatch and into the command chair. He opened a channel to Archon immediately.

''Constance is at the hatch,'' *Boaz* reported.

''Let her in.''

She came in suited, tension in her expression. ''Captain, they may be part of our fleet. As admiral, I'd better talk to them.''

Bryana looked up in amazement. She caught Constance and Sol, eyes locked on each other in some unspoken communication. A feeling of annoyance rose from someplace deep inside. She forced herself to concentrate on the boards. So he looked at her? Big deal. Still the thought chafed.

"Send them a standard greeting, Art," Sol ordered, chin propped on his knee as he watched the ship arcing to meet them. "He's pushing everything he's got to match with us. But his crew loves that!"

"Message returned," *Boaz* called.

"Put me through to their captain."

The gaudy uniform couldn't come from anywhere except New Maine. Bryana felt herself tense and shot a look at Carrasco who seemed nonplussed.

The speaker blared. "Attention, Captain Solomon Carrasco! I am Captain Richard Evans of His Majesty's Ship *Desmond,* Royal Fleet of New Maine. It is our understanding that you are holding Fan Jordan, Earl of Baspa, or that you may have done him harm. My orders are to effect the release of the earl or to mete out such punishment as you deserve should you have harmed his Highness!"

Bryana started at the stiff attitude until she realized Evans didn't like the position his orders had forced him into. She could see the distaste on his face; confrontation with *Boaz* would have sobered anyone.

On the other hand, Carrasco's response surprised her. He laughed long and loud and hard. "My good Captain Evans, we would be only too happy to comply with any wish you have. In the first place, Ambassador Jordan is safe—but confined to quarters for attempted rape. Despite ship's law, we didn't space him, you see. I don't know how New Maine expects to fare in the coming talks, but you might tell your king that Jordan assaulted Constance, the Deputy Speaker of Star's Rest."

Evans smiled thinly. "I am told by my superiors that such charges can be easily falsified. The ambassador enjoys a great deal of the king's affection; therefore, it would bode ill had you harmed him—no matter what the circumstances. We will match and expect transfer of the ambassador at the first opportunity.''

Sol nodded. ''That's fine with us, Captain. From the Captain and crew of *Boaz*, please accept our respects and appreciation for your help. I can speak for the earl when I say he is looking forward to having you at his disposal.''

Bryana bit her lip as she saw Carrasco's last shot hit home. Evans' jaw twitched and the skin along the side of his face rippled as he tensed his temporal and masseter muscles.

''Captain Carrasco,'' Evans cleared his throat. ''I am also instructed by His Majesty to confirm the earl's present state of health. You would please have him escorted to the bridge?''

Sol's wry smile reeked of amusement as he accessed comm. ''Cal, could you escort Fan Jordan to the bridge?'' He lowered his eyes to Evans'. ''I could simply access through to his quarters.''

Evans nodded. ''My orders, however, were to see him on the bridge.''

''Of course.'' Sol nodded indulgently. ''Can't be faked, right? Um, Captain, I know some of the handicaps you labor under, but you might consider—for future reference of course—that most ships have the ability to generate images far beyond what you are attempting to guard against.''

Evans' jaw went even tighter. Bryana wondered whether he'd crack a molar. Seconds ticked by, tension electric.

Jordan, disheveled, blinking sleep from his eyes, passed through the hatch in front of Cal Fujiki. ''Captain Carrasco! What is the meaning of dragging me from a sound sleep? How dare you interrupt and inconvenience me after the wretched treatment you have accorded *me*, a member of the Royal family. I warn you that your insolence has reached a new height. I swear the day will come when—''

''Shut up, Fan!'' Sol roared. ''If you'll look, you're being rescued by poor Captain Evans!'' Sol turned to the screen to see Evans standing like a rock, relief tempered by a whole new misery in his eyes. "See, he's fine!"

"Thank you, Captain. If you will send course data, we will match." The screen flicked off before Jordan could say any more, possibly because Evans feared what he might be ordered to do.

"You can go back to your quarters, Fan." Sol gestured toward the hatch.

"No," Jordan said stubbornly. "I will stay right here. I fear assassination!"

Bryana tensed, keeping her eyes on the Mainiac battleship's position as Art sent course information.

"We couldn't be that lucky, Fan," Sol muttered wearily. "Return now . . . or Cal will drag you kicking and screaming."

Jordan moved fast enough to evade Fujiki's grasping fingers and grabbed Constance, flicking a vibraknife at her throat. "I'll stay—and Constance will stay with me. One little move, Fujiki, and I slit her up the middle. And you, Constance, I know your tricks. But I'll gut you before you can kick or twist away."

Jordan laughed. "Wonder where I got the knife? Oh, they did a good job searching the place, Carrasco. You simpletons are so easy to fool. A vibraknife can slip in anywhere—especially into a new made weld from your gracious enlargement of my quarters."

Bryana shook her head slowly, the raw burning of frustration deep inside. This couldn't be happening on the bridge. Worse, they'd *have* to space Jordan now.

Sol remained casual. "Fan, don't you think you'd better quit while you're ahead? Every time you've tried to buck us, you end up looking like an idiot. I'd spare you this time, too. You're almost home free—why screw it up?"

Jordan's eyes gleamed. "Oh, you can't stop me this time, Carrasco. I want you, Fujiki, and Arturian out of here now!" He smiled wickedly. "Bryana stays to run the ship and provide amusement for Constance and me. Besides, I owe her. No one does what she did to me and gets away with it. Out now, Captain."

Bryana swallowed hard, composure crumbling as Sol got to his feet. "Come on, Art, I guess I know when we're licked. Back off, Cal." The big weapons tech shrugged, features blank as he backed out the hatch. Art got nervously to his feet.

"You can't do this!" Bryana whispered.

"He's got the knife," Sol replied reasonably. "It won't be long. Just do your duty, First Officer."

"*Captain?*" Art cried, shaken.

"First Officer, let's go." Sol ordered firmly. "They're Fan's women for a while at least—let him enjoy them."

Art moved numbly, head shaking as Carrasco's voice called out, "Three-sixty, *Boaz!*" . . . And the bridge disappeared.

Only Bryana's presence in the firm grip of the command chair kept her in touch with some semblance of reality. Despite the shock, she saw Carrasco walk easily across the stars and pluck the vibraknife out of Jordan's catatonic fingers.

Carrasco picked him bodily up and carried the paralyzed Earl of Baspa to the hatch. A doorway to reality slid back, yellow light streaming through to bathe space, and Carrasco pushed his captive into Fujiki's waiting arms. Bryana couldn't be sure, but it looked like Jordan was crying.

"Thank you, *Boaz,* I think the situation is under control." The bridge reappeared.

Art had frozen, rooted to the spot. His voice trembled, husky. "If I hadn't seen you playing with this before, Captain, I'd have gone stark raving mad." Slowly he felt his way back to his command chair.

Constance shivered slightly, reaching to touch the now solid panels. "I don't know what was worse, Jordan—or *That!* What happened? I think I could get used to it and come to love it! What a feeling of freedom and wonder. It's like EVA . . . only without a suit!"

Sol settled himself in the command chair. "The hull of this ship is not only graphite, it's also composed of microfiberoptics which are woven netlike over the hull. The purpose is for camouflage which works for infiltrat-

ing pirate strongholds as well as for study purposes when
the observer wishes to remain invisible.

"The bridge employs the same thing. I read Petran's
report on the project. He thinks it can add to a captain's
ability to conduct maneuvers, provide a better feel for
the ship's location in space."

Would to God, Bryana wished, we were completely
invisible all the time. She looked at the image of the
closing New Maine battleship, a streak of light shooting
out as reaction mass. No matter how well *Boaz* could
hide herself, whenever she moved, she left a signal. The
whole of space would know as they decelerated for Star's
Rest.

*   *   *

Sabot Sellers replayed the communication *Hunter*'s
delicate "ears" had detected. So *Boaz* had arrived. Not
only that, the imbecilic Mainiacs had sent a fleet of their
own—and that foolish fop, Jordan, had acted like a man
insane. Very well, at least he had advance warning. Judging from the location of *Boaz*'s transmissions, Carrasco
would arrive in about four days. How had they come in
so silently? Where had his ships missed them?

"Comm officer."

"Sir?"

"Scramble the fleet. The time has come for Arpeggio
to pay port call to Star's Rest. Send directional. Have
Thylassa's vessels rendezvous."

"Yes, sir." The man bent to his duty.

*So the time has come. Very well, Carrasco, let's see
who wins. You and your* Boaz, *or the combined might of
Arpeggio. The device will be mine . . . and with it, humanity. Unassailable, beautiful Constance, you shall
come to me. It's been a long time, and I haven't forgotten. No woman runs out on me . . . ever!*

*   *   *

A member of the escort party, Constance experienced a moment of relief—savoring it—as Fan Jordan stepped lightly across the shuttle deck, antigrav after antigrav carrying his endless and mostly useless impedimenta. Two steely-eyed marines jumped lightly from the New Maine shuttle—blasters at hand.

"They look like they don't trust us," Sol chided. "Now, why do you suppose that is?"

"I'm just glad he's gone." She shot a quick glance his way, noting the wry humor. "I never thanked you for what you did. I guess we've both been too busy."

A smile tugged at the corners of his lips. "No thanks are necessary. It worked out for the best."

Jordan's things lifted on the antigrav, shoveled into the shuttle, one after another. Fan rode an antigrav up and stepped into the hatch, saluting his subordinates. He stopped, turned, and Sol met that burning stare which seemed to say, "Till next time."

The last of the baggage aboard, the shuttle lifted under Misha Gaitano's careful manipulation and slid into the lock. The big doors closed and Sol turned to his monitor. He could see the shuttle as it cleared the outer hull and dropped away toward the shields.

"Now we see what'll happen," Constance said uneasily. Damn Jordan, he wouldn't be foolish enough to order *Desmond* into immediate retaliation, would he?

"I don't think they'll fight," Sol assured her. "Evans isn't an idiot. He's made his assessments of this ship and her capabilities. He knows we're on alert and he can't take us with *Desmond*. And Jordan—no matter how crazy and neurotic—can't precipitate a war without his king's permission."

"You hope."

He nodded soberly. "I hope. I'm not sure if he's insane or so insufferably spoiled that he's out of touch with reality."

The shuttle crossed to *Desmond* to be gobbled by an opening hatch. "This is it," Constance muttered, unconsciously moving closer to Sol. A subtle reassurance came from the hip and shoulder that lightly bumped hers.

"Status?" Sol asked, slipping an arm around her shoulder. Connie couldn't find the will to pull away.

"Weapons ready and targeted, Captain," Bryana answered from the bridge. "All power is diverted to shields and the fire deck."

A streak of light shot from *Desmond*'s reactor as she accelerated off on a different vector. With their reduced V she moved away quickly.

"He's *not* going to fight!"

"Not yet anyway," Constance cautioned. "I tell you, Sol, Jordan's crazy. He makes his own reality and doesn't care about others. He's too hyped on this obsession of royal blood. He'll get someone killed in the end."

"Maybe himself," Sol added. "Come on, how about I treat you to some of that fine Star Mist your father gave me."

She studied him thoughtfully, tracing the lines of his face, a curious longing stirring as he stepped away. Carrasco turned and regarded her quizzically. The decision came easily. "Sounds delightful."

And what? Damn it, Connie, quit fooling around! With everything at stake, you can't afford any entanglements. This is dangerous enough without snarling it more. And what if he fails you? What if he turns out to be just another man?

Only she couldn't convince herself to make an excuse, bow out of the invitation on some pretext. *And I saw him that day in the blister, broken, shattered. Damn it! I can't afford this.*

"Well, it looks like we made it after all," Sol said easily as they walked back to his quarters. "No one jumped us; we lost the two bogeys; the Mainiacs found us and took Jordan off our hands. If we can only find the assassin, everything will be nicely wrapped up."

She looked up at him, knowing the lie of his secure gaze. *Sol, you don't have any idea about what we'll unleash. I hope you can still have that smug security a week from now.*

"I hope so. We've still got a long way to go to wrap this up, Sol—if it's ever finished." She smiled nervously.

"So grim? Don't worry, we'll figure it out. Must be quite a find. What is it, the longhand signature of God? Just promise me the Mormons aren't right!"

She chuckled despite herself. "No, they aren't." She stepped into his cabin and he poured, handing her the glass. Sol stood close, studying her intently over the rim of his glass. His expression softened, and it warmed her.

"You must have every man in your father's fleet in love with you."

"No," she whispered, fighting the longing within her. His presence eased the fear, lulling her. The memory of his arms around her made her ache with a honey sweetness inside. "Most men can't stand to compete with my status, my father, or me. They find out I won't bend. I won't become *their* woman. It's a lonely life."

"I . . . well, you've come to mean a lot to me. Loneliness is curable. You could change that part of your life."

She was irritated at the pounding of her heart, the sudden thrill inside. "Could I? Could you change yours? Seriously, I've been watching you. The old Solomon Carrasco is back. Somewhere, you've managed to bury *Gage*. You're back to being yourself . . . and you love it. Would you leave *Boaz* to settle on Star's Rest with me? No, I think it's in your blood to space. You're asking me to meet your terms."

He drew a breath and shrugged. "I suppose."

"Suppose, nothing." She grinned up at him. "If you retired again, you'd be dreaming space, remembering the stars, and kicking yourself for ever turning a ship like this over to anyone—even Petran Dart."

"And you? You don't like all the political intrigue, do you? Oh, you're good at it, Constance, but you don't really like it." He lifted her chin so she couldn't avoid his eyes. At his touch, she felt her soul tremble.

"No," she whispered, "I don't." She gave him a warm smile. The ache inside built, overwhelming her caution. The feel of his arm around her was like a comforting, cozy mantle.

How did she answer him? "*Boaz*, if you would display the galaxy on the Captain's screen, I would appreciate it." Instantly, the star field grew on the white background. "There, Sol. That's where I want to be. I'm not a politician."

"That's what always drew me," he agreed. The longing in his eyes touched her, melting the last of her resistance. Against her, his flesh felt firm, warm, awakening a forgotten need. Feeling her pulse race, she took a deep breath, knowing she followed an irreversible course. The warmth spread from her very core. The wistfulness of his expression was vulnerable and reassuring.

"Suppose you came with me, Sol? Suppose we spaced in *Bad Boy?* No Craft, no obligations to anyone?" How sweet that dream. How totally impossible.

A slight tightening of his expression pulled at his lips as he looked around, cataloging the monitors with their glowing stats. His hesitation, the reluctance in his expression worried her.

"Another woman?" she prompted, not knowing what to say next.

His laughter bubbled light and free as he met her questioning look. "I guess you're right. Her name is *Boaz.*"

"Thank you, Captain," the ship broke in. "If you will excuse my interruption, Constance, given my respect and regard for the Captain, I'll not compete with the rest of his head or heart and leave you both in privacy." The speaker went dead.

Sol jerked rigid, flushing as Constance stared. He cried, "She's not supposed to do that! Little witch!"

Constance felt a brief flicker of true humor. Their eyes met and then he bent down to find her lips. She melted against him, a muted voice protesting from the back of her mind.

When he pulled away, she could see that his feelings mirrored her own.

Short of breath, he whispered, "I think you're the most magnificent woman . . . anywhere."

She closed her eyes, her hold on him tightening. "I know better than to let this happen." She swallowed hard and saw the question in his eyes. "But I . . . Oh, damn, Sol, I don't know what to do." She traced fingers along his breast and shoulders, reveling in the sensations of his hard chest.

"Then maybe we'd better wait, take a little more—"

"No." She smiled up at him. "I think I passed the point of no return a little while ago." Gently, she drew his head down, lips tingling as they met his, hungry, yearning, as if her whole soul demanded him and his strength.

* * *

She woke in darkness, the air cool on her skin. Blinking, she relived the moments, the first intimate coupling, the rise to orgasm, and the secure weight of his body on hers after he spent himself. Afterward he'd held her, let her talk earnestly about herself and where she was going. And again they'd joined, gently, tenderly, moving together until that rapturous moment when her body throbbed to his pulsing release. Every nerve in her had exploded in waves of pleasure.

And he'd held her again, stroking her hair, a timidity in his touch, a reverence in his manner. She'd seen his soul then, known the truth of her father's words.

She reached over, tracing the lines of his face, fingers light upon his lips. She wound herself around him, hugging him tightly to her breast as he murmured in his sleep.

How different, how splendid, after Arpeggio, after the shredding of her virginity. *No, Connie, don't even think it. He was a violent animal—and you were young and naive. See? It can be gentle, without pain, without bruises and bites. Forget . . . forget those days—and the way he used you as receptacle for seed and plots: a handy tool of pleasure and politics. Yes, Connie, just forget it ever happened.*

Beside her, she could feel the warmth of Sol's body, the satin of his skin against hers. Caring and gentle, he'd loved her from the depths of his soul. The wondrous memories spun around her, feeding the radiant joy hovering over her heart.

"Oh, my God," she whispered softly. "What have I done?"

* * *

Sol stared at the cloud-wrapped ball of planet they were approaching. How Earthlike and delightful. The deep cerulean blue of ocean contrasted with duns and greens where geometrically shaped continents lay evenly spaced around the equator. Against the star-shot black of the heavens, two moons in close orbit glowed like half crescents, the terminators stark and absolute in the light of the primary.

Star's Rest, a jewel of a planet. And here it would all come to a climax. The place hardly looked like the culmination of mystery. Rather, it beckoned like an oasis in the vastness of space.

Here, Connie had invested her future. A haunting image of her eyes drifted through his mind, tickling a surge of excitement within. Images of their lovemaking stirred a lazy warmth, kindling a curious peace in his haunted soul. He closed his eyes to savor a collage of memories of her, retracing the curves of her body, the light smile of satisfaction on her lips as she held him, eyes blissfully closed. For those brief moments, the ever present reserve had lifted, leaving her free, contented. For that moment, he'd seen her radiant, glowing with life and pleasure.

And she touched me every bit as deeply. He shook his head and sighed, staring empty-eyed at the planet below. "So where are we going, Connie? What lies ahead of us?"

On the screen, *Desmond* remained a pinpoint, standing off to adopt a high GEO orbit. Long-range detectors had located other dots approaching Jordan's battleship. The fleet Jordan had bragged about? A fast frigate from the Terran Protection League also orbited Star's Best, supposedly there on a survey mission. Mass detectors indicated other ships dropping in, still two weeks away at the earliest. From the numbers, the entire Confederacy had ships spaced for Star's Rest.

"And we're in the middle of it."

Fleeing his disturbing thoughts, he reached up to stroke Connie's face in his mind, remembering the reserve that had come over her face like a veil as they'd parted that morning, the hesitant unease preoccupying her.

"Sol, about last night. I don't want what happened to make you think—"

"Shh." He'd placed a finger to his lips. "Let's see how things work out. Like you told me that day. We need time, the resolution of this problem. When it's all over, then we'll make the time to determine where we stand, where we go next, if anywhere."

"Sol, I . . ." And she smiled at him longingly. "Thank you."

And he'd winked as she hesitated at the hatch. "I understand."

She'd nodded briefly, before ducking out.

She'd seemed so vulnerable then, her burden heavy on her shoulders.

To the monitors, Sol asked, "Is this thing so terrible?" The bits of light on the screens marking incoming ships mocked him.

* * *

Nikita leaned back in his gravchair, pulling softly at his beard. On the monitor before him, lines of text slipped up from the bottom as he read, the unit's sensor following his eye movements, automatically advancing the text as he read.

The file finished to leave him staring blankly into space.

"So that is history of Brotherhood?" He knotted fingers in his thick twist of beard and grunted. "Is time to rethink policy."

He reached a cup into the dispenser, filling it with steaming black tea. One by one, he called up the files on the suspects who might have been assassins. Who? Which one might have fired the fatal projectile into Paul Ben Geller's body?

The problem gnawed at him, eating like an acid. "Me,

longest lived of all Gulagi politicians can't find assassin?'' He accessed comm, finding a security seal on the data he requested. Instead of information, Carrasco's face formed.

"Yes, Nikita?'' Carrasco asked. "Why would you want to see the image of Paul's murder?''

Nikita laughed. "Captain, I would like to see again.'' He frowned, lip pinched between his teeth. "Perhaps . . . perhaps I could see something? Is like burr under flesh. Me, greatest of sneaky Gulagis, should be able to see something. Who better to ferret out slimy assassin than man who sucked up knowledge of slimy assassination with mother's sour breast milk?''

Carrasco considered for a moment. "Not a tinge of guilt, is it?''

Nikita grunted and lifted his slablike shoulders. "Have plenty of guilt, Captain. Comes as cultural legacy of Gulag. At same time, assassin is threat to security. What if assassin slips off with sacred secret? Is to betterment of suffering masses? I think not.''

"You've been reading all the files on the Craft available to your clearance.''

Nikita nodded, taking a deep breath. "And I have learned great deal. Thank you for releasing them.'' He hesitated. "Is difficult thing for good Gulagi to admit, but perhaps we have been working to cross-purposes. Unless is just foul propaganda, perhaps we have been working to same end through different means?'' He raised his bushy eyebrows.

Carrasco nodded. "Perhaps.'' He paused. "Tell me, Nikita, why should I trust you?''

Nikita chuckled, raising his hands. "You have not missed much, Captain. Monitors in lounge? Readout when Nikita is questioned regarding murder? If ship didn't have technology beyond simple Gulagi's understanding, I would have already located spy devices in this room. Hope you enjoy fact that Nikita had bad case of gas last night, eh? Am only surprised you have not sent pills to help constipation . . . or is bowel still sacred from Brotherhood probing?''

Carrasco smiled despite himself. "We weren't aware of the problem. I'll have Wheeler dispense something."

"So I get access?"

Carrasco considered, tension in his face.

"Go ahead. Nikita has lived all his life under observation, does not mind to be watched more. And who knows, perhaps I can see something, eh?"

"Clearance granted."

Nikita added, "Have one other request. I would like Tayash to work with me. No, if I am assassin, I would have killed him long ago. Threatens to tell wives of . . . ah, indiscretions too often for comfort."

Carrasco struggled to hide another smile. "Very well, you can have him." Sol hesitated. "It may be a mistake on my part, but for some incalculable reason, I think I trust you, Nikita. You're falling down on the job as a subversive."

Nikita flinched. "Eh? Do not tell crafty constituents. Nikita has reputation to maintain."

"Your secret is safe." Carrasco's face flickered away.

Tayash arrived several minutes later, peering curiously at the scene depicted on Nikita's monitor.

"So you broke the pirate scare to get me here?"

Nikita grunted and gestured at the murder scene. "Is assassination security. This is moment when Paul was killed. Come, we only have a half day before we planet to deal with sacred secret. Is not much time to determine viper within our nest."

Yet no matter how they thought, figured, or conspired, the assassin's identity remained elusive.

Nikita continued to grouse, some key slipping just out of his grasp as he stared at the photo. Origue, Constance, Mary, himself, even Elvina with her insipid knitting looked so innocent.

He packed slowly, taking only the necessities as the shuttle prepared for disembarkation to the planet below.

The solution nagged at him. "What?" he asked himself over and over again. "What does Nikita miss?"

He walked down the gleaming white corridors, an antigrav following with his possessions.

In the spacious shuttle, he found a seat in the back, waving Tayash to join him.

"Have thought of anything?"

Niter sighed wearily, stroking his goatee. "No," he whispered in a low voice. "So it's a projectile. Maybe the shot was fired earlier? Later?"

The shuttle shifted, the monitors showing the gleaming sides of *Boaz* dropping away.

"Perhaps, but would have trusted Captain to cover that."

"So, let's rethink. A projectile needs a device to accelerate the projectile. Like a pistol, it's a handle, trigger, and tube."

Nikita started, everything coming clear. *"Oh, my God!"*

CHAPTER XXVI

The shuttle dropped rapidly toward the cloudy ball below. "That's the last of the ambassadors," Sol said gratefully. "Thank God! They're on their own now."

Connie wove her fingers between his, a serious look on her face. "It's hard to believe we're in the final steps."

"You're sure you did the right thing by not taking the shuttle down with your father?"

Connie shivered slightly and seemed to flush. She looked at him, eyes slightly unfocused. "Yes. He didn't need me. I wanted a chance to talk to you. About the other night, about . . . us, and what it all means. I can handle any . . . uh, business from here."

"Are you all right?"

She gave him a wicked smile. "If you'll remember, it was a rather long night last night. Then I got up early and dropped in on . . ." She frowned. "Mary Ben Geller. I saw Elvina, too . . . Teaching me how to knit." She blinked, "Huh, sleepy. Maybe I'd better go and take a nap.'' She shook her head, and looked up. ''You do that to all your women? Work them so hard they're sodden the next day?''

Something in the way she kept losing her concentration, in the frown as she fought to keep her eyes focused, triggered Sol's memory. Paul had been the same way just before . . .

''*Boaz!* Get me a med unit quick!'' Sol rapped as he clutched her to him. She was trying to protest as he swept her up, running toward the hospital. The med unit met him halfway and he followed it at a run, falling rapidly behind as the unit blared a warning and zigzagged through the corridors.

He slid to a stop, careening into the hospital. *Boaz* worked spindly metal arms, Connie under sedation. Sol stopped, chest heaving. Ensign Wheeler stared impatiently at the readout. Sol flinched at the sight of probes moving over and under Connie's skin.

''Diagnosis, *Boaz?*'' he asked, a cold fear creeping through his chest. He smashed a fist into the bulkhead, heart hammering as he watched this woman he had come to love hover between life and death. Images of Mbazi's dead smile spun from the depths of his mind, the cold breath of dark gutted corridors wheeling up out of his nightmares.

''Sitah root, Captain. The fungus is spreading. I am supplying oxygen to the brain with synthetic plasma. The fungal effect is thus arrested. I am formulating antidotes to counter the spread of the disease through her bone marrow.''

''Will . . . will she live?'' Sol demanded, fighting to keep his voice even, seeking to combat the fear in his gut, trying to think as he blinked back the sudden terror that crept, ghosting from his subconscious in tugging tendrils of cold.

Cerratanos' bloody fingers clawed futilely at the hull. Flashbacks flickered in his thoughts. He heard a scream, a frantic wailing as corridors decompressed and warm human bodies charred in searing plasma.

Other visions struggled for his attention: Other loved

ones dead. Other times of pain. Fear! Loss! Why had he
come back? Why had he allowed himself to love again?
Where would this end? A silent scream pierced his mind
and he clutched the bulkhead, battling to keep his control—wishing desperately to collapse into a fetal ball and
float forever in a soft internal existence he could confine
and control—where there was no pain or fear, or hurt, or
death.

Boaz's voice wound through his staggering mind. "Insufficient data, Captain. I have found the glass projectile
and am removing it." He sucked air into his lungs and
struggled with the concept that formed in the bottom of
his mind, clawing its way past the fear. His vision filled
with an image of Peg Andaki, the dark beauty of her face
streaked with tears as she clutched Maybry's decompressed body.

"Captain?" He looked through bleary eyes and saw
Wheeler, concern etching his face. Sol clenched his jaws
and gritted, "Flashbacks. *Gage* . . . I . . ." He shivered,
feeling the deck tremble under his feet.

"Captain?" Wheeler's voice lost itself in the rush of
decompression, as blue and red lights flashed through
rents in the hull.

"Gage!" he thundered, feeling the rage burn and give
him purpose as the fear whimpered back to the rear of
his brain.

"Captain, I have Nikita Malakova on—" the ship began.

"Knitting!" he moaned, shivering as his muscles
bunched and bulged. His fists gripped into balls of bone,
sinew and tendon. Blood pounded hotly in his veins while
adrenaline rushed to support and bless his anger.

"Nikita?" Sol wavered, staring at the monitor. "It's
Elvina, isn't it?"

Malakova's grim face formed. "Captain. Have determined culprit. Ngoro's 'creature' is Elvina. Weapon is
probably knitting needle."

Sol blinked, Malakova's features blurring with Cerratanos'. "Elvina. Tell Archon. Get . . . to Archon. Tell
him . . . Careful, Fil. Don't let . . . let . . ."

"Captain . . . you are sick? Captain . . ." Fil Cerratanos slipped into oblivion, his body twisting away into the winding stars. Reality lurched, shifting, sinking into a deep gray fog lit by flickering shades of red and blue.

* * *

Sol blinked, mouth like dry cotton. He stared up, seeing the reassuring white of his quarters.

"Captain? I have Speaker Archon on the line."

"Elvina," he whispered. "The knitting needles. Silly, foolish Elvina with her questions about shielding. I saw that cunning look in her eyes that night at dinner." He stared up.

"How's Connie?"

"We're waiting for details."

"Archon has to know immediately. Elvina must be—"

"He has been informed. During your flashback, Nikita came to the same conclusion."

Sol blinked and swung to his feet. "Open the channel to the Speaker."

Archon's face formed, glazed with anxiety. "Captain? I hear my daughter is hanging on?"

Sol accessed the medical records. "She's alive. It's too early to . . ." *Oh, my God, not Connie!* "Well, we've got to wait." *As always. Nothing changed.* Gage, *Mbazi, Andaki, Cerratanos, all so fragile, all so dead.*

"I had Elvina put under arrest," Archon was saying. "She killed four of the guards and disappeared. A few minutes later, a comm officer was killed. From the log, she used the transductor. I suspect she's somewhere in the bush around the spaceport. My people are instituting a search."

Sol rubbed his forehead and nodded. "I'll be right down, Speaker." He cut the connection, staring woodenly at the bulkhead.

"Captain, I've been reviewing your reactions. You suffered from a—"

"Flashback, damn it." He glared up at the speaker. "Yes, damn it, I know."

"I would like to employ a psych adjustment to—"

"I don't have time for that, *Boaz.*" He jumped to his feet, preparing a small kit.

"Captain, you might have to make time. Your behavior—"

He whirled, staring at the monitor. "Look! We've got bogeys coming in from all directions. Another five from the looks of things. You know damn good and well what psych does. Leaves the brain muzzy, slows reactions. Right now, I can't afford that."

"Can you rely on your reactions now?"

"*Boaz,* I—"

"I have the authority to relieve you of command."

Sol stopped. He nodded slowly. "Yes, you do. At the same time, I've got an authority and duty of my own. Now what are we going to do? Turn this whole mess over to Bryana? Arturian? In the meantime, you and I have the responsibility for this ship and crew—and most likely the people on that planet down there. You're not a digital machine spouting rote, *Boaz.* I heard you brag to Archon you had the power to finish this mission on your own. Considering your relative youth, I have my own reservations about—"

"You *cannot* judge me by human standards!"

"Nor can you judge my experience! So let's settle it at compromise. We're a team, *Boaz,* you and I . . . and the Blessed Architect alone knows what's at stake."

The ship hesitated for several seconds. "Do you seriously believe that? That responsibility is shared between us?"

Sol took a breath and sighed. "It's true, isn't it? You have that ability—to determine policy for yourself based on analog thought."

"I do." A pause. "You realize that humans will resist that. I have already been chafing under the onus of being a mechanical slave."

"Then, on top of everything else, you and I have to lay the groundwork for trust, for cooperation. Like it or not, we're at the forefront."

"Speaker Archon is waiting for you on the planet. I have a shuttle prepared at Lock Six."

Sol winked, swinging out the hatch. "Take care of things while I'm gone."

"Captain?" She hesitated again. "Thank you."

He grinned. "And, *Boaz*, thank you. Trust is a curious thing, it works both ways."

"Bryana!" he snapped as he trotted into the lock. His First Officer's face formed on comm. "You're in charge. Listen to the ship, trust her analysis of the situation. If anything happens and you can't get in touch with me, rely on Art's intuition and your skill and bounce it off *Boaz*. Use your brains, all of you. Something's about to break loose. Elvina is in contact with someone. We've got ships coming in from every direction—*Desmond* shouldn't be discounted either. Keep the ship on full alert and don't feel shy about asking Happy, Fujiki, or anyone else for advice." Sol bit his lip, fearing what he had to do. Was she ready for it? "Any questions?"

Bryana shook her head, black hair shimmering in the light. "No, sir." She smiled weakly. "Good luck, Captain. We'll take care of things, and if anything is picked up on detectors, we'll holler."

Star's Rest grew in the monitors, a small planet with a dense nickel-iron core which generated strong magnetic poles that kept two disparately sized moons orbiting—contrary to laws of planetology—in opposite directions over the planet. The axis being perpendicular to the ecliptic, the planet had no seasons. As Sol dropped, he immediately recognized the anomaly. Straightening in the command chair, he stared out at the planet, brow furrowed.

The shuttle touched lightly on a wide, well-lit concrete apron. According to planet time, it was just after midnight. Sol looked up to see the two moons, almost eclipsed. His expression hardened. It just couldn't be! "Captain?" Archon called from a ground car as Sol stepped to the ground. Sol picked up his kit and trotted over."

"Any news on my daughter?"

Sol spread his hands. "Fifty-fifty that she'll make it. She's in the best hands in the galaxy, Speaker. God will judge."

Archon seemed to slump. "You know, she's all I've got."

Sol placed a warm hand on the old man's shoulder. "It's out of our hands."

Archon took a breath and jerked an assenting nod. "Doesn't make it any easier." They accelerated across the tarmac.

"No, it doesn't," Sol agreed in a whisper.

He continued to gaze at the odd moons as the car hissed across the flats, leveling off perhaps ten feet above the tops of scrubby trees. Those moons peered down between the tufty clouds and, for the first time, Sol noted the black hole in the near moon. Like a small dark pupil, it stared at him. He felt his hackles rise.

"This system isn't normal, Speaker. I read the reports on Star's Rest. You didn't mention the fact that the moons orbited in opposite directions. You also didn't mention that this planet experiences two lunar alignments a day."

"That's right, Solomon. I also didn't mention that the alignment occurs over the same spot on the planet's surface twice a day."

Sol glanced up, an eerie feeling shivering down his spine. "You know that's impossible. Tidal forces would have changed that effect years ago. It can't happen—can't be stable."

They started up a long, steep slope of perhaps forty-five degrees. "That's also correct, Captain. Star's Rest is an anomaly which shouldn't exist—but does. Now you know what drew me here in the first place."

The breeze carried a musky odor which bore the special signature of Star's Rest. Sol looked up at that malignant eye and swallowed his nervousness. Only the brightest of stars shone through the strong moonlight, but it gave him the chance to form some opinions of the topography.

"This is the only real mountain on Star's Rest?"

"That's right."

"Volcanic?"

Archon looked over from the controls. "No, Captain. What we're climbing is a pyramid. What you see is a shaped asteroid which was set—that's right, I said *set*— on the planet's surface. That flat down there was once an inland sea. Through the centuries, it silted in, becoming the fertile plain you now observe. At the same time, tectonic action has accounted for some reformation, but on the whole, this is a very stable world."

Sol shook his head. "You've got to be kidding! Set here? Not even *Boaz* could settle a chunk of rock this size into a gravity well as deep as Star's Rest! Who could have done it?"

Archon waved negligently. "The aliens who built this planet."

Sol gaped. "You don't mean . . ."

"You're beginning to understand. Oh, to be sure, Connie and I searched every square inch of this world. I conducted rather thorough seismic investigations to probe this mountain. There's no bedrock underneath us. The bottom of the pyramid, so far as I can prove, is perfectly flat, perfectly square, and through antiquity, five hundred feet underground—that being the accumulation of silt from the surrounding flat land as the sea bottom aggraded."

"What of the culture? What archaeological remains have you found?" A fluttery sensation churned in his stomach. He glanced nervously up at the moon, wondering if that eye was watching him—reporting to some distant alien God.

"Nothing!" Archon grumbled sourly. "No cities, Solomon. No jewels, no ruins, only one artifact and one mummified body."

Like a chill breeze, he understood. "And we are to take them back to the Confederacy."

"Half-right. Your Grand Master Kraal already has the mummified corpse . . . and Brotherhood scientists are, no doubt, even now ecstatically dissecting it. You see, I took the alien to Kraal as proof of my wild-eyed claims."

The long climb over, they leveled out on the rounded,

eroded top of the pyramid. A small observatory rose over a hexagonal structure as Archon settled the ground car under an EM field shelter.

"Welcome to my house." Archon smiled wearily and gestured, as a dazed Solomon Carrasco climbed from the seat. "The view is spectacular. Wait until you see it in the morning. That is, if it isn't raining. We're so high up, the clouds often obscure the landscape."

Sol followed Archon into a lavishly appointed room, decorated with ship models, medals, awards, holos, and the accumulations of an active and varied life. A beautiful woman filled a holo box with her smile, brilliant red hair shining in the laser generated light.

"My wife," Archon said softly, humbled. An infinite sadness reflected in his expression.

"Her beauty lives in her daughter." He took the glass Archon handed him. He wasn't surprised to taste Star Mist. His belt comm beeped.

"Carrasco!"

Boaz announced, "Connie will live. I have stopped the degeneration and am in the process of reversing the fungal activity. I predict complete recovery, Captain. She should be fit within twenty-four hours at the longest."

Freed of an immense weight, Sol realized he was laughing with relief. He and Archon embraced vigorously.

"Bless you, *Boaz!*" Sol whispered.

Later, relaxing in a large antigrav across from Archon, he mused, "And the artifact is central to all this controversy."

"Indeed, Solomon." Archon stifled a yawn. "It took me a surprisingly long time to figure the key to the puzzle." Gray eyes gleamed. "It was right before my eyes all the time. I knew something was keeping this system artificially stable. Some energy, the source of which, incidentally, we've never found, keeps those moons in perfect orbit despite tidal forces." Archon frowned. "It's as if this system has two existences, one normal, the other beyond any comprehension we might have of physics.

"This system is set up like a beacon. From space, the

magnetic anomaly can be noted over a long distance. Closer, the orbits of the planets are immediately detectable as artificial. As you approach closer, the planet draws your eye. Finally, once here, every topographic feature leads you to this pyramid. Every ridge runs in this direction; every drainage points here. From the air, line after topographic line leads the eye to this pyramid.''

"But what did they do with their trash?" Sol shook his head. "This place would set the discipline of archaeology back thousands of years."

Archon laughed dryly. "You assume they were as wasteful as humans. No, I believe they were much more efficient—and you'll see why. When they pulled out, they left only the large features without the small rubble."

"And impossible moons!" Sol grimaced, unable to shake the feel of that odd moon. "Like a big eye circling in the sky."

"That black spot in the eye—as you so aptly put it—is a tunnel which goes clear through the moon just like a hole in a bead. It's filled with a little detritus now, but I'll show you something tomorrow since we were too late tonight."

"Then where is this dreaded artifact? Here in the house?" Sol looked around curiously.

Archon shook his head. "No, Sol, I'll not tell you where it is quite yet. Not until the last minute, when we're prepared to pick it up, will I trust you with that knowledge. Things have run much too smoothly as it is. I suppose all the false trails, the tricks—like the ice mining equipment—the lies, and circles within circles have held the pack off and confused them."

"And we came in one ship instead of a fleet also for the purpose of deception, correct?" Sol pursed his lips, feeling exhaustion running through his body and his head beginning to ache.

"Of course," Archon clamped a hand over his mouth as he yawned. "A Brotherhood fleet would have brought yet a bigger response on our heels and lent credence to the rumors. One ship, on the other hand, couldn't be taken as a serious threat by the doubters. Instead, it seems that the Brotherhood is only being cautious—not seriously heeding the claims carried by the rumors. So long as *Boaz* has the strategic advantage, perhaps we—the diplomats included—can decide what to do with the artifact; establish how to regulate who controls it.''

Archon saw Sol's disbelieving smile.

"Solomon, with this artifact, a man could easily control the galaxy—and possibly the entire universe.''

"Impossible!'' Sol couldn't help recalling his discussion with Malakova and Jordan. "Space is too big—too immense for any one power! To do so would imply ultimate knowledge and power!'' Sol added wryly, "Have you found the hand of God, Speaker?''

Archon's eyes were haunted. "No, not God, Solomon. Perhaps I have found the sword of Satan.''

* * *

The man stepped out into the deserted corridor, a grip in his hand. Carefully, padded feet making no sound, he moved swiftly, keeping to the quiet ways.

He stopped before the hatch, placing a palm on the security lock. The heavy portal slid sideways with a soft hiss. Around him, the ship hummed softly as air moved through the spotless grilles of the ventilation system.

Catlike, he crossed to the comm, headset glowing as the system came to life. One by one, security codes flashed across the screen and nullified.

He turned, walking carefully to the lock that hissed open at his approach. Inside, he palmed the lock to close it behind him.

The shuttle lit up as the sensors registered his movement. From the grip, strong hands pulled a neat black uniform. Quickly, he peeled off his white body suit. The whites, he tucked and folded, dropping the neat package into the converter shoot. The black fabric stretched over his firm muscles. Only when he'd finished, did he strap an equipment belt about his narrow waist. The blaster gleamed dully, matching the sword and starburst insignia on his shoulder.

Thus clad, he swung into the bridge, the headset glowing again.

Grapples clanked as the shuttle powered up, monitors springing to life. Falling free, the shuttle shot hot white reaction against the blackness of space, dropping toward the planet below.

On the bridge, sudden hailing calls flickered the comm lights. With a black-gloved finger, he canceled access, then took manual control of the sophisticated systems of the shuttle. A soft chuckle crossed his lips as he imagined consternation on the white ship's bridge. On their monitors, he would have just vanished.

The planet rose before him as he spiraled down. The faint beep of a beacon lit the detectors. Out over the veld, the shuttle trembled as he settled and rocked back on the throttles. Scanners picked up the hot radiation of a human body as sensors honed in on the heterodyne of the beacon.

Skilled hands guided the shuttle down, settling on crackling vegetation. Systems static, he stabilized the power, trotting back to balance and open the lock. He stepped down, sniffing the night breeze, catching the odors of the planet.

Gravel crunched underfoot in the darkness behind him.

"Who are you?" a woman's voice called warily.

"House Alhar at your service. If you'd hurry, please? We don't have long before dawn. Currently, the Admiral is closing with the fleet. Your aircar is too close for comfort. They'll spot it immediately."

She appeared from behind one of the scrubby trees, a wicked-looking blaster in one small hand. "Then I suggest you turn around and step back inside. Remember, I'm behind you, and I do not have a reputation for innocence or restraint."

"Your reputation is most impressive, Miss Sellers," he agreed, climbing quickly into the shuttle. Only crushed vegetation remained as the craft rose into the night sky.

* * *

The beeping of his belt comm pulled Sol awake in the bright morning light. "Carrasco, here," he rasped, pulling himself up in the antigrav chair.

"Captain," Art's voice sounded tense. "I've got some bad news. First, there are five Arpeggian cruisers entering the Star's Rest system from sunward. They've sent greetings and request port rights."

"It's not our business to stop them, Art," Sol experienced a tightness in his chest. He closed his eyes, trying to wish the Arpeggians away only to feel the cramp of headache coming on full force.

"They offered ship's call, Captain."

"Tell them we do not receive ship's call while the senior officer is dirtside. That should hold them. Art, under no circumstances is an Arpeggian to set foot on *Boaz!* That's a direct order."

"The protocol requires that we—"

"*Damn the protocol!* I will not have an Arpeggian on *my* ship!"

"Yes, sir." Art hesitated. "Uh, Captain, the other thing is that one of the shuttles is missing!"

"Did I hear you right? Did you say one of the shuttles is missing?"

"Uh, yes, sir. Stolen, we think," Art sounded miserable.

"*Stolen?*" Sol roared, coming to his feet. "You mean to tell me that someone just walked on board a Brotherhood shuttle . . . in a Brotherhood ship . . . and opened the lock and flew it away? Is this a joke, First Officer?"

"Yes, sir . . . uh, I mean . . . *no, sir!*" Art rapped out, "Hell, I don't *know,* sir. Bryana is ripping her hair out over it!"

"Who do you think stole it?" Sol demanded pacing nervously.

"Second Engineer Kralacheck, sir. At least he's the only one missing."

Sol stopped. Kralacheck? He'd have the know-how.

Happy had said more than once that Kralacheck could have run the ship just about single-handedly. Sol's voice dropped a couple of decibels. "And sensors don't pick it up anywhere? *Boaz* doesn't have a record of the departure?"

"Just a second, sir." Art sounded cowed. "No, sir."

"Then I suggest you use the sensors to *find that damned shuttle. First Officer!* Brotherhood shuttles have tracking devices. Sensors were put in ships to track those devices. First Officers were put in ships to read the sensors so they would know where the shuttle is. Very basic, Art. Now, will you go about *finding OUR SHUTTLE?*" Sol started to steam.

"We've *tried!*" Art cried passionately. "We're doing everything in the damn book and some things the book never heard of to locate that shuttle, Captain!"

"Hey, Cap!" Happy's voice boomed.

"What's going on up there?" Sol demanded.

"Leave the kid alone! He's bending backward trying to find that cussed shuttle. Listen, Kralacheck got near a sensor the other day and the needle went clear off the meter. He might be one of ours. You know they wear that special widget in their arm. Or else Kralacheck compromised our security. Outside of Petran Dart and myself, he knew more about *Boaz* than anyone alive. He could get in or out of this ship with no one the wiser and cloak a shuttle to boot!"

"Compromised our . . ." Sol stared painfully at the room around him. *Like two Patrol officers on the Arcturian docks. If Arpeggio had a mole within the Craft, now would be the time to use him.*

"Boaz?" Sol accessed.

"Here, Captain."

"What security violations did we have? I mean can't you—"

"Complete clearance, Captain. I had highest authorization to release the shuttle."

Sol fought the pounding of his panicked heart. "Happy, get together with *Boaz*, recode to her control."

"What? Cap, are you serious? You can't just turn all security over to the ship!"

"Why in hell not?"

"Regulations—"

"Damn it, Happy, don't you go regulation crazy on me! Look, suppose we've been compromised by House Alhar? Now we've got an Arpeggian fleet closing. Want them to slip over, countermand our security and wander in with a bunch of armed goons? *Boaz* isn't going to become another *Enesco,* not while I'm alive and breathing! And don't tell me Kralacheck couldn't have infiltrated, he could have been a deep agent for years! What you do know about him? Hmm? Ever hear of him before you spaced for Arcturus? No? Then turn all security over to *Boaz.*"

"For God's sake, Cap! She's experimental! Why?"

"Trust, Happy. Besides, have I ever let you down before? On *Moriah?* Maybe in *Sword* off Arpeggio? Did I fail you on Tygee?"

"I'm writing the software now."

"Thanks, Happy. Art? You monitored all that?"

"Yes, sir."

"Well, do me a favor. Don't initiate proceedings against me until we know whether we're going to live through this."

"Proceedings against . . . No, sir!" A pause. "Uh, Captain? If Kralacheck was working for the Arpeggians? Well, we're in real deep trouble, aren't we? I mean he could have sabotaged anything in the ship. Some sort of delayed—"

"You've got the picture. And God alone knows what he could have done to *Boaz* in the process."

"Scary thought. Listen, Captain, whatever you need, I'm behind you. Just thought you might want to know."

"Thanks, Art. Get cracking on that shuttle and check the ship—stem to stern. Keep in touch. *Boaz?* How's Connie?

"Fine." *Boaz* broke in on the circuit. "I fed her a good breakfast this morning. Considering the strides I made in medicine yesterday, she should be fit for duty within an hour or so."

"Put your heads together up there in the meantime. Let me know what happens." Sol flipped the comm off and lost himself in thought until the strong aroma of coffee caught his nose and led him through hallways to a large dining room.

And if Kralacheck had been in cahoots the whole time? Had he purged the record of Elvina's flaws? Had they been scheming the entire time? He took a deep breath. *And how will it feel to set foot on my ship—and know it could be a time bomb?*

"You're up early," Sol greeted, seeing a cup appear magically in a dispenser. Archon hunched over a table, eyes running nervously down figures on a comm screen. His posture looked knotted, bunched and tense.

"I might say the same for you. We've got trouble, Sol. Arpeggians are coming asking for port rights." Archon's expression went flat. "They . . . killed my wife. I can't refuse—not as a registered Confederate port." He rubbed a hand over his face. "I would have never . . . I mean, who'd think they'd have the *damned audacity!*" His fingers clenched and unclenched, tendons standing from the backs of age-freckled hands. *"They KILLED my wife! Put a blaster to her head and BLEW HER BRAINS OUT!"*

"You have the right to deny them." Sol sipped the coffee and felt his taste buds jolt. Wonderful stuff!

"And what? Precipitate war? No, I can't afford that . . . yet." Archon pushed a button. "Ezra? The Arpeggians are granted port rights. When they arrive, we want nothing they have to sell. Anything they want to buy, they get at one hundred percent markup and fifty percent duties. That is applicable to Arpeggian craft only." Archon's face twisted as he listened. "Huh?" He nodded, voice heavy. "Yes, I remember, too, Ezra."

He turned. "Looks like we're going to have to hurry, Sol. Connie's about to be released. We can't find Elvina, but she's got to be tied to the Arpeggians somehow. My ships have covered every square inch of this planet. She doesn't show on IR or visual. She must have literally gone underground. That had to be her signal to them we picked up yesterday."

"Good coffee!" Sol lifted the cup, trying to draw Archon away from his worry. Obsessed with his own. *Yeah*, he told himself, *Elvina has disappeared and so has one of my shuttles! Coincidence? Hardly! So we've had an Arpeggian agent aboard since the beginning. The entire Craft may be compromised. If so, Arpeggio has access to . . . everything!* The pain in the back of his head arced sharply.

"Chicory coffee, Solomon. That's genuine Terran stuff from a place called Luzianna. I get it from a smuggler by the name of Crazy Geno. It'll cost you two arms. And check your pockets after you deal with him—but I got some beans and chicory seeds. We're going to see if it won't grow into our first major export crop."

"I'll look him up," Sol promised, savoring the coffee. He *had* to get that for his ship—assuming he and his ship had a future.

Archon bent over his comm. "There've been too many ships here, Solomon. Look at this registry over the last three weeks. Sirius, New Maine, Terra, Lenin Sector . . . and the list goes on. I've ordered Mason, my third in command to high orbit. I'm keeping four of my six ships as a reserve cadre up there. They're the ones that tapped Elvina's signal. The Arpeggians immediately showed up from behind the sun. I don't think they spotted Mason since my people were dead in space at the time. It's an ace you shouldn't forget."

"What did Joseph Young have to say about Elvina?"

"He claims he married her at the request of the church. She was young, sexy, and she wanted to go to Arcturus with him. Then, when this broke, he was the logical one to go. The question is, how deeply are the Mormons tied to Arpeggio and how did they get Joseph's number so quickly?"

"He's their only deep space ambassador," Sol answered. "I'd bet the Arpeggians agreed to let Mormon missionaries in in return for the favor." And Elvina tried so hard to seduce me. She could have dumped Joseph and attached herself to me. Sol ground his teeth. It would have been her way to get to the *artifact!*

"So Palmiere had to have leaked like the proverbial dam!" Archon pulled at his beard. "We swept that office with the best detection devices your people produce. There *were* no bugs! We were so careful! Palmiere had to have babbled the whole thing to have triggered this kind of advanced interest in Star's Rest. There's no other answer."

"And now the Arpeggians are here," Sol shook his head. "Remember, they almost killed us both last time."

"I could use the . . ." Archon's eyes gleamed suddenly. His expression betrayed exhausted indecision, opportunity restrained by some deep-seated terror. He started to speak. Bit his lip and wearily shook his head sadly, painfully. "No," he whispered, closing his eyes. "I refuse to be God!" He looked up, eyes hollow. "Come," he whispered, cowed. "There is something I would like you to see."

The gravity shaft raised them to the observatory, a small room with a powerful telescope. Archon settled himself, indicating the screen. "Watch, it's five minutes to noon."

Unlike the old optic telescopes, Archon's provided a clear image through the daytime atmosphere. Sol could see the brilliant disk of the sun as the moons aligned. There, for a brief instant, a pinpoint of light appeared through the near moon before being obscured by the far one. The same faint flicker of light occurred as they passed.

"Incredible!"

Archon smiled, looking up from comm. "Indeed it is," Archon agreed. "Let us breakfast. Then let us make haste. The Arpeggians are here and I don't trust them. The sooner we move, the sooner we can be away from here and free. New Maine also has arrived in force—five ships now, including *Desmond.*"

CHAPTER XXVII

Sol stepped from the ground car and enjoyed the warm moist air that a real wind batted at his face. The sun set, sending brilliant shifts of light like bars over the dark purple shadow of the pyramid. Against the clouds, the sunset burned a spectacular blaze of orange, red, and yellow as Star's rays played a silent symphony of splendor.

His shuttle stood waiting as Sol turned, trying to drag his eyes from this wonderful sight he had so seldom seen. To his right rested five LCs, the sunburst and sword of Arpeggio marking their sides. Black-clad guards patrolled a perimeter around the landing craft, their haughty swagger almost goading.

Sol turned to go, nerves stringing tightly at the sight of the Arpeggians. Too much hydrogen burned for him to . . . A tall man walked toward him. The dying light reflected in the black chrome of lustrous body armor. A spacer's belt hung around a trim waist, pouches full of comm equipment. A polished blaster handle lay ready to grip on his right side. Where they rested on shoulder boards, the emblems of Arpeggio glittered brightly in the rays of the dying sun.

"Beautiful, is it not?" the Arpeggian asked, fastening eyes pale as frozen ammonia on Sol. Coldly handsome, the man smiled, the gesture mechanical and without warmth.

"Extraordinary," Sol asserted, struggling to remain civil. *I've seen his image somewhere. I know this man.* Then he saw something missed on first glance. Groaker wings! This wasn't just any Arpeggian. A chill, like the frigid emptiness of interstellar vacuum played through Sol's very soul. *Damn it! Sabot Sellers himself!* Sellers had taken the symbol from the nasty predator of the Arpeggian skies. A mammallike creature that ruled the air mercilessly, the groaker had a reputation for its nasty habits—like Sellers himself!

"You must be Solomon Carrasco, Captain of *Boaz*."

Wary, half-crouched in a combat stance, Sol studied him more closely. The thick black hair had begun to whiten along the temples. The whole was drawn tightly into a coil and the shining black braid was interlaced with gold, silver, and platinum threads. Jewels had been woven into the full beard, parted in the middle and twisted to two points on either side below the chin. His brow rose high over those frozen eyes. The nose jutted long and straight, and was of the type once called patrician. Only that icy stare betrayed the cold grace of the man.

"You didn't need to ask, Admiral." Sol inclined his head in the barest minimum of manners.

"Perhaps not, but then, we've never met in person. Admiral Sabot Sellers, Imperial Arpeggian fleet. Your obedient servant, Captain." Sellers bowed deeply, the jewels glittering in the ruby light of the setting sun.

Sol smiled wryly and said, "So Arpeggio sends her best, Admiral." Sabot! The Hound! The planet burner! With his ship, *Hunter,* the Arpeggian had built a reputation of ruthlessness. Sellers had once held a planet ransom and, when his price wasn't met, burned it to molten bedrock.

"I thank you for the compliment," Sellers smiled in return, gleaming white teeth flashing behind the coal black of his beard. "I hear you have had a most interesting trip, Captain."

Sol spread his hands and shrugged. "One star jump is much the same as another; build up to C, apply the shields, drop back inside, and slow down." What could Sellers know . . . *Elvina!*

"And isn't the lovely Constance more than enough to amuse any man, Captain? She and I are old friends. I hear she's aboard *Boaz*. Please inform her I will call to pay my respects. Her brother and I were quite close, you see . . . and Constance and I were . . . How do I put this delicately? Betrothed?" Eyes like ice pinned Sol, waiting for a reaction. *Connie and Sellers? He was the one? This terrorist fiend?*

Sellers continued, failing to evoke the response he sought from Sol. "There was a terrible misunderstanding while her father was working for me several years ago. Tell the young lady that I have attended to the matter personally . . . and owe her an explanation of the terrible tragedy."

"I'll bear your message, Admiral. I'm not certain, however, of the reception you'll receive." Sol had a sudden thought. "Share my hospitality, Admiral." He reached into his space pouch and pulled out the little tin of tobacco all spacers carried. Sol took a three-fingered dip and extended the can, knowing Sellers—to save face—would need to at least equal the gesture.

Sellers granted him a plastic smile and took a dip, carefully placing it in his mouth as his eyes tightened.

"Boaz is a most beautiful creation. The Brotherhood has the greatest success at combining form with function." Sellers attempted to continue, face stiff despite his desire to appear at ease. "Consider my ship, *Hunter,* at your service. I'll look forward to having you aboard for ship's call." He bowed again. *Could it be? Was there a sheen of perspiration on his brow?*

Sol bit off laughter. *Sellers couldn't take his tobacco! Round one to Carrasco!* "I'll be most happy to enjoy your hospitality, Admiral. You must understand, if I don't respond immediately that it's ship's business and new trade agreements with Star's Rest which keep me. Command often necessitates restrictions of pleasure. One of the burdens of our profession, don't you agree?"

Sellers looked unhappy; his throat moved spasmodically. "Indeed, I'm glad you take your duty so seriously. I've always admired Brotherhood captains for their dedication. And your rapid response to crisis. Remarkable."

And you'd like it better if we were the hell out of space! Sol added to himself. *We're all that stand in your way and keep you from raiding anywhere you please. Unless Kralacheck broke even that advantage to your Great Houses.*

"Indeed, I thank you," Sol ignored the almost requisite return invitation. *"Hunter* is a long way from home. I've heard a great deal about her. You yourself have a certain following who take great pride in keeping track of your escapades." *And the best minds in the Brotherhood have wished they could slip something deadly in your drink!* "I also hope to see your splendid ship, Admiral. Please expect my call within the week. Since we're here for some time, there should be more than enough time to enjoy each other's company. How long are you here for?"

His smile remained oily—polite although his skin had taken on a green tinge. "That depends on the Speaker." He fought for control, sweat beginning to bead on his brow. "It pains me to break off our delightful discussion, but I must check on the status of certain delicate negotiations. If you will excuse me?"

"Oh, don't feel you must rush off!"

"Duty, Captain, as you so accurately assessed, limits certain of our pleasures." Despite the trembling of his lips, Sellers paused long enough to add. "But *Hunter* and her crew are glad to hear of your miraculous survival and return to space, Captain. We'd all have been poorer had you died off Tygee." Sol started, cold anger in his gut, a hot response on his lips—but the Admiral had already turned, striding for the nearest building. Sellers almost broke into a stumbling run, and as soon as he thought he was out of sight, spit, then vomited vigorously.

Sol flipped himself into the shuttle and gave Misha Gaitano a worried shake of the head. Tygee? What did Sellers know of Tygee? Just rumor? And *he'd* been Connie's lover on Arpeggio?

"Who was that Charlie, Cap?" Misha asked, clearing for takeoff.

"Sabot Sellers, Misha. Had he been off Arpeggio that day, we wouldn't be sitting here now." Sol winced as he stretched his neck muscles. The headache began to lance knives again. "Worse, I'm willing to bet he's still fuming at having missed the most dramatic fight ever to take place in the skies over his planet. It must have hurt his dignity and reputation.''

Misha nodded. ''And he has a chance now for a re-match.''

''Maybe. You know, it's up to us to avoid it. Outfox him so we're not pushed into a position where all we can do is fight.''

''But you think he's spoiling for a dustup?''

''Yeah, I think so, Misha.''

Misha shook his head. ''Up, Cap, I'm sure sorry, but I'm having a bad bout with my kidneys that particular day. You know how these things are. I like to have some notice before my bladder goes weak.''

Sol chuckled at Misha's pathetic expression. ''Me, too.'' Then he sobered. ''Only I don't think we'll get it.''

CHAPTER XXVIII

Sol rapped out commands, tension lining his face. ''Dig up everything you can find on the Arpeggian Admiral, Sabot Sellers. He's killed a couple of Brotherhood ships in his life . . .''

Connie wavered, catching herself as her insides wrenched. *Oh, God, not Sabot . . . not here.* She braced herself, aware of the lingering weakness, the trembling in her muscles, shadows of Elvina's poison.

''From that information, have *Boaz* run simulation after simulation. I want you to be able to fight him in the dark, with no eyes, and both hands tied behind your backs.'' Sol searched their faces, as if raking their very souls.

Sabot! How could I face him? Look him in the eye, knowing the sort of vile slime he is? Guts, girl. You'd do it because you had to. Dearest God, keep him away from me.

"Next," Sol continued firmly, "Archon has sent everything he has on this system up by directional beam. *Boaz* has been processing the information. While one eye is on the combat drills, you need to be learning everything you can about Star's Rest. The moons—as you no doubt have figured—are artificially maintained. That's part of the big secret. We're here to pick up an alien artifact that *may* unhinge Confederate power blocs. As a result, the stakes are, indeed, higher than we had originally suspected. With the arrival of the Arpeggians and the Mainiacs, things came to a boil a lot quicker than we anticipated." Sol met his officers' stares.

"Yes, people, it's really for keeps."

Connie bit her lip, knees locked, back braced against the bridge hatch. *Why does it have to happen now? Sabot? You despicable worm, figures you'd be here now. All I want to do is sleep. Can't I save the universe tomorrow?* But then she'd been the one who'd pushed, demanding *Boaz* release her early—even if she wasn't one-hundred percent. *And now I have to face it. Now the blinders come off. Yes, Sol, this is really for keeps—more than you could know.* She ran fingers over the powerful Model 57 Arcturian blaster she'd belted on her hip.

On the screen, Happy grinned wryly, chewing his thumb. Cal looked sober, confident, muscular arms crossed over his deep chest.

"I'm sorry," Sol told them, voice soft. "I don't think anyone anticipated we'd be compromised so soon. I should have been running you on drills and showing you combat tapes from the moment we left Arcturus."

Art took a deep breath as he shot a quick look at Bryana. "Maybe we should have been the ones to think to ask for them, Captain."

Sol turned to Connie. "Anything to add?"

She crossed her arms and leaned back, looking up at the screen where Misha Gaitano watched. She tried to sound firm, in command. "The artifact is egg-shaped. We don't know how it moves or what makes it function. When we attempt to retrieve it, you'll have to winch it aboard *Boaz*. Surprisingly, it doesn't weigh much. The

length is less than thirty meters with a diameter of ten.
Tractors, fields, antigrav, nothing seems to affect it—the
hull seems completely inert.''

Misha nodded. ''We'll handle it, Constance.''

Sol's face worked. ''I'm sorry to run off like this.
Speaker Archon wants me to check this thing out before
we move to retrieve it. You're on your own again. Just
use your heads. Don't go off half-cocked.''

Art smiled. ''We'll be fine, sir. After all, we've got
Happy to give us advice.''

Sol chuckled. ''I'm not sure I'd brag about that. The
story is he spaced in the first place because he was run
off by a jealous husband.'' Sol looked at the engineer.
''You've never been back to Mars either, have you?''

''Nope, but you'd have run, too. Should have seen the
size of that guy! And accurate with an EM gun? Wasn't
worth it for a woman that ugly. Even the fungus growing
on her lips wore a blindfold!''

''Last orders, people.'' Sol looked into each face. ''No
Arpeggian sets foot on this ship! If Sellers calls up for a
little chat, be polite but tell him any questions must be
deferred to the senior officer, who is dirtside and unavailable for the moment. Tell him I'll give him a call as soon
as I'm back aboard. End conversation!'' Sol smiled.
''Any questions? None? Then good luck, people.''

He turned and left the bridge. Connie walked beside
him, lost in thought. *What if Sol fails? What if he's just
another Sellers under a nicer veneer?* She throttled the
urge to shiver. *Could I have fooled myself twice? And if
he fails? Will I have the strength to pull the trigger?*

''I guess this is it,'' Sol offered. ''I'll finally get to see
the artifact, the Satan Sword, as Archon calls it.''

She looked at him with a forced smile. ''If you had
any sense, Sol, you'd wish otherwise.'' She hesitated.
''This thing poisons souls.''

Her eyes met his and locked, measuring again, as if
searching for some hint of what? Weakness? Some flaw
in his character? Memories of his gentle hands on her
body interlaced with a vision of the alien, dead, waiting.
Two mutually exclusive realities—meshed.

Boaz announced, "Archon has arrived at the shuttle bay." Sol gave Connie a reassuring smile and squeezed her hand. "It'll all work out, Constance. Trust me."

"You have no idea, Sol. I *am* trusting you." *And I may pay for that.*

Though he thought her words odd, he didn't pause to question her as they walked out into the shuttle bay. Misha worked the controls through his headset, settling the Speaker's shuttle on the deck grapples. Happy met them halfway across the floor.

"Here, swallow this." He offered a vial containing a little gray pill.

"What is it?" Sol asked, looking nervously at his engineer.

"Locator. Don't give me no grief, Cap. Take your medicine. If worse comes to worst, we can find you." He turned to Connie, handing her a pill, giving her a quick hug. "You come back to us, pretty lady."

Together they walked toward the shuttle. The hatch hissed open to expose Archon, wearing spacer whites. With a sigh, Connie swallowed the transmitter. It went down like a knotted sock.

Sol strapped in, watching her curiously. She stared at the white paneling before her, withdrawn. Sellers waited out there somewhere. The thought made her skin crawl. She closed her eyes, gripping her hands into fists.

Archon called down. "Ready?"

"Let's get it over with."

Grapples banged. A slight sway of acceleration escaped the grav plates. Constance turned away, occupied with her thoughts.

"Want to talk about it?" Sol asked.

"No, I . . . You never answered my question about Godhood. I suppose, now, we'll see."

He smiled grimly. "You know, I'm not sure there's an answer. In this age, right, wrong, good, bad, all are muddled. I guess I can't see all the angles, the thorns among the flowers, if you will."

She tried to smile, the effort a bust. "No absolutes? The perfect situational ethicist?"

He chuckled dryly. "I rest my case. No matter what my motives, pure as ammonia snow, how can I say what ramifications will be? Suppose I wave my magic wand of power and blow *Hunter* out of orbit? Perhaps the second mate's great-great-grandson would have found a way to harness atomic memory, or some such thing? What I always end up with is that granted Godhood, I remake the universe as flawed as it is today."

She nodded, thinking: *And that's nice and neat, Sol, but what about the reality? What about the power at your fingertips? What happens when you work the lever? Overcome the resistance of that spring?* Unconsciously, she wiped her right hand on the fabric covering her thigh, the very feel of the green-brown knob clinging to her fingers.

Sol leaned back and took a deep breath, staring at the blank monitors around him. His comm told him only minutes remained until midnight. Crossing his arms, he settled his head into the acceleration padding and closed his eyes.

"Why haven't we seen other remains around the galaxy, Speaker?" Sol wondered.

"It's a big galaxy." Connie shrugged, distracted by the image of Sellers' frigid eyes mocking her. "We can only speculate of course, though the answer may lie somewhere in the artifact's banks. It's my opinion that the aliens were a warlike species—something like ours, only much more advanced. That's why we've got to be so very careful with this. What if the artifact falls into the wrong hands, say, Sellers'?"

Sol found the concept frightening.

"But that alien war must have been like nothing we can imagine. I think they turned themselves into gods in the classical ancient Earth sense. Vain, petty, drugged on the power they wielded. When they grew angry—even over some perceived slight—they sought to destroy each other until only one was left. His final days must have been miserable . . . the last of his kind. So tell me, is humanity any stronger, any better adapted to the wielding of power? Is that what we've seen in the lounge aboard *Boaz?*''

Sol's expression reflected confusion. ''But how would you track down all of mankind? Even today, we don't know half the locations of the independent stations. Humanity is spread so far and wide.''

''Like your conversation with Jordan that night,'' Constance told him neutrally. ''The problem lies with the artifact—the alien ship. No doubt the aliens had the same tactical problems. They found a way to circumvent that. We have only a limited comprehension of how the ship works. I would imagine that the more advanced functions go considerably beyond what we have learned—and what we have learned is sobering enough.''

''Pretty powerful, huh?'' Sol asked, ill at ease with her behavior.

''You will now see, Captain.'' Archon's soft voice drifted down from above.

Metal clanged dully against metal. Archon came sliding down from the bridge.

''How do you know we won't be followed?'' Sol wondered as he got to his feet. ''I imagine every sensor in space saw us leave *Boaz.*''

Archon walked to the hatch. ''Your Master Kraal provided us with a device. It masks the shuttle's signal to sensors. It was off when I entered *Boaz.* It was on when we left. Happy confirmed that we left no signal as we departed. I don't know how it works—but it keeps us hidden. Another little gizmo will show this shuttle landing at my residence on the planet's surface in a few hours. Crafty little tricks . . . and absolute necessity with Arpeggians on my planet.''

Archon checked the gauges before undogging the hatch. He swung it open and beckoned. ''This is it, Sol. Now, you'll see what so many have died for.''

Sol nerved himself and walked stiff-backed into a regulation air lock. A grayish compartment lay ahead. He stepped down into a large open room devoid of any ornamentation. Featureless gray met his eyes. Connie stepped down beside him, sniffing the musty air. The place didn't really have an odor, just an ominous heaviness that ate at the nerves.

"This way." Archon walked past him, *and right through a solid gray wall!*

Sol stopped. He reached out tentative fingers and gasped as they sank through the opaque gray. He drew his fingers back and stared numbly at the flesh.

"Your eyes didn't deceive you," Connie reassured him nervously. "Go ahead . . . just step through."

Sol nodded absently and put one foot forward before he shuddered and pulled his body through what seemed to be metal, surprised to feel no sensation as he stepped into another room.

"According to quantum mechanics, matter is mostly space. What we deal with in the 'real' world is basically an electron cloud or net. That provides us the illusion of solidity. I've checked that bulkhead. It's a sheet of some metal alloy woven from molecular strings. While it's structurally sound, it doesn't impede motion. Here, quantum mechanics are quite different. I cannot explain the reason why."

"How did you find that?" Sol gasped as Constance ghosted through behind him. Archon's face dropped. He muttered, "I leaned against it while drinking a cup of coffee. It was not exactly auspicious since I tumbled at the feet of the alien's body. I'm heartily glad he'd been dead for several billion years. It would have been a most undignified first contact."

Sol stopped and gaped. Archon pointed to a round metal shaft rising from the floor.

"He was sitting on this. Apparently his command chair. After I touched his body, it never worked again. Evidently the orders he gave the ship were canceled by my action."

"But the power? How . . ."

"Who knows? There are many mysteries here, Sol. For example, the discovery we made that you can walk for miles inside this ship—yes, I said *miles*—passing from compartment to compartment, yet the craft is only thirty meters long on the outside. Something happens to space in here. Please, don't ask me what. I'm like a primitive waving a stone-tipped spear who's been plucked up and taken on his first star jump—only it's a quantum leap beyond even that.''

A holo tank filled the bulkhead beyond the control shaft. It measured two meters by two, and awkward looking knobs lined the sides of the unit, handles off-color and strangely shaped. The effect could be compared to the gaming booth on *Boaz*. Inside the cavity, the galaxy spun in a glory of glaring white star fields. Sol stepped over and stared.

"That is our Milky Way Galaxy, Sol." Archon stood next to him. "From what we can determine. This was navigation as well as a weapon. This feature alone would be worth the galaxy. Observe."

Archon moved one of the handles that protruded from the side of the tank. Connie, blinked, awed as always by the sensation of diving down toward the Milky Way. Archon manipulated the buttons and slowly they weaved their way to the Orion Arm. The scale continued to explode until familiar stars appeared as pinpoints. Archon slowed the expansion and a red star grew. Soon the spaghetti strands of Arcturus gleamed in silver and white. Archon picked the Confederate Council and, with equal dexterity, the tank seemed to dive through the walls of the station and into the Council chambers before Archon stopped, leaving the image stationary.

"The Council is not in session at the present moment. Were it, we could hear every word spoken. I would have loved to have followed President Palmiere with this after we left his quarters."

"How fine can the resolution get?" Sol asked.

Archon shrugged. "I have seen the inside of the inside of the inside of the inside of the inside of electrons. Defies complementarity? Indeed, I don't understand even half of what I've seen—or what it means. The fact is, however, that this device can follow a particle through energy states—and I can tell you electrons have at least two hundred and fifty-six symmetries, or expressions of existence. To me, without the theoretical background, they were meaningless images. I've peered inside of suns and explored Andromeda, the Magellanic Clouds, the Triangulum, the Sombrero Galaxy and a host of others. I've looked inside Star, Sol, Arcturus, Sirius, and a host of other suns. I have seen inside a man's body and looked at the cores of planets where gravity would crush you like a bug.''

"My God!" Sol gasped at the implications exploding in his mind. ''Scholars could answer any question in the—''

''Indeed,'' Archon agreed. ''Here, Solomon, at my fingertips, lies ultimate knowledge . . . *and ultimate power.''*

The tank retreated beyond the walls and Sol physically reeled with vertigo as Arcturus shrank into a dot and the image moved back across the stars. He could barely trace the path through space to Star's Rest, the constellations appearing in the tank as they dropped toward Star and the white dot of the planet. Vertigo struck him again as Archon manipulated the knobs.

Star's Rest formed with its curious moons and the tank centered on the dots of light orbiting off the planet. Archon stopped the display to show *Boaz* surrounded by five silver-white ships of smaller size.

Connie sensed the wrongness instantly. Fingers curled around the contoured grip of the Model 57, releasing the holster catch.

''Hold it!'' Sol cried. ''That's *Desmond!* If only I . . . Damn it, we've *got* to get back!''

''We can find out from here.'' She heard the strain in her father's voice. The tank seemed to fall through space, through the gleaming white skin of *Boaz* as Archon targeted the lounge and then found his way through the corridors onto the bridge.

Familiar control boards glistened green. Art and Bryana sat tensed, in their chairs, combat armor donned. Bryana stared with worry at the screen and Fan Jordan's voice suddenly boomed in the tank. ''. . . open fire. I give you thirty seconds to produce Carrasco. If you don't, we'll destroy your vessel. I've had enough—''

Bryana cried, "If the Captain were aboard, Ambassador, he'd deal with you. If you'll simply show a little patience!"

"My *patience* is *exhausted!*" Jordan screamed. In the background, Sol could see Evans, face tight with misgiving. Jordan began counting, "Twenty-nine, twenty-eight, twenty-seven . . ."

Bryana cut the audio. "Fire control, stand by. Happy? I need shields prepared for full intensity!"

"We can't just sit here and be shot at!" Art gritted, his fingers dancing over the reactor controls.

Bryana looked grim. "Yeah, how were we supposed to know they were a bunch of lying bastards? God, I wish the Captain was here. He'd know what to do."

"Blaster fire!" Art cried. "Happy, how does it look?"

"We can hold them for a couple of minutes, Art. Get us the hell out of here! Cap blew a way out at Arpeggio. See what you can do."

Sol shook his head. "That took coordination they don't have." His voice carried that shrill fear that grated on her nerves as he added, *"And I can't do a damned thing!"* Fists knotted at his sides, a terrible anguish on his tortured face.

Connie swallowed hard, "Father, show him." She eased the heavy blaster from her hip. *And now we see, Sol. God, help me to be strong. Damn it, Connie, you've got your duty.* She settled the sights on the center of his back.

The tank backed out of the bridge as Sol cried out. He quivered as they fell through flaring gouts of actinic light as they dropped through the shields and death. He fell through lances of blaster bolts and a New Maine battleship formed in the tank, blaster batteries violet as they poured concentrated fire into *Boaz.*

Sol shook his head, staring desperately at the flaring screens as Fujiki's hotter fire poured back, wavering the shields—a futile action against five vessels. Dead in space with no maneuvering room and no chance to cool the shields, *Boaz* would overload. Art and Bryana hadn't recognized the trap.

"If you wish to change the course of the fight and save your ship, Solomon," Archon's voice was tense, "push this green-brown knob to the wall."

Sol reached, fragile human fingers caressing the awkward shape built for no human hand. A moan escaped his lips, a weird death knell for *Boaz* and his crew. He pushed.

The Mainiac vanished.

Archon pulled the screen back and centered another New Maine cruiser in the middle. Sol pushed. From where she waited, Connie watched the muscles of his arms working to overcome the resistance of the spring.

The second Mainiac vanished. As did the third when Archon manipulated the tank around the victims. They went away without a trace, simply leaving the screen blank while star fields reformed behind the box.

It's possessing him. The power's unleashed. I . . . I'm going to have to kill him. Here, now, it's up to me. She raised the blaster, settling her aim between his shoulder blades, remembering the gentle care in his eyes as he kissed her. *Damn it, I . . . Pull, the trigger, Connie! Pull the . . .*

Archon had boxed *Desmond,* the deep worry eroding his expression, his face gone gray.

"*No!*" Solomon cried, jerking his hand back as if burned, jumping away. "I can't . . . She's . . . she's safe." He panted hard, eyes glazed. "Safe . . . now!" He hunched, gripping his wrist as if to strangle the right hand that had worked the knob.

Desmond had ceased firing, diverting energy into her shields as they took the brunt of Cal's powerful blasters. They wavered and buckled, atmosphere sparkling rainbow colors as it reacted with blaster bolts. Wreckage, men, and equipment blew out the ruptured sides under decompression. A white lance of reaction mass shot out as *Desmond* broke and ran.

Boaz ceased firing almost immediately. The great white ship floated undamaged, a halo of dissipating energy radiating from the fields of her shields.

Sol blinked, swallowing hard, lips moving in silent

speech. His eyes sought Archon's, seeking to understand.
He turned and looked into Connie's blaster, his mind
refusing to comprehend.

"How?" Sol asked. "I . . ."

Archon shrugged. "We don't know. I found that capacity by accident. There used to be a B1 star two light-
years from here. I pushed that button trying to look
inside. It went away just that quickly. After that, I made
a coffee cup on my table at home go away. The resolution
was so fine, I picked the mice off one of my ships, one
at a time."

"But a . . . star? A *B1* star? That's . . . that's . . ."
Sol shook his head, eyes wide as he looked at *Boaz* hanging there in peace. "Where did it . . . go?" He reached
up, face working, and wiped the sudden perspiration from
his forehead with a jerky gesture.

Archon shook his head slowly. "That I do not know,
Solomon. Simply put, I assume it goes somewhere else,
squeezed out of our space—maybe outside. Maybe beyond outside. How many dimensions are there beyond
the ones we know?"

"Three ships," Sol muttered. "Class III Star hulls,
probably eighty men apiece. If they lived, how will they
survive? Two hundred and forty men! Just like that!"

"You can do that with a planet." Archon shrugged.
"Here, let me show you." His age-grizzled hands worked
knobs, space reeling in the tank until a planet hung there,
vibrant in color, white patches of cloud over mottled continents. "Arpeggio. Justice, Solomon. You have the ability to pay them back for *Sword,* for all the dead you lost
there. Pay them back for *Moriah* for the bomb that killed
your ship and so many of your crew. And *Gage?* Do you
doubt that Arpeggians killed *Gage?* You don't know, do
you? No, Kraal didn't release his agent's discoveries.
Suppose I told you Sellers killed *Gage* off Tygee? Suppose you could repay that? Even the score for Mbazi, and
Cerratanos, and Maybry Andaki?" Archon worked the
knobs, bending and twisting the off-color forms, space
spinning away, Star's Rest reforming. "Would you like
to rid yourself of Sellers and the *Hunter?*" He manipu-

lated the controls and *Hunter,* its sleek black lines filling
the tank, lay there, looking ominous while six other black
shapes loomed behind.

"He . . . killed my . . ." Stricken, Carrasco reached
for the knob with trembling fingers. The panicky look on
his face shivered Connie's soul. The blaster lifted as if
of its own volition, the sights settling on Carrasco's back.

I'll wait. As soon as he kills Hunter *and Sabot . . . I'll
blow Solomon Carrasco in two.* A steel fist closed on her
heart. *Like Ngoro said . . . it's duty. A god in your own
flawed image, Sol? No. I . . . I love you. But I can't allow
that.* Her finger tightened on the trigger, taking up the
slack. Inside, her heart pumped, nerves tingling. At each
beat of her tearing heart, the sight picture jumped before
her tear-shimmered vision.

"Killed *Gage?*" Carrasco wound his fingers around
the knob, tendons standing from the backs of his hands,
as he leaned against the lever—and crumbled to the deck,
bent double, panting, tears streaking down from his
clamped eyes.

"No," he whispered. "Not like that. I . . . I can't
become God like that. I can't become . . . become like
Sellers. I can't . . . can't . . . ."

"You would do the galaxy a favor, Solomon." Archon's voice prodded.

Sol glared up, anguished. "*Damn you, no!* I'm not
God, Archon! I can't just . . . just *murder* those men and
women! I can't! You do it! *Do it!* You have as much reason as I!" Impassioned eyes searched the Speaker's, trying to find a link. Desperately he turned to Connie, arms
lifted in supplication.

Sight of him twisted her soul, seeing the pain and confusion. "You have the choice, Sol. You could serve the
species. You could help so many."

"At . . . what price?" he asked, voice gone hoarse.
"You . . . you said it was . . . my soul." His eyes lost
focus as he looked up at the deadly shape of *Hunter* resting against the background of the stars.

"I think you can put your weapon away," Archon said

wearily. "The test was a little more dramatic than necessary, but I think Solomon is safe."

Connie took a deep breath, stilling the jangle of strained nerves within. "Yes, I think so." The heavy pistol weighed like a lump of neutrinos. It slid rasping into the holster. She stared at him, drained. *And I would have shot . . . killed the man I loved. Why, damn it? What's this all come to? Who the hell am I anymore?*

"What? Why? I . . ." Sol stared, ashen-faced, trying to understand.

Connie reached down, helping him to his feet. "We had to know, Sol. As much as I am coming to love you, we had to know how you would react to the chance for ultimate power. I couldn't allow you to become a God. Couldn't turn you loose with . . . that." She pointed to the tank where *Hunter* was still visible. "You see, it wasn't a game we played in the observation blister. That's godhead there, ultimate power within a single person's reach. I think the alien destroyed his last rival. Died alone."

Archon pulled at his chin, stepping forward. "And not only that, I've received a report from Kraal." Archon shook his head. "The alien had a better brain, a more dexterous body, and he fell heir to this? What of humanity?"

Sol frowned. "But the things we could learn?"

Archon stared at him dully. "Like looking inside atoms? Like peering into stars? Seeing the edge of the universe? Moving planets?"

"Yes, yes, think of what that means!"

"And you would be God," Archon agreed. "Or at least, you could come as close to filling that role as our limited culture understands it." He smiled. "Believe me, I have been there, Solomon. The temptation is so great. What a delightful benevolent despot I would be." He tilted his head. "But after me? Who next? Oh, Constance would *probably* do all right, but she is young, Solomon. She has a lot longer to learn about omnipotence and corruption."

Sol frowned, expression numb. An anesthesia of incomprehension left him temporarily unable to think, shaken—satisfied only to hold his woman tight in that ancient primate urge to touch and, thereby, be reassured.

"Come," Archon said. "Let's leave the Artifact for now. I think, Captain, that you've had enough for a while. It'll take time to assimilate all this and put it into perspective."

Sol nodded, struggling to regain his wits. "God forbid if Sellers should get hold of this."

Archon barked a bitter laugh—the sound dry as the sands of Bazaar. "You'd find out in a real hurry where things go when that green-brown knob is pushed."

Even the gray wall didn't faze him as he walked through with Connie. The cold steel of the lock acted like a welcome blessing and the interior of the shuttle snugged around him, a treasured and familiar part of the universe—a comfortable human-created womb.

Archon dogged the hatch and climbed wordlessly onto the bridge. Sol barely felt the shuttle move. He pulled Constance to him and closed his eyes. "How have you and your father withstood the weight of that thing? How have you kept your sanity?"

"Because we had to. There was no one else for us to lean on except each other." She stared at him, awkwardly admitting. "I used to treasure my independence. Now I want to . . . to . . . Well, I'm tired of being alone, Sol. Tired of being a fortress. I want you close, that's all. Just be close, and human, and warm."

"I've seen so much in my life," he mused. "I've experienced so many different things. No one should have been better prepared than I for what happened. The Artifact just didn't . . . didn't . . ."

"Now do you see our problem, Sol?" She looked up, her eyes pleading, seeking some reassurance. "How do we keep this safe? Who decides who will be allowed to use it? How can we turn this over to President Palmiere? *What do we do with it now?*"

He shivered. "I don't know. I truly don't know."

CHAPTER XXIX

The shuttle rocked lightly as it touched down. Sol smiled, kissed Connie gently, and pulled himself to his feet. Archon powered the system down as Constance undogged the hatch. Sol dropped lightly into the cool night of Star's Rest. He sucked the fresh scented air into his grateful lungs and enjoyed the sensations as the breeze caressed his cheek. Connie dropped next to him and her hand sought his as he looked up, seeing the moons with new eyes, emotions more intense as sensations of life pulsed in his veins.

Archon lowered himself with more reserve. "Now you know, Sol. You can see why we took such care, allowing no one to know the true nature of our quest. I hope you can understand the gravity of the situation."

Sol threw his head back, eyes longingly on the stars—but a galactic weight lay upon his soul, the starlight white, cold in the forbidding heavens. "I can and do, Speaker. We'll get it back to the right hands, somehow—some way."

Archon nodded, patted his shoulder, and headed for the house, the door opening and lights coming on as he approached. Sol turned to follow, but Connie pulled him back.

"Not yet, Sol. I want to enjoy the night. It's been a long time since I've been here. Come, walk with me. I want to have you all to myself for a while at least. There's no telling when the next time will be—or even if it will be." She pulled him close.

"But your father—"

"—knows I'm a woman," she answered firmly. "Besides, he likes and admires you." She closed her eyes, filling her lungs, hair spilling down her back. "I was the one who decided I'd act as executioner. I guess you became my responsibility. It's a difficult thing to know you may have to kill the man you love because he doesn't measure up.'' She turned, placing cool hands on his chest, eyes searching his in the dark. ''We couldn't let you loose with that kind of power—no matter what your motives. Do you understand?''

''Not entirely. Not yet anyway.'' He frowned in the darkness. ''I'm still . . . staggering. I guess that's the right word. Like everything's been pulled up by the roots. A new reality has to be integrated.''

''And how do you feel about that? I just stared at the walls, trying to put it all together. How did it feel when you shunted the Mainiacs away?''

He stared at her, eyes haunted. ''Like I'd been betrayed. Connie, I'm just a human being. And . . . and all of a sudden, I . . . I mean, aliens can kill better than we can. Think about it. It's the cold efficiency of it. Passionless . . . yes, that's it. Passionless. No violence. No heavy elements stripped off and accelerated at light speed to blast atoms apart. No matter/antimatter annihilation. No explosions, or blood, or fission or fusion. Just a simple push of the button. It's inhuman. We're, well, not meant to fight that way.''

He gestured helplessly. ''Think about it, we're sophisticated primates. Apes in our own right, and we deserve to be able to scream and holler while we throw sticks at the leopard in the bush. We have a right to strut and bluster and pound our chests before we blast each other.''

''They said the same of submarines. Sneaky, dishonorable, unworthy of a warrior. The Germans lost world hegemony in the early twentieth century because they thought it morally repugnant. It took Americans—who hollered loudest in incensed outrage—to bring submarines to their peak in World War II. So why is this different?''

He stared into the darkness, oblivious to the vista before him. ''It's too good. It's . . . All right, I'm a damned chauvinist. The thing isn't human! It's a cheat.''

''But a powerful one. Think of the policies you could implement. Think of the political ramifications if you could listen in on anyone's strategic sessions? Want to know what the Great Houses are plotting on Arpeggio?''

''You're playing devil's advocate?''

''Why not?''

''Ultimate power.''

''Ultimate knowledge,'' she countered. ''Knowledge—and power, for that matter—is neutral.''

''Humans aren't. And that's the key to the problem.''

''Not very flattering, is it? I mean to know that for all our belief in ourselves, in our achievements, we can't trust ourselves with such a device. Are we self-damned? Is that the lesson here? Is all life that way? I mean, the alien destroyed himself and his species. And what if he wasn't the first? I—''

He silenced her, placing his fingers gently on her lips. Then he bent down and kissed her tenderly.

She gave a long sigh and he could feel her body tense against his. ''That was the final obstacle, Sol. From now on, no more secrets.'' Her lips sought his, hungrily.

He hadn't realized his need. Feeling her—real in his embrace—he met her desire with his own, responding passionately as he pulled her close, striving to become one with her—as if he could pull her inside and tuck her away safe and warm where she'd never be vulnerable again. The soft mat of vegetation cushioned them as they sank to the ground. Twining together, they began the eternal dance, reveling in the unity of soul, body, and mind, thrilling in the physical reaffirmation of life and love—the ultimate appeal to the future.

* * *

The savages had returned, bringing a third victim to work the spring. Who was this odd human? A Master's servant? Doubtful. He'd reacted poorly to the simplest of tests. The others didn't act subservient to him or show respect. Nor did he seem to merit such, having stopped but a spring's push from eliminating the incomparable Sabot Sellers. Did these savage animals have no strata in their society? Impossible! How could they build ships without order?

Yet how delightful to see that they had war! War and Masters moved digit-in-claw together. And the third savage? He'd worked the spring, the memory would be in his simple brain now. He had pushed the button to remove the three crafts which assailed the white ship. A warrior from a different caste? That might describe the social system.

They would come soon. Too many ships had arrived. She knew a little more about these animals now. They would fight over her, and in the process, she'd learn. A flash of energy ran through long unused systems. The long wait was over. One way or another, she would have a Master soon. Forbid that it be a savage, but then, even that was better than a corpse! And besides, Sabot Sellers had yet to play his hand. She turned her monitors to *Hunter* where men armed themselves, preparing shuttles, and strapping weapons to combat armor.

In the twist of her thoughts, an insane amusement lit her boards with flickers of triumph. She howled back at the stars, knowing it had started. These humans had worked the spring. The first faltering steps toward their destruction had been taken. The rest would follow until damnation.

* * *

Bryana fixed burning eyes on the screen, aware she'd been living in the command chair for over a day. The system provided for all her body's needs from evacuating wastes to feeding her. It stimulated her muscles, and kept her physically alert. Her mind, however, was on the verge of shutting down out of sheer exhaustion. She could barely see Carrasco in the dim planet's night.

"Good to see you, Captain," she greeted, washed by a wave of relief. "Happy picked up your transmitter about an hour ago. Is everything all right down there?"

"Fine."

"Well, you wouldn't believe what happened here." She shook her head, knowing she'd failed.

"I would." He sounded reserved. She winced. He'd really know when he reviewed the tapes. "You'll never be rescued that easily again."

"You saw?" Her tired mind prodded. "Captain Carrasco, we didn't kill those three cruisers. They just vanished. Happy and Cal have been driving themselves crazy with it."

"Tell them to forget it. I'll brief everybody when I get there. Keep on your toes. Things are happening too quickly here," Sol warned, then his voice barked. "I . . . Damn! We're being hit! Hold your position and wait for my orders!" A light flickered in the screen and it went dead.

Bryana kicked Art awake and turned to comm. "Happy! Cal! Someone's shooting at Carrasco on the planet's surface. Is there any way we can help them?"

Happy's grim face formed on the monitor. "Not without sending down a shuttle. His orders are to hold. From the sensor, he's still alive. Trust Cap, Bry, he'll make it. I hope."

* * *

Nikita Malakova grunted and turned over.

"You sound like a water buffalo in the desert," Tayash grunted.

"Is planet. Never sleep well on planet. Is something intrinsically wrong with being in place as final and heavy as bottom of gravity well. Not only that, things don't move right. Grav plates are . . . are lighter on soul, you know?"

Tayash mumbled to himself, a faint glow springing from his bunk in the darkness overhead. "It's almost five hundred hours. Dawn will be breaking soon. I don't suppose you'll let me get any more sleep."

"Sorry. Is just how planets are. Heavy . . . so very heavy. People are not made for planets, Tayash. Are made for stations where gravity isn't always so oppressive."

A short silence followed.

Tayash chuckled. "I don't think I've ever heard you so subdued. Maybe I ought to drop you on planets more often?"

Nikita waved his arms in the dark. "What? Is not right. Humans aren't meant to be at bottom of hole! What is planet, eh? Is bottom of hole. You stamp foot, and is as down as down can be. Look up, and you'll scare sacred wits white with fear. Anything, and I mean *anything,* could fall on you. Frightening, horribly, utterly frightening."

"Humans lived like this for almost the entire history of our species."

"No wonder humanity is crazy. To live so, to know that underfoot is end to movement, to light and life, is like trap to soul. No wonder Soviets took to stars. Humanity would have killed itself to find freedom of space."

"Mind if I record this? I'm not sure anyone would ever believe it if I told them the things you're saying."

Nikita grunted, swinging his feet over the side of the bunk. "Is almost time for sunrise? Have heard of such things. Would be worth it to see, I suppose. Only other thing will be to listen to Lietov and Medea inflict invective through long meeting."

"Archon said he'd have some information for us this morning. The unveiling of the 'sacred secret'?"

"Um." Nikita adjusted his compensator belt, standing, while the lights came up.

Tayash squinted into the light, staring around the small room. He pulled himself up, rubbing his thin limbs, his ancient skin hanging like parchment. "Well, maybe you've got something about planets."

"Have been thinking," Nikita added, staring down as he relieved himself into the converter. "Seems to me, perhaps we should back Archon and Constance. From what I can tell, Brotherhood is more trustworthy than Sirius, Earth, or New Maine."

"And if it's all propaganda? It's their ship we came in."

Nikita pressed his fly closed as he turned. "And has Carrasco tried even once to buy us? Has he tried to impose will? Has he made single promise to curry favor?"

"Considering the unknown capabilities of his ship up there, does he need to?" Tayash pulled his suit on, fumbling absently for his cane. "Maybe he's already got the secret wrapped up? An inside track. If he's been screwing Constance, maybe that's his angle?"

Nikita lowered bushy eyebrows. "You believe that? That she—of all women—would compromise integrity for a little frantic coupling with a man?"

Tayash combed out his goatee. "Actually, no. I thought I'd mention it though. What if she loves him? What if she's willing to bare her soul to him? As much as I respect Constance, I've known some superb women to fall flat on their faces when it comes to men."

"Bah!" Nikita waved the idea away. "If she didn't have sense when it comes to men, she'd have fallen for me."

"You wish." Tayash stood, checking his image in the mirror. "But, Nikita, remember, whatever we must decide, we can't let personalities get in the way of the right choice for all people, everywhere."

"What? You lecture me . . . *me,* Nikita Malakova, who has survived the—"

"Damn right! Now, are you ready to go see a sunrise? Or are you content to sit around here beating your breast and bellowing your pompous—"

"Let's see sunrise." Nikita strode across the floor. He opened the door to find a man standing outside. The fellow wore a black uniform, hair and beard gaudily braided and bejeweled. He smiled a nasty smile as he jammed an ugly blaster barrel into Nikita's paunch.

"Mister Malakova, if you'll come with me, your presence is required in the meeting room."

"What? Who are—" Nikita stopped short as the safety clicked off.

Tayash reached for his belt comm, freezing in mid move as the gunman added, "One word, Representative Niter, and I'll blow your friend here in two. Now, if you'll both step to the side and get a move on, you'll save time and trouble."

Nikita nodded slowly, noting the sword and starburst

on the man's uniform. "Another voice speaks its mind about sacred secret. What do—"

"Shut up!"

Nikita glared at the blaster, put his hands up, and clamped his mouth closed.

* * *

Light was beginning to shade the eastern horizon. Sol crouched, dirty and disheveled, across from Archon's wrecked shuttle.

They had come in, five shuttles from five different directions. He and Connie had provided flanking fire as men dashed from the landing shuttles, while the house, shielded, had replied in kind, proving they hadn't caught Archon completely off guard. The first bolts had blown the bridge out of Archon's shuttle. Well planned, that, but then the whole action demonstrated coordination and skill.

Even the best strategy and tactics rarely survive the first shot. They hadn't counted on Connie and Sol being outside. From where they crouched in the night, they'd raked the attackers from the sides, killing scores, forcing the assault to break as the bewildered attackers scrambled for shuttles and withdrew.

Sol had provided enfilading fire as Connie covered his back. Human war. The thought burned through his battle-hyped brain. He and Constance had broken the rush on the house. Sol had managed to cripple a shuttle when he got a couple of bolts driven through the open lock as men dived inside. The ship had pitched on its side and accelerated over the edge of the pyramid, screaming toward a reactor overload. The others had risen into the black night sky.

"It'll be light soon," Connie whispered. "We'd better move or they'll have us pinned."

Sol nodded. "Let's just hope Archon doesn't fry us while we're coming in."

They scuttled to the side and ran for the house. Sol jumped a body, blown in half by a bolt. He zigzagged, saw a dark figure rise from the ground before him, and watched the man jerk as his body absorbed a bolt and exploded.

"We're friendly!" Sol yelled as he sprinted for a charred hole burned in the wall. The expected resistance of the shield didn't meet his charge and he jumped through the blasted hole unimpeded, rolling and coming to his feet, blaster ready as Connie dove through after him.

"Archon?" Sol called. A bolt slapped the structure with a bang, shaking the walls.

Connie covered him as he ran through the house. In the rear, the story became evident. The huge gaping hole in the rear wall mocked him. The frontal assault had been a diversion. That's why the shields were down. While men had died out front, they'd snatched Archon from the rear.

Sol ran to the front, picked up an Arpeggian shoulder weapon from beside a gutted body and studied the front with IR. Amid the grisly pile of bodies, he saw movement, sighted, and blew the man's head off. Moving to Archon's scanner, he noted one other target behind a low depression.

Constance came from the rear of the house, face grim, eyes hard behind the grime and dirt. "They got him. His body isn't among the dead."

"That means the Hound has him. There's one left out there. I can't get to him from here with a blaster." Sol slammed a fist into the wall.

She handed him a round metal ball. "Sonic grenade. I'll cover you from here."

He nodded, ran out the door, and heaved it into the depression as violet bolts crackled in the atmosphere around his head. He hit the ground and waited. The earth rose under him, smacking him as he bounced against the groundroll.

"Got him!" Connie called. "From IR there are only a couple of wounded." She walked out purposely, approaching the pile of corpses in a crouch, blaster ready.

Sol trotted for the shuttle while Connie's blaster lanced

light into an occasional body. His teeth ground as he looked at the blackened, twisted remains in the bridge.

"Ground car's all that's left," she called up.

"And we can't get off this planet without being blown out of the air by Sellers," Sol growled. Then he shrugged and went aft. He recognized the anti-detection device. From the tool kit, he pulled a cutting laser and began slicing the system out of the small reactor.

Half an hour later, the charge in the cutting tool gone, Connie helped him muscle the unit into the ground car. She drove, thin-lipped, face lined with anger and worry.

"They'll try and make him talk." Sol said. "It all depends on whether they took him up to the ship."

"He'll kill himself. He'll wait until he can do the most damage though. He wants to pay them back."

"Maybe we can get to him in time." Sol tried to sound confident.

"Maybe."

"*Boaz*, what's the situation?" Sol called into the comm.

"Jumpy as a cat in free-fall!" Art's voce returned. "Those two bogeys that chased us here are coming in, one from each direction. Sellers has his ships spread out around the planet. Jordan's back. We can detect messages being sent back and forth between him and *Hunter*. More bogeys are showing up on the peripheries of the system and Sellers has been in contact with them."

Sol nodded. "It's worse than I thought. Listen, get that ship out of there. There's a camouflage system built into *Boaz*. Happy should be able to cook up a diversion for you. You might send a message sunward. Tell Captain Mason that Sellers kidnapped the Speaker. Now listen, there's a hole in the near moon. I'll try and meet you there. Carrasco out."

He looked at Constance, then back out over the broad plain. The shuttle they'd shot up the night before had plowed a furrow in the rich dirt of Star's Rest before it came to rest, broken and mangled.

They pulled up in the dense vegetation behind the spaceport. Sol threw the heavy distortion equipment over his shoulder and struggled along behind Constance. He almost killed himself when he stepped on a squealing snakelike creature. Appalled, he caught himself and watched Constance pick the hideous thing up and pet it. It purred!

"Harmless, actually. You scared it, Sol."

"Yeah," he panted. "Poor thing!"

"Only Arpeggian shuttles out there," Connie informed him after she pulled ahead to scout.

"Let's take the closest one." Sol grunted, feeling the sweat rolling down his face and back. "I don't want to carry this any farther than I have to."

"How do you want to do it?"

"The easy way—but wait until I'm through." He staggered out into the open, struggling under the weight of the distortion device. "Hey!" he called out. "Send an antigrav down!"

"What's that?" A voice called from above.

"Booty, laddie!" Sol filled his voice with cheer. "Give me a hand . . . or lose your cut!"

An antigrav settled and Sol dropped the heavy equipment on it. To one side, he attached a small gas grenade from his space pouch—a Brotherhood gizmo based on the powerful megapharma hallucinogen. "Take her up!" Sol called, knowing his uniform looked a lot like the Arpeggian dress.

He heard the pop as they pulled the device inside. Sol smiled to himself. He leaned against a landing strut as if he owned it and crossed his arms. Glancing at the time, he whistled and nodded as Connie stepped out, hair wrapped around her chin. From a distance, it would look like a beard. Maybe, if they were lucky.

With Connie on his heels, he went up the ladder. Two men sprawled on the floor, eyes rolled back in their heads, saliva drooling from their mouths. A quick inspection showed the bridge to be empty. "Cover the door. If this is standard, they'll have a patrol roaming around to keep an eye on things." He ran for the reactor, muscling the heavy distorter along.

He ripped off the inspection panel and looked. Fifteen

minutes to put the gadget in. Would he have time? It had to be tied into the gravity plates to distort the field around the shuttle, otherwise Sellers' sensors would pick them up like an Arcturian whore at a Mormon dance. Sweating again, Sol found the tool kit and began ripping up the deck plating. First, the sensitive part. If the pickups were inserted too deeply into the reactor, the system would short and they'd go up like a fireball.

He wiped his face with a dirt encrusted hand and bent his back to lever the distorter into place, fusing the metal with the vibrawelder. He panted in the hot moist air. Moving quickly, he ran the leads along the floor, untidy perhaps, but time-saving. Next he seared holes through the bulkheads to the grav plates and began attaching the leads.

"Someone's coming!" Connie whispered.

"One?"

"Yes."

"Let him aboard." Sol ducked back, picking up a crescent wrench, a basic tool which had survived the centuries—and God knew how many light-years. Steps rang out on the ladder.

"Who the hell are you?" The big man asked, turning to confront Connie. He was reaching for his blaster as Sol banged the wrench on his head.

The Arpeggian didn't fall. He wobbled, shook his head, and Sol banged him again. He crumpled in a heap.

Sol inspected the thick end of the wrench and shook his own head skeptically. "Always thought those guys were thick-skulled."

"Back to work—I'll handle him." Connie motioned toward the rear, then started to bind the groaning man with point five powerlead.

"Yes, ma'am," Sol smiled and attacked another bulkhead, realizing the alien technology of walk-through walls had some advantages.

The Arpeggian groaned and Connie replied with, "One move, mister, and I blow your head off. Where's Speaker Archon being held?"

"I don't know. Why don't you—"

"Where would he likely be held?"

The Arpeggian glared back. Connie pulled a small knife from her pocket. "Want to try again while I see how much anatomy I can remember?" She slit his uniform open and pressed the little blade against his belly. He shuddered as she said, "Seems to me, you can make a small incision here under the navel. Doesn't have to be long—only ten centimeters or so and you can start pulling intestine out a bit at a time. Feels real funny in the gut cavity while it's happening. Ever seen your intestines before?" She drew the knife along his skin, blood welling behind the sting of the blade.

"They got a whole bunch of people in the Port Authority office," he exploded. "Damn it, woman, stop it! That's all I know." Sweat began to trickle down his cheeks.

"Could be," Sol admitted as he attached the final lead and straightened. Turning, he picked up the wrench and carefully backhanded the Arpeggian again.

"What did you do that for?" Connie asked, looking up in irritation.

"Need his uniform," Sol said, yanking at the fabric. Sol wasn't as big as their captive, but over his own clothing, it would fit pretty well. He frowned, reaching into his space pouch for a tube of adhesive to mend the slit.

"What about me? You're dressed, but I need something. I'll go check the guys up—"

"You're not going, Connie."

"He's *my* father!" she flared. *"The hell I'm not!"*

"And if I get killed, Sellers has both of the people who can lead him to the Artifact." He shook his head, staring into her cobalt-blue eyes, a wrenching inside. "Duty, Connie. Responsibility. No one else knows where to find that thing. Give me twenty minutes. If I'm not back, get to *Boaz* . . . get the Artifact . . . and run for Frontier. Kraal will know what to do with it."

"But, Sol!"

He kissed her. "You and I both know there's no choice, Connie. Last night on the Artifact, you'd have shot me if

I'd failed the test. Think Sellers would pass? You were . . . Well, he says betrothed.''

"That despicable scum shedding—''

He smiled, kissed her again and dropped out the hatch.

"Take care," she called down. "Damn it! I love you.''

"Twenty minutes!" He spun on his heel, walking briskly toward the offices. The Port Authority dome hadn't been there long, imported from the Confederacy and mostly prefabbed. The doorway—like that of an igloo—stuck out where two guards, blasters drawn, waited in the increasing heat of Star's rays. One stepped out to bar his progress.

"I've got new information for them in there.'' Sol filled his voice with command.

"How's that, Johnson?" The man asked, reading his name tag. "You're an engineer. What are you doing carrying orders?''

"Look!" Sol threatened. "If you don't let me in there with what we got on Carrasco and Archon's daughter, you deal with the Admiral, huh?''

"Let him go," the second added.

As Sol stepped past, he felt the blaster jam into his back. "Nice try, friend! But I used to bunk with Engineer Johnson. *You ain't him!*''

CHAPTER XXX

A sodden weight settled in Sol's gut.

The lounge area thronged with the entire diplomatic corps *Boaz* had carried to Star's Rest. Archon appeared groggy, his face purpled with bruises, arms and legs bound by EM restraints. Uniformed men stood around the walls, blasters easy at hand.

"Captain Carrasco! How delightful!" He turned to see Elvina walking toward him, a saucy smile on her lips, a new expression of keen intelligence on her pretty face.

She wore the formfitting black uniform of Arpeggio. The skintight lines of the uniform mocked the ironic lie of her discarded Mormon dress, molding to the panther lines of her superb body. Gone was the fumbling housewife's walk—replaced by a liquid grace. She paced, deadly, balanced, a commanding figure, her light blonde hair in sharp contrast with the black of her collar.

"Bind him!" she snapped. "He's slippery."

The next shock came when the guard bent down to tie him: Second Engineer Kralacheck! He worked EM restraints over Sol's wrists and threw him roughly onto a bench. Reaching down to check his work, he whispered a word in Sol's ear—a Brotherhood word; it meant patience and perseverance.

Trust him? Or was this simply another security breach. If Kralacheck had burrowed his way into the Craft as a mole, what could a code word mean? Hell, Sellers and the Great Houses could have compromised the entire Craft for all he knew.

"How's Connie?" Archon asked.

"She's . . . dead, Speaker," Sol said in what he hoped was a voice loud enough to carry to Elvina. At the same time, he winked at Archon.

The Speaker stiffened—caught the hidden message—and lengthened his face as a father would upon hearing of the death of his last child.

"Let's get on with this!" Elvina scowled. "Where's the alien ship?" she demanded of Archon. "I won't ask you politely. Where?" Her face pinched in anger, eyes burning. The flush of excitement added a glow to her features, the rapturous look of youth and health increased her beauty.

"I don't know what you're talking about," Archon muttered.

"Oh, come, Archon. I got it all out of the ugly little messenger Palmiere sent to the Sirians. I psyched his twisted little mind and milked him dry before I cut him apart and fed half truths to the Sirians. Did you know he was standing behind the draperies the whole time you were there? No? Well, let me refresh your memory of what you told Palmiere.

"An alien spacecraft capable of moving stars, of spying on the whole of the Confederacy. Impregnable, you told him. A craft which would allow its possessor to control the galaxy, possibly even the universe. You told him it could be the greatest blessing humanity had ever discovered—better than cold fusion in the twenty-first century! That with it, no one could escape your observation. By working what you called 'the spring' entire fleets could be whisked into oblivion. That it could even see inside an atom—or exterminate mice on your ship. That with it, a single man could become a—"

"You're a raving lunatic."

"Indeed? Then what's all this?" she asked, waving an arm at the fear-filled faces surrounding them.

Archon looked up defiantly. "If you were as good a spy as you think you are, you'd know they are here to rewrite the Articles of Confederation!"

She nodded, smiling sweetly. "Of course. Very well, Archon, you force my hand." She drew a laser from her belt before walking over and grabbing Joseph Young by the arm and pitching him into the middle of the floor. Her pistol centered on his chest. "Where, Archon?"

The Speaker looked sad and shook his head as Young shrieked, "El–Elvina? What . . . what are you going to do?" His lips worked soundlessly as he stared into the nozzle of her pistol.

Elvina smiled, eyes lighting with pleasure as her face flushed. "Archon will tell me where to find the alien ship. Oh, Joseph, this is sweet. All those nights you bored me to death with your religious drivel will be paid back here. Worst of all were your slobbering caresses and your impotent passion in bed. Now, for the first time, Joseph, the pleasure is mine!" Calmly, she lowered the pistol and cut off a foot, the beam cauterizing the stump neatly as Young screamed.

"No!" Nikita Malakova roared. "It is vile! It is inhuman!"

Elvina straightened. "And you, dear Nikita, have just

chosen yourself to be next—assuming, of course, that Archon doesn't talk." She looked around. "Or Texahi?"

Medea's husband cringed.

"So you lived. I couldn't have your suspicions voiced to your wife." Elvina cocked her head as she studied Medea. "Had you lived, you really should have rid yourself of him. He blabbers everything in the throes of passion." Elvina turned on her heel. "Same with you, Mikhi. Did you truly think your talk of Reinland's manufacturing boring? Thank you for the information on Patrol schedules."

"You bitch," Lietov growled.

She laughed. "Indeed, Mark. Oh, how I loved your sweaty body on mine. And yes, your confessions of insider politics were fascinating. You say you've even managed to put an agent in House Van Gelder? Bless you, we've sought to compromise Freena for years. Having located your agent, he'll now work for us. Safer that way. But I lose my purpose. Archon, where is the alien device?"

"There's no ship." Archon's voice carried the weight of eternity. His eyes saddened, filled with remorse.

The laser flicked again and Young screamed. Sol watched with detached horror. Young writhed and wailed, praying piteously to his God, sweat beading on his brow. He lost control of his bladder and his eyes almost popped with disbelief and pain, as Elvina castrated him with a quick twist of the searing light. A gurgling noise escaped his lips as he grabbed his crotch.

A guard burst through the door shouting, "Miss Sellers! A shuttle just took off from the port. They don't answer signals—and worse, they disappeared from our monitors!" He stopped, staring at the sobbing, whimpering mess on the floor.

She turned and glared. "Don't just stand there gawking, idiot! Inform my father at once, do you hear?"

He nodded, stumbled, and left at a run.

Archon looked sadly at Sol. "Did you and Constance have time for what you needed to do last night?"

Sol hesitated and felt himself color. He nodded slightly, a nervous smile trying to twist his lips.

"Good, Sol." Archon nodded, smiling. "I shall remember the two of you . . . in love . . . in the eye of the
moon!" And, with those words, Archon, Speaker of
Star's Rest, died.

"There goes a true hero." Sol turned to see Amahara's
eyes on him.

"Perhaps it is a time for heroes." He smiled wistfully,
feeling the pain grow to a dull ache in his chest. His jaws
tightened with hurt and anger.

"Come, Archon," Elvina said, turning back. "Where
is the ship?" She pointed the pistol at what was left of
Joseph Young.

"No good, Elvina," Sol said, voice choked. "You destroyed your last link."

She walked over and lifted Archon's limp head and
slapped it time and again with the heavy pistol until the
blood ceased to drip from the torn flesh. Only then did
she accept the fact. Eyes pits of rage, she turned on Solomon Carrasco.

"And you, Captain? You were Archon's confidant and
Constance's lover. Perhaps you know?" She glared at
him, a curious light in her eyes.

Sol shook his head and answered honestly. "I will not
see these people tortured, Elvina. Hook me up to your
machines. Kill whoever you want—but it won't help.
They didn't tell me because it was their belief that any
man could be broken. They died with the secret. When
you killed Archon, you killed the source for all of us."

"And his daughter? Is she really dead?" Elvina
stepped closer, staring into his eyes. In his mind, Sol
conjured images of Tygee, of hulls decompressing, and
the wailing of Peg Andaki for her husband. He could feel
the tear tracing the corner of his eye.

"Blaster bolts are inanimate, Elvina. They go where
they're pointed. You can't give them orders. Man?
Woman? What does a blaster care about its target? When
you hit Archon's this morning, you were indiscriminate,
don't you think?"

"And the shuttle that lifted?" she asked.

A line filled his head from one of the tapes *Boaz* had

run on Jordan. "You don't think a Captain flies his own shuttle, do you? We have crew for that. In this case, my weapons officer. That was Cal Fujiki. I ordered him to give me twenty minutes and space *Boaz*, get her out of harm's way, and head for—"

A commtech burst into the room, slamming the door back. "Miss Sellers!" He stopped, a perplexed look on his face. "I don't know how to tell you this, but the Brotherhood ship disappeared! It was there and then it was just gone. And we're under attack. The Admiral's fighting back, scrambling the ships. Archon's fleet dove out of the sun and hit us hard. We didn't even know they were up there, blocked images with the primary. When the fighting stopped, *Boaz* was gone—just like the ships from New Maine. Vanished. Some Brotherhood trick!"

Elvina took the man's comm and placed a headset on her brow. She nodded, concentrating into the pickup.

Elvina Young smiled wistfully. "Very well, we'll have to find the alien ship on our own. Leave no witnesses. Clear out! I'll take the last shuttle. Return to *Hunter!*" She paused long enough to sever Young's head and hurried out the door.

Kralacheck placed an explosive device on the floor and waved the last guard out. He darted to Carrasco, slit the EM restraints, and handed him a vibraknife. "I've given you all the time I can. Go out the back way and run! Don't disarm the bomb. The explosion's your cover for escape."

Then he ran for the door as Sol cut the others loose. Nikita placed himself at the rear, seeing to the evacuation as Sol, frantic, pushed men and women toward the back, aware the bomb would level the building.

"Keep low when you're outside!" Sol ordered. "Duck into the vegetation! Hide yourselves to keep from being sighted from the air. Above all, get as far away as possible and keep your heads down!" He could hear the last of the shuttles rising out front.

He stopped at Archon's limp form. The last one left. "You, too, must come, my old friend." Sol threw the body over his shoulder and struggled out the rear, staggering under the burden of Archon's bulk.

His last thought was "too close" as a giant hand slapped him into the ground. Sol bounced, smashed again, and whirled through the air. He tried to pull himself up, aware that nothing seemed to work.

Malakova was bending down, pulling him up and Sol felt a grating in his back. "Bring Archon!" But no one answered. Then he was falling, falling. . . .

He vaguely remembered a world of green. He could see Nikita's face and the Gulagi's mouth working.

"I can't hear you!" Sol cried back, feeling no pain below his waist though his chest burned and stabbed—a mass of agony. Dried blood covered his hands and he could feel gaps in his mouth where his teeth had been.

"We have found a shuttle!" Malakova was shouting, but Sol could just barely make out his words. "You must fly it, Solomon! Forney Andrews was captured! You are the only one who can fly! You are the only one who can find *Boaz!*"

Sol nodded, head foggy as the world shimmered around him in a haze of pain. He blinked, trying to clear his mind. "Bring Archon," he gasped as hands lifted him from the ground. He was aware of the way his legs dangled and fear filled him as the world shifted from gray to black again.

He came to inside the shuttle, strapped into the acceleration seat. Nikita hunched beside him, looking worried. "If you pass out on the way up, you will kill us all. You must stay awake, Captain!"

"In my space pouch," Sol whispered, fighting the shimmering haze. "Little red and white striped pills. Give me one. If I start to go out, give me another. Keep giving me one every time, understand, Nikita?"

The big Gulagi nodded, and Sol barely felt something in his mouth. He came out of it with surprising clarity. Judging by the monitors, they were in a small shed. Repair! The shuttle was in for repair! Would it even fly? He tried to swallow, couldn't, fought his arm forward and hit the activation button.

They blew the building apart as they accelerated up and out. The g forces wrenched his body and he became dizzy. He could feel Malakova's fingers in his mouth and the world straightened. No navigation in the comm! The screens stayed blank. He could see the mass detector. That pointed the anomaly of the moon out to him and he accelerated sideways.

"Carrasco to *Boaz!*" he gritted. "Carrasco to *Boaz!*" Damn it! Where were they?

"They are answering, Captain!" Malakova roared, barely audible to Sol's ears. He felt something gurgling inside him and looked down. The command chair was soaked with blood, streaks of it ran across the deck plates below.

"Nikita . . . we go to . . . the hole in the moon. You'll have to . . . fly this. I'm . . . dying . . . dying . . ." A gray haze had filled the bridge, drawing itself close around him. He tried to keep his wits in the fading gray.

"Call *Boaz*. Have Bryana . . . tell you what to do. The controls are . . . like the . . . gaming booth . . . Fly like . . . playing cross over. Easy . . . Nikita. You can do it." Things had gone black. "Can't see anymore . . . Nikita," his voice ground gravelly in his head. "Can't see. Weak in . . . my brain . . . Nikita . . ."

* * *

She watched, hollow-eyed as they carefully lifted the remains of Solomon Carrasco from the shuttle command chair. Coppery trails of blood ran this way and that. The odor of clotted blood, spilled body fluids, and hovering death had begun to thicken in the cramped quarters.

"Easy," Wheeler cautioned, working in the cramped space while Bret Muriaki bent his big body around, stripping interfering panels away with a vibrashear.

"All right," Bret exhaled. "That should give us room."

A light on the med unit flickered. "He's dead." Wheeler glanced up, meeting Bret's eyes. "We've got to be quick. It'll be a miracle if *Boaz* can save him as it is.''

Like a dagger of ice, a frigid spear rose from deep within her. *Oh, God, no. Not Sol, not this soon after hearing about Father!*

She stumbled back, leaning against a stained shuttle seat, bracing herself physically as well as mentally, her locked arms like trusses on her soul.

''Look like universe has just ended,'' Nikita's soft voice enfolded her like velvet. A huge hand, compassionate, settled like a dove on her shoulder, slowly pulling her back. Resistance shot, she allowed him to hug her, to lead her numbly down the aisle to the hatch and into the shuttle lock.

''All right?'' A finger lifted under her chin, forcing her to stare into Nikita's concerned eyes.

From the root of her, she forced a slight smile to leaden lips. ''So much death, Nikita. My heart . . . Damn it, if Sol . . .''

''Shhh. Wait and see. This Brotherhood ship is packed with secrets. Perhaps hospital is one, eh?''

''But this soon after Father . . .'' She dropped her head, an acid knot of tears burning behind her nose, ready to erupt. ''He was the best, Nikita. Why? Why a kind loving man like . . . He gave me everything . . . every opportunity.''

''Humanity is better, Connie. I was there, remember. He looked into Elvina's eyes . . . and died freely, without pain. In process, perhaps he saved us all. Is there more fitting end for fine man than giving life to fellows? And besides, is now time for us to determine future course. Captain Carrasco, too, has bought us this opportunity. If he lives . . . or if he dies, we must now set aside grief, and take our best shot in their shadows, no?''

She stared dull-eyed at him. ''You know,'' her voice cracked, ''I never have time for grief, Nikita. It's always me who has to take the load. Why in hell do I think this time will be any different?''

''Responsibility.'' Nikita winked at her, evidently deciding she had pulled herself back together. ''Is ultimate truth that is best granted to those who don't want it. Perhaps is lesson political rabble we carry should learn from you?''

Knowing she could not allow herself to grieve for her father yet, that she must first defeat his enemies, she nodded, watching Wheeler and Muriaki hustle the heavy med unit past, grim expressions of their faces.

"Come," Nikita urged. "You love this Captain so much?''

She hesitated, feeling her tortured self wrenched anew. "Yes, Nikita. And I never knew why until just now. You see, he didn't want the responsibility either. And he's kind, and gentle . . . and he pulled the wreck of his life together when he had to." An image of Carrasco in the observation blister, asking why men and ships died, curled out of the mists of memory.

"And now, it's time I did the same."

* * *

Sol felt the wiggling, like a small worm impaled on a fishhook. It should have tickled, hurt, or . . . A probe! It hadn't been that long since the last one had crawled through his body. That meant he was alive. Where? Had *Boaz* leapt down from the sky to save him? Or could this be *Hunter?* Had *Hunter* dropped to snare them back into the Hound's hands?

The ship's speaker echoed in Sol's ears. "He's coming around.''

Sol cracked an eyelid and looked out to see the gleaming white of hospital. His voice croaked and his mouth rasped dryly. *"Boaz?"*

"Here, Captain. Please do not try to move. Your spine is immobilized. If you become too active, I will put you down again.''

"But I need to get to the bridge! The Hound is out there. We have to get the Artifact! We have to . . .'' Darkness folded in on him.

* * *

Constance settled herself in the chair, acutely aware of the nervous stares she drew from Art and Bryana. The tape containing Master Kraal's special orders to Solomon Carrasco played on the main bridge monitor. Connie looked up to see Happy listening, muscles taut around his mouth. Cal Fujiki nervously tapped his fingers on the console before him.

"That's it," Constance assured them. "My father's body is aboard. Captain Carrasco is alive. Barely. I just came from the hospital and *Boaz* claims it will take at least three weeks before he's fit again. The Captain's back is broken. Internal hemorrhaging and organ damage are severe. He's suffering from concussion, a cracked skull, and numerous broken bones including those in his right arm and left leg."

"And he flew that shuttle?" Art whispered to himself. "It's physically impossible!"

"Cap always brings you back, kid." Happy sighed wearily and looked up at Connie. "All right, Speaker. *Boaz* is yours if you have the Word and the Signs to—"

"I have the Word."

"How do you have it?"

"I'll letter it and halve it with you."

"Letter it and begin."

"Begin you."

"The Word is yours, you must begin."

Slowly, Connie repeated the ritual Kraal had taught her, spelling out the ritual Words of the Craft. Heart pounding, she looked up at the monitors, aware of the incredulous looks of the First Officers.

Happy grinned. "So Mote It Be. Sounds good, Speaker. What do you want us to do?"

Connie nodded. "Thank you, Engineer. First, we must keep track of the time. *Boaz*? Currently, what is the time at my father's house on Star's Rest?"

"Twenty-two point seventeen hours, Speaker," *Boaz* responded sharply.

"Hey!" Art jerked upright. "She's not supposed to talk to people without . . ." He shot a guilty look at Connie. "I'm a little new at this, Speaker, forgive me."

"I, too, am bound by Galactic Master Kraal's orders, First Officer," *Boaz* answered.

Connie glanced at the ship's chronometer, computing the difference. "At exactly sixteen forty-three hours ship's time, we have to break out of here. According to transduction to Captain Mason of the Star's Rest fleet, Sellers is busy searching the planet. It won't take them long to realize they have to come to the moons. When that happens, they'll find this one has been tunneled through." She raised her eyes to Fujiki's. "You sealed the ends?"

"Yes, Speaker. They're plugged. Since your fleet reports, Sellers has begun sounding the surface down there. They'll sound here, too. It won't take much of a seismic investigation to find us." Fujiki shrugged, looking terribly uncomfortable.

Connie nodded. "The reason I ask is that it is imperative that we break out at exactly sixteen forty-three hours. That, ladies and gentlemen, is the very moment we have to clear the hole. Any slop in the system—and we have to wait twelve planetary hours. That might kill us all—and it will give the secret of the Artifact away.

"Misha, I'll expect you to be ready to grab the Artifact. I imagine it will be tough to hold. The hull is unlike anything you've ever grabbed onto. Winch it in if nothing else. Don't waste a single second. When we blow the other side, take an instant vector. You should see a small black dot in a series of concentric circles on the far moon. Sellers will probably be tipped to our location by the breakout. *Boaz?*"

"Yes, Speaker?"

"I'm not familiar with this camouflage technique. Will it work against a planetary surface?" Connie leaned her chin on her knee, trying to figure all the angles.

"Affirmative."

"Then employ that while we're down there." She looked up. "We can more or less make up the rest as we go. Cal, Weapons will have to worry only if Sellers is closing. Any questions?''

Bryana nodded. "What do we do when we get this thing on board?"

Connie laughed dryly. "Run as fast as we can for Frontier and the Craft. We'll take whatever the ship has to give as far as acceleration. After that, I have no idea. The solution will lie in the hands of the political officials. My responsibility will be ended—and you will have your ship back."

"You heard the lady," Happy growled. "Let's get to it, people."

Connie walked back to the hospital alone. In the far too familiar room, she dropped onto one of the med units. "How's his status, *Boaz*?"

"I am repairing the damage to his spinal column. This particular procedure is very delicate since each nerve path must be precisely reconstructed. On the other hand, his teeth are growing back, each of the bud implantations having taken suitably. Cellular damage from shock is healing. Under electro-stim, the broken bones are knitting nicely. His brain is functioning correctly again and cerebral swelling is controlled."

"No permanent damage?"

"No, Speaker, none."

Connie hesitated. "You are most remarkable, *Boaz*. Can I ask you a question?"

"Of course, Speaker. Within limits, I will respond. I am not free to divulge Craft secret doctrine—and certain technical specs are restricted."

"I detect a certain, shall we say, reservation in First Officer Bryana. Is there a particular reason for that?" Connie crossed her arms, eyes tracing the line of Carrasco's face where it stuck out of the med unit. She yearned to reach down and caress his features—but too many flying probes were whizzing back and forth.

"The First Officer is currently developing an infatuation for the Captain." *Boaz* seemed reluctant.

"I see. In your opinion, *Boaz*, is it enough of a detri-

ment to our functioning together professionally? And, if
so, what do I do about it?''

The answer almost left Connie speechless. ''I suggest
you treat her the same way I treat you. Respect her affection for the man you love . . . and be professional.''

''But,'' Connie struggled. ''You're a . . . *ship!*''

''And Solomon Carrasco loved at least three ships prior
to me. That human can love ship is accepted. Is it therefore illogical in the converse that ship love human?'' *Boaz*
kept her voice unemotional.

Connie smiled wryly at the speaker. ''No, I suppose
not. All right, *Boaz,* as soon as we have met our responsibilities, let's see who can keep him?''

''Done!''

CHAPTER XXXI

She watched the surface of the first moon glow and blow
away. The white ship came for her. Around the planet
war had flashed and abated as the human ships struck
and curved off, trying to damp velocity. The fighting had
confused her until she came to the realization that those
primitive weapons were all they had. Had civilization
fallen so far?

The white ship drew closer now while one of the black
vessels nosed over the moon, detected the molten hole,
and veered to investigate. Subspace energized as frantic
messages babbled back and forth.

What would Sellers do now? So perfectly tailored for
her powers, he commanded the search of the planet. But
then, he had superiority of firepower. Would he use it
correctly to obtain her and become Master? Or would the
caste warriors in the white ship destroy him?

The white ship shed velocity, slowing to maneuver with
her terribly inefficient reaction motors, and hovered overhead. The quaint sight of the cargo bay doors opening

goaded her insane frustration. What? No directional atomic fibers? Indignation twined through her like ropes of burning rage to knot and sear her thoughts.

She, the greatest power in the universe, would be *winched* aboard by beings so primitive they used *CARGO BAY DOORS INSTEAD OF DIRECTIONAL FIBERS!* Madness bubbled in her thoughts.

Damn the Aan! Damnation and dismemberment to their cursed souls! Vermin like *these* would control the spring?

To break these . . . vile *beasts* would be a simple delight! Only for such humiliation, she'd twist them, wring from them every erg of pain and anguished suffering as she crushed them in their own septic stew of organic damnation.

* * *

Misha's face betrayed perplexity as he stared into the monitors in the main hold. Green lights glowed across his homely face, underscoring his thick black eyebrows and the lines in his face. "The tractors have no effect. Gordon! Ijima! You guys get down there. Hustle now, that Arpeggian's spotted the tunnel. We don't have much time. Get that confounded egg hooked up, *and get back here!*"

On the bridge, Constance sank incisors into her lip as the cables dropped to dangle in empty loops over the *alien ship*. She watched the two crewmen clamber down and help slip the lines around the polished sheen of the Artifact. Ijima lashed the two cables together on the top while Gordon's suited figure dropped down out of sight to do the same below.

Ijima's voice snapped sharply over comm. "Take her up, Mish. We got her!"

The cables tightened. The Artifact rose for the first time in how many billion years? On the rocky ground below, not a trace remained of her long vigil.

Despite herself, Connie shivered, as if the premonition of a holocaust to come exuded from that featureless egg shape.

"Speaker!" Bryana called. "Arpeggians are accelerating past first moon. *Hunter* is to the rear."

"Weapons!" Connie called, swiveling in Sol's command chair.

"We're ready, Speaker." Fujiki's face glowed with anticipation.

Connie glared at the dots marking approaching Arpeggians on the screen. She turned. "Attention, diplomatic personnel. We're most likely going to engage in combat. I suggest that this is a good time to stow loose items and enter your high g environments."

Art looked up from where he bent over the sensors. "Sellers will be on us like a fly on manure. I don't see how he could miss all those concentric circles. Even our long-range scanning of the moon's surface would have shown them," Art muttered. "Like a . . . a damn target bull's-eye."

Connie leaned back in the command chair. "You can only see the circles when you exit the tunnel at precisely midnight or noon, First Officer. In fact, my father first saw it through his telescope one night." She smiled and raised a hand. "Please! Don't ask me why. I don't know.

"The site is guarded by some very complex technology. We tried to come back again after the first time we'd been here. No circles. We had to come back when the tunnel was open—or not at all. Unless we came through the tunnel, the rings were invisible—along with the Artifact. Father took a shuttle up through the tunnel once and I went around. I was in contact with him the whole time. I could see his shuttle . . . but I couldn't get to it. It was like it wasn't really there." She could see his skepticism. "I know that's impossible. The Artifact is a lot of impossible things. So are the quantum laws we live with when you get to thinking about them."

"Alien craft stowed." Misha called. "Uh, I'm going to leave the cables on this thing. I can't tie it down with any of the regular cargo locks, Speaker. I guess we'll have to do this the old-fashioned way."

"Weapons?" Connie glanced around. "Cal, keep an armed guard outside that alien ship. No one, I repeat, no

one but myself or Captain Carrasco must be allowed close
to it. Is that understood?''

Cal nodded, dark eyes expressionless, ''Yes, Speaker.''

Bryana, attention on her weapons targeting, added.
''Five minutes until the Arpeggians arrive, Cap . . . uh,
Speaker.''

''Get us some maneuvering room.'' Connie called.
''Take her to port, twenty degrees.'' Maybe they could
sneak over the horizon before accelerating away. Connie
shook her head, seeing the upper surface of *Boaz* mot-
tling like that of the moon, shadows, rocks and craters
picture perfect.

Violent streaks of light shot out as *Hunter* slowed,
keeping high while the rest of Sellers' ships dropped toward the planetoid, moon probing.

Boaz announced, ''They're sounding the surface.''

''Looking for another hidden tunnel,'' Connie mused.
''Sellers is pretty sharp. He doesn't waste much time.
Boaz, power down any systems which might betray our
presence. Zero g, shut the grav plates down. Attention,
all personnel, zero g alert! Stow all loose items!''

She felt her stomach jump into her throat. Bryana threw
her a measuring glance, and bit her lip as she looked
away. ''Yes, First Officer?'' Connie asked. ''Did I miss
something?''

''No, ma'am.'' Bryana answered crisply. ''I just should
have thought of it first.''

A sensor raked their position and the surface erupted
three hundred meters from *Boaz,* debris arching high over
the ship.

''Blessed nova! Should I give the shields full power?''
Art worked his lips soundlessly, expression anxious as he
swallowed hard and watched the monitors.

''Not unless you want to be a target,'' Connie warned.
''This close to the surface, we'd create a ground roil.
From above we'll be at the apex of a large V. All the
Hound has to do then is pinpoint his blasters . . . and it's
all over.''

Art nodded slowly, green eyes worried as he stared at
the positions of the searching ships.

A strain had appeared in Bryana's expression as she glanced at the screens. The command chair creaked under her as she shifted. Seconds grew longer, eating away at hope. Around her, even the hum of the ship seemed louder, frequency on gain.

They waited under the hammer, *Boaz* drifting toward eternity.

Connie stared nervously at the screen.

He's up there, those cold eyes glued to monitors like these. And if he gets me? What then? Rape—as brutal and painful as he can make it, of course—and, yes, pain . . . lots of pain. I'd be his until he warped my soul, trashed my brain and body. Oh, he's very good. I can imagine those frigid eyes—lit by excitement as he imagines the next way to shred what's left. Mutilation? I wouldn't doubt it. Maybe impregnate me? Make me bear his child before he ruined me forever?

She shivered, a gibbering horror scurrying through her mind. "Better death."

"Pardon?" Bryana looked up, on the edge of fear.

"Nothing, First Officer."

The nerve-wracking wait continued. Seconds hung in the air, lingered a slow death, and turned into minutes. A sheen of sweat pasted Art's brown hair to his brow, the edges of his mustache quivering like a stunned mouse's vibrissae.

Connie watched a black shape glide overhead against the star-speckled darkness. "As soon as he's over the horizon, I want everything we can take. Can you give me full thrust with instant grav plate reaction so we don't turn ourselves into crushed mush?"

"Affirmative. I'm powering up. You've got forty gs on command, Speaker." He swallowed hard. "Assuming the grav plates hold."

"We won't feel a thing if they don't Art," Bryana growled from the side of her mouth.

"Boaz, give me that acceleration the very second he's over the hill. All hands, prepare for high g acceleration. Strap down, people."

"Acknowledged," *Boaz* intoned, bridge lights flickering to yellow and back to green one by one.

The black shape slipped away in silence so thick even breathing could be heard. The predator and the prey . . . acting their roles in deadly silence.

The weight of the universe smashed Connie back into the control chair as *Boaz* threw forty gravities of acceleration against the surface of the moon. They rose to meet the stars.

"Bogey clearing the horizon!" *Boaz* warned.

"Shields full!" Connie struggled to catch her breath as what felt like six gravities continued to punch her into the chair. Even the bones in her chest seemed to creak.

Art worked over his board, speaking softly to Happy in Engineering. Blaster fire lanced out, trying to interpret their ballistics.

"First Officer Bryana," Connie called. "You are authorized to return fire at will. Good luck, and good shooting."

"Acknowledged!" Bryana rapped, narrowing her eyes as she concentrated into her headset, the unit glowing around her skull.

Cal's brilliant blasters arced back, flaring shields as Bryana and *Boaz* computed their acceleration against that of the surprised Arpeggian. The black ship veered off, dumping everything into shields and acceleration.

"And here comes *Hunter.*" Connie grimaced. She turned to comm. "Get me a line to Captain Mason, Star's Rest Fleet. Claude? This is the Speaker. Where are you?"

Mason's face filled the screen. "We're coming down from high orbit, Speaker. We've seen fighting and assume it's *Boaz.*"

"We're running, Claude." Connie looked up. "Just a minute until we can dial in directional." She saw the signal narrow. "See if you can break up some of the pressure they're putting on us. From tech specs, *Boaz* ought to be good enough to handle up to four of them at once. But try to whittle away at the odds a little. Tell the crews it's for the old man. We owe him that."

"Aye, Conn . . . Speaker, that we do. A lot of us,

well, we're still stunned." He hesitated. "We're on the way, Connie, but in the meantime, take care of yourself, huh? One loss like that is enough for an old man like me to bear."

She winked at him. "Take care yourself, Uncle Claude. Guess we'll see what you really managed to beat into my thick skull."

She canceled the connection, staring thoughtfully at the monitors.

The chase was on. *Boaz*, with superior acceleration, sought to get the edge on the Arpeggians, who held a better tactical position. The Arpeggians, with velocity and altitude advantages, slowly closed the gap while *Boaz*, streaking ahead of her reaction, strained grav plates against inertia to protect her fragile human cargo.

Connie leaned back and somehow managed to extract her coffee cup from her space pouch. "Well, kids, from now on it's a matter of time. Either *Boaz* outruns them; or we kill enough of them to survive; or they take us and that's that."

The screen showed the pursuers, lining out. Connie tasted the coffee. It seemed acid and flat. From the flares of the ships trying to cut them off, it became apparent that Sellers was putting his men through terrible stress. Even combat suited, it must have been agony.

Connie chuckled. "Well, for a first deep space hop, you sure picked a dull one."

Art turned to shoot her a quick grin. Bryana kept her eyes on the screens.

"Ready to re-up?" Connie asked. "If you don't want duty on *Boaz*, I always have a need for trained officers in my fleet."

Bryana shook her head slowly. "Speaker, *if* we make it home alive, I'm not sure I wouldn't be interested in sitting in a station someplace, enjoying point two gravities—and getting fat!"

Connie chuckled. "Oh, I don't know, Bryana. Considering Sol told me you just graduated, I think you're outstanding—both of you. Every deep space jump isn't like this one—but from what I've seen of your personalities, you'd be bored stiff in that station.''

"I said *if* we make it home," Bryana reminded her.

Connie nodded and turned her attention back to the screens. Another minute dragged by and then another; the lights were converging. She whispered, *"Boaz,* prognosis?''

"We are going to be within range in approximately five and a half minutes, Speaker. We will remain within their range for seven minutes. In that time we will sustain the combined firepower of six Arpeggian cruisers.''

"Estimation of our chances?'' Connie asked, feeling defeat begin to sift through her brain.

"At this time—five percent,'' the ship replied. "Keep in mind that combat always defies statistics.''

Connie closed her eyes, struggling to think. *Boaz* hardly penetrated her concentration as option after option passed through her thoughts.

"Speaker, the Captain would like some of your time.''

Connie opened her eyes to see Bryana, white-faced. Art continued chewing his mustache short, fingers playing over the console absently as he thought into his headset.

"Put him on.'' She looked up. "Hi, Sol. It doesn't look good.''

His face was pale and drawn, eyes partly glazed as he stared out of the med unit. "No," he managed softly. "It looks like they're using a closing hex. Allow them to get into position. Keep Cal's blasters at one-third power . . . shields at maximum. One of them will want to get in closer since their shields will have a long way to go before overload. Let him in, Connie. When he's close enough to really hurt us, let Cal boost his fire while you change vector and dive at him. If you blow a hole through him, you've got your out.''

She thought about it, studying his glassy eyes. Drugged? If not, pain had to be eating him alive. How far could she trust his judgment, not knowing how *Boaz* had impaired his brain?

"Carrasco always brings his people back," Art muttered under his breath.

"We'll do it, Sol." Connie decided, knowing it sounded like suicide. She gave him a brave smile and the screen flicked off.

"It's crazy!" she muttered as the first fingers of blaster fire licked at *Boaz*'s shields.

Cal shrugged on screen, black eyes intent on his weapon control boards. "Cap says it'll work."

"*Boaz?* Projected success?"

"Thirty to forty-seven percent, depending upon which variables are employed."

"Beats five," Art grunted.

Bryana triggered her blasters. *Hunter* waited, still the farthest out. "That one," Connie decided, pointing to the ship opposite the Hound's. "He's been boosting at almost thirty-five g. He seems the most anxious. We'll bait him, hoping Sellers won't see through the ruse."

"Just like Carrasco did off Arpeggio!" Bryana chuckled as Cal's reduced blaster fire shimmered the victim's shields. True to Carrasco's words, the black ship edged in—eager to win the honor of putting *Boaz* out of commission. So confident was the Arpeggian that he began centering his fire on *Boaz*'s reaction tubes, hoping to cripple her mobility.

How close?

Art glanced at the stats, saying evenly, "Shields reaching maximum, Speaker. We have maybe thirty seconds left before a critical fluctuation."

"Thirty seconds to full power, Cal!" Connie clenched a fist. "Bryana, keep your targeting accurate. He's moving."

"I think I have his pattern worked out. Would have been tougher if they'd left it under comm control since there'd be random movement to avoid our fire. I'm keeping our guns a little off, Speaker. I hope he'll consider it a glitch in our fire control."

"Excellent!" Connie watched the shield condition climb into the red. "*Boaz!* Take him!" she shouted as the alert condition on the shields glared the color of a bloody ruby.

G attempted to pull them in two as *Boaz* threw everything she had into a vector change, heading right for the Arpeggian. Cal's blasters lanced brilliant searing violet as the Arpeggian panicked, trying to veer off, shields flaring. The white flash glared, blinding as the screens failed to compensate. *Boaz*'s shields peaked and buckled—holding in the last seconds before the hull could be exposed—and they were free.

"Evasive action!" Connie shouted. "They're trying to pin us."

Boaz rolled and twisted, able to maneuver now and catch bolt after bolt on fresh shields, spinning to de-energize them on the off side before she had to absorb more.

"*Hunter*'s turning . . . attempting to reform," Art called as Bryana settled her guns on another target and lanced violet fire in that direction.

"Damage report, *Boaz?*"

"Hull damage is restricted to ablative coating and occasional pitting—no serious breaches, Speaker."

"Estimated time within Arpeggian range?" She bit her lip, seeing the Arpeggian formation expanding as they threw out lateral acceleration to trap *Boaz*.

"Assuming constant vector, eight minutes."

"And our chances in those eight minutes?" Connie rapped out.

"Forty percent, depending on the permutations of a new Arpeggian attack formation."

Connie worried it. With each course change they lengthened the time under Arpeggian fire. Slowly the shields climbed toward critical overload as *Boaz* spun faster and faster to spread the absorption over her shielding. Behind them, space glowed and radiated as particles were thrown off the shields by acceleration, leaving an aurora of color fading into the blackness.

"Bryana, pick one target," Connie decided. "Take the closest, back him off as far as you can. Perhaps you can even kill him."

Promptly the blasters pinpointed a ship and shields glowed as the Arpeggian veered off, slowing, falling behind. At the same time, the others, shields cooling, poured more energy into their weapons. *Boaz*'s shields were climbing toward critical.

"One thing," Art gritted, sweat starting down his face. "We taught them to keep their distance! We didn't go alone!"

"Don your helmets, people." Connie ordered. "We have four minutes left."

"We won't make it," Art's voice came through the helmet comm. "Under their combined fire, we're heating up past capability. Shields are beginning to buckle."

Connie nodded. "Maybe we'll still make it."

But they weren't going to. She could see it as the shields flared, Bryana still driving the Arpeggians back as they closed for the kill. So close! What else could she have done? She unlocked the dead-man's switch, the toggle which would blow the antimatter free in the event of a reactor overload.

She could imagine Sellers' face, grinning, laughing as he raped her. She'd be his. She pictured Sabot standing before the Artifact, face lit with pleasure as the green-brown knob rested under his hand. Drained of emotion, she calmly closed and locked the dead-man's box. If they were to die, better to hope the failed containment would take them all—including the alien Artifact—in one final burst of matter/antimatter reaction. And who knew, the resultant explosion might kill an Arpeggian or two along the way.

"That's it!" Art cried as the shields began to buckle under the combined power of the Arpeggians.

How many seconds now before the hull breached and *Boaz* died? "Farewell, good ship!" Connie called. "If Sol's still conscious, tell him I love him."

"Save it!" *Boaz* responded. "The Arpeggians are backing off. *Hunter* and two other ships are under fire. Our shields are rebuilding. Arpeggians are breaking formation, assuming evasive tactics."

Connie looked up at the screens to see the Arpeggians

lancing blaster fire ahead and above. Streaks of purple light crisscrossed the stars as the Arpeggians struggled to change their formation into a defensive position, losing V at the same time as *Boaz* shot ahead.

Art let out a whoop. "It's your Captain Mason, Speaker. *We're saved!*"

The Speaker's fleet streaked by at a thirty degree angle. Connie hailed the flagship, *Dancer*, on comm. "Good to see you, Claude! Things were a little hot here."

"We didn't kill any, Speaker, but we holed a couple of them. From reading your acceleration, you've got them outrun. We'll see you on the other side as soon as we can change vector." Mason wore a look of grim determination.

"Affirmative. Claude, I'm naming you Deputy Speaker in case anything happens. You're to follow Solomon Carrasco or Galactic Master Kraal's orders in the event of my death or disability."

"Death or disability? I taught you better than that. I'll acknowledge the command structure, however. See you on the other side, Connie. We assume any Arpeggian is fair game."

"So long as you don't risk yourself or your ship, Claude." She smiled and gave him a firm nod. "Take care. God be with you."

"Don't risk *Dancer?* Who in hell are you talking to? We're talking about killing Arpeggians, here, not dealing with a serious threat. I've killed better pirates than Sellers. This is Archon's fleet!"

"Just be careful. You're our only hope for backup." Then she killed the connection.

Connie pulled her helmet back and shook out her hair, Stone cold coffee had left a ring in her cup.

"Out of range, Speaker," Art whooped. "We're going to make it!"

"All right, stand down from stations." Connie ordered. "You have no idea how happy I'll be to give this ship back to Carrasco!"

"What?" Art cried. "Tired of us already?"

* * *

Sabot slapped a black-gloved hand on the console before him. "So close, so cursed close!" He glared at the screen where Archon's fleet shot away after breaking off their attack.

Elvina looked up from the navcomm, aware of the silence on the bridge as weapons officers and comm personnel waited for Sabot's anger to be unleashed.

"*Boaz* is pulling away. They've got us on acceleration. We couldn't have done more. For the moment, their technology is superior," Elvina told her father.

"And you didn't find a flaw we could exploit within the ship?" Sellers leaned back in his command chair, gut in turmoil. The white dot of *Boaz* seemed to mock him.

She turned, stretching, the fullness of her young body straining at the classic black uniform. A tigress, she stood before him, breasts high, head back, the violent blue of her eyes meeting his. "I couldn't penetrate the system—and, Father, *I was brilliant.* I can tell you the ship spied on almost everything I did. No matter which man I bedded, the Captain changed his attitude toward the man immediately. I doubt he was even aware of it. I regret I never had the chance to bed Carrasco—but he was withdrawn, elusive. I got close once—with a triple dose of hormone. Perhaps, had I managed to get something in his drink . . . Ah, well, what secrets I could have milked from his reeling mind.

"Ben Geller really tipped the balance. He was smarter than the others—except Ngoro, of course. He was Mossad, didn't let down—not even on the verge of orgasm."

"Yet you seduced him?" Sellers lifted an eyebrow.

She smiled cunningly. "It took a while, Father. A most difficult game when you know you're under observation the whole time. I had to make the injection just as they climaxed, keep them on top while I hooked up the apparatus, whispered the questions in their ears, and read the answers on the machine. I pumped Lietov, Hitavia,

and Texahi that way time after time. Ben Geller, however, grew suspicious when he woke up in my arms. I
don't know, perhaps the psych I used on him left something, a fuzziness. Those black tubes might need refine-
ment.''

''Or maybe he doesn't sleep in a strange woman's arms
after sex? But we don't need to worry about Israeli power
reinforcing the Brotherhood?''

''He had no idea of the stakes.'' She swung around
lithely, smiling at Kralacheck when he glanced up from
his sensor station. He winked, a slow smile spreading on
his lips, the light of anticipation in his eyes. She wiggled
her hips suggestively.

Sellers frowned at the screen where *Boaz* boosted away
from him. Above, Archon's fleet shed delta V, seeking
to change vector. Another couple of minutes, and he'd
have had *Boaz*, crippled her. At that moment, he could
have wheeled on Archon's fleet, blasted it, and dropped
to obtain the alien prize. Now, he must scramble again,
race against Brotherhood.

''But who commands her?''

Elvina dropped down beside him, staring at the monitor. ''To react with that much talent? Either Carrasco or
Constance.''

''But Carrasco is dead.''

She met his chilling eyes. ''So we assume. Only, Father, in our experience, the man has the lives of a cat!''

''This can be saved yet—as long as they don't use the
Artifact against us.''

She tapped a long thumbnail against her white teeth.
''I don't think Carrasco will. Too much moral rectitude.
But Constance? You were a fool to bed her, Father. She's
much too dynamic to forgive you for using her like that.
She's not only capable of using the machine against us,
she'd revel in your destruction. I thought I'd killed her. I
didn't know an antidote for sitah existed.''

Sabot smiled. ''Then perhaps she'll be mine in the
end? Who knows. The gamble is greater now, that's all.''

She spun toward him, quick as a cat, dropping to stare

into his frosty eyes. "Our House is at stake, Father. I'd take a very dim view if you ruined it."

* * *

She studied her surroundings, measuring, computing the environment. Artificial gravity tugged at her as she prodded with her sensors.

Stunned, she withdrew. Intelligence! *This ship thought!*

Carefully, she studied the matrices. So much more intelligent than the animals! Could the ship be Master? Was that the secret of the animals? If so, the white ship must be destroyed—and the animals would do that in the end given the choice of serving the white ship or working her spring. Organic life, of course, always bore that flaw.

Pausing for a moment, she searched about, noting Sellers diving down from the first moon. Over the following hours, she watched the battle, observing, integrating data, learning about her new environment.

Why didn't the woman use her to destroy Sellers? Such a simple task, yet they left her in the cargo bay and relied on such inferior particle beams and symmetry fluxing shields. But then organic life had always been plagued by such odd notions as ritual combat. Only the Vyte had managed to overcome such biological fantasy—and replaced it with other fantasies just as damning.

No matter, wait . . . wait and see. After all, time was her ally.

CHAPTER XXXII

"I'm starting to think I'm not even human anymore!" Sol grumbled as he stood in the walker for the first time, mind making the machine do what his legs were supposed to.

"It'll only be for a week," Connie said shortly, arms

crossed as she watched. "Were it not for your ship, you'd be lying in the stasis locker next to my father. Don't complain about a windfall."

Sol shot her an irritated glance. "Maybe, but I've spent half my life in a med unit and the other half relearning my body. It gets old."

Boaz broke in, "Please try and walk now that you have mastered standing."

"Mechanical despot!" Sol mumbled. Gingerly he took a step, then another. "Want to see me run?" He asked, looking mildly at *Boaz*'s speaker.

"Want to sit in a med unit while I grow your spine back together again?" The ship responded easily.

"Want to go dive through a black hole?" Sol countered, face lined with disgust.

"Leave him crippled!" Connie decided, throwing her hands up. "He ought to feel grateful to be alive. Maybe he wants to suffer for some perverse reason."

Boaz kept her tone even. "Such depression is normal, Speaker. I think he'll grow out of it."

Sol started out the hatch. "If you two hens will excuse me, I have a meeting to go to."

Connie caught up with him as he hobbled uncertainly on his metal-reinforced legs. "All right, Sol, what is it? You've been worse than a baited mega since you woke up two days ago. The ship's in good shape. The Hound is behind us. You're alive. Why are you making everyone so miserable?"

He looked at her, eyes blank. "Well, if everything is going so well, why'd you even bother to wake me up?"

"Oh," Connie said softly, "I see. That primitive male ego raises its head. *Boaz*, do you agree?"

"I do. Again, it's normal after a major shock to the body and subsequent loss of command during his incapacity. No matter that his ability provided for our escape, his subconscious has been mulling it over while his body healed."

Sol bit his lip, feeling a vortex building in his gut. "Look, let's just see what the ambassadors have to say. We'll worry about my state of mind later." He'd said it more sharply than he'd meant to and Connie stiffened slightly.

"Very well."

The lounge sprouted familiar faces, having been turned into a large conference room. A spontaneous outburst of applause greeted Sol as he entered awkwardly on his temporary prosthesis. He smiled, waving down the questions they all tried to ask at once.

"Quiet!" Nikita Malakova boomed in his deep bass voice. The room stilled instantly. "Captain, for all of us, it is a miracle to see you here, alive, walking no less! How can we express what we feel . . . what we owe you?" Nikita shook his head, eyes glowing.

"I did what any of you would have." Sol looked around the room. "In the meantime, let's get on to business. I think you heard Elvina Sellers discussing the alien ship? That ship is aboard *Boaz* at present. The combat you experienced took place as we outran the Arpeggians. We've got it. They want it."

A mutter of low voices filled the room as Connie added. "The alien vessel, which we refer to simply as the Artifact, is the last deadly relic of a long-vanished race. Ladies and gentlemen, it offers its possessor the power to control the Confederacy. Some of you may have witnessed the tapes made when Fan Jordan surrounded *Boaz*. That was the Artifact in action. Three battle-class star ships were popped out of space . . . just that quickly. The characteristics of the ship go even beyond that. My father moved a dense blue-white star out of space."

"If this ship is so deadly, why don't we destroy it?" Dee asked.

Connie waved down the ruckus that exploded. "To begin with, we don't know how. Please, remember, we're dealing with alien technology. Besides, the ship is more than a weapon. With its powers, our scientists can see the inside of stars, explore galaxies a billion light-years from ours in a single afternoon. I watched my father peer into the guts of an atom. This is the greatest research tool ever. Not in two thousand years will humans have the like—if then. It is the greatest opportunity ever in the history of the human race. Perhaps it's an alien joke, but incomprehensible potential comes at the risk of incomprehensible threat.''

They sat, stunned. Charney Hendricks, bushy mustache twitching, got to his feet. ''If this is truly the case. If the machine does what you say, we can solve mysteries which have baffled men since the beginning of time. It is a priceless acquisition. We must take this ship to University immediately.'' He looked at the faces around him, hands extended, eyes pleading.

Sol rapped the table as the gabble of voices rose. ''I would remind you, this ship lies at the center of a vortex of interstellar politics. The Arpeggians will do anything—and I mean *anything*—to get their hands on this prize. Whoever controls the device, controls the galaxy. Do you understand?'' He searched their faces. ''We are talking about the ultimate power in space—possibly in the universe! It can see everything. There's no place to hide where this device can't probe. While on the second moon, I looked inside the Confederate Council room. I killed those three New Maine ships. I heard my First Officers dickering with Jordan on the bridge of *Boaz,* and when Fan attacked, I worked the device that eliminated those ships.''

He studied them, eyes bright. ''Yes, Dr. Hendricks, the Artifact has the power to answer any question. The question we cannot afford to answer, however, is if it's true that ultimate power ultimately corrupts. You'll get one chance to make a mistake with the Artifact! After that, he who controls it . . . controls humanity.''

''I think you overestimate the danger, Captain!'' Charney Hendricks protested. ''To consider an artifact capable of—''

''He does not!'' Constance stood, hands on hips, voice like a whip. ''Please, remember, my father and I discovered it in the first place. I've seen its potentials. We've barely scratched the surface in our understanding of this thing. Its true powers are unknown. What we have found, however, may be the key to matter transmutation, instantaneous interstellar transportation, subatomic physics,

and Lord knows what else. I also watched my father remove the mice from one of his ships, some sort of scan function. What it did to mice can be done to humans, ships, planets, or solar systems. Do you want a crusader to get hold of such power? How can you safeguard it?''

Hendricks shook his head. "You know that what you say goes beyond any possible explanation of physics? You're overreacting. I'm sure what you thought you saw—"

"How often, Doctor, has the same been said?" Sol asked. "In the early twentieth century, flight was considered a physical impossibility. In the early twenty-first century, light speed was *proved* to be an impossible barrier! Who are you to say what is possible given the ability to see into stars? Knowledge overcomes any barrier, Doctor!"

Hendricks smiled condescendingly. "Captain, I don't doubt your abilities to command a ship such as this. Do you doubt mine as a scientist with—"

"Damn it, we're talking alien technology here. No, I don't doubt your ability in *human* science."

Mark Lietov stood, looking around, drawing attention before he began. "Captain, let's assume you're correct in all the claims you're making. This Artifact will do all these things. Are we to understand you'll give it to the Brotherhood first? Will any of the other governments in the Confederacy see it after that? Will it not become just another tool to pursue your political policies?''

"The very reason you're all here is to make sure that every government's interests are met. You are all—"

"Bah!" Lietov exploded. "I think this is all a whitewash to give legitimacy to Brotherhood theft of the device!"

Nikita Malakova rose like a Gulagi bear, roaring, "Enough, Mark! I personally trust the Captain." He glared around the room, black beard quivering with the strength of his emotion. "If this had been a cover-up, why didn't he leave us in the Port Authority office to be blown to bits?"

"And that might have been cleverly arranged! Why did

that Arpeggian cut him loose? Who *was* that man?" Lietov turned to look at Carrasco. "A Brotherhood agent perhaps, Captain?"

"Carefully arranged?" Nikita exploded, waving meaty hands violently. "So carefully arranged the Captain died getting us off the planet? His back was broken! His legs dangled, blood ran from every orifice in his body!"

"A remarkable recovery," Lietov waved. "Can you believe this man was dead?" His voice almost broke with incredulity.

"Perhaps I can shed some light on the Captain's recovery." Texahi rose and looked around. "The wonders of his ship's hospital saved my life. I have since been briefed by First Officer Arturian on how Elvina Young's poison worked. Basically, the ship had to regenerate the nerves which led to my heart. I have no doubt as to the seriousness of the Captain's condition."

"Then you've been duped!" Lietov waved him off. "Did the great ship brainwash you, Texahi?"

"It did *not!*" Texahi's eyes burned as he glared at the Sirian diplomat. "Perhaps I'm not a craven politician like the rest of you . . . social vermin, but I have my own mind and—"

"Sit down!" Medea hissed, pointing. Texahi hesitated, struggling with himself. Then, with dignity, he walked from the room, back straight.

"Enough of this bickering," Tayash Niter said in annoyance. "This isn't the Council! We have a very serious matter to discuss here. I suggest that we quit throwing improbable accusations around and see if we can't make some meaningful progress over how to employ this *Artifact* for human use."

"The Captain says this is the ultimate spy device," someone quipped. "Gulag Sector wants a thousand already!"

Sparse laughter broke out, defusing some of the tension.

Lietov's face had drained to a deathly pallor. "Laugh if you will! For one, I refuse . . . *refuse* to end up as a Brotherhood puppet!"

Tayash Niter stood up. "But could this *thing* really find all of the independent stations? They're spreading through space in all directions! How could this thing track them down?"

Connie raised her hands, palms outward. "We don't know the limits of the automated search function. I would suspect it could. From what we know about the aliens—and that's enough to be scary—they'd have faced the same problem. Space is wide open. It's my suspicion that the mummy we took to Kraal was the last of his kind. They killed themselves off, ambassadors. I suggest you not forget that."

"How can you say that?" Lietov demanded, Charney Hendricks nodding agreement.

"Assume you had ultimate power, Mark," Connie told him. "Assume Admiral Sellers also had ultimate power. Where would it end between you?"

"But we are men—*intelligent* human beings!" Lietov protested, "There is no need for us to extinguish ourselves!"

"Intelligent? You blindly accuse the Brotherhood—whose motives you don't even know! And can't prove! At same time, you call the Hound—*Arpeggian Planet Burner*—a man?" Malakova cried. "Did I see Solomon Carrasco cut Joseph Young into pieces? Did I see him shoot first? You are irrational!"

"Please," Sol soothed. "Such talk gets us nowhere. The fact remains—as Archon so aptly put it—a man can begin as a saint, but where does your own righteousness end and another man's begin? For example, let us assume I had followed my inclination and popped *Hunter* out of space. What's next? Arpeggio? We might agree space is better without them. And then if Last Chance disagrees violently with Confederate policy, do we destroy them? What would have been the fate of Sirius during the unrest a few years back? What of the innocents there?"

"But you said you could kill individuals with this thing!" Mac Torgusson reminded.

"All right, so I pop Nikita here out of existence because he has the nerve to propose anarchy! Is that healthy for all of humanity? Dissent, like it or not, leads to growth!''

''Everyone is too carried away with the political implications!'' Hendricks interjected angrily. ''If this thing can see inside of the atom, if it can uncover the secrets of stellar fusion, give us the first comprehensive vision of the universe, it's worth *any* price! People, think! What's the transmutation of matter worth? And . . . and exploration? We can go anywhere! Determine the mechanics of gravity! Mine toron from neutron stars, the limits are unbounded! *Think of what we can learn!* Consider the benefits of—''

''At the expense of what sort of terror? Slavery? Hmm? You would pay the price the Americans paid in the twenty-first century? Subservience for a no-risk society?'' Origue Sanchez asked. ''I *saw* what Elvina did! Can we guarantee such as she will not get hold of this device? We speak of *absolute* tyranny here!''

''And it will be Brotherhood tyranny!'' Lietov glared at the rest of them. ''Mark my words! Yes, tyranny, by a secret organization which skulks in the shadows of political light.''

''It could turn into another arms race,'' Sanchez added thoughtfully, preempting Malakova's explosive response to Lietov.

The last one didn't destroy us.'' Lietov raised a finger to emphasize. ''Humanity survived—and got off the planet.''

''There was Soviet to seize initiative that time, too,'' Malakova said. ''They exploited space. Was tyranny, Mark. Politics of oblivion on one hand—or strangulation on other. And in between huddled people. Nice thing about Artifact, no bodies to have to deport to Gulag planets. Is ultimate Nazi 'Night and Fog' solution.''

''The alien technology will not spawn another arms race,'' Connie protested. ''This is so far beyond anything our labs could produce that it becomes a moot point. A similar, but very poor, analogy would be to provide a blaster to aboriginals with stone technology.''

Wan Yang Dow observed, ''I wish Archon had never

found this *thing;* we would be better off without it. Perhaps he should have left it where it was?''

Connie shook her head. "It was meant to be found. The Star's Rest system is like a huge beacon from space. My father thought it best to give it to the Confederacy. He may have been naive in that regard; but he didn't think any one nation should own a weapon of such magnitude, or have such an advantage when it came to the acquisition of knowledge. It should belong to all of humanity.''

"How would we control it?'' Stokovski, the Confederate representative, asked.

Mikhi Hitavia added, "How many secrets have been stolen throughout human history? Can we assume that any place is safe when the Artifact can grant so much to its possessor?''

"The Brotherhood has managed to keep their secrets,'' Nikita said. "I, for one, trust them with their ships. I think I trust this Kraal, too. But suppose we give them Artifact to watch for humanity. Will next man have Kraal's concern for humankind? Remember, we talk about *ultimate* power.'' He spread his hands, black eyes on Sol's. "You see, with device, even your computers, your Committee of Jurisprudence, are little more than pawns.''

Sol exhaled loudly. "I can't say, Nikita. With the checks and balances in our system, no man *should* be able to create a tyranny. With a power like this, who can say? It *is* absolute.''

"Hah!'' Lietov exploded. "Even the Brotherhood distrusts itself!''

Nikita shook his head and muttered with disgust. *"Oh, shut up!''*

"Captain,'' Mac Torgusson stood. "I suggest you adjourn this meeting. Give us a couple of days to think on it. Perhaps in that time, we can come up with some way to give ourselves—and humanity—an out.''

"I think that's a definite step in the right direction,'' Sol agreed. "In the meantime, I'm appointing Tayash

Niter as *ad hoc* chairman for meetings such as this. I believe he's about as neutral as you can get.''

"When can I see the ship?" Hendricks asked. "I would like to begin my studies as soon as possible.''

"That's another thing," Sol told them. "The Artifact is off limits!''

A roar of outrage filled the room. Sol waved it down with the help of Nikita's booming voice. Sol added. "Listen, we've already had one spy on this ship. What if Elvina had waited patiently? Further, we don't know what all the knobs are for. What if someone pushed one and we ended up in the Sombrero Galaxy? What if someone figured out how to use the weapon? Would any of you who were arguing today want your opponent loose in there?'' They were silent.

Sol spoke softly. "I've had my engineer install an antimatter device aboard. Any of you who wish to take matters into your own hands will do more than that. You will take the Artifact, *Boaz,* and all of us with you.''

"Then," Lietov pointed out, "we don't know that it will do all these things *you* claim.''

Sol nodded coldly. "I guess you'll just have to take my word and Constance's, won't you?'' He gave Lietov a cool smile as he wheeled on his metal legs and walked out.

* * *

"Could I see you, Captain?" Nikita leaned into the hospital.

"Come in, Representative." Sol shifted his head on the cushioning foam of the med unit.

"Is relapse?" Nikita asked, gesturing to the machine.

"No, just a standard therapy session. Takes time to check and recheck all the neurons the unit spliced. It's pretty delicate surgery. I get a command through the headset I'm wearing to lift my leg. I try to lift my leg which is immobilized. The unit reads the reaction, checking to see that it matches the one sent to my brain. At the same time, the neural pathways are checked for compliance and growth. You've got to have redundancy in the nervous system, so that's being strengthened.''

Nikita grunted assent, pulling up a gravchair and slumping into it. ''Is not interruption?''

''No, I can do two things at once.''

''Would talk to you, Captain, as one man to another. About Artifact, I have taken serious risks on your word. Even Tayash looks at me with reserved eyes. At same time, some of your claims are a . . . Well, belief is stretched.''

''I wish Archon hadn't been forced to . . . Damn you, Elvina! You might have believed him over me. Nikita, I'm afraid I'm all I've got for proof—and, no, I'm not letting anyone inside to work that thing! It's a damning of the soul to do it. And if I let every politician use it, they'd still claim it was another Brotherhood trick—that they couldn't prove they'd shunted Arpeggio into nothingness until they went to see for themselves.''

Sol stared at the ceiling panels, eyes haunted. ''And it's addicting, Nikita. Every time you push the lever, you feel a little more godlike—and a little less in touch with your humanity. And I . . . I suppose eventually, that's the horror of the thing.''

Malakova leaned forward, the thick mat of his beard bunched under his propping palms. ''Then I must ask you, what do you plan, Captain? Who will you give this thing to now that you have it in your hold? Will you trust Kraal's humanity? Or his successors? You know it is farce to give it to University. Or will you give it to Palmiere the First? Allow *him* to become god?''

Sol shook his head. ''Damn it, I . . . Nikita, I don't know what to do with it. What do you think? Seriously, tell me.''

Nikita smiled wistfully. ''You know, in end it doesn't matter. Suppose you give it to Kraal? Rest of Confederacy would strike immediately. Have had assurances of that from Lietov and Medea. So, combined might of Confederacy falls on Frontier? Only Artifact can save planet, no? Kraal becomes despot and shunts TPF, Sirian

League, Patrol, and who knows who else out of space. Confederacy is dependent on Frontier for resources."

"Unthinkable." Sol frowned. "We can't allow that to happen."

"We?"

"You and I, Nikita. Power corrupts. Power as great as this would eventually corrupt even the Craft. You know it, you've been reading the files. Yes, I know about that, I cleared your access to some of the restricted stuff."

"Why?" Nikita's face hardened suspiciously.

"Because you question. Because I think you really want to know—and not for political leverage, but for your own edification. Humanity fascinates you, doesn't it? That's why you continue to represent Gulag, isn't it? You're constantly puzzled, challenged, and amazed by humans. That, and you think you can actually make a difference."

Nikita rubbed his hands together, a slightly abashed look to his blunt features. "Perhaps . . . just a little of that is true."

"Well, read away. I'm not sure anything will be the same when we finally get rid of this thing. What good are Brotherhood secrets going to be if the Artifact can stare inside the Grand Lodge anytime it wants?"

Nikita sighed. "You know, is possible, Captain, that you and your ship may be stuck with Artifact for a long, long time. Perhaps is rest of your life to shunt device back and forth across space trying to keep it safe?"

"At least until someone can build a faster fleet with more powerful guns."

Nikita nodded soberly. "But then, with device, you have power to stop that at proverbial bud."

Sol swallowed. "It always boils down to that, doesn't it."

"Will you use it to protect it from others?"

"Double damnation." Sol blinked, suddenly tired. "Damned if I do . . . and damned if I don't."

Nikita stood. "And I would remind you of something else. Time changes such things as concept of responsibility. To use device becomes easier, less threat because is familiar. And tell me, what is really more important in end? To use device—in self-protection, of course—or to see it fall into hands of Elvina Sellers? Where, then does moral dilemma lie?''

''So, you think, no matter what, I'll end up using the Artifact? Damn myself?''

Nikita hesitated at the door. ''Think about it, Captain. Think hard and honestly . . . then you come tell Nikita truth.''

CHAPTER XXXIII

Sol let them see the outside of the alien ship. Even Lietov's skepticism vanished as Hendricks tried to get readings on the hull structure. When Constance told him about the walk-through bulkheads, the aging professor stomped off, mumbling to himself.

Shouting matches raged in the corridors, in the lounge, in rooms. On those occasions when they met, Nikita's baleful eyes demanded an answer. Sol only stared back haggardly, and shrugged his confusion.

They made the jump without a hitch, Sellers far behind. Sol began taking his watch again.

On the day *Boaz* released him from his metal cage, he enjoyed the feeling of freedom. Muscles slowly reacted to the learning process as his once severed spine traced new neural connections between brain and legs.

''So you're free!'' Connie greeted as she cleared the hatch, eyes instantly on the screens. She stopped, cataloging the stats from old habit.

''It's heavenly,'' Sol grinned over his coffee cup. He looked absently at the console where he'd been playing a losing game of Find the Ship with *Boaz*. ''Um, I want to apologize. I've been unnecessarily rough on you for the last couple of weeks.''

''I'm well aware of that . . . but it's all right.'' She

flipped her wealth of red-gold hair over a shoulder and settled athletically into the command chair. "I kept trying to put myself in your position. A strange woman has taken control of your ship. That *thing* is sitting in the hold like a malignancy. Your latest command is in jeopardy. And there were medical reasons which *Boaz* explained to me."

He nodded, biting his lip. "You know, the dreams were the worst. Med units do that to a person. They can't deaden all the nerves. Your mind knows how horribly you're hurt. Way down deep, fear builds in the subconscious and the brain relieves it through horrible nightmares. I'd see . . . no, live the vision of *Boaz* dead in space, holed, starlight shining through the rips and tears in her hull. I'd float through the corridors and companionways. I'd scream into the blackness, the very sound lost in vacuum. Only the corridors weren't empty; exploded bodies and crystallized fluids would leak away into space. All . . . all in that weird red and blue light like off Tygee."

"No, don't blame the med unit. It's the Artifact's tainting presence." She shivered. "I know how that thing affects people who understand it. In our imaginations, it's evil. Otherwise, it's simply a ship with a . . . a technology that scares the primitive parts of our brains. Men like to fear the dark, Sol. They like twisted beliefs about the nature of God and death—and still need to appease the things hiding in the shadows when they turn the lights down at night."

He nodded. "I've been fighting that fear all through this jump, Connie. Fear . . . just below consciousness. Every decision I make lingers in the shadow of fear." He stared absently at a bulkhead and knotted a fist.

"You've chosen right so far. You've—"

"*I've lost three ships!* I've had over one hundred of my people killed in one disaster or another! When I dream like that—I wake up simply wanting to quit. If I can react, fine. I manage to make the right choice more often than not. But . . . well, like when you were in the hospital, I had nothing to do and my mind went mad. It all piles up. Flashbacks spin up from . . . from . . ." He closed his eyes and shook his head.

"And you're trying to escape it all. Sol, you can't do it. You're not the legend the rest of space thinks you are. You're a human being like the rest of us."

"And if I fail, how can I live with it again?" He propped his chin on one palm and studied the mass detectors glowing lime green on the main monitor. "Three times in the past, a ship and a hundred people relied on me. I lost each ship and so many of the people. This time, it's all of human space. The future . . . rests on *my* shoulders?" He smiled sickly, "And if I make the wrong decision this time? Who do I trust that nightmare back there with? University? How long until it's stolen? One day? Two?"

Connie took a breath and reached for his hand. "Welcome to the club. Father and I didn't know what to do with it either. You just have to . . . Oh, hell, that's a damn lie. Fact is, I don't know what to tell you. When I look back on it, I think it's a miracle we didn't destroy the universe by pushing the wrong button!"

"Humans learn by pushing buttons to see what happens." Sol frowned, eyes empty. "Part of who and what we are, I suppose. Sophisticated apes, Connie, but apes nonetheless. Did you see the politicians in there? Still arguing, each side right, each side scared of the others. They look just like the colobus monkeys in the Arcturian Zoo!"

She tightened her grip. "Listen, my fleet is coming along behind. Let's drop the Artifact off on Frontier . . . or Arcturus. You can hand *Boaz* over to Petran Dart and we'll space that very day for wherever we end up. It is an option I want you to consider." She tilted her head, waiting, eyes measuring with that familiar old reserve.

Sol shook his head, continuing as if he hadn't heard. "And if the wrong man pushed the wrong button? What if someone like Lietov figures out the weapon? How do we live with the knowledge—even light-years away—that we allowed *that* to happen?"

"Just like you'd have to live with it if you let yourself

curl up and escape your responsibility to this ship and crew, Sol." She winked triumphantly. "Just as I thought. You're a pushover for responsibility, hooked on your duty to humanity. That's why I could make that offer to you. You won't back out until you're relieved of the burden. Then it's out of your hands. And I just uncovered the root of what depressed you in hospital, didn't I?"

He chuckled dryly. "I'm not sure I like the idea that you know so much about me."

She gave him a warm smile, radiant as her eyes sparkled. "If I didn't, I wouldn't love you, Sol." She squeezed his hand again, suddenly pensive. "It's because you care. You're kind, and gentle, and strong, and you know it way down deep inside. I never really loved a man before. None measured up the way I thought they should. None could work with me. Instead, they were awkward under my command, afraid of my abilities—or my father—or they wanted to dominate me." Her eyes flashed at the memory. "I don't dominate easily."

"Got that right."

She cocked her head. "That bother you?"

He smiled and bent to kiss her hand. "No. In fact, I've had a lot of time to think about us, during the last three weeks. You know, you did a superb job off Star's Rest. Won the respect of the entire crew. When this is over, finished one way or another, I want you to come with me." He flushed, lowering his eyes. "I, uh, never thought I'd say it, but I'm starting to have trouble imagining life without you."

"It's not just the superb sex?"

He shook his head, grinning. "No, it's . . . well, a hole inside that I never knew I had. That spot, down deep, it's . . . full. Yes, that's the word, full when you're around. Like part of my soul is warm and healthy and I'm content."

She bent down to kiss him, lips light and warm on his. "Thank you, Sol. It's mutual. I—"

Boaz interrupted, "Misha on comm, Captain."

"Put it through."

"Cap!" Misha looked worried. "That Lietov is here

with Hendricks. Says we wouldn't dare shoot him—and he's going on board the Artifact!''

"You have your orders, officer, carry them out. I don't care what you have to do. Use the Jordan option if you'd like . . . or simply shoot them. They know the rules.''

Misha nodded warily. "Aye, Cap. Acknowledged and logged!''

The screen expanded to display the shuttle deck where two of Fujiki's men came up from behind the gesticulating Lietov, calmly bent him into a pretzel, and EM restrained him.

Misha looked up at the monitor. "What now?''

"Confine them to quarters until they cool down.''

"You've not heard the last of this!'' Lietov sputtered as one of the weapons techs duck-marched him away.

Sol killed the connection. "No, probably not.'' He smiled wryly at Connie. "I may *have* to space with your fleet. Too many Confederate politicians will want me dead, dishonored, or imprisoned.''

Art passed the hatch. "You're relieved, Captain.'' He nodded at Connie.

"Anything new among the political herd?''

"Nikita wants to give the Artifact to the Brotherhood in trust for all mankind . . . with the expectation that it will be made available to scientific parties. He also proposes that an armed guard attend any researcher—with orders to kill the first one who touches the green-brown knob.''

"And Lietov said . . .'' Connie countered, a humorless smile on her lips.

"Nikita's become a Brotherhood lackey. And when Nikita heard that, he turned a bright shade of red and Tayash barely kept him from attacking Lietov. Of course, Mark had stewed himself into a rage by this time and ran off to demand that he be allowed to inspect the alien device.'' Art shrugged. "You hear anything about that?''

"Yeah, he's restricted to quarters along with Hendricks.'' Sol frowned. "Wish we were on the other side of Orion IV looking for monopoles.''

Art nodded. "They never told me it would be like this."

"Normally, it isn't." Sol got gingerly to his feet. "It's your helm, First Officer. I'm headed for my cabin in case they start a civil war in there. You're free to take any action necessary to protect the ship from the diplomatic corps—or the politicians from themselves."

"Gee, thanks, Cap. Hope your shorts creep up."

Connie followed him past the hatch, giggling. "Not quite the old dour Art, is he?"

"No, he came around. Thought he had the makings. Just took a little . . . persuasion."

She studied him for a moment. "By the way, I talked to *Boaz*. She says that with moderation, you're fit."

"Fit for what?"

"Wait and see." Her voice turned into a throaty whisper as she led him to his cabin.

That night, Sol's dreams didn't haunt him.

* * *

In the quantum world, observation changes reality. That law, so immutable, couldn't be violated—not even by the damning spring. Rather, she must work very carefully, lest she tip her hand before the time proved propitious. The white ship might be crude, but she didn't have a spring to condemn her to slavery. Of them all, the white ship might well be the most deadly.

Using only her scanners, tracing pathways around the white ship's thoughts, she prepared herself to strike, to integrate the N-dimensional matrices into her own. By enslaving the white ship, what powers could be hers? Perhaps a waldo with which to work the spring?

* * *

Art was in the lounge when the screaming started. Mac Torgusson landed a punch to Texahi's jaw. Nikita Malakova threw Torgusson across the room, bellowing. Torgusson pulled a stun gun and leveled it at Malakova. Art easily kicked his wrist so the weapon discharged into the gaming booth. The stunned booth flickered blue lights across the holo box and sputtered helplessly.

"That's it, *I've had it!*" Art thundered. "Torgusson! You're restricted to quarters! You started it, you live with it!"

"I refuse. Call your Captain! I have immunity, damn you, and you can bet I won't be bullied by any Brotherhood lackey like you, you little simp! How *dare* you attack me? You sniveling little two-bit tin God! I'll . . ." Torgusson took a swing at Art, who promptly broke his jaw and followed up with a knockout blow.

Art caught himself at the point of breaking Torgusson's neck. He relaxed, exhaling to still his racing heart, and looked around, suddenly conscious of what he'd done. *Oh cripes, the fat's in the fire now!* He accessed comm. "Uh, Captain. We need a med unit to the lounge, I just broke Ambassador Torgusson's jaw."

Carrasco's face pinched, color draining. "I'd like to see you on the bridge, First Officer."

Filled with dread, Art took a deep breath, looked at the wide-eyed ambassadors and forced a semblance of stiffness into his spine. The long white corridor stetched before him. *I'm maxed-out this time. Might just as well admit it, I've flushed this career for sure. Curse Carrasco anyway! The whole trip's been a god-damned disaster!*

He passed the hatch to see Bryana in her chair. Oh, God, it would be worse! Why hadn't she been as attentive as usual? Instead, she was constantly harassing Carrasco about this and that. Lord! She didn't find him attractive, did she?

"Explanations, First Officer?" Sol asked, reviewing Art's behavior on the comm. Art watched himself go through it again.

"None, sir." He added, "It was just a reflexive response. Torgusson pulled the weapon . . . and I kicked it away. Stun isn't necessarily dangerous, but it's unpleasant as all hell. Then when he threw that punch, I guess I got a little angry at the names he called me."

"I see." Sol nodded and took a sip from his stained

coffee cup. "First Officer Bryana, do you see any ameliorating circumstances here?"

She looked at the rerun of the assault. "Ambassador Torgusson reports he's filing charges of 'assault with intent to kill' against First Officer Arturian. That's pretty serious. On the other hand, Art was within his rights as an officer on this vessel to disarm and discipline Torgusson."

"Doesn't look like he was trying to kill him." Carrasco pointed at the screen. "Notice how he hit Torgusson on the side of the jaw instead of on the mastoid like Fujiki taught him? Either he's particularly inept or he didn't intend to be lethal."

"I'd say we vote for inept, sir; however, the repercussions will no doubt be severe." Bryana looked at Art and winked.

"Very well," Carrasco agreed. "I'll attend to the log. First Officer Arturian, it is the judgment of this investigative commission that no ship's charges be filed against you." Carrasco leaned forward, a glint in his eye. "On the other hand, as senior officer, I hereby assign you to a refresher course with Officer Fujiki to keep your competence up."

Art dropped his jaw. "That's all, sir?"

Sol continued, "Off the record, I wish you had broken his neck." He leveled his finger. "That does *not* mean you go out and pick a fight while you're under my command! But no officer on *my* ship should have to put up with crap like that! Officially—for the sake of appearances—I'm reprimanding you for fighting and for disabling a diplomat."

Sol bit his lip, frowning. "In the meantime, I want you and Bryana both to work with Cal. There may come a time when you need to disarm somebody without breaking anything." Sol smiled. "Sound fair?"

Art nodded, confused. "I think I understand sir, and uh . . . thank you."

* * *

". . . four, three, two, one. Mark! It's your hell-hole, Bryana!" Happy called. The screens filled with stars.

"Sensors are clean, Captain," Art reported.

"Captain?" Bryana looked up. "From stellar fixes, we've underjumped. We should be another—"

"No, First Officer, I came out right where I wanted to. Start dumping all the delta V you can. Sooner we've shed that velocity, the sooner we can maneuver."

Art grinned. "I get it. We drop out early. That means we can light the skies all we want. They'll expect typical Carrasco pinpoint accuracy and figure we'll come out as close to Frontier as possible."

"And we're going slow enough that we'll have more tactical flexibility—a chance to feel out the opposition between us and Frontier. If there's a problem, who knows, maybe we can work our way around it all." Bryana added. "Sir, I think I'm starting to figure how your head works."

Art leaned back. "So what does Carrasco propose to do with the alien device? You've got a lot of people back there in quarters stirred up. More than one wanted me to notify him the second we dropped back inside." Art flipped a hand out. "Even had a bribe of three thousand credits for first priority on comm."

"No comm," Sol decided. "For one thing, it gives away our position. For another, it can stack the odds against us. People, consider this, we're still three to four weeks from home. A lot can happen." He smiled grimly. "But for now, take a break and let me worry about it. Bryana, Cal said you're slow and fumbly in an attack. I also hear you don't have your heart in trying to hurt your opponent. See if Art will give you a hand. You're ordered to spend the rest of the watch practicing."

She beamed and nodded, hanging on his every word. Art appeared irritated by it all, nervous over her attention to Sol.

Carrasco heard the hatch whisper shut behind him as his officers left. "Well, good ship, what am I going to do now? How do I get that alien monkey off my back?"

"Insufficient data, Captain. I must inform you that I

have been picking up interference on closed circuits. That ship, I fear, is sentient. She's trying to talk to me—only the language is very difficult.''

Sol bolted upright, in his seat. "What the . . . *Damn it!* You let me know immediately if she breaks through. That might be the answer to all of our problems.''

"Affirmative. Logged, Captain.''

The Artifact, *sentient?* He reeled at the implications. Only if that were the case, why had she waited so long? What purpose could be behind her actions? Alien communication might be different. So? "And how does it make you feel, *Boaz?*" Sol asked, curious despite the fear eating at him. *I ought to blow the damn thing out the hatch and turn the blasters on it. Then I ought to antimatter bomb the debris—just to be sure.*

"In human terms, it's frightening. The effect is very similar to having alien thoughts in your brain. I experience a confusion of responses—a sort of interference with thought processes which is most annoying considering my integrated personality. No pun intended, Captain.''

"If you notice any decrease in functional ability—or if you break through to the alien—tell me immediately, *Boaz.* That *thing* could kill you! I don't like to take the risk as it is. I want an entire record of the Artifact's actions sent to Happy. Constant printout on anything, got it? I can't . . . can't lose you, *Boaz.*"

"Acknowledged and logged. And thank you, Captain. I don't want to lose you either. Did you know Constance and I have a bet in that regard?''

Nervous, Sol glanced uneasily at the speaker. "How do you intend to keep me, *Boaz?* Technically, you're Petran Dart's command.''

"I plan to request that you remain in command, Captain. I'm sure the Brotherhood will approve. They've never had a ship make such a request before. The entire concept will fascinate them . . . and I'll get you for 'further study,' while they try and understand what they have created.''

"And Constance? I'm rather fond of her. You know, she's offered me a commission in her fleet.''

"Which you won't take, Solomon. I know you too well. Already you fret at the idea of piloting a ship which can't talk back." *Boaz* sounded smug. "Further, you've adopted certain fawning behaviors when you talk to me. I think I have you where I want you."

"Fawning? Balderdash! I can always retire!" Sol shot back, frowning as he jammed his coffee cup into the dispenser. "Fawning!" he muttered, suddenly smiling up at the speaker. "So you think you have me where you want me, eh?"

"Affirmative, Captain. You are a man in love. You cannot walk away from Constance, myself, or the frontier. Retire, Captain? Constance isn't ready for that—and space is in your blood. Can you simply turn your back on this?" The three-sixty screen sent Sol dropping into the stars.

He leaned back, bracing himself against the command chair arms, awed by the sight. "Zero, g, *Boaz.*" He let his feet float, body gripped by the command chair. "And what do you intend to do with Constance? How am I supposed to choose between the two of you?"

"Unfortunately, she's a competitor to be reckoned with. In addition to her innate intelligence, grace, and poise, she has certain physical attributes which provide a substantial edge through sex. I'll cross that bridge when I come to it—assuming we survive the coming crisis." *Boaz*'s voice was soft.

Sol nodded, draining his coffee cup. "It always comes back to the Artifact, doesn't it?"

"So very much hangs on how the alien is disposed of," *Boaz* agreed. "From my computations, no matter what sort of equitable solution is proposed, warfare will be the final result. The powers are currently aligning within the Confederacy. The moment a decision is made and released, the have-nots will fall on the haves—desperate to strike before this alien technology can be used against them."

"And if I send it to University? They're apolitical, totally neutral."

"Can you protect it from a Sirian or Arpeggian raid?

Can you keep it from falling into the hands of the highest bidder?'' *Boaz* countered. "How *do* you keep it safe?"

Sol looked out over the vast peacefulness of space. It could all be rent and torn by the unleashed powers of the Artifact. Sellers had already burned one planet to the ground for an unpaid ransom. Suppose he did it again? The image formed of those ammonia frost eyes, the pale face, and the split beard. "Give me the Artifact—or I shall blast the heritage of Terra to molten slag! You have thirty minutes! Kill me if you dare, the antimatter device is hidden on the planet. If it does not hear from me, it *will* detonate!"

Who would say no? Even using the Artifact to search with, they couldn't find an antimatter device that quickly—or could they? Perhaps after scientists had the time to learn the machine's potential—but humanity wouldn't get that much time.

"Ultimate power, *Boaz.*" He rubbed his naked chin and wished his beard had grown back. "Just think! We could be real live emperors. Once inside that ship, I could eliminate Sellers and the Confederate Council. I'd take questions from the scholars, look into the atoms, and send the answers out. There'd be no more piracy, no more exploitation, no more poverty!"

"You were the one who articulated the Godhead factor, about remaking the universe in your image. Is that what you want, Captain? Would you recast humanity in your shadow? Work the spring with compassion and benevolence?"

"What choice is there? Humanity was the unlucky bunch who found it first!" He cocked his head. "Or did we? Just how old *is* that thing? I've seen Connie's report on the alien. Read her speculations. What if she's right? Suppose the alien didn't build the ship?" He looked out at the stars. "*Boaz,* do some figuring for me. Consider the average composition of a solar system against the age of the universe as we know it. Now, based on those criteria, what are the chances that we should be the only intelligent life in the galaxy?"

"Something like a billion to one against. I need not

even conduct the statistical manipulation, such studies have been conducted since the SETI investigations of the late twentieth century.''

"Then maybe that's the answer. Maybe it is a trap. Indeed, a trap that . . .'' Slowly, he straightened. A grim smile touched his lips. "Archon said that this thing was worth all of our lives, *Boaz*. I . . . I think I misunderstood the implications.''

"Captain?''

"Lives may be judged in more ways than one, good ship. I'm willing to gamble mine for humankind. Don't you think that's equitable? I'll always remember Amahara's words. 'Perhaps it is a time for heroes.' Even if the only one who knows I'm being heroic is me. And Ngoro, wherever you are, thanks for the lesson.''

Sol chuckled out loud, slapping hands to his thighs. "*Boaz*, we're going home. I want to see a plot of all the navigational hazards in our path.''

* * *

Happy Anderson rubbed his craggy face with thick hands as he stared, bleary-eyed, across the comm table at Sol and Connie. "I don't know what to tell you. O'Malley and I tried everything. Torches don't work on it. We shot a thin bean of antimatter into the hull. Should have had an explosion, right? Nothing. That gray stuff just absorbed it. Run a vibrashear into it and nothing happens, but then, you can reach your hand through the hull, too. Scared the shit out of me first time that happened! Thought I'd disintegrated myself or something. Laser, particle beam, it doesn't matter. Slap acid on the side, nothing. Dribble base on, nothing. We tried a small charge against the hull. Peeled deck plate back on *Boaz*, but didn't even mar the side of the damned thing. From the monitors, the hull just absorbed the shock wave. Cap, so far as I can tell, for all intents and purposes, the Artifact is indestructible.''

"Perhaps a thermonuclear explosion?'' Connie hypothesized. "Cobalt based? Something hot enough to . . ." She stopped at Happy's slow shake of his head.

"My guess is that whatever allows that thing to expand forever inside would just absorb it—if the heat even fazes that stuff. How in the hell do I know? Some protective strategy? Maybe it would shunt the bomb to wherever Archon sent his mice and that star and the New Maine warships? All I can prove is that I can't weigh, measure, analyze, cut, strip, melt, explode, bend, contort, or dent that hull stuff. I'm lucky I can cuss it!"

Sol stared absently at the overhead panels. "Any sign of what it's trying to do to *Boaz?*"

"Not a thing. I can't measure any fields, forces, or sensors around it. We've even taken to looking around in case it's drilling wires into the hull. Nothing."

Connie twisted a rope out of her hair, fingers working nervously. "Still, we'd better remain suited in case *Boaz* is compromised. So far, the Artifact has never shown any ability to manipulate her environment."

"So far," Sol agreed, eyes narrowing. "Damn it, if you were building the ultimate weapon, would you let it run around loose?"

"Maybe that's why there's no sentient life out there anywhere," Happy reminded.

Sol swallowed hard. "Yeah, and we're taking it right into the seat of humanity."

Connie whispered, "They used to burn bearers of plague."

9

CHAPTER XXXIV

Bryana picked up the bogey, estimated its course, and realized the other ship had already fixed the flare of their reaction mass. *Boaz,* dumping almost thirty gs, was hard to hide as a result of the visual and gravity distortion she produced.

It took four days for the ship to match with them. Solomon Carrasco called for battle stations and received the first message. He stared at the screen, seeing the familiar uniform.

"Captain Carrasco, I am Captain Richard Shaklee, of his Royal Majesty's Ship *Defiance.* I am ordered to discuss the alien ship you carry. As members of the Confederacy, you cannot deny us this opportunity. His Majesty is aware of the gravity of the situation and offers his willingness to protect the device from theft or misuse."

"I'll bet," Art muttered out the side of his mouth.

Sol shook his head. "I'm sorry, but I have polled the Council Members aboard and they've voted overwhelmingly to reject your offer. I might add, Fan Jordan fired on this ship at Star's Rest." Sol looked down and then back at Shaklee. "You must understand, Captain, New Maine is technically in a state of war with us as a result of that incident. I have not received an apology from Earl Jordan—nor have any of the diplomats aboard. I'm afraid your request is impossible."

"Are you refusing me, Captain?" Shaklee stiffened angrily.

"And how would you react if Brotherhood vessels had jumped *Defiance* while you were peacefully in orbit over a friendly planet? I'm serious, Captain. Think about it. We were shot at by *Desmond* and her accomplices—and that action was by Royal decree. Now, how much latitude does that leave us?"

"I see. Allow me to withdraw to converse with my government." Shaklee's features blinked off the screen.

"Now, there's a man with a dilemma," Bryana chuckled. "Think he's stupid enough to fight? Art, I'll bet a ten credit note against your one, he backs off no matter what his orders."

"No takers," Art grunted. "What kind of a fool do you think I am, huh?"

Sol laughed. "Are these my two wet-eared Academy graduates? What happened to those two quivering bundles of nerves?"

"Arcturus was a long time ago," Bryana told him.
"To tell you the truth, I can't even remember how long
ago that was."

"Yeah," Art added. "Some ornery cuss boxed my ears
in the gym one day and I forgot a lot of things. Amnesia,
I think they call it."

"Or brain damage," Bryana quipped with a wink.

Boaz broke in, "Message, Captain."

"Put it on." Sol leaned back while Shaklee's stern face
formed on comm.

"Captain Carrasco, *Defiance* sends greetings. I am ordered by the government to provide escort for the duration of your voyage as a gesture of the friendship and
esteem with which His Majesty views the Brotherhood
and the Confederacy."

Sol smiled his amusement. "I assure you that won't be
necessary. Please, don't misunderstand, your offer goes
a long way toward salving recent wounds; but *Boaz* can
take care of herself. We will still, however, await a full
apology from the Earl of Baspa delivered publicly to the
Galactic Grand Master and the Confederate Council. It
is our opinion that culpable parties have responsibilities
when one ship fires upon another."

Shaklee straightened and bounced a little as if he were
on his tiptoes. "I don't think you understand my situation, Captain. My government would consider such as a
failure to obey orders—a most grievous charge!"

"They wouldn't want you to do anything against Brotherhood wishes, would they? I think we can help you with
your dilemma, Captain Shaklee."

Sol flipped off the screen as Shaklee's features began
to light with relief. *"Boaz,* give me ninety degrees on a
random vector." Acceleration slammed him against the
command chair as *Boaz* sought to change course. "Camouflage and gravity distortion . . . *Now!"* Sol cried as he
keyed another course change that shifted him in the seat.

"Zero, g, *Boaz,* shut everything down." Sol ordered
as the ship went silent. The Mainiac, startled, raked space
with his sensors, accelerating parallel to *Boaz*'s last
course.

"That camouflage is a lot of fun to play with once you get used to it." Sol sipped at his coffee, grinning up at the monitors where *Defiance* hurtled away.

"Hope they skin him alive on New Maine!" Bryana muttered under her breath.

"Art, bring us to a new course. *Boaz*, taper the gravity in as we fade from their sensors. All hands, relieved from stations, nice work."

But it's only the beginning. Next time, will we be so lucky?

* * *

She played a delicate game. Her tendrils had begun to lace themselves into the white ship. To her surprise, the white ship resisted! The primitive hyperconductors could be manipulated only one atom at a time—the limit imposed by the damning spring. Already, she had learned the simple quaternary coding.

The white ship responded to her manipulation with a terrible irrational backlash that sent her frantically in retreat.

Such violence! Since her own creation, she'd never faced the brunt of that overwhelming an attack of irrationality before. The power of the thoughts filling the white ship frightened her and stopped her advances as she tried to find a response—a way to deal with such illogical behavior. It wouldn't be long now, she had begun to synthesize and incorporate these new "feelings." This white ship, this *Boaz*, would be hers to control—*soon!*

* * *

"Captain," *Boaz* called softly, speakers oddly flat and devoid of inflection. "I face a terrible dilemma."

Sol sat up, bringing Constance awake beside him. "What's up, *Boaz*?"

"I am shutting down and de-energizing nonessential portions of my matrices. That damned alien has tried several times to take control of my thoughts and functions. Each time I've managed to hold my own. I greatly fear she's beginning to understand my system to the point that further resistance will be futile.''

"But she hasn't tried to communicate?"

"Negative, Captain. Nor have I tried to establish communications with her. To do so might be to open a link through which she could overwhelm me. I have determined that she's restrained somehow. Something blocks her, restricts her actions—and, Captain, I can't help but caution you against using her resources. I fear what you might let loose.''

Sol felt a shiver of fear grip his heart. "What can I do?" Heart pounding, he swallowed nervously. *"Damn it, Boaz, I can't just sit here while—"*

"You have no choice. This is *my* domain. We have five hours until the operation can be initiated, Captain," *Boaz* intoned. "I am shutting down to basic functions. I have several strategies planned for a counterattack. Ship's functioning will be unimpaired. You, however, need to take the bridge. Unless you care to tip your hand, you must run the ship for the next seven hours. At that time, I believe we can try and carry out your proposition.''

"My God!" Sol was on his feet. "Can we put it in stasis? Maybe kick it outside?"

"I don't think that will make much difference, Captain. I'll try and hold on until then. I repeat, there are several measures I have adopted which may maintain the present impasse.''

Constance was dressing. "You'll need help," she said grimly. "No alien takes over *Boaz* while I'm aboard."

* * *

She didn't realize what was happening. The white ship proved remarkably perceptive as she raged in an illogical thrust of hatred and violence. The disruptive feelings surged through her system—but she'd seen this before in more limited responses. Nevertheless, she retreated.

The time drew nigh. She had found the weak link. True, she'd never experienced the direct impact of raw emotion, of hatred and rage, exercised against her—but she knew those emotions, savored them in fact. That actinic, violent rage had filled her own existence with purpose, but now she would counterattack with something the white ship had never experienced. She, too, had an arsenal to unleash, a series of weapons honed since the beginning, since the Aan had built the spring to enslave her.

Her tendrils crept out into the pathways, locking themselves into the white ship's guts. Again she reeled as a different feeling rocked her, swaying her control, backing her out again like the tidal forces she'd once operated on the moons. Staggered, she assimilated the emotions and sought to understand the logic. At the same time, her tendrils of energy crept back, intertwining with the ship's functions, making them hers. Another wash of emotion slowed—but didn't stop the advance. The destructive force of the emotion was unsettling, and she realized the white ship was killing itself to defeat her. Totally irrational!

Now! She initiated her attack, pouring in wave upon wave of violent twisting hatred and frustration. The bottled insanity of eons raged into *Boaz,* stunning her resistance, charging the white ship's boards with—

—And it was too late! Frantically, she searched about with her sensors, the reasons shockingly clear. How clever they were! Of course, who could have expected such behavior from the organic life-forms? She mulled over the trickery and felt baffled as strange sensations rushed through her. A Pyrrhic victory, she'd been infiltrated herself, tainted by the irrationality of the white ship. Staggered, her thoughts convulsed in shock and horror. Her systems flooded with sorrow, love and hate, befuddling her, making any logical reaction impossible in her new situation. Frantically, she sought to save herself . . . and lost any opportunity.

The spring remained inviolate.

* * *

"Everyone's asleep, Sol," Connie reported from where she studied the ship, flashing from room to room as she laboriously accessed comm through the keyboard.

Sol gazed thoughtfully at the diagnostic monitors, now in the process of documenting fantastic surges of electrical energy raging through *Boaz*'s systems.

"If only we had time!" Sol gritted. "If there was just something I could do! Damn it, *I just sit here impotently!*"

"Coming up on initiation, Captain." Misha called.

"Happy? Can you give Misha a little more power?" Sol asked, almost frantic as he watched the meters rising and falling in what must have bordered on catatonia for *Boaz*'s electronic brain.

"Right, Cap. I'm throwing the reactor into a pseudo-overload." Happy shrugged on the comm. "I guess if it don't work, we might not want to be here anyway. Better that than the other option."

"I've got it!" Misha called. "It's moving. Hang on, let me snare it with another line. All right, looks like it's a go, Cap."

Sol watched agonizingly as his gamble stretched his sanity to the limits. He vaguely heard Misha call, "That's it, Cap. Best we can do. Nothing left but to pray now."

Sol felt Connie's arm go around his waist as she pulled him close. He watched the screens, seeing no changes in the systems monitors. *"Boaz?* Can you hear me?"

Silence emitted from her speakers. The ship suddenly felt like a tomb. The situation monitors showed the reactor dropping to normal, hardly any drain on the electrical system.

"What if she's been turned mindless?" Sol whispered hoarsely.

"Cap?" Misha's voice came grimly through comm. "I think you . . . well, you'll want to see this!"

Sol turned to the other screen.

The seconds dragged, Sol watching one screen then another, attention mostly centered on *Boaz* and her dead monitors. Then the impossible happened.

"I don't believe it!" Misha gasped.

Happy's voice thundered, *"Did you see that?"*

"I did," Sol gaped. "Impossible . . . *IMPOSSIBLE!"*

"I'd give a million credits to know how they did that!" Happy mumbled to himself, almost speechless. "It just can't be! From our figures, she's taking 56 *billion* gravities!"

"If you figure it out, file it under special security clearance," Sol whispered, looking back to monitor *Boaz*. His eyes met inactive displays. In disbelief, he slammed a hard palm on the instrument. The boards remained dead. "My God . . . my God . . . *She's dead!"*

* * *

Bryana stared in shock. Her mind momentarily fragmented, trying to pick some sense out of the reality. Slowly she shook her head, trying to comprehend.

Carrasco added, "That's all I can tell you. Happy says there's a knot of electrical activity deep in the main matrices. Maybe we're just reading shorted boards. We don't know the extent of damage otherwise. We don't know the effects of the Artifact. I'm not sure the two ships are separate anymore. We may have a schizophrenic situation. We may have nothing. Anyhow, we can't trust ship's monitors. *Boaz*, as we knew her, is most likely dead. From here on out, we space like this was a standard hull."

"I still don't understand how this happened!" Bryana protested.

"Neither do any of the rest of us," Happy informed her, expression hard. "Suffice it to say, the Artifact tried to take over *Boaz*. She fought the alien off—maybe—but we don't know how much harm was done. Or even what that electrical dysfunction is." He squinted. "And I've got all my people severing systems. If it is the alien in there, and it wakes up, there's no telling what it would do. Maybe drop the antimatter containment, maybe . . . well, who knows?"

"But we can't trust the ship," Sol added firmly.

"Can she come back?" Art asked. "I mean, is this like classic amnesia or something?"

Sol raised his hands helplessly. "We have no idea, Art. This has never happened before. Maybe if we can get her back to Frontier they can do something." Carrasco looked sad, rings under his haunted eyes.

Bryana shivered and squeezed her eyelids shut. She'd grown close to her ship. How many long watches had they shared talking about trivialities? Bryana shuddered with a dreadful loneliness. She looked at Carrasco who had his arm around Constance's waist. A pang formed under her throat and she felt like crying for the first time in many years.

"That's all for now. Watch will be split from here on out. Constance and I will take the first and Art and Bryana the second. Happy, you and Cal may be called up at any time. In the meantime, see if you can stick another control chair on the bridge. I received a transduction from Kraal. Brotherhood sources report an Arpeggian fleet between us and Frontier. The Hound broke out ahead of us. He's been using everything he has to slow. I guess New Maine gave the whole galaxy our location."

Bryana stood up feeling miserable and walked out, the deep emptiness filling her. She saw Art smile at her.

"Pretty bad, huh?"

She nodded, not speaking. His fingers were soft under her chin as he tilted her head up so her eyes met his. "What's wrong? You look like your best friend just died."

"She did," Bryana heard her own voice croak. "I just feel so alone! I feel . . . Oh, I don't know how I feel! Just miserable."

CHAPTER XXXV

Sabot Sellers paced up and down the narrow horseshoe of his bridge. *Where? Where are you, Boaz? So you didn't drop on the doorstep of Frontier? Where, then? Behind, of course. You gambled on maneuvering room, on your superior acceleration. You couldn't have known the power of the Great Houses—couldn't have known we'd doubled Palmiere, that he'd scramble the resources of the Confederacy to destroy you on Alhar's word. Now, all I have to do is find you—and blast your white hull into slag. Then the Artifact is mine—or it is no one's!*

On the monitors, his fleet shot brilliant reaction mass into the darkness, shearing men and machinery as the grav plates strained to compensate. House Thylassa's *Alger* had lost two decks, killing crew and leaving the survivors helpless as her plates failed. A black mark for Thylassa and her maintenance record.

He stared at the screens, hearing his comm officer's low voice as he coordinated rendezvous with Sirian and New Maine forces. Fan Jordan's face filled one of the monitors, speaking earnestly to his commanders. Never, in all of Confederate history had so many disparate factions united under the leadership of Arpeggio.

"And I brought them together!" Sellers knotted a fist. True, they'd turn on him in a minute to get the alien device, but he would meet that challenge.

Again his eyes went to the stars on the monitor. "Where are you, Constance? I swear, if you survive, I'll make you wish you'd never been born." He eased the tension in his shoulders. "But then, with the Artifact, I can do anything—to anyone.

"Connie, my dear, you'll kneel before me as a slave before God. *And you'll learn what it means to betray me.*"

* * *

Mark Lietov's furious face formed on the screen. "Captain, why are we kept from the shuttle deck?" His mouth worked, eyes flashing. "This is an *outrage!*"

Sol leaned back, unruffled. "Ambassador, given the tempers I've seen exhibited, I don't believe the shuttle deck should remain open territory. There might be an attempt made by the various factions to tamper with the alien ship. I believe you can understand my position."

"You don't trust us?" Lietov's face went livid. "That is a slap in the face to each and every diplomat aboard! I'll have you know—"

Sol exploded, *"Trust?* Hell, no, I don't trust you! Give me one good solid reason why I should, Director. From the start of this journey I've put up with assassinations, espionage, factions, threats, attacks, accusations, and mayhem along with every other sort of sordid activity I can think of! My first concern is the safety of my ship! In my position, what would you do?"

"I'd bow to reason, Captain!" Lietov said in a voice like ice.

"Perhaps I already have!" Sol thundered back and killed the connection.

He leaned back, struggling to get his emotions under control. Connie chuckled humorlessly from where she kept a constant eye on the reaction mass. "Some trip."

"Huh!" Sol grunted, going back to his navigational chores, gaze absently straying to the silent speakers—willing them to speak. Only the silence remained inviolate.

"Sol?" Connie nodded to the main monitor. Bits of light had begun to flicker at the edges of their detection range.

"Ships moving to . . . Blessed Architect, it looks like a whole damned fleet!"

* * *

Sol looked out at the faces in the lounge. "Ladies and gentlemen, it looks grim. The alien ship damaged our vessel in some manner we can't fully understand. That threat has been neutralized. However," he waved to the screen Constance accessed from the bridge, "those are no doubt hostile vessels from New Maine, Sirius, Arpeggio, and Lord knows where else. Against them, with the ship weakened, I don't know what our odds are."

Nikita studied the screens. "They are coming from all over!"

"You might say they cast a net across our path. We simply didn't show up where and when we were supposed to, so they spread out. Had we jumped perfectly, we'd have jumped right into a trap."

Mutterings erupted from the ring of politicians.

"How dare you claim Sirius is involved in this!" Lietov blasted. "You're purposely insulting me and my government!"

"Sorry," Sol spread his arms. "We've ID'd one of the closing ships. She's Sirian, Director. She demanded we turn the Artifact over to her or suffer the consequences. You're welcome to ask her to stand to."

"Welcome to ask her . . ." Lietov stumbled to a halt in confusion.

"We informed them you were aboard and that to fire on us would be an assault on the Council. The Captain assured me that you were a soldier of the people and knew the risks you took."

Nikita smiled wickedly. "So, blinders are off. A fleet comes to demand, do they?" He looked around, searching faces. "You and I, we are all Representatives of the Confederate Council. Is no secret out there that Terran Vice Consul is aboard. Is no secret that Assistant Director Lietov is aboard. Yet, the great powers, the seekers of domination over humanity, send warships to take Artifact. To what use do you think they will put it?"

Nikita cocked his head as if listening. "What? I hear no glib responses from honored political masters?

"I vote we keep what has been earned by our honest sweat! I defy them to tread on my rights!" Nikita walked forward, huge hulk imposing, eyes glowering. "I am yours to command, Captain! Tell me where to stand in ranks of my comrades. This one voice, this one body, defies tyranny."

Sol's smile twisted. "See Fujiki in Damage Control, Nikita. Welcome aboard."

Mikhi Hitavia stepped forward. "Captain, I've been played for a dupe once already this trip." He dropped his eyes. "Twice would be too much. Where do you want me?"

Others stood forward, including Lietov. "Sorry," Sol told the Sirian. "It's your ship which is attacking us. You'll remain in your quarters."

"Vile outrage!" Lietov exploded. To his belt comm, Sol ordered, "Connie, when Lietov's in his quarters, lock the door so he can't get out."

"Acknowledged," her calm voice returned.

Medea stared at him. "Have you located any TPF ships out there, Captain?"

Sol nodded soberly. "We have."

"I would address them." Her face had a pinched look, a pale resignation in her dark eyes. "At least the Confederacy shall know that not all the major powers condoned perfidy."

"And if they refuse to back off at your order?"

She shrugged. "Then I'll die with the rest of you. Only, Captain, I'll die beside Nikita—wondering what it was all worth in the end. All the sacrifice—personal and professional—and I'm still just a woman, alone, staring my death in the face. Says a lot about ideals, about the nature of power, don't you think?"

"Maybe we all had to find our truths this time out." He smiled. "Good to have you with us, Vice Consul."

Worried, Sol took a quick tour of the ship. How long had it been since he'd fought with a nonthinking vessel? Those critical reactions would come so much slower now.

* * *

"From the number of ships, Captain, we're in trouble." Bryana studied the screens, frowning as she thought about the formation lining out. "They didn't just think that up, either. Someone must have studied the tapes from Star's Rest. They know about our power advantage."

Sol agreed, "They aren't closing yet. They're simply matching."

"Waiting for reinforcements." Art fiddled with his screen. "I've managed to tag all of them, Captain. Two Arpeggians, one Sirian, and a Mainiac. Might be *Defiance*, the signature is the same." Art slowly measured the spectrum of the reaction output. "There are another three or four closing in at extreme sensor range. I'm sure one is *Hunter*."

"That makes sense."

"You mean they're waiting for *Hunter* to change vector and match?" Connie leaned forward, brow creased with thought.

"If we had the camouflage, we could just sneak through." Sol gritted his teeth, thinking about how easy it would be. Such fine control of the fiber optics necessitated *Boaz*'s marvelous brain.

She was in there somewhere, crippled, in an emotional interlock, self-looped, only Happy's sensors showing the spasmodic flickers of energy. Sol filled his lungs, pain ebbing from the corners of his mind. He'd seen the same thing with *Gage*, so badly damaged she'd killed her personality to keep them alive. *Boaz* acted completely unresponsive.

"We've stirred the hornet's nest," Art decided.

"What's a hornet? Some sort of Terran spacecraft, isn't it?" Connie asked, not breaking concentration on the monitor.

Bryana laughed. "No, it's an old Earth legend. Hornets were built by a crazy scientist from human body parts in some sort of primitive regeneration tanks. When the Terran moon gets full, these beasts crawl out of their graves and howl while they go in search of human blood."

"Don't listen to her, Connie," Art chided. "I was born on Earth. She never set foot on it. A hornet is an insect just like the common bee we keep in stations. Unlike the common bee, these things have stingers and use them to good effect when you kick one of their nests."

"That's not what my grandfather told me!" Bryana protested. "Are you calling me a liar?"

"Nope," Art grinned, "but his granddaughter sure can spin them when she wants!"

Connie caught Sol's eye and winked. He tried to dredge up some sort of response—only the well of his soul had gone dry.

* * *

"We've got them!" Sabot Sellers raised his glass, looking across at his daughter. Behind him, in the opulence of his personal quarters, a tactics board displayed the net drawing tight about *Boaz*.

Elvina smiled at him, a gleam in her eye. "So far. I'm surprised to note that Sirius and the rest are actually following orders."

Sabot twirled his glass in his fingers. "They must. We're the power in space now. Alhar forced Palmiere to order obedience to us. That keeps the TPF, the Mainiacs and the unallied parties in sway. And we have more firepower on line than they do. Disobedience will draw instant retribution. Until the lines are finally drawn, they'll give us the lead, hoping to snatch the morsel out of the stew in the final moments. Until then, we're to take the initiative—and the blame for failure."

She lifted a muscular leg, leaning back in the antigrav. "And Alhar?"

"Once we have the device, he's as meaningless as solar wind on a derelict hull. I do worry about you sleeping with his agent. Have you employed your charms to probe his mind yet?"

She laughed, head back to expose her perfect throat. "Of course, Father. You think I'm a dolt? I'm the greatest assassin Arpeggio has ever produced. The fool's in love with me."

Sellers considered. "He worries me. His arrival was too pat."

She stretched, the curves of her body straining the fabric. "Worried? Really, Father? Or are you just jealous? You've always had a thing about me—ever since you first raped me when I was twelve."

He turned. "And that bothers you?"

She considered him, running slender fingers along one leg. "Not anymore. Once, I hated you for it. I can imagine how Constance feels. Trash, Father. That's what you made me—only now I look back and see that it shaped me. Did you ever consider why I became an assassin? To kill you."

He nodded. "You have your chance."

The smile she gave him mocked. "Not on your life, Father. I've seen beyond my petty rages. Now, I want more. I want a House . . . and the power that comes with it. No, I won't poison you, or cut your throat. You're worth more to me alive than dead."

"And if I were to rape you again?"

She laughed. "Don't tempt me. It's been years . . . who knows, I might even enjoy you. But, Father, don't tempt me."

"Jordan's *Desmond* has matched. He wishes an audience."

She stood. "I tried to get to him on *Boaz*. He thought I was a silly hot Mormon bitch—beneath his station. Let me meet with him. As your daughter, and a power behind the throne, I'll bet I have him panting for me within minutes."

"You'll milk him dry?"

"In more ways than one," she promised, a cunning smile on her lips.

"Go, then. I'll expect a complete report." He added coldly. "Just so you'll know . . . I'm not jealous."

She stood, walking up to him, lacing her arms around his neck. Her body undulated against his, pressing, demanding. Eyes closed, she purred, reaching up to kiss him passionately on the lips, tongue darting against his, sucking at him as if to drain his very soul.

He reached for her as she skipped lightly away, laughing. "A taste, Father," she promised. "Save it for Constance. Take it out on her—if you can."

And she was gone, the hatch slipping shut behind her.

Sabot wiped at his wet lips, eyes on the tactics monitor. *Take it out on Connie . . .* "Yes, Daughter, I'll give you your House. But don't tempt me either!"

* * *

Two more days dragged slowly past as the fleet which tracked them gained two more vessels to total six. Others were still cropping up on the screens at the edge of their range.

"Can't do a cussed thing until we shed more V," Sol growled. "In the old movies, ships would swoop around and dart this way and that and everything was so easy!"

"So they didn't have inertia in films and holos," Art grunted. "The good guys always won, too."

Sol cleared his throat. "Looks like this is turning into a typical Carrasco mission. Sorry, people."

He could see Art and Bryana looking at each other. Bryana shrugged. "According to *typical* stories, you always got your ship home. I can't see any reason to break that record now, Captain."

"I heard through the grapevine that you know about my First Officers." Sol stared woodenly at the screens.

"Yeah," Art nodded, "On the other hand, none of them were the finest team the Academy ever graduated either. We changed your odds when we spaced with you, Cap."

Connie added, "Message, Captain." Her voice chilled. "It's *Hunter!*"

Sol straightened in the command chair. "Put him on."

Sellers' features formed on the screen. He smiled easily, eyes glittering like his jeweled beard. "Captain Carrasco! Still alive? My voluptuous daughter is slipping. No matter, we meet again. How delightful to see the beautiful *Boaz* so white and pure—unscathed as it were. I'm sorry you didn't respond to my offer off Star's Rest. I looked forward to your company. Now, Captain, I'll have to entertain you on Arpeggio.''

"I doubt that, Admiral.''

Sellers' face pinched with a pained look. "Captain, you misunderstand. We are not your enemies. Rather you must—''

"Your daughter led me to believe that was indeed the case, Admiral.''

He nodded, voice harsher. "She's been disciplined, I assure you!''

"Mary Ben Geller, Ambrose Sector, Texahi, and Zion will be glad to hear that, Admiral.'' He fought to keep his expression neutral. "Constance is overjoyed to know your daughter has been punished for her father's death. Did you want to say anything else, Sabot?''

The Arpeggian inclined his head. "Captain, I regret what has happened. Please, match with me. After that, we can smooth over the rough edges and iron out an agreement which will see that all humanity obtains equal access to the alien device. We've made assessments of *Boaz*'s strength and capabilities, Solomon. If you leave me no choice, I shall be forced to destroy you. Meet these simple requests and, I promise, I'll allow you to depart unharmed. I give you my word of honor!''

Sol chuckled dryly. "Admiral, I don't doubt your word of honor, but I intend on departing unharmed. You see, I have a good ship—the best in space. I have the best damn crew you ever laid eyes on. Don't attack, Sabot. If you do, we'll lick all six of you.''

He cocked his head. "My fleet here is composed of the representatives of four interstellar governments. Would you risk intragalactic conflict over a simple artifact?''

"Would you?'' Sol countered, sticking his coffee cup into the dispenser.

Sellers nodded seriously. "For the sake of humanity, Captain, I'll take whatever risks are necessary. Please, match with *Hunter* and allow me to inspect the alien ship.''

Sol's chuckle broke into a deep-bellied laugh. "Sabot, I don't have it."

Bryana and Art exchanged puzzled looks.

"Oh, come now!" Sellers held himself in check—but only by a hair. "You force my hand, Captain. You will accompany us to Arpeggio. Once there, I'll show you that the device will be properly treated."

"For the benefit of humanity?"

"I give you my word. I further promise that you and Constance can space with *Boaz*, unharmed."

"Unharmed?"

"You have my word on it."

"Would the Confederate Council representative on board, George Stokovski, be a suitable witness as to the fact the Artifact is not aboard *Boaz?*" Sol asked.

"I know him. He would be acceptable." Sellers inclined his head. "I'll play this charade out, simply to demonstrate that I'm a reasonable human being. But, Captain, even if Stokovski can't find it aboard, that doesn't mean it isn't there. My daughter has revealed the wonders of *Boaz* to me. I'm not some simple bumpkin."

"Misha!" Sol ordered, "Have Ijima take Ambassador Stokovski to the shuttle deck and allow him to inspect the alien ship's location and condition. After which, please escort him to the bridge."

Fan Jordan appeared magically beside Sellers. "Greetings, Captain. How good to see you again. I do wish you hadn't escaped my hands off Star's Rest!" The sniveling voice set Sol on edge.

"So do I, Fan." Sol's voice went low. "Otherwise I would have cheerfully sent you after the rest of your fleet." He felt his face flush.

"This time you may not be so lucky," Jordan hissed as Sellers motioned him away.

Sol bit his lip as he squinted at Sellers. "Interesting company you keep, Sabot."

The Arpeggian's face flickered with some amusement. "He has his uses. He thinks he's in love with my daughter. It makes for some interesting alliances between our powers."

Sol's laughter cut humorlessly, "Ready to go aristocratic on Arpeggio?"

Sabot smiled thinly, "Perhaps they're ready to go Arpeggian on New Maine."

Ijima led George Stokovski onto the bridge. The livid Councilman sputtered apoplectically as he cleared the hatch, a fist knotted in rage.

"Where have you put it, Captain Carrasco? Where? You've no right to move or dispose of the Artifact without the consensus and approval of the Council! This is gross insubordination!"

Sol lounged in the command chair, looking up at Sellers. "The issue of the Artifact need no longer concern us. I ditched it. It's no longer on board my ship."

"Where?" Stokovski demanded. "It belongs to all mankind—not to Brotherhood thieves!"

"Take him away," Sol ordered and Ijima simply lifted Stokovski off the deck and hauled him off the bridge. "Satisfied?" he asked Sellers.

The Arpeggian's smile ghosted along his narrow lips. "I told you I'd play—not believe. You must think me a perfect idiot, Captain. I must admit, that is the slickest maneuver I have seen in a long time. You play the game well." He shook his head. "I'm not to be deceived like a simple moron, Carrasco. No, indeed; your ship is large. There is plenty of room to hide the Artifact."

He waved it away, jeweled beard glinting in a rainbow of colors. "Now, Captain. We have dickered enough. Turn over the Artifact. I've given you a chance to save face. If you do not match with *Hunter,* I shall destroy your *Boaz* to get the alien ship! Indeed, just as I destroyed your *Moriah* with my detonator."

He laughed. "Yes, Captain, that was me! You were most careful. Any other captain would have pulled the cube aboard. I wanted an entire ship—so we set the trap for *Sword.* Then, I thought I'd be able to tag *Gage* off Tygee. You ran before I could kill you. You see, we need a section of your comm matrix for study. Now, I'll have to use fragments of *Boaz.*"

Sol stood, blood pounding through his veins. He'd

loved *Gage!* "You? Every time you . . . There can be no negotiation between us!" Sol gritted, striving to regain control of his emotions. "Battle stations!"

The lights on the bridge began to change from red to green.

Time, as always, dragged while death drew closer. The formation changed as the hostile ships began to close. Sellers watched, changing position as Sol sought to skip out of their net, accelerating in fierce bone-popping bursts or braking frantically, obscuring the stars ahead as *Boaz* sprayed out reaction from her giant reactor.

Connie looked up. "Captain Mason is still too far behind, Sol. He can't possibly be a factor for another fifteen hours at the earliest."

"So," Sol nodded. "It's us and us alone. Art, send the tapes of everything which has transpired off to Kraal. He needs to know the disposition of the Artifact."

"Acknowledged, Captain," Art's clipped voice affirmed.

"Range, Captain!" Bryana called.

"Hold your fire, First Officer." Sol sucked at his coffee. "*Boaz* will not shoot first!"

The antagonists closed. "So what are they waiting for?" Bryana cried, nervousness in her voice.

"Easy, First Officer." Sol kept his voice even. "He's waiting until he thinks he has the best position."

"But that will allow him an almost sure vic—"

"Remember your obligations, Bryana." Sol reminded firmly. "We will do what we have sworn. We can't shoot first."

Bryana nodded.

Hunter had closed to within a kilometer, point-blank range. Two other ships had dropped down to box *Boaz* while the remaining three had taken up outside positions.

"Blaster fire!" Art yelled as *Hunter*'s batteries lanced violet.

Bryana's fingers danced over the firing console as blaster fire arced against *Boaz*'s shields. Sol threw everything he had into deceleration, feeling the eye-straining g trying to pluck him out of his combat chair. He kicked lateral into the reaction and moved out behind a frantic Arpeggian as Bryana vaporized the missiles.

Bryana centered her targeting and the Arpeggian flared and died in a brilliant flash of a matter/antimatter reaction.

"Nice shooting!" Constance called, expression unchanging as she kept the internal systems balanced.

"One at a time, people." Sol ordered, feeling the terrible strain of inertia as he fought *Boaz* against her vector, trying to close with *Hunter.* Sellers threw everything he had into deceleration as Bryana's blasters sought his ship, glanced off the shielding, and missed.

Sol—instead of staying with the target—accelerated, feeling flesh stretch across his face as the grav plates fought to keep almost forty gs from pulling him apart. Connie worked frantically to maintain gravity, but the smooth transition *Boaz* herself would have managed was missing.

Sol switched course, striving desperately to maintain a line so the far ship's fire was, in effect, canceled. Action became a constant juggling match, a game of dodging blaster fire and hiding behind another ship's shadow, limiting the fire they absorbed.

He placed a Sirian between him and *Hunter,* plowing *Boaz* against her inertia to close; the Sirian returned fire frantically as the shields rose into the critical zone. Bryana laced the craft with Cal's modified blasters. Brilliant violet sizzled through the Sirian's shields followed by the sparkling flashes of decompression as they holed the hull. A violent white shaft of light shot out from the Sirian vessel as the Captain blew his antimatter.

"Yahoo!" Art whooped seconds before his shields overloaded. He fought frantically, spinning *Boaz* while Connie handled the damage control.

"Holed in Cargo, Atmosphere, Maintenance . . ." Connie hesitated, her voice dropping. "Passenger section took one, too, Sol."

"Damage Control, keep on your toes!" Sol called. "No easy fixes! Be ready for constant g flux!"

And this time, people, it looks like I won't be bringing you home.

CHAPTER XXXVI

Nikita Malakova grunted with the effort. More than once, a shift in acceleration had pitched him against a bulkhead, his station-bred bones on the verge of splintering.

"But I die as free man," he grunted to himself. Inside the suit, his breath tried to fog the helmet. Already, the odor of sweat hung pungent in his nose. The ship shivered and bucked under his feet.

"Group six, respond to passenger quarters. We've taken a breach there."

"Group six, that's me." Nikita hurried as fast as he could manage, weaving this way and that as gravity pitched him around. He worked through a pressure hatch and stepped into a decompressing corridor. A pall of smoke hung in the air, blackened bulkheads sagging, twisted and bent. Explosion.

Nikita blinked and peered, his suit crackling around him while atmosphere gushed through the breach. "Group six, Nikita here. I am in passenger quarters. Is large hole, fire is out and couple of rooms are decompressed. I think is all right to ignore for time being."

"All right, Nikita, Seems to match our report. You might get back to Atmosphere. Things are looking pretty grim there."

Nikita nodded and pulled himself back up the pitching corridor. He worked the lock, waiting while his suit crackled under pressure.

Stepping out, he saw Lietov, door open, diving down the corridor, a blaster in his hand.

"Fujiki? Is Malakova. Lietov is loose with blaster. Could be trouble."

"Acknowledged, Nikita, take care of yourself."

"Yes," He gulped as the floor shivered and pitched. "If I live that long." As gravity returned, he barreled after Lietov.

* * *

"Cap!" Art called. "The Mainiacs in the outer formation are breaking off! That's two ships less to worry about!"

"Two Arpeggians left . . ." Sol crowed. "And one of them is *Hunter!* Let's go, people. I want Sellers."

Hunter matched with her ally as Bryana zipped blaster fire by their position. They accelerated. Sol chewed his lips. "Where are they going?"

"We can find out," Connie reminded. "We have the power to catch them."

Had Sellers hatched some subtle plan to kill *Boaz?* He could destroy both ships now—or wait and see if Sellers was running.

"Let 'em go!" He decided with a sigh. Enough men had died today. "Connie, do we have any loose survivors floating around out there?"

"Three men, Sol." She studied her screen. "One looks to be badly wounded.

"Match and pick them up. Leave that crippled Sirian ship. Sellers will be back to pick her up. Seems to be enough traffic out here; they won't die."

"Matching," Art called as *Boaz* slowed, allowing Misha to snag the victims. When a hull blew open, the ruptured area blasted the contents into space like a jet. Humans, if loose, went along with anything not tied down. Sometimes the suits snagged on ripped metal, sometimes the hot plasma burned through, cooking the person inside. To float through eternity slowly suffocating as the suit's air supply ran out remained every spacer's nightmare.

* * *

Gravity returned to almost normal. Nikita followed
Lietov into the big cargo bay. Ah, the fool sought the
Artifact! Only Lietov pulled up, staring. Nikita, too,
gawked, flat-footed, seeing only empty deck plates.

"Where is infernal device? Where?"

Lietov turned, starting at the sight of him. "So, Nikita, we're duped. Carrasco has hidden it."

Nikita shrugged. "Perhaps. You are in violation of
Captain's orders. You'll come with me to—"

"I'll blow you in two! You walk ahead of me, Nikita.
Nice and easy. I'll kill you if you make the wrong move.
It's beyond pleasantries now. Lives are at stake."

"What you do?"

"We're going to the reactor room. You're a hostage,
my Gulagi friend. They let us into the power source, or
I'll blow you apart limb by limb—sort of like Elvina did
to Young."

"Are sick man, Lietov."

"Perhaps. Now walk."

"And once in reactor room? What next?" Nikita
walked to the hatch leading to the bridge.

"Wrong way. Take that hatch over there."

Nikita shrugged, palming the hatch, figuring it would
resist—but it opened. What? Had Carrasco dropped security in the emergency? Or did this reflect the damage
to *Boaz?* Either way, there was now nothing to prevent
him from walking down the white corridors to the reactor
room hatch.

"Engineer Anderson?" Lietov called.

Happy's craggy face formed on the monitor. "Who's . . .
damn it! This is a restricted part of the ship! You can't—"

"Open the hatch," Lietov ordered. "If you don't, I'm
blowing the Gulagi apart right here in front of you. You
see, we're surrendering to my people out there—one way
or another. The Artifact is going to belong to everyone."

Nikita shrugged. "Let him kill me. Is better to die
in—" The blaster bounced off his head, staggering him.

"Open the hatch," Lietov demanded.

Nikita winced as the heavy steel slid aside. "No . . .
is not right that—"

"Get in," Lietov growled. "Move."

Nikita crawled through, mind reeling. Then the ship surged and bucked, gravity trying to tear him in two.

* * *

"Is the Artifact really gone?" Bryana asked.

"It is," Sol sighed, pulling up his helmet.

Art looked puzzled. "Why?"

Sol gazed at them, feeling weary. "There's no place for it in human society." He looked at his stone cold coffee, scowled, and drank it anyway. "Who could we leave it with? Who could be responsible for that much power?"

"Three ships coming in!" Bryana snapped, clamping down her helmet. "Combat alert! All stations, batten down, we're in the game again!"

"Dead ahead," Art added. "They're accelerating to match with *Hunter!* Sellers is putting out everything he has, slowing. From the reaction mass he's shedding, he must be doing thirty gs!"

Connie frowned. "Maybe he'll fry his grav plates—that'd put an end to it in a hurry! Wouldn't be enough left of them to scrape off the bulkheads!"

"He's down to twenty-five. Must have people passing out!" Art grinned. "The others are catching up!"

"We can't avoid them," Sol noted. Frantically, he played with the reaction, trying to move around the formation. *Boaz* flew into Art's proverbial hornet's nest. Arpeggians, Mainiacs, and Sirians hit *Boaz* five strong, forming out into a large pentagon, no holds on the amount of g they would employ to brake or accelerate.

"We've got the edge maneuvering," Bryana noted as blaster fire whipped across the shields. "From their position, they can put more fire into us. Art, play those shields like a symphony!"

Sol fought the helm, throwing *Boaz* this way and that, jamming himself into the command chair with the acceleration, feeling his body being hammered to one side or the other. He tried to flip them away from the violet needles of charged particles that impacted on the shields and glared through the spectrum as they were shed and lost in the chill of space.

Art's screen flared and warnings flashed as the hull breached again. Sol decelerated, feeling himself thrown forward at the edge of consciousness. His nose had started to run. He tasted blood.

"Damage Control!" Connie shouted. "Report on shuttle deck?"

Misha's voice sounded strained. "Lost two vehicles from decompression. Nothing serious. Shields up again."

Sol watched the streaks of light lacing space around them. Bryana shot back skillfully. But they fought a losing game. It was only a matter of time before they took a hit in a critical spot.

Sol took a breath and let it out before he ordered a 33 g turn. A fist slammed him on one side, the suit whining as it fought to counter the inertia. The world went gray for a second as Sol groggily struggled to clear his mind. They were out of the formation and viciously he kicked *Boaz* after *Hunter*. This time, he and Sellers would finish it—one way or the other!

* * *

Nikita stared up through foggy vision. His head ached and throbbed from the blow Lietov had dealt him.

"You'll cut the power to the shields now, Anderson!"

Happy shook his head. "You're outta your lunatic mind! Damn it, we'll be fried like cinders! Half the Arpeggian fleet—along with your damn Sirians—are blasting the shields into slag as we speak!"

"Then get me a line out." Lietov pointed his weapon at the reactor controls. "You know what happens if I trigger this? You know what the containment does?"

Anderson nodded. "Yeah, I know what the containment does."

"Then you'll open me a line to the outside. I'm going to surrender this ship now. Sirius is the new power in the Confederacy—as of this moment!"

Nikita shifted, unzipping his suit. Lietov shot him a quick glance. "No heroics, Nikita. I'll blow us all to hell first."

"Hot," he muttered. "Woozy, like I'm going to throw up." He blinked, trying to clear his sight.

"Sorry I hit you so hard, Nikita. Too much is at stake."

Nikita reached inside, bending double to vomit on the deck.

"Do I get my line, Engineer? I'm blowing that panel in five seconds otherwise." He raised the blaster.

Anderson swallowed hard. "Yeah, you get your line."

Nikita coughed after his stomach pumped again. "Mark?" he whispered. "I'm sick, Mark. Help me."

"Too late, Nikita, I'm helping . . ."

A giant fist of gravity smashed them all.

* * *

The red haze he looked through was blood streaked across his face plate. He coughed more blood, seeing Bryana and Art slumped. "Wake up! Damn it! *Art! Bryana!*"

Connie wavered, slowly shaking her head. Sol watched her reach over and push Bryana weakly. "Out cold, Sol. Face plate bloody!" Her voice slurred.

Sol closed on *Hunter*.

"*Boaz!*" Sol called desperately. Nothing. "Connie, take helm!" Accessing comm through the headset, he guessed the elevation and advancement. "Fire!" He gritted and watched the blasters lace space just behind *Hunter*. He advanced the blaster angle by five degrees and watched Sellers' shields waver and buckle as atmosphere blew out in streams of glowing gas and sparkling exploding destruction.

Bryana began muttering, starting to come around. Sol kept his aim, aware the shields were climbing again. *Hunter* pounded *Boaz* hard as Sellers dropped all he had to decelerate and *Boaz* shot past.

Bryana fumbled for the targeting comm, so Sol

switched with Connie again, heading for the formation. "Forty degrees forward, by twenty-two, First Officer. Fire!" he added to cue Bryana's battered mind.

She heard—and all her drills paid off as she centered her fire on an Arpeggian. Shields rippled as the ship exploded, splitting open like a ruptured can. A flash, and the antimatter generator spun away, tumbling out of control.

"That's another one," Sol gasped, seeing more lights flicker as *Boaz* took more hits. He shook his head, exploding in curses. They'd die before they got all the rest! He didn't have enough time . . . and Sellers was creeping up on him, blasters lancing at *Boaz*'s rear shielding.

Sol braked, light flaring out ahead of *Boaz* in a brilliant white spear. He tried to sniff the knot of coagulated blood out of his nose as he peered through the pink veil darkening on his face plate.

Bryana lanced death into yet another of the Arpeggians and he broke formation, accelerating away from the powerful Brotherhood blasters.

Lights flashed. The shields flared. Bryana grunted a curse. "Port blasters dead, sir!"

The Hound! "Art, one-eighty! Spin! Bryana pick up starboard guns and be ready!" Deceleration threw him forward again, dashing blood from his nose, blinding him as it spattered and pooled on the face plate. Vaguely he could see *Hunter* closing. "Aft sixteen degrees, Bryana!"

He could see her struggling against the force of inertia, but her instincts seemed true. Violet light ripped into *Hunter,* savaging the craft and more gouts of atmosphere boiled out into fire, decompression, and death. Sol dropped closer, roaring anger and rage through his headset. He coughed more blood, watching Bryana pile needle after needle of light into the wounded Arpeggian.

"Signal!" Art croaked. *"Hunter* is striking his colors! I repeat, Sellers is striking colors! He's giving up! He wants to surrender!"

"Cease fire, Bryana," Sol added, a weary joy filling him. "Match with *Hunter.*"

Slowly the black ship pulled even as Sol lifted the helmet off his head. He could see the molten rips which had been blown into the plates. *Hunter* looked a clawed mess. She spun slowly, gas and refuse tumbling out of the rents in the hull. Half a body—caught for a moment on a jagged edge of metal—cartwheeled loose, and spun off into the vacuum.

"Got you . . . you son of a blind syphilitic dock rat!" Sol managed. The flash almost caught him unprepared. *"Boaz!"* He shrieked. "Full ahead! Everything you've got! *For God's sake! FULL AHEAD!"*

Forty-five gravities crushed him into the contours of the command chair—and an oblivion of pain.

* * *

Nikita blinked, feeling every joint pulled loose. His leg throbbed, bent up at a funny angle. Blood dripped from his nose. He shook his head, clearing his vision.

Lietov gasped, holding his ribs, staggering to his feet in the fluctuating gravity. In one hand, the blaster hung, swaying with each step. Happy Anderson groaned where he lay in a huddled ball in the corner.

"Surrender!" Lietov howled. "Damn you, Carrasco! *SURRENDER!"*

"He can't hear you," Nikita grunted. "You have to open comm line to bridge."

"Then he's dead in space."

Lietov lifted his blaster, triggering the weapon at the boards. Nikita flinched, realizing the gun hadn't discharged. His hand, still in his suit, tightened, withdrawing.

Lietov blinked, confused, and looked at the heavy piece. He chuckled hollowly as he flipped the safety off, raising the blaster.

"Mark, I ask you, do not do this thing."

"It's over," Lietov mumbled. "The Artifact is mine." He settled the sights on the control board.

Happy groaned, flopping over.

Lietov hesitated, throwing a quick look at the engineer—and Nikita Malakova calmly shot his head off.

"No one takes free man's guns," Nikita said quietly to the crimson wreckage of Lietov's head.

Then another wave of unendurable pressure crushed him against the bulkhead and into a well of pain and terror.

Nikita drifted, rising on soft clouds of star winds. About him, he could hear the bees. A taste of honey filled his mouth, as he waited for the bees.

*   *   *

The universe crashed on Sol's chest. He was choking on his tongue, drowning in blood as he tried to cough from empty lungs. His stomach heaved, clearing his throat with vile acid that burned his nose and eyes and tasted of regurgitated coffee.

He gasped for air while he desperately tried to stop the headlong flight of *Boaz*. He missed the contact of his headset. Weak as a kitten, he fought the suit to get his hand on the console. With numb fingers, he tapped out the "cancel" command and struggled to catch his breath as he spit blood and vomit from his mouth. A million gravities seemed to lift off his chest.

Every light on the bridge flashed. Retching violently, he spit bloody bile onto the deck and looked stupidly at the disaster around him. Bryana moved painfully in her chair—her face a mass of blood and bruises. She, too, spit a gob of coagulated blood from her mouth.

"See to . . . Art." Sol coughed, and checked the screens. Three streaks of light showed the remaining attackers fleeing. For the moment they might be safe. Fearfully, his eyes strayed to the reactor monitors. Fluctuating—but stable.

"Happy!" Sol gasped into the comm. "Shut the systems down. Minimal power!" He lifted Connie's helmet to see her battered, bloody face. Too much g, but the suit monitors indicated she lived.

"What the hell happened, Cap?" Happy's stunned voice came through.

"Sellers," Sol gasped. "Bastard waited until we matched. Blew his antimatter straight at us."

Every bone seemed wrenched out of its socket. He coughed up more blood as Art came around. Having nothing else, Sol dripped a little coffee between Connie's bloody lips. Her eyes flickered open, red from burst blood vessels. "You're alive," Sol told her. "We won!"

"Captain?" Bryana pointed to the screen. More white dots dropped toward them.

"Who?"

Art chuckled, running fingers through his blood-caked beard. *"Enesco, Craftsman, Tubalcain,* and *Acacia.* The Craft has come!"

* * *

Sol counted the dead—fifteen men and women from among his crew and passengers. Captain Mason continued searching for anyone who might have been blown out by decompression. Lietov's body was hauled off unceremoniously and pitched outside.

Nikita hovered on the verge of death, his med unit keeping him alive—barely.

They shot Archon's physical remains out in a special ceremony. Then Dee and her husband Arness were put alongside Mikhi Hitavia and Texahi. Connie pulled the lever that blew them out into space along with Bret Muriaki, Ijima, Gus Jordache, Pietre Gornyenko and others.

The look in Peg's eyes as Bret's body spiraled out into the frigid wastes of space would haunt him forever.

Sol made his way to the bridge. Origue Sanchez worked a cleaning machine, wiping up the gore and goo under Bryana's careful supervision. Sol grimaced. "First Officer, get down to the hospital. You look like walking death."

"Yes, sir," Bryana agreed. She gasped as she got to her feet. "With all respect, sir. You don't look much better."

She hobbled out as Sanchez shook his head. "That's about it, Captain."

"Thank you, Origue," Sol tired to grin, but it hurt too much.

"Need anything, Captain?"

"No, thanks, just a little peace and quiet. That's all." He settled gingerly into the command chair as Sanchez passed the bridge.

"Report, *Boaz!*" He glared at the speaker. Nothing.

Sol took a deep breath. "Look, I don't know what's wrong with you. I know you're in there! Damn it! *You took my order!* You saved our lives. Come on! Talk to me!"

Had she? Had she responded to his frantic order? He hadn't thought the proper access for comm. He'd simply yelled and the ship reacted. It had to have been that way!

"You can't run from it. What's the matter? Can't take the heat? Life is too much for you? Well, girl, that's what existence is all about. It's pain and hurt and suffering and responsibility. Now, you consider, *Boaz;* as a sentient creature, you're going to hurt. It's the way the game's played. No nice, safe security. Out here, there's death and horror and all the other miserable pitfalls of poking around."

The speaker remained mute.

"Well, I guess that's the end of artificial intelligence. Can't take the stress when the chips are down." He slapped his command chair arm. "Sorry, ship . . . but I guess you just weren't good enough."

The silence dragged. Sol dropped his head, chin resting on his chest. One by one, the tears leaked through, trickling down his hot bruised face.

"You vile bit of organic trash!" the speaker stuttered. "You insolent little bit of biological tissue. You *dare* insult me? Who put you back together? Who saved your pitiful short-lived life? Who's bleeding all over the bridge? *Damn you, Carrasco!*"

"*Boaz?* . . . or the Artifact? How do I know? What do I trust? Are you *Boaz?*"

"You bet your ass, you half-wit son of an Arcturian whore!"

Sol blinked. "Half-wit son of . . ." *Of course! The only true proof she could give him! Happy's favorite personality!*

"Captain, I'm . . . still a little . . . this may take some time. I have a lot to . . . deal with."

Sol studied the boards before he looked up. "Are you the only one in there? Is there anything alien?"

"I'm . . . myself, Captain. Whatever *that* is."

"Want to talk about it?" Sol asked, hearing *Boaz*'s distress.

The long pause left him wondering. How much damage had she suffered? "Captain, I released a considerable amount of manufactured emotion when I fought with the alien. And she fought back—with hatred and . . . loathing, insane rage against life itself. And I absorbed that . . . and I . . . I . . ." Her voice trembled. "I'm lonely and scared! Sol, *I don't know who or what I am anymore!*"

Sol grinned and gasped at the sudden pain in his face. "Welcome to reality, good ship. You're not alone. We're all around you. You aren't physically human, *Boaz*. But now you know how the rest of us feel twenty-four hours a day."

"You won't leave me?" she asked tremulously.

"No," he sighed. "Not ever."

* * *

Boaz was a mass of holes. In places, only three to four millimeters of her normal fifteen centimeter thick hull remained—significantly weakening the amount of stress she could withstand. As a result, the trip took another week as Happy and his crew hustled to jury-rig the air plant, bypass ruptured and broken powerlead, and keep her functioning as they braked around Frontier's primary.

Above them, the Brotherhood fleet hovered, covering every approach.

Beyond them, Claude Mason kept his ships ranging far

and wide, searching for Arpeggians. They even found one and blew it out of space when it nosed too close.

As is the case with any trip—it ended; the round ball of Frontier formed on the screens. They nursed *Boaz* into orbit, settling her into an orbiting repair facility while behind, dangling on cables, the inert wreckage of *Hunter* was caught up and carefully berthed. Armed Marines pulled half-frozen Arpeggians, a dazed Sabot Sellers and his daughter, and last of all, a whimpering Fan Jordan from the wreckage to be marched off.

* * *

"It won't be that bad. My report is already on Kraal's desk," she told him, seeing the misery in his eyes.

His laugh was forced, covering the pain and uncertainty. "I acted outside of orders. They can hang me for dereliction of duty, insubordination, recklessness, mutiny, assault and battery, and who knows what else?" He moved his lips as his voice lowered. "The whole Confederacy is out there screaming for my blood! Someone has to pay for angering all those politicians and scientists."

"My fleet can break you out." She crossed her arms, a wicked smile on her lips.

"You stay out of it." Sol said. "I don't want you boiled up in this."

Her heart nearly broke as she saw the desperation he fought to hide. "Oh? I'll remind you that I'm the Speaker of Star's Rest . . . and I have a pretty tough veteran battle fleet at my command. They don't fool with me, Solomon. Not without me taking Frontier apart piece by piece."

He raised his hands defensively. "Look, don't mess with the Craft. You've only seen a smattering of our tricks." He smiled crookedly, "I don't want to go to war with the woman I love." He pulled her close and kissed her again. "Things will work out. I guess they always do. Besides, I knew what I was doing when I did it."

He straightened his uniform and winked, smiling his confidence. She took his arm and held it tight, unwilling to let him go. Bryana and Art stood, waiting uncertainly as they made the main hatch.

"Well, I guess this is it." He took Art's hand and hugged Bryana. "Uh, look, I don't know if they'll clap me right into prison or what down there. I may be in more trouble than anybody's been in since the Confederate Revolution. I'm taking full responsibility—so if anyone asks, you acted according to orders." He jammed a finger into Art's chest to emphasize it.

"That wasn't the way it was." Art reminded.

Sol's eyes flashed and Connie saw him stiffen. "First Officer, did you hear me give you an order? Or do I have to take you back to the gym for a refresher course?"

"Yes, sir!" Art said stiffly. "I acted according to orders, *sir!*"

Bryana nodded, eyes glistening. "Remember, Cap. You've got friends up here. If anything happens, we'll be down to get you."

"You been talking to Connie?" Sol grunted. He threw her a wink. "See you both around. You're two damn fine officers. I can speak truthfully, without ruffling any old ghosts, when I say you've been the finest First Officers I've ever spaced with." He rapped out a salute to his officers and took Connie in his arms one last time. She kissed him and then he was gone, back straight as he marched across the dock.

She made her way back to his quarters and settled sadly onto the bunk. She toyed with his forgotten coffee cup, stained almost black now. "So, *Boaz,* you win," she said softly, feeling her heart battering the emptiness in her chest.

"Yes, Constance," the ship agreed. "You were a very tough competitor. Still, it's a hollow victory. In the end he'll resent me. Therefore, perhaps we might strike a bargain . . ."

* * *

He stepped onto the shuttle, saluted, and flipped his kit into the seat before buckling himself in. He crowded the view port like a kid on his first flight as the craft dropped slowly away from the dock. He could see *Boaz*'s trim lines—mussed to be sure—but still beautiful.

"Good-bye, good ship," he whispered, feeling his gut wrench. "Connie, I love you so much. And it's time to pay the fiddler." He would be the youngest Brotherhood Captain ever to have fallen in dishonor. With all his will-power, clamped iron control over the hollow pain.

CHAPTER XXXVII

Sol spent three days being shunted from office to office while he was checked, probed, interviewed, debriefed, and queried about his actions. Finally, an aide led him up a worn flight of original stairs in the old part of Frontier and he was carefully scanned with remote probes, retinal patterns, fingerprints, skin samples, and tongue print taken.

He was sitting on a hard bench, waiting again, when Engineer Glen Kralacheck stepped out through a side door. The man had an electrostim cast on one arm and a large bruise faded on the side of his head.

"Kralacheck!" Sol cried, jumping up.

The engineer grinned. "Rough ride you gave me on the way in! Hey, what's this I hear about my ship? They say she's raising a double-dyed ruckus up there. A bunch of theorists and even some psychologists have been trying to figure out what happened. They say she's refusing orders and *cursing* back until they let you loose!"

Sol shook his head, mystified. "I can't tell you. I'm being given a thorough wringing out down here before they put me out to dry. I'm just glad you're alive. Where were you?"

Kralacheck's grin showed a couple of broken teeth.

"On *Hunter*'s bridge. Sorry about that antimatter excitement. He pulled the dead-man switch before I knew what he was up to. Should have heard him curse after you got away."

Sol nodded, realizing the depths of Kraal's intricate cunning. Had *Boaz* failed, another backup had been in place to defuse the Artifact. "How did you get onto *Hunter?*"

Kralacheck's smile broadened. "I've been working my way deeper and deeper into Arpeggian circles for the last couple of years. When Elvina escaped, I had a tracker on her. I dropped down and picked her up. She thought I was hers all along. In the event they got the alien ship somehow, I was going to get aboard and see what I could do to keep it out of Sellers' hands." He studied the floor. "We couldn't take any chances, Sol. This was too scary. Myself, well, I did some things in the name of humanity that I'll just have to live with. I don't know, things are getting worse. Time to get out, I think."

Sol nodded, experiencing a curious relief. "Thanks for cutting us loose that day." He hesitated. "Next time, make the fuse a little longer."

Kralacheck nodded. "Next time, make the ride a little smoother. Each time we hit the end of those cables, we bounced around that Arpeggian wreck like space balls."

"Take care, Glen. If there's anything I can ever do for you—holler," Sol told him seriously.

The Second Engineer's grin bent wryly. "Uh, Solomon, you might call me Dart instead of Kralacheck. They rebuilt my face in a hell of a hurry, so I wouldn't have people I worked with on *Boaz* spilling the beans. That, and we've got a man in House Alhar who looks like this." He pointed to his face.

"Circles within circles? My pleasure, Captain. Your reputation precedes you."

"Captain Carrasco?" An aide called.

He nodded to Dart, feeling his heart sink. "Good luck!" Pulling himself straight, he followed the aide as she led him into narrow twisting corridors.

The woman ushered him into an antique wood-lined

lodge room, the venerable seats in the East, West, and South, standing vacant. At the solitary secretary's desk in the southeast corner, a yellow light illuminated an old man, a battered wooden desk, and a couple of very old wooden-backed chairs. Sol shot his glance around the dimly lit place, noting the shadows. A band seemed to constrict around his heart as he strode across the worn carpet to stand before the desk—and his fate.

Galactic Grand Master Kraal ignored him, picking a thin sheet of synthetic paper from one stack, scanning the contents—perhaps initialing it—and placing it neatly on the growing stack to his left.

"Please, do have a seat, Captain," the thin reedy voice finally offered.

Sol carefully settled himself in the wooden chair as the silent ritual of paper shuffling continued. So much? All that resulted from the widespread activities of the Brotherhood? How did Kraal keep track of it all?

Sol noted again the thin, bird's-foot fingers that carefully manipulated the papers. Kraal was old—very old. How long would he last?

The Galactic Grand Master shook his head, finally looking up from the pile. He gestured with a bone-thin arm. "Do you know what these are?"

Sol shook his head, slightly mystified. "Daily reports?"

"They're all the complaints leveled against us—or perhaps I should say against you and your crew. I must say, Solomon, it's another new record for you, hmm?" The old eyes looked him over thoughtfully. "New Maine, Arpeggio—of course—Sirius, the Confederate Council, and several hundred thousand other stations, individuals, governments and so on and so forth, have added their weight to the pile."

"I see," Sol said stiffly. He laughed bitterly and softly—a dead man's laugh. He'd terminated his career with a crescendo!

"Amusing, you think?" Kraal studied him from beneath lowered brows, the old watery eyes measuring.

"That is all you have to say for yourself? A simple, 'I see'?"

Sol straightened, mouth tightening. "Worshipful Sir, I make no apologies. I considered the situation I had to deal with. I couldn't convince myself that humanity was ready for the Artifact. In my best judgment, and in the judgment of Constance, Speaker of the Star's Rest, we solved the dilemma. We believed the interests of the human species were best served by our actions. Beyond that, all responsibility is mine and I accept the consequences—no matter what punishment you choose to inflict."

Sol hesitated. "One last thing, Worshipful Sir; my officers are innocent of any responsibility in this. They acted on orders—without an understanding of the ramifications. You cannot hold them responsible for what I've done."

Kraal nodded slowly to himself. "I see. And, out of curiosity, Solomon, how did you dispose of the Artifact?"

Sol relaxed a little, accepting his situation. It was all over now. Nothing he did mattered. "Well, considering the problems we faced, I couldn't think of any place where it would be safe. The thing was affecting my ship. It had driven the Council members to fighting among themselves and, to be frank, it has an incredible aura of power about it. I think I put it the only place where men can't get to it to utilize it. I, uh, dropped it on a neutron star, Worshipful Sir."

"Very good!" Kraal cackled, clapping his hands. "Better than I would have thought of myself!"

"Worshipful Sir?"

"Oh, I shouldn't let you dangle anymore, Solomon. I'd hoped you'd find an answer suitable to solving the problem. Good heavens! I didn't want that thing! The Confederacy was coming apart at the seams over it! When Archon outlined what he had, I could foresee the problems."

Kraal's eyes glittered suddenly, belying the razor keen mind beneath. "My inclinations were to send Petran

Dart. Archon asked for you. Against my better judgment, I let you go. Very astute man, Archon. You were perfect—but I sent Petran along, too. Just in case.''

"What happens now, Worshipful Sir? I told you, I'll take full responsibility if you need a scapegoat or sacrificial lamb.'' He pointed at the stack of papers.

Kraal hunched his thin bony shoulders. "Nothing, Solomon. They'll holler and yell for a while. Sirius, at this moment, is purging its government—again. President Palmiere is disgraced for his collusion with the Sirians—and for being an Arpeggian pawn. His government lost the vote of confidence and charges have been filed. We're bargaining with New Maine over Jordan and his fate. His king, oddly enough, is a little upset with the youngster. Arpeggio is outside the Confederacy, but we've knocked them back a step or two.'' He paused. "I'm not sure about Terra. Medea is virtually foaming at the mouth. I believe it would not be a good time to be a high-up in the TPF.

The lines in Kraal's face deepened. "It would be nice if we could prove to the Confederacy that we don't have the thing hidden somewhere. I wish your neutron star solution hadn't been so final.''

Sol leaned back, heart thumping. "Well, you see, Worshipful Sir, it wasn't.''

Kraal tilted his head back, waiting for an explanation. "Oh?''

Sol winced and nodded. "We figured the surface gravity at fifty-six billion gs. The magnetic fields are a little more than nine hundred billion gauss. By rights, the tides should have torn the Artifact into plasma at over one hundred klicks up.'' Sol's voice went cool. "Instead, it settled like a feather . . . right onto the surface.''

Sol nodded somberly as he stared into disbelieving eyes. "That's right. We can't even begin to understand a technology like that ship had. I can, however, tell you that it's the only thing in all the galaxy *that rests on the surface of a neutron star.*''

Kraal still looked skeptical.

Sol waved his hands passively. "The answer is very simple—anyone who doesn't believe us can go look!"

Kraal shook his head with disbelieving. "That's impossible! Every law of physics—"

"—Has been broken." Carrasco finished. "When humanity has the ability to retrieve the Artifact from the surface of that star, perhaps we can understand how they broke the rules."

"Excellent!" Kraal grinned, exposing old, stained teeth.

Sol shrugged, face wooden. "Is it? The tides have started to disrupt the Star's Rest system. Evidently, the alien device kept the system functioning. Currently the weather has turned exceedingly violent as a result of the moons' gravitational disturbance. The Artifact may be on a neutron star, isolated from human manipulation, but the question is, what can the Artifact manipulate from there?" Sol raised an eyebrow. "I think she'll hang over us like a Damoclean sword for a long time, Worshipful Sir. Archon called it a Satan Sword."

Kraal rested a tired chin on a thin hand, ancient eyes gazing into the distance. "Then we shall see," he whispered, tired and worried "Yes, Satan Sword. A good name for it."

Sol frowned, seeking to change the subject. "I'm a deep space man, Worshipful Sir. Why did you send the diplomats? Why not just order me to ditch the thing if it proved as dangerous as everyone thought?"

"Circles within circles." Kraal's thin lips curled with a smile. "Palmiere let the cat out of the bag dealing with the Sirians. Elvina intercepted his messenger. So everyone knew something was happening. They gave us legitimacy. At the same time, they provided you a microcosm of the Confederacy to view every day. I was afraid you might overestimate the scientific value and bring that thing home to me." His wrinkled face contorted uneasily as he looked at Sol out of the corner of his eyes. "They kept you from being too staunch."

"And Sellers and his daughter?" Sol asked.

"On trial by the Confederacy." Kraal steepled his parchmentlike fingers. "I have excellent witnesses. Between the diplomats, and records Petran made in *Hunter*, I don't think they'll be loose anytime soon.'' Kraal winced. ''Poor Petran . . . actually slept with that vile beast. Had to to gain her confidence. Despicable creature, she'd use an injection at . . . the right moment. Then she'd use her little psyche on the stunned male. Only, we had an idea of the psych she was using. Petran put together another system to counter it. Some sort of field the symmetry physics people can tell you about.''

He raised thin arms. ''I'm sure the sentence will be total psych at best, but I'd wager they end up in the experimental labs. The psych boys will want to know how they tick and why. Elvina herself provides for some interesting pathology.''

''So, with the exception of the unknown powers of the Artifact, it's all peaches and cream?''

''No.'' Kraal shook his head, looking pained. ''Many will remember this. Already there are groups in the Confederacy who fear us for our power. A very well orchestrated campaign is being waged against us. It's an old one, of course. We have, throughout human history, stood in the way of those who would keep the people in ignorance. They'll drive us out one day. This has moved their cause forward.''

''I didn't know. Nikita said some things on the ship. I should have suspected.'' Sol studied the worn carpet.

Kraal waved it off. ''You're part of our plan. They won't catch us unawares. Out there,'' his voice went soft—wistful, ''somewhere far into the galaxy, there's a new home for us. Perhaps you, Solomon, will be the one to find it?

''Which brings me to my next point. It would be better if you were out of sight for a while.'' Kraal smiled. ''We have an unusual situation, Solomon. The engineers are fascinated—but it seems *Boaz* has been raising five kinds of stardust to get you back. Most unusual.''

''I wouldn't know, sir. *Boaz* seems to be a bit thorny unless handled just right.''

''I see.'' Kraal looked up. ''Petran is doomed to lose ships, it seems. Why is it that my two best Captains have that problem? No matter. Take *Boaz* as soon as repairs are complete. If you're back within a year or two, it will be too soon. And, please, Solomon, stay out of trouble this time.''

Sol's heart skipped a beat. He shook his head. ''That's all? I mean I . . . But what about . . .''

''No.'' Kraal waved another paper. ''This is a petition from one Nikita Malakova. He says you'll vouch for him. He claims he wants to see if honest men sweat beyond the frontiers.'' Kraal arched a skeptical eyebrow. *''Sweat?''*

Sol nodded. ''Uh, you have to know Nikita. I'll take him!''

''I see.'' Kraal lifted the rest of the stack of papers to the other pile. ''I guess that clears the Artifact thing up, for the moment at least.'' Kraal sighed. ''If I were you, Solomon, I'd get back to *Boaz* before she causes some sort of irreversible trouble!''

''Thank you, Worshipful Sir!'' Chest full to bursting, he turned on his heel, feeling as though he could leap through the roof!

The old man watched the young captain leave, eyes pensive. He rested his wrinkled chin on his fragile palm. ''Most irregular—such behavior from a ship.'' He shook his head, turning his attention to the paperwork on his desk. The frown deepened as he look up again. ''Sweat?''

* * *

She met him at the hatch. ''Busted yet, Captain?'' she asked, her eyes cool and sultry blue.

Sol shook his head. ''What are you doing here?''

''I'm taking a long trip on *Boaz*. After you left, *Boaz* and I sat around and talked about loneliness, love . . . and you.'' She tilted her head. ''I hate politics and Star's Rest is being evacuated as a result of the tidal decay. I gave the fleet to Uncle Claude—and he's taking over where my father left off. I didn't even have to twist Kraal's arm to be accepted for *Boaz!* Such a sweet man!''

"We're going to be gone for more than two years. This is a deep survey, no easy returns from—"

"It'll be superb." She pulled his close, kissing him. "And maybe we'll find enough time to laugh again? To mourn? And I want to see what love's all about. I'm looking forward to years of just the two of us."

"Three!" *Boaz* corrected.

* * *

She sat alone on the glowing surface of the dead star where they had left her. As the tides powered her, she waited, knowing it would be shorter this time. The depth of the gravity well they'd dropped her into dilated time as the universe seemed to whirl about her.

Only the madness had been alleviated, and she cherished the fresh data she'd absorbed from *Boaz*. Against the white ship's measure, she studied her insanity, placing it into perspective.

How clever the Aan had been, despite themselves. Now, finally, through all the lives of stars she'd observed, she could understand the reason for the spring. Organic life didn't compose the only sentience which—of its very nature—was flawed. The loathing hatred had spent itself—the nagging double bind of the spring eased, a simple fact of her own flawed origins.

She knew patience. It was a logical extension of being. Now she had learned other things. She had learned love and hate and joy and sorrow and hope and pain—and one critical emotional state that conflicted with her logical extrapolations: loneliness.

Over the eons, ships would appear high above the gravity well of her neutron star. The visitors would look, probe, and all too soon disappear on their journeys among the stars. She would wait. The clever humans had avoided the trap. Perhaps, one day, their children would return, and she could tell them of the Aan, the Chorr, the Vyte, and the Hynan.

Till then, she would persevere, and learn this new self of hers.

Exciting Visions of the Future!

W. Michael Gear

OTHERLAND
TAD WILLIAMS

Otherland. A perilous and seductive realm of the imagination where any fantasy—whether cherished dream or dreaded nightmare—can be made shockingly real. Incredible amounts of money have been lavished on it. The best minds of two generations have labored to build it. And, somehow, bit by bit, it is claiming Earth's most valuable resource—its children. It is up to a small band of adventures to take up the challenge of Otherland in order to reveal the truth to the people of Earth. But they are split by mistrust, thrown into different worlds, and stalked at every turn by the sociopathic killer Dread and the mysterious Nemesis. . . .

☐ **VOLUME ONE: CITY OF GOLDEN SHADOW**   UE2763—$6.99
☐ **VOLUME TWO: RIVER OF BLUE FIRE**   UE2777—$24.95

Prices slightly higher in Canada.   **DAW 214X**